"From alternate realities . . . [?] . . . on the wildest adventures . . . [?] . . . he characters that keeps t[?] . . . [?] . . . m-pelling."   [?]

"Koch still pulls the heat [?] . . . [?] plot threads that go unrecognized until they start tying together—or snapping. This is a hyperspeed-paced addition to a series that shows no signs of slowing down."   —*Publishers Weekly*

"Aliens, danger, and romance make this a fast-paced, wittily written sf romantic comedy."   —*Library Journal*

"Gini Koch's Kitty Katt series is a great example of the lighter side of science fiction. Told with clever wit and non-stop pacing . . . it blends diplomacy, action and sense of humor into a memorable reading experience."   —*Kirkus*

"The action is nonstop, the snark flies fast and furious. . . . Another fantastic addition to an imaginative series!"
—Night Owl Sci-Fi (top pick)

"Ms. Koch has carved a unique niche for herself in the sci-fi-romance category with this series. My only hope is that it lasts for a very long time."   —Fresh Fiction

"This delightful romp has many interesting twists and turns as it glances at racism, politics, and religion en route . . . will have fanciers of cinematic sf parodies referencing *Men in Black*, *Ghostbusters*, and *X-Men*."   —*Booklist* (starred review)

"I am a huge fan of Gini Koch, and this series. I adore the world building. I love the sarcasm, banter, romance, mystery, action, and a slew of superhero-like characters that stand up against evil wherever they go."   —Gizmo's Reviews

DAW Books Presents GINI KOCH's
Alien Novels:

ALIEN
NATION

GINI KOCH

DAW BOOKS, INC.
DONALD A. WOLLHEIM, FOUNDER
375 Hudson Street, New York, NY 10014

**ELIZABETH R. WOLLHEIM
SHEILA E. GILBERT
PUBLISHERS**
www.dawbooks.com

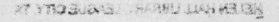

First Printing, December 2016
1 2 3 4 5 6 7 8 9

DAW TRADEMARK REGISTERED
U.S. PAT. AND TM. OFF. AND FOREIGN COUNTRIES
—MARCA REGISTRADA
HECHO EN U.S.A.

PRINTED IN THE U.S.A.

To Kenny—welcome to your own personal Alien Nation. We're glad you're a part of our Alien Collective.

ACKNOWLEDGMENTS

It's that time again—time to say "thank you" to the many people who make both writing and the career that goes along with it worthwhile.

Infinite thanks to Sheila Gilbert, the most patient and excellent editor anyone could have and same again to my wonderful agent, Cherry Weiner, neither of whom screamed "Finish the book already!" once, even though I'm sure they both wanted to multiple times. You're the bestest in the Westest to my super critique partner, Lisa Dovichi, and the fastest beta reader around, Mary Fiore, both of whom, Lisa especially, screamed "Finish the book already!" multiple times. Couldn't have made it through this particular challenge in deadline extension without all of you, and I'm grateful that I get to work with all of you all the time.

Love and thanks to Alexis Nixon, Kayleigh Webb, and the other good folks at Penguin Random House and everyone at DAW Books, especially Josh Starr, Sarah Guan, and Katie Hoffman for being excellent and awesome all the time. Same again to all my fans around the globe, my Hook Me Up! Gang, members of Team Gini new and old, all Alien Collective Members in Very Good Standing, Members of the Stampeding Herd, Twitter followers, Facebook fans and friends, Pinterest followers, the fabulous bookstores that support me, and all the wonderful fans who come to my various book signings and conference panels—you're all the best and I wouldn't want to do this without each and every one of you along for the ride.

Special love and extra shout-outs to: my wonderful assistants, Colette Chmiel and Joseph Gaxiola for continuing to fight the good fight of keeping me reasonably calm, on schedule, and somewhat coherent; Edward Pulley for continually allowing me to steal Joseph away all the time with good grace; Al Barrera for doing such a great job of helping me with social media; Kathi Schreiber for many things including being the light at the end of the tunnel; Museum of Robots for making such awesome licensed products of my works; Chrysta Stuckless, Kevin Bowman, Craig & Stephanie Dyer, Jan Robinson, Marsheila Rockwell, Anne Taylor, Koleta Parsley, Missy Katano, Erica Singleton, MJ Nicholson, Lynn Crain, Terry Smith, and Richard Bolinski for lovely and delicious prezzies that always make me feel like the Queen of the World; Joseph Gaxiola, Edward Pulley, Brad Jensen, Kathi Schreiber, Al Barrera, Megan Nash, Julie Hargraves, James Wilson, Chris & Anette Hansen, Vicki Kung, Duncan & Andrea Rittschof, Javier de Leon, and Chris "Delicious" Swanson for help, sweat, and support at cons; Summer Brooks and Slice of SciFi for giving me things to review so I still get out of the Casa, into the world, and continue to experience popular culture; Doug & Gen Cook for the opportunity to be "home" and eating well while on book tour; Kelly Mueller for keeping me apprised of things I would never see or know about and therefore ensuring I know about them; Javier de Leon for being there and Robert Palsma for ensuring that he could be; Chris "Delicious" Swanson for awesome concert experiences; Scott Johnson for still having the best little B&B in San Diego and adding on best turkey meatloaf maker to his already impressive list of skills; Michele Sharik, Brian Pituly, and Brianne Lucinda for going long distances to see the me all the time; Adrian & Lisa Payne, Duncan & Andrea Rittschof, and Hal & Dee Astell for always showing up and making every event all the better for your presence; Dan & Emily "Amadhia" King for constant love and support; the Authors of the Stampeding Herd—Lisa Dovichi, Barb Tyler, Lynn Crain, Hal Astell, Terry Smith, Sue Martin, Teresa Cutler-Broyles, Phyllis Hemann, Rhondi Salsitz, and Celina Summers—I literally would not have finished this book without the competition with and support from all of you, and I'm proud to pound hooves with every one of you (psst, buy their books); and last but not least, Matt Rich, Mark Settell, and all the good folks at Right Toyota in Scottsdale for being the place I get the most writing done (true story) and for not only letting me stay at the dealership all day long, but encouraging me to do so even when my cars don't need servicing.

Last in the listings but always first in my heart, thanks to my husband, Steve, who listened to far too many songs on continuous repeat without complaint, and our daughter, Veronica, and her brand new husband, Kenny, for giving me one of the best reasons in the world for being distracted. May you two be as happy as Kitty and Jeff and save the world all the time in your own ways.

"DON'T TREAD ON ME" is a great rock song from Metallica. However, it's about to become the third rock from the sun's theme song.

There's never been a more exciting time to be living on Earth, by which I mean never have so many different alien species of varying intelligence and talent levels been more interested in our lonely little blue marble. It's as if Earth just became the galactic vacation hot spot, formerly only known to a select few but now offering special getaway packages on the cheap.

Of course, it's also nice that we've been invited into the galactic community as a whole. We're getting help with interstellar ships and all sorts of weapons and other really cool stuff. I'm certain there's going to be a price to pay that we can't afford down the road, but right now, it's all great.

Well, other than the fact that all the anti-alien hysteria is really ramping up. And, seeing as I'm married to the current Alien of Aliens—aka Jeff Martini, whose parents were born on Alpha Four of the Alpha Centauri system and who is now, despite his wishes, the President of these United States—that means we have a whole lot of hysteria going on worldwide.

On the plus side, much of that hysteria is focused on the Z'porrah, our very own dino-bird boogeymen from far, far away. They're real, they hate us, and they make great fall guys. Of course, I know the price for this is also going to come due later on, right when we least expect it and can't handle the balloon payment, but, as with so many other things, that's a worry for another day.

On the not plus side, the rest of the hysteria is focused on us, on American Centaurion, Centaurion Division, and all of our various allies, especially those allies from other solar systems. So, you know, business as usual.

On the other plus side, we're certainly living in interesting times. Yeah, I know, it's a Chinese curse for a reason. But, as experience has enthusiastically taught me, things can always get worse.

In other words, once again, I should probably strap everyone in for another bumpy ride. And cue up some music. "Ready, Steady, Go" by Meices sounds about right. Though Panic! At the Disco's "Ready to Go (Get Me Out of My Mind)" might be more appropriate.

Because any version of "Leave Me Alone," be it by Shaggy, Jewel, Pink, or The Veronicas, is not a song that anyone—friend, enemy, frenemy, or uninterested casual bystander—ever pays attention to in my particular patch of the multiverse.

CHAPTER 1

"IS IT A GOOD DAY for America and the world at large? In addition to the Stars and Stripes, we now have a flag from an alien nation flying at the White House. Does this mean that President Martini values an alien planet more than Earth?"

The newscaster had a total Serious Face on. Which was hilarious in one sense, because when said newscaster had been live at our scene, he'd been pretty darn thrilled.

"It's not 'flying,'" my husband, Jeff, aka the President of These United States fumed, as pictures from the treaty signing we'd done the day before flashed onto the screen. "It was in one room and it was standing there. And since when have I not valued Earth? I've risked my life to protect Earth!"

Managed not to say that I'd mentioned that the flag's photo op might be problematic. I'd been overruled, my first career being in marketing or no. Now wasn't the time to toss out a big Told You So to the room.

"Not only is the flag of Alpha Four flying at the White House, but it's also been added to the United Nations," our Serious Newscaster shared. The image changed to the outside of the UN. Sure enough, there was the black and white flag of our people flapping in the wind, right next to the American and Australian flags. I had no idea if this was a new position for the flags or if ours had just been inserted into the regular lineup, but it probably didn't matter.

"It's not even the flag of Alpha Four," Christopher White, Jeff's cousin, added, while glaring at the TV monitor. "It's *our* flag, the flag of our people, and a flag we created when we went into exile here, so it's the flag of the A-Cs of Earth."

A-Cs loved their black and white so much that not only did

they wear it practically 24/7 in what I called the Armani
Fatigues—black Armani suits and ties with crisp white shirts for
the men, black Armani slim skirts with crisp white oxfords for
the women—but their flag was black and white, too. Sometimes
wondered if they couldn't see colors, but experience showed me
that they could.

The flag was definitely an homage to the Stars and Stripes. It
was set up in a similar fashion, with thirteen alternating bands
of black and white and a square in the upper left-hand corner
that had one large gray star on a black background, with twenty-
one white stars superimposed over this big one, going from
smaller to larger in a spiral pattern. The stars were to honor the
original families who'd broken off from the main Alpha Four
religion way back when. For a monochromatic theme, it was
quite attractive.

"Who approved that?" Jeff asked the room at large. "I didn't
approve that! I haven't even heard from the UN!"

"No one at the White House approved that," Rajnish Singh
replied. He was Jeff's Chief of Staff and, like Jeff and Christopher, talented above the norm.

Jeff was an empath, most likely the strongest one in the galaxy, meaning that he probably had his blocks set to high so that
he didn't collapse from feeling all the tension that was currently
in the Large Situation Room. Unless people in here were wearing emotional blockers or overlays—created by our enemies to
keep Jeff and all the other empaths in the dark about bad guys
and their plans—which I doubted.

Christopher was an imageer, meaning he could touch a picture and know everything about the person in the picture. Or he
could have, before our enemies snuck in a virus that had damp-
ened or destroyed the talents of most of our imageers.

Raj, however, was a troubadour—someone who could affect
people with his voice, facial expressions, and body movements.
Early on in my time with the Gang from Alpha Four I'd been
told that troubadour talent was useless. I'd found out, however,
that it was the best stealth talent around, and since our enemies
were indoctrinated into the mindset that troubadours didn't matter, no one had attacked their talents yet. I hoped that would last.

Since Raj was a troubadour, I normally expected him to
sound soothing in stressful situations like this one. But he was
clearly upset, because he wasn't trying to exert any talent at all
and sounded as pissed as Jeff and Christopher.

"Will other alien flags soon be flying all over our country?" the Serious Newscaster asked. "And are these aliens the reason the Z'porrah attacked our world again? Stay tuned for the first of our twelve-part investigative report: Aliens Among Us."

Charles Reynolds cleared his throat as the show mercifully cut to a commercial. Chuckie was my best guy friend since 9th grade, always the smartest guy in any room, and also now the Director of the CIA. "It's not an issue for us to say that the photos were shown out of context," he said, sounding calmer than anyone else had so far. "And I'm sure we can get someone at the UN to share that the flag was their idea. However, this is highlighting one positive thing—the press and therefore the public at large have bought that the attacks at Camp David were caused by the Z'porrah."

The Z'porrah were an ancient race of nasty dino-birds who had the longest-running feud ever going with the Ancients, who were an ancient race of shapeshifters. The Ancients were on the side of Earth and the Alpha Centauri solar systems—and by "on the side of" I mean "had meddled with everyone's evolution but because they cared"—versus what the Z'porrah were doing out this way, which was still mourning the death of our dinosaurs and wishing the rest of us were long gone.

So, during our last frolicsome fun of less than six weeks ago, we'd taken the advice of the Planetary Council and blamed the created in-control superbeing and android attacks at Camp David on the Z'porrah. That our spin for the events of Operation Madhouse had started biting us in our butts far sooner than expected was just par for our particular course. We were, as always, stuck in the sand trap, and only a miraculous hole-in-one was likely to save us.

Serene Dwyer, who was the strongest imageer after Christopher, a stealth troubadour, and the Head of Imageering for Centaurion Division, nodded. "That the press is attacking is no surprise. That's what they do these days. However, what Alexander and our other galactic advisors told us is still accurate—LaRue Demorte Gaultier was, is, and always will be a turncoat Ancient and a Z'porrah spy, and every action against us can be traced back to her, directly or indirectly."

"Can we honestly confirm that?" Jeff asked.

Serene nodded. "We can, Jeff. Believe me."

I believed her, since I knew that Serene was also the head of the very clandestine Centaurion CIA made up of troubadours around the world. I was the only person not involved in their operations who knew they existed. Therefore, if Serene said she had proof, we had proof.

"However, some of that proof can never be shared with the general population," James Reader said. Reader was the Head of Field, a former top international male model, and the handsomest human I'd ever met. In a room full of A-Cs he looked normal, because the A-Cs were truly the hottest people on Earth. So far as I'd seen, they were the hottest people in the galaxy, but I was prepared to find other alien races just as good-looking out there. That was me, always willing to take one for the team.

"Leave the spin to us," Doreen Coleman-Weisman said. She was the current American Centaurion Ambassador, a job I'd done for what had seemed like far too long and then, the moment I became the First Lady, far too short a time.

She'd grown up in the Embassy, and though her parents had been traitors, Doreen was loyal to Earth and the rest of us. However, she was the best qualified to be doing the Ambassador's duties. Well, other than one other person.

Richard White was the former Supreme Pontifex for the A-Cs of Earth, meaning their Pope With Benefits. He'd retired to the active lifestyle when my daughter, Jamie, had been born, and he'd been my partner in butt-kicking ever since then. However, due to the events of Operation Epidemic, where one of our most virulent enemies had launched a bioterrorist attack that had killed half of our country's leadership, White was now the Public Relations Minister for American Centaurion.

White nodded. "Yes, Jeffrey, this falls to us. Doreen and I have been preparing a statement to counter most of this. With the help of the Planetary Council, of course." He nodded toward the other aliens in the room, of which we had a lot, since the Alpha Centauri Planetary Council had come to visit at the start of Operation Epidemic and literally hadn't had time to finish their business and leave yet. We liked to keep our guests busy, go team.

The news came back on. "Welcome back. In a related story to the alien flags flying over the White House, our next story deals with the religious summit taking place in Rome right now." We switched from the bald-faced lying Serious Newscaster to a shot of Vatican City. "We've learned that the Pope and religious leaders from all parts of the world are indeed in agreement that they will be encouraging their flocks to join together in order to face the 'brave new world' we find ourselves in."

The Pope was outside along with a variety of other religious leaders, including ours—Paul Gower. Gower had been groomed by White for this position, and he was reasonably comfortable with it these days. He was also Reader's husband. The camera zoomed in on him. Sadly, it probably wasn't because Gower was big, black, bald, and gorgeous, but because he was the A-C's Supreme Pontifex and, therefore, the person getting all the "blame" in this situation.

Sure enough and right on cue, the Serious Newscaster shared his so-called thoughts. "Is the Pope being negatively influenced by the head of the aliens' religion?"

"Where is this coming from?" Jeff asked. Though this time he wasn't asking the room at large. He was asking the two members of the fourth estate who had unlimited access to us—Mister Joel Oliver and Bruce Jenkins.

Oliver had been the laughingstock of the media for decades, because he'd insisted that aliens were on the planet. He remained the best investigative journalist going, and these days, he actually had the respect of his peers.

Jenkins was known as the Tastemaker, and he had tremendous influence. He'd been after us in a bad way during Operation Defection Election, when Jeff had been running as Vice President to the late Vincent Armstrong. But events of that particular frolic had made Jenkins switch sides in a very fast and permanent way. Discovering that one of the candidates you're supporting is an android did that to some people.

"I believe that the answer is simple," Oliver said.

Jenkins nodded. "Follow the money."

"Excuse me?" Jeff asked.

The answer dawned on me. "Oh. This station is owned by YatesCorp, isn't it?"

CHAPTER 2

OLIVER NODDED. "Yes. Recently added into that media conglomerate."

"Recently as in the last two weeks," Jenkins added. "You know, right after the attacks on Camp David that we managed to spin well, and the inauguration gala and Club Fifty-One Gratitude Ceremony, which also went far better than could have been expected."

"Mergers happen all the time," Elaine Armstrong said. She was Armstrong's widow and now Jeff's Secretary of State. As such, she was fully on Team Alien. "Not that I am for one moment suggesting that this isn't part of a concerted effort against us."

"YatesCorp is trying to gather as many affiliates as possible," Oliver said. "And as Bruce pointed out, that's only started since the last actions against the A-Cs were salvaged."

"So, Amos Tobin is making his move." Looked down the table to Thomas Kendrick, the head of Titan Security and one of the newer additions to Team Alien. "Thomas, your thoughts?"

He shook his head. "I realize I used to be sort of 'in' with Amos and the others, but I don't think they ever trusted me fully, since I came over from the Department of Defense. None of this is something I know anything about."

Based on what had gone on during Operation Madhouse, I believed him. That the others did, too, was confirmed by heads nodding around the room, including Jeff's. And if Jeff felt that Kendrick was telling the truth, then Kendrick was telling the truth.

"However," Kendrick went on, "I can guarantee that they want to harm your ward. That, they never tried to hide from me."

My ward was Elizabeth Jackson, now Elizabeth Vrabel. Lizzie had been adopted by Benjamin Siler, who was the first human-alien hybrid, being the son of Ronald Yates and Madeleine Siler Cartwright.

Yates was the exiled former Supreme Pontifex who happened to be White's father and Jeff and Christopher's grandfather. Yates had built a media empire and then some, which was now being run by Tobin.

He'd also been an in-control superbeing named Mephistopheles. Mephistopheles had allowed Yates to die, with the idea that he'd then move to me. But I'd killed Mephistopheles before that could happen. Operation Fugly might have been six years ago, but there wasn't a day it didn't find a way to rear its head and add into whatever else was going on.

Cartwright had been one of the many female Brains Behind The Throne we'd encountered over the years. She was dead now, too, thanks to the fact that we had talented allies. But Yates, Cartwright, and her sister and brother-in-law, Cybele Siler Marling and Antony Marling, had done experiments on Cartwright's son.

As such, Siler aged far slower than everyone else and, in addition to the standard A-C abilities like hyperspeed, super strength, and faster regeneration, he could "blend," meaning he kind of went chameleon. That blend could extend to those he touched, and while he couldn't hold the blend for all that long, experience had shown that he could hold it long enough.

His uncle had rescued him from the torture his parents were perpetrating upon him and had raised Siler in his trade—assassination.

Due to a variety of things that had happened during Operation Epidemic, Siler had moved himself and Lizzie into the Embassy, and they used the name Vrabel for anything public. But the events of Operation Madhouse had put Lizzie into the White House with the rest of us and made her my ward, just because things hadn't been complicated enough already.

Despite all that had happened to her—including her parents being traitors who'd been ready to kill her when she wasn't willing to go along with a plan to murder millions of people—Lizzie was a great kid. She was also a protector. Tobin and the others were after her because she'd schooled their kids on why picking on people weaker than yourself was a bad thing to do.

"I get that they don't like that Lizzie kicked their kids' and their friends' kids' butts. But the only reason I can see for them continuing the vendetta is because they want to hurt Amy and blame it on Lizzie."

Amy Gaultier-White was one of my two best girlfriends from high school. She was a tall redhead, a lawyer, and still fighting to get control of her late father's company, Gaultier Enterprises. She was also in the room, because we were nothing if not the most unconventional and chummy administration the White House had seen in a long time if not ever.

"Well, the Fem-Bot Initiative certainly indicates that." Amy was going to say something more, and it looked like Siler wanted to say something, too, but Tim Crawford ran into the room. And he really had to run to get close enough so that Jeff could see and hear him.

In a normal presidency, this meeting would have been taking place in the official Situation Room. But that room only held about twenty-five people and, as such, was far too cramped for the numbers we seemed to drag with us.

So, we'd done what we always did and adapted. The much larger State Dining Room was converted into what we now all called the Large Situation Room, or the LSR for short. This had been met with some resistance by the White House staff, but we'd shut them down by sharing that we'd eat in here, too.

And, frankly, even though it was more ornate than the Original Situation Room—aka the OSR—it was a lot airier and more relaxed. Sure, the many TV screens weren't embedded into the walls and such, as with the OSR, but rolling A-V equipment was easy enough to set up when you were dealing with people who had hyperspeed, and in this room we could seat a heck of a lot more people. This meant that we were doing these meetings in the White House Residence instead of the West Wing, but it was a small price to pay to not have to tell various members of our extended team that they had to sit on the floor or, worse, not attend the meetings at all. I'd personally have done a lot to be allowed to miss these meetings, but I was in the minority.

Tim was doing the job that was still the favorite one I'd ever held—Head of Airborne for Centaurion Division. "Where have you been?" Jeff asked, before Tim could speak. "I asked you to be here thirty minutes ago."

"Sorry I'm late, but you'll be glad I am. Or at least interested in why." Tim didn't sit. "I was at Andrews with the rest of my team, getting briefed on more of what Drax's helicarrier can do."

"Where is he?" Jeff asked. "He was supposed to be here as well."

Tim rolled his eyes. "Jeff, if you'd let me finish, I'd be happy to tell you. Unless you desperately need someone to berate for some reason."

"He does, we just watched the news and they were, as so frequently happens, mean to us, and Jeff's tender feelers are hurt. However, I'm here. Tell me whatever it is, Megalomaniac Lad. I care and currently feel no need to berate anyone."

Tim grinned at me. "Thanks, Kitty. Anyway, a request came through to Colonel Franklin and he felt that we needed to discuss it, so I could brief all of you."

"And that was?" Jeff asked, sounding annoyed. "I'm not trying to berate you, Tim. I just want to know why you're late."

"Jeff," my mother said sharply, "relax. And that's an order."

That my mother was both in the room and telling the President what to do wasn't so much because she was a meddling busybody as much as it was her job. As I'd discovered six years ago, my mother wasn't a business consultant. She was *the* consultant for anti-terrorism and the Head of the Presidential Terrorism Control Unit, a division almost as clandestine as the one Serene was running, but with a lot more power. The P.T.C.U. reported directly to the Office of the President, and most of the other Alphabet Agencies reported dotted-line into the P.T.C.U. somewhere.

"Ah, Angela has experience with this, Jeff," Fritz Hochberg, our newly instated Vice President, mentioned. "More than you or I do, frankly."

Jeff ran his hand through his hair. He had dark, wavy brown hair and I liked when he did this, because it managed to make him even more handsome than normal, which, considering he was the hottest thing on two legs, should have been impossible. But it wasn't.

Jeff must have picked up my lust spike, because he glanced over at me and gave me a very personal smile. He also relaxed. That was me, keeping the top man stress-free by wanting to constantly keep him in the sack. This was, sadly, probably the only FLOTUS duty I was actually going to be good at, but at least I had this one firmly under control.

"You're right," Jeff said. "Tim, I'm sorry, please go on."

Tim shook his head. "Too much caffeine? Anyway, while I realize that the media attacks are making everyone tense—and yes, I know about them because they have TVs over at Andrews—this may make it a little better."

Resisted the urge to tell him to hurry up. We all liked to own our dramatic moments now and then.

Reader felt no such compunction. "Tim, seriously, stop dragging it out. What's going on?"

"We have a whole lot of people asking to enlist." Said as if this was the coolest news in the world.

That sat on the air for a moment. "Um, in the Armed Forces?" I asked politely. "Don't we usually have that? I mean, I'm sure it ebbs and flows and all that jazz, but people wanting to enlist isn't all that unusual."

Tim grinned. "For Army, Navy, Air Force, Marines, the National Guard, and the Coast Guard? Sure. But that's not what I mean. I mean that we have people, many, many people, who want to enlist to serve in Centaurion Division. And they're all humans."

CHAPTER 3

TIM'S NEWS STUNNED THE ROOM into silence. The A-Cs were normally quiet when they were thinking, but a quick glance showed that they were probably not thinking all that much, because to a one, they all looked shocked out of their minds.

White recovered fastest. "Ah, are you certain they want to join Centaurion Division?"

"Positive," Tim said as his grin got wider. "And they're not just from the U.S. We have requests coming in worldwide."

"Why?" Jeff asked flatly.

Tim shot Jeff the "really?" look. "Because they want to fight evil aliens and they want to go into space to do it."

"Oh, wow, it's Heinlein's *Starship Troopers*, isn't it? Only we're fighting dino-birds instead of bugs."

"I have no idea what you mean, baby," Jeff said. It was obvious that most of the other A-Cs weren't getting this one, either—they weren't really up on any science fiction books, movies, or TV shows, presumably because they didn't think those were works of fiction so much as historical documents about their lives. The other aliens in the room looked equally confused, but several of the humans all started to come around.

"This could be wonderful news," Hochberg said. He was a former four-star Army general, so he'd definitely be one who'd know.

We had other former and current military personnel in the LSR with us, and they all started to look kind of excited. "Something like this, combined with the religious leaders being in agreement, could really bring worldwide cohesiveness," Senator Donald McMillan said. He was a former war hero, the senior senator from Arizona, one of the few honest politicians we knew, and, by now, a good friend.

Hochberg nodded. "And this allows America and American Centaurion to lead the way. A win-win."

"Or a lose-lose when things go wrong." Chuckie said.

"Charles, is right now the time to be negative?" Hochberg asked.

"He's right and it is." I'd spent most of our lives defending Chuckie, and even though we were in top-level positions now, I still ended up doing it far more often than not. "Things are going to go wrong. They always do. We need to be prepared for that and plan for that. And before anyone tries to give the optimistic arguments I can see forming, I'd like to go on record that I told you all that the flag thing was going to be an issue. I was ignored and overruled. Note that the American Centaurion flag is now an issue. Meaning, don't ignore me, or the smartest guy in the room, when we tell you that we'd better be prepared for anything and everything to backfire right into our faces."

Okay, so, so much for the mindset of not saying "told you so." Apparently, some in the room needed the reminder.

"Charles and Kitty are both right," Elaine said. "And I, for one, feel that while we want to work for the best, we'd damn well better be prepared for the worst."

"I agree with the naysayers," Jeff said. "And not just because my wife told me to." This earned a laugh that definitely reduced the tension in the room. Jeff was just so good at leading. "In my experience, we never get to have things go the easy way. However, I'm definitely of the opinion that we'd better work for what we want. And I think world peace, if it's possible, would be in our best interests. And I still have no idea what you mean about *Starship Troopers*."

"In its simplest form, humanity joins together to fight alien bugs."

Jeff shook his head. "We don't want to start a galactic war."

Heard a snort behind me. "You're already in one." This was from Malcolm Buchanan. He was built a lot like Jeff—big, broad, and handsome, though he had straight brown hair and blue eyes. Despite being a human, he also had Dr. Strange powers—if he didn't want you to see him, you didn't see him. As always, I'd forgotten he was in the room until he'd spoken.

"But we don't want to be," Elaine said.

"What we want and what we get are two very different things," Buchanan said. Rightly.

"Well, we've got a lot of people who want to be prepared for it," Tim said. "And we need to determine how they're going to enlist and how we're going to organize that division."

"Keeping in mind that by our telling the world that the latest attack on us was instigated by the Z'porrah pretty much means that we're saying they're our enemies and we need to be prepared. Which, in case the rest of you have forgotten Operation Destruction, they are and we do. I'm not willing to let them come back to destroy our world or steal my children or anyone else's."

Serene nodded. "Frankly, this enthusiasm is what we want. If we can get enlistments from all the countries in the world, then every one of them has a reason to care."

"Having skin in the game helps," Chuckie said. "However, losing someone in battle means that all that goodwill and cohesiveness can turn around in an instant."

"We're going to lose against the Z'porrah if we're not prepared," Raj said. "And by 'we' I mean our solar system and the Alpha Centauri system." Heads around the room nodded, particularly those from the Planetary Council.

"Is arming for war really what we want to show the world and the greater galactic community?" Jeff asked.

"That depends on what you expect to find outside of your solar systems." This comment came from Rudolph "John" Wruck, aka an Ancient and the only survivor from LaRue's attack on her own crew decades prior. During Operation Epidemic I'd discovered that Wruck wasn't actually a Yates progeny, as we'd first suspected, but rather someone going deep undercover on his own to try to stop LaRue and her allies. I'd turned Wruck to our side, and even though he hadn't been with us all that long, there wasn't a minute where we weren't glad to have him.

"What do you mean, John?" Jeff asked.

Wruck shook his head. "I mean that here, on Earth, the goal of a cohesive human community is a good one. To have humans and any aliens living on Earth be cohesive is also something to work for. However, you need to understand that part of why all of these," he nodded toward the Planetary Council, "want your help isn't because they want to lead you toward peace. They aren't giving you interstellar flight to be friendly. They're doing it because they want you to lead them into war."

The room went still, and now all heads turned toward the Planetary Council. Specifically, toward Alexander, titular emperor of Alpha Centauri, definite king of Alpha Four, and Jeff and Christopher's cousin.

Alexander stood slowly. "I will not deny this, because it's true. Events have repeatedly shown that we must work together to repel the biggest threat to all of our worlds. Information received from elsewhere in the galaxy confirms this need—either you are with the Z'porrah or you are against them. Neutrality is not recommended, because if the Aligned Worlds leave you alone, you become an easy target for Z'porrah to conquer."

"So, people wanting to enlist with Centaurion Division is a good thing," Tim said cheerfully. "Meaning we're back to my original point—we need to figure out how to handle this, who's in charge of it, and how we ensure that we can register people from other nations into it."

Chuckie and I looked at each other. "In other words," I said slowly, "we actually need to create the War Division."

CHAPTER 4

"I'D SAY I CAN'T BELIEVE IT," Chuckie said dryly, "only I can, I really can." He shook his head. "And the worst of it is—we need this."

"Why are you two so upset?" Jeff asked us. "I may have my blocks up, but I can read both of you really clearly right now."

"Well, it's just the irony we're having difficulties with, Jeff."

"What irony, baby? Seriously, all I'm getting is that you're both resigned and upset. I'm just not sure why."

Heaved a sigh. "Probably because of all that's gone on in the last six weeks. But, to explain, I've literally spent my entire career with Centaurion doing my best to keep you guys from becoming the War Division. Prior to Operation Madhouse, Chuckie was the Head of the CIA's E-T Division, and he risked his life over and over again to also keep the A-Cs from becoming the War Division. And now, here we were, about to gleefully become just that."

"I wouldn't say we're gleeful," White said. "However, while we A-Cs are pacifistic at our cores, frankly, humans are not. And, clearly, the Z'porrah are not, either."

"They are not," Jareen, my Reptilian Soul Sister said. She was here with the Planetary Council representing her planet, Beta 13, and, due to all the crazy that had been going on since the Council had arrived, we'd had almost no time to just hang out and catch up. Wasn't sure if she was as bitter about that as I was, but I kind of figured she was. "First they attacked Earth, and then they attacked the entire Alpha Centauri system. This will not end, unless or until we end it."

"If it's been going on as long as you're all indicating, it's unlikely we're going to end anything," Chuckie pointed out.

"However, we do have experience with never-ending war on this planet."

"Plenty," Mom said dryly. "Which is probably helpful."

King Benny cleared his throat. "I believe Richard has misspoken slightly." He was a giant walking otter from Beta Eight and one of the new official leaders of that planet. And he was probably the cutest thing we had on Earth right now. But, he was also a warrior. He bowed his head toward White. "Some of those on Alpha Four are pacifistic, just as those here are somewhat pacifistic. However, the former rulers of that planet were quite willing to be ruthless."

"He has a point," McMillan said. "And, frankly, while Centaurion has always tried to find the non-lethal way of dealing with issues, we'd all be dead already if you hadn't been fighting superbeings with deadly force and intent."

"So, if the need is enough and the monster is bad enough, you guys will fight. And, frankly, keeping our planets, let alone our galaxy, free of Z'porrah rule is a pretty big need." And if I was honest with myself, while the A-Cs were thinkers and creators, they were also very good at being warriors as well.

Jeff sighed. "Good points all. I think the difference is that we're making this choice willingly, as opposed to being forced to fight for an ideology or a leader we don't agree with."

"Does everyone agree with us, though?" Reader asked. "I mean, there's no way we're going to get a hundred percent of Americans, let alone anyone else on Earth, to agree with us. But do we feel that we're representing the majority, or even a large minority?"

Tim rolled his eyes. "Raj, could you turn on the TV screens?"

Raj pressed some buttons on the super-duper remote he controlled when we were in here. The curtains over the windows automatically closed and the screens jumped to life. Some had regular programming. But several had news reports. All of them showing a great number of people holding signs that said, "Let Us Fight," "Stop The Evil Aliens," and similar sentiments.

"Gosh, it's just like a Club Fifty-One rally, only with positive statements. Assuming the evil aliens they're talking about aren't, for once, all of the A-Cs."

"Some of those people *are* Club Fifty-One," Tim said. "Their schism has been very good for us. The majority of them are now pro our aliens and, based on today, getting more and more pro aliens on our side all the time."

"The rest are more virulently anti, of course," Chuckie added. "And we need look no further than Harvey Gutermuth and Farley Pecker for who will be leading the charge against this."

Gutermuth had taken over as the head of Club 51 after we'd taken out its first leader, Howard Taft, during Operation Drug Addict. Due to the schism, Gutermuth was now the head of Club 51 True Believers, which was what the remaining anti-alien Club 51 loons had become.

"Well, we should never expect the head of the Church of Hate and Intolerance to ever promote any kind of togetherness." Between Pecker and Gutermuth I wasn't sure who I despised more, though Gutermuth was far more politically sneaky than Pecker. They'd both served time for attempting to blow us up at the end of Operation Infiltration, but they'd both gotten out early for supposedly good behavior—though intel had shown it was because they'd both bought their way out—and were back at their respective hate-filled posts. We were lucky that way.

"I think we need to be sure that we're also representing the majority of the A-Cs," Doreen said. I was going to chime in and agree, but the communications system came on. "Excuse me, Mister President."

"Yes, Walter?" Jeff asked. Walter Ward had been our Head of Security at the Embassy and was now doing the same at the White House. His older brother, William, was in charge of all Security worldwide, and based out of the Dulce Science Center. Walter was dedicated, eager, and a slave to titles.

"Is the First Lady with you?"

Jeff shot me a What The Hell look. Shrugged. I had no idea what was going on, either. "I'm here, Walter, what's up?"

"We have an incoming message."

"Okay," Jeff said. "From whom?"

"Ah . . . I'm not entirely sure, Mister President, sir." Walter sounded confused and worried. This probably boded.

"Walt, do you have any guesses?"

"Not really, Chief First Lady." He sounded evasive.

"Walt, I think you have a really good guess that you're afraid to share with the room. Am I right?"

"Yes." While Walter was still in his mid-twenties, he was incredibly competent and dedicated to his job. He also wasn't normally this coy. Something was up in a big way.

Jeff's mouth was opening, presumably to tell Walter to spill the beans. Put up the paw. Jeff's mouth slammed shut. Amazing.

I'd been testing out my Talk To The Hand gesture, and prior to my being made the First Lady it had had no real effect. The moment I became the FLOTUS, though, the paw had power. It was always nice to have something, anything, in the win column.

"Walter, who would you feel better sharing this particular communication with?"

There was a pause. "Only you, Chief First Lady."

More mouths opened. Put the paw right back up. Mouths slammed shut. It wasn't the coolest power, but it was one I apparently had in spades, so I was keeping it. "I'll be right there, Walter. Is it okay if Malcolm comes with me?" Asked because I knew without asking that Buchanan was going to come with me whether Walter wanted him there or not.

"Yes." The com went dead.

"What the hell?" Jeff asked the room in general and me in particular.

"Do you think we're infiltrated?" Chuckie asked, before I could reply. "Because this doesn't seem like Walter but it does seem suspicious."

"It does seem suspicious, but I don't think Walter would willingly or knowingly ask me to walk into a trap. I think he's completely unsure of the correct protocol for whatever situation he thinks he or we are in and is, therefore, asking for the one person he knows doesn't give a crap about protocol at all."

"I agree," Buchanan said. He drew back my chair and helped me up. Jeff glared at him but it was only about a three on his jealousy scale, or, as I thought of it, Jeff's base reaction to any man doing anything with me that Jeff felt he should be the one doing. "If we're infiltrated, we'll let you know."

"How?" Chuckie asked flatly.

"I'll run through the White House complex screaming."

"Sure you will," Jeff said, sarcasm knob at about eight on the one-to-ten scale. "But fine, we'll carry on with Tim's news here, you find out what the hell's going on with Walter."

Buchanan and I headed off. Wruck and Siler followed us. I chose not to complain about this. Instead, I decided to ask Team Tough Guys a pertinent question. "Any guesses?"

"Many," Siler said. "Too many to waste the breath, since we'll find out soon enough."

"I assume that you three don't think this is as benign as I do."

"I assume there is no immediate threat," Wruck said. "But

Walter sounded very stressed, meaning a threat is coming. Potentially."

"Anytime someone only wants you, Missus Executive Chief, it means that something's going down and they want the person most likely to come up with the best plan of attack or retreat to weigh in first."

"Wow, Malcolm, when did you add sucking up to your repertoire? I don't mind, but it's kind of a surprise."

Buchanan chuckled. "There are people who are more loyal to you than to anyone else, even Mister Executive Chief."

"Three of them are with you right now," Siler added dryly.

"I'm all kinds of flattered. And I'm sure you feel that Walter's one of those."

"You're the reason he went from handling gate transfers at the Dulce Science Center to two of the top Security positions Centaurion has," Buchanan pointed out. "You're the reason his brother has the topmost Security position. Yes, he's loyal to you, first, and the rest of Centaurion's core teams second."

"Same with his brother," Siler added. "Frankly, if you ever leave your husband it will cause a schism as dramatic as the one Club Fifty-One's gone through."

"Not that I'm planning to leave Jeff."

"Right now," Buchanan said with a laugh. "It was a near thing though."

"True." I'd been really mad at Jeff during Operation Madhouse, after all. Him allowing warheads to be aimed at the ship I was in had that effect on me. Not to mention him making deals with terrorists. And him buying the idea that I was big in the helpless victim department. Decided I should stop thinking about this because it still had the potential to piss me off, even though I understood what had driven all those bad decisions. "But it was all a big misunderstanding."

"Keep in mind that misunderstandings like that can and do happen all the time," Siler said. "And when they happen on international and galactic stages, they can have far longer-lasting ramifications than a familial spat."

"Or," Wruck said, "they can have exactly the same ramifications."

CHAPTER 5

"MIND EXPLAINING THAT, JOHN?" I asked as we wandered the White House Complex. I sucked at mazes, and while the White House wasn't that bad on the maze scale, we hadn't been here all that long and we'd been hella busy our short time here, so I still tended to get lost and wander into the wrong room more often than not.

"The Ancients and the Z'porrah weren't always enemies."

This news was so shocking that the rest of us literally stopped in our tracks. "Come again?" I asked when I could find my voice.

"Tens of thousands of years ago, we were friends. Our races are two of the oldest in the galaxy, and we were encouraged by races even older than us to go forth and help the younger races. Originally, the Ancients and the Z'porrah worked together to uplift various species."

"Any we know of?" Siler asked.

Wruck shook his head. "Our galaxy is teeming with life, and all of these were far closer to the Core. Over time, though, arguments happened. There's no clear answer for why we became bitter enemies—each side has their own story, but experience has taught me that the true answer lies somewhere in the middle."

"That's why there are so many Ancients who are Z'porrah spies, isn't it?" I asked. "The relationship goes back far enough that, to some Ancients, whatever the Z'porrah think is right."

Wruck nodded. "It goes the other way, as well. There are Z'porrah who are our spies, for example."

"I learn something new every single day. Glad I'm open to it. Speaking of which, though, there's no way your people call themselves the Ancients. As far as I knew, the A-Cs here on Earth named you guys the Ancients."

"In a way. However, the sound of the name we call ourselves is very close. Anciannas is our real name. It's not surprising the A-Cs translated that to Ancients. And these days, it fits."

"Yeah, it does. You know, LaRue—well, the LaRue on Bizarro World—told me that the name you had for yourselves was unpronounceable for humans."

Wruck shrugged. "The Z'porrah refuse to use our name. She was a Z'porrah spy."

"Gotcha. She didn't want to say the name so told me I couldn't say it and we moved on. So, was the book we found and translated a religious text?"

"Yes, it was. We traveled with it for reasons similar to why an Earthling would travel with the Bible or the Koran."

"Always nice to be right." Not that there was anyone here who I could lord this over, but when I had some time, I was definitely going to share this with Jeff, Christopher, and Alpha Team and be as smug about it as possible. "Speaking of formerly held beliefs, we all thought that the crew your crew came to check up on died here due to pollution. The crew whose crash we know about, I mean."

He shrugged. "LaRue hid our ship with someone, Yates, I'd assume, because she didn't crash it."

"How did she think she'd killed all of you if you weren't in the ship?" Buchanan asked.

"She shot us all, then lit us on fire, and tossed our bodies into the Superstition Mountains in Arizona. Something she did right before this gave me a warning. I didn't have time to avoid getting shot, but I was able to alter into a race that can survive pretty much anything. I believe you met them."

"You turned into an Alpha Seven Cleophese? I'd think LaRue would have noted one of her crew turning into a Cthulhu lookalike."

He managed a smile. "I maintained my appearance but took on some of the Cleophese properties. I wasn't able to shift into a full Cleophese—it was why I had to recover from my injuries before I could start tracking LaRue, and why those injuries almost killed me anyway. I'd have died like the others if I hadn't had that one moment's warning." Now he looked sad. "I had no time to warn anyone else."

"We all hate her, and even though the original is dead, trust me, I'm all about finding any and all of her clones and destroying them sooner as opposed to later." Had another thought. "She had a Z'porrah power cube with her, right?"

"Yes. I saw it, the glitter of it, right before she attacked us. That was what warned me. And I assume that's what she used to hide our ship."

"Meaning there's an Ancient spacecraft somewhere on Earth." Something else for us to try to find. Mentally added it onto our to-do list. It was a long list, and getting longer daily.

"This didn't answer Kitty's actual question," Siler pointed out.

"True. Regarding the crew, we came to find, as shapeshifters, that we can adapt quickly to circumstances, including polluted ones. In fact, adapting to pollution is easier than what I had to do in order to survive LaRue's attack. We can adapt to breathe underwater. Pollution is unpleasant but survivable. As far as I know, the first ship didn't crash so much as it was shot down."

"Wouldn't that have given them time to shapeshift, though?" I asked.

"If it had been a conventional shot from an Earth force, yes. It was from a hidden Z'porrah power cube and, as far as I've pieced together, the shot essentially paralyzed the crew. They had no way to avoid crashing and they were unable to shift into a form that could survive the impact."

After Operation Destruction and all the hidden tunnels, rooms, and power cubes we'd found, the assumption had been just what Wruck was describing. But it was different, hearing Wruck tell us about how people he would have known—his people far more than we were or could ever be—had died. He sounded dispassionate. I knew in my gut that he wasn't.

"That must have been horrible," Buchanan said quietly. "Knowing you're about to die and being unable to do anything to save yourself."

"We're at war," Wruck said, as if this answered everything. Sadly, it probably did. "At any rate, the paralysis would be why the bodies would have been in a good state of preservation, and probably why death from pollutants or just Earth's atmosphere was the presumed cause of death."

We stopped talking about this cheery subject as we reached Walter's White House Security Command Center and went in. Walter had set this up similarly to how we did it all over Centaurion Division, meaning it looked nothing like a normal human would expect. Because Security A-Cs, especially those who were in command positions, were expected to sleep on the job.

This was probably because the original Head of Security, Gladys Gower, had been a combination of a dream reader and empath, meaning that she could feel and see things going on in her sleep and was basically on the job 24/7. Therefore, the security command center in the main A-C facility, the Dulce Science Center in New Mexico, had several bedrooms connected to its futuristic eye in the sky setup, because Gladys had had a support team.

At the American Centaurion Embassy, Walter had been a one-man operation. He'd made the sitting room portion of his bedroom suite into the command center and had put a cot next to his equipment. Here at the White House the setup was similar, but because there were a lot of humans around, the bed was in the connecting room. The eye in the sky equipment, however, was in full force. TV screens, computers, audio equipment, and things I didn't bother to try to identify were all over this room. Walter was in a big, comfy executive chair on wheels. I was about ninety-nine percent certain he slept in the chair more than his bed.

That the A-Cs still expected their various security chiefs to be 24/7 and essentially leashed to their command center was something I'd given up arguing about. Pointing out that having people trying to follow in the footsteps of a talented rarity fell on deaf ears, particularly the ears of those I was trying to relieve. Walter, who had no talents, William, who was a top imageer, Missy, who was now the Head of Security at the Embassy and whose talent situation I was unaware of, and every other A-C given this duty worldwide were all adamant that making changes was not in their manifesto. They were going to be as close to Gladys as they could be or die trying. The Security A-Cs were possibly the most dedicated of all the various divisions.

Walter was—true to expectations and despite the vast number of Secret Service agents we had hanging about—alone except for his Poof, Teddy, who was perched on his shoulder, and his Peregrines, George and Gracie, who were sitting near him.

Poofs were adorable alien animals, small round balls of cuteness with black button eyes and no visible ears or tails because of how fluffy their fur was. They were considered the Royal Pets of the Alpha Four Royal Family, of which the Martinis and Gowers were a part and into which the Whites had married. However, I'd discovered that they were really animals from the

Black Hole Universe, and therefore they all technically belonged to the person who'd brought them with him to this universe when he'd taken off for Crimes in Support of Free Will.

This was probably why the Poofs could go Jeff-sized with a mouth full of razor-sharp teeth whenever danger threatened, and why they were able to ingest things—Z'porrah power cubes, weapons, anything they wanted or I asked them to—without feeling any ill effects. They also attached to whoever named them, and they had a really wide view of what constituted a name. I tended to consider that whoever had a Poof as a pet was approved as an ally.

The Peregrines, on the other hand, looked like peacocks and peahens on steroids, complete with really nasty claws and beaks and total brawler attitudes, and they were truly from Alpha Four. They were also Royal Protectors and tended to work in mated pairs. Alexander had sent us a dozen such pairs when Jamie was born, and by now we had a whole lot more. Walter had had George and Gracie from the start, and while my Peregrines Bruno and Lola were the Head Birds, George and Gracie considered themselves the Chief Security Birds. Peregrines took their jobs seriously.

Like Siler, the Peregrines had the ability to go chameleon, where they blended into the surroundings and could only be seen by those they allowed to see them. As such, when Bruno went visible I didn't jump so much as feel I should have mentioned to Jeff that I'd have Attack Bird support in case of trouble in addition to the dudes with me. By now, even Jeff had admitted that the Peregrines were great protection.

Bruno and George started to have a quiet bird conversation. I caught bits of it— basically Bruno was getting George's views on the situation. What I couldn't catch was what George's views actually were, though he seemed to be matching Walter in the worried department.

That I could understand any of it was because I'd somehow become Dr. Doolittle and could talk to the animals. The animals always understood me, but I could only understand them if they wanted me to. Right now, Bruno and George didn't care if I heard them, but they weren't going out of their way to ensure I could comprehend. No worries. I had an A-C here that I could get all the pertinent info from anyway.

"Walt, what's going on?"

Walter didn't look upset to see Siler and Wruck. Interesting.

He did, however, look deeply worried. "Several things, Chief First Lady." He cleared his throat. "Ah, I think the four of you should prepare yourselves."

Well, presumably I could get information out of him. "It's Anticipatory Statement Day, I see. I didn't get the memo, but I can roll with it. What, exactly, should we be prepared for, Walt?"

"Potentially an invasion."

Let that one sit on the air for a few moments while I ran through the countries crazy enough to try to invade the USA right now, when we were on, essentially, an Extremely Touchy High Alert and had been for a couple of months now. "Okay, so I'm going to focus on the word 'potentially' and assume this is why you wanted me to come here and didn't want to share this with everyone else in the LSR."

"Yes." Walter pointed to several of his screens. We all got closer to him and them and took a look-see.

"Huh." Honestly didn't know what else to say. Because what I was seeing wasn't on Earth. No, what I was seeing were spaceships. And they weren't Earth or Alpha Centaurion spaceships.

CHAPTER 6

THERE WERE A LOT OF QUESTIONS I wanted to ask. To their credit, the men with me were utterly silent. Checked. Nope, none of them had run off to share this news with the rest of the team. Good. This was news that was going to take a diplomatic touch to disseminate. I probably was not the girl for this job, but I'd also likely have to muddle through because that *was* my job. Always the way.

"Um, my first question may surprise you. How can we see what we're seeing?"

"We were given long-range viewing by Alpha Four," Walter said. "Something the Planetary Council brought with them."

"Ancient technology at its core," Wruck said. "Though they probably don't realize it."

"Does all of Earth have this Ancient At Its Core Alpha Four Technology?" Because if they did, the entire planet was going to go to DEFCON 1 in a matter of moments.

"No. It's restricted to being wherever Mister Executive Chief is, which is why I have this and Dulce does not. I am the only one with this equipment right now, Chief First Lady."

Meaning no one knew about this right now other than Walter, me, Buchanan, Siler, Wruck, a Poof, and three Peregrines. Actively chose not to contemplate Jeff and Chuckie's reactions to Walter's choices, just hoped Mom would approve.

"Walt, I know it's hard for you, but no titles right now. Do it for me. You can use them again when we've worked through this particular Gordian knot."

He heaved a sigh. "Okay . . . Kitty."

"Good man. Okay, so, are these all coming from the same directions?"

"No, they're not. The equipment scans space for signatures of traveling ships. Once it spots such, it hones in. We can see about a hundred light-years in any direction."

Buchanan whistled softly. "Does NASA know about this?"

"Not yet," Walter admitted. "Right now, Emperor Alexander wants this under Jeff and Kitty's control and no one else's."

Meaning Councilor Leonidas, who was basically Alpha Four's version of Winston Churchill, didn't want just anyone using this equipment. Couldn't blame him—with this we could apparently check in on the A-C system as easily as we could check in on Japan. Checked Walter's Earth Screens. All seemed reasonably okay all over the world. For the moment. Had a feeling that moment was going to be gone really quickly.

"So it sees what's going on in the Alpha Centauri system?" Siler asked.

"Yes, and other systems as well. But as long as it's normal space traffic, I keep scanning. These aren't normal. In that they aren't traveling within their own solar systems, but are in the space between systems. I tend to ignore those, too, because they're usually traveling between systems far from us. However, these appear to be heading for Earth."

"I remember we had a star chart from the Ancients." Looked at Wruck.

Who nodded. "Every ship travels with a galactic map. And, to anticipate your question, there are a large number of inhabited star systems within a hundred light-years of Earth." He studied the screens. "And, based on the ship designs, all these five are from nearby systems, as in, systems Walter can observe."

Let the idea of a hundred light-years counting as "nearby" pass. I wasn't living in a world where that distance was insurmountable. I lived in a world where entire fleets made hyperspace jumps from the Galactic Core without issue. Usually to come and try to destroy us.

"How close are the ships that you're worried about?" Buchanan asked.

"They're all between us and the Alpha Centauri system," Walter replied. "I didn't contact anyone until I was sure that they weren't going there."

"They have their own scanning. Did anyone from Alpha Four or any of the other planets give us the heads-up?"

No sooner asked than a weird beeping noise came out of something that looked kind of like a computer, but not one made on Earth. Walter put on a headset and started writing at hyperspeed.

He stopped, took the headset off, and turned back to the rest of us. "Yes, Kitty, that was them just now. They've determined that the trajectories are clear and they feel that these ships are absolutely heading for Earth."

"Lucky us. John, you seem to know the ships."

"Yes. They're from different systems." He pointed to the rightmost screen with a ship that looked like a large manta ray, complete with its wings or flaps or whatever moving slowly up and down as if it really was a ray swimming through space. "This one belongs to the Vrierst. They're farthest from home here."

"Per what everyone's said and our knowledge of where we sit in the galaxy, they're all far from home if they're in our neck of the woods, even though they're in our neighborhood, so to speak. I'm going to refrain from asking if Earth has somehow gotten onto the Galactic Hot Spots list and instead ask if everyone else thinks the ship that's fairly close to the Vrierst ship looks like a hand trowel with a wide handle or if it's just me."

Wruck managed a chuckle. "I suppose it does. That belongs to the Yggethnia System. There are several inhabited planets in that system and they tend to work together. They're one of the two closest to Earth, after Alpha Centauri, that is."

Another screen had a ship that was ball-shaped, with what looked like a variety of neon-blue rings encircling it in various directions—all spinning so fast that I could only see them moving because I was enhanced with A-C abilities thanks to the mother and child feedback I'd had when Jamie was born—so that it resembled our depictions of atoms. "Who's in the funky Death Star Atomizer?"

"That would be a ship of the Themnir. They're from Sirius, so the next closest after Yggethnia. And they're extremely pacifistic. That's not a Death Star, it's what they call a Roving Planet."

"What about the one that looks like a tree?" Buchanan asked, before I could make another *Star Wars* comment, pointing to the next screen. He wasn't wrong, but it was a tree that was definitely a spaceship. A giant treeship.

"That's a Faradawn ship," Wruck said. "And it's the type of ship they use to collect survivors of battles, disasters, and so forth."

"So, are they like the Shantanu?" The Shantanu were the colorful penguin people from Alpha Seven. They essentially functioned as the Alpha Centaurion System's version of the Red Cross.

"Not in looks, but if you're asking if they're the people who go out and help others, yes, they are." He looked worried.

"So, why are they, and all these others, coming here?" Bingo, Wruck looked more worried by this question of mine.

"I can only assume something bad is happening in the galaxy," he said finally.

"You mean more bad than normal?" I asked.

Wruck shook his head. "I honestly have no guess."

"I'm fond of the Borg ship myself," Siler said, indicating our fifth entry, which was a cube.

"That belongs to the Lyssara, and they'd call it a comb, not a cube." We all stared at Wruck.

"Um, John? I don't see anything that would indicate that said ship was like something any of us would use on our hair."

"Oh. No. Not a comb like that. A comb like bees create. They're like giant honeybees. As you'd understand them."

Was about to come up with a really snarky retort when Walter shifted a bit in his chair and I finally caught sight of the last screen showing in outer space. That ship in this section of our neighborhood really caught my eye. "Is that a Z'porrah ship?"

CHAPTER 7

MY QUESTION WAS RHETORICAL, since there wasn't a one of us that wouldn't recognize what I was looking at. On the screen was a lone ship that looked like what we humans typically called a flying saucer—with lights along the circumference, and a dome on top. That was where the power cube sat, inside the dome.

"Yes," Walter confirmed, voice tight. "I haven't found any other Z'porrah ships, though."

"So, does this mean that we're under attack?" Buchanan asked, sounding far less interested in talking and a whole lot more ready to lead a battalion against our enemies.

"The Z'porrah never attack singly," Wruck said, sounding confused. "Ever."

"That's it. Walt, need to go live to the LSR, please and thank you."

He shot me a worried look. "Are you sure?"

"Yes. I'll be discreet."

All of the men shot me looks that indicated they didn't believe discretion was in my wheelhouse. Chose to ignore them and gave Walter the "do it" look. He did. "Excuse me, the First Lady would like a word."

"What's up, Kitty?" Jeff asked.

"Jeff, I'd like you, Christopher, Richard, Alexander, and Chuckie only to come to Walter's security center. No Secret Service need apply, and no one else needs to come along for the ride at this precise time. Just something I want to show you select few. Everyone else can carry on with the business of the Centaurion War Division."

Jeff grunted. "We'll be right there."

They were right there by the time I'd turned around to look at the door. Hyperspeed was the best, and Christopher was essentially the Flash. "What's going on, and why didn't you want James or Tim?" Christopher asked as they reached us and he and the rest of them disengaged from their hyperspeed daisy chain.

"Because, as so often is the case, I want no one reacting or doing anything until we're done and you all do what I want you to do." Brought them up to speed, fast, on what was on Walter's screens, and Walter shared that Alpha Four had also alerted us.

"I'm relieved these are not heading for my system," Alexander said, "but we now consider any attack on Earth to be an attack on us. Do I need to ready our fleet?"

"Not yet. I think we want to be as sure as we can be of what's coming. That's why I only wanted you guys here and we haven't shared this with the full team in the LSR."

"So, why are we here?" Christopher asked, shooting me Patented Glare #2. He was a glaring champion, after all, and this was a prime opportunity to brush up the skills.

"I want you and Jeff to do a Go Team move on these ships before we do anything else. I want the others here to do some of the heavy thinking and additional panicking as necessary."

"Always nice to be needed," Chuckie said.

Jeff grunted again. "Fine, we still have time to get all of Earth in a state of readiness for attack. I hope, at any rate. What ship do you want us testing first?"

"The Z'porrah's. Duh."

He managed a quick grin. "Good point."

Walter and the animals moved out of the way and Jeff and Christopher got next to the screen. Christopher put his hand on the monitor and Jeff put his over it. This was a combo empath and imageer move, where the imageer got the picture of the being or beings and the empath picked up their emotions. It had worked well during Operations Fugly and Destruction and more, and Christopher and other powerful imageers had been able to get reads on beings in ships that were far, far away, and despite the virus, Christopher's talent was still reasonably strong. So I had faith we'd learn something this time.

They were quiet for a few long moments. Then they removed their hands slowly. "They feel like no Z'porrah I've ever felt before," Jeff said.

Christopher nodded. "It's not all Z'porrah in that ship. There are some Ancients, too, at least going by the fact that they look kind of like John."

"They felt like John," Jeff agreed. "Basically, the overriding emotions on that ship are fear and hope."

"What does that mean?" Buchanan asked.

"I have no idea," Jeff admitted.

"Test the other ships," I suggested. "John, tell them about the people in those ships, too."

Wruck explained the giant honeybees thing, so they tried on the Lyssara's Comb next. Jeff shook his head. "I get nothing. I haven't met any of these in person, and I think it'll take time to adjust to them."

"They look like giant bees, though," Christopher said. "Walking and talking, but bees."

"Hope their honey's good. Check the Faradawn Treeship."

"The Faradawn resemble living trees," Wruck said, as the guys put their hands on the screen. "Mostly willows, as Earthlings would see them, but others as well."

"So they're dryads from Greek myth?" White asked.

"Similar, yes," Wruck said. "They might have come out here long ago."

"Seems like everyone has."

"Is it truly time for sarcasm?" Christopher asked me.

"It's always time for sarcasm, as you know. You feeing alright?"

"This takes a lot of focus. Lots of trees in that ship, but there are a lot of other races, too. And I mean a lot."

"Yeah," Jeff said, as they took their hands away. "Far more than I can get a read on right now. General feelings of fear and hope, though, from the few that registered as close to other races I've read before."

They checked the Vrierst ship, which were, per Wruck, sort of ethereal and cloud-like while still having shape and substance, and the Yggethnian ship, where the races resembled lemurs and sloths and other rather cuddly Earth creatures. Same thing—not enough history for Jeff to go on and lots and lots of different beings there, particularly in the Yggethnian ship.

"I don't get what's going on," Christopher admitted. "Why are any of these coming here, to Earth?"

"Especially since none of them seem aggressive," Jeff added.

Time to put on my Megalomaniac Girl cape and make the leap because this was actually my real job. "Would we think news of our repelling the Z'porrah more than once has gotten around the Greater Galactic Expanse?" I asked Alexander.

"Yes, it has. We've been approached, as we've said, to join the greater galactic community mostly due to our handling of the Z'porrah. Especially when we repelled them so effectively from our solar borders."

"Yeah, Operation Civil War was fun, wasn't it? So, anyway, I think I know why these ships are heading here, and it's not to rain down fire on us from the sky."

"Why then?" Jeff asked.

Looked over at Chuckie. Could see the wheels turning as he studied the screens. "Why does anyone come to America?" he asked quietly.

"Yep." This earned me blank looks from the rest of the room. "Really, guys? Let's put it another way. Richard, why did you guys come here?"

"We were exiled and seeking asylum." White jerked. "Oh. Oh really?"

"Yeah. I don't think we have attacking races. I think we have six ships full of refugees."

"Don't you mean five ships?" Siler asked. "The Z'porrah are our enemies."

"Yes, they are, as a whole. But as John just told us, all the Z'porrah don't hate the rest of us, just like not every German was a Nazi. I think they're fleeing, just like the rest of these ships."

"Why are they coming here?" Jeff asked. "We have one inhabited planet. Alpha Centauri has ten."

Thought about how Wruck had described the Vrierst. "Could those ethereal people live on a planet like Jupiter, John?"

"Probably. Their home planet is a gas giant."

"And I'll bet some of the others could handle being on the moon or Mars or whatever. Maybe most would have to be on Earth, but still, we have seven or eight other planets, depending on who you ask about Pluto and Planet Nine."

"So does Alpha Centauri," Jeff said flatly.

"But we are not who was perceived to repel the Z'porrah," Alexander said thoughtfully.

"Um, you guys are the only reason Earth isn't a smoking crater overrun by dino-birds." Well, them and ACE, our benevolent superconsciousness currently housed in Jamie. I was going to need to talk to ACE the moment Jamie went down for a nap, which didn't happen a lot these days.

"Yes, from that attack. But Earth forces came to rescue us from our own civil war and to help us to repel the Z'porrah. And it was Earth who created the alliances with the Shantanu and Cleophese."

"You mean it was Kitty, Alexander," Chuckie said, turning around. "Kitty created those alliances. She's created every alliance Earth has made with any alien race we've met, starting with you."

"And she flips your enemies all the time," Siler added.

"Right," Chuckie said briskly. "Meaning they aren't going to Alpha Centauri and they're not really coming to Earth, either."

"Now you've lost me, dude."

Chuckie rubbed the back of his neck. "Kitty, they're coming to *you*."

CHAPTER 8

LET THAT ONE SIT on the air for a few moments. "Um, excuse me?"

Chuckie heaved a sigh. "Look, when I was strapped to that mind-expanding machine the Rapacians had, I could see everything in the galaxy. And everyone. Every living thing."

"I'm amazed your mind didn't explode," White said, as he patted Chuckie on his shoulder. This wasn't new news, and White was aware of all that had gone on and the harm that had been done to Chuckie. But we were all still waiting for Chuckie to have another Migraine Meltdown Experience. He'd been doing great since Operation Epidemic, but none of us wanted to just assume he was cured simply because the Mastermind had been exposed to the world.

"It would have, except for Jamie and Kitty." Chuckie looked directly at me. "I know you saw it too, when you were protecting me, Kitty. They're all out there."

"Yeah, I'm not going to argue that there are probably more living beings in our galaxy than we can all comprehend. But I don't see what that has to do with this situation."

Chuckie shrugged. "I'm not sure, either, but who's to say that we didn't project as well as perceive?"

"You mean you think all those people know about you, Kitty, and Jamie?" Jeff growled protectively.

"Jeff, I have no idea. I'm just hypothesizing right now. But I think it's possible."

Had a feeling Chuckie was more than hypothesizing. I'd known him over half our lives and I could tell when he wasn't telling the entire truth. Took the assumption that he was lying to keep Jeff from overreacting, a sentiment I heartily agreed with.

"We have a Rapacian in the Large Situation Room," Alexander pointed out. "One who is very loyal now to our empire, but who would stop being loyal if Kitty said she didn't care for Alpha Four's leadership anymore. He may be able to tell us if the hypothesis Charles has shared happened or is possible."

"I'm all kinds of flattered that all of you think I'm that influential, but before we race to drag our own Hawkman into this, and therefore everyone else as well, I think we need to accept that Lakin may not have any idea of what that machine could do. Or, more importantly, what it could do with a mind like Chuckie's strapped into it."

"I think we need Drax and the other Vata," Siler said. "They can mentally connect to machines. Let's see if they can do what you two," he nodded toward Jeff and Christopher, "did, or if they can do so through your link."

"Before we do that we need to have Alpha Team in here," Jeff said. "This falls under their bailiwick. In fact," he looked at me, "I'm going to echo Christopher's earlier question. Why didn't you ask for James, Tim, and Serene to join us?"

Contemplated my responses. Honesty seemed the best policy. "It's the same reason Walter asked for only me at first, I think. It's because this isn't actually their bailiwick. Not anymore. If we have new aliens coming to Earth, we can't hide them, and I sincerely think that we don't want to kill them clandestinely, either. I don't think we want to kill them at all."

"What if they're coming to kill us?" Jeff asked.

"Then we'll handle it. But if they're coming to attack, that requires a political and military response from the entire world, not just Centaurion Division. And if, as we suspect, they're coming here for help, that demands a political and humanitarian response from the entire world, or at least from the United States, not just Centaurion Division. I didn't want you guys instantly going into an attack and defense mode that we're comfortable with."

"Why have my dad and Chuck come for this meeting, then?" Christopher asked. "I get why I'm here."

"Because I want the smartest guy in any room around for things like this, and because Paul isn't available. Richard was the Supreme Pontifex for decades, and I think we need the religious body chiming in."

"In other words you want to know if we should show mercy, compassion, and generosity," White said. "And I would be a hypocrite to say otherwise. Your father and Stanley Gower would agree with me on that, too, Jeffrey. We were the three who came asking for the United States to give us asylum, which they did, with reservations. But still, we weren't turned away."

"Though it was close," Chuckie said. White nodded. Wondered if White had given Chuckie the Early Earth A-C History Lesson, because many times since we'd come back from Operation Civil War, Chuckie said something that made it seem as if he'd been there with them when they'd first come to Earth. Which, considering he was only a few months older than me, was flat-out impossible. Of course, I'd switched universes not too long ago, so who was I to question the possibilities in our vast multiverse?

Jeff ran his hand through his hair. "It's a different world now, though, Uncle Richard."

"No," Wruck said. "It's the same world. But as we're seeing, it's a world that might be ready to unify, for the first time since its beginning."

"You think we should let them come, don't you, John?"

"Yes, Kitty, I do. I think that if they're all fleeing, then they need a safe haven."

"The Z'porrah are our enemies," Christopher pointed out. Rightly. "We just got everyone to agree to that, all over the world. That's why we have that potential for unification. And now you're saying that we should welcome a ship full of them with open arms?"

"If they're coming as refugees, that usually means they don't agree with the regime that's in power. They also might be able to tell us what's going on with the Z'porrah in relation to our systems."

Chuckie nodded. "Kitty has a good point. But we also need to consider that most refugees are fleeing war or oppression or both. We know the Z'porrah are at war, and have been for millennia. But these refugees may not know anything other than that they want to get away to some form of safety."

"Which is why we presume they're heading here," White said. "Earth could have viewed us as enemies or a threat. We certainly have the ability to be both. But we came in peace, and these others may be doing so as well."

"Which boils down to: we won't know until they get here," Jeff said with a sigh. "Walter, how long before the first ship gets into Earth's solar space?"

"I honestly don't know, Mister President. I haven't really bothered to focus on speed calculations, since this is the first time since I got this equipment that any ships have been headed toward us."

"And he's only had this for a very few weeks," Alexander added. "We brought this with us when we first arrived, but due to everything that happened, I was not able to give any of the equipment to Walter until after we returned from Camp David."

"And I didn't get it set up until after the inauguration party," Walter added. "I needed to focus on all the security gaps you and Chief First Lady found."

"What a great spin, Walt. Seriously, I meant it before. No titles right now, dude. Not even for Mister President here."

"I agree," Jeff said.

"I think I can figure it out," Chuckie said before Walter could whine about the cruelty of No Title Time. "With John and Alexander's help. But it may not matter. If they're using hyperdrives, each ship may be able to jump here."

"No," Wruck said. "The Z'porrah fleet has a controlled wormhole device to allow them to jump thousands of light-years at a time. However, the individual ships do not. And I would sincerely doubt that a fleeing ship would have managed to get one."

"Then figure out the timeline," Jeff said to Chuckie. He, Wruck, and Alexander went into a Science Huddle. My ears turned off quickly—this wasn't where my skills were needed or helpful.

"Apparently I'm going to do my old job and represent Alpha Team until one of you breaks down and advises them," Christopher said, shooting Patented Glare #3 at the portion of the room that wasn't involved with higher math. "But has it occurred to anyone that the Z'porrah ship could be a ruse or a trap? We're supposed to think they're refugees, but what if the moment they land, they attack us?"

"That's not what I felt," Jeff said. "And they don't know that we know they're coming. Do they?" he asked Walter.

"Not to my knowledge. But I don't know what equipment their ships do or don't have."

"The Trojan Horse idea isn't one we should ignore," Siler said. "Because while appearances make it unlikely, it's still very possible."

"Look, I realize that empathic blockers and overlays have

limited my abilities for the past few years, but you're all acting as if we have no information." Jeff sounded annoyed and just this side of pissed. "I may not have been able to read the people in the other ships well or at all, but I'm telling you that I know what the Z'porrah and Ancients feel like empathically, and I'm saying that there is no one on that ship who's thinking bad thoughts against us."

"You said they felt like no Z'porrah you've read before," Siler pointed out.

"Yes, because I'm used to feeling nothing but hate, disdain, contempt, superiority, and bloodlust from Z'porrah. And these feel nothing like that. They're afraid and they're hopeful as their main emotions, but they had the rest of the usual emotions in there, too, meaning they aren't faking it or using some kind of empathic shield to fool me. If you want, I could waste time and tell you what each one of them is feeling, but I'd prefer that you all trust me when I say that I know what hope and fear feel like, even when they're coming from races we haven't interacted with all that much."

"So, basically, you feel that they're refugees without ulterior motives and without spies in their midst."

"Yeah, baby, that's exactly what I'm saying. Spies wouldn't be bothering to hide their emotions from an empath when they're in the middle of space far away from the planets with the empaths on them. If they even know we have empathic talents."

"They know," Wruck said, while pointing to various things on the Spaceship Screens. "Believe me, the Z'porrah know all about every sentient race in the galaxy. We do as well. However, knowing that there are empaths and knowing how to hide from them are two very different things."

"I agree that it would be a leap to assume that any spy on the Z'porrah ship would be expecting Jeff to know they were coming, be able to reach the ship, and be able to read anyone on the ship," Chuckie said, still looking at the screens and scribbling things down on a pad Walter had provided. "It's possible, but highly improbable."

"Based on the condition these ships are in," Alexander added, "I would feel that any of them being an attacking force is also highly improbable."

"So, we're back to the idea that they're refugees, Christopher. Can we show them a modicum of mercy now?"

This question earned me Patented Glare #5. But before

Christopher could reply, Buchanan cleared his throat. "I think you're all missing the bigger, far more worrisome, question."

That got the room's attention, even Team Science's. "Which is?" Jeff asked.

Buchanan nodded toward the screens. "If we have six refugee ships headed toward us, with the potential of many more behind them that Walter just hasn't picked up as out of the norm yet, then I think what we really need to ask is: Who are they all fleeing *from*, and is that enemy coming after them?"

CHAPTER 9

THE ROOM WENT SILENT for a few long moments. Then Jeff nodded. "That is definitely the right question, thank you." He shook his head. "We can't keep this a secret for too much longer, and I mean minutes, not hours or days. We need to make a plan of action, and that requires a good chunk of those in the LSR."

"They're fleeing from the Z'porrah. I mean, that seems like the obvious choice to me."

Chuckie shrugged as he turned back to his calculations. "Maybe. But just because the big war is between the Z'porrah and anyone else they don't like, that doesn't mean that smaller conflicts aren't causing issues."

"True," Wruck said. "We tend to let the individual solar systems deal with their issues themselves. We step in as needed, but less and less once species are on a path toward full sentience and civilization."

"Do you mean spaceflight?" Alexander asked.

"No, not wholly."

"The Shantanu are hella sentient and hella civilized and they only care about spaceflight because they had to in order to help their solar system and because helping the Cleophese to survive on land and, as an extension, space was something important to them."

Wruck nodded to me. "Exactly. Sentience requires a full understanding of not just the world around you but that there is a vast galaxy filled with other beings out there. Whether you desire to meet those others or not isn't the defining characteristic. For us, at any rate."

"What's the defining characteristic for the Z'porrah?" I had a feeling I knew, but it was always nice to do the double check.

"They want races that will strengthen them. They don't care about sentience and civilization, or even the potential for such, so much as they care about creating a stronger fighting base." Wruck shook his head. "Originally, when we were allies, they didn't feel this way. They agreed with us on how to uplift."

"That must have been one hell of a spat."

"They start small," Siler said. "They always start small, and then get larger and larger until they're all-encompassing. You've seen that here on Earth. And if you're not sure, look no farther than Stephanie."

Jeff groaned. "Speaking of my niece, we have an extra layer of issues."

"You mean you think Cliff Goodman and his Crazy Eights and Stephanie and the Tinkerer are going to try to take advantage of the current and upcoming situations?"

"It's a safe bet," Siler said.

Chuckie nodded as he appeared to finish perpetrating higher math. "We need to assign more resources to tracking them down."

"Maybe. Maybe not." This statement earned me the room's attention.

"Mind explaining that?" Christopher asked.

"Sure. I enjoyed being ahead of our now dethroned Mastermind. And, frankly, we're currently ahead of Stephanie and the Tinkerer, too."

"How?" Jeff asked flatly.

"She means that we know what's coming and they don't," Chuckie said. Rightly. "However, they do know about the current push to join Centaurion Division. Meaning they have a great way to infiltrate."

"Yeah, join up as a World Protection-Minded Citizen, undermine from within. Only, we know what all of them look like."

"Do we?" Buchanan asked. "We have no idea what the LaRue and Reid clones are looking like right now, nor how old they are. You know that Goodman isn't going to try to become a recruit. And while we have descriptions of the rest of them, most of them are average-enough looking that it'll take one of us to identify them. And we don't have the time to do that."

"Meaning at least some of them are already trying to enlist." This time, the rest of the room was with me, at least if I took the morose expressions to be accurate. Heaved a sigh. "Really, guys, why so serious? We have A-Cs. A-Cs who have seen these people. A-Cs with hyperspeed who can look at everyone at every recruiting station in a matter of minutes, if not seconds. I think it's a fabulous way to grab whichever Crazy Eights are out to do active dirty work duty."

Jeff nodded slowly. "That makes sense. And that falls to Alpha Team."

"Geez, I'm not trying to distance us from them. I just want us telling them what we want them focused on, not the other way around."

"Why?" Christopher asked, clearly speaking for the majority of the room. "They've never ignored you before."

"Really? Every single one of you ignored me when I said that letting the press see our flag was a bad idea. Alpha Team works independently from us—if you'd care to recall when you, Jeff, and I were in charge, we almost never advised the President of anything. We ran whatever we needed through my mother or Chuckie and then just did whatever we wanted. James, Tim, and Serene are continuing that fine tradition. And I'm saying that, in this case, we cannot have them doing that. They need to follow direction from the Office of the President, period."

"That didn't work so well a short while ago," Chuckie said quietly.

Managed not to roll my eyes, but it took effort. "Yes, I know. You guys were all fooled and the Office of the President was stupid. However, to toss all modesty to the wind, I'm here right now. I'm not presumably kidnapped and you're not watching fake torture porn. I am not going to allow us to be stupid."

"Other than when we're following your plans," Christopher snarked.

Siler turned to him and shot him a look worthy of the Glaring Throne. "Before you insult her one more time, I'd like to mention that regardless of what goes wrong in her plans, they work out in the end. What plan of *yours* has worked out recently?"

Christopher looked shocked, and Jeff looked ready to try busting Siler's head. Cleared my throat and, thankfully, got their attention again. "Once more all kinds of flattered, and Nightcrawler, I cannot tell you how much I appreciate your support of my planning, or what Richard and I call Going With The Crazy. However, I think Christopher was joking, hard as that sometimes is to tell. And his plans work, too."

"Occasionally," Christopher said. He eyed Siler. "Your loyalty to her has never been in question. Your loyalty to the rest of us, however . . ."

"Doesn't matter," Chuckie said firmly. "Unless Kitty's planning on leaving Jeff, which I doubt, this particular family fight is over. And I mean that in a very Director of the CIA way."

Looked at Wruck. "This is how it started, isn't it? The big fight between you guys and the Z'porrah. Someone made an unfunny joke, someone else got offended, and here we are, thousands of years later, dealing with the fallout."

He nodded. "I assume so."

"Let's learn from other people's mistakes for once, then, gang, what say?"

"I agree," White said. "I also believe that we're about to restructure an entire division with existing bases worldwide. Meaning we're about to take an agency that works for the good of the world, change it, and essentially shove a very American agency into every country where a Centaurion base already exists. Some won't mind. I'd anticipate that most will."

"So, what do you suggest we do to soften that blow?" Jeff asked.

White looked at me and smiled. "I suggest we send our best diplomat out on a conversion mission."

"I'm against Kitty traveling the world without me," Jeff said firmly. "For a variety of reasons."

"First ladies travel without their husbands frequently," Chuckie said without any indication that Jeff's tone was something he was going to pay attention to. "It's something the job demands."

Jeff shot him a betrayed look. "You think Richard's plan is what we should do?"

"It's not a plan yet," Chuckie said. "Currently it's a suggestion that has great merit. We will have to form a plan, which Kitty and her team will then totally ignore, but still, at least we'll have an idea of what they're not doing when and where."

"I resent that. I totally can't deny it, by the way, but I also totally resent it."

Chuckie grinned. "I'm going to make everyone happy. Among the people going with Kitty are going to be Alpha Team. So that way, when they're being mavericks, they're with the Maverick Queen and will, we all hope, be following the Crazy that works."

"That's sound," Buchanan said. "We'll be with them, of course." He indicated himself, Siler, and Wruck.

"As if we could stop you?" Chuckie asked. "I realize we

could assign you elsewhere, but I highly doubt that Angela will want the three of you too far from Kitty. And the kids."

"WHAT?" Jeff bellowed. No one bellowed like my man. This was, for him, a rather quiet bellow in that Walter's many TV screens didn't all shatter, but it was a bellow nonetheless. Teddy dove into Walter's pocket, all three Peregrines squawked in pain, and every other person jumped. "Sending my wife off to do whatever it is you're planning is one thing. And it's a thing I don't like. But sending my children, too? No. They stay here, where it's safe."

"Oh, Jeff, calm down. I'm going to point out that the big kid going with us is able to kick butt with the best of us, and you know that Lizzie's going."

Siler nodded. "She'd never forgive us if we benched her for this."

"What this are we talking about, exactly?" Christopher asked, presumably to keep Jeff from popping a vessel.

"A worldwide recruitment tour," Chuckie replied. "I'd tell you to go, Jeff, but we're still too volatile for the President to be absent for a week, let alone longer. She'll visit the countries where Centaurion bases are, talk to their leaders, get them to agree to the divisional change, and then do some recruiting at the same time."

"Chuckie, that all sounds grand, but I think I do better with aliens and good guys who've been seduced by the Dark Side. I'm not so great with regular, normal people in the diplomacy department."

"Which is why Richard will be with you."

Christopher's turn to show what apoplexy looked like. "Why are you always so fast to risk my dad?"

Chuckie shot me the long-suffering "why me?" look. White chuckled. "Son, I appreciate your concern, just as I'm sure Missus Martini appreciates Jeffrey's hysterical overprotectiveness. However, I feel that Charles is right—Missus Martini has the best chance of doing what we need, she and I work very well together, and it's not as if you won't be monitoring us constantly."

"And it's also not as if you can't use a gate and get to us if we need help," I added. White was clearly jazzed about being on this show—he only called me Mrs. Martini when we were in action situations. "Heck, Christopher, these days you don't even need a gate."

"I just worry," Christopher grumbled softly.

"By the way, I want Camilla with my team, too."

"Done," Chuckie said.

"You two know I can just veto this, right?" Jeff asked.

"Yeah? Let's see what my mother thinks before you toss your Presidential muscle around." Other than in the bedroom. Jeff could toss the muscle in the bedroom better than anyone else in, by my estimate, the entire galaxy. The only downside to this plan was that I wouldn't be with him, so I would miss out on countless orgasms.

I found this thought depressing, and Jeff clearly picked it up because he shot me a look I was both familiar with and totally loved—his Jungle Cat About To Eat Me look. "We'll discuss it later," he said quietly, right before he put his Serious Leader Of The Free World look back on his face.

"What about the flyboys?"

Chuckie shook his head. "I'm not sure. I don't want Jeff without plenty of people we know we can trust implicitly. Just because we've foiled a variety of assassination attempts, and haven't foiled others, doesn't mean that more aren't in the works."

"It doesn't mean that more aren't on their way in six spaceships," Christopher snapped. "One spaceship in particular."

"I'll try to reach ACE tonight, I promise."

Christopher heaved a sigh. "I don't want to hurt Jamie just for intel."

"But in this case, it's vital intel. ACE is very good about ensuring that she doesn't hear us talking when she's asleep." And I did have at least one other option, too. It would be just as tricky to get information out of him as it would be from ACE, but for entirely different reasons. Still, this appeared to be the right time to try to reach our various Powers That Be Hangin' Out On Earth.

"Tonight would be good," Chuckie said. "As long as Jamie's not at risk."

Took a good look at him. He looked tense and kind of excited and also just a little worried. "Huh. Those ships are going to be here a lot faster than we'd like, aren't they?"

Chuckie nodded. "Less than a week, if none of them use a hyperjump of some kind."

CHAPTER 10

THE ROOM WAS once again stunned into silence. Chose to be the one to break it. "Always the way. Well, at least we have the forewarning. Such as it is."

Jeff grunted. "I officially hate this new plan and don't want anyone doing this, let alone Kitty and the kids. But I also see that, despite supposedly being the most powerful man in the United States, I'm going to be overruled by my wife, my uncle, and my friend."

White laughed. "Yes, Jeffrey. Or as we call it, routine."

"Don't worry, my mom will probably overrule you, too."

"Great." Jeff ran his hand through his hair. "So, before we go back to the meeting and have Walter send what we're seeing here over so that everyone can share in the stress, and then tell them how fast this is all going down so everyone can share in the panic, do we know of anyone still alive who dealt with our arrival here in any kind of meaningful way? I'm looking for someone to advise us."

White and Chuckie both chuckled. "Yeah, we do," Chuckie said. "Many, but you'll be happy to know that the one I and, I'm sure, Richard are both thinking of will be more than happy to help."

"You know him as the new Chairman of the Joint Chiefs of Staff," White added.

"Wow, my Uncle Mort really gets around." Uncle Mort was my father's older brother and a lifelong Marine. He was also totally badass and I enjoyed the rare times when I got to work with him. It didn't hurt that he was my favorite uncle and I was his favorite niece.

Uncle Mort was hugely pro-alien, at least pro our Earth

A-Cs, and if there was anyone you wanted around when aliens were coming to either defect, beg for asylum, or attack, it was Uncle Mort.

"Well, that's a relief," Jeff said. He looked at Walter. "Please reach General Mortimer Katt and let him know we need him to gate it over here. Ask him to meet us in the Large Situation Room."

Walter nodded. "Anyone else?"

"Let's get Colonel Franklin, Drax and the other Vata, and the flyboys here, too. You know, so we can make it a real party," I suggested. "The other Joint Chiefs might be a good idea, too, but only if we can keep them from declaring World War Three or *Independence Day Three-D*."

Walter looked at Jeff. Who shook his head. "Franklin, all the Vata, and the flyboys, yes. The other Joint Chiefs, no. I haven't worked with any of them enough to know how they'll handle this news."

"Yes, sir, Mister President," Walter said, clearly completely done with No Title Time.

Jeff took my hand and led us off. "I can't believe you're all okay with Kitty leaving for a world tour right now," he grumbled as we walked at human speed.

"Well, it's not like I'm desperate to escape your clutches or anything, but Richard and Chuckie's plan makes sense."

"For the job we need done it would be either Kitty or Elaine," Chuckie said. "And I think you need Elaine here with you right now."

"I need my wife more." Jeff heaved a sigh. "Have I mentioned how much I never wanted to get into politics in the first place?"

"Once or twice," White said, clearly trying not to laugh and showing zero sympathy.

Jeff grunted at him. "You're the reason all this started, Uncle Richard. I blame you for all of this."

White grinned. "I know and I'll take that blame happily because I'm incredibly proud of you, Jeffrey. You're everything I knew you would be."

Jeff stopped walking, let go of my hand, and hugged his uncle tightly. "Thanks," he said as they pulled apart. "It's nice to know that I'm not failing everyone's expectations."

Christopher, Chuckie, and I exchanged the WTH look. "Um, Jeff? Who do you think you're failing?"

"He's listened to the media," Alexander replied before Jeff could. "And if you allow it to, what people who have no idea what you have to do on a day-to-day basis in order to keep things running will say about you can be hurtful."

Gave Alexander a hug, just 'cause, since I had to figure he was speaking from experience. "Ah. Well, haters gonna hate, Jeff. You're an awesome president."

"Yeah?" Jeff said as we started off again. "Let's see how everyone feels when I share that we know we have space invaders coming and they'll be here in a week or less."

"I'd ask how that's your fault, but apparently it's my fault, so I'll brace for the haters to turn on me. Which I expect no matter what, anyway."

"Fault is the wrong word," Chuckie said.

"Not if they're coming to attack," Christopher muttered.

"Stop it," White said calmly. Christopher looked sulkily at his father. Who was apparently having none of it. "No one is going to allow anyone to land on this planet without vetting them first. We have allies here who are more than capable of doing that vetting, including Jeffrey and every other empath on the planet. Your sulking about not getting included in Kitty's entourage is embarrassing."

"Is *that* it?" Chuckie asked, as Christopher had the grace to look embarrassed. "We need you here, with Jeff, for a variety of reasons, but the main one being that I just don't want one of our best secret weapons far away from the President."

Christopher perked up at this. "Secret weapon?"

Chuckie didn't roll his eyes but I knew he wanted to. "No one moves faster than you. If there's an attack on the President or any other official, who is the person most likely able to save them? You. If we need to evacuate, who is the person we all want everyone else linking to? You. Our enemies seem unaware of how fast you can move, and even if they know, there's not a lot they can do to stop you."

"Short of tossing out a bucket of glue in his path. Or flypaper."

"Hilarious, Kitty." Chuckie turned back to Christopher. "You've somehow managed to avoid the same level of scrutiny that Jeff, Kitty, Paul, and several others have, and even if the press knows about you, they can't *see* you if you're moving fast, let alone at your top speed. Why in the world would I want the fastest man on the planet far away from the most likely target we've got for attempted assassination? The Secret Service are fine. They're not A-Cs. And the other A-Cs aren't you."

Christopher seemed mollified. "Why am I still assigned to the Embassy, then?"

"What part of 'secret weapon' didn't you catch? If you're assigned to the Embassy, the assumption is that you will be there. Meaning no one's prepared for you to be wherever we actually need you to be. And," Chuckie added, "you're still needed at the Embassy. That we feel you can manage to do both jobs is a compliment, not an insult."

"Yeah, okay. And I'm sorry. I'm just worried and not feeling at all trusting about anyone in any of those ships, let alone those in the Z'porrah ship."

"Caution is wise," Wruck said. "But caution and hatred are not the same things. If we're correct and those in the Z'porrah ship are coming to Earth as refugees, then they aren't our enemies."

"In fact, there's a good chance they're our friends." We were outside of the LSR now. "And, Christopher, trust me—I'm not going to let anyone get Becky any more than I'll let them get Jamie or Charlie. Or any of the other kids, talented or not."

Christopher didn't look convinced. "I remember how many times they've tried to get Jamie. And the other hybrid kids. And Lizzie. They want our children, Kitty."

"I know. But what they want and what they'll get are two very different things. Despite our track record, I realize the temptation is to lock everyone in a Centaurion base and just hide. But that doesn't work anymore."

"And hasn't worked for quite a while," Chuckie said quietly.

Took his hand and squeezed it. No one said anything else, though. Two of the Gower siblings, Michael and Naomi, had both been killed because it had turned out that we hadn't been safe in our bases. Gladys Gower had died because of that, too. And Chuckie and Naomi had only been married six months when she'd died.

Or, rather, when everyone other than me thought she'd died. Naomi had ingested so much Surcenthumain—what I called the Superpowers Drug, which had been created by our enemies to use against us and everyone else—that she'd literally become a superconsciousness. But the other older and more powerful superconsciousnesses out there—some of which we'd had the "pleasure" of meeting—had decreed that she couldn't come back to Earth and couldn't let on that she was still alive in a very different way than she'd been before.

However, Naomi was watching over us, in every universe where we existed. I'd learned this during Operation Bizarro World. Jamie knew Naomi was out there, too, I was pretty darned sure. The Jamie in Bizarro World had certainly known, and she'd said they all knew to call on Auntie Mimi for help.

But Chuckie and the remaining Gowers couldn't know Naomi was still out there somewhere. Because the Gowers might and Chuckie would spend all their time trying to find her. And that way led to nothing but heartbreak and the wasting of lives. And we'd had enough of that already to last several lifetimes.

"I'm sorry," Wruck said quietly. He'd been undercover with the Mastermind and his cronies when Operation Infiltration went down. He hadn't been with LaRue when she'd murdered Michael, nor had he been around when Naomi had taken the Surcenthumain. But that didn't mean that he, like the rest of us, didn't wonder what he could have done differently.

Chuckie nodded. "I know. We all are. But that doesn't change anything."

"No," White said gently, "it doesn't. The dead are at peace. It's the living we need to protect."

"And watch," Christopher added.

"Vigilance will be our watchword, Christopher, I promise." My phone rang before I could say anything else. And my phone tended to ring at inopportune moments when it was one of our many enemies calling to share the wonder that was their insanity.

CHAPTER 11

PULLED MY PHONE OUT of the back pocket of my jeans—
sure, I was the FLOTUS now, and also sure we'd been in a
high-powered meeting and all that jazz, but I'd chosen comfort
over conformity today.

Took a look to see if I was going to be staring once again at
unfamiliar digits. Thankfully, and surprisingly, the call wasn't
from an anonymous number. "Hey, Squeaky, what's up?"

Squeaky was the nickname I'd given to Nancy Maurer during
Operation Defection Election. She had a very squeaky voice I'd
thought was faked when we'd first interacted. It wasn't fake, and
circumstances being what they were, we'd ended up saving her life
and, ultimately, her son's life, too, though he was now an in-control
android. We'd also rescued her grandchildren from their mother,
who had apparently willingly become an android herself. Due to
all of this, Mrs. Maurer had ended up as my First Lady's White
House Social Secretary. Conventionality was not our watchword.

Hearing it was someone we knew who made sense to be calling me—versus the Standard Opening Gambit Call from one of
our many crazed enemies—Jeff gave me a quick kiss on my
cheek, indicated to Siler, Buchanan, and Wruck that he wanted
them with him, then he and the other men headed back inside to
presumably start sharing the wonder that was heading our way.
I stepped away from the door just to be polite.

"Madam First Lady, I need you to come to your office as
soon as possible." I had my own staff and, unlike Walter, they
accepted that I hated titles and only wanted them used when
necessary, when giving clues to each other, or when tossing our
weight around. Meaning something was up. Or I'd screwed up.
Either option was likely.

"Why? Crap, have I forgotten a meeting or something?"

"No, not a scheduled meeting. You have . . . a package here. I believe you'll want to open it as soon as possible." And with that, she hung up.

Stared at my phone for a few long moments. "Huh." Said to no one in particular. Shoved my phone into the back pocket of my jeans and contemplated what might be going on.

Formality indicated something was up. Sure, maybe someone had sent a present and Mrs. Maurer just felt I'd want to open it immediately. But if so, why be formal? Could be a bomb, but in which case, why be so calm? The phrase "not a scheduled meeting" sort of indicated that someone else might possibly be there with her, meaning the only answer I could come up with was that the "package" was a person and she was being formal to give me a warning of some kind.

Meaning whoever had dropped by, snuck in, gated over, or beamed in was most likely sitting with Mrs. Maurer right now, over at the East Wing of the White House Complex, aka where I was expected to hang out more of the time than I actually did.

The White House wasn't inaccessible, but it was pretty darned secure. Though, as Walter had tactfully pointed out, when we'd first gotten here, Jeff and I—and most of our extended team of friends and family—had circumvented the security measures with ease and frequency.

However, White House tours were still suspended due to the various terrorist attacks we'd had during Operations Epidemic and Madhouse, and due to us thoughtfully pointing out all the weaknesses and such, security was running on Extra Crispy. Meaning no one should have been able to waltz onto the White House lawns, let alone into the East Wing entrance, up the stairs, and into my offices at the end of the long hallway without going through a variety of security personnel, starting with Walter and his Eye in the Sky technology.

Of course, Walter had been focused on our potential Outer Space Trespassers, versus the mundane Earthbound ones. But even so, the Secret Service was supposedly on the case, and we had other security measures in place as well, including the standard Snipers on the Roof Plan that quite a number of presidents before Jeff had been using with supposed excellent success.

Additionally, pretty much anyone who was able to just drop in without an appointment was already in the LSR or their various rooms or offices within the complex. Meaning that no one should be with Mrs. Maurer unless we'd been expecting and willing to receive them. And she'd just confirmed that the expectation had not been in place.

Contemplated my options. She'd sounded calm, but had gotten off the phone quickly. Wasn't sure if this indicated she wanted me and the cavalry or didn't want to give anything away in case someone was listening in on our phone call.

So, did I bother those in the LSR with this? Especially since this had the potential to really just be a package from some head of state somewhere trying to curry favor? Mrs. Maurer hadn't sounded panicked. Didn't mean there wasn't an enemy in there with her somehow, but under the circumstances, decided not to disturb anyone in the meeting at this precise time.

Thanks to becoming enhanced due to the Surcenthumain Boost I'd gotten by carrying the mutated hybrid baby of a mutated A-C, I had all the A-C bells and whistles, which included hyperspeed and faster regeneration. Christopher had been working with me on my Super Skills since Jamie had been born, and I was finally good enough to avoid unintentionally slamming into walls at hyperspeed.

So, I kicked up the speed and zipped over to "my" side of the White House complex. Hyperspeed being what it was, I was out of the Residence section, through the East Wing, upstairs, and outside of my office in just a few shakes of an ocellar's tail. I did a fast check to see who of my staff were in their offices.

None of my staff were where I expected them to be. I had Mrs. Maurer functioning as both my Social Secretary and the head of the Graphics and Calligraphy Office—the existence of and need for which I was still having trouble accepting as necessary in the modern age of the internet and social media—but she'd indicated she was in my office, so her not being in either her office or in the G&C, as I called it, wasn't a surprise.

Because I wasn't trying to win the Overstaffing Award, I also had Abner Schnekedy doing double duty—as both Chief Floral Designer and Chief Decorator. He had one office, but he wasn't in it. While it was always possible that his wife, Lillian Culver—who'd wisely kept her maiden name for business, and who was the top lobbyist for the defense industry and, somehow, now a loyal ally—had requested Abner's presence in the LSR, the likelihood was slim. Barring someone wanting input on the design of our War Division recruitment posters, Abner would have no necessary input into affairs of state.

Because I had a Chief of Staff, too, and because that job required diligent attention 24/7, Vance Beaumont's office was
right next to mine. Him not being in his office wasn't a shocker,
though—because of his position he was actually in the LSR,
sitting in between Culver and his husband, Guy Gadoire, who
was the head lobbyist for Big Tobacco and also, somehow, a
droolingly loyal ally, emphasis on "drool" when he was kissing
anyone's hand, mine in particular.

I had no doubt that Vance was representing the FLOTUS Input in a far classier and on-point manner than I would have.
Vance could enjoy the pomp and circumstance while I dealt with
the weird, which was a wise division of labor as far as I was
concerned.

My last main team member, however, was also nowhere on
the floor. Colette Alexis was my Press Secretary and an A-C
troubadour. Because we'd originally thought that I wouldn't be
making any kind of statement about the A-C flag situation, Colette had stayed in her office, working on the many things I was
supposed to be making statements regarding.

So, either Abner, Colette, and all the sweet young things
who'd scored interning duties in the East Wing were in my office with Mrs. Maurer, or she'd had them evacuate the area. Had
no idea which option I should hope for, so instead decided to go
for a move that might make Chuckie proud and listened at my
door.

Heard absolutely nothing. No talking, no movement, no typ-
ing, nada. So, either no one was in here or everyone was doing
their best to be silent. Or someone was causing them to be silent.

Because of how our luck rolled, I chose to bet on my surprise
visitor insisting on or creating the overwhelming quiet. Also
chose to not wait any longer. Presumably I was expected, and
hyperspeed should mean that I could get out of the way fast.

So I opened the door to my office. And was instantly knocked
down.

CHAPTER 12

MY ASSAILANT SLAMMED AGAINST ME, hitting me right in my chest. Fortunately for me, I'd spent years in kung fu and tucked my head automatically. Which was good because I didn't hit my head. It was not so good because it put my face far closer to my assailant's.

I was instantly covered in dog slobber.

"Prince, buddy, chill out," I managed to get out between happy German Shepherd love licks. I tried giving him the rough petting a manly dog such as Prince felt was the right kind of greeting in order to sort of flip him so I could get to my knees.

Did not achieve this goal because my speaking alerted Prince's pals, Riley and Duke, that I was fine and, therefore, needed to be licked as well while they, too, received their enthusiastic petting from me. So, I was at the bottom of a dog pile. Prayed there were no reporters lurking about, because this would be, for me, the typical kind of press that I got.

Three men barked three sharp commands and three German Shepherds reluctantly stopped assaulting their perp with love and backed off. Officer Herman Melville trotted over and helped me up.

"Kitty, I'm so sorry. They were waiting for you and were being really well behaved. They were acting like someone was skulking around, though, so we had them on alert."

"Yeah, thanks, it's okay, Officer Moe. I was said skulker. Nancy's short, spy-speak call seemed skulk-worthy."

Melville winced. Due to how we'd met during Operation Assassination, I'd nicknamed him and his closest pals in the D.C. K-9 unit after the Three Stooges. Larry, who handled Duke, and Curly, who handled Riley, didn't seem to mind their nicknames.

Or else those were their real names and they just hadn't ever felt the need to tell me I was a good guesser. Melville, however, really hated being called Moe. Under the circumstances, though, I felt he could take the hit for the team and find the will to go on.

"I'm sorry. Prince knows your scent."

Bent down and gave him more loving. "Yes, he does. *Yes*, he *does*! Who knows Kitty? *Who* does? Prince does! And Riley does! And Duke does!" Gave all three dogs more loving, which they received enthusiastically while pretending they'd gone deaf and couldn't hear their handlers telling them to back off.

Doggy greetings finally over, and me ready for a shower and a change of clothes, I got fully into my office. Mrs. Maurer wasn't alone with a quarter of D.C.'s K-9 team—Colette and Abner were in here with her—and everyone was having tea and cookies.

"Squeaky, why all the stealth? And where are all the interns?"

Mrs. Maurer shrugged. "The stealth you'll find out about. It seemed prudent to tell all the children to go see to things in the lower levels." The White House had a lot going on underground. Not as much as an A-C facility, but still more than the average place that wasn't a Disney theme park. "And you do have a package. It was here when I came into your office." She pointed to my desk, which had a very large cardboard box sitting on it.

"The stealth can't be because of the dogs. They love you." Prince had, in fact, saved her life during Operation Defection Election.

"Oh no, not at all."

Clearly I wasn't going to get anything specific out of Mrs. Maurer about why she'd been all Moneypenny with me. Meaning it was time find out what was really going on.

Chose to find out what was really going on with the box first. "Did anyone check this for bombs?"

"Yes," Melville said. "The dogs all sniffed it. Nothing dangerous." Prince had the best nose east of the Mississippi, so if he felt the box was safe, then the box was safe.

Opened it up to find a rather large turtle statue, about three feet tall, though it was lying down, made out of what appeared to be bronze. At least I thought it was a turtle. It looked kind of like one, though also a lot like Jiminy Cricket, but a frog-like Jiminy Cricket with a turtle shell. Decided to go with turtle and call it good.

Picked it up and only managed it because I was enhanced. "Wow, this is heavy as lead. Well, bronze, I guess." Put it on the floor next to my desk. Did not plan to keep it there, but figured I should find out who the giver was—and send them pics of me looking thrilled with this gift—before I put it away in storage forever. That was me, FLOTUSing like a pro.

Prince padded over and took a deep sniff of my new statue. Snorted. Per Prince, this smelled like metal. Nothing to see here and nothing to worry about. He dutifully trotted back to Melville.

"What a . . . lovely gift," Mrs. Maurer said, clearly trying for the positive spin.

"Yeah, and I wonder who sent it. Does some country count weird turtle frogs as their mascot?"

"Sports team, maybe," Officer Larry suggested.

"Good point." I was into sports. Perhaps some team wanted me to endorse them. Any team who were called The Weird Turtles or similar could probably use all the help they could get.

Looked inside for a note. There was none. Looked at the box. No return address. No mailing label, either. Was about to ask about this when Vance entered the room.

Vance did not get the same greeting as I had. Vance got eyed by the three dogs, sniffed suspiciously from a distance, then snorted at, so he was aware of their feelings on the subject of him. He was not the K-9 Favorite.

Vance, being Vance, did indeed find the will to go on. "Officers," he said with a nod, "Nancy sent me a text sharing that you needed our First Lady and only our First Lady. I've kept those in the LSR unaware of who's come to call, but why are you here? More to the point, why are you here undercover?"

By now, anyone who I considered to be in our Circle of Friends knew that Vance was my Chief of Staff. So, Melville wisely didn't argue about Vance being with us. He just shrugged. "We have a . . . situation at the main precinct and I don't want to cause the usual media circus."

Decided this could take a while. Moved the box off my desk and put it in front of the statue because why get into the whole "who sent this?" thing now, then grabbed some tea and cookies for myself and indicated that Vance should do likewise. "Usually the crazed lunatics come right to me."

"I agree. Not that we're complaining about you using discretion." Vance shot Melville a friendly look. "Which puts you in the vast minority. What circus that wants to center around the First Lady are we avoiding?"

"We're not sure, and this one might have come straight to you," Melville said. "But she made another stop first, which is why we have her."

Wondered if the "she" in question might be Stephanie. She was an A-C, though, and it was unlikely that she'd give herself up to anyone, let alone human police officers. And only humans working with and trained by Centaurion would have a chance of catching her if she didn't want to be caught.

"She went to Harvey Gutermuth, dear," Mrs. Maurer said, presumably to hurry Melville up. Apparently he wasn't allowed to be a part of the Anticipatory Statement League today. "That's why I knew you'd want to be involved as soon as possible."

"Good thinking. So, who out of our Rogues' Gallery do you have? My bet would be Casey Jones if Gutermuth was her first stop."

Melville nodded. "We think that's who it is. She won't give her name."

"She's been arrested a ton of times."

"She has. However, she doesn't . . . match up to our records."

"How so?"

"Altered fingerprints for one. And she doesn't look the same as the photos we have of her from the P.T.C.U." .

"As you said, she's been arrested more than once," Officer Larry added. "And while those pictures show a natural age progression, how she looks right now . . ." He made a face. "It's not good if it's really her."

"How do you mean?"

"She was a decent looking woman before," Officer Curly replied. "Now?" He shook his head. "Now, it looks like she's been rode hard and put away wet for the past decade."

"Kudos for your likely apt Old West saying. Being from Pueblo Caliente, I really appreciate, and understand, the description." This earned me a big grin from Officer Curly.

"How did you get her into custody?" Vance asked, presumably before Officer Curly and I could start bantering.

"Gutermuth," Melville replied. "He called us to share that he had a stalker with a gun following him around. He's a public person who espouses some nasty views, so it's not a shock that he could have someone following him, and after the last few months, our Chief takes any complaint like this more than seriously."

"Did he send you guys to apprehend her?"

"No, K-Nine was not involved. Six cars were sent, she was surrounded and apprehended easily, without a fight. The moment she was captured she started asking for you, Kitty. By name and title."

"We haven't received any calls from the D.C.P.D.," Mrs. Maurer said. "At least not officially, and all calls come through me."

"I'm sure you haven't." Melville shrugged. "Half of the crazies we arrest ask to talk to the President or First Lady."

"So your Chief sent you to bring me down to the station?"

"No," Melville said, sounding just a little angry. "We're not supposed to be here."

CHAPTER 13

"EXCUSE ME?"

"This isn't officially sanctioned," Melville explained. "The Chief doesn't want you bothered over some nut job. But we," he indicated himself, Larry, and Curly, "think you need to talk to her. She's saying that she has information you'll want."

"We want to sneak you in," Officer Larry said. "So that no one knows you're coming to the police station. And then sneak you back here."

"I approve of the sneaking," Vance said.

"So, Potentially Casey is still in the station?" I asked.

Melville nodded. "She's still being processed and if she's who we think she is, we'll have to turn her over to your mother's agency anyway."

"Good point. Okay, so I'm all for verifying if it's her. Because if it *is* her, then she may indeed have a message for me. That said message might just be 'we all still hate you' is likely, but, hey, it could be worthwhile intel."

"I'd like to know why Gutermuth threw her under the bus," Vance said. "You verified that she was still working with both Club Fifty-One and the Mastermind. Why would they disown her now?"

"Yeah, because I can guarantee that Casey's still a True Believer. Well, I guess that's part of why I'm going to go to the police station. So, we need Len and Kyle, and I'd like Manfred, too."

Len Parker and Kyle Constantine were, officially, my driver and bodyguard and had been since we'd arrived in D.C. They worked for the CIA and reported to Chuckie. Well, now everyone reported to Chuckie, but back in the day, they'd reported into his division and him directly. I'd met them in Vegas during Operation Invasion, they and the rest of the USC football team had helped me out, and they'd chosen the career of Kitty Wrangling over going pro. There were many days I questioned their career choices, but never a day I wasn't happy they were with me.

Manfred was an A-C troubadour assigned as the head of my Centaurion protection detail, meaning that he, like Colette, undoubtedly answered up and into Serene's A-C CIA. He was a great guy and rarely if ever complained about who he was stuck babysitting.

"What about the rest of us?" Vance asked.

"Nancy and Abner will stay here." Neither one was good in a fight, neither one knew Casey or any of our other potential Crazed Lunatics who might be this prisoner, and I preferred to leave the easy hostages safely at home, call me overcautious. "Vance, you'll need to go back to the meeting and run interference while representing our FLOTUS interests. Colette, you'll be with me." Keep the A-Cs close was my motto, and it was a good one because hyperspeed remained the best superpower going.

"Sounds right," Vance said as he sent some texts, while Colette looked pleased, Mrs. Maurer looked disappointed, and Abner visibly relaxed.

"We also need to bring along my Secret Service detail, at least some of them. Though I know we need to ask them to allow us to be stealth rather than trumpeting that I'm coming or going."

"I'm ready to faint to hear that you plan to bring us along on whatever the latest mad scheme of yours is." Evalyne, the head of my Secret Service detail, definitely had a sarcasm knob and, like my mother's, hers went well past eleven on the one-to-ten scale.

"I think we misheard." Phoebe was the second in command of the detail, and she, too, was honing her sarcastic abilities. "There's no way Kitty was saying she wanted to bring us versus ditch us."

"Wow, I'm almost sorry I was behaving, since you both seem so disappointed." Looked behind them. I had four male Secret Service agents, too, but they were nowhere in evidence. Well, realistically, I had a lot of agents assigned—no one worked 24/7 unless they were A-C Security. I always had a team of six if I left the White House Complex unless, as mentioned, I'd managed to ditch them. However, due to the fact that Jeff and I were pretty much winning the Worst People To Guard Ever Award on a regular basis, there were times when it was just easier to have them come along, and this certainly seemed like one of them.

"It's just the shock of it all," Evalyne said. "I'm waiting for the roof to collapse or something."

"Hilarious. Anyway, where are the dudes? Not that I think we actually want them along."

Len and Kyle trotted in, and Manfred zipped in right behind them. "You wanted us, Mister Beaumont?" Len asked, while Kyle gave a little wave in Colette's direction. She beamed at him, but quickly went back to looking professional and nodded to Manfred, who I figured she'd advised to show up pronto. Len looked at Melville. "What's wrong and what's going on?"

"Never let it be said that my boys are slow or stupid." The situation was explained for all our new arrivals. "So, I think we need to get over there as unobtrusively as possible. Which probably means via a gate."

Gates were devices that resembled airport metal detectors but sent you wherever in the world you needed to go in a matter of seconds. They had been, were still, and probably always would be the bane of my existence, because I'd never gone through one yet that hadn't made me totally nauseated, or worse. My suggesting the gates, especially when Jeff wasn't going to be along to hold me through the horror, was me totally taking one for the team.

"What about Mister Buchanan?" Kyle asked.

"Or Mister Wruck and Mister Siler," Len added. "You know they don't like you leaving without them knowing."

"Dudes, seriously. I have three K-Nine units, you two, Manfred and Colette, and Evalyne and Phoebe, and we're going to a police station that will be loaded with cops. Frankly, I feel that I'm working on the Overkill Level for security right now. We will be in and out fast. Just check out the new crazy chick prisoner, see if we know her, determine who of our Rogues' Gallery she happens to be, interrogate or additionally incarcerate her, and leave. This is our plan. It's a simple plan and, hopefully, a fast plan. Why bother those dealing with other gigantic issues? We'll be back before they notice we're gone if we're using gates."

"We have a gate where we're going," Melville said. "Your

people installed it when your husband became the Vice President. So you can get back as unobtrusively as we'll be going over."

"See? Easy peasey. So let's get going." Realized I'd let slip that something big was going on and hoped no one had picked that up.

"What gigantic issues?" Mrs. Maurer asked. Dang, someone had noticed that particular informational slip.

"Um, I'm not sure if I'm at liberty to say at this precise time."

"You're not," Vance said flatly. "I was still in the LSR when your husband shared what's coming. We're supposed to keep it on the DL." The rest of those in the room looked at him balefully. Vance was unfazed. "You feel free to take it up with the President, his Chief of Staff, and the Director of the CIA."

"DL means down low," Abner said quietly to Mrs. Maurer.

Who shot him a look that could freeze milk. "Thank you so much for sharing, young man. I'm sure that I've never heard that abbreviation ever before in all my days, which are double all your days."

"Sorry, just wasn't sure you knew," he mumbled, blushing.

Mrs. Maurer sniffed. "I'd wager I know what more acronyms mean than you do, worldwide. However, we'll let it slide and stay here in ignorance together."

"I can tell you once they leave." Vance jerked his head toward the K-9 crew.

"What?" Melville asked, sarcasm knob clearly heading toward eleven. "Are more aliens invading or something?"

CHAPTER 14

"LOOK AT THE TIME!" Grabbed Len and my purse, which I'd left in my office earlier in the day, and started to head toward the nearest gate, which happened to be in the bathroom connected to my offices. "We need to get moving."

"Oh my God, more aliens *are* invading?" Melville didn't sound freaked. Well, not *too* freaked. He sounded kind of excited. Hoped he was going to represent the reactions of the majority of the public, but sincerely doubted it. Our luck so rarely ran that way.

"Cool," Officer Larry said as I stopped my escape attempt and let go of Len. Put my purse over my neck, though, because it was always a good idea to live by the Scout Motto and Be Prepared.

Officer Curly nodded. "Especially if they look like the A-Cs."

"Ah, per what little I know, they do not. No idea if they're better or worse, by the way. Now that I've already breached Jeff's latest security directive, can we go while you guys shut up and share this with no one?"

Vance sighed. "I think I have to take them into custody, Kitty. Based on what Chuck said."

"It's cool." Len was looking at his phone. "I already advised Mister Reynolds of what's going on. He feels that we can trust the K-Nine unit, these three officers in particular, to protect national and international security."

"You can," Melville said. "But it's nice to know that the CIA actually trusts us."

"No," Kyle said strongly. "The CIA trusts no one. *Mister Reynolds* is trusting you, which is, frankly, a huge honor. And Kitty is, as well."

The three officers looked at each other. "You can trust us," Officer Curly said. "I don't think we've ever done anything against you."

"Yeah," Officer Larry said. "We're on your side and have been since well before you knew it."

Melville nodded. "Kitty, you know we've got your back, just like you've got ours. Huge honor of trust or no."

Prince, Duke, and Riley, meanwhile shared with me that they were, of course, going to keep this news to themselves and would, also of course, take down anyone who tried to share it without authorization.

"Super-duper. Believe me—Chuckie trusting you is indeed a big deal. Let's not share this with the rest of your squad, though, please and thank you. You three I know I can trust. The rest of your gang I have the utmost faith in. But since no one's supposed to know yet . . ."

"Agreed," Melville said briskly. "So, are we advising the President of what you're doing or not?"

"I didn't share why the K-Nines were here," Len said. His phone beeped. "However, Mister Reynolds has guessed at least somewhat accurately. He says that as long as you're taking me, Kyle, at least two A-Cs, and some Secret Service with you, it's okay to do, and I quote, 'whatever the hell they want from her this time.' So we seem cleared."

Chose not to ask if Len had really only shared part of what was going on with Chuckie. Also wondered if the person Kyle was texting was Buchanan. Assumed it was. Actively chose not to complain about the boys doing what they felt was right. Was well aware that they got private tongue-lashings I wasn't privy to and saw no reason to try to ensure they had another.

Decided I was heading to the main police precinct in a clandestine manner and so didn't need to change clothes. Did wash the dog slobber off my face and hands while Manfred calibrated the gate. The K-9 teams went through first, each human officer holding their canine teammate. Then Kyle, Evalyne, and Phoebe stepped through to verify that all was well wherever we were landing.

Colette and Len received a go-ahead text from Kyle, so she went next, leaving me, Manfred, and Len. But before we could step through, Mrs. Maurer stuck her head in. "You have an additional teammate coming." She backed out and said addition joined us in the bathroom. A very handsome, human addition.

"Jeff, Chuck, Buchanan, and your mother want me going along, Kitty," Kevin Lewis said, flashing me a grin. He was a former pro football player who my mother had recruited into the P.T.C.U. early on in his career. He was tall, with dark black skin, twinkling dark brown eyes, fantastic teeth, and literally bags and bags of charisma. "I'm the most expendable right now in terms of what's coming. No offense meant toward you," he added to Len.

Kevin was married to Denise, who, besides being blonde and fair skinned, matched him in everything. They both had the best smiles and charisma to spare. Their children, Raymond and Rachel, were beautiful blends of their parents. Basically the Lewises were representing in the Humans Can Be As Hot As A-Cs department.

Kevin was also Mom's right hand in the P.T.C.U., so if Mom wanted him along on this trip, then along Kevin would be.

"I never argue when I'm forced to travel with extra hot guys, Kevin."

"Frankly, I'm flattered that Mister Buchanan sent you instead of coming himself," Len said.

"I'm flattered, Kitty. And Len, I'll try not to take that as an insult."

Len laughed. "Never, sir."

"Oh, stop the sir stuff with me. Like Kitty, I prefer informality, and you know it."

"Let's get this goat rodeo rolling, though. The faster we go over, the faster we get back." That was me, Ms. Expedient. Len put his arm around me then stepped us through. I squeezed my eyes shut. It didn't help.

As always, the feeling of the world rushing past me, visible out of the corners of my eyes if I was trying to be macho, and felt even with my eyes closed when I wasn't, played havoc with my stomach. Happily, the journey was incredibly brief, and Len holding me helped considerably.

Opened my eyes to find out that, sure enough, we were in a bathroom. Nice of the police to keep to the A-Cs' theme. Len moved us out of the way as Kevin stepped out behind us, Manfred bringing up our rear. No one looked surprised at our location. Yeah, we'd all been with Centaurion long enough—most gates were in the bathrooms of every airport, train station and, these days, bus station or any other potential transport hub we could think of.

This bathroom turned out to be in the basement level, near the holding cells. So nicely convenient for us to pass the least amount of people who might recognize that the FLOTUS was around down here, too. So far, so very good.

"Remember," Melville said quietly, "the Chief didn't want to bother you with this, Kitty. So we want to stay as low-key as possible. I only want to let him know you're here if this turns out to be legit."

"Word. And we're all with you."

Evalyne nodded. "Phoebe will stay with Kitty. I'll go with the officers to secure the area." I'd managed to get those agents assigned to my detail to accept that when it was just us, or we were with those in my inner circle, or we needed to be cool, they should use my first name, not my title. Thankfully, Evalyne and Phoebe were quick studies and had seen the wisdom of this early on. Chummy first names for others, however, weren't necessarily on their docket.

So, Evalyne and the K-9 team headed off. Manfred nudged me. "I'll go make doubly sure that we're all okay in here." He zipped off at hyperspeed, presumably to check out the entire building, not just this floor.

Looked around, for lack of anything else to do. It was a unisex bathroom with five stalls and five sinks and not much else, other than décor that didn't seem necessary. Whoever had sent the weird turtle statue to me, though, had either sent the same to the D.C.P.D. or else the gift had been from the K-9 squad and they hadn't shared—perhaps I hadn't seemed enthused enough or something. But there were three rather large turtle statues in here, two of them on either side of the sinks, one near the back of the room.

All looked similar to the one I'd gotten. In fact they looked enough alike that they could have all been the same—the only difference was that they were each posed a little differently. Why anyone wanted turtle statues in here I had no idea, let alone ones about three feet tall. Of course, why I would want one was just as much of a mystery. However, right now, this wasn't my circus and, therefore, these weren't my monkeys. Or turtles.

Unsurprisingly, Manfred was back first to distract me from the D.C.P.D.'s odd decorating and possibly gift-giving choices. Hyperspeed rocked as always. "They're ready. No one's down here but those who came with us." He shook his head. "I looked at all the prisoners. None of them are familiar to me."

"Well, you haven't spent as much time up close and personal with most of our enemies as I have. Let's go see what's what and who's on first."

"We'll go at hyperspeed," Phoebe said. "That way no one other than the one prisoner we want to see will get a glimpse of Kitty."

This plan made sense, so we hooked up and did the Hyperspeed Daisy Chain. Meaning we were with the others in an instant. Only, as I looked around, Phoebe's plan wasn't actually going to work because while the cells were metal and sturdily made they weren't exactly private. The design was sort of doubled-up chain link, but there was enough visibility for the prisoners to see who was in the other cells.

There were five cells down here—two were large and had people in them, women in one, men in the other. There were three smaller cells in between the two larger ones. Two were empty, but the middle one had someone in it. We stopped in front of the middle one.

Looked into the cell. There was definitely a woman in here but, as Manfred had said, she didn't look familiar. Casey had been a stewardess, and she was an attractive brunette who was around my age. The woman in this cell had scraggly gray hair and looked like she'd chain smoked 24/7 since grade school.

She knew me, though, because her eyes widened and she came closer. And as she did, I realized that I did know her and it was indeed Casey Jones—at least as I'd expect her to look about sixty years in the future and, you know, after smoking all the cigarettes in the world.

"Casey, what the hell happened to you?"

"Cliff Goodman's insanity happened to me," she rasped out. "You have to stop him."

CHAPTER 15

LET THIS ONE SIT on the air for a bit. "Um, you know, that's almost funny, coming from you. Since when do you think we're on the same side and since when do you ask me for help?"

Casey grimaced. "I went to Harvey first. He refused to see me, and that's why I'm here. I asked for you, but they said you weren't coming and that no one would contact you."

"I have friends in all the places. Your request was shared, and here I am, representing for Amnesty International. Gimme a mo, though." Pulled Melville back and turned us both toward the wall, away from Casey. Kevin joined us. "Has anyone tested to see if she's in heavy makeup and/or wearing a wig?" Spoke very softly, so Casey couldn't hear me.

"I have no idea," Melville replied in kind "We don't normally wash prisoners' faces. She was searched for weapons by female officers, so if she was in a wig I assume they'd have found that."

"Maybe." Wigs were easy to find—after all, at the start of Operation Drug Addict, when we'd first had the pleasure of meeting Casey and her set of Club 51 loons, two of them had been wearing wigs to make themselves look old. There were other ways to make your hair look like crap, of course, and Casey was a dedicated lunatic, meaning that if she felt the need was great enough, maybe she'd sacrifice her great hair for the cause. "We need to figure it out, and fast. Casey could be dying and all that, but she's a decent actress. And I find this entire scenario highly suspicious."

"Do you want me to go talk to the Chief?" Melville asked.

"I will," Kevin said. "Because this just became a federal situation."

"Take Manfred with you, just in case."

He grinned at me. "Always nice to know you care." He nodded to Manfred and those two headed off.

Went back to Casey, ensuring none of us were within her arm's reach. "You look flat-out awful and like you've aged decades since I last saw you. What gives?"

"Whatever you did to Cliff the last time he saw you is what 'gives.'"

"Seriously, time's a'wastin', especially for you, at least based on what you're looking like right now. What are you talking about?"

"You infected him with something."

Per intel we'd gotten from the CIA and Serene's assumptions during Operation Madhouse, Cliff was indeed likely infected due to what I'd done to him. It was nice to have the confirmation, though.

"Huh. I slammed some dirty needles into his ass. If he's whining about my infecting him, that's all his own fault for releasing his Death Virus. You're saying that my doing this to Cliff somehow made you into someone I should try to fix up with the Crypt Keeper?"

"No. I'm saying that he's sick, in mind and body. He found out that I was still tight with Club Fifty-One. So he made me the guinea pig for all their attempted cures."

Attempted. Interesting. "So, how contagious are you?"

She shook her head. "I have no idea. I may be deadly. I may not. I'm not clear any longer on what's been done to me."

Evalyne was talking quietly to Kevin using her Standard Issue Secret Service Via *The Matrix* equipment. "We need Doctor Hernandez ASAP. Advise that we may be in another contamination situation. Yes, more A-Cs, too, but only in case we have to lock it down fast. No, no more P.T.C.U. on-site than you right now, I don't think. It's one prisoner and she's contained."

Wrenched my attention back to our prisoner. "Fantastic. So, Casey, what is it you want to share with me?"

"I want to give you the location to Cliff's hidden base."

Contemplated my responses. They seemed limited. Sure, I could snort loudly and leave. Or I could gather the relevant information. If we could believe whatever she said, which I doubted. Sure, I'd flipped a lot of our enemies. But none of those enemies had been dyed-in-the-wool alien haters like Casey was. And I knew how things worked—my instincts said that if

Casey was coming to me, then she was coming to lie to me or send me to a trap in some way. The real question wasn't if she was lying to me, but whose orders she was actually acting on and what was really waiting for us at the location she'd give for the "hidden base."

Decided that I was here and therefore getting the relevant info was the Plan of the Moment, so went with the obvious reply. "And what do you want in exchange for giving us that information?"

"I want you to save my life and, whether you can save me or not, end Cliff's."

She could be telling the truth—it was possible, after all. But that didn't mean she was. And there was a really easy way to find out. "So, I'm just curious—how did you get away from Cliff and the rest of the Crazy Eights?"

"The crazy who?"

"It's my affectionate nickname for all of you loons. Answer the pertinent question. If you were the guinea pig, how did you escape to get here to relative safety?"

Her eyes shifted right, left, up, then down. Quickly, but still, I was watching her closely. "I saw an opportunity and took it." She looked back at me and she looked angry and sincere. "They thought I was dying and left me alone. I got out and made my way here."

The majority of A-Cs couldn't lie to save their lives. Only troubadours and the very rare and specialized Liars could manage it well naturally. Some, like White and Doreen, had practiced enough over the years that they could lie rather effectively when it mattered. But Jeff and Christopher were each a master class in how to easily spot someone desperately trying to lie. Meaning I'd spent many years now honing my skills at spotting tells. And Casey was definitely lying.

I had several options, but chose to go with the one I figured she was hoping for. "Gotcha. So, where is Cliff's newest Secret Lair?"

"Outside of Paris."

Ensured I kept a poker face on. "Does he only have one or is he shuttling between locations?"

"There's one in Paraguay, but he's not there right now."

Proof, as if I'd needed it, that Casey was lying. Paris and Paraguay had been hot spots for anti-alien activity and supersoldier creation using superbeings years ago. But we'd stopped all of that during Operations Confusion, Assassination, and Destruction. There was no way in the world that Cliff was going back to any of these locations—he knew we knew where they were, and even if the "new lair" was supposedly "close by" the old ones, it made no sense to go to these locations—all his allies there were dead, gone, or turned to the side of good, with an emphasis on dead for the majority.

Plus, I knew that Cliff had last been in the Middle East, which made far more sense, especially if he wanted to get foot soldiers in the form of the remaining remnants of the Al Dejahl terrorist network.

However, someone or something was currently in Paris. And conveniently, I was about to go on a FLOTUS World Tour with Alpha Team and plenty of others who were happy to kick butt at the drop of a hat. Sure, I'd have the kids along, but their current crop of babysitters and protectors were well up to the task, so I could leave my children in safety while I and the others looked for the Parisian trap Casey was hoping we'd walk right into.

"Got it. Well, you give us the exact locations and all that jazz and we'll see what we can do for you."

Casey eagerly shared the supposed location while Len and Kyle both took notes. The location sounded like it was near to the Gaultier Enterprises facility outside of Paris, which again meant that whatever or whoever was there, it wasn't Cliff.

Tito arrived now. He was in a full hazmat suit and carrying a big medical bag. "I'd ask what's going on," he said to me, "but I'm sure I'll find out soon enough." Melville let him into Casey's cell and Tito proceeded to perpetrate medical procedures upon her.

Prince, meanwhile, got close to the bars and started sniffing intently.

Tito finished up fast and exited the cell. While Melville locked it back up, Tito studied his phone.

"Missed a call from Rahmi?"

He shook his head. "We have new apps that allow me to diagnose what's going on at a molecular level."

"Wow, what will they think up next?"

"Ask Alfred. This came out of NASA Base." Jeff's father was one of the few male A-Cs with scientific aptitude, of which he had tons. I'd discovered that most of the advances we had were due to Alfred, though the Dazzlers—which was what I called the female A-Cs to myself—were no slouches in this area, either.

"Of course it did." Managed not to say aloud that it was only because of White that the A-Cs hadn't taken this planet over. Yates had tried for that, after all. But the son wasn't like the father, and for that I was incredibly grateful.

Sadly, Stephanie had taken up Yates' mantle. She was incredibly determined, quite talented and, as Jeff's niece and Alfred's granddaughter, had a level of safety most of our enemies didn't—she wasn't someone any of us could kill easily. Most of the A-Cs couldn't even contemplate doing so. I could, but I didn't want to devastate Jeff's entire family. And Stephanie knew this, and used it to her advantage.

Thinking about Stephanie sent my mind right back to our Lunatic of the Moment. Cliff had been sleeping with Stephanie as well as with other women—this was why Stephanie had ultimately turned on him, the old hell hath no fury thing. But Cliff hadn't been overly discriminating, and he was a master manipulator.

"What are you getting?" I asked Tito softly.

"She's not contagious. I don't even think she's actually sick, though she looks horrible. There's something wrong with her blood though. I'm getting weird readings."

Turned to Melville. "We need to hose down our girl there. Immediately if not sooner. FLOTUS order and all that."

"What?" Casey said. "Why are you suggesting that?"

"I think you're faking." As I said this, another option for why her eyes had been flickering around when she was lying presented itself, just as Prince started to growl. Knew that his growl was confirming what Tito was about to realize—most versions of the androids we'd encountered had blood of some kind inside.

Didn't question my gut. If I was wrong, so what. But if I was right, this was one of the typical opening gambits. And we'd walked right into it.

Either Casey had become a willing android or they'd made one in her likeness. Or they'd cloned her for this in some way. Didn't have time to find out. And I knew this because Casey looked straight at me and smiled. "See ya."

Then her eyes started blinking in a way I recognized—in the Android About To Self-Destruct way.

CHAPTER 16

"**EVACUATE IMMEDIATELY!**" I did my best to channel Jeff's bellow. No one bellowed like my man, but I was pretty good. I was also stupid, trusting, and had made myself and my team literal sitting ducks, but I'd go with pretty good on the bellowing and call it even right now.

Happily, everyone here had been in an action situation with me before. The K-9 guys scooped up their dogs, Len and Kyle went in between the K-9s and took hold so they were all connected to each other, and Colette grabbed Melville's arm and headed back for the bathroom gate.

I grabbed Tito and Evalyne, who grabbed Phoebe. I zoomed us back to the bathroom in time to see the last part of Riley's tail going through the gate. Didn't stop to think, just threw the three of them through the gate behind the others. Either Colette had taken the time to calibrate it, or they were all headed to the Dome, which was where the majority of gates recalibrated to after each use.

Didn't go through myself because I still had Kevin and Manfred here, plus however many A-Cs had answered Evalyne's call, as well as all the rest of the D.C.P.D. that might be hanging about. The prisoners might not want to be blown up, either.

Happily, there was a fire alarm in the bathroom. Chose not to ask why it was here and instead pulled it, thanking whoever had designed this place for having some foresight. More foresight than me, at any rate. Then I ran back into the holding cells, Rage riding shotgun, which was always a good thing for me in these kinds of situations.

The Casey-Bot hadn't exploded yet, but I had to figure it was just a matter of time. Of course, she was bending the bars of her cell, so she might have been holding off in order to create more damage. Or catch me, since it was obvious I'd been the target. Totally obvious. Now. Rage shared that I was indeed an idiot, but being stupid made me madder and that was fine.

Left her there—she hadn't achieved much yet in terms of bar bends and I had a lot of people to clear out. I'd deal with her sooner or later, probably sooner.

Found the stairs and ran up, pulling my iPod and earbuds out of my purse as I did so. Some people wouldn't have practiced this move for a danger situation, but those people weren't me. I worked a lot better with tunes. Got the iPod clipped to my belt and the earbuds in before I reached the top of this set of stairs. Hit random and was rewarded with "Speak of the Devil" by Sum 41 hitting my ears.

Turned out there were several floors above where we were, and I checked the first one I came to, pulling any fire alarms I passed along the way. I had no idea if this added anything to the general cacophony or what, but figured it couldn't hurt. Didn't bother me because Sum 41 was handling ear protection, so to speak.

No people were in evidence. Ran up to the next level. No people again. Headed up the next set of stairs and ran into Kevin and Manfred at the top, literally.

"Ooof!" Managed to grab Manfred so I didn't fall down, and he somehow was able to stay upright and not lose either me or Kevin.

"What's going on?" Kevin asked.

"Casey's an android of some kind and she's going to blow."

"Why are you still here?" Manfred asked, sounding shocked. Thought he knew me better than that, but then again, panic situations tended to focus a person on core personality traits, and Manfred was a protector.

"Um, because you two are still here. And, you know, everyone else."

"Why ask why?" Kevin said to Manfred. "It's Kitty." He took a firm hold of my hand. "Get us to the gate."

"But there are people in here!"

"We had A-Cs on-site," Kevin said as we headed back the way I'd come. "The fire alarm meant they went into action. Everyone's evacuated other than us, and we were coming back to make sure you'd gotten to safety." Well, that huge relief explained why I'd found no one so far. Go team.

"What about the prisoners?" There were men and women in

these cells. They might have been in for DUIs or prostitution or much worse, but still, they might be innocent, and even if they weren't, this wasn't the way they should go. Cliff's insanity had killed too many people—innocent and guilty alike, indiscriminately and with much happy malice aforethought—for me to want to let him or his minions kill anyone else.

"I don't care about them," Kevin said. "I care about the First Lady."

The Casey-Bot was out and blocking us. Manfred managed to come to a stop before we reached her. She smiled at us, one of those nasty smiles all the bad guys seemed to adore. "And here I was trying to help you."

Wrenched out of Kevin's hold as "Thanks for Nothing" came on. My iPod wasn't on general random, it was on random for Sum 41. Worked for me. "Be right with you, Casey." Looked back at Kevin and Manfred. "And I care about all of you. Get those people and yourselves out, and that's an executive order or whatever. I'll handle our Casey-Bot." With that, I flipped myself forward.

Hit her in the chest with both feet and congratulated myself on the skills working to optimum. Not that it was hard when I was this angry. And not that there was anyone around to witness it, because, thankfully, Manfred had taken my direct order to heart and was wrenching the cell doors open while Kevin collected prisoners, so they were a little occupied.

The Casey-Bot went backwards and as she hit the floor I sprang off and flipped into a crouch facing her. She flipped up from a prone position onto her feet. If she somehow wasn't an android, she was a world-class gymnast. Voted for android without a lot of contemplation.

She swung a roundhouse kick at me, which I dodged while I swept her legs, which she jumped over. This landed her closer to me, though, so I sent an upward blade kick into her stomach and she flew back into her cell.

Kevin slammed the cell door shut and grabbed me. Then he pulled a gun and started shooting, right at her head. Six shots in, her head crumpled and I knew what was coming for sure now. Chose not to wait around and took off for the bathroom.

Arrived as Manfred was shoving what I hoped was the last prisoner through. Heard the explosion and it sounded massive. Didn't look around, just shoved Manfred through as well and kept on going, dragging Kevin with me, hoping the heat I was feeling was just my imagination.

CHAPTER 17

THIS GATE TRANSFER was longer than the previous one, but that wasn't a surprise. We were most likely heading for the Dome, and New Mexico was a lot farther away from D.C. than the police station had been to the White House.

On the plus side, when I was this high on adrenaline, the gate transfer wasn't as bad. Finished stepping through and didn't even gag too much, but we hadn't ended up where I was expecting. Based on the general ages of the faces looking worriedly at me and the fact that we were in what I recognized as a typical A-C main gate transfer area, we weren't at the Dome, or even the Dulce Science Center. We were at Caliente Base.

Caliente Base was in Pueblo Caliente, Arizona, where Chuckie, Amy, and I had all grown up. It was a decent-sized A-C facility, in this location because the Southwest had been number one with a bullet when we'd had parasitic superbeings littering the planet. During Operation Drug Addict, I'd sort of led a secession and most of the younger A-Cs had moved here. Caliente Base was to American Centaurion a lot like the A-Cs in general were to the U.S. and the rest of the world—separate but equal.

Made sure Kevin was unscathed, then ensured that there was no scathing on anyone else. We all appeared okay. "Nice to see everyone. Why are we here?" I directed this question to Colette, since it seemed likely that she'd been the one spinning the calibration dial.

She shook her head. "I didn't change the setting because I didn't feel we had the time. I expected to go to the Dome."

"Then I ask again, why are we here?" This time I was asking the A-Cs that were surrounding us. Some of them looked familiar. Three in particular. Did my best to force myself to try to remember if I knew any of them beyond having seen them in the halls over the past years. My lack of paying attention to things that mattered to other people—like remembering names and occupations of the people working with me—was amplified when I was around this many unfamiliar A-Cs. I was like a chameleon on plaid and about as useful.

Six years ago, if someone had told me that I'd start to think that a sea of beautiful people was normal and almost mundane, I'd have laughed my head off. But reality was that being surrounded by as much beauty as I was on a daily basis—in all its many varieties of skin tones and body types—ended up making it even harder for me to differentiate who was who if I didn't know the people well. And, these days, I didn't know anyone at Caliente Base all that well. It had been quite a while since we'd lived here, and we hadn't lived here all that long, either.

"We don't know," a young woman I was prepared to say I'd met before replied. She was in her early to mid-20s, typical Dazzler gorgeous with long, curly, light brown hair and a perfect hourglass figure. "My science teams showed nothing that would indicate anything untoward."

Memory did me a solid and tossed up that the reason this gal was saying "my" was because I'd promoted her to the head of science and medicine here during Operation Infiltration. Meaning this was, by my decree, the Top Dazzler On Duty, Viola Sciacca. "Viola, it's good to see you."

She beamed at me as the music changed to "Handle This." I was definitely on the Sum 41 channel. Worked for me and the current situation. "It's wonderful to see you, Madam First Lady."

"Oh my God, don't you start, too. First names right now, please and thank you."

Viola laughed. "Sorry . . . Kitty. We're in contact with the Dome to determine if the gate at your last location was tampered with."

"I think we should ensure that the location still exists," Kevin said. "That was a huge explosion. We barely got through in time."

"But we did, Donald Downer, so let's be happy. Speaking of which . . ." Turned and took a look around. "Where are the prisoners we brought with us?"

"Here," Melville said from off to the side. There were three women and six men who were surrounded by A-C Field agents with weapons drawn. The K-9 units were nearby but not surrounding. The women all looked like they were working the streets. The men I couldn't get as easy a read on—none of them were in micro-miniskirts, five-inch heels, and tiny tank tops. They ranged from kind of ragged and potentially homeless to jeans and t-shirts to suits. Two of each. Chose not to make a Noah's Ark comment, but it took effort.

"Why aren't you all on guard duty?" I asked Prince.

"We—" Melville started, but Prince wuffed, growled, wuffed again, whined, and wuffed one last time.

"Got it. They're all still dealing with the effects of the gate transfer and have just finished being sick. They're also clear they're surrounded with nowhere to go, so at the moment, a low enough security risk to just allow the A-Cs to handle it. Good boys."

Dug around in my purse. Charlie hadn't quite started teething yet, but it was coming any day now, meaning I was carrying teething biscuits just in case. A-C baby teeth came in all at once, and based on Jeff's reactions to Jamie's teething, I kind of hoped Charlie would start ASAP so we could be on that world tour and far away from Jeff when he was in the worst of it.

Gave each dog a pet and a biscuit, figured I needed to focus and so stopped my iPod when the song finished and put it and my earbuds back into my purse, then turned back to the people. Took another close look around. Was pretty sure two of the guys were also people I knew. Both were, like Viola, in their early to mid-20s. One was about Christopher's size and build and on the fairer side, while the other was taller with a darker Mediterranean look going. Both were, as per usual, incredibly handsome.

Memory again did me a solid and shared that the shorter one was Romeo Ruggero and the taller Carmine Giordano. I'd also put Romeo in charge of military and Carmine in charge of the gates during Operation Infiltration. This wasn't as big a deal in most bases, but Caliente's odd status made being the main Gate Agent an important position.

"There's no tampering from our side," Carmine said.

"Good to know. And good to see you again, Carmine, and you, too, Romeo." Both dudes beamed and I saw their eyes dart around—not to look at those with me, but at the other A-Cs. It dawned on me that the FLOTUS visiting—regardless of your relationship to her—was perceived by many to be a big deal. Meaning this was kind of a test run for my world tour. That was me, getting a double any time I could.

"We need to regroup and advise the President that you're alright," Kevin said.

"True enough. Viola, lead on to a convenient conference room."

"What about them?" Melville asked, pointing to the prisoners.

Considered options. A-Cs were fast but trusting. "Bring them with us."

Kevin shot me the "really?" look. "Because you want them in a high-level meeting why?"

"They were down there. Besides, what else are we going to do with them?"

"I'd like to put them into a cell," Melville said. It was clear that Larry and Curly agreed. The prisoners were far too busy looking around to share their opinions, though I was willing to bet "not a cell" would be what all nine of them would vote for.

"I'd personally like to make sure that they're not contagious," Tito said, still inside his hazmat suit. "Sure, we were dealing with an android or something, but she could have brought a virus along with her."

"Let's get into a room with a door we can close, then, just in case. Carmine and Romeo, I'd like you with us, too." If we were contagious, we'd just infected all of Caliente Base—and therefore the majority of the Earth A-C breeding population—but I chose to keep that worry to myself.

We trotted off. Caliente Base was a smaller version of the Dulce Science Center. Dulce went down fifteen stories. Caliente only went down ten. We'd landed on what I considered the Base's Bat Cave Level—where there were all sorts of computers, screens, terminals, and more, with tons of people dashing about doing things that it would probably make my head hurt to know about. Most were A-Cs, but there were always U.S. military personnel around as well.

We reached our conference room. In a human-run building, that room would have walls and perhaps some windows to look out at the view. In an A-C facility there was no view, so that was out. They seemed to adapt by giving all the conference rooms low walls with glass all the way to the ceiling. It was like being in a fishbowl. I still had no idea why A-Cs felt that they didn't need to sequester themselves where they couldn't be seen when having top-level meetings, but I'd given up worrying about it. Mostly because, based on new information we'd gotten during Operation Madhouse, I had a feeling it was influence from the Tinkerer.

Tito tested each of us as we entered the room. First he checked everyone with the OVS—the Organic Validation Sensor—which looked like the wands used by airport security to do the closer body checks, only with a lot more blinking lights.

Once each person was verified to be mostly organic and so not an android or Fem-Bot or whatever, it was shots time. Tito had a plethora of needles in his bag and seemed happily content to stab each and every one of us with them. No one complained—Operation Epidemic hadn't been that long ago.

"If we're infected, we'll have to lockdown this Base," Evalyne said quietly to me. "But D.C. is the bigger issue. We have no idea how many local LEOs were in contact with whatever that thing was."

"Android, Fem-Bot, clone, some combo. The possibilities are really endless. I'm just glad we have no androids or robots or whatever with us right now."

Tito studied his phone. Then frowned and shook his head.

CHAPTER 18

FELT THE WHOLE ROOM TENSE as Tito went back into his medical bag. He pulled out something that looked like a hand can opener, loaded something I couldn't see into it, then put it up against one of the female prisoners' upper arms. From the way she jerked she was getting a shot.

Tito did this with all the prisoners other than the two guys in suits. Then he put the pseudo can opener away and relaxed. "Nothing contagious. Well, nothing contagious anymore. We're not dealing with any kind of plague or supervirus."

Everyone in the room let out their breath. Decided we didn't need to know what venereal diseases and other things the prisoners were dealing with. Also decided that telling Tito he could have shared that there was nothing dangerous going on a hell of a lot earlier could wait for later. There were more pressing matters at hand.

"Super, so the Casey-Bot was full of it?"

"No idea," Tito said. "As I told you, her results were off because I was testing for a human and, since she wasn't fully human, there could have been something in her that would have infected others."

"I think she was created to give us the distinct impression that she was dying," Kevin said. "Presumably to get Kitty into exactly the position we were just in."

"Great, that's part of the reason for us to powwow. So, let's sit and get in touch with Jeff and the others."

Settled in while Tito got out of his hazmat suit. Barring the Fishbowl Effect, A-C conference rooms were nice—big oval tables, cushy seats, individual TV monitors set in the table from the days when Imageering would have been showing real and altered footage at the same time. Missed the good old days.

Thankfully we'd gotten a big room because we had fifteen counting the three Caliente Base A-Cs, plus the nine prisoners, and three big German Shepherds. There were only twenty chairs, so the working girls got to sit and the two guys in suits claimed the other chairs.

Two of the remaining prisoners looked fine to stand, but the two ragged-looking ones clearly needed a seat. "Carmine, can we get four more chairs in here?"

Everyone looked at me in surprise. "There's not really room," he said. Correctly.

Len and Kyle stood up. "They can have our chairs," Len said, indicating that the two ragged men should sit. Both of those looked shocked, but they took the chairs as offered. Len and Kyle went over and stood near the two remaining guys.

"Thank you," one of the ragged men said. He looked around. "Are we part of your meeting?"

"Were you down in the cells with the woman who exploded?" Waited until all nine of them met my eyes and nodded. "Then, yes, you're part of this meeting. I have no idea why you were down in the holding cells, but you may have seen or heard something that can help us, so, right now, you're all part of the team."

"Don't expect it to last," Melville said. He pointed to the girls. "Soliciting."

"I guessed." Looked at the two ragged men. "Vagrancy?" They both nodded. Took a look at the men in suits. "DUIs." They looked surprised but nodded as well. "And our two younger dudes?"

"Disturbing the peace," Melville replied. "Drunk and disorderly. The usual. They're frat boys on vacation."

"Awesome. So we have nine people with different viewpoints and different ways of looking at the world. Excellent. We're just going to confirm our living status with the President and then we're going to discuss what went on in minute detail."

"Told you that was Code Name: First Lady," one of the working girls said smugly to the other two. The other girls looked impressed. So did the rest of the prisoners. Figured the awe was going to be short-lived and didn't get cocky.

"That movie is not really happening," I said to the room at large. No one looked convinced. "Is it?" I asked Kevin.

Who grinned. "We can't really stop Hollywood, Kitty."

"Ugh. Moving on, let's call Jeff before he loses it. I'm sure they've heard about the explosion by now."

"They have," Kyle said. "But I sent Mister Reynolds and Mister Buchanan a text already, letting them know we're all alive and unharmed and that we'd be calling shortly."

"Great. Then let's make the call."

"Do we want to video conference?" Romeo asked.

It was a good question, which I pondered. "Probably?" Wasn't sure what the fallout would be with the nine prisoners joining in.

Kevin leaned next to me and I leaned over as well. "The A-Cs can give them a different memory, remember?" he said softly.

"Not if they're intricately involved," I whispered back.

"The CIA's helped make some advancements with that. Trust me, if we need to erase this memory, we can."

"How *Men in Black* of us. Again. But fine." Straightened up and looked at Romeo. "Good call. Video conferencing it is." While Viola and Carmine were getting that set up, my phone rang. Happily, it was my Carly Rae Jepsen "Call Me Maybe" ringtone. Dug the phone out of my purse. "Jeff, why are you calling me directly? We're about to be calling through on the hotline or Bat Phone or whatever."

"Baby, are you alright?" He didn't sound freaked out, which was good, presumably because he'd been able to emotionally read me and the others and none of us were panicked anymore.

"Yes, I'm fine. And it wasn't my fault."

"It's never your fault. What happened?"

"I'm planning to tell you all about it on the about-to-happen joint video conference call."

"That's fine, but I wanted to talk to my wife, one on one, to verify her well-being privately first. Call me a caveman."

"Happily, every night in bed. Touched and all that. But the game's afoot and I'm fine. We're all fine. No one's hurt and, despite our worries, per Tito it appears that we don't have Death Virus Two launching."

"Good." He didn't sound like he felt all was good.

Contemplated what to say. "Miss you."

"Miss you, too. And you've only been gone less than an hour."

That was it. He was already stressing about me and the kids heading off without him. "It won't be all action while I'm gone."

"Any action when I'm not there to help you and protect you, baby, is too much."

"Right back atcha. You'll have your own crap to deal with, too. And I'm not leaving yet."

"Feels like you've already left."

Heaved a sigh. "Look at it this way—Charlie's going to be teething soon. If it all works out, we'll be far enough away from you that you won't be in agony from his pain."

Jeff chuckled. "Love the spin. Okay, I'm getting glared at by pretty much everyone. I think we have to get off and be official."

"Yeah. Oh, be aware that we have nine people who were in the holding cells with us, so be sure no one over there spills any beans we don't want shared."

"Why do you have criminals with you?"

"We had to rescue them so they weren't killed, and we didn't have time to take them anywhere else. Besides, they may have seen something."

"Only my girl. Fine, but I want to be on record that I'm not giving any of them jobs and you're not bringing them onto the team."

"I'm not planning to do so, Jeff."

"You never plan it, baby. It just happens."

"Blah, blah, blah. Love you."

"Love you, too." He sighed. "This is a terrible time for this kind of action against us."

"Is there ever a good time?"

Jeff laughed. "Good point. Just be careful, baby. Something's really off about all of this, and you're the focus of whatever's coming."

CHAPTER 19

WE HUNG UP and I turned back to the center. The table was now one big screen showing us the other room and, presumably, they were seeing us on the many video screens over there. Didn't ask how the A-Cs did it, because I only cared that they could.

Did the usual pleasantries, then brought the folks in the very crowded Large Situation Room up to speed on what had gone down. When we were finished there was silence.

Chuckie broke it. "Why?"

"Why what?" Melville asked.

"We told you," Manfred said. "The gate was calibrated for Caliente Base. We didn't come here intentionally."

"Why the elaborate ruse is, I think, what Chuckie's asking about." He nodded. "And I agree." I'd had some time to calm down and think. Not a lot of time, to be sure, but some, and things didn't add up, regardless of who'd sent the Exploding Casey-Bot to us. "Though us being here is another part of the confusion."

Jeff nodded. "Let's deal with the bomb first. There was absolutely no guarantee that anyone would actually bring Kitty to the station."

"No," Siler said. "There's precedent for it. They know that she'll run right to our K-Nine friends and vice versa. That relationship is as old as your time in D.C."

"So we were patsies?" Melville asked, sounding pissed. Not that I could blame him.

"So was the Casey-Bot. In that sense."

"She was confused." This came from one of the working girls, the one who'd marked me as the real FLOTUS. Couldn't guess her age—could have been eighteen, could have been thirty. Makeup and the hard living of being a streetwalker had aged her for sure. She had frizzy blonde hair and looked like she weighed about eighty pounds. Didn't see any track marks, though, so I had a little hope that she wasn't a junkie.

"What's your name?" I asked her.

"Star."

"Right. What's your real name, babe? No one here is going to be one of your johns, so let's be who we really are, okay?"

She looked embarrassed. One of the other girls, this one a black girl who looked a hell of a lot less downtrodden and who I thought was probably around twenty, rolled her eyes. She had tight curls, a short 'do, and a voluptuous figure. Same amount of makeup as the others, but it looked better on her. "Her name is Jane. I'm Rhonda, and this is Meriel. She's from the Czech Republic."

The girl indicated as Meriel had long, curly black hair, big eyes, and was tiny but top-heavy. Unlike Jane, who looked like she'd been on the streets for a while, or Rhonda, who looked completely confident, Meriel didn't look experienced or confident.

"How long has Meriel been in the country?" I asked Rhonda.

"Not too long. Came with a boyfriend who dumped her on the street with nothing. Our pimp took her in." Rhonda looked at Jane. "I don't think that thing was confused, though. I think she was scared. At least until she," she nodded toward me, "showed up."

"Explain what you both mean, please," Chuckie said. "Jane, you go first."

"Okay. Well, she just didn't seem like she knew what was going on. She was in the middle cell, which was odd, because she should have been in with us, don't you think?" she asked Rhonda.

But it was Officer Larry who answered. "She would have been, however based on who'd called to have her arrested, and who she was then asking for, the Chief wanted her alone. We have enough holding cells that we could do it."

"She didn't seem right," Meriel said quietly.

"Accurate," I said. "But how do you mean?"

"Her reactions . . . I am new here but I know English, it's why we came. She seemed more lost than I was when Sergei left me. She seemed normal when the police were with her, though."

"Yeah," Rhonda said. "She was all up in their faces about how she needed to speak to the First Lady and it was life or death. The moment they left, though, she sort of turned off."

"Android, do you think?" Chuckie asked. Others in the room

started talking and he shook his head. They stopped. "I'm asking Kitty. She's had by far the most experience with them."

"Yeah and it does sort of say android or Fem-Bot. I think we can rule Fem-Bots out, though, because as far as we know, there aren't that many models."

"Was she an android like . . . Joe and Randy?" Lorraine asked slowly.

"Or more like the first ones you dealt with?" Claudia added.

Lorraine and Claudia were my two best A-C girlfriends, Captains on Alpha Team, typically Dazzler brilliant and beautiful, and they were married to Joe Billings and Randy Muir, respectively, who were two of my five flyboys. During Operation Epidemic the flyboys, along with many others, had been captured—first by Gustav Drax, before he'd become our Royal Vatusan Ally, and the second time by Stephanie and her Android Army. They'd definitely preferred Drax.

Stephanie had been turning Joe and Randy into very unwilling androids in a method that seemed to have worked in some ways. The guys were now more like the *Six Million Dollar Man* than a regular human. However, they were still them, and still, per Tito, more organic than not. However, they were a lot less organic than they had been, and my team and I had basically found them just in time.

"No idea," I admitted. "She blew up too fast. But I can say that if she was turned into an android by the same method, then either it didn't agree with her or she was really at death's door anyway."

"She didn't register as non-human, so I can't tell you if she was actually sick or not," Tito said. "I didn't use the OVS because I was expecting an epidemic situation, and by the time we realized that there was something wrong all hell was breaking loose. However, I want to stress that there's something distinctly different about whatever we want to call that thing that exploded than from what we've seen from androids or Fem-Bots."

"She looked and sounded like she was dying," Evalyne said.

Phoebe nodded. "And she did say that it was because of Cliff."

"That could easily have been programming," Kevin pointed out.

"Programming or not, I think someone tossing out our known boogeyman is not to be trusted. Frankly, I think we have three main suspects—Cliff and his Crazy Eights or however many are left, Stephanie and the Tinkerer, or Harvey Gutermuth."

"Why would you think Gutermuth is a suspect for this?" Jeff asked. "He refused to help her, didn't he?"

"That's what he told the police. But if the plan was to get me into a small area where the Casey-Bot blowing up would have the best chance of killing me, I can't think of a better way to get the cops to do what you want than to pretend that your assassination tool is stalking you and has to be arrested."

"That she'd be put down in holding would be a given," Melville said. "But you actually showing up wasn't a sure thing."

"Yes, it was," Chuckie said. "As Benjamin said earlier, the K-Nine unit requested it, and Kitty went."

"But there wasn't a guarantee that any of us would go to her," Melville argued.

"Dude, come on. You guys focus on the weird. Our enemies know that. I'm on the side of thinking it was a pretty sure thing that this would catch your attention."

Chuckie nodded. "I think the question is how they expected it to work."

"Well, everything our enemies toss at us tends to be doing double duty. So, could it all have been an elaborate ruse just to get us to go through the gate and end up at Caliente Base? And if so, why?"

"I find it hard-to-impossible to believe that our enemies would have tried to blow you up but have ensured that, should you manage to escape, you'd end up in one of our Bases." Jeff's sarcasm knob was heading for eleven. "Unless everyone over there has been turned or mind-controlled, it makes no sense."

"I was the first one through the gate," Colette said. "I didn't stop to calibrate it, because calibration for the Dome means we can send as many through as fast as we need. But that's not true of going elsewhere. We should have had difficulties coming here. But we didn't."

"So it's safe to assume that whoever changed the gate calibration wasn't the same as whoever put Casey into action," Chuckie said. Might not have been in the room with him, but I could still see the wheels turning. Just didn't think he was getting anything, based on how it looked like a migraine might be on his near horizon.

"Why make Casey or whatever it was look so bad that I was called in?" Tito asked. "An epidemic scare would have resulted in a lockdown—is that the only reason? Because if it is, why did she explode?"

"Because," one of the frat boys said, "you didn't fall for it."

CHAPTER 20

THE GUY WHO'D SPOKEN reminded me a little bit of Len and his pal reminded me a tad of Kyle, at least as they'd been when I'd first met them. These two were in a frat, meaning they were in college, and they were likely jocks. Whether they were like Len and Kyle and therefore *smart* jocks was the question of the moment.

"Name, rank, serial number," I said to him. "As in, where are you from, where do you go to school, and which frat are you two in?"

"I'm Bud, this is Cujo," he indicated the bigger guy. "We're from Chicago but we live in Tallahassee now. Alpha Tau Omega fraternity at Florida State."

"Not PIKEs?" Kyle asked suspiciously. Knew why. Kyle ran my Cause which, when I was the wife of the Vice President, had been getting antirape programs into colleges across the country, modeling the program on what Kyle had created at USC after he and Len had run into me in Vegas. Kyle, therefore, knew every problem frat on every campus. He'd recently mentioned that the Pi Kappa Alpha chapter in Florida had been getting in trouble a lot.

Bud shook his head. "No, we're in a good frat."

"That remains to be seen," Len said.

Bud and Cujo glared at him. Decided I had more questions. "Seriously, no one's mother named them after a Stephen King killer dog or a beer. Real names, dudes, now."

Bud grinned. "I'm Barnaby Ramsey, he's Carlton Shepherd."

"Better. We can go back to Bud and Cujo now. So, what team are you two on?"

"Football," Cujo said. "On scholarship. I'm on special teams. Bud's a running back."

"Called it." Okay, so they weren't exactly the same as Len and Kyle, but they were damn close. "Bud, you said that the Casey-Bot exploded because I didn't fall for it. You have any more on that?"

He shrugged. "If we're going with her being some kind of robot or android or whatever, then she was programmed, right?" Most of the room nodded. "So, those chicks are right—she acted weird when the cops weren't around. When they were, she was all raving. When they weren't she was just quiet and sitting there on her bench."

"Like she was turned off," Cujo added.

The ragged man who'd thanked us for getting them chairs leaned forward. "The boys are right. I'm Mickey and this is Garfield," he indicated the other homeless man. Chose not to demand their last names or anything else—they weren't in any condition for me to be snarky or hard on them. "We were watching her 'cause she was interesting."

"She didn't try to talk to no one," Garfield said. "She didn't even look at the other girls."

"She looked at the men?" Chuckie asked.

Mickey nodded. "She looked us over once or twice while she was sitting but that was it."

"She smirked at us," Garfield said, sounding offended. "Like she was so superior. But we wasn't roughed up by the cops when they brought us in. We went like gentlemen."

Mickey nodded emphatically. "We did. We don't argue with the police doing their jobs."

Melville heaved a sigh. "Mickey and Garfield are regulars, Kitty. So are Star, sorry, Jane, and Rhonda. Meriel, it's her first time in."

"You guys keep track of all that?"

Officer Larry nodded. "We try to stay up on all our repeat offenders. For various reasons."

Would have questioned this more, but the K-9 unit was quite specialized and, frankly, knowing them, I didn't really doubt that they and the rest of their squad were tracking everything they could. They looked for patterns beyond normal police work. It was the reason we'd become allies, really. And the reason it made sense that our enemies would figure that they'd have contacted me right away. As had been pointed out more than once, we had a predictable playbook.

"The jocks and the classy drunks are first-timers," Officer Curly added. "At least around here."

"We're visiting friends in town," Bud said. "But we don't have records at home or at school."

"Jocks never do," Melville muttered. Len and Kyle both rolled their eyes at me. Managed not to laugh, but only just.

Looked at the guys in suits. They both looked about forty, normally decent looking, the blond in a navy pinstripe and the black-haired one in charcoal. They looked like any typical businessmen or political movers and shakers—dressed well, well coiffed despite being in lockup, and, unlike the hookers, the homeless men, and the frat boys, totally bored.

"You two gentlemen have anything to add to this?"

The blond opened his mouth, but words didn't come out. Instead, there was a shrieking sound.

CHAPTER 21

EVERYONE JUMPED, the homeless men and the working girls in particular, as the man slammed his mouth shut without ever getting to say a word and winced, along with the rest of the room. Not that I could blame them—the alarm was loud and insistent.

"I know that sound," Reader said from the LSR. "That's a bad sound."

"Scramble," Jeff said to him, Commander in Chief Voice on Full. Didn't have to ask who was scrambling where, as Reader, Tim, Lorraine, and Claudia got up and disappeared from view. Checked out the rest of those in the LSR. Couldn't see Buchanan, Siler, and Wruck and assumed they were either already on their way or possibly here already.

Prince, Duke, and Riley also scrambled, right over to me. They were trying to guard me, but they were in pain from the sounds. Tried to cover their ears, but they had six ears and I only had two hands. Seeing the dogs' distress Kevin covered Riley's ears and Evalyne covered Duke's while I did my best for Prince.

A-Cs were pouring out of various rooms and hallways, all Field agents as near as I could tell. Some of them were older, so I assumed this meant that they'd been sent over from Dulce. Sure, Caliente Base might be considered separate, but there was no way the rest of Centaurion Division was going to ignore an emergency at this Base.

Sure enough, Buchanan came in and made a beeline for me. An A-C I didn't recognize at all raced into the room right behind him and headed for Romeo. "We're under some kind of attack," he shared, sounding very worried and a little confused. Was amazed any of us could hear him, but presumably he'd learned to project from his diaphragm.

"Some kind?" I asked, as the alarm kept on singing us the song of its people. Refused to stand, even though Buchanan was tugging on my arm. Not only did I not want to leave until I knew what was going on, I had a dog's ears to try to protect.

Romeo hit something on the table and we got the LSR on our individual screens and an exterior view on the rest of the table. The term "some kind" was actually appropriate.

There were what looked like hundreds of tiny dirigibles sailing down from the sky. Well, tiny wasn't quite right—they looked to be about three feet or so in length and probably around two feet in diameter.

"Is there a steampunk fair or festival happening around here that we weren't informed of?" I asked as Alpha Team came into the room. We were at Marx Brothers territory. That happened to me a lot. Figured now wasn't the time to mention it, however.

"No," Chuckie shouted from the LSR. He had to shout—the alarms remained hella loud. "No kite festivals or hot air balloon events, either."

"Shut those alarms off," Kevin thundered. Romeo did something and the sounds muted. The alarms were still going, but now they were at elevator music level. "Thank you."

"Make that quadruple for me and about a million-fold for Prince, Duke, and Riley." The dogs heaved huge doggy sighs of relief. They licked Evalyne and Kevin, then buried their heads in my lap. Rubbed their necks, with assists from Evalyne and Kevin. "Our favorite law officers want you two to know that they love you both almost as much as me right now."

"I'm flattered," Evalyne said.

Kevin grinned. "Me, too. It's always nice to have more friends."

"We need to get you back to the White House now," Buchanan said, interrupting our doggy lovefest.

"No." Looked closer at the images. Some of the dirigibles, those already on the ground, were turning into what looked a lot like turtles. Memory nudged. "Did anyone else notice the turtle statues that were in the D.C.P.D. bathroom?"

"We have no statuary in our bathrooms," Melville said.

"Yeah you do." Looked more closely at the screen. "Or rather, you did. Lorraine or Claudia, can anyone other than an A-C calibrate a gate?"

"Sure," Lorraine said. "It's not that complex. Seeing through the cloaking is a bigger issue than turning the dial."

"Well, that would depend, though," Claudia countered. "I don't think Kitty means could she do it or could Kevin do it or even if one of these new, ah, temporary team members could do it. I think she means could *they* do it." She pointed to the screen.

"Got it in one. I saw three turtle statues in the bathroom. And they looked a lot like the space turtles landing all over the outside of Caliente Base."

"It's time to go," Buchanan said in a tone that brooked no argument.

Pity, because I was going to ford that brook. "Again, Malcolm, no, and I mean that in my totally FLOTUS Willing to Declare Sovereignty Again way of mine. Ev and Pheebs, did either one of you notice the turtle statues?"

"I didn't," Evalyne admitted while Buchanan cooled his jets. He'd been with me when I'd declared the helicarrier I was in as its own nation. Knew that, brave as he was, he didn't want to be the focus of my wrath.

"I did," Phoebe said. "But I was waiting with you and Evalyne wasn't."

"I saw them, too," Kevin said. Len and Kyle also chimed in with turtle statue sightings.

"So, those of us who waited in the bathroom saw them." Looked around. "Where's Siler?"

"Here." He appeared out of nowhere. I enjoyed jumping due to being startled and watching the rest of the room do so, too. I knew that he hadn't used hyperspeed for this—he'd blended. He grinned at me. "I like to make an entrance when the opportunity presents itself. And to anticipate your question, I'm sure that others can do what I can. The Peregrines can, chameleons on Earth can—that another race from another planet can blend or give themselves the appearance of being inanimate isn't surprising at all."

"Super-duper. Malcolm, despite your growling at me and muttering under your breath, the only place we're going is outside. Jeff, that statement goes double for you if you're still on audio with us. I don't think this is an attack. And not only because I literally see no weapons being waved about."

Heard some talking from the LSR, but it was clear they were speaking amongst themselves and weren't trying to talk to us.

Reader and Tim exchanged a look then looked back at me. "You thinking what I'm thinking, girlfriend?" Reader asked.

"I sincerely hope so. I don't think this particular part of the Upcoming Alien Invasion was spotted by our lookout because they're all too small."

Reader nodded. "And the rest of what I'm thinking is that they want an audience with you, Kitty. Specifically."

"That tracks," Buchanan said from behind me, sounding as if he'd accepted reality and had given up trying to remove me from the situation.

"Which is why you all ended up here," Tim added. "They wanted you here for when the rest of them landed."

"That makes sense. We'll worry about how they can see and calibrate the gates later. Where is John?"

"No idea," Buchanan said.

Siler shrugged. "He's fine, wherever he is."

"I honestly wasn't worried. I was wondering if he could give us a rundown on who's arriving in droves. Oh, and by the way, and I'm seriously just spitballing here, but have we done anything, anything at all, to alter what the rest of the world might be seeing on their TV screens and such?"

"Yes," Jeff said, sarcasm knob already at eleven and threatening to go to twelve shortly. "Amazingly enough, we managed to figure out that we needed to take action. Serene and Christopher are handling it, in coordination with Dulce."

"Our imageers are capable of this work," Romeo said, just a tad stiffly.

"Yes, they are," I said quickly. "But your base is the one under attack. Normally, it's okay when your friends, families, and allies try to help out and protect you."

"Deal with internal politics later, please," Chuckie said. "We have a galactic issue that needs to take precedence and requires everyone's focus."

The issue didn't look like much. The turtles were landing and then just sort of standing there, looking around. Wasn't sure if I was reading their expressions correctly, but if I was, they looked hopeful and expectant, not threatening.

"We need to go out there and determine if we bring them in here or not. Christopher and Serene on this particular case or not, someone's going to spot this and we're going to have a lot of media here soon."

"Not you," Jeff said in the Growly Man Voice he still persisted in believing I obeyed outside of the bedroom. In all the time we'd known each other, I never had, but apparently his base emotion was optimism.

"Of course me," I replied as I finally stood up. Stood up to get going but mostly because I knew Buchanan was clear that if he tried to grab me and run I'd kick him in the tenders. "Alpha Team is here. Doctor Strange and Nightcrawler are here. The Martian Manhunter is around somewhere." I mean, I presumed Wruck was still around, since he'd come over with the others. "The K-Nine squad is here, and Prince, Duke, and Riley are ready to bite down hard."

Interestingly enough, it was the mention of the dogs that caused Jeff to relax. Not that this was a surprise. Prince had saved Jeff's life at the end of Operation Defection Election, and despite what he might want to insinuate, Jeff loved the animals as much as I did, and he believed in their willingness and ability to protect almost as much as I did.

"Fine," Jeff said in a resigned tone. "Just be careful. All of you."

Prince wuffed.

"Oh, good point. Prince wants to know what we're doing with the sorta prisoners who are sorta on the team right now."

"I supposed saying that they should go into cells in the facility will be met with complaints, derision, and whining," Chuckie said. "So just ensure that they're under guard and don't allow people who were in lockup to be the first Earthlings these new aliens interact with."

"I resent that," Rhonda said.

"Me too," Cujo agreed. "We're not bad people."

"Duly noted. It's field trip time, gang. Let's go see what the new turtles in town have to say for themselves."

CHAPTER 22

WE HUNG UP WITH THE LSR, then headed for the door. Buchanan barked some orders, so the K-9 guys took the three streetwalkers, Len and Kyle had Bud and Cujo, Lorraine and Claudia took Mickey and Garfield, and Siler and Manfred took the two dudes in suits.

Buchanan, Evalyne, Phoebe, Kevin, and the three dogs took me. Actively had to work to neither be offended nor annoyed.

The rest of the team were determined to be able to walk without escorts, so they went on ahead.

The Base was on Full Alert but, thankfully, Romeo gave some orders and the alarms all went to low, though they didn't stop.

We wended our way through the floor and headed for elevator banks. As per usual, I was lost within about a minute. Sure, I'd lived here for a while, but that had been years ago now, and Centaurion Bases were far more maze-like than the White House could ever hope to be. Maybe Buchanan wasn't wrong to have me surrounded. I certainly didn't have to worry about getting lost this way.

Viola joined me and my particular part of the entourage. "What do we do?" she asked me quietly. "We haven't had an issue like this before."

"You mean other than every other attack and similar?"

She looked down. "I mean that *we've* had to handle. Not since . . . you put us all in place."

Considered my response. If I advised them incorrectly it could have terrible ramifications, not the least of which would be everyone losing confidence in Viola, Romeo, and Carmine.

But, I had no clear idea of what to do with all the personnel.

We were at high alert but the threat didn't seem all that terrible at the moment. On the other hand, looks were often deceiving.

When in doubt or unwilling to give a reply, I'd learned to go with my father's sage advice of answering a question with a question. It was advice that was quite flexible in terms of the situations it would work in. "What do you think you all should do?"

Viola didn't hesitate. "I don't believe we should take this threat as benign. Just because these new aliens look cute doesn't mean they aren't here to cause problems."

Dad's wisdom was once again shown to be the right call. "Good thinking. What else?"

She was quiet for a few moments while we walked along. "We should be ready to evacuate, in case of emergency."

"I agree. I'd give the 'pack up anything that matters' order and have everyone err on the side of overstuffing the suitcases. That includes any and all pets and the humans."

She laughed. "We don't leave our friends and family behind."

A reminder that I'd turned Caliente Base into the Hybrid Breeding Facility. "Take Romeo and Carmine with you. I think this will require the Top Dawgs to ensure that no one panics, everyone obeys, and those with hyperspeed use it."

She shot me a small smile. "Thank you, Kitty."

Gave her a fast hug. "No worries. And let's hope that we're just being Nervous Nellies right now."

Viola grabbed Romeo and Carmine and they headed off, taking the Field agents we'd had with them.

We reached the elevators as the Field agents assigned to us returned. They assured me they were all packed and that others had their belongings and loved ones accounted for. Hyperspeed was the best.

Particularly with the extra Field agents along there were a lot of us and, needless to say, not all of us could fit into one elevator at a time. Frankly, we were at a bank of three elevators and there was no way all of us would fit into three cars. For safety reasons, we went six to a car, though Siler, Manfred, and the two DUI Dudes went in their car alone. The Field agents decided to speed things up and they took the stairs.

The first sets went on up and the agents headed off, leaving me and my current protection detail along with Claudia, Lorraine, Mickey and Garfield waiting for the next cars.

Was about to ask the girls what had been going on in the LSR that we'd missed—since pretending that aliens weren't showing up seemed kind of pointless now—when I heard a sound.

"Hist!"

Looked around. "Um, did someone just sneeze or hiss or something?"

As I asked all three dog started sniffing like mad.

"No one spoke that I saw," Buchanan said. "Though your mouth was open, Missus Executive Chief."

"I'd been about to talk."

"I guessed. The silence was a special rarity."

Before I could ask Buchanan if Christopher had asked him to keep me on my snark toes, Prince growled. Then Duke and Riley joined him. They were growling at nothing as far as I could tell.

Of course, this was reminiscent of how Prince and I had met Siler, so I didn't tell the dogs to cool their jets. "Don't attack," I said to them. "We want to be sure before we bite."

At this the rest of those around me, Mickey and Garfield included, started looking around in a protective manner. Felt the love. Also felt that they probably weren't making whoever had tried to get our attention feel confident about making any more noise.

Looked for turtle statues, or a sign of someone blending. Due to having spent a lot of quality time with Siler when he was blending, I'd gotten decent at being able to spot the way someone blending looked—just like the disguise Sherlock Holmes wore in one of the Robert Downey, Jr. movies—hidden but just a little more there in the space than should be.

However, I didn't see any signs of this. And from the way the dogs were sniffing and growling, they weren't sure where the hisser actually was.

"Whoever just sneezed or whatever, we have no idea who or where you are, so if you want to talk to us, now might be a good time to, you know, speak up."

The dogs broke rank and trotted off. Decided to follow them. Because I had hyperspeed, I used it to avoid anyone being able to grab me. Because they weren't stupid, the others followed us.

The dogs headed into another room that was close to the elevators. If I'd ever been in this room before I didn't remember the experience. There was nothing amazing about the room— there was a small conference table and a few chairs and far less of the usual A-C bells and whistles than the rooms I was normally spending time in—it just wasn't familiar.

But the dogs felt there was something very special in here. They spread out to surround the table as best they could, with Prince staying in front of the door and Duke and Riley taking the long sides of the table.

Dropped to my hands and knees to see a turtle-ish person standing there under the table, hunched over just a bit, hands out in that "don't attack me, doggies" kind of way, looking freaked out. Close up, it looked kind of like a bright green Jiminy Cricket crossed with a frog, with two long fingers and one long opposable thumb on all four limbs and huge, teardrop-shaped teal eyes. However, the shell on its back said turtle. And it also looked familiar.

In fact, it looked like the statue that had been delivered to my office.

CHAPTER 23

"**H**EY THERE, JIMINY, want to explain what you're doing here before my big, brave puppies have some turtle soup?"

The turtle turned its head fully toward me. "I'm here to escort you."

Well, that was a new one. "Um, escort me where?" The rest of those with me were also down on their hands and knees now, and Prince had come a lot closer to our newest visitor.

"To meet my people. We've come to ask for asylum."

"Hey," Garfield said, "we seen you before!"

"Yes," Mickey agreed, "we did. They were scuttling around before your people came in. No one believed us when we pointed them out."

"Because they're drunks," Kevin said quietly. "No one listens to the ravings from the drunk tank."

"Apparently this time someone should have. What's your name?" I asked our visitor. "Because I'm just betting that though you kind of look like Jiminy Cricket, that's not what your parents named you. And I'm presuming you have parents, so if that's wrong, too, just let me know."

"I do have parents. My name is not Jiminy Cricket, but I don't think you can pronounce it." Sounded male, though I had no way of being sure if this was an accurate assessment or not. The females could sound like this for all we knew at this time.

"Wow. I'm going officially on record that everyone on Earth is sick and tired of every visiting alien race sharing that we can't pronounce their fabulous names. We have a lot of weird names on this planet, including those from countries that seem like they either don't use vowels or don't use consonants. So, you know, try me. Just for grins and giggles."

"Okay." He opened his mouth and made a sound that reminded me of bubbles going through a water dispenser. He looked at me expectantly.

"Um, yeah, okay, I have no idea what that was. Anyone else?" The general comments were that no one could translate whatever that sound had been. And the Universal Translators I'd discovered we all had implanted weren't coming up with anything, either. "Well, while we may be sick and tired of it, in your case, at least, you're right. So, what should we call you?"

"Based on your many languages, I believe my name would translate to Muddy."

"Like Muddy Waters?"

"I suppose so." Muddy sounded unsure. "Fifteenth child born in mud is what my name means in my own language. If Waters is an ending name, however, that would not translate. I am from what I believe would translate as the Cabbage Clan."

I was unsure that Muddy Cabbage was as good a name as Jiminy Cricket. It certainly wasn't as good as being Muddy Waters. However, I chose to use some of my hard-learned diplomacy, such as it was. "Then Muddy would be fine for us, and yes, Waters is a last name in the example I was using. But, do you like how that name sounds to you? Because if you don't, now's your chance to change it."

He stared at me. "You can change your names here?"

"Um, yeah, in a lot of ways. But, since you're new here and we literally have no idea of what to call you or your people, if you want us to call you something other than Muddy, we're okay with that."

"I'd really like to know what planet Muddy is from," Kevin said.

"Oh, good point." Waited. Muddy said nothing. He looked at me expectantly, however. "Fine. Who are your people and where are they from? Oh, and please respond to any of our questions, not just mine."

"As you wish. We are called the Turleens from the planet Tur. It's in the system I believe you call Sirius."

"Are you the only sentient race on your planet or in your solar system?" Kevin asked.

"No, there are others." Muddy looked uneasy and sounded underwhelmed.

My turn to ask a question that I didn't have to repeat. "How many of them are coming to visit Earth?"

"I have no idea. Do you feel we should change our names to be accepted by Earth?"

I found the subject change back to naming conventions interesting, but Buchanan spoke before I could say anything else. "Can we get off the floor anytime soon? I'm sure Muddy or whatever he may choose to end up calling himself can tell us what his new name will be when we're all standing."

Muddy looked at him. "Why do you need to stand up to have a meeting?"

"You're standing," I pointed out.

He nodded. "That's true." He took a step closer to me. Prince shared that Muddy was damn well close enough via a very intimidating growl. "I mean her no harm," Muddy said. To Prince. Directly.

Prince growled again, this time a little less threateningly. He wasn't convinced.

"There are indeed traitors in your midst," Muddy said quietly. Wasn't sure how many of the others could hear him. "But I'm not one of them."

"Where are your friends, the other two who were pretending to be statues in the police bathroom?"

"They're with your other friend," Muddy said. "They are all searching the premises to make sure that there are no other traitors here."

"Do you mean John?"

"I mean the Old One."

Old One was close enough to Ancient, and since the Ancients and Z'porrah had meddled all over the galaxy, Muddy knowing about them wasn't a shocker. Which side he and his people were on was a far more important question. But it was one I figured I needed to sneak up to.

"How did you deliver yourself to my office?"

"My friends and I brought the box in, I got inside of it, and they sealed me in. I was hoping to speak to you privately."

"Interesting choice. Most people just call and make an appointment. Why didn't the dogs smell you as anything organic?"

"When our shells encase us or when we freeze, as I did while waiting for you, we appear to be made of metal. The metal is from our world, but it smells like metal on your world as well."

"You were in the police station," Kevin said.

"Good point. How did you get into the bathroom before we did, Muddy?"

"My friends were in your bathroom, waiting by your transference system. When the others arrived," he nodded toward the dogs, "they froze. They went to the police station once they realized you would be going there as well. It is imperative that we are able to plead our case to you and we wanted to ensure that you were safe. I followed behind you."

Couldn't argue. The third turtle statue had indeed been behind me and near the gate, so this matched up. "Okay. So, how did you get in here, in this building, without the dogs knowing?"

"We used your transference machine, the one at the police station. We felt it important to test first, to ensure we had adjusted it correctly."

"You were able to recalibrate the gate without issue?" Kevin asked suspiciously.

"Yes. I and the two with the Old One did indeed do so. We needed to ensure that you would come here when you left."

"How?" Kevin asked. "It's hard for a human to do, let alone someone who's never seen a gate before."

"But we are not humans. We can see through your cloaking and we were careful. The calibrations are not that complex."

Felt that this wasn't quite true, but then again, maybe calibrating a gate wasn't hard for Space Turtles.

"You know that place blew up, the police station," Buchanan said casually.

Muddy looked horrified. "But . . . but there were others in there! Not traitors, just people! Who would do that?"

"Are you saying that you didn't?" Kevin asked.

"Absolutely we did not! We are here to request amnesty, not to harm anyone. As I told you, I was coming to escort you. However, I saw that the traitors were with you and felt that I should be cautious and not present myself until I was sure that it would be safe to do so."

"Who are you accusing of being traitors?" Buchanan asked.

"The ones who were working with the . . . thing . . . that exploded."

"Anyone with us in this room right now?" I asked.

"No, they have gone with the others." Muddy looked worried. "If they meet my people first it will not be good."

Thought fast. Sincerely doubted that any of my people were who Muddy felt were traitors. Besides, if they were people he'd spotted before, he'd only had his time in the police station for traitor spotting. "Were they in the cells or outside of the cells?"

"Inside. They knew the thing. I saw them pass signals to each other."

"How many?" Kevin asked, sounding pissed. Felt his pain.

"Two. Two males."

Process of elimination was fast and fairly simple. "If it's not Mickey and Garfield here," I indicated them and Muddy shook his head emphatically, "then that leaves the jocks or, as Melville called them, the classy drunks. Were they young men or older?"

"I can't tell your ages yet." Muddy sounded apologetic.

"Were they dressed like him," I pointed to Kevin, who was, like all the other men who worked with Centaurion in some way, dressed in the Armani Fatigues, "or like me?"

"Him," Muddy said confidently.

"Crap. My canine protectors, did you smell anything off about those DUI Dudes?"

Prince wuffed, Riley whined, and Duke barked softly.

"Huh. So they smelled human. But then again, so did the Casey-Bot. At least for a while."

Prince wuffed, whined, wuffed, and growled.

"Interesting."

"What did he say?" Buchanan asked, in the long-suffering tone Jeff normally used when I had my Dr. Dolittle cape on.

"That the dogs gave everyone in the conference room a thorough sniffing and everyone was what they presented as, human, A-C, hybrid. So while the DUI Dudes might be androids of some kind, I'm inclined to doubt it. Oh, and Muddy smells like a person now. Well, like a Turleen person. That's how they were able to find him—he wasn't 'frozen' and so had a living organism scent, versus metal. It takes a little while for the metal scent to wear off when they 'unfreeze,' so that causes some delays as well."

"Whatever that Casey Thing was, she looked human," Kevin pointed out.

"Yeah, but Prince picked up that she was wrong. It took him a little bit, but he did notice it. And the best officers of the law here were around the other prisoners a lot longer and they didn't give off the wrong kinds of smells."

"So, does that mean that the Mastermind has infiltrated us again?" Kevin asked, sounding ready to bust some heads.

Pondered this again. "No, actually. I'm pretty sure I know who the DUI Dudes are working with. But we need to get upstairs and outside, before they do what I'm betting they want to do."

CHAPTER 24

UNDER THE CIRCUMSTANCES, speed was of the essence, and that meant elevators were too slow. Lorraine called for more A-Cs, who arrived in a moment. Apologized to Mickey and Garfield in advance as the A-Cs picked up the dogs, then the rest of us linked up and we all hypersped off to the entrance into Caliente Base. We were outside in the Arizona heat fast. Wished I'd had the foresight to put on extra sunscreen but since I hadn't, just hoped that what I wore on a regular basis back in D.C. would suffice. It never had before, but hope liked to spring eternal.

Unlike Dulce and most of the other A-C bases that all had a "ground floor" that made the building look mundane, Caliente technically started underground, with a wide tunnel that led into what looked like a low hill, which was the top level of the Base. The way in and out was camouflaged—not all that artfully hidden, really, but the entrance was just in the right spot to be missed if you weren't looking exactly right. And I was sure there was some cloaking going on as well. Chuckie and I had searched in this area for years when we were teenagers, looking for signs of aliens. Well, he'd searched and I and our family's dogs had gone along for the ride. But we'd never found anything.

The Turleens seemed to know where the entrance was, however, since they were massed around it, still looking expectant. Their ability to see through cloaking that no human nor a wide variety of other aliens could see through seemed proven.

Reached the others just as Reader was about to make first or, since I had Muddy with me, second contact. Stopped in between him and the Turleens. Lorraine and Claudia wisely stopped a bit away in a decent patch of shade so that Mickey and Garfield didn't barf on our newest visitors. The dogs stayed with them, in a communal barfing pack. The dogs weren't stupid, and shade was the best thing in the world in Arizona in the summertime.

Took a look around. "Where's Siler and Manfred?"

"No idea," Reader said. "I thought they were with you."

Managed not to curse as a new race's first introduction to us, but it was a near thing. "Malcolm, Kevin, take some Field agents and find them. The two guys with them are Club Fifty-One True Believers."

They didn't argue or ask if I was sure, just nodded and took off. Turned back to the Turleens, noting that Muddy wasn't puking. Interesting. Wondered if they had hyperspeed and figured we'd find out. Up close I realized many of them weren't green—some were yellow, yellow-green, and green-yellow, which Crayola had taught me were two very different colors. All neon, though.

Was about to say hello when Muddy stepped forward and raised his hands. The rest of his people all came to what really looked like military attention. "My fellow Turleens, I rejoice to share that we have been granted an audience!"

The Turleens patted themselves on their backs. Literally. Hands up over their shoulders, patting away. Based on the sound this made—metallic bongo drums—realized that what they were doing was banging on their shells. Presumed this was how this race applauded and decided to roll with it. Wondered how hot this felt to them, or if they were like the A-Cs and considered Arizona's summer weather to be pleasant-to-cool.

The back patting stopped. Muddy, arms still raised, spoke again. "Now we plead our case for asylum!"

More weird bongo drumming. Wondered when he'd get around to saying my name. Realized I hadn't actually given it to him. Figured it would be part of their introduction ceremony, whatever it was.

Muddy's hand were still up. "My fellow Turleens, I give you . . . the Queen of the World!" With that, he spun toward me and flipped his arms down in a very I Am Your Loyal Subject manner, accompanied by the most enthusiastic back patting yet from the rest of the crowd.

The realization that being called Code Name: First Lady wasn't nearly as bad as being called the Queen of the World hit me. Took a look around, just in case actual royalty had arrived. It hadn't. Then again, Jeff was, technically, actual royalty, and I

was his wife. Had a horrible feeling about where all this was
going and that at least half of my diplomatic tour would be spent
explaining that no one in the U.S. actually thought I was the
queen of anything, let alone the world.

Checked out Alpha Team's expressions. Claudia and Lorraine were trying not to laugh. Reader and Tim appeared to be
weighing the benefits and risks of laughing while trying to also
look official and in charge, with limited success. Expanded to
the perusal of my team. Everyone else looked shocked or, in the
cases of the working girls and homeless men, impressed. At
least I had five people who were finding this awesome.

Turned back to Muddy. "Ah . . . thank you?"

He straightened up. As he did so, the rest of the Turleens all
stopped banging their shells and now did their salaams to me.
Found this incredibly unnerving and prayed there were no news
helicopters or such nearby.

"No," Muddy said once the others were all bent over in sup-
plication, "it is we who thank you. We have come to beg for your
assistance. Assistance we know you have given to many."

Couldn't deny that one, standing at the entrance to an A-C
base, so I didn't try. "Um, you do know that the decision isn't
only up to me, right?"

"You are the Queen of the World. Of course the decision is
up to you." Muddy didn't sound like he doubted this. I found this
complete faith in my assumed role suspicious, especially since
it was clear that he and his people had been observing us for
quite some time.

Leaned down and spoke quietly so, hopefully, only he would
hear. "You're all running from something really terrifying, ar-
en't you? So terrifying that you're willing to do just about anything to get protection. Including pretending to be completely
naïve as to who's in charge of what and where. And I'm not
buying it."

Straightened up, and stared at him.

To his credit, he stared back. However, he wasn't Mom and
he wasn't Chuckie and, to date, only those two had ever been
able to outstare me, and even Chuckie couldn't do it all of the
time.

Muddy was a fine stare opponent, but in the end, he blinked
first. "You're right," he said softly. "We have observed your
planet for centuries. Some of us have visited over the years, as
well, pretending to be one of your Earth animals. We don't stay

too long, but we enjoy your planet. However, mass exodus has never been considered."

"Until now."

He nodded. "Until now."

"There are others on their way here, too, did you know that?"

"Yes. They flee what we flee."

Always nice to be right. I'd share that with Buchanan whenever he finally returned. "Just what are you fleeing?"

"The Aicirtap."

Spun toward Reader and motioned for Muddy to come closer, which he did. Tim did as well, so we were in a small huddle. "You hear any of that?"

Reader now looked grim, so his answer wasn't a surprise. "All of it, girlfriend, I know when to eavesdrop. The question is—do we believe what we've been told?"

"Six ships headed this way give some credence."

"What do the Aicirtap look like and where are they from?" Reader asked Muddy.

Muddy sort of scrunched up his face, so I assumed he was trying to come up with a description we'd understand. "I believe you would see them as large beetles. They are about his size." He pointed to Kyle. Which was not good, because Kyle was a big guy. "Only broader."

"Fantastic. It really is *Starship Troopers*. And they're from?"

"The system you call Tau Ceti."

"So in our 'neighborhood' but not as close as your system or Alpha Centauri."

Muddy nodded. "They have spaceflight, but not as we do. More as the others do."

"You fly through space just the way you landed here, wrapped up in your own shells?"

Muddy beamed. "It has been said that you have understanding beyond others. Yes, our shells encircle us and allow us to hibernate while traveling through space."

"Flattery will get you nowhere, but keep it up, I love it." Considered what he had and hadn't said when we'd been under the conference table together. "So, here's a question. My first thought was that these Aicirtap were from your planet or system, based on how you talked about the other sentient life there. But you say they're from Tau Ceti, not Sirius. So . . . who on Tur and in the rest of the Sirius system are you Turleens not fond of?"

Muddy looked surprised by this question. "We do not dislike

the other races on our planet or in our system. However, we do not agree with them, either."

"Agree with them about what?"

"About uplift. The Z'porrah came to Tur and said they would uplift us. We Turleens did not accept their help. We are aligned with the Old Ones."

"And they just let you say thanks but no thanks and didn't try to destroy or enslave you?" Tim asked, sounding as if he believed this as much as he believed in the Tooth Fairy.

"Well, we might have said that we would eagerly consider their offer and then have pretended not to remember the offer."

"I think I get how your people work," Reader said. "But they didn't come back for your answer?"

"They moved on to the rest of the sentient races in our system. Despite the example, most seem to be considering taking the Z'porrah's offer. Meaning we Turleens will be surrounded by enemies who used to be friends."

"Why are you against the Z'porrah's offer, Old Ones alignment or no?" Really hoped the Old Ones Muddy meant were the Ancients, not Cthulhu and his pals, but I took nothing for granted these days.

"Because we saw what happened with the Aicirtap. They used to be very calm and loving, happy in their world, and welcoming to other races. We used to have trade with them. But when the Z'porrah came to them not with war but with supposed peace, the Aicirtap allowed them to state their case. They were eager for uplift, excited about the possibilities. But their uplift went wrong. Perhaps not wrong as the Z'porrah intended, but wrong for what the Aicirtap expected. They tripled in size, ferocity, and hunger. The Aicirtap were peaceful and loving once. They are no more."

"That sounds horrible," Tim said.

"It was, and it is. We Turleens cannot allow it—to be turned into monstrous versions of ourselves. But the other races in our system . . ." He spread his hands. "They believe that the Aicirtap wanted to become as they are now, and believe it will not happen to them."

"Okay, so the Aicirtap are warlike and such now. But why are so many fleeing? And, from what we know, also fleeing from systems that are on the 'other side' of Tau Ceti from where Earth is?"

Muddy shuddered. "They eat us. They eat everyone."

"All the Turleens?"

"Yes. But not just us. *Everyone*. They will eat anything and they will nest in anything they cannot eat. They are voracious and vicious and they are spreading out throughout the galaxy. They must be stopped. And we are not equipped to stop them."

"Aliens and *Starship Troopers* combined. Does it get any better than this? And how is it you think Earth is better equipped to handle this than your system? Why in the world do you think we're the planet to run to?" Why did everyone think we were the planet to run to? It truly couldn't just be because of me.

"You've repelled the Z'porrah," he said as if this answered everything. Knew that it probably did, so didn't choose to argue. "You have repelled them more than once, you have dethroned an emperor, you have stopped a systemwide civil war, and you are a God." Okay, apparently, it was just because of me. "We wish to align with you, because the Aicirtap are deadly and they have aligned with the Z'porrah."

"And," Reader said slowly, "all of the inhabited planets in Sirius are about to align with the Z'porrah, too."

CHAPTER 25

"**WE NEED TO GET BACK** to the LSR," Tim said. "Jeff and Chuck and the others need to know what's going on and what's coming."

"No argument, but we have to handle things here first." Besides, I wanted all the answers I could get right now, before a million people would interrupt me to ask their questions. "Muddy, why would a Z'porrah ship be coming to Earth? Not the fleet, a lone ship."

"I told you, the Aicirtap eat anything. They will eat Z'porrah, too, if those Z'porrah are not well protected."

"But you said they've aligned with the Z'porrah," Tim pointed out.

"They have, but if they're hungry . . ." He shrugged. "The Aicirtap are dangerous, and though they are aligned with the Z'porrah, they are no longer controlled by them."

"And you don't think anyone else being uplifted by the Z'porrah will be controlled by them, either, do you? You think your entire system is about to become a larger version of what the Aicirtap are."

"We do. The others fleeing most likely do as well. The Z'porrah particularly want to uplift the Q'vox."

This was a new race I hadn't heard mentioned before. "Who are they?"

Muddy scrunched his face up again. "I believe you would describe them as half man, half bull. But they are huge as compared to humans."

"Minotaur people? Why not, right? Complete with horns and hooves?"

"Hooves on their feet, yes, and very long, large, sharp and strong horns."

"So, they sound scary." Minotaurs weren't known as the cuddliest creatures from Greek mythology.

Muddy shook his head. "Most Q'vox are peaceful and placid. They love art and music and food and they do not eat other sentient life forms."

"And whose ship would these Q'vox be in?" Reader asked.

"Most likely they would be with the Faradawn."

Well, that tracked, at least based on Jeff and Christopher saying that the Treeship was packed. "So, why uplift them? Why uplift any sentient races that already have spaceflight? It seems like overkill."

"It is," Muddy said. "For we younger races, the hope is longer life—both the Old Ones and the Z'porrah have found the secret to longevity."

Based on what we knew, this was true. And I could see how it would be tremendously appealing. Apparently the Turleens were suspicious-minded. Meaning I already had an affinity for them.

"Does it work?" Tim asked flatly.

Muddy shrugged. "Who can tell? We Turleens are not willing to give up our autonomy and what we consider ourselves to be in order to become the Z'porrah's slaves."

"You just said that the Aicirtap aren't listening to the Z'porrah," Reader pointed out.

"True. However, there is no proof that, should the Z'porrah trigger something, the Aicirtap would not become mindless automatons. We Turleens are not trusting of the overall motive, because we know the Z'porrah want an unstoppable army. And, if the uplift worked on the Q'vox as it did on the Aicirtap . . ."

"Yeah, we have gigantic minotaurs destroying everything and everyone." Made a mental note that the Z'porrah wouldn't be the only ones trying to get their mitts onto the Q'vox, and the other races, too. We had to neutralize Cliff and His Crazy Eights and Stephanie and the Tinkerer far faster than as soon as possible.

Kevin and Buchanan took this moment to return. But they didn't have Manfred or Siler with them. Decided Muddy didn't need to hear whatever they were going to tell us. "Muddy, would you please ask your people to stop genuflecting?" He smiled, nodded, and went to the rest of the still-bowing Turleens. Turned back to the others. "Malcolm, what did you find?"

"No need to sound so worried, Missus Executive Chief. Siler and Manfred realized something was wrong with their prisoners."

"Mostly because those prisoners tried to overpower them in the elevator," Kevin added dryly. "As Siler put it, that was something of a clue. There was no issue with our side winning, of course, and instead of bringing them out here to cause more problems, Manfred and Siler took them to a holding cell."

"Well done. Has anyone seen John?"

Both men shook their heads. "And Siler hasn't seen him, either," Buchanan added, sounding just a tiny bit worried. He looked behind me at the Turleens. "You sure we can trust them?"

"Seems that way. As always, events will tell."

We indicated that the Field agents in attendance should be guarding the other prisoners and had Claudia and Lorraine come over so we could update everyone on what Muddy had told us and ensure that we all got sunburned together, though I presumed Reader would tan perfectly, as would the girls. And everyone else. Maybe Tim would sunburn to show solidarity with me, but I doubted it. I was always the lobster in any group.

"Do you think we can believe them?" Kevin asked when we were done. "They could just be telling us what we want to hear."

"Like the DUI Dudes? I don't think you fly from the Sirius system just to spin a bunch of lies."

"Apparently anyone can travel across the galaxy like it's nothing," Reader said. "Other than us."

"Well, that's why it's nice to have friends who can give you a lift. And all that." Was about to ask if anyone had a theory as to why the DUI Dudes were okay with being around a robot that was set to explode when Tim nudged me.

"Uh, Kitty?" he said, sounding a little freaked. "I think you want to see this." He was looking behind me.

Turned back to Muddy and his people. But I wasn't seeing Muddy and his people anymore. I was seeing what looked like hundreds of desert tortoises. Calm, placid, dull desert tortoises, all looking as dull and uninteresting as a tortoise possibly could.

"Um, wow. They can shapeshift, too. After a fashion, at least." Thought fast because the question was—why had they done so right now? "There are either enemies or reporters nearby. Lorraine, Claudia, we need the teams to fan out."

Lorraine nodded, barked some commands at hyperspeed, and the girls and the rest of the A-Cs who were with us took off. Thankfully she'd only spoken a few short sentences, because hearing A-Cs speak at their normal speeds tended to make humans sick to their stomachs. Len had pointed out that this was a weapon we'd never actually used. Filed this thought in the front of my brain for review sooner as opposed to later. Hoped my brain would do me a solid and share when this was needed, but placed no bets that this would actually happen.

Len and Kyle moved Cujo, Bud, the working girls, and the two homeless men nearer to us. "What do you think's going on?" Len asked me.

Was about to answer when Cujo jerked. "Listen. Do you hear that?"

We all listened intently. "Sounds like a sprinkler," Rhonda said slowly. "Do you guys water out here or something?"

"Ah, no, we don't water the desert," Reader replied. "I don't hear anything yet."

Garfield jerked. "I do now." He went pale. "We got incoming!"

I'd heard the flyboys use this term before, and they were always right. Noted that Garfield had a dirty patch on his jacket that indicated he'd done military service. Chose to err on the side of paranoia. "Everyone, link up, and that's an order."

Lorraine, Claudia, and the Field agents returned. "Apache helicopters coming," Claudia shouted. "We need to get inside!"

"Get them all inside," I told the girls, as I spun and ran over to the Turleens. "You guys need to follow the others and get inside *now*. We have a likely attack coming."

One of the tortoises transformed into Muddy. "We know. We can survive it in these forms."

"Awesomesauce and I don't care. Get inside where it's safe."

"Why would being trapped inside be safe?" he asked me, sounding genuinely confused.

Had a horrible thought that made far too much sense. Gave up on worrying about how I was introducing us to a new alien race and cursed. "They don't care that they're caught."

"What do you mean?" Buchanan asked from behind me. Took a fast look. Thankfully—or not, under the circumstances—everyone else was no longer visible.

"The DUI Dudes. Their job was to do exactly what they did—be rescued by us so they'd show whoever's got the other side of the trackers I guarantee they're wearing exactly wherever we went. We just exposed Caliente Base to attack."

Sure enough, as I said this, the choppers appeared in the distance, probably several miles away, though anywhere near us was far too close. And while I couldn't tell if the warheads were armed, decided to take the leap and assume they were.

"Malcolm, the hell with me. The majority of the A-C breeding population is in this base. Get inside as fast as you can and get them evacuated, and *not* outside, or I will tell my mother that you made a pass at me."

He snorted. "She wouldn't care." He looked at Muddy. "Anything happens to her and I'll destroy your entire race with my bare hands. Got it?"

Muddy nodded. "We will guard the Queen of the World."

"Bring me the DUI Dudes because I don't want them rescued so they can give their pals another one of our locations," I shouted to Buchanan as he took off. He waved a thumbs-up at me and I turned toward the choppers. There were a dozen of them if there was one. "Muddy—are you and your people maneuverable when you're in the air, can you carry anyone else, and how much weight can you carry?"

"We are far more maneuverable than you would think, and we are far faster than we've shown. And I could carry you on my back. Easily."

Hoped that the Turleens shells weren't really metal, because they'd been out in the sun for quite a while now. However, being a cat on a hot tin shell was the least of my worries currently.

"Then, let's make it so and show the most anti-alien humans on the planet that the Alien Nation will not go down without a fight."

CHAPTER 26

"YOU ARE CERTAIN these are enemies?" Muddy asked.
            With perfect timing, as the lead Apache fired. Right at
the hill that was essentially the roof of Caliente Base. We were
just far enough away that we weren't hit by spraying dirt, but
only just.

Caliente Base wasn't outside of the Pueblo Caliente metro
area, and it wasn't in a deserted part of town, either. It was in the
desert, yes, but near to plenty of homes and businesses. Far too
close, since these were war choppers and they were firing real
weapons of mass destruction. There could easily be people and
their pets out in this area hiking or biking, not to mention the wild
animals that lived in this area. And these assholes were potentially
going to destroy or kill them in the name of alien hatred.

My good friend Rage arrived and shared that it was time to
stop these people sooner as opposed to later.

"Next question?"

"I see why no one argues with the Queen of the World."
Muddy shouted some orders in Turleen. As with his name, it
sounded like so much watery gurgling to me. However, that
didn't matter because the Turleens all went back to their natural
forms. For a moment.

Then their shells grew and slid around them and most of
them took to the air—a fleet of tiny dirigibles against a dozen of
the most formidable helicopters ever created for warfare. Chose
not to question our odds.

Instead I put my earbuds into my phone and my ears and hit
random play. No time to choose one of my now many Fight
Songs lists.

But it didn't matter. "Safer on the Outside" by American Hi-Fi hit my ears. Really hoped I was on the Algar Channel but even if I wasn't, I was always better with music than without.

"Please let my purse be a portal again," I murmured as I reached back in. "Because goggles would be awesome right about now. As would any other help the King of the Elves might want to toss my way. Like sunscreen."

Algar wasn't a real elf, but that's what I'd nicknamed the Operations Team way back when, because they always did everything at what seemed like the moment you needed or asked for it. Had found out during Operation Infiltration that there wasn't actually a Team, but just one individual. The one the rest of those from the Black Hole Universe were hunting with definite intent to incarcerate.

So far, they hadn't found him. Hoped that would last because, despite his protests to the contrary, Algar helped us, me in particular, far more than his Free Will Manifesto would indicate that he would or should. I firmly believed he had a Master Plan he was following to try to right the wrongs he'd inadvertently allowed to happen to this particular universe.

It was because of Algar that every A-C and human working for and with them believed there was a full team of other A-Cs providing all the maintenance for every A-C facility worldwide. The most constant "proof" of this were the refrigerators—you asked for what you wanted, opened the fridge door, and, voila, whatever you wanted was sitting there waiting for you.

There was a supposedly scientific explanation for how these were portals—using a subatomic, spatiotemporal warp process, filtered through black hole technology causing a space-time shift with both a controlled event horizon and ergosphere that allowed safe transference of any and all materials and so forth—that had never made as much sense as there being Magical Elves hanging about. And one Magical Elf it turned out to be.

The Poofs had come with Algar, so they knew who and what he was. I and a few others—Gower and White specifically—were the only non-Poofs who knew Algar existed, though I was pretty sure the Peregrines had figured it out. Whether William, Walter, and/or Missy had been clued in yet to his existence I didn't know. Because we were prevented from talking about Algar to anyone at any time unless he was there and allowed it, by his power. Jeff couldn't even pick up what any of us were feeling when we were with or thinking about Algar.

Happily, either Algar was on the case or he'd never actually turned off my purse's portal ability since Operation Civil War, because I pulled out a nice pair of goggles. They weren't the super-duper ones that we'd used during Operation Epidemic, but they'd protect my eyes, and that was the important thing.

Additionally, I found SPF 100 sunscreen and a pair of thin gloves. Clearly the Turleen shells were going to be hot and Algar didn't want me getting third degree burns all over my face and arms. Slathered the sunscreen on then put on the goggles, which had the added advantage of the strap helping ensure my earbuds would stay in my ears. Pulled the gloves on quickly and was happy to find they were a kind of thin neoprene, meaning they'd help me hold onto whatever I could manage to grab with less slipping.

Muddy and a yellow-green Turleen, who was identified as Lily, were with me. Each turned into their own dirigible. Lily was along to act as wing turtle and to catch me should I fall off of Muddy's back. "Turn your face toward the ground if you fall off," Lily instructed just before her shell encased her. Chose not to worry about that. I'd ridden katyhoppers on Beta Eight—I could handle this.

"Where do you want to go?" Muddy asked. His voice was muffled, but I could still make it out through his shell and my music, though the sound of the helicopters was going to make him hard to hear shortly.

"We need to take out the lead helicopter and, if at all possible, take control of it or any of the others."

"Ah, we have some experience with that." And so saying, we lifted off.

It was different, flying via Space Turtle. Due to the shape, it wasn't uncomfortable, and Muddy's shell wasn't all that hot. But the katyhoppers had had legs for me to brace against, and horses normally had saddles and reins, and manes in the case of bareback riding. But Muddy was a smooth ovoid. Tried to bring back ancient horseback riding lessons from when I was little. Your seat on the horse mattered more than anything else. Decided that didn't help much in this case and reminded myself that I'd fought Rapacians in the air while standing on the backs of katyhoppers and chose to tell myself that I'd be good.

Which was immediately put to the test as the choppers started firing at us and the Turleens, Muddy in particular, had to take evasive action. We turned on our side, or what I assumed was Muddy's side and certainly was mine, and, as "Spin" by Splender came on my personal airwaves, I fell off.

Flipped in the air so I was facing the ground as I'd been

instructed. Hoped Jeff would still want to have sex with me should I become permanently disfigured. Tried to move my purse so that it would hit the ground before my face did, but didn't have a lot of success.

Thankfully, I landed on Lily, who swooped under me just in time. Sure, I hit kind of like a sack of potatoes, but I wasn't too badly winded. And I discovered there was a small rim that went around the outside of her shell. It wasn't much but it was enough to hold onto.

"Thank you!" Managed to shift around so that I was holding onto the rim near the front of Lily's dirigible shape, but at ten and two, versus holding on at noon on the clock, so to speak, so she'd be able to see. Not that I knew how any of them were seeing in the first place.

I was lying flat but kind of curved, since she was kind of curved, and finally realized what this felt like. Swung my legs back and around, staying bent over, just like I did when I was riding a sport motorcycle. Lily was actually perfectly sized for my knees to hit at her rim, and I tucked my legs under what I was going to assume was her belly until told otherwise. Managed to shove my purse between my torso and her shell, too.

In this position, I was far more secure on her back, and we zipped around bullets at what wasn't hyperspeed but was still pretty darned fast. Was definitely grateful for the goggles. And the gloves and sunscreen, because it was still hot as hell up here, and flying through hot air was just as comfortable as it sounds.

The cockpits were set up with the gunner in front and the pilot behind. Each was in his or her own compartment. Couldn't make out much in terms of who the various pilots and gunners might be. They were all wearing sunglasses, caps, and headsets, which pretty much ensured that I wouldn't be able to pick any of them out of a lineup. My only takeaway was that they were all dudes or chicks who were on the manly side of the house.

The other Turleens were causing issues for the helicopters. The Turleens were small and maneuverable, and that made them thankfully hard to hit. Muddy hadn't been lying, either—the Space Turtles were working together to get the choppers to shoot at each other in a variety of ways that involved a lot of swooping and what looked like a lot of near misses.

My music changed to "It's My Turn to Fly" by The Urge. Wasn't sure if this was a clue or not, but by zipping, swooping, and swerving Lily had gotten us up to the cockpit of the lead chopper.

We were sort of sitting on the nose. Well, not really sitting. We were hovering but keeping pace with the chopper so that was the next best thing. Our staying low enough not to be taken out by the blades was the other best thing.

Lily was somehow flying backwards, since I was looking in at the guys inside the cockpit. I was hella impressed, not that I had time or ability to share this with her. Was thankful for the goggles because they were also keeping my hair from whipping around in my face, at least somewhat.

The positive of this was that the bad guys stopped shooting since I was in front of them but in a spot where they couldn't hit me. The other choppers didn't fire at us, either, in part because they'd be more likely to hit their own side and in other part because the Turleens were keeping them very occupied. All of this was good because they'd stopped firing at Caliente Base.

The bad part was that I had no idea how long we could last like this, the chances of one or more Turleens being hurt or killed was high, and at any moment the gunners might decide that they didn't care about us and start firing on the Base again.

The wind in this position wasn't awful, but chose not to look down because I sincerely doubted we were low to the ground. Not that I could tell. Lily was doing a great job of being a remora to this particular great white shark, and I honestly had no idea where we were in the not-so-friendly skies. Looking up at the blades was also right out—I didn't need any more stress than I already had in this situation.

Knew the glass was reinforced, but we had to get through it somehow. Well, I had to get through it. Because it didn't take genius or a song cue to tell me that the best way for me to protect everyone was to get inside this cockpit and take over. Not that I had a lot of helicopter flying experience, but Jerry Tucker, my favorite flyboy, had trained me how to fly pretty much anything, choppers included. I'd be fine. If, you know, I could get inside.

We were basically as steady as we were ever going to get. If there was ever a time to try to reach my Glock, this was it. Besides, if I fell off of Lily I'd land right on the chopper anyway.

Gripping her shell even tighter with my left hand and locking my legs as much as I could, let go with my right and started digging around in my purse. Being faced backwards helped keep the wind resistance on my side, so to speak, and the gloves weren't a hindrance, for which I was ever so grateful.

Wasn't sure if the crew in the chopper were aware of who I

was and why I was trying to stop them, or if they just wanted to get me and Lily off of their machine, but the gunner flipped me off, then opened what looked like a side window, put out a gun, and started shooting.

Dug in my purse faster. Was rewarded by getting my gun in my hand. Didn't have time to worry about extra clips right now, but that did mean I couldn't shoot wildly.

Unlike the guy in the chopper, because he was laying down a steady stream of bullets. All his shots missed, but far too many of them came too close for comfort. Meaning he probably wasn't going to miss with the next clip.

He pulled his arm back inside, presumably to reload. Took aim, for his head, and fired. Was shocked to see the glass take damage. It didn't shatter, but it would after a couple more bullets. Fired those bullets.

My shots did break the glass, but none of them hit the gunner. The glass was also shatterproof, meaning it was now a pretty mosaic that was hard to see through. The current *Enemy Mine* kicked the glass out and it sailed over us—I ducked just in time to not get hit by any of it.

However, the next bullet did indeed hit, right by my left hand. I yelped and let go. Try as I might, started sliding off Lily's back. My music appropriately changed to American Hi-Fi's "Save Me." Was now about ninety-nine percent sure that Algar was at the musical controls—he enjoyed his little jokes, after all.

The dude fired and he hit Lily's shell again, very near to where my head would have been if I hadn't been slipping.

Had no idea how much firepower Lily's shell could take. Muddy had indicated they weren't afraid of what was coming, but that didn't mean they were correct in their assessment of the choppers' weaponry. Besides, I needed to get into the cockpit.

Let go with my legs and slid back. Landed on the front of the chopper, feet first, which was something of a shock. Flipped flat as soon as possible, keeping a tight hold on my Glock.

Managed to keep myself on the chopper's nose, but it was a lot harder than staying on Lily. Sure, I had all the room I needed to stretch out and luxuriate and all that, but the chopper's ride wasn't nearly as smooth as Lily's. It was about the same as being on top of a runaway train, with almost the exact same terror and adrenaline rush, too. Traveling by Turleen was by far the better way to go.

On the plus side, as dangerous and ridiculous perches went

this one wasn't so bad, mostly because there was some kind of turret on the nose that worked nicely as a brace. However, the turret wasn't all that large and it was the opposite from the way I needed to go, so didn't choose to snuggle my butt into it.

Could try to crawl into the cockpit while the dude was shooting at me or I could shoot at him from this position. Decided this was choosing between the lesser of two evils. But I wasn't slipping around at the moment, and that was definitely one for my meager win column.

Tried to ignore his bullets, which were getting closer to me. Instead, forced myself to relax and let the movement of the chopper become natural while telling myself that I wasn't moving—the target was. Relaxed even as a bullet ricocheted right by my head. Aimed and fired.

Hit my target, though not in his head. However, a shoulder hit was darned good enough, especially since I'd hit the arm holding his gun. He fell back and, based on mouth movement, cursed.

Shot him again. Once again, missed his head, but hit his torso. Not a killing shot, though. Couldn't tell if he was wearing a bulletproof vest or not, but while he was hit, he wasn't stopped. However, he was out of ammo and had to reload again.

Each clip for my gun held fifteen rounds. I'd used five shots so far. I could keep on shooting at him then have to search for a clip, or I could try to get into the cockpit before the pilot decided to bank the chopper. "Fight from the Inside" by Queen came on my airwaves. Clearly Algar supported Plan B.

Figured that the pilot had to be thinking what I was thinking or would be so thinking sooner as opposed to later. Managed to sort of scramble into a blocks position, just like at the start of a race. Though most track meets weren't held on flying helicopters, but I liked to really test the skills.

Decided I was in a good enough position for government work and shoved off as hard as I could. Because the chopper was coming toward me, in that sense, and I was leaping toward the open window using enhanced strength and a hyperspeed boost, sailed into the cockpit and hit the guy who I'd exchanged gunfire with.

The positive was that I was inside. The negative was that he'd had time to reload. And, you know, based on how I'd landed in the cockpit, his gun was shoved into my stomach.

Always the way.

CHAPTER 27

ONE OF MY BETTER QUALITIES, at least in my opinion, was that I could both think very fast and not think at all and merely react. While the latter doesn't sound like the greatest skill, in hand-to-hand situations, she who reacts fastest has the most likely chance of surviving.

So, didn't think about it. Just slammed my head into the gunner's head. As hard as I could. At hyperspeed.

This slammed his head back against the cockpit. My head hurt, but not as badly as his, because he was knocked out. Got lucky because his hand went limp and I had the time to grab his gun and move it away from my body, using my left hand, too. Hyperspeed again. Took a moment to wonder, as I always did, why the Flash wasn't a bigger, more popular hero. Truly, superspeed had it all goin' on.

There wasn't a lot of room in here. Shockingly, the Apache's cockpit wasn't designed to host a kegger. Had a momentary moral quandary of what to do with the unconscious dude. I could toss him or sit on him, but until I got him out of here, I couldn't do much else.

Looked up to see the pilot gaping at me. Made the "put the chopper down" sign, which was me pointing down emphatically. The pilot responded by flipping me off. Clearly that was this team's go-to move. And so much for that quandary. I had a gun in each hand, and the gun I'd taken from the unconscious guy had a full clip in it.

Braced myself by putting one foot onto the unconscious guy's chest and my butt against his instrument panel. Hoped this didn't mean that I launched rockets but decided I'd deal with that later. Then I started shooting at the glass that divided the cockpit.

Took a few more bullets than the front window had, but the glass shattered. Dropped my Glock into my purse, picked up the unconscious guy with my free hand, and tossed him at the broken window. Hard.

Which turned out to be the right choice for two reasons. One because his body knocked the glass out and onto the pilot, and two because the pilot also had a gun he was firing at me. Only the bullets went into his gunner.

The now presumably dead body hit him. The pilot lost control, which wasn't all that surprising, really, because he had a ton of broken glass and a dead body on him. The chopper started to spiral, nose heading toward the ground.

Decided that jumping and taking my chances with the ground was in my best interest. Didn't even need the song change to Van Halen's "Jump" to tell me that, but it was always nice to get confirmation. Dropped the empty gun and dived over the side.

To land stomach first on a Turleen.

Wasn't sure who this was and didn't care. Just grabbed on as best I could as my new ride zoomed away from the crashing chopper.

The chopper hit and exploded, with dangerous debris flying everywhere. Whoever I was riding on flipped and spun to avoid it. And I wasn't able to hold on.

Landed on another Turleen, who flew me farther away. This one had to avoid both debris and bullets and—at this point, surprising no one—I fell off again.

Hit another Turleen and started to slide almost immediately. But this one was joined by a buddy, who was able to sort of shove me back up. Managed to get a hold and straddle my current ride while the other stayed with us. They were side-by-side, and while I wasn't able to lie across both of them, having the one on my right was sort of comforting.

Three more arrived, so we were in a formation with me and the one Turleen in the middle and the other four covering me slipping off to either side or front to back. Had no hopes that this formation would last the moment one of the gunners in the remaining choppers decided to shoot at us, but for right now, I'd take it.

Unfortunately, the crashing of one chopper appeared to remind the others of what they were here to do. The shooting increased, and several loosed missiles hit what I was pretty sure was the top of Caliente Base. It was hard to be certain from my current vantage point, which was pretty high up.

My music changed to "Here Come Cowboys" by the Psyche-delic Furs. Took a look—sure enough, there were five jets on the horizon. "I think the cavalry's coming," I shouted to the Turleens around me. Had no idea if they heard me or knew what I meant.

Recognized the flying signatures—Matt Hughes, Chip Walker, Jerry, Reader, and Tim. Wondered where the hell Joe and Randy were while at the same time I sort of pitied the pilots in the choppers—no matter how good they were, they were no match for Reader and Tim, let alone any one of the flyboys.

My phone rang, interrupting the Psych Furs. Hadn't gone hands-free, but my earbuds allowed me to answer calls, so I risked it and let go with one hand so I could answer the phone. "FLOTUS Airlines, how may we help you?"

"Commander, it's always so fun to join you in your work."

"Jerry! So good to hear your voice. The metallic dirigible-looking things are the good guys."

"Yes, James and Tim explained that."

"Where are Joe and Randy?"

"With Matt and Chip. They're going to be following your lead and destroying the enemy from within."

As he said this, saw that the planes I knew were piloted by Hughes and Walker had something extra underneath—Joe and Randy were in what looked like giant hammocks holding them to the bottom of the planes.

"What the literal hell, Jerry?"

"Kitty, we liked what you were doing," Hughes said.

"Are we on a group call?"

"We are," Walker replied. "James felt you'd enjoy the nostal-gia. And our Six Million Dollar Men said they didn't want to be shown up by a girl."

"They did not put it that way."

"You're right, Kitty," Joe said, sounding as if he was in a wind tunnel which, under the circumstances, he was. "That's not how we said it."

"We said we wanted to live up to your example," Randy shared from his own wind tunnel. Had to figure that I sounded this way, too.

"Awesome. That's two of you and me, sort of, for eleven choppers. What's the rest of the team planning to do?"

"Kicking butt and taking names," Tim said. "You and the Turleens seem to have reached an understanding."

"Hilarious. Is anyone planning to get me or anything or do you all want me to try to take on another Apache by myself?"

"Yes to getting you, no to your acting like *Walker, Texas Ranger*," Reader said. "However, we have to neutralize the threat first, because I can guarantee that our enemies will be shooting at you if we try to grab you right now."

"They're shooting at me and the Turleens, and now you guys, regardless."

"Not for long," Joe said.

"Seriously have no idea how you think you're going to drop from a jet onto a helicopter without being shredded by the blades."

No sooner were the words out of my mouth than I saw several Turleens fly up under the jets with Joe and Randy underneath.

"We're not doing it the stupid way," Randy said, as his net released and he dropped onto a Turleen. "I told you—we want to live up to your example."

Joe followed suit, and both of them were riding the Turleens like I'd ridden Lily—as if the Turleen was a sport bike.

Had no idea if the Turleens could hear us, had telepathy, or had been observing us long enough to know that the jets and the people in them were on our side, but they were functioning as if all three were the case. The Turleens with Joe and Randy on them zipped off for the nearest helicopters.

The guys didn't take as long as I had to get off their respective Turleens. Of course, they had android-enhanced limbs now. Meaning they could hold onto the choppers much more tightly than I could.

Joe and Randy were moving pretty much at hyperspeed as they quickly reached the cockpits, broke through the glass, tossed the gunners out, broke through the next part of the cockpit, threw the pilots out, then took control of their two choppers.

Normally it wasn't safe or comfortable to fly without the protection of the glass and metal that made up a cockpit. Joe and Randy apparently were ignoring the discomfort or their android enhancements meant they weren't affected. They took on two other choppers.

Meanwhile, the five jets were focusing firepower on five of the Apaches and the Apaches were returning fire. The Turleens around those choppers broke off fast and clustered around the two remaining unengaged choppers.

The set of Turleens surrounding the chopper that had the highest altitude started swirling around it. It looked kind of pretty, like a weird, gigantic brass merry-go-round or flying wind chime, but it was effective. There were enough of them that the pilot probably couldn't see and they were able to cause the chopper to start swirling as well. Didn't take too long before its nose was pointing down. The Turleens disengaged and zoomed to safety just before the chopper crashed into the desert.

The other set of Turleens had focused on the last chopper, which was flying low, clearly set on bombing the hell out of the Base. They were doing the same maneuver as the others but weren't really slowing it. Either the pilot was better than the other, more determined, suicidal, or hoping to score a lot of points by taking out extra aliens, because he was just barreling through them.

The positive of this was that he had to bank and come around again, so they bought our side some time. But the Turleens he whizzed through spun what looked like out of control. They all recovered, but they disengaged and came over to me and my Dirigible Entourage.

The roof was still holding up, as far as I could tell. However, I had no idea how much more it could take. Maybe it could withstand a nuke. And maybe one more hit was going to cause it to tumble down. I wasn't willing to find out. Rescue be damned—it was indeed time to be, if not *Walker, Texas Ranger*, then at least *Lone Wolf McQuade*.

"I need to get into that cockpit!" Had no idea if the Turleens could hear me or not, but all of a sudden they spread out, but in a straight-ish line. And that line was heading for the chopper.

Decided that they were right—the fastest path was to use them as stepping-stones. Didn't think about it—now wasn't the time to contemplate anything other than getting to the last chopper before it was able to destroy anything.

"Kitty, do *not* engage!" Reader shouted. "We'll handle—"

My call disconnected and Sweet's "Fox on the Run" came on. "I'm flattered and I copy that, My King of the Elves."

Time to use the skills and hope that Algar's faith and Christopher's training was going to be enough. One of the things Christopher had worked on with me for years now was to make me not think about anything "new." I didn't think about breathing; I shouldn't think about using hyperspeed. When I was enraged, this happened naturally. When I wasn't—and Rage had taken a breather and was watching the show, munching on popcorn at the moment—it was a lot harder.

There was no time to get angry. There was only the now, and the race that had to be won. Pulled up into what, a day ago, I'd have called a turtle position, and took off.

Happily, didn't fall flat on my face or even slip, despite the smoothness of the Turleens' shells. Did have to hurdle to get to each Turleen, but this was absolutely in my wheelhouse. I was a hurdler with a perfect four-step, meaning I could lead with either leg. Never before had this been a more important ability than right now, because the Turleens were spread out about one leap each.

Hyperspeed didn't mean you took less steps—it meant you took them faster than the human eye could see, but you still had to take them. Meaning I had to hurdle the entire way. Not a problem, really. I'd trained under the most sadistic track coaches any high school or college had ever seen. This was an actual exercise I'd had to master in freshman year of high school—every step was a hurdle. I'd been good at it then, and I was better at it now.

The chopper was heading right for us and began firing—bullets as opposed to missiles. Presumed the pilot wanted to save the bombs for the main target.

I was going so fast now that I could see the bullets coming. It was very much like being in a *Matrix* movie only I wasn't in a cool leather trench coat.

Had to leap to my right to avoid a bullet. There were no Turleens to my right.

CHAPTER 28

WELL, there had been no Turleens to my right, but one swooped up from who knew where and I landed on its back. Leaped again, to my left this time, to get back onto my path. But had to move into a somersault to avoid some more bullets.

Saw two Turleens heading for me, side-by-side again. So, did my best to land with my feet spread apart so that I had a foot on each one. It worked but I took no time to marvel. Bullets were peppering the air and most of the Turleens had had to stop being a living bridge to avoid getting hit.

Wondered at this for a moment, only because Muddy had seemed so unconcerned. Saw a bullet hit a Turleen and ricochet into one of our side's planes. Realized the Turleens were breaking off to avoid inadvertently causing friendly fire more than to avoid getting hit themselves.

I was close enough to my target to feel the wind from the main rotor blades. Wasn't going to be able to stay upright like this much longer. My Turleens realized it, too, and swooped underneath the chopper. Saw my opportunity and took it— jumped up and grabbed onto the landing gear.

Time to use the gymnastics skills I didn't possess.

Was on one of the wheels and the leg that attached it to the chopper. This wasn't a great place to be in that I didn't have Joe and Randy's android-enhanced limbs, and so couldn't rip out the undercarriage and crawl in that way.

Could, however, reach the Hellfire missiles that were right next to me. Well, the term "right next to me" was overstating it a bit. I could see them and the right jump would mean I could grab onto a missile.

Had no idea how securely the missiles were clamped in before they were launched, but had to figure they were pretty secure since no one wanted a missile falling off just because the aircraft had hit turbulence.

Had lucked into jumping onto the side with all four missiles still in place. However, there was no doubt in my mind that the gunner was going to let all of them fly at Caliente Base as soon as possible.

This was confirmed by a missile from the other side firing. Watched its trajectory. Wasn't aimed at the Base. Squinted and could make out bodies on the ground. Moving bodies. Meaning they were firing on either civilians or people coming to help. Time to stop worrying about the weakness of my plan.

Flung my legs up so that they wrapped around the wheel. Moved my body so that I was now sitting on the wheel, which sounds easy, but wasn't. Thankfully, no one was around to hear my grunting. Holding onto the leg as tightly as possible, maneuvered myself so that my feet were on top of the wheel. Did this all at hyperspeed but it took longer than I liked because of how precarious my position was.

Finally managed to get where I wanted to be. Chose to not think about this at all and leaned out for the pylon holding the missiles. It was closer in this position than it had appeared when I was hanging off the wheel, so had that going for me.

Didn't spend time marveling and instead climbed up the pylon to get onto the wing. Had to hold on because the wind resistance was incredible, with gusts coming from all directions.

My music changed to Pink's "Blow Me (One Last Kiss)." Considered what Algar might be trying to tell me. Was in a good enough position so, left hand clamped onto the wing, reached into my purse. And came out with what certainly looked like a bomb that attached to metal.

Chose to say "thank you" in my head and slammed the sticky bomb onto the side of the chopper. The timer was set for fifteen seconds. Hit the green button and saw the counter go down to fourteen. Time to go.

Let myself slide off the back of the wing so I'd fall straight down and not risk getting sliced by any of the blades, main or tail.

However, this meant I was plummeting straight down. Tried to turn around in the air but couldn't manage it. Had a great view of the rest of the aerial fighting. Our side appeared to be winning, with choppers on the ground or blown up. Winced in anticipation of slamming into the ground or, if I was really lucky, another Turleen.

Did hit, but not the ground or a Space Turtle. I hit a pair of strong arms.

"Oof!" Jeff said as he hugged me.

Looked up. "The chopper's above us and it's going to blow really, really soon."

Jeff didn't question—instead he ran us out of range. Just in time, as the chopper exploded and debris once again fell out of the sky.

"What are you doing here? Not that I'm not thrilled to see you and relive some of our nostalgic moments and all that." We were far enough away, so took off my goggles and gloves and dropped them back into my purse.

"I'm here because, as usual, I didn't want to watch my wife die. I know it's a terrible failing, but I've learned to live with it."

He didn't put me down but flipped me so that he was holding me. Wrapped my legs around his waist. "Seems like old times. And they let you out of the meeting, let alone the complex?"

Jeff rolled his eyes. "Just who do you think could have stopped me?"

"Good point." Hugged him tightly as I turned off my music, just to be polite to my heroic husband and all. "It's great to see you. I'd totally make out right now because, as always, you saving me from going splat is a total turn-on, but we have an attack we need to ensure is over."

"That's what the armed forces are for." And with that, Jeff kissed me, hard. Kissed him right back, because who was I to argue with the Leader of the Free World?

To his credit, Jeff ended our kiss sooner as opposed to later, but not so soon that I wasn't ready to go for it right here. He looked more than a little smug about this, which was amusing in that I was pretty much always ready to go for it with him. But it was nice to know that he never took that for granted.

"Who else is here? I saw a bunch of bodies that one of the missiles was aimed for. And was anyone hit or hurt?"

"Chuck, Lorraine, Claudia, Christopher, and Serene came over with me, along with far too many Secret Service agents and about a dozen Field agents. No one was hurt, but only because we'd assigned Field teams to the Secret Service."

"I thought Christopher and Serene were handling media stuff."

"They decided helping everyone save the First Lady's life and the lives of everyone at Caliente Base took precedence."

"No need to sound so snippy, I wasn't complaining that they were here." Looked around. "Where is everyone?"

"Christopher is confirming that Caliente Base is cleared out. I sent Chuck and Serene off to ensure that law enforcement keeps people away from here, and they're also wrangling the Secret Service. Lorraine and Claudia are handling the ones who refused to leave the area. In other words, the main details for you and me."

"They're doing their best."

Jeff sighed. "I know. I think we need to assign A-Cs to those positions, though. Because no human Secret Service agent can do what the greenest Field agent can."

"I could. Tim and James could, too. Don't sell them short. Maybe we should train them like we train our human agents instead of trying to circumvent them all the time."

"This from the woman who pointedly circumvents everyone all the time?"

"Blah, blah, blah, I just know their hearts are in the right place and I don't want to just dump them from their life's work because we're faster than they are."

"I don't want to fire anyone. It may not matter soon, anyway."

"What do you mean?"

"The world is about to change, baby. Speaking of which, how do we get your newest friends to regroup over here?"

"Sadly, I have no idea. Put me down, would you?"

"If I must."

"You must." Jeff complied and I waved my arms. "Muddy! Lily! Other Turleens. Come to Kitty!"

"You talk to them like you talk to the Poofs and Peregrines?"

"Um, no, only just now." Had a thought. "Poofs Assemble!"

Several Poofs including Harlie, the Head Poof, Poofikins, which was my official Poof, and Murphy, which was Jeff's Poof, who he pretended wasn't his special favorite with absolutely no success. They all purred at me.

"Kitty appreciates your support. Are you able to help me get the nice Space Turtles to disengage from the enemy? As fast as possible?"

Harlie mewed, then the Poofs disappeared. Sent a text to Lorraine telling her roughly where we were.

"What are they doing?" Jeff asked.

"I have no idea. I just hope whatever it is works." Whatever it was did. The Turleens broke off and zoomed to where Jeff and I were standing. We were surrounded by little dirigibles in moments. Noted that several of the dirigibles had a Poof riding on them.

Lorraine, Claudia, Evalyne, Phoebe, and the first and second in command of Jeff's Secret Service detail, Joseph and Rob, arrived at the same time.

"Poofs rock. Muddy, are you there?"

A dirigible near to us changed into Muddy and the Poofs bounded over and into my purse. Muddy bowed to Jeff. "It is an honor to meet the King of the World."

Jeff groaned. "Please don't call me that in front of anyone else."

"We'll work on that later." Did fast introductions for Joseph and Rob. "Muddy, I want to get the Turleens to safety."

"We are safe here, and will not desert the King and Queen of the World, or their retainers."

"Why is he insisting on calling us that?" Jeff asked me.

"Haven't had time to ponder that, Jeff. We've been busy." Though I was certain that Muddy had a reason for it, because I was also certain that Muddy did not, for one moment, actually *believe* that Jeff and I were the king and queen of anything.

"Yes. Why were you up on that helicopter?"

"Which one are you referring to?"

"You were on more than one?" Jeff sounded ready to pop a vessel. Evalyne and Phoebe merely exchanged long-suffering looks.

"Not my fault you weren't paying attention. And I'd like to point out that this entire situation is also not my fault."

"It's never your fault. Look, we need to get everyone out of here. Airborne will handle the cleanup."

"Okay, but I think my team handled things well. The Turleens and I held off the opposing force until Airborne could show up."

"True. And none of the crashed aircraft landed on top of Caliente Base, either, or in or near any other civilian areas. By a miracle I'm willing to ascribe to any deity who'd like to take the credit." Jeff ran his hand through his hair. "But I want to get you out of here, baby."

"Blah, blah, blah. This is now a disaster scene. Us being here shows how seriously we take any attacks on American soil."

"Love the spin," Jeff muttered.

"Kitty's right, Jeff," Lorraine said. "And you know it."

"It's a gift and a skill." Took a look around. Sure enough, the fight was over, all choppers on the ground or blown up. Watched the team land the jets. "I don't want to leave, and not just because I think we need to do the Frowny-Faced Photo Op to show that we're taking anti-alien attacks seriously. We need to interrogate whoever's still alive, and I don't want them taken back to any of our bases. To anywhere, really. The DUI Dudes had trackers on them, which is how they found Caliente Base in the first place."

"I understand what you're saying only because Buchanan briefed me during Caliente Base's evacuation. And before you ask, everyone is at Dulce, including the police dogs, except for the two Club Fifty-One True Believers. They're with Buchanan, Siler, and Manfred, regretting the days they were born."

"Where are they at?"

"Guantanamo, via a gate in Caliente Base. I can guarantee that they're not going to get attacked there, but if they are, the Navy is primed and ready to shoot whoever down with extreme prejudice."

"Go team. Where is John? And the two Turleens who were with him?" I asked Jeff and Muddy both.

"I have no idea," Jeff said. "Wruck is confirmed to not be in Caliente Base or at Dulce. And there are no, ah, Turleens there, either."

"I don't know where they might be, either," Muddy admitted. "The rest of our people are here, with you."

Jeff looked around. "You aren't a populous race, or are you the only ones seeking asylum?"

"We are quite populous, but we are the force chosen to ask Earth for asylum. The rest of our people are still on Tur."

"Waiting for the other sentient races to take the Z'porrah's offer? That seems kind of foolhardy."

Muddy shook his head. "No, it is a precaution. The Aicirtap are heading for Earth."

CHAPTER 29

LET THAT ONE SIT on the air for a moment. "Um, Muddy, are the Aicirtap coming to Earth because they're following the ships that are fleeing, or were they coming here all along?"

"We assume both, but are not certain. The Z'porrah want Earth destroyed."

"Oh, good. Well, at least we're once again back to using the right boogeyman for the job."

"I don't understand you," Muddy said politely.

"So few ever do. Jeff, we need to get me on that world tour sooner as opposed to later."

"Suddenly you're excited to be doing the diplomatic job?" Jeff sounded as if he not only didn't believe it but never would.

"I'm excited to do our version of *The Russians Are Coming The Russians Are Coming*—which is an old movie versus an old TV show, which is why you won't know it, Jeff, but my dad loves it—and get the planet fired up for the aliens coming to help us defend our world against the Z'porrah's shock troops."

Jeff and Muddy both stared at me. Everyone else looked impressed. Felt very kindly toward everyone else. "Wow," Jeff said finally. "I'll take your word on it for the movie reference. But, you came up with that spin already? When did you have time? While you were falling from great height?"

"I'll be insulted later. I came up with that spin just now, thank you very much. Again, marketing hires and creates spin doctors. I realize I haven't been active in that career since we met, but, trust me, I was a natural at it."

"You are only somewhat correct," Muddy said. "Some of those fleeing are unable to help in the fight."

"Everyone can help the war effort in some way."

Jeff groaned. "It's war for certain, isn't it?"

Muddy answered before I could. "Yes. The Aicirtap will look at this planet as a, I believe the correct word is 'buffet.' And the Z'porrah will be right behind them if it looks as though they're winning."

"What about if it seems as though they're losing?"

"Then I believe they will hold off. The Z'porrah are tired of losing to you."

"Earth has done a decent job of repelling them, I guess."

"No." Muddy shook his head emphatically. "They fear *you*, Queen of the World. And those who support you. But you, most of all. They want you destroyed. They believe that with you gone, both the Earth and Alpha Centauri systems will fall easily."

"Wow, they sell everybody else really short."

He smiled. "No. They understand how effective you have been. Even now, you have formed another alliance." He indicated the Turleens surrounding us. "An alliance willing to fight by your side."

"True, baby," Jeff said. "And this is exactly what Chuck said earlier, so I don't know why you're arguing it even a bit."

"It's one thing for us to guess. It's another to have it confirmed. So to speak. All kinds of flattered, of course, but that just means I need to get moving on Mission: Get The Rest of the World Ready."

"That will take both of you," Muddy said.

We stared at him. "Just how closely have you been observing Earth?" I asked.

"Assume that she's asking that for me, as well, and in an extremely formal capacity," Jeff added.

"That does not affect my reply." Muddy shrugged. "As I have already told the Queen of the World, we have been observing, and visiting, for centuries. Not me, personally. Our lifespans are more like yours than those of the Z'porrah or the Old Ones. However, Earth has been a very interesting place to watch. There is so much otherworldly activity here. We have always had the ability to travel through space, discovered this planet millennia ago, and have enjoyed observing what goes on here in person as well as from a distance."

"I'm officially tired of being the galaxy's stealth vacation destination. How much did the Turleens meddle with our evolution?"

"Not at all!" Muddy seemed shocked I'd even asked. "Only the Old Ones and the Z'porrah have the means and the inclination to uplift. The rest of us understand and accept that."

Knew this was untrue, but then again, I was one of a handful who knew the Black Hole Universe existed.

"Really?" Jeff asked, sarcasm knob heading toward eleven. "No one else tried to affect things to their benefit? No one in all the thousands of years that intelligent life has been around?"

"Wanting to uplift and having the ability to do so are two very different things. The most non-Z'porrah or Old Ones meddling, as you call it, happened when your people came here."

Jeff looked upset. Looked at Lorraine and Claudia. Yeah, they looked upset, too. Trotted over and gave the girls a hug. Then went back to Jeff, took his hand, and gave it a squeeze. "If that's what Muddy calls meddling, I and the rest of Earth will take it, you guys."

He managed a grin and squeezed my hand back. "Thanks, baby, I just don't want to be the cause of harm to the planet that took us in."

"You haven't harmed this planet," Joseph said. "You've helped us."

"It's why we want to do a good job," Rob added. "Not that we feel that we haven't been. But you're the future. And it's a future that matters."

"As the others have said, you have not harmed this planet," Muddy said. "And I must stress again that what you hope to achieve will take you both."

"They don't want Jeff leaving the country right now. Due to all the things I'm sure you guys know from watching the Earth Channel."

"Yes, however, those reasons mean nothing now." Muddy looked at us and sighed, presumably because we all looked blank. "Galactic war is coming. The King and Queen of the World must both go forth to the lands they rule and explain why all must put aside their differences and band together."

"You know we're not really the king and queen of anything. I know you do, so don't try to play dumb, Muddy."

He smiled at me. "The Z'porrah are not a democracy. Neither are any of the planets in the Alpha Centauri system. The idea of royalty is something that our galaxy is filled with. Yes, there are plenty who are in other forms of government. However, more of those have fallen against the Z'porrah than not."

Another chance to let a big statement sit on the air. We were just chock full of this kind of luck today.

"You're insinuating that worlds with some kind of royalty in charge fare better against the Z'porrah?" Jeff asked finally.

"The numbers do not, so far, lie. Yes."

"Why?" Claudia asked.

"Possibly because when the King of the World says 'this must be done' it is done."

"He has a point," Rob said quietly.

"You're therefore also saying that when a world has a variety in charge, they're more likely to argue points of protocol, or vote for the Z'porrah's uplift than not?" Wanted to be really sure of what Muddy was telling us.

Muddy nodded. "Tur is one such planet. We fear that the other sentient races will choose the Z'porrah. The Aicirtap were, I believe you'd say, communist. The Old Ones are theocratic, but that theocracy is based on bloodline and so falls more toward royalty. The races fleeing to Earth are, for the most part, democratic, with a few that would fall into the Earth categories of socialist and communist. The Z'porrah, however, are triumvirate."

"That's not a form of government," Jeff said.

"On Earth? No, not really. However, on other worlds? Yes, it is. Three chosen or who have proven themselves in whatever ways matter. Those three make all the decisions until one dies and a replacement is found."

Thought about Operation Destruction. "Three Z'porrah came to officially tell us to surrender."

"Yes. They work in the threes in terms of leadership, both high and low. And if all three are in agreement, none under them question."

"Some do," Jeff said. "Because we have a lone Z'porrah ship heading for us, too."

"Did you read their emotions?" Muddy asked politely.

Jeff ran his hand through his hair. "How much about us do you know?"

"Much more than your enemies do."

"Let's hope. I did read them, yes. They were scared and hopeful, just like the rest of those in the ships." Jeff concentrated. "Your people aren't scared. Your people feel . . . determined. Some are exhilarated, some are angry about the attacks, some are looking forward to sightseeing. But overall, determined seems to be the Turleen feeling of the moment."

"We are determined. We will not allow the Z'porrah to win. Ever."

Realized just what Muddy and his team really were. "You're the Turleen version of Mossad or the CIA or MI6 or Navy SEALs, Army Rangers, or Marine Special Operations or similar, aren't you? The strike force that goes in first to assess the situation and make a beachhead."

"More like the Marines," Muddy said. "And Mossad."

"Have the rest of the races on Tur and in the Sirius system gotten this much intel on Earth?"

"No. We are the only ones with natural spaceflight ability. We don't share information on other races unless or until it becomes necessary."

Jeff studied Muddy. "The other races on your planet have no idea how formidable your people actually are, do they?"

"What would make you say that?" Muddy asked, with no denial in his tone.

"Might equals right a lot on our world," I answered. "Size tends to be thought of as might, as well. And they're not listening to you in regard to the Z'porrah."

Muddy spread his hands. "But we are not mighty. We are small and frail and like to spend our time in enjoyments, relaxing in the beautiful lakes and rivers of Tur, not taking part in the democratic conventions the other sentient races seem to love so much."

"None of you?" Jeff asked suspiciously. "As in, no Turleen has ever decided to get involved?"

"We have those who don't conform, of course. And in the past we were far more focused on rule. But as other races matured, we realized that we preferred to lay low, as you Earthlings put it, and just be happy in ourselves."

"I don't buy it," Jeff said flatly. "At all. Especially because of your saying you're like Marine Special Forces and Mossad combined. Those people are never just 'happy in themselves.' They're always focused, always training, always ready."

Muddy grinned. "You are far less trusting than those we share Tur with. The majority of Turleens would prefer to do as I said—stay home and enjoy the pleasures of our own abundant world. However, in order to ensure that this happens for the majority, a minority must be willing to plan and fight."

"What about the others who are coming here? How willing or able are they to fight?" Needed to know if we were really getting additional troops or just new people who wanted to hide behind us.

"As I said, some will be. Some will not be. Just as on Earth. Some of those fleeing literally cannot fight, particularly against the Aicirtap. Some are fleeing because they are pacifistic and wish to remain so."

"The Q'vox? Or, as I guess we'll think of them, the Minotaur People?"

"Yes, they are pacifistic. They dread war and will do all they can to avoid it. The few Q'vox who have chosen to become warriors have also become . . . unstable. A Q'vox who chooses to fight is a Q'vox who goes insane in some or all ways."

"Wonderful," Jeff muttered. "Anyone else coming merely to hide?"

"I assume most who are fleeing are coming to hide," Muddy said. "They are coming to Earth to ask for help, protection, and asylum. Some will choose to help you fight. Some will not."

"So people remain people wherever they are and whatever planet they happen to be from, be they Space Turtles, Naked Apes, or Cannibalistic Beetles?"

"Yes," Muddy said. "Just so. But the Space Turtle strike force is here to help you, in whatever ways we can, so that our planet can remain safe."

"And to move here if it can't, right?" Jeff asked.

Muddy shot him a wide smile. "If the King of the World will allow it, yes." He winked at me. "I believe the Queen of the World and I have already reached that agreement."

"Muddy, this is indeed the start of a beautiful friendship."

Was about to ask if Muddy had any guess for when the other ships would arrive, as well as if he had any suggestions for how we could convince almost two hundred countries to let us be in charge without them having any say, when my phone rang. And this time, it wasn't Mrs. Maurer calling.

CHAPTER 30

"A NUMBER I DON'T RECOGNIZE. What perfect freaking timing." Jeff groaned as Evalyne handed me a tracking insert. Shoved that into my phone, then answered. "Whom do I have the pleasure of speaking to at this inopportune moment?"

Buchanan had installed software on my phone that easily allowed me to record any conversation for however long it might run. Triggered that software because I was sure we'd want to record whatever opening or continuing gambit this call happened to be.

"Madame First Lady, how good it is to hear your voice." It was a man, eliminating half the population and another version of Casey at the same time. The voice was familiar, but I couldn't place who this was.

Looked at the phone number again. Nope, it wasn't one that was logged into my address book, so this wasn't Ansom Somerall, the only remaining head of Gaultier Enterprises, aka the man Amy was fighting against for control of her father's company. Somerall tended to feel that he was a ladies' man of the highest order and persisted in flirting with me whenever he called, despite receiving absolutely no encouragement in return. Some men really didn't know how to take no for an answer. But this caller wasn't him unless he was calling from a new number.

Process of elimination was going to take too long. "If I knew whose voice I was hearing I might share the happiness."

He chuckled. "I'm hurt that you don't remember me."

"I hate this game, in case you weren't sure. People who were raised right say, 'hi, this is John, may I please speak to Mary?' They don't expect the person they've called to telepathically know who they are, nor do they act butt-hurt when their dulcet tones aren't immediately recognized. So I'm now trying to think of who I know who was raised badly. That's a reasonably short list, but I'm just going to bet that when you finally tell me who you are your name will already be on said list."

"It's Amos Tobin," he said, sounding mildly offended. "And I was most certainly raised right." Tobin was a nice-looking, middle-aged black man, just starting to show some paunch around the middle, who went for a folksy look. Originally from Texas, he always wore cowboy boots, a bolo tie, and a Stetson. The boots, tie, and Stetson varied in color to match whatever he was wearing. Had no idea what color he was in right now, but if it was black, I expected a bad joke. "You know me—good guys always wear black."

And there it was. "Of course it is, you don't appear to have been, and supposedly they do." And right on time, in that sense. After all, it was his media outlets that were trying to stir up anti-alien sentiments right now. "And in case you wanted confirmation, your name was indeed on my list of rude people."

"I beg your pardon?"

"You should be so begging. Just loved your station's attack this morning." Was it only a few hours ago? Checked Mr. Watch. It was a special model that altered to whatever time zone it was in, the same as cell phones. It was now High Noon in Pueblo Caliente, meaning, yep, only a couple of hours had passed since I'd been in the LSR dealing with stress about the American Centaurion flag. How long ago and unimportant that seemed right now. "And I'm busy."

"I know, that's why I'm calling."

"Because I'm busy or to apologize?"

"Both, actually. I had no idea that my most recent media acquisition was so virulently anti-alien. Steps have already been taken and people have been fired. And if you'll allow it, I'd like to send you an apology gift, as well."

Thought about this. "You want access you know I'm not going to give you."

He chuckled again. "Well, I hope that you'll change your mind. I don't want us to be enemies, Missus Martini, if I may speak to you in a familiar way. We started off as friends, and I'd like us to remain that way."

The way Tobin was talking you'd have thought that I'd worked under him when he was building his fast food empire or something, as opposed to my having met him at the start of

Operation Infiltration, after he'd been chosen by the Board of Directors to take over YatesCorp. Considering when we'd met, and how, only an eternal optimist or a lying sack would have considered us pleasant acquaintances, let alone friends. And I knew he wasn't that level of optimistic.

I also wasn't going to willingly let him send me a "gift" that would contain bugs, bombs, or both. "No gift is necessary, and we're not chummy enough for you to get the pass to be so familiar. My friends call me Kitty. People I don't know well but who I like get to call me Missus Martini." Or White, when we were kicking butt. And Tobin was absolutely not in White's special category. "Madame First Lady will do for you right now, Mister Tobin."

"As you wish. I'd prefer that you call me Amos. It breaks my heart that strangers have caused a rift between us, but I'll be doing everything I can to repair it."

"Sure you will. Amos, what is it you actually want?"

"Other than to apologize? I'd like to ask that news crews be allowed in to interview those involved in the firefight above Pueblo Caliente."

Hit the mute button. "Jeff, how have we managed to hold off media from getting close to what's happened?"

He shot me the "really?" look. "I told you. The CIA, the FBI, Secret Service, and our Field agents. We may have evacuated Caliente Base, but we didn't all leave the area in general, and Chuck and Serene are here running point. I pulled in more Secret Service to ensure that the FBI would do what we wanted and just to have more bodies. Why are you even asking?"

"Just trying to find out what's going on that I didn't know about." Unmuted my phone. "Sorry, Amos, but right now, no press of any kind will be allowed in."

"Not even your Mister Joel Oliver or the Tastemaker?"

There was something in the way he asked that made me be very cautious in how I replied. "Why would you be asking about them specifically?" Noted the four Secret Service agents communing and looking worried and pissed.

"Oh, I just purchased the outlets they work for," he replied cheerfully. "So they now work for me. Therefore, I'm asking on their behalf if they can come in and get the scoop."

Hit mute again. "It's worse. Jeff, you need to contact MJO and Jenkins and see if they know that YatesCorp just bought their outlets. And Ev, what's going on with you guys?"

Jeff growled as he pulled his phone out and made a call.

"We can't track this," Evalyne replied. "The device is working, but it's blocked. And that should be impossible."

"Nothing, in my experience, is impossible. Check in with Chuckie and Malcolm." Unmuted and went right back to my new dear friend who appeared to have a lot of stealth under the hood. "I'm hoping you're about to give both men a raise, Amos. They're the best."

"Well, if increasing their salaries would make you feel more kindly toward me, consider it done."

"That was an off-the-cuff comment, Amos, not my asking for a bribe in any way, shape, or form. Frankly, I'm sure every employee you have could use a pay increase and more paid time off." If he was going to try to trap me then I was going to go all *Norma Rae* on him. "I think it's time big business stopped treating its employees like cogs in a wheel. Corporations aren't people—people are what make up corporations."

"If you say so." He didn't sound nearly as happy. Presumed he was recording this call, too, and while he could take me out of context, since I was also recording, he'd lose that battle. Assumed he was assuming I was recording as well. Stopped this line of thought before it made my head hurt.

"I do. Raises for all, not just top management. All the way up and down every business you own, from the top dudes and dudettes down to the people doing the worst-paid jobs and all stops in between. Everyone gets more than a cost-of-living increase and more paid time off, regardless of who they are."

"Ah, while I applaud your support of the working man and woman, why do you want me to do that?"

Ensured I sounded shocked and completely sweet. "Why, so that I know that you only have this country's best interests at heart. Our country is only as strong and prosperous as her people, Amos. You know that."

"I was hoping to serve the war effort in other ways."

War effort. Meaning he knew that there had been some kind of fight between armed forces here. And/or that he knew that we had aliens arriving. No time like the present to find out.

"What war are you referring to?"

"The one that just began."

Not enough to go on. "Which one is that?"

"The one that started over your hometown when foreign forces attacked an American Centaurion base."

Hit mute again. "Lorraine, need to know if the dudes in the Apaches were foreign or not." She nodded and made a call. Claudia started texting. Unmuted. "Amos, my understanding was that the attack was perpetrated by our homegrown terrorists, Club Fifty-One True Believers."

"Ah, how interesting. But, you see, no one is allowed in, so we can't verify that. Or anything else."

We were playing verbal chess, and he'd just moved his piece and called check.

Jeff nudged me. "Oliver and Jenkins have no idea and are verifying what's going on."

"James and Malcolm both confirm that the DUI Dudes and the living crews from this attack are working for Club Fifty-One True Believers," Lorraine said.

"I've verified that we have no interference," Claudia added. "The tracker should be working. Dulce shows the tracker to be online and functioning, it's just not getting any readings."

So much information, so little of it helpful to my current situation. "Amos, the people in charge do feel that the attacks were perpetrated by Club Fifty-One True Believers. You can roll with that story. Otherwise, they don't feel that press will be helpful at this time."

"So you're saying that the Office of the President doesn't want press in at this time?"

Damn, he was good at this. Better than Somerall. I'd had no issues diverting and ignoring Somerall. The YatesCorp Board of Directors had chosen really well when they'd picked Tobin.

"No, the Office of the President is not in charge of specific battles, skirmishes, and so forth. The CIA, FBI, and local law enforcement are on the scene. We need to bow to their authority since this is their bailiwick."

"Ah, I do understand. Tell me, though—out of the CIA, FBI, local law enforcement, Centaurion Division, and the Office of the President, who has the authority over the new aliens who just arrived?"

Checkmate.

CHAPTER 31

TIME TO ONCE AGAIN follow my father's advice of avoiding answering a question with a question of your own. "Amos, if I may ask, where are you located right now?"

"Me? I'm in D.C."

"In which case, I'd like to know your thoughts on the fact that a D.C.P.D. precinct was blown up earlier today."

Silence. Possibly Tobin was hitting mute to ask his cronies or advisors what to say.

Hit mute myself. "I need Chuckie here, faster than fast."

Claudia zipped off at hyperspeed while Lorraine sent a text. Claudia was back with Chuckie, Reader, and Tim in three seconds. Christopher arrived immediately after, asking Lorraine what was going on and why she'd asked him to get here ASAP. Sadly, Tobin came back to our call as they arrived, so I had no time to share. Indicated that the others should share what they knew amongst each other. Jeff and Muddy did most of the talking, albeit quietly.

"Are you saying that the bombing was done by aliens?" Tobin asked.

"Hardly, Amos. The bombing, like the attack, was done by Club Fifty-One True Believers."

"He's friendly with Gutermuth," Chuckie said quietly.

Nodded and spoke again before Tobin had a chance to reply. "Harvey Gutermuth and Farley Pecker are friends of yours, aren't they, Amos?"

"Well, I'm friendly with a lot of people," Tobin said in that backpedaling way so near and dear to most politicians' hearts. Wasn't sure who'd learned it first, captains of industry or captains of countries, but the effect was the same. Prepped myself to start hearing a lot of BS.

"True enough. But I'd like to know where you stand in terms of your relationship with Gutermuth, Pecker, Pecker's church, and Gutermuth's anti-alien organization. And I'd like to know now, and in exact detail."

Hit mute because I'd managed to salvage my chess match with a pawn and now was the time to put all my sales training into effect. Once the offer was made, the question asked, or the definitive statement stated, whoever talked next lost. I was not about to talk next.

To Tobin. To the others, hell yeah, I was going to talk.

Everyone was caught up with what was going on with the Turleens and all the other alien races coming to hide, help, or eat, so it was time to get caught up on everything else. Double-checked that the phone was on mute. It was. And presumably Tobin was, unlike most of his cronies, trained in the same sales technique I was and was no more willing to lose than I was.

"All prisoners are at Guantanamo now," Reader said. "We used a floater to get them there, and the flyboys did the escort. Your Uncle Mort is there, too. The flyboys will join us here once the handoff is officially complete."

"Good, that should mean our homegrown terrorists will be having the Worst Day Ever. Is Serene alone at the scene, though?"

"No," Claudia said. "She called in troubadours and they're assisting Field agents along with all the CIA and FBI agents and local law. She's got it under control."

"Caliente Base is completely cleared," Christopher shared. "Looks like minimal damage, though there is some. It'll take the Operations Team to fully determine what needs fixing and what doesn't."

"Tobin is still not responding?" Chuckie asked. "It's been at least two minutes since you stopped talking."

"Nope. And the call is still live." Triple-checked. "And still on mute."

Chuckie rubbed the back of his neck. "I'm not used to any-one outlasting you, Kitty. Are we sure he's not dead?"

"No, but I'm sure I don't care."

"He said he was in D.C.?" Christopher asked slowly.

"Yeah, why?"

"Media centers are New York and L.A. If he just took over

Oliver's paper, they're L.A. based. Jenkins is syndicated out of New York, but they have a satellite office in L.A., too." Christopher looked thoughtful. "And they're not the only ones."

"Meaning Tobin was lying and is in California. What does that mean or matter?"

"Means I'll be right back." Christopher zoomed off.

"What is he doing?" I asked in general.

Jeff sighed. "Give him his moment in the sun."

"Not trying to deny him sun moments, Jeff. Just have no idea what he's thinking."

"I'm sure it's relevant," Reader said. "I'm also sure he's gone to California."

"Guess we have time to wait," Tim said.

"He can run around the world without any issues these days," I pointed out.

"Your people are most amazing," Muddy said politely. "So many things you can do that others cannot." Pondered why he was saying this at this precise time. Muddy might look cute and goofy but that was an act, his race's protective coloration. Muddy was quite sharp, and he reminded me a lot of White, meaning he wasn't saying anything without a reason.

"Thanks," Jeff said. "We try."

"You succeed," Phoebe said. "And since we're waiting for whatever we're waiting for, I have to mention that once again being saved by the people we're supposed to be protecting is, at best, humiliating."

"Yeah, I've given up feeling that I can ever be good at my job again," Joseph agreed. Evalyne and Rob both nodded emphatically.

"Apparently any alien can do more than a human," Evalyne added.

Rob looked at me. "Well, a normal human."

Felt bad that, once again, we were making these people feel inferior. "Inferiority." Looked at Muddy. "That's going to be the issue we have to deal with."

"I don't follow you," Muddy said.

Wasn't sure that this was true—in fact was willing to bet he'd started this particular conversation to lead us right to this conclusion—but chose not to argue. "Humans feel inferior to most aliens. That's the underlying emotion behind all the anti-alien groups—they fear that the aliens are better than them."

"They're better looking," Tim said dryly. "Some of us learn to live with it."

"And some adapt," Lorraine said, pointedly looking at me.

"Didn't really have much of a choice in that."

"Why hasn't Amy mutated?" Claudia asked. Everyone looked at her. "What? I figured we were just hanging out, waiting to see who blinks first between Kitty and Tobin, discussing inferiority issues and adaptation. I can't be the only one wondering."

"You're not," Chuckie said. "I have a theory but I haven't been able to speak to the people who would be able to confirm it."

"Who can't you reach?" I asked.

Chuckie shook his head and sighed. "You were there, with me and Christopher, and you're asking?"

Considered this. "Oh. You mean you want to talk to one of the katyhoppers on Beta Eight."

"Yes. But I think my theory is sound, even if we don't get to confirm it with Boz or the others."

"And that theory is?" Jeff asked, Commander in Chief Voice on Full.

Chuckie rolled his eyes, but before he could answer his phone rang. "It's Christopher," he told us as he answered. "What's up? Oh? Really?" Chuckie's eyes narrowed. He reached out, took my phone from me, and hung up the call. "Yes, you're authorized. Consider yourself an official CIA consultant and an official agent should anyone ask. See you shortly." He hung up, eyes flashing.

"Do we want to know?" I asked.

"Well, Christopher's hunch paid off. Tobin wasn't in D.C. but in Los Angeles. Not at the headquarters for where Oliver works but at the YatesCorp offices that are right next door."

"Why did I hang up on him?"

"Because he was tracking the call. That's why he was willing to play the 'don't speak' game—the longer you were on the phone, the more accurately he could pinpoint our location. And, as we already knew, he was also blocking his location, via some very sophisticated equipment."

"I should have thought of that."

"No," Reader said. "That's not your job. It's mine."

"Frankly," Evalyne said, "it's also ours."

Chuckie rolled his eyes again. "Stop it with the blame game. I'm the Director of the CIA now. Seriously, if we want Jeff to be angry with someone, choose me."

"I'm angry with Tobin, not anyone here," Jeff said. "What did you authorize Christopher to do?"

"Arrest Tobin on charges of wiretapping the First Lady. And to confiscate all of his surveillance and scrambling equipment."

"That's a serious charge," Joseph said.

"As I recall, it's along the lines of treason. And that should carry a penalty with it." I sincerely hoped, at any rate.

"Not that we're saying he doesn't deserve to be brought up on that charge," Rob added.

"Glad we're all in agreement. Was Tobin alone, do you know?"

"Christopher didn't say," Chuckie said, "but he'd called in Field agents. We have every Centaurion base in the world on high alert right now. He didn't have to wait long."

"Where did Christopher take Tobin?" I asked Chuckie.

"Why?" Jeff countered.

"Because he wasn't in on the Blow Up Caliente Base Plan, which is probably more of a Blow Up Kitty Wherever She May Be Plan, so I'm curious as to what his game is. As in, is there more to it than just whipping up the ol' anti-alien frenzy or trying to accuse Lizzie of being a teenaged terrorist?"

"Oh, good point," Chuckie said.

"I'm not following it." Jeff heaved a sigh. "Explain what you mean. And someone find out where Christopher's taken Tobin. And anything else we actually might need to know." Claudia, Lorraine, Reader, and Tim nodded and all started texting. Apparently not to be outdone, the Secret Service agents started texting, too.

"Tobin was tracing my phone to find out where I was. If he was part of the Club Fifty-One True Believers plan, then he'd know already. There's no logical reason for him to try to track me if he's a part of it, because even if they were trying to send a specific bomb to blow us all up, they already freaking know where we are."

"You should be back in the White House," Joseph pointed out, still texting.

"Yeah, but let's be real. If Tobin has been doing what the rest of our enemies have—you know, memorizing our playbook— then there's no way he'd expect me to be back in the White House. Any of us, really."

"So he wasn't a part of this attack, he's just taking advantage of the situation," Jeff said. "Which sounds like the usual multiple plans going against us at the same time."

"Alien invasion, Club Fifty-One True Believer attack, and one of the Land Sharks making a move. Sounds like Wednesday."

Claudia snorted. "True enough. I win the Christopher lottery. He hasn't taken Tobin anywhere—he's concerned that Tobin's got hidden tracking on his person or equipment and Christopher doesn't want our locations given away."

"I wasn't trying to win," Reader said. "I was anticipating where to tell Christopher to either take or move Tobin to. Have him brought here, to Caliente Base. It's already been breached, Christopher confirmed it as deserted, and the damage was minimal."

"And I was telling my team to not come here but to go help Christopher," Tim added. "The flyboys are already with him. Floater gates are great."

"And I told Malcolm what's going on so he's not flying blind," Lorraine said. "He's back on-site here at Caliente Base, with Manfred and Siler, since your Uncle Mort's cut them loose."

"I've confirmed that the children are all safe, including Lizzie," Phoebe said. "I'm keeping day shift with them and have pulled in night teams as well. Your father is with them, too, Kitty."

"White House and Embassy are secured and have shielding up," Joseph said.

"Have advised the head of the P.T.C.U. of what the current situations are, including that we're taking Amos Tobin in for questioning in regard to espionage," Evalyne shared.

"I've also advised Kevin Lewis of our situation," Rob added. "He's running point at Dulce."

"See? Everyone has a part to play." Eyed Muddy. "That's what we're going to need to do, isn't it? Convince almost two hundred countries that each of them has an important role in our brave new world."

"Possibly," he said. "Many of you move fast, but you may not have time."

"Do we have time to question Amos Tobin?"

"Probably not," Chuckie said looking at his phone. "Because I think it's time for the two of you to be seen here."

"Why so?" Jeff asked.

"Because Serene just told me to get the two of you and your very obvious Secret Service details to her." He gave us a weak grin. "It's time for your close-ups."

"Should I change clothes?"

"No," Claudia said. "Raj just told me that the production company that wants to make Code Name: First Lady has asked for a meet and greet with you and the, ah, steampunk turtles."

"I'd suggest brushing your hair, though," Muddy offered. "Unless the windblown look is one you're happy with."

Heaved a sigh while I dug my brush out of my purse. "Christopher, tell your dad we need him here, pronto."

"Why?" Christopher asked, as he dialed. "For his diplomatic skills? Or because Paul is still at the religious summit?"

"Oh, all those things and more besides, I'm sure. But mainly because I really want him to meet Muddy. I think I've just found Richard's new best friend."

CHAPTER 32

THE LESS SAID about our time with the press the better. Thankfully, when you're the President of the United States, you don't actually have to answer any questions you don't want to—well, as long as you have someone running interference.

Since we had Serene and her team on-site, they did most of the reporter wrangling, which meant that we had troubadours influencing everyone, so things went far better than we probably had a right to have hoped for.

The questions were just what you'd expect—were we being invaded, were we being attacked by terrorists, what were the terrorists aiming for, why were the President and First Lady in Arizona—but troubadours were made for this kind of thing. My press secretary was at Dulce and Jeff's was in D.C., but Serene and her team were great, and we were actually able to get out by merely having Jeff say that there had been an anti-alien attack, confirmed to have been perpetrated by Club 51 True Believers, confirmed that we were on-site because we were taking the threat very seriously, and that was all we could share at the moment. It didn't satisfy the press, but it was good enough for government work.

The Hollywood contingent were harder to shake off. How they'd gotten here so fast was a question I'd answered for myself when I saw several helicopters parked in the near distance, including one that had this production company's name emblazoned on its side.

However, the phrase "call my agent" still worked, and once I'd shouted it at them enough, they backed off, and then we took off, though sadly not at hyperspeed.

We'd chosen to have everyone else, Turleens especially, go

into Caliente Base to wait for us. So it was just me, Jeff, Serene, a whole herd of Field agents, and all the Secret Service agents one could ever want. Meaning that the moment we were done answering the press evasively and putting the Hollywood types onto the scent of an agent I didn't possess, the Secret Service did one of the things that they did best and hustled us away from the madding crowd while keeping said crowd away from us.

The Secret Service was better at this than the Field agents, in part because they had no compunctions about pushing someone out of the way, and in other part because they couldn't use hyperspeed, no matter how much they might have wanted to. In most cases, this wasn't great. However, when you needed to be seen leaving in a protected manner, it was spot on.

We headed back to the "attack site" and went into Caliente Base. In addition to all those who'd been on the ground with us already, Viola, Carmine, and Romeo were back on-site, to go over their Base for damage and so forth. Our K-9 squad was back, too, because there was no way they were missing this. Plus, Prince, Riley, and Duke had missed me.

Tobin had apparently been working alone, because Christopher and his team hadn't found anyone else with him in his private office at the YatesCorp location, and if he had accomplices he was the only bad guy I'd met who wasn't willing to throw them under the bus to save himself.

He'd been brought here as requested, meaning it was time for us to do the old Good Cop, Bad Cop, Oh My God Cop routine. In the olden days, Jeff and I would have been involved with this. However, it wasn't a great PR move to have the President involved in interrogations and, sadly, the same went for the First Lady. This gig took all the fun out of things.

On the other hand, PR said it was A-okay for the Top Man and His Woman to watch from a vantage point that the prisoner couldn't see. Caliente Base hadn't had a police-style interrogation setup before today, but it was amazing how fast A-Cs could put that kind of thing together, especially with input and assistance from the K-9 unit.

One big fishbowl conference room—one of the few with two entrances—was divided into sections. A third was given to the interrogation side, two-thirds to the watch and listen in secret side. Considering how many people and dogs we had on the watch and listen side, this was a wise choice.

The interrogation side was blacked out or, as I thought of it, the fishbowl had been made hella dirty. One-way glass divided the sections. Had to figure this was one of the nicest interrogation setups around. The chairs were certainly the cushiest, and I had that confirmed by Melville.

Chuckie, Reader, and Tim were doing the interrogation. We'd also scored the *Matrix*-style earpieces, courtesy of the Secret Service. So, Chuckie, Reader, and Tim could hear what Jeff, I, White—who'd come over as requested—Lorraine, Claudia, the flyboys, Buchanan, Siler, the K-9 team, the Secret Service, and Muddy were saying to them or each other. Jeff in particular, since he would be reading Tobin's emotions.

We'd included Muddy because he was both interested and might have a viewpoint that would be helpful. We'd also promised the guys on the interrogation side that we'd talk softly because the earpieces were small, shoved into their ear canals, and extremely good, meaning a whisper would sound like a normal voice and a shout would cause them all to scream in pain.

The usual interrogation pleasantries began. Tobin didn't seem worried, or afraid, or even angry, which I found both interesting and worrisome. Jeff confirmed that Tobin was, overall, calm, with a bit of amusement and even a little glee here and there. Tobin had been searched for trackers and emotional blockers and overlays and been declared clean, but that didn't mean that he really was.

"I'm getting the right range of emotions," Jeff said while Chuckie and Reader paced around the room and Tim sat opposite Tobin. "So if he's got an emotional overlay on, it's the next generation, because he feels right. Unworried and unafraid, but otherwise, he's got the normal gamut of emotions going on."

Tim had the Good Cop role and—after Jeff had confirmed Tobin's emotional state, and Chuckie had then outlined the crimes that Tobin had committed, and their accompanying penalties—he started in.

"Look, Mister Tobin, we just want to know why you were trying to track and trace the First Lady."

Tobin shrugged. "I wasn't. That equipment was planted by your agents."

"Lying," Jeff said instantly. "Unconcerned about it, unconcerned if it will be traced back to him, too."

"Now, why would anyone, let alone any of us, do that?" Tim asked.

"I have no idea," Tobin said. "But I assume it's to hide that you're bringing in dangerous aliens to do some sort of world-wide coup."

Looked at Jeff. "I seriously want to know where he's getting this idea. It can't be from Muddy and his people. They don't look threatening."

"Could he have seen the others who are coming?" Muddy asked.

"It's possible," Jeff said. "But highly unlikely."

"Unless he has an alien helping him." Everyone in my room looked at me.

Jeff nodded. "Tobin firmly believes what he just said. That wasn't a fishing question—he feels that he knows."

"Oh, wow. Um, Chuckie? Go for the 'who's giving you this intel' line of questioning, because I'm betting that some or all of our A-C traitors may be working with Tobin."

"Now," Chuckie growled, "why would you think that?"

Tobin shrugged again. "There are aliens all over. We know it. The President tells us aliens were what attacked at Camp David last month. So, what's to stop you from bringing in more aliens to combat them?"

"That sounds suspiciously like he's trying to pretend he'd support that idea," Claudia said.

"I think that spin would be a bad tactic for us to use," Lorraine countered. "Though I'm sure Tobin would love us to give him something that big to work with."

"He's trying to lead Chuck, to make Chuck give something away," Jeff said. "Tobin doesn't feel that he knows that this is why aliens are coming, he's just guessing."

"Despite Claudia and Lorraine's concerns, that could be a good reason for us to allow the refugees safe haven, Jeffrey," White said.

"Only not all will be in a position to fight," Muddy pointed out for those new to this news.

"Why would you think we need to do that?" Reader asked Tobin.

Tobin rolled his eyes. "We needed to do that the last time we were invaded. Why would this time be any different?"

"Just what kind of telephone system do you think we have?" Tim asked with a grin.

Tobin chuckled. "One good enough to bring a boatload of aliens here who are still sticking around."

"He means the Planetary Council," I said, "and don't anyone

say 'duh.' Someone remind him that those aliens came to welcome us into the Galactic Community."

"Duh," Jeff said quietly. I shot him a glare and he shot me a
very sexy grin. Decided to forgive him for the duh. "Kitty's
right, that's exactly who Tobin's thinking of. And he's aware that
we view them as friends. Interestingly, he's not feeling that
they're enemies—it's just something to use against us."

While Jeff was doing his explanation, Reader shared what I'd
asked. Tobin didn't look impressed. "Or they came to plot with
you against us," he said dismissively.

"You know that's not true," Tim said.

Tobin shook his head. "No, son, I don't know that. All I know
is that you all consort with any and all aliens and leave the regular humans out."

"That's real," Jeff said. "He's jealous that he's not in our inner circle."

"I feel the love. Not my fault he hasn't done anything to earn
our trust."

"I'm a regular human," Tim said. "So is Thomas Kendrick.
Neither one of us are left out."

"Thomas drank your Kool-Aid."

"Just what is that supposed to mean?" Reader asked.

"I mean you're trying to take this world away from the humans and give it to aliens. Any alien, as long as they're not a
human."

"He means it," Jeff said.

"Sounds like the typical Club Fifty-One True Believers rhet-
oric," Chuckie said. "So, you're basically one of our homegrown
terrorists. You were tracking the First Lady to try to finish what
your cronies started—her assassination."

"No one else speak," I said urgently. "That's the definitive
statement." Tim grinned, Reader rolled his eyes at me, and
Chuckie didn't react. But none of them spoke.

Tobin didn't stay silent too long. Well, at least not in comparison to how long he'd stayed silent before. A good thirty seconds
passed—during which time Chuckie looked deadly, Tim looked
bored, and Reader looked pissed—before he finally spoke.

"No."

Jeff grunted. "He doesn't want to kill Kitty. At least emotionally she's not a target. He feels . . . amused by the idea."

Chuckie rolled his eyes. "Right." He looked at Reader. "Tell the cops we'll be taking this one. I presume he was involved with the attack on the precinct, too."

"I have rights," Tobin said.

Chuckie got right in his face. "Not in this room, you don't. You've been involved in a terrorist attack on American soil and American targets, as well as on American Centaurion soil and American Centaurion targets. News flash—that makes you a terrorist. There will be a fight between the CIA, the FBI, and Homeland Security for which Agency gets to grill you. I'm betting we'll play nicely together and share the love, though. Because you and your lunatic friends attacking our President and our First Lady under the nauseating purity of the race idea just moved you up to Public Enemy Number One."

Tobin snorted. "I'm not a terrorist, son. And you can't disappear me—I'm a powerful public figure."

"We can," I said. "YatesCorp has the Bloodline Clause. And we have several people who can prove blood ties to Ronald Yates. All we have to do is announce that we've found Yates progeny and the Board will have to be focused on that."

Chuckie smirked. "Really? Well, I hope you can prove that you're related to Ronald Yates, then."

Tobin blinked. "Excuse me?"

Jeff sat up. "That has his attention and, for the first time, he's worried."

"YatesCorp has an interesting clause in its governing documents," Chuckie said. "All someone has to do in order to take a full seat on the board, with all the salary and rights and so forth, is to prove a genetic connection to Ronald Yates. Now, you're not going to sit there and tell me that you don't know about that."

"I have no idea—"

"Bull," Reader said. "There's no way you don't know about it. You're not trying to stop a supposed alien invasion. You're trying to remove anyone you think might have a blood tie to Ronald Yates."

Looked at Jeff. "Starting with you."

CHAPTER 33

THAT TOBIN HAD AN ULTERIOR MOTIVE wasn't a shock. That it hadn't dawned on us before that he'd probably be looking to protect his interests was the shocker.

There were a lot of people with provable Yates bloodline out there. All the Martini clan other than Alfred and the men who'd married Jeff's sisters, due to Jeff's mother, Lucinda. All the White clan other than Amy. Serene and her son, Patrick. Mahin Sherazi, who was a hybrid. Siler, if his DNA hadn't been too altered by his parents. Nerida Alfero and any other hybrid Crazy Eights or Yates Family Players that might still be alive. Heck, even the Ronaldo Al Dejahl clone who was on Beta Eight, aka Ronaldo 2.0, probably could make a claim that would stick. Basically, there was a lot of competition for board seats, and it would make sense that said board would be fully in support of Tobin ensuring that there was no competition left alive.

But it wouldn't take all of them. It would only take Jeff. Because if the President of the United States was now on the Yates-Corp board and shared that he didn't care for the dude running the corporation, then said dude would be out faster than Tobin could utter one of his folksy sayings.

And if the President couldn't serve due to the requirements of office, well then, his uncle and cousin certainly could. Meaning Christopher and White were also on the Assassination Roll Call List.

Missed the Dingo and Surly Vic fiercely right now. Because they'd have known what was going on and either stopped it or told me how to protect against it.

"How would my talking to the First Lady have any bearing

on this?" Tobin asked, shaking me out of my mourning for my dead "uncles."

"All assassination requests against you and yours are still being ignored by the community," Siler said to me, speaking softly. "I don't know how long that will last, but for right now, there's no assassin that would take a hit on you or anyone else you care about for fear of retaliation. And the Cuban Mob was schooled and has decided that you're far more work to kill than you're worth."

"I feel the love."

"You weren't talking to her," Reader snarled. "You were tracking her. And you were tracking her with intent to harm."

"Now, son, there's no way you can prove that. And it's untrue as well. And, under these antagonistic circumstances, I'm not saying anything more without my legal team present."

"James is dead on," I said to the room and earpieces at large. "Tobin's trying to get rid of Jeff, and anyone else he thinks might have a Yates blood tie, in a believable fashion. And nothing's more believable than a terrorist attack, particularly one started by the Club Fifty-One Loons."

"We can't prove it," Jeff pointed out. "And I can feel him clearly—he's not going to say another word to Chuck, James, or Tim."

"We don't need to prove anything right now. Suspicion of terrorist activity is more than enough for Chuckie to do exactly what he said he'd do. What I want to know is this—how did Tobin know that Jeff was a direct descendent of Ronald Yates?"

"Aren't you making a leap with this?" Jeff asked. "That he's trying to kill me or knows who is or isn't related to dear old granddad, I mean."

"Does he even know Yates was an A-C?" Christopher asked.

"No idea. But my so-called women's intuition is insisting that he likely does."

"Stephanie might have said something," Lorraine added.

Claudia nodded. "Or someone else. We just said that Tobin might be getting his intel from others. What if it's not from an A-C but from a former human agent, one of those loyal to the former Diplomatic Corps?"

"The girls have good points, Jeff, and besides, I know I'm right—Tobin's figured out that the most potent risk to his keeping his position at YatesCorp is you."

Jeff sighed. "You're rarely wrong."

"True enough. Chuckie, we need to know why Tobin thinks an invasion is coming as well as how he knows that Jeff is part of the Yates bloodline. Without, of course, confirming for him that Jeff or anyone else is indeed part of that bloodline."

Chuckie tried. So did Reader. So did Tim. But Jeff had called it right—Tobin wouldn't speak.

"Guys, let him sit for a while and come into the room with us." Once again everyone looked at me. Shrugged. "It's a standard cop show tactic."

Chuckie shot me the "really?" look, but the three of them left Tobin handcuffed to the table and joined the rest of us as requested.

"He's not going to crack," Jeff said when they joined us. "He's got a very strong will, and he's unwilling to talk to any of you anymore. And he doesn't want to talk to an alien, either."

Considered our options. Decided they were few and the one I wanted to go for was the right one. "Then let me talk to him."

Mouths opened. Put up the paw. Mouths shut. Enjoyed my FLOTUS Power for a moment. "Regardless of anything else, the person he called was me. The weak link is presumed by our enemies to be me. So, let me do one of the many things I do best."

Jeff didn't look happy. "I don't like it," he muttered.

"He can't hurt me," I pointed out. "He's shackled to the table and, besides, I'm more than capable of taking him. And we're loaded with Secret Service and Field agents burning to be of service."

"I don't want you going in there alone," Jeff said.

"He's not going to talk with other people in the room. Is he aware the rest of us are watching?"

Jeff concentrated. "He feels he's being watched, so yes."

"Fine. Then let's move him to another location."

"He's going to feel he's being watched anywhere you put him," Tim pointed out.

"Possibly. But not if we switch it around and put him in this side of the interrogation chamber."

"I don't want him observing us," Jeff said dryly. "If that's okay with you and all."

"So picky. Fine, then all of you wait elsewhere. But bring Tobin in here. Jeff, I'll pretend to be Mister Smith and use an earpiece, you can all be on a group call nearby and feed me intel, but I really want to know what he's thinking."

"The room's set up for this," Reader confirmed. "We keep Secret Service and Field outside the conference room, we all go to Imageering and observe. We'll have the Secret Service ensure that Tobin sees we're gone when he's brought to Kitty."

"I don't want her alone in here, period," Jeff said, Commander in Chief Voice going strong. "I realize he isn't armed, but since we have androids and robots running around all over the place, call me a caveman but I don't want my wife left alone with someone who could attack her or worse."

"Oh, I won't be alone." Reached down and petted Prince. "I'll have three big German Shepherds right here with me."

Prince nudged up against Jeff, who sighed and petted him. "Fine, I'll trust you all on this. Because we either need to get Tobin's information, arrest him, and therefore let him advise his legal counsel, or let him go. We can't take too much more time with this—we have a world to warn and prep."

"And he seems far too aware of that, so, barring Chuckie having truth serum on hand, I think we need to try my plan."

"I'm far more willing to take Tobin to Guantanamo than I am to give him sodium pentothal, and I'm less willing to let him lawyer up, so while I share Jeff's concerns, I think Kitty's track record says we give her interrogation skills a shot."

"Just don't do a lap dance this time," Tim said with a grin.

"Oh, that was so Operation Drug Addict ago, Megalomaniac Lad. I have a different approach in mind."

"And that is?" Jeff asked, sounding and looking unamused.

"I plan to fight folksy with folksy." And then I'd play hardball, but that didn't need to be said aloud.

Jeff and Chuckie both groaned. "I can see so many ways this can go wrong," Chuckie said.

White chuckled. "Or, as we call it, Charles, routine."

CHAPTER 34

"I BELIEVE THAT I RESENT all your insinuations." Definitely not the time to tell them that I was going to play hardball sooner as opposed to later. They wanted a show, they'd get a show.

"This I gotta see," Jerry said. The rest of the flyboys indicated that they were looking for popcorn and front row seats as well. Chose to feel that they were being supportive, but it took effort.

Despite Jeff's begging for ideas to the contrary, no one could come up with a better option for how to get Tobin to talk again, so I was given my *Matrix* earpiece and everyone other than Prince, Duke, and Riley trotted off. Tobin was unshackled and brought in to me. The Secret Service agents tried to shackle him again, but I stopped them.

"You're not worried I'll attack you?" Tobin asked, sarcasm knob definitely at eleven and threatening to go higher.

Shrugged as I waved the Secret Service out of the room. Then I patted Prince's head. "I have protection if you try anything funny."

"Yes, I've heard how fond of animals you are." Tobin seated himself next to me. "And as they say, money can't earn the wag of a dog's tail."

"True enough. I tend to feel that dogs are a good judge of character." Well, Prince, Duke, and Riley were. Our dogs, the ones we'd inherited when my parents had moved to D.C. and into a no pets building, were not nearly so picky. All Tobin would have needed to do to get three out of four of them into his lap was offer a doggy treat of any kind.

On cue, Prince growled softly at Tobin. Who patted his head

without seeming to have any concern. "He's a good dog, guarding his mistress."

"These aren't my dogs. These are trained police officers."

Tobin chuckled. "Doesn't mean they don't think that, when push comes to shove, you're theirs and vice versa."

"I can't speak for the dogs," Jeff said in my ear, "but Tobin is far more relaxed with you. Still on his guard, but this is exactly what he wanted, to sit down with you. Stay sharp, baby, he's smarter than the average enemy you have to confront."

Apparently it was time to move on from the small talk. "I'm curious, Amos."

Tobin stared at me. "Beg pardon?" he asked finally.

"I'm curious about what in the world is going on. Why did you call me?" He opened his mouth. Put up the paw. He shut his mouth. Wondered if all the other First Ladies had enjoyed this power as much as me. "Don't tell me you wanted to chat, Amos. We both know that's a lie, and if you want to be my friend, you won't lie to me. You were tracking me. Why?"

"I was concerned for your safety."

Managed not to roll my eyes. "You're a hugely successful businessman who has literally no experience in espionage. And yet, here you are, at the middle of a huge conspiracy and, frankly, looking at a frightening few months wherein you're taken to a hole in the ground and the YatesCorp Board finds your replacement and then forgets about you. I'm curious as to how you got here. I didn't figure you for a Don Quixote type."

"His worry spiked," Jeff said. This earpiece thing was working nicely. "He hadn't considered the option you just raised."

"I'm not tilting at windmills, Madame First Lady, and you know it. I know you'll do whatever you need to in order to protect your husband, whether he's right or wrong."

"Where is my husband wrong?"

Tobin shrugged. "I understand why the A-Cs are here. But having one as President is too much."

Leaned back and crossed one leg over the other. "Interesting viewpoint, coming from a black man."

"My race has nothing to do with this."

"He's telling the truth as he sees it," Jeff shared. "He's honestly worried that aliens are going to replace humans on this planet."

"Which is a legitimate concern," Chuckie added. "Be careful what you share, Kitty."

"Actually, it does," I said to Tobin. "Because race is about to become a thing of the past. We're all humans and we'd all better act like it, sooner as opposed to later."

"And I point out that the president isn't a human."

"You sound like Gutermuth and Pecker."

Tobin shook his head. "I understand why you'd think that. But I don't hate aliens."

"You just want them kept 'in their place,' right? You know, like blacks, Jews, women, gays, and so on. Or you want them to leave the planet. But only if they leave all the things they do for us and gave us that help us. Those you want sticking around." Didn't even try to keep the disgust out of my tone.

"No, that's not what I want."

"Oh, sorry, forgot who you like to hang out with. What you actually want is to control the A-Cs and, barring *that*, you want them enslaved or killed."

"I am not your enemy, young lady."

"He's mad," Jeff said. "He started getting angry when you compared him to Pecker—though not Gutermuth, which is probably significant—and he's gotten angrier as you've continued to speak."

"Well, old man, you haven't exactly acted like our friend."

Tobin's jaw dropped. "What did you call me?"

"Old man. Seemed appropriate since you called me young lady. I presume that was to put me in *my* place, but, in case you haven't been paying attention, I don't cave for that crap." Leaned forward, while the three dogs did the low growl thing. "Understand me, *Mister* Tobin. I am the First Lady of these United States and you will treat me and my husband, your President, with respect, or I will personally ensure that I find every single person in the galaxy with Ronald Yates' genetics and get them all onto the YatesCorp Board. And then I'll next ensure that they remove you and the rest of the Board in a New York Minute."

Got and held eye contact with him. Time to see if he was up to Mom and Chuckie's standards. He was good at the Stare Contest Game, but Rage had joined my party and there was no way I was blinking first.

Sure enough, Tobin finally blinked. Then he leaned back. "I see that everyone's sold you quite short."

"Yeah, it's got to be hard for you to have that Come to Jesus Moment wherein you discover I'm not the weak link." Narrowed my eyes. "In fact, you might want to consider just who you're screwing with and rethink your various strategies."

Jeff chuckled in my ear. "Yes, he's reassessing you as fast as he can. He's also impressed. He wasn't before, but he is now."

"Who *am* I screwing with?" Tobin asked.

"Self-control," Chuckie said urgently. Knew he didn't want me to share anything key, such as the fact that I was the person responsible for Ronald Yates' death. Sure, Mephistopheles had let Yates die so Mephs could try to move to me, but that was likely nuance I had neither time nor inclination to share.

"The woman who can send you into the darkest hole you can imagine, or who can ensure you get to continue doing whatever it is you actually do."

"You're threatening me," Tobin said mildly.

"No. 'I'm going to rip your balls off and shove them down your throat if you ever try to track me again' is a threat. Stating reality isn't threatening, it's sharing the full situation."

"Where is Janelle Gardiner?" Tobin asked. Presumably to throw me off my game.

But since I actually knew where she was, this wasn't derailing but merely intriguing. "Somewhere safe. Which I'm sure will disappoint the hell out of Ansom Somerall."

"He's not trying to throw you so much as he really wants to know if she's alright," Jeff said. "And his reaction when you mentioned Somerall is interesting—Tobin doesn't like Somerall. At all."

Tobin's eyes flashed. "Just what did you do to her?"

"He's emotional, for the first time," Jeff said. "It's complicated, but, I think . . ."

"You're in love with Janelle, aren't you?" I asked.

Tobin stared at me. "She's an esteemed colleague and a friend. And Ansom told me that your people had taken her."

The moment of truth. Did I trust him with the truth or not?

"I'm not sure what you should do," Jeff said. "You threw him, though, and his emotions are completely jumbled."

Siler appeared behind Tobin. Managed not to jump out of my skin but only because I'd been focused on keeping a poker face. He looked at me, nodded, then went back to blending. Realized he'd been in the room the whole time, since the dogs didn't react at all.

Knew what Siler was telling me to do. And, really, what did we have to lose?

"You're right. We did take Janelle."

CHAPTER 35

TOBIN STARED AT ME. "What have you done to her?"

"Us? Nothing untoward. I think she'd describe our taking her as a rescue. She was being held prisoner by Ansom and Talia Lee so they could create Fem-Bots in her image. I and my team rescued her just in time. Oh, and there's a Fem-Bot of her wandering around, or at least there was, so unless you're seeing Janelle in the company of a confirmed P.T.C.U. agent, be careful, because the Bots like to blow up."

"Just like his mind," Jeff said, "which is officially blown. He doesn't know whether to believe you or not."

"Why aren't Ansom and Talia under arrest, then?" Tobin asked, sounding dazed but trying to rally.

Gave him a good dose of the "really?" look. "Why would you think?"

He actually appeared to be giving this consideration. "You didn't catch them red-handed."

"He has no issue believing that Somerall and Lee were behind doing something terrible," Jeff shared. "And he also has no issue believing that we were the good guys. But he wants to see Gardiner."

"Correct. We have only Janelle's testimony and, until we feel that we have an ironclad case, neither she nor we want to risk allowing her out of protective custody." Cocked my head at him. "Would you like to see her?"

"I would. Very much." He seemed to catch himself. "Just to reassure myself that she's well and you're not telling me a whopper of a tale."

"You know I'm telling the truth, just like you know that Somerall and Lee are more than capable of doing what I just described. It's interesting, though."

"What is?"

"I was under the impression that Quinton Cross was Janelle's, ah, protector, supporter, mentor, and champion."

Tobin's eyes flashed and I recognized the look in them. But Jeff's confirmation was nice. "He's incredibly jealous of Cross. Who's jealous of a dead man?"

Heard Chuckie snort and the rest of the room chuckled. Yeah, Jeff was the King of Jealousy, but now wasn't the time to point that out. I'd leave that for the others.

"Quinton was a good man," Tobin said, sounding reasonably insincere.

"Who was or wasn't banging the chick you wanted?"

Tobin gaped at me. "Excuse me?"

"I'd swear I thought you were married."

"I was," he said stiffly. "My dear wife passed away due to the bioterrorism attack that put your husband in the President's seat."

"My condolences. Losing the person you love most is never an easy thing to go through."

"You're working him over," Jeff said. "To the point that I may not be able to keep on reading him. He was interested in Gardiner while his wife was alive but made no advances, at least as far as I can read. So there's guilt and lust and panic, plus everything else he's feeling. You have him on the ropes, baby, keep going."

Confirming Jeff's readings, Tobin was the most flustered that I'd ever seen. Time to continue pushing. "So, are you still a good guy in black if you were lusting after another woman when you were married to someone already? I'm just curious again."

"I never strayed," Tobin said staunchly.

"Right. I'm sure that you, the King of Fast Food and then some, never once considered stepping out on your wife. Other than, you know, with Janelle Gardiner. Seriously, was Quinton Cross that much of a smooth operator?" I'd always pegged Cross as a perverted deviant, but some people liked that sort of thing, and I was never going to try to guess what our friends, let alone our enemies and frenemies, were into.

"What would you know about my private life?" Tobin demanded.

"As much as you know about mine."

At this, Tobin jerked, just a little, but enough for me to notice.

"He's spied on us," Jeff growled in my ear. "And now he's panicked that we've done the same to him."

"It sucks when turnaround equals fair play and all that jazz, doesn't it?" I asked Tobin nicely. "But the relevant conundrum isn't whether or not you and your cronies were spying on us. Or if we're doing the same to you. No the question I still want answered is what your relationship with Harvey Gutermuth and Farley Pecker is."

"Huh?" Tobin seemed utterly thrown. Either he was still focused on Gardiner or I was that good. Had to figure he was having issues due to being caught out as an adulterer in his mind or whatever, rather than that my interrogation skills had gone nova.

"Kitty, I'm moving Jeff to an isolation chamber," Chuckie said. "He's fine, but Christopher feels he won't be for too much longer if he doesn't get away from the emotional impact. Richard is going with him, along with his entire Secret Service detail, so don't worry."

Managed not to panic about Jeff's condition. Just hoped they wouldn't have to give him the adrenaline shot to his hearts. One person had never been able to hurt Jeff unless he was already weakened. Of course, the entire day had probably been an Empathic Stress Test, so it wasn't hard to believe that if I was affecting Tobin then it was going to affect Jeff.

"I want to know your relationship with Harvey Gutermuth," I said briskly to Tobin, so as to focus on interrogation and not worrying about my husband, "and I want to know now."

"I'm not interested in Harvey!"

Didn't need Jeff to tell me that Tobin had taken my question to be about sexual interest. Managed not to laugh or roll my eyes, but only because I was in the moment, so to speak. "Interesting place your mind went to. I want to know what your relationship is with Gutermuth—in detail."

"We're business associates." Tobin still seemed shaken, but he was recovering.

"Is he in love with Janelle, too?"

Tobin jerked. "What in the world? Do you think everyone's zooming each other?"

"Depends on who you're talking about. I'm fascinated, personally, that you're taking anything I say as being sexual in nature. I wonder if the YatesCorp Board is aware of your deviant nature."

"Now you listen here—" Tobin started.

Prince, Riley, and Duke all started growling, stood up, and moved in between us. "I believe my precious puppies want you to check your attitude. Fast."

Tobin took a deep breath and let it out slowly. "Fine. Excuse me." The growling didn't stop. "I'm not going to try to hurt her," he said stiffly to the dogs.

Had to give him a modicum of credit—he was treating the dogs with more respect than I'd expected. "If only you treated me, my husband, and the rest of those trying to protect this country and world with the same respect you just gave three police dogs, we might be able to reach some kind of understanding."

Tobin opened his mouth, then his eyes bugged. "Gah!" His eyes rolled back and he went down.

Moved fast and caught his head before it hit the ground. Then looked around. To see Siler standing there. "Wow, Nightcrawler, I think you gave Tobin a heart attack." Put Tobin on the ground and checked, but his heart appeared to still be beating.

Siler chuckled. "He just fainted."

"Did you know he would?"

"No. I told you, I can't hold a blend forever. I'd been behind you so I could see his expressions and didn't have time to get behind him when I lost the blend. At any rate, it's convenient that he passed out. I want us moving him to a secured location now, and by that I mean to where Janelle Gardiner is. Your mother can decide what we do with him."

As he said this Christopher, Chuckie, and Buchanan arrived. "Jeff's fine," Chuckie said reassuringly as Christopher barked some orders and two Field teams came in with a stretcher. "But I think, based on what just happened, we probably got him into isolation just in time."

"I feel bad. Okay, not that bad, but still, kind of bad. It's not every day we watch someone faint on us."

"He was just emotionally battered," Christopher said. "And Siler here appearing out of nowhere was the last straw. Per the empathic Field agents we had outside the room."

"Works for me. What's the plan for the rest of us?"

Chuckie sighed and rubbed the back of his neck. "Your mother wants a full accounting. Immediately."

"Um, are we in trouble?"

Chuckie managed a grin. "I doubt it, but she's concerned and wants everyone back in D.C. Can't blame her. But that means we either leave the Turleens here or bring them back with us. Neither option is what I'd like."

"Leave the majority here, but I want Muddy coming back with us. And I gave that order as the FLOTUS, by the way."

"Not as Mata Hari? Good to know." Chuckie went to the Secret Service agents who were nearby and gave them some instructions.

Buchanan, meanwhile, was talking quietly with Siler. Joined them. "Okay, I want to know why Nightcrawler chose that exact moment to show up. Because I don't buy your whole 'I lost my blend' line."

Siler grinned. "You're not the only one with an earpiece. I lost the blend because I lost focus, due to the news Malcolm's going to share with you."

"We've heard from Wruck, Missus Chief," Buchanan said.

"And?"

"And he and the two Turleens he's with feel that they've got something you need to focus on far more than whatever Amos Tobin has going on."

"And that is, Malcolm?"

Buchanan grimaced. "They've found a race of aliens who are not only on Earth, but have been here possibly longer than the A-Cs."

CHAPTER 36

LET THAT SIT on the air a bit. "Um, come again?"

"Aliens are among us," Siler said. "It's not really that much of a surprise. If Muddy's people can travel here without most Earthlings knowing, and the Ancients and Z'porrah can travel here, again without most Earthlings knowing, and A-Cs can land here and be hidden for decades without most Earthlings knowing, why not a race that wants to hide here and just never bothered to check in with the authorities?"

"Is that what they found? A hidden race?" Wondered if Jeff was going to be able to take this news once he got out of isolation, or if it would just put him right back in. I wasn't an empath and the isolation chambers terrified me, but right about now, they were looking pretty good.

"Somewhat hidden," Buchanan said. "Hiding in plain sight, so to speak."

"Either you're trying to be coy—which isn't a good look for you—or you don't want to tell me. Which is it, Malcolm?"

"Neither. I only want to tell you, your mother, Mister Executive Chief, Mister White the Elder, and Mister Reynolds."

"God, I hate it when you get all official. It only means bad things."

"Exactly." Buchanan took my arm. "Let's get your husband and Mister White, grab Reynolds, and get to your mother, pronto."

Put Alpha Team in charge of getting Tobin to wherever we were getting him. Put Christopher in charge of finding out what Serene and her team were now up to. Had a brief argument with Buchanan about bringing Muddy along with us. Siler backed me, though—if we had two Turleens with Wruck, then one Turleen with us was probably the way to go.

Muddy put Lily in charge of the rest of the Turleens, and I put Viola, Carmine, and Romeo in charge of ensuring that the Turleens stayed inside Caliente Base. Thusly set up, Muddy, Siler, Buchanan, Chuckie, and I headed off to get Jeff out of isolation, my Secret Service detail and the K-9 squad coming along as a matter of course.

Isolation chambers were a combination of an iron maiden and the Mummy's Tomb, with a lot of scientific-like extras tossed in to make them really hit eleven on the creepy scale. And every Centaurion Base had a full section devoted to them, because Jeff wasn't the only empath who needed the regenerative fluids and the total emotional calm the isolation chambers provided.

So far, Jamie hadn't needed to use one. Neither had Charlie. Continued to hope that my children would be spared the need. However, the isolation chamber in our rooms in the White House was rather cozy, with comfy beds that made it look more like you were staying at an austere Sheraton than going to bed with a zillion needles stuck in you.

Jeff's Secret Service detail were guarding the door, Joseph on one side, Rob on the other, with the rest spread out a bit to watch all potential avenues of entry. Since the isolation area was basically rows of chambers, this made sense. Resisted the urge to shudder—this place and all those like it kept Jeff alive. My being creeped out by them, therefore, wasn't important.

The beds in standard isolation chambers weren't cushy nor comfy. They were more like large metal trays that were movable into whatever position the patient needed. Normally it was at an angle, with the head higher than the feet, and that's what I expected to see.

Instead, we found Jeff sitting in a chair, looking reasonably relaxed. This was a new one. White was in there with him, also in a chair.

Knocked on the window. White got up and opened the door. "Are we ready to go?"

"Wow, I'm not used to seeing anyone so casual in one of these, Jeff in particular."

Jeff stood up and shrugged. "I wasn't at a point of collapse, baby. I was heading that way, but I could have lasted for quite a while more. It just made more sense for me to get into a chamber and relax."

"Jeffrey saw the light of reason when Charles pointedly

asked who had adrenaline with them." White's eyes twinkled. "I chose to come along to keep him company."

"Uncle Richard is rarely an emotional issue for me," Jeff added, as he gave me a hug. "And before you say it, yes, baby, you are an emotional issue for me, but for all the right reasons."

Hugged him back. "Good. I sincerely hope you're really all rested up and such, because we have some news we need to share with you and my mother at the same time. And Mom would like that time to be pronto."

We headed for the main gate, which, as per usual for most Bases, was on the ground-level floor, which was currently packed with Caliente Base residents returning home. "Where are we heading?" Jeff asked Buchanan.

"Dulce. Then Bermuda."

We all stared at him. "We're going on an impromptu vacation?" I asked. "I'm not against it, but I kind of thought we had issues going on and all that."

Buchanan sighed. "Trust me, we won't be there long. At either location."

Jeff grunted as we went to one of the larger gates that would allow several of us to go through at the same time. He shared our destination with the gate agent, said agent calibrated the gate, Jeff swung me up into his arms, I buried my face in his neck, and we all stepped through.

As always it was nauseating and, also as always, it was a hell of a lot less nauseating because Jeff was holding me. It wasn't a long trip from Caliente Base to the Dulce Science Center, so that was good. It was going to be a lot longer to Bermuda. Made a mental note to reapply my sunscreen before we left.

As per usual when arriving at Dulce via the gates, we exited onto the Command Center Level, aka the Bat Cave, where a lot of The Future: NOW! looking science-y stuff was being used and everyone, human and A-C, was bustling about like the busiest of bees. It was a lot more crowded here than normal, because of Caliente Base being evacuated.

The majority of Earth's A-Cs worked in the Science Center. NASA Base had the second highest A-C population, with the rest of the A-C population spread out to the other Bases worldwide. Meaning that many of the people living in the Science Center had children who'd moved to Caliente Base. So there were a lot of family groups hanging out talking, working, hugging, and so on.

Apparently we were stopping at Dulce to leave the K-9 unit with their remaining prisoners. Though it didn't seem likely that any of them—sorta prisoners or K-9 squad—was going to be leaving any time soon.

Bud and Cujo were being shown around by Len and Kyle, who had apparently forgiven the younger guys for going to a school that wasn't USC, playing on a rival football team from the Trojans, and being in a frat other than whatever frat Len and Kyle had been in as undergrads. Realized I didn't know. Realized I currently didn't care, either, but added it to the Worst Boss Ever List that I was keeping for myself.

Bud and Cujo also had expressions I was familiar with—the "I can't believe there are this many hot chicks in the world!" looks. They were getting eyed by several of the younger Dazzlers who hadn't gone back to Caliente Base yet. Had a feeling we'd just scored two new recruits, because if the Dazzlers were interested, it meant Bud and Cujo were smart.

Mickey and Garfield were in medical, getting treatment, and Tito refused to allow them to be taken back into custody. Melville didn't argue much, probably because the Dazzlers on Duty were a great distraction, and also because Jeff made the "what Tito wants, Tito gets" statement and no one felt like arguing with the Top Man.

The working girls were a different situation, however. Because they were insisting they needed to come with me.

"I want to help Code Name: First Lady," Jane said emphatically. She'd been told my name but refused to use it. Decided that there were more important battles to be fought. "We helped already. We want to help more."

Rhonda nodded. "I think we added our share. And we'd be dead if the First Lady hadn't saved us. We heard it was part of the plan, that the weirdo robot thing knew she'd rescue everyone, but I gotta tell you, we aren't taking that for granted. Plus, we're ready to kick some ass if anyone tries anything."

"I just do not want to go back to jail," Meriel said quietly. "Or back to our pimp. And I would like to be helpful to the people who have helped us."

"I knew this was going to happen," Jeff muttered. "The new jocks aren't leaving either, and the old men aren't going to be allowed to leave until they're already so integrated in they won't want to go."

"How is this my fault? How? Just because they're jazzed about helping out? That's a good thing. Citizens need to be involved. Look at it as a great way of getting the recruiting process started." Which gave me an idea. "Girls, I'd like to ask you to help work on a really important project."

The three girls gave me their utmost attention. "Whatever you need," Rhonda said. Jane nodded enthusiastically. Meriel looked suspicious.

"We need to create a recruitment campaign that encourages people to sign up to become a part of Centaurion Division to protect Earth and her allies, whether they're here on the planet or far away."

Meriel brightened up. "Oh, a propaganda campaign! I know about those, my grandfather told me all about them."

Decided now wasn't the time to get all the pertinent details, especially when I took a look at Jeff and Chuckie's expressions. "Super! So, um, you guys get started on that. You'll have to integrate your ideas in with the larger team's but well begun is half done and all that other Mary Poppins stuff."

Waved Len and Kyle over, explained the new assignment, and added them, Bud, and Cujo to the mix, meaning that the prisoners would be under Len and Kyle's guidance and watchful eyes. Gently suggested that if Officers Melville, Larry, and Curly had input they should share it as well, but made it clear that the team leader was Len with Kyle as second in command.

Working girls now put to work on something other than sexual favors, potential new jock recruits also put to good use, Len and Kyle not feeling totally left out, K-9 unit officially watching their prisoners, so to speak, and my sunscreen reapplied, we headed to the elevator bank in order to get to the main gate level, which was where Buchanan wanted us leaving from.

While waiting, a nose nudged at my knee. Sure enough, Prince was there and shoved in between me and Jeff.

Who heaved a long-suffering sigh. "Someone let Melville know that his dog wants a trip to Bermuda."

Gave Prince some major loving while Buchanan sent a text. "He just wants to protect us."

"I just want to know what's going on," Chuckie said. "Why are we going to Bermuda when Angela wants to meet with us?"

"Because she's there," Buchanan said as the elevator arrived and we all loaded in. It was a tight fit, and Buchanan forced our Secret Service details to take other elevators.

Evalyne shook her head. "You're planning to go to Bermuda without us, aren't you?"

"I'm not," I said loyally.

Buchanan shrugged. "Yes. Because the Head of the P.T.C.U. has another assignment for all of you. However, I'll give that to you upstairs."

Dulce went down fifteen floors. Way back when and what, these days, seemed a lifetime ago, Jeff and I had lived on the fifteenth level in what I called his Human Lair. There were many days I still missed the Lair, though our family was now too big to live there comfortably. But I'd have been willing to give it a try and, based on Jeff's expression when Buchanan hit the button for the top floor and Jeff looked at the button for Floor 15, he'd have been willing to try, too.

We exited and, true to his word, Buchanan waited for the Secret Service contingents to arrive. As they did, Buchanan sent another text, and two more A-Cs joined us.

One of them I knew—Francine Alexis was Colette's eldest sister, one of Raj and Serene's most experienced troubadours, and the A-C we used as my body double. Which was a total compliment to me, because Francine was a Dazzler and therefore far hotter than me. But if you're told it's the FLOTUS and the double looks close enough, rarely does anyone question.

The man with her wasn't someone I'd met. However, he did resemble Jeff. He was clearly an A-C, though he wasn't quite as handsome as Jeff was. Then again, I felt that Jeff was the hottest guy in the galaxy, so I might have been a tad biased. He was introduced as Craig Rossi. Showing incredible self-control, I didn't make any Martini & Rossi jokes, but it took a great deal of effort.

Craig was dressed like every other A-C or human agent working with them—in the Armani Fatigues. Francine, however, wasn't dressed like me, but instead was in my FLOTUS Uniform—an iced blue blouse, black skirt, and comfortable black pumps. Her hair was down and actually styled, and she had makeup on. Clearly the idea was that I'd changed and primped after fighting Apache helicopters in the desert. Could not argue with the mindset.

"You're escorting these two," Buchanan said to our Secret Service details, nodding at Francine and Craig, "back to the White House. In a very obvious manner."

"Are we flying?" Evalyne asked.

Buchanan shook his head. "No, it's too dangerous right now. However, you're going to go back to Pueblo Caliente and make a brief appearance where the President will shake hands with the mayor to show continued support. Then you're going to Sky Harbor and being seen to be getting onto a private supersonic jet."

"But we'll use hyperspeed and actually go to a gate in the airport," Francine said. "So everyone needs to be prepared for that because we have to exit after we're all on board but before the exit ramp goes up."

Joseph nodded. "We're used to that kind of timing these days."

"Then you'll all go back to the White House complex and wait for when you have to 'arrive' at Andrews," Buchanan continued. "Colonel Franklin is prepped for all of this."

"Who's providing the jet?" Chuckie asked suspiciously.

Buchanan grinned at him. "You are."

"I don't own a private jet," Chuckie said flatly.

Managed not to share that in Bizarro World Chuckie and his family did indeed own a private jet. "Private jets are cool, and I'm sure someone can pay you back."

Chuckie shot me the "really?" look. "I can afford to buy one, Kitty. I just never saw the need."

Buchanan shrugged. "It's a need now, and Pierre says to tell you that he got you a fantastic deal using contacts provided by Beaumont."

"You know Vance has all the right contacts," I said quickly. "And I can promise that he didn't let Pierre buy some drug dealer's used plane."

Chuckie relaxed. "True enough. And, okay, if Pierre approved this, then I'm fine with it."

"Who's actually flying the jet back to D.C.?" Jeff asked.

"Airborne," Buchanan said. "So it'll be in good hands." He shot the Secret Service a stern look. "And you know these two will also be in good hands, so no complaints about your assigned roles. The Head of the P.T.C.U. expects you to ensure that this fiction flies in all circles."

The agents all nodded, then they encircled their new charges. Buchanan had them go off to Pueblo Caliente first. Once they were confirmed to be with the mayor and so forth, he gave the gate agent our coordinates.

We did the whole sordid gate transfer thing again, and this time was definitely longer, so worse for my stomach. However, where we landed wasn't what I was prepared for. At all.

CHAPTER 37

WE WERE ON THE DECK of a large boat in what sort of looked like the middle of the ocean. I could see islands in the distance, but Jeff and I weren't about to discover if we liked Bermuda's beaches more than Cabo's.

All the various things we'd had to handle in Pueblo Caliente and at Dulce had taken several hours, and by coming back to the East Coast we'd lost an additional three. The sun wasn't setting yet, but it was definitely thinking about it. Figured we had no more than an hour of good light left, if that.

Had a pang of worry, since the sun set late at the start of July. Jeff and I had undoubtedly missed dinnertime with the kids. Sure, that just meant that Colette and Francine's middle sister, Nadine, had ensured that Jamie, Charlie, and Lizzie all ate at the Embassy, which was where the kids did dinner anytime Jeff and I weren't able to be with them. And sure, the kids enjoyed their now-special time with Pierre fussing over them. But still, it wasn't the same as having their parents there.

Shoved all the Bad Mommy thoughts away. Right now, I had to meet an alien race. Another alien race. Before meeting a lot more alien races. And trying to get the entire world to be enthusiastic about all these other races. Yeah, time to focus on the things going on in front of me. Plenty of time to beat myself up later.

The boat was definitely government-issue, but also just as definitely the kind of government-issue that was supposed to be under the radar. It had at least three decks and looked like any other rich person yacht—unless you noted the gun turrets all around. And you had to actually look to note said turrets. Had no idea which drug lord this had been confiscated from, but was glad the boat was now on the side of good.

Mom was here, looking official in her P.T.C.U. baseball cap and vest. Jeff put me down and I trotted over and gave her a hug.

She hugged me back tightly. "You've had a busy day, kitten."

"Yeah, it's been a thrill a minute, Mom. Meet Muddy." I indicated the Turleen.

Mom reached down and shook his hand. "I hear you're the man in charge."

"Of the contingent here, yes." Muddy looked around. "I do not see my two friends nor the Old One."

"They're in the water," Mom said briskly. "Rounding up the aliens." She shook her head. "It's been an interesting time here." With that she led us to the port side of the boat.

There was what looked like a very large seal and two sea turtles in the water, and they appeared to be herding just an absolute tonnage of tiny blue and white creatures. Each one had a body that resembled a gecko with six rounded and spiny limbs or fins or whatever they were. They looked familiar, as if I'd seen them somewhere before.

"*Glaucus atlanticus*," Chuckie said. "Why are we here to look at sea slugs?"

"Right! Those natural sciences classes I made us take at ASU really keep on paying off, don't they?"

"Because they are not only sea slugs, apparently," Mom said, ignoring my comment on my college curriculum. "They're not from Earth originally."

The realization that the hidden alien race we were coming to meet were tiny, lovely, little creatures that floated on the surface of the ocean nudged into my brain. "Um, they're pretty and they eat jellyfish. How does that make them aliens?"

The seal leapt up onto the deck of the boat in a way no seal was actually able to do and shifted into Wruck. "They're ready to speak with you," he said to me and Jeff. "The Turleens are going to need to translate, however."

"The sea turtles are your missing pals?" I asked Muddy.

Who nodded. "Their names translate for you to be Dew and Mossy. Dew is a female, Mossy is a male."

"Good to know. And you all speak *Glaucus atlanticus*?"

"No," Muddy said politely. "We all speak Mykali. Which is what they are."

"How long have they been here," Chuckie asked, "and how long have you Turleens known they've been here?"

"For centuries," Muddy replied. "It's why we speak their

language—if you plan to travel to Earth, it's suggested you learn Mykali so that you can communicate with the natives who will not, ah . . ."

"Try to kill you," I supplied.

"Exactly. But only recently did we realize that humans had no idea that the Mykali were here. It is because of that, and because of the others who are coming, that Dew and Mossy took the Old One to meet the Mykali."

"After searching for more enemies," Wruck added.

Chuckie looked at him. "And what about the Ancients? Or the Z'porrah? How much did you affect with all of this?"

Wruck shook his head. "I had no idea the Mykali still existed. We know of their solar system, which died, but what happened to the races that lived there was unknown."

"To the Ancients only, or the Ancients and the Z'porrah?" Jeff asked. "Because it seems unlikely that your two races just ignored a bunch of others you could meddle with."

"This happened when our races were still friends," Wruck said. "At that time, we were still young enough races that we were unable to help with uplift or rescue. This system's dying spurred us on to greater achievements."

"If you can call what your two races have done to this galaxy achieving," Jeff said.

"You mean the Mykali here are the only ones left?" I asked, lest Jeff and Wruck get into an argument we didn't have time for and that didn't matter anyway—what was done was done.

Wruck nodded. "Yes, we just confirmed it with this group. The Mykali's home planet was running out of water hundreds of thousands of years ago, due to their star beginning the first stages of its death. The planet was heating up and the water was evaporating. Earth was discovered, and it was determined that they could live in Earth's oceans. They came here in a mass exodus."

"That's sounds far too simple," Chuckie said. He looked down on the water. "I'm not saying that the Mykali might not be playing possum and just pretending they have no scientific knowhow in order to remain under humanity's radar, but if so, how did something without any actual limbs or digits create spaceflight?"

"Who did their uplift?" I added. "Because that seems to matter quite a bit right about now."

"Neither Ancient nor Z'porrah uplifted anyone in that solar

system. As I said, this happened well before we had the capability."

"So how did they get here?" Jeff asked pointedly.

"They can't survive out of the water for too long, nor can they stay congregated like this for too long a time—this high a concentration of Mykali will bring predators," Wruck said. His meaning was clear. We were going to get this info straight from the sea slugs' mouths or we weren't going to get it.

"Great. I hope that the Elves have the contract for this boat."

Was relieved that Buchanan and Mom had kept the Secret Service away because the argument we'd have gotten for this plan would have been extreme. As it was, we all just trooped into a lower deck and changed into swimsuits that were neatly laid out on the beds in each guest cabin.

"Thanks," I said quietly to the suits. Had no idea where Algar's portal was on this ship, other than potentially in my purse. Which was not going to be going swimming with us.

Jeff sighed as we got undressed. "This would be a great place to relax."

"If by relax you mean have wild sex for hours, yes, I agree. Of course, I think the various new aliens around and aboard, not to mention my mother, would probably suggest we wait for another time."

Jeff pulled me to him and kissed me deeply. As always, I was grinding against him in a moment. He ended our kiss slowly, eyes smoldering. "Well, it's something we should definitely keep in mind, baby."

"Mmmm, I love how you think."

Swimsuits on, Jeff slathered the rest of me with sunscreen. Looked around the room. "I wonder if there are any goggles or such around?"

"Why are you asking in such a loud, weird way?"

"No reason." Wandered over to the small dresser. Opened up the top drawer to find goggles and snorkeling equipment for five. "Huh, lucky us."

Gave Jeff a set of goggles, a snorkel, and flippers, took a set for myself, then went in search of the others. Found them all on the main deck with Mom and handed out the rest of the gear.

Had to admit, as impromptu outings went, getting to be with Jeff, Buchanan, Chuckie, and White all in swimsuits made up for a lot of other things. I had one-third of a best-selling swimsuit calendar in front of me. Did my best to think about flowers, because Jeff was really able to pick up my lust, and though I didn't have any desire to do anything other than look and drool a little, it had been a tough day for both of us and I had no desire to get into any kind of jealousy argument.

Jeff snorted softly. "I know you think we're all hot. It's a compliment that you're trying to decide if I should be Mister January or Mister December."

"Wow, that flowers thing doesn't work at all."

He kissed the top of my head. "Most of the time it does, because I ignore you as best I can when you start thinking about carnations, tulips, and roses. Figuring out what you were trying to avoid me noticing wasn't really a challenge in this instance, though."

"Blah, blah, blah. I just hope the water's warm."

"It's Bermuda in the middle of summer," Chuckie said. "That water will be warm."

"You're not swimming with us?" I asked Siler.

"Nope. I'm staying on the ship with your mother and the dog. Where it's dry."

"You don't like water?"

"I don't like swimming in water where there might be sharks."

"I literally didn't think you were afraid of anything."

Siler shrugged. "I saw *Jaws* at a formative age."

"You know that it's rare for great whites to swim in these waters," Chuckie said.

"And I also know that they do," Siler replied cheerfully. "I'll be here, manning the shark torpedoes, waiting to hand you all towels."

The yacht had a ladder that allowed us to climb down into the water, though the flippers we were wearing made it a little difficult, so all of us jumped in when we were still above the water-line. Happily, Chuckie was right again—the water was perfect. Really would have liked to have a chance to swim and actually snorkel, but didn't figure that request would be met with anything resembling enthusiasm from anyone else.

Once the rest of us were in the water, Muddy and Wruck both dove in from the upper deck, Muddy going to Sea Turtle Mode and Wruck again choosing Giant Seal. The seven of us swam to where Dew and Mossy and hundreds of Mykali were gathered.

Fast intros were made and then the fun of translations began.

Dew seemed to have the best grasp of what the Mykali were saying, so she was the main focus of conversation.

"How long have they been here?" Chuckie asked.

Dew relayed the question. Heard nothing but what sounded like faint music, but she nodded and turned to the rest of us. "Since before you walked upright."

"How did they get here?" Jeff asked.

Question relayed and what might be musical answers given. "In natural ships." Dew sounded uncertain. "They are balls of earth that fly through space."

"Meteors or meteorites?" Chuckie asked.

Dew nodded. "I believe that's what they mean."

"How did they create them?" Jeff asked.

More consultation. The noises the Mykali made were very soft, but when they were together it was louder. "Are they a hive mind?" I asked Muddy and Mossy.

Mossy nodded his head up and down and back and forth. "In a way. They are individually sentient but when together like this, they can combine their minds to create a higher sentience level."

Would have said wow, but Dew was speaking. "The Mykali did not create the spaceflight. They come from a world that was once abundant, as Earth is. Others on the world found a place to try to live and those sent the Mykali to Earth, long, long ago. The Mykali have waited for thousands of years for the others from their world to join them." She looked sad, in as much as a sea turtle could. "They fear that the others were not able to leave their planet in time."

"Or they found another one, or ones, to test," Chuckie said, and I could see the wheels in his mind turning. "So, a race of higher sentience decided to send the Mykali out first, just like the Russians sent a chimp into space before they sent a human."

"That makes sense," White agreed. "Our people did the same with sending my father here, for example."

Chuckie nodded. "It's a tried and true formula. How long were the Mykali flying through space to get here?" he asked Dew.

More consultation. The Mykali's voices sounded like singing and the more they spoke, the louder it was getting. "Their voices are beautiful. Are they what gave rise to the idea of siren songs?"

"Possibly," Mossy said, once White explained what I meant by this. "They have on occasion tried to communicate with humans. You're too far removed from them. We Turleens know of them because we have visited Earth often enough. Most of us don't go to your oceans—Tur has only lakes and rivers, though we have an abundance of those, but no salt water. So your oceans are a bit . . . frightening to us. Some are excited by the challenge, though, so they have gone, as Dew and I are right now, in these forms. And in these guises they have met the Mykali."

"They don't know how long it took for them to reach Earth," Dew said. "They were in suspended animation inside their ships. They do know that some of their ships did not arrive. Whether they reached a different planet or were destroyed during flight they also do not know. They cannot live on land and so have no comparison, but say that your oceans feel like home."

"If they've truly been here longer than humans have been sentient, then it's difficult to think of them as aliens," White said. "They technically could have more claim to the planet than humanity."

"Which is not the way to lead with their story," I pointed out. Remembered from college that they could eat poisonous jellyfish and literally saved that poison for their own use, which was their only form of defense. "Because humans have a tremendous inferiority complex thing going, and these Mykali are basically defenseless against anyone wearing really thick gloves." Or any scientists with traps, or hunters of any kind.

"So," Buchanan asked, "what do we do about these Mykali?"

Jeff sighed. "We leave them alone."

CHAPTER 38

"BUT THEY'RE AN EXAMPLE** of another sentient alien race," Buchanan pointed out. "It could help with what's coming."

"How, exactly, would that help?" Jeff countered. "Look, I understand why everyone's excited about this. Only there was a reason my people hid in plain sight for years on this planet. If we share that this race—this basically helpless race, particularly as compared to humans and A-Cs—is here, and has been here for longer than we have, then I know what will happen."

"They'll be hunted, dissected, captured, and killed into extinction." Everyone looked at me and I shrugged. "Look, humanity isn't the nicest form of sentience out there. It's why everyone's running to us right now—we're vicious, even in our curiosity. Sure, we can show incredible kindness and care, but basically, Naked Apes are really effective at destroying. I agree with Jeff—these people need to be protected, and to do that, we have to go back to saying that they're pretty sea slugs."

"I agree," White said. "Wholeheartedly, Jeffrey."

Chuckie sighed. "I agree as well." He eyed Buchanan. "And you agree, too, and so does Angela. It's why you wanted Richard with us, just in case Jeff was vacillating, and ensured that the Secret Service and everyone else didn't come with us."

Buchanan grinned. "I hate being so transparent, even to one of the boss men. But yes. Angela feels the same as you do. She just wanted confirmation before we told Dew to warn the Mykali about humans and to stay far away from as many of us as they can."

"Tell them that if we ever find their other people, we'll let them know," I said quickly. Once again, everyone looked at me.

"Look, they're still waiting for them to arrive. They may have been sent out first, but that means, to them, that they were saved first. They've tried to communicate with us because that's what they were used to—talking to other sentient races. It's got to be a weird form of loneliness, but still—imagine if you used to talk to all the animals on the planet and then you couldn't. It's a loss, and apparently it's a loss that generations of Mykali still feel, because I sincerely doubt that they live for ten thousand years."

"They do not," Dew said. "Lifespans are short, between an Earth month and a year. But they all still remember their first home world." She turned back to the Mykali and relayed what we'd just told her.

"Shared mind, shared memories," Chuckie murmured. "Fascinating. And I completely agree with Jeff—there's no way our scientists would let these people be. Kitty's right—we'd destroy this race within one generation."

Dew finished and several of the Mykali swam over to me. I was careful when I moved my hands toward them because I didn't want to get stung.

But stinging didn't happen. Five swam into each hand, making me really glad I had flippers on to help keep me upright in the water. Looked at them and listened. And realized I could understand them, in the same way I could understand the other animals.

They were thanking us for being kind, thanking me for understanding their loneliness, pledging their fealty to us, as they had so long ago to the others who'd sent them here to Earth to pave the way to save their home planet.

Wanted to hug them, but didn't because I didn't want to hurt them. Instead, I nodded. "I don't know how and I don't know when, but we'll find out what happened to your original world and all the different people that were on it. And if there's a way to safely reunite you with them, we'll make it happen. I promise."

The Mykali sent love and thanks thoughts to me and shared that if I ever wanted to find them, just go out far from shore and call to them and whoever was nearby would come to me.

"Thanks," I said softly. "And if you need us, hopefully there will be some Turleens on the planet who will be able to share it with me."

The Mykali started to disperse slowly, when suddenly they began to move swiftly, while shouting one word. Prince started barking at the same time, and he was barking the same thing as the Mykali were shouting.

Dew and I shared that word together. "Shark!"

Looked around fast. We'd floated rather far away from the boat, which so totally figured I didn't even choose to comment on it. Didn't see a fin in the water, which might or might not be a good thing. As the Turleens leapt out of the water and flew back onto the ship, decided that Algar had given the humans and A-Cs snorkeling equipment for a reason and looked underwater.

The water was clear and beautiful. Meaning I had a great view of the great white heading for us from below.

Fortunately, or not, depending, my reaction to a fight or flight situation appeared to always be fight. Unless it was a snake, in which case my reaction was Freeze In Terror. Reality said that a great white shark was a hell of a lot more dangerous to me than any snake in the world, but while it was hella scary to be looking at, I could see its trajectory, and the shark wasn't aiming for me or the other swimmers.

It was aiming for the gigantic seal, aka Wruck, aka the only Ancient on this planet. Who also happened to be trying to help the Mykali get away, meaning he was a really fantastic meal on the flipper as far as the shark was concerned.

An arm went around my waist and I was practically flying through the water. Jeff had me up onto the deck in seconds, White had Chuckie up there in the same way, and Buchanan apparently used his Dr. Strange powers to move almost as fast as A-Cs could. Either that or Buchanan was as scared of sharks as Siler, who was indeed manning a gun. White, once he had Chuckie on board, hauled Buchanan the rest of the way up as well.

However, my Dr. Doolittle skills were running on high and I could feel the shark's mind. It wasn't as bright as the dogs or cats, but it wasn't nearly as mindless as movies like *Jaws* would suggest. She wasn't a vicious killer trying to eat an entire sentient race and an unlucky shapeshifter. She was just hungry. And I knew it was a she, just like I knew she was pregnant.

Knocked Siler away from the gun. "No, don't shoot her! She's preggers!" Then I dove back into the water.

Thankfully my parents had spent money on ensuring that I learned to swim and to dive and all that jazz. And I was enhanced and the water was great and while I wasn't necessarily an Olympic-level swimmer, what I lacked in skill I was definitely making up for with speed.

The shark wasn't racing toward Wruck and the Mykali, but

she was going fast. Didn't matter, I was revved and the skills were working at optimum. Got in between her and Wruck in record time.

"John, get out of here! The shark wants a Wruck Snack!"

Wasn't able to really talk to her—how I'd picked up her thoughts I wasn't sure, but it might have been how Jeff picked up emotions. The shark was really focused on the fact that she was going to get a fantastic meal, and that idea sort of radiated from her. So I wasn't sure if I could tell her to stop in the same way I'd tell one of the animals who lived with me to cease and desist.

Of course, now that I was between her and the giant seal, the shark took notice of me, analyzed the situation, and decided that the thing in the water that was flapping around just like a scrawny seal might make a good appetizer.

Time to think of what they taught during Shark Week, which was a quick exercise for me since I'd never watched. However, I'd seen *Tomb Raider II*, and that meant it was time to channel my Inner Lara Croft. Balled up my fists together and hit the shark as hard as I could on her nose.

Amazing me in a very positive way, my punch pushed her backwards, shocked her, and made her shake her whole body. A-C super strength wasn't as great as hyperspeed, but it surely had its moments.

She recovered, and came at me faster. Slammed my fists harder against her snout. Results were the same—shoved her backwards, shocked her, and made her shake.

Didn't want to cause her a pregnancy issue, but knew I had to stall her because I had no idea how many guns were now aimed at this pregnant shark. Focused as hard as I could on the shark's mind and tried to tell it to swim away because all this food was dangerous.

She came for me again, but at the last minute she sheared off and dove, getting away from me as fast as possible.

Was about to congratulate myself on now being Aquawoman, when I felt something watching me. Turned around to see a gigantic orca whale. Right behind me.

Always the way.

CHAPTER 39

TRIED TO FOCUS on the orca's mind, but got nothing. It dove down and I watched it chase the great white away. Then it resurfaced right by me again. And turned into Wruck.

"Oh. And I'll just give myself the 'duh' on this one."

He smiled. "Wanting to protect the innocent and helpless isn't a bad trait. And I appreciate you leaping in front of a great white shark to protect me." He turned back into the orca, swam under me, and gave me a fast ride back to the boat. Which was totally cool. Wondered if I could ask him to do this again, and if I could bring Lizzie, Jamie, and Charlie along for them to enjoy it, too. Decided I didn't feel like hearing everyone else's reaction to this idea, so kept it to myself.

Jeff helped me up and off the orca's back. "You really like to see how strong my hearts are, don't you?" He clutched me to him, hearts pounding.

"Wasn't intentional, Jeff, I'm sorry. But the shark is pregnant and—"

"We got it," he said, as he reached down to help Wruck, who'd shifted back into human form, up onto the deck. "And I'd like to mention that I'm not punching Chuck because your mother said I can't."

"Chuckie did the Vulcan Nerve Pinch to keep you immobile?"

"Yeah. Per your mother's orders."

"I feel the love."

"I knew that a shapeshifter was in the water with you," Mom pointed out. "Why you leaped back in was beyond me, but Benjamin and I did determine that John was likely waiting for everyone else to get to safety before he transformed into something that would scare the shark."

"Sorry, just didn't think about it."

"I know." Mom took me from Jeff and hugged me, her breath-stopping bear hug. "You're a protector, kitten. And despite there being no real need for it, I'm proud of you for risking your life to protect things weaker than yourself."

"Thanks, Mom. Air . . . need air . . ."

She chuckled and let go of me. "I'm relieved the Secret Service weren't here. I can guarantee that this incident would have put them over the edge."

"We all rejoice, then."

Chuckie grabbed and hugged me next. "I only stopped Jeff because I realized that Wruck was probably going to shift into a Cleophese or similar."

"Yeah, a giant Cthulhu monster would definitely make a great white run."

White's turn to hug me. "I'm relieved that Jeffrey and I didn't have to do anything overly heroic."

Laughed. "As if that's not something you do naturally?"

Buchanan shook his head at me. "You definitely keep life interesting, Missus Chief."

"It's a gift and a skill. Nightcrawler, how are you holding up?"

"Resolving to never, ever put a toe in an ocean again, but otherwise, okay." He smiled at me. "Thanks for stopping me from killing the mother-to-be, though."

Wruck nodded. "Yes, I think we're all glad. Not only that the shark's life was spared, but she was a tagged fish, and that means if we'd killed her we'd have to answer a lot of questions we'd all prefer to avoid."

"Go team." Heaved a sigh. "So, now what?"

"Now," White said, "you prepare yourself and your team for your world tour."

"I wonder, can the shark come back?"

Mom shook her head. "Trust me, there's no time for you to play around."

Chose not to whine about this, because I figured there was more going on and, besides, my mother never put up with it.

Turned out that Mom had been the one to pilot the ship. Chose not to ask how she knew how to handle a boat like this, though there was undoubtedly a great story that went along with it. Also turned out that she'd taken a gate down to Miami and had piloted the boat from there, pretty much confirming my view that it had originally belonged to a drug dealer.

Seeing as how the President and First Lady were considered to already be in D.C., instead of getting to take the boat back, Jeff called for a floater gate while the rest of us gathered our things. Chose not to be bitter—there was no way this boat was soundproofed enough for us to have sex in it unless we were the only two on board.

Kevin Lewis and a small team of P.T.C.U. agents exited the shimmering that was the most obvious indication of a floater gate. Kevin reassured Jeff that all was well in Dulce and other areas, then we walked through the floater and exited into the closet of our family suite in the White House Complex.

Chuckie, White, Buchanan, and even Wruck all had clothes hanging up for them in the closet, so the hint was clear. They each showered and changed in our bathroom, while Mom and Siler filled us and those waiting for showers in on what we'd missed elsewhere and Prince demanded petting from everyone within reach. Muddy, Dew, and Mossy didn't need to change. Realized they didn't wear clothes so much as their shells adapted to whatever they needed.

"There's still a hullabaloo about the American Centaurion flag," Mom said as she scratched behind Prince's ears. "Only the terrorist attack in Pueblo Caliente has overshadowed it. There's enough footage of the Turleens as to make it pretty impossible for us to deny that something went on beyond an attack."

"I miss the good old days."

Mom nodded. "Christopher and Serene did their best, but honestly, the entire world is going to know what's going on sooner as opposed to later."

White joined us, dressed and pressed, so to speak, because hyperspeed rocked. Chuckie went in next, while White settled on the sofa.

Was hungry and had to figure everyone else was as well. Jeff and I were still in bathing suits, and I didn't bother to change. Just made sure I used hyperspeed and zipped across the hall to the family dining room. The Elves had this contract for sure.

"Snacks and such that I can carry over to the other side without being seen so that all of us can get some sustenance into our systems, Turleens included, please and thank you."

Opened the fridge to see two good-sized packed bags. Didn't question, just took them. "You're the best." Closed the fridge and zipped back to the others. Passed sandwiches and sodas around, which were accepted gratefully by one and all. There were some bizarre-looking kinds of big food bars that the Turleens greeted with great joy as well. Set aside food and a Coke for Chuckie, gave Prince the ten dog biscuits provided, then settled onto Jeff's lap.

"In other words, there may be no reason to lie," White said, in between munching.

Siler nodded. "Exactly. Some of the spin is that the helicopters were trying to stop the dangerous aliens. All that's coming from YatesCorp-owned stations."

"Fantastic. What have we done with Amos Tobin, by the way?"

"He's where you requested, with Janelle Gardiner." Mom heaved a sigh. "Based on what I'm hearing from the agents watching them, I don't think you've flipped him, or her, so much as it's clear to them that they're both better off aligned with you than with Ansom Somerall."

"Yeah, I'm not counting on making either one of them our best friends forever."

"I'll read them when we have time, but I'm sure you're right, Angela," Jeff said. "I'm just glad Kitty's flipped those she has."

"Speaking of someone you're never bringing back to the good side of the Force," Siler said, "Kitty, I think your hunch about what the Casey Thing was telling us is going to pay off. We sent some Field agents from Euro Base over to investigate, with strict orders not to get too close. There's definitely something untoward going on in the area of France you were told Cliff's hideout is."

"Only, based on what you just said, you don't think it's Cliff. You think Cliff sent the Casey Thing to us to give me information on where Stephanie's hiding, right?"

Siler nodded. "Exactly. That she had Gutermuth ask for her to be 'arrested' just means they were playing the Club Fifty-One True Believers card."

"Which also makes sense," Chuckie said, as he came out and Buchanan, who'd just finished wolfing down two sandwiches, went in. Chuckie sat and I brought him his food. "Gosh, and Jeff's not even jealous. How things change."

Jeff grunted. "Don't push it. Or yourself. Eat, Chuck. You need the food."

Chose to actively not worry about whether or not Chuckie was taking care of himself and instead focused back on Stephanie. "Did the agents think we have a chance of catching her?" I asked Siler.

"No idea. We kept them far back. But we don't want anyone just randomly going after her anyway. Frankly, it's going to need to be me, Malcolm, and John, and no one else."

"Why so?" Jeff asked.

"No one else is capable of capturing her at this time," Wruck said. "She has no compunction about hurting any of you, but you're all reluctant to hurt her."

"And we aren't," Siler added, presumably for Jeff's benefit, because I knew that everyone in the room already knew this to be true, Jeff included.

Jeff heaved a sigh. "I know, I know, saving or rehabilitating her is a stretch. But I can't help hoping that we'll manage it."

"Which is why we want you kept far, far away from wherever she is," Siler said briskly.

Mom nodded. "And that's a direct order, Mister President."

Jeff didn't argue, and neither did White. Instead the conversation turned to whether or not Jeff should go with me on the FLOTUS World Tour. Buchanan finished and Wruck went in for his shower and change of clothes. He was done before we'd finished arguing about this one point. Muddy's thoughts about world royalty were shared, but Mom didn't seem convinced. At all.

"Why are you resistant?" Muddy asked her.

"Because the President needs to be here, taking care of his country. No one is going to like your King of the World idea, least of all if Jeff is in their country. Plus, that leaves him far too open to assassination."

"This job is so great," Jeff muttered.

Mom ignored him and went on. "Plus we have alien ships arriving. We have no idea where they're going to land, but if they're coming to the United States anywhere, just as happened today, the President needs to be around, not presumed to be off on holiday."

"Where do you think the others will land?" I asked Muddy. "Near where all of you did?"

"It's possible. Your desert areas are very uncrowded normally, and they make fine landing sites."

"Marvelous," Chuckie said under his breath.

"The area we were just in is also popular," Muddy continued. "Though I believe landings are preferred farther from land."

Chuckie sat up straight. "You mean in the Bermuda Triangle?"

"If that's what you call it."

"We do." Chuckie was almost vibrating with excitement. "Why there?"

Muddy looked surprised. "Many ships prefer a water landing, and that area is clearly marked for such."

CHAPTER 40

THE ROOM WENT SILENT. Broke it. "Um, excuse me? What do you mean by the area being marked?"

"For landings," Muddy said patiently. "There are clear indications for where to land if you know what to look for."

"How long have those markings been there?"

"To our knowledge, forever." Muddy shrugged. "I realize by your expressions that for all of you this is shocking. For us, it's not so much. Your desert area is marked for landing, too."

"Hang on." Got up and ran to the family dining room again and went to the fridge. "Odd request. Need a map of the peaks that the Planetary Council landed on right before my wedding, and I also need a map of the Bermuda Triangle. And any other triangular places that you think or, rather, know are marked as freaking alien landing sites."

Opened the door. There was an atlas sitting on the shelf. Took it out to see that there were bookmarks placed throughout. "Thank you once again for all you do." Closed the door and ran back to the others. "Found this atlas that I've been prepping to show the kids where we're going."

Flipped it open before anyone could mention that I'd had zero time to prep anything other than my introductory speech for a Code Name: First Lady marathon. Made a mental note to talk to Raj about that whole Hollywood situation before it blew up in our faces. Again.

The page was the Bermuda Triangle. "I see no markings," Chuckie said. "And this atlas has pictures taken from space."

"They don't photograph well, perhaps," Muddy said politely. "However, they are there. We Turleens come here enough that we didn't need to choose an official landing area. Plus, we were coming specifically to meet with the Queen of the World."

"Seriously, call me Kitty, and also seriously, stop using that title. We get it, your hints are landing hard. We just know humans and we all know how badly everyone in the world is going to take the assumption that Jeff and I are their sovereign lords."

The next bookmark was for the area I'd asked about—the section of southern New Mexico and Arizona that had Hatchet, Animas, and Chiricahua Peaks, which formed a very shallow triangle. This area was a hotbed of alien activity and always had been.

Apparently, we now knew why.

Because Muddy nodded rather enthusiastically. "Oh yes, that's the landing area."

We all looked at Wruck. "So, did the Ancients provide landing strip information on our planet, or was that the Z'porrah?"

He had the grace to look embarrassed. "I believe that was done long ago. We both used to mark the worlds so that our observation teams and, as you'd call them, missionaries would be able to land safely."

"And you never thought to mention it because?" Chuckie asked.

"Because it never occurred to me. I'm sorry, I've been here a long time, and in that time, I've been aligned with you for only a few weeks. I haven't thought about the landing areas since LaRue attacked and almost killed me. That information was never something I'd have even considered sharing with those I was associating with."

Most of the room didn't look happy with this answer. But it made sense to me. "That's fine, John. We have to remember that we're lucky you're here, alive and well and with us. We're just already so used to having you around that we forget that you were alone, behind enemy lines, for decades."

Jeff sighed. "Kitty makes a good point, and I apologize for being upset with you for forgetting to tell us something key."

"I'll do my best to remember what you all don't know," Wruck said, earning chuckles from most of the room.

"How many of the ships coming to us will prefer a water landing, do you think?" Jeff asked Muddy and Wruck.

"The Faradawn Treeship will, most likely, as will the Vrierst ship," Muddy replied. "As for the others, we're unsure."

"My data is out of date on anything like this," Wruck said. "I had no idea the Mykali were here. I don't know that any of us, Ancients or Z'porrah, know."

"Probably for the best, at least in terms of keeping the Mykali safe. But back on topic, the Shantanu definitely were water landers. A manta ray ship landing in water makes sense, and I guess a tree heading for water does, as well." Thought about the other ships we'd seen. "The Z'porrah tend to be hoverers. Will any of the others do that, hover impressively overhead?"

"Hovering overhead is usually reserved for an attack or is done as part of an official welcome," Muddy said. "Though we can't speak for those coming to Earth just now."

"Doesn't matter," Jeff said. "What it means is that we need to be prepared to have these ships land in our deserts and our oceans."

"Are we sure they're coming to our deserts and oceans?" I asked. Looked at the atlas. There were a lot of other bookmarks in it.

Every head, including the three Turleen heads, nodded. "They are coming to seek protection from the King and Queen of the World," Muddy said. "As I keep reminding you."

"Chuckie, we need the mind working on how we spin this, because I'm fresh out of cool marketing ideas. All I've got as a blueprint is *Independence Day*, and I'm hoping we're ready to have our experience go better when the Aicirtap arrive."

"I hated that movie," Chuckie said, but I could tell he was thinking. He shook his head. "Give me a little time."

"I'm not sure that we have it," Mom said. "The estimates for arrivals are just that—estimates."

My phone beeped. Got off Jeff's lap and went over to dig it out of my purse. Noted that my music app was open and the song cued up was V.V. Brown's "Shark in the Water." Snorted a laugh but kept myself under control. Either Algar had had that hint up for me and I'd just never looked at it or else, as I suspected, he was sharing a joke with me.

Looked at the text that had just come in. "Huh, Nadine says that all three kids want to stay at the Embassy tonight."

"They don't want to be with us?" Jeff asked, sounding hurt.

"Apparently Pierre is having some kind of elaborate sleepover for all the Daycare Kids and ours don't want to be left out." Checked to see if I had any other texts. I did. "Mom, Dad's there, too, and wants to know if you're okay with him staying with the kids."

"Tell them all yes," Mom said. "You and Jeff need to get cleaned up and dressed and then everyone needs to get back to the Large Situation Room. When aliens are arriving, the government doesn't get to sleep."

Sent confirmation texts to Dad and Nadine. Wasn't sure if I should be hurt or relieved that the kids didn't want to hang with us tonight. Settled for both.

Chuckie called Serene and Jeff called Raj. Craig and Francine were eating an official dinner and then would be heading to the LSR. Those who needed to know what was really going on did. All others would remain unaware that Jeff and I had taken a side trip to Bermuda.

Since the Planetary Council were still on-site, Mom decided that the Turleens would go with her and the others and get introduced while Jeff and I cleaned up.

"What time is it?" I asked as Jeff closed the door that led out to the main hallway. "I'm totally jumbled from going back and forth across the country and I didn't think to actually look at the time when I was looking at my phone."

Jeff turned and shot me a look I was very familiar with—his Jungle Cat About To Eat Me look. My breathing got heavy.

"It's time," he said, as he locked the door, "for you to change out of that bikini."

CHAPTER 41

JEFF STRIPPED OFF my bikini quickly. "Mmm, looks like you didn't sunburn."

"You'd probably better check me all over just to be sure." Yanked his trunks down just before he picked me up and stepped out of the trunks.

"Gladly," he purred. "I plan to check all over. In a very detailed manner." With that I wrapped my legs around his waist, his mouth covered mine, and we went from zero to a hundred in less than a moment.

Jeff was grinding against me and I was doing the same to him, while his mouth ravaged mine and I ran my hands through his hair. Rubbed my breasts against his chest, felt his hair rubbing against my nipples, and I was ready to go for it.

In the olden days, before kids, we'd take a long time on foreplay. Tonight the kids weren't around, so we should have been able to take our time, but we had a huge room full of people waiting on us. So we didn't wait.

Jeff slid into me and all the rest of the crap that was going on faded away. Aliens, bombs, haters, sharks . . . those things didn't matter right now. It was just the two of us, slamming together at hyperspeed, which sounds like it would be a disappointing sexual experience but was, frankly, the complete opposite.

My orgasm hit hard and I triggered Jeff. Howled into his mouth while he growled back into mine. Our bodies shuddered in time together and I enjoyed the feelings of sexual satisfaction that washed over me.

For normal men, that would be it. Great, but it. But Jeff was far from normal in all the good ways, and A-C regenerative powers were never more impressive than during sexy times.

Still inside me, he carried me into our bathroom, continuing to make out the whole way. He turned the shower on with one hand while we ground together again and pretty much just like that he was ready to go again. I was pretty much always ready to go, and right now was no exception.

The shower was one of our favorite places to do the deed, and the soundproofing at the White House was, thankfully, as good as it was at the American Centaurion Embassy, meaning I could yowl my head off and the only person who would know about it was Jeff. Had the distinct impression he really enjoyed my sounding like a cat in heat and was a connoisseur of the various noises I made, because he sure did his best to make sure I was symphonic every single time.

Once we were under the water, Jeff moved his mouth from mine and onto my breasts. He'd brought me to orgasm at second base the first time we'd ever slept together, and he liked to ensure he batted a thousand every time.

However, it took more effort if I'd orgasmed already, which was fine with me and, apparently, also fine with Jeff. He put my back up against the shower wall, then sucked, nipped, and licked my breasts and nipples, while his hands massaged my butt in a way that was erotic without being sexual, and I continued to grind against him.

Unsurprisingly to me after all this time together, I was heading toward the edge in good time, and, as Jeff nibbled the space between my breasts, I went over the edge.

He waited until my howling was done, for the moment, at least, then let me slide down his body. "Time to wash up, baby," he said in a low, sexy voice.

"Happy to." Getting clean had become one of my favorite things in the world when Jeff and I met, and it remained on my Top Ten Best Things To Do With My Husband List.

One of the many plusses about being attached to American Centaurion were the bath products. They'd always been good, but when Pierre had come on as the Concierge Majordomo of the Embassy, he'd upgraded all personal care products to his standards, and he'd insisted we have these products at the White House Complex, too. Per Pierre, they weren't always the most expensive, but they were definitely the best.

Our soap selection was vast, and our shower had very nice built-in shelves that held it all. Chose a sandalwood and vanilla combination soap along with a soft sponge, and started to soap Jeff up.

He grinned and followed suit, choosing a lavender and vanilla combo for me. Soon we were covered in soap, soap bubbles, and sexual desire. "Can I take a picture of you like this in case the vote goes for you to stay in D.C. when I go on my tour? Just, you know, so I have something to stare at?"

Jeff laughed. "Only if I get the same shot of you." He bent down and kissed me. Dropped my sponge and started soaping certain parts of him up with my hands only. He dropped his sponge, too, and did likewise.

After a few erotic minutes of this he rinsed us off, and I did as well—soap was great but not fun in the intimate areas. Once the soap was gone, however, Jeff knelt down and made really sure that I was rinsed clean.

Grabbed his head and just held on while his lips, teeth, and tongue reminded me why it was great to be his woman and the water flowed over us.

Finally, he sucked in just the right way at just the right time and I hit High C. He delved his tongue deep inside of me, then worked his way up my body licking me everywhere. My neck was my main erogenous zone and, once he was there, he spent some time ravaging it, just to ensure that I had a kind of double orgasm. I was too busy feeling the rapture to determine if it was one huge long one or two or more, but decided to forgive myself for the lapse.

I was almost unable to stand anymore when he picked me up and slid back inside me. Was still able to wrap my legs around his waist and, in order to again take an active role in all of this, bit down right where his shoulder met his neck. Diligent hunting over the years had shown that this was an area that made Jeff go harder and faster and, true to my experience, he growled and thrust into me—fast but not at hyperspeed, just fast for a human.

Moved my mouth from his neck to his ear and gently bit his ear lobe. This was also something he liked, and him thrusting faster was confirmation.

We were like this for a good long while, alternating between who was nipping and nuzzling whom, but even the greatest things have to come to an end. Jeff sped up, just a little, but it was enough, and I went over the edge again and he came with me.

Our bodies shuddered in time, then he once again let me slide down his body. Nuzzled my face in between his pecs. "Mmm, I love being married to the Alien Sex God."

"I just take those marriage vows to always make you happy seriously."

Rubbed my face against the hair on his chest when something occurred to me. "Hey, you know, we haven't washed our hair yet."

Jeff chuckled as he kissed the top of my head. "Well, we'll have to rectify that immediately if not sooner. Can't go to an important meeting with unwashed hair."

"Decorum is our watchword."

Jeff grinned at me. "And here I was thinking our watchword was orgasm."

"Good point. I like your choice better."

CHAPTER 42

SEVERAL MORE CLIMAXES LATER, we were both shampooed and conditioned and clean. We dried off then headed to the closet to get dressed.

Jeff was, of course, in the latest set of the Armani Fatigues, and I was in my FLOTUS Standard Issue—the exact same outfit Francine had been or was still in. Managed not to heave a sigh. The benefits of being married to Jeff far outweighed our somehow having become the top couple of the United States.

Jeff wasn't using hyperspeed to dress, meaning he was as excited about the next round of Stress Meetings as I was. He was going so slowly that I finished dressing first, which was quite the rarity.

"You okay?"

He nodded. "Just don't feel like rushing." Jeff kissed my cheek. "But thanks for worrying about me."

Thusly reassured, headed out of the closet to see that the atlas was on the floor. Which was not where I'd left it. And it was opened to one of the bookmarked pages. But not one that we'd looked at already.

Took a look. The page was one for part of the Middle East. And there was a faint triangle drawn on it.

Picked up the atlas and took a closer look. "Huh."

"What are you doing?" Jeff asked, as he came out fixing his tie.

"Studying places to go." Realized I needed to have a chat with whichever Powers That Be I could reach, meaning I needed to be alone. Leaned up and gave Jeff a kiss. "I'm sure this isn't your preferred plan, but are you okay going down ahead of me?"

His eyebrow raised. "Want to tell me what's going on?"

"Sure. I have a Secret Boyfriend I want to hook up with. He's been waiting patiently and, since we're all done here for now, it's his turn."

Jeff snorted. "Got it, I'll mind my own business."

Hugged him. "I just want to make sure I don't lose this thought. It relates to my fun FLOTUS World Tour and, as I'm sure you can tell, I'm nervous about doing a good job."

He kissed me deeply. "You'll be great, baby, you always are."

"Thanks and right back atcha, especially when it comes to sex. I promise not to take too long to join you and the others in the Fun House."

"That's a good name for the Large Situation Room, as long as you mean it sarcastically, and I know you do."

Jeff left, and I waited for a few moments, just to be sure he hadn't forgotten something. My coast apparently clear, took the atlas and headed into the closet. Stood in front of the hamper. "Thanks for all the help today."

Waited. Nothing.

"Um, I'd love to ask a couple of questions, starting with the page the atlas was opened to. If you have time and all that."

More nothing.

Heaved a sigh. "Look, I'm about to head out around the world trying to ease everyone into a 'most aliens are good' mindset while at the same time prepping the world for galactic war, along with trying to find and stop Stephanie, Cliff, and you and ACE alone know who else. I'm also not sure if I should be supporting Muddy with the idea that Jeff should come with me, or supporting Mom with the idea that Jeff should stay here, and I have literally no idea which option is better in the short or long run."

Nada.

Heaved another sigh. "Okay. Well, um, thanks for the goggles and such. You know I'm aware that you won't always come when I call, right?" Turned around. "I'll check my iPod and phone for more musical clues. Maybe ACE will be feeling chatty tonight, should Jamie actually slumber at Pierre's slumber party."

"Except that I usually do come when you call."

Turned around to see a handsome, rakish dwarf with tousled dark hair and eyes that were just a little too green to be natural for Earth sitting cross-legged on top of the hamper.

"So, were you in the shower or something?"

"No. There are just times I enjoy seeing what approach you're going to use."

Rolled my eyes. "I'd say ugh and something else unpleasant, but I'm sure that would mean you disappeared, so I'll just laugh hollowly and play along."

"I also always find it interesting that you're worried that you'll manage to overcome the obstacles in your path."

"Dude, seriously, I don't know why that's a shock to you."

"You beat a great white shark away from helpless sea slugs."

"You mean I slammed my fists into a shark's snout until the shapeshifter noticed I was being stupid and then saved me and the others."

Algar cocked his head at me. "Why would you think being a protector, in any way, is stupid?"

"John was right there."

"John was distracted."

"He'd have noticed how close the shark was before I got there."

"Would he have?" Algar shrugged. "Maybe he would have. Maybe he wouldn't have, and another universe would create because of the fact that he was eaten by a great white shark."

"Is that how they create? One incident? And, if that's the case, did another universe create because I stayed on the boat instead of going back into the water or because I considered staying or whatever?"

Algar raised his eyebrow. "Is that what you wanted to talk to me about, the multiverse?"

"Well, no, not so much. Not that I'm against that talk, but I kind of have a lot going on in this particular part of this particular universe. And I could really use some advice or suggestions or even just a playlist with answers."

Algar chuckled. "You know you don't really need my help."

"Oh my God, not this again. I need something. Earth and the galaxy need something. I have no idea how to handle what's coming. I'm not sure what to focus on, and I know I'm totally out of my depth."

He sighed. "What would you do if I told you that it would be impossible for you to handle things incorrectly?"

"I'd say you were lying like a wet rug. I've heard the whole 'you can't make a wrong choice because your choice is right at that time' thing. That's fantastic in terms of choosing what job to take, or what dress to wear, or what city to move to, but it's not quite as easy when you're dealing with a galactic issue that involves multiple races, including some who, point-blank, want to eat us."

"There is that, yes."

"Is Muddy correct in terms of what he told us about the Aicirtap?"

"He is, as a matter of fact. The Turleens travel all over the galaxy, sometimes openly, sometimes stealthily."

"In other words, ask Muddy some more questions about what's going on."

"I always recommend being curious."

"I'm curious about why the atlas was opened to a page showing the United Arab Emirates, Saudi Arabia, and Iran. Complete with a triangle drawn around an area where the points of said triangle are, I believe, the three tallest structures in the Middle East."

"Why would you think that was significant?"

"In addition to the fact that the book was opened to that page? Because apparently the Bermuda Triangle and the triangle formed by the three peaks that the Planetary Council landed on right before my wedding are both landing strips for alien spacecraft. And I want to know if there are others, where they are, and how they will or won't affect what's heading to us from space."

Locked eyes with Algar. Did not figure I had a chance in hell of winning a stare-down competition with him, but still felt up to giving it a try because I really wanted some answers.

Algar smiled at me, blinked slowly, and suddenly I saw things in his eyes. Triangles all over the world, each one marking a safe place to land for a variety of different aliens. Some no longer used, some used all the time.

The images flashed through his eyes, just as images had flashed through Jamie's newborn eyes during Operation Confusion, when I had to find her father and everyone else in order to save them and the day. I'd thought ACE had done that, possibly even Jamie herself, but now it was obvious that Algar had been the one to give me those vital clues.

The triangle that connected the three tallest structures in the Middle East had something unusual in the exact middle, which happened to be in the Persian Gulf—it had a structure deep under the water. And that structure didn't look manmade, at least not by any man from Earth. It resembled a gigantic block that was made up of a bunch of inverted tentacles, only not really. But that was the closest I could get. Really hoped that it wasn't where Cthulhu and his pals hung out, because that was possibly the very last thing we needed.

There were also other images that flashed through Algar's eyes, including the tallest structure in the world and one of the Middle Eastern Triangle Points—the Burj Khalifa.

Algar blinked again and the images were gone. I was looking back into his normal eyes, if they could ever be considered normal.

"Wow. Um. That was . . . intense. Oh, and thanks, by the way, for helping me save everyone when Jamie was born."

He smiled. "I don't do it for your thanks, you know."

"I know. But for whatever reason you *do* do it, I appreciate your support." Considered all I'd seen. "Paris wasn't 'there.' Nowhere that looked like France was."

Algar shot me a very innocent smile.

"Huh. You don't want me wasting time on Cliff's lame 'go capture Stephanie' clue. Why not? Siler's pretty much confirmed that she's there."

"Benjamin is rarely wrong, and he's not wrong now. However, I know you know how to prioritize."

"Yeah, well, stopping the bad guys feels like a priority. And you know I'm going to have to hit Paris, London, Sydney, and any number of other major cities."

Algar sighed. "You asked for help. I give it to you, and you discount and ignore it."

He had a point. Pondered it while I looked through the rest of the bookmarked pages. Most of them related to the area in the Middle East that the atlas had been opened to. Clearly Algar felt that a lot of action was going to take place in this area.

Thought some more. "The triangular areas are actually landing sites, right?"

"So Muddy told you, yes."

"I'm asking for your confirmation, please and thank you."

"Fine. Yes."

"Wow. A straight answer. I may faint. Later, when there's time for it."

Actively chose not to mention that he was being far less obscure in his helpful hints than normal—why push my luck? Also actively chose not to wonder if Algar was being more clearly helpful than usual because what was coming was so horrendous that he felt he had to give us more of a fighting chance, mostly because I had a horrible feeling that this was indeed his reason for being a Helpy Helper.

Instead, ran over everything that had happened so far during the Kitty's Current Big Day Show. "What was Casey, the Casey in the police department, the thing that blew up? Android, robot, something else?"

"Ah, and now you ask the right question." Algar sounded pleased but in no way ready to actually, you know, answer the right question.

Resisted the urge to sigh and roll my eyes. "Okay, so she's the key to whatever it is you want me focused on, right?"

Algar nodded.

"Argh, you're killing me, Smalls. Okay, so there has to be something significant or off or extra-weird about her or you wouldn't be having so much fun with this. So, lemme ponder some more, since I know you love making me work for it."

"This is how you learn."

"Thanks, Professor Algar." Considered why Casey had looked so bad. "So, here's a thought. Androids are so well made they can pass for humans, both externally and emotionally. But Casey looked flat-out awful. We stopped Stephanie's android-ization of Joe and Randy mid-process. They're changed internally, but they still look the same."

"And?" Algar asked leadingly.

"And that means that Casey wasn't an android, unless said android was made to look awful, and I kind of doubt it. Though, it's a great excuse for why she wanted to 'turn' on Cliff."

"Go on."

"Okay, Fem-Bots are made, currently, to look like specific people. And neither Cliff nor Stephanie are involved in their creation or manufacture. Or, rather, if the Mastermind Complex started the Fem-Bots, someone else finished them. Meaning that Casey was not a Fem-Bot gone wrong."

Received yet another nod. Once again had to actively choose not to make a smartass comment. Just tried to channel Chuckie and look at this as a cool way of exercising my mind.

"Therefore we can rule out Casey being a Fem-Bot, and she probably wasn't an android, either. But she smelled human, or human enough, to the dogs, and she didn't register as non-human to Tito's tests, though she did register as 'off.' Sure, he didn't use the OVS, but Tito made a point of saying that she registered as distinctly different from any android or Fem-Bot we've seen."

"And?" Algar was definitely in Teacher Mode. Lucky me.

Focused back on things that had bothered me about Casey at

the police station. And thought about what I knew about her. "I can't believe that Casey signed on for a suicide mission. I mean, seriously, she's a survivor. And I also can't believe that Cliff did some weird test on her and then let her go. The testing as punishment I could believe, but not that they allowed her to escape. Them allowing her to escape I could believe if she didn't know she was wired to explode. But it was clear that she did."

"What else was unusual about her or the situation?"

"She looked awful, and it was real, not makeup. Whatever was done to her was a real thing."

"So, what might all that mean?" Algar asked.

"Will you answer a question first?"

"If you insist."

"I really do, because I can't answer the Big Question without this confirmation. Was whatever that Casey Thing was sent to us by Cliff and/or someone acting on his direction?"

Algar shook his head. "The things you waste your specific questions on amaze me."

"Amaze *me* and give me the answer, please and thank you."

"Yes."

It was amazing what some simple confirmations could do, though, regardless of whether or not Algar approved of my specific questions.

"I know what that Casey Thing was."

CHAPTER 43

ALGAR COCKED HIS HEAD at me. "And just what was she?"

"Please tell me if I'm wrong, but I think she's a clone. A badly done clone, but a clone nonetheless."

"Why do you think that?"

Well, it wasn't a flat-out "you're wrong" so held onto the idea that I was right. "Because the Mastermind Collective has perfected cloning. Or, at least, they had perfected it. I know we destroyed their main cloning facility during Operation Infiltration, and we also stole all their manuals. Maybe Cliff's brilliant enough to have all that memorized, but I'd wager that LaRue added at least fifty percent of whatever the process was, and I don't think the LaRue Clone is going to be as on the ball as the Original Model. Based on The Clarence Clone and Ronaldo Two-Point-O, the clones have a strong degradation from copy to copy, at least the ones hastily created do. And these days, I'm betting every clone has been hastily made, whether due to lack of proper equipment or a safe place to complete the cloning process."

"What do you perceive as wrong with those two clones?"

"TCC is simple. Not stupid, but he wasn't given the memory dump. Two-Point-O got memories, which is why he's a better cloned version. But he wasn't given enough, in that sense, because he knew the memories weren't his own and so rejected them. But Casey seemed like Casey, only she looked horrible."

"How well do you know Casey?"

"Not well at all. Okay, all she had to be was unpleasant and spout whatever Cliff told her to and I'd believe it was her. Cliff knows us well—far better than Stephanie does, in that sense—and he has our playbook memorized."

"Well done."

"So, I'm right? She was a clone?"

"Yes. Now, what does *that* tell you?"

Considered why Algar felt that focusing me on an area in the Middle East would be important. We were all pretty sure that Cliff was in the Middle East, so his new hideout could conceivably be within the triangle. In fact, based on my seeing the Burj Khalifa more than once, it was a safe bet he was somewhere in the UAE, probably close to Dubai.

My brain nudged. The real thing that Algar wanted me to note was that Cliff was cloning again. Sure, the Casey Clone had looked horrific, but if I took that to its most logical conclusion, then it showed that the process wasn't working well.

But it worked well enough to get her into the D.C.P.D. station so she could blow it up and get the DUI Dudes into one of our facilities. It probably hadn't mattered to them which one. Wherever we'd gone, they'd have had us pinpointed and Club 51 True Believers had plenty of supporters all over the country. Even if we'd gone to the White House, my playbook said that I'd flip the prisoners onto my side and therefore take them along with me. Which was exactly what I'd done.

"I hate being so transparent."

"It's worse to be evil. Just saying."

"Thanks for that. Okay, so Cliff is back in the cloning business."

Algar nodded. "His form of uplift."

That was absolutely a clue so I didn't speak. Instead I thought about why Algar had said the words he just had.

Algar felt that Muddy was giving us good and accurate intel, meaning that whatever Muddy had said I could take as gospel, at least for the moment. He'd described how the Z'porrah's current version of uplift—sold as making an already sentient race "higher" on the evolutionary scale and extending their lifespans—had backfired on the Aicirtap. And the Q'vox were terrified of what might happen to them if they were uplifted in this manner.

In point of fact, I'd noted to myself so many hours ago that we wanted to keep the Q'vox far, far away from Cliff and Stephanie, because cloning minotaurs that were billed as unstoppable when enraged sounded like a really bad idea that the League of Evil Geniuses would undoubtedly embrace.

"Wow. You're right. I actually had the answer already."

"And yet you persist in demanding my time and attention."

"I like feeling special. You're worried that Cliff will get his heinous mitts on the new aliens, the Q'vox in particular, and that will spell the end of this planet and, most likely, this galaxy." Thought some more, specifically about what Algar had shown to be hidden at the bottom of the Persian Gulf. "Crap."

"Excuse me?"

"I just realized what the building at the bottom of the Gulf looks like. Besides a vacation home for the Cleophese. So, um, I need to ask another question that you're going to berate me for asking. But a girl really likes to be sure before she panics."

"I'll allow it."

"You're too kind. Muddy expects the Faradawn ship—the ship carrying however many fleeing Q'vox on it—to land in water. Muddy and everyone else would expect that water to be in the Bermuda Triangle. Only . . . if I think about what you showed me and I consider what little I saw of the Treeship, said ship possesses roots, or things that look like roots. And roots resemble tentacles. And I think the Faradawn ship is actually going to dock itself in the Persian Gulf. Is that correct?"

"Most likely, yes."

Algar saying most likely meant one hundred thousand percent yes. "And, just spitballing here, but you also firmly feel that Cliff's found a new base of operations in the Middle East, nice and near to this landing site, most likely in or around Dubai."

"It's a very welcoming country. Quite modern for the area. Lovely hotels. Amazing architecture."

"I'll recommend you write for their Tourism Bureau. So, do we invade the UAE, ask for their help with extradition of America's Literally Most Wanted, or what?"

"You have a tour you need to go on," Algar said, as if the rest of this conversation hadn't happened. "You need to focus on that, not bothering a foreign country with America's little problems."

Stared at him. He stared back, expression pleasant. Resisted the urge to strangle him. Instead, took a deep breath, held it, and let it out slowly.

Looked at the atlas again. The triangle cut through Iraq as well, and there were three other countries included inside the triangle. Fully included, which the UAE, Saudi Arabia, and Iran were definitely not. Qatar, Kuwait, and . . . Bahrain. "It's time for me to talk to our friends at the Bahraini Embassy, isn't it?"

"It would make sense for the First Lady to visit the country from which one of her dearest friends comes."

"Check. And we'll manage not to insult Israel with this decision because Mossad will handle that for us in some way. So, you'd suggest that I start the tour in Bahrain, right? Just go for the gusto without passing go or collecting two hundred dollars?"

"It would seem wise."

"Jeff needs to stay home, doesn't he? Not because of all the official reasons, but because of Chuckie. If Jeff goes with me, then Chuckie will come with us, too. And he'll murder Cliff or, worse, give Cliff an opportunity to hurt or kill him, because I don't care what he or anyone else says—Cliff is the reason Naomi's dead and there's no way that Chuckie doesn't still want to avenge that."

"See? You really don't need to come running to me to chat all the time."

"Oh, but I enjoy the mental workout so very much. You know, I'm supposed to bring the kids with me. Sure, we'll have full protection details on all of them, but this just took on a whole additional dimension of risk. I'm not sure they should be coming along. I don't care about my looking like the worst mother in the world, but I do care about my kids or Lizzie getting snatched by the Crazy Eights. Or anyone else, for that matter."

Algar shrugged. "As to that, I recommend you focus on getting to sleep as soon as you possibly can. I'd also suggest eating some rich dessert prior to going to bed. It should ensure you have vivid dreams."

And with that, Algar snapped his fingers and disappeared.

CHAPTER 44

"THANK YOU," I said to the hamper. "I really do enjoy our talks." Sorta. Some were definitely less painful than others. This one was threatening to give me a migraine.

Put the atlas back onto our coffee table. Considered putting it into my purse, but it was kind of heavy.

Algar's "chat with ACE" hint made me just want to blow off the LSR and try to sleep. However, there was no way that Jamie was asleep enough for me to safely talk to ACE—it was just turning nine at night. Her bedtime was seven whenever we could manage it, but there was no way she was asleep yet, not with Pierre in charge of the festivities. They were probably into the second movie in whatever Disney marathon he'd planned.

Meaning I had to cowgirl up and join the others in the Stress Meeting. Joy.

Considered what relieved stress. Had had sex with Jeff already and that wasn't an option right now. Couldn't cuddle the kids because they were elsewhere having fun. Looked in my purse. Sure enough, I had Snoozing Poofs on Board. But only Harlie and Poofikins. Had to figure that the other Poofs were with their owners.

Stroked the two Poofs gently. They made happy sleeping noises. Could have woken them up, but just the act of petting them made me feel better.

Wished Algar hadn't left already. I needed guidance for how to handle things in the LSR, since I couldn't very well say that The Great God Algar had shared some wisdom with me. Eating one of Chef's desserts wasn't going to be a problem, but it would be hours before I could legitimately try to talk to ACE in my sleep.

Pondered my options. There were two people in the world who I knew for certain were in the extremely limited Algar Club. White was undoubtedly in the LSR, so my calling him would be suspicious.

Had no idea of what time it was in Italy, but it was probably really early in the morning. Then again, he always insisted that if any of us needed guidance, he was there 24/7. Time to put that to the test. Pulled out my phone and made the call.

He answered on the fourth ring. "Kitty?" Gower sounded tired but not necessarily asleep. "Is everything okay?"

"Um, in some ways yes, in some ways no. Are you able to talk privately? And I apologize for most likely waking you up."

"I was awake. I've had trouble sleeping for a variety of reasons. Just didn't have my phone near me when you called."

"Are things okay with you?"

"Yes, it's just a difficult time, wrangling all these different religious leaders into one cohesive mindset. Officially we're all together. In reality, it's taking longer than we probably have."

"Yeah, as to that . . . I kind of need Supreme Pontifex guidance."

"Really?" Gower sounded a lot more awake. "What's wrong? Are things okay with Jeff and the kids?"

"Oh, yeah, this isn't a domestic issue. It's more of an 'I know what to do but cannot tell anyone *how* I know what to do' issue."

Gower was quiet for a few moments. "You talk to . . . him . . . regularly, don't you?"

"Yeah, I do. Do you?"

"Not as much as you. I think you're his favorite, but he does visit when I really need him." He cleared his throat. "I'm amazed we can talk about him at all."

"I think he knows we need to be able to not pussyfoot at this precise time. So, get comfortable, I have a lot to catch you up on."

Spent a good fifteen minutes talking fast and nonstop. The beauty of sharing with an A-C was that Gower could hear faster than I could talk, so I could talk as fast as possible. I still wasn't able to talk at hyperspeed, but I was a fast talker by nature, and when I had my Recap Girl cape on I was even faster.

Finished up. "So," Gower said slowly, "we should be realistic and admit that you're not really going on a FLOTUS world tour so much as you're going to use that as a cover to stop Cliff before the Faradawn Treeship lands and all hell literally breaks loose."

"Got it in one. I therefore need to start this tour in the Middle East. I can get Mona Nejem to help me start in Bahrain and, hopefully, use that as the excuse to talk to people in the region. But I'm sure that will meet with a lot of resistance."

"And jealousy, too, I'd imagine."

"Probably. More because it's 'The First Lady' visiting rather than anyone wanting me, specifically, to come hang out."

Gower chuckled. "Oh, don't sell yourself short, Kitty."

"Thanks for the vote of confidence. Not sure that makes any of this more workable."

"I can help you with the reason for why you need to start in Bahrain. We're having a lot of pushback from the Muslim leaders, more because they fear that their extremists will fight this tooth and nail than because they're not willing to move forward into the brave new world descending on us."

"Just like our extremists will. Yeah, I truly feel their pain. So, what, we're going to say that I'm going to the Middle East first to soothe the Muslim leaders? I'm Jewish. I'm not so sure that will fly."

"You may be Jewish, but your reputation precedes you, and you're considered someone essentially neutral."

"Pull the other one, it has bells on. My mother was in Mossad. For all we know, my mother is technically *still* in Mossad."

"Yes, and yet you can count the Ambassadress of Bahrain as a close friend. You're responsible for continuously breaking up the Al Dejahl terrorist network, which is not aligned with Islam in any way but which, due to the name and the region where the majority of recruitment is done, reflects badly on everyone in said region."

"Wow, you're as good at the diplomatic spin as Richard is." Had a happy thought. "Um, Paul? Would it be possible for you to go with me on this tour?"

He chuckled again. "Yes, I was anticipating the request. James isn't going to like the idea, though."

"Well, all of Alpha Team is supposed to go with me, and you're part of Alpha Team still, so . . ."

"That spin won't fly with him. However, the religious summit has voted to head to Saudi Arabia in an attempt to sway the hearts and minds of as many as possible. Europe seems to be the most willing to go along with us, but Russia and all those surrounding countries aren't so sure."

"Meaning I need to get Olga Dalca involved as well."

"Yes, again, your being close friends with the Romanian Ambassadress is a huge help and yet another example of your neutrality."

Chose not to ask how I'd become the poster girl for We Are The World. "Whatever works. Speaking of the region, though, I'm sure that Cliff has a benefactor of some kind helping him out, because if he's embedded himself in that area, and I'm really sure that he has, then he didn't do it without assistance."

"There are always remnants of Al Dejahl around, just waiting for their new leader. I'd assume that's who he's with."

"Figure one of them has money, because Hacker International cleared out of most of Cliff's holdings along with those of anyone else connected to him that they could find."

"Our enemies rarely work alone."

"Which is why I don't want to, either. So, does Jeff go with me or stay here? And what about the kids? I was told, gads, only this morning that the kids were going with me on the world tour, but I'm worried about taking them."

Gower was quiet for another few moments. "I think your mother is right—the President needs to stay put. I understand why Muddy thinks otherwise, but while the Turleens may have visited a lot, what they haven't done is interact with humans, and observation is different from interaction. Plus, as you mentioned, we don't want Chuck on the front lines with Cliff if we can help it."

"I kind of wish ACE was still riding shotgun with you."

He chuckled. "I know. He won't allow anything to hurt Jamie. Or any of the other children, either."

"I know, but as the memory of the two of you trapped in an airless chamber in a baggage car of the Paris Metro is still vivid, we need to remember that ACE and Jamie both are vulnerable to any variety of attacks."

"Attacks on your mothering skills aren't going to help the situation, though."

"True enough, but I'd rather have those attacks come at me than have my children in danger. And while Lizzie is more than capable of kicking butt, she's still a kid, too."

"Can't argue any of that. I'm going to call into the Situation Room. I'm awake and it sounds like my input could be useful."

"It always is. Call the Large Situation Room, by the way—we've got all hands on deck."

Gower chuckled. "Will do."

"Are we telling them all about the real plan?"

"No. If Jeff knows you're planning to take on Cliff he won't stay in the States, and Chuck will try to get there first and handle it himself, which we know we don't want. I think we keep the real plan to ourselves and those who must know until we're in the Middle East."

"Works for me. I'll have to tell Mona what's going on in order to get her help, and Olga will probably already know most of it."

"That's fine, but for the Large Situation Room, we're doing this as a joint political and religious action."

"Works for me. Tell them I'm on my way, please and thank you."

"Will do, and I'll see you soon, Kitty."

Hung up and considered my next moves. Figured it would be a lot better if I already had things set up, so I called Mona first. She was awake and, since I could tell her what was really going on—excepting the assistance from one of the Powers That Be—she was quickly amenable. And she was clear that the real mission was on a need-to-know basis and most, Jeff included, wouldn't actually know about it until we'd either succeeded or needed help.

"Anything we can do to end that madman once and for all is something I wholeheartedly support," she said after I'd given her all the pertinent details. "Give me a few hours, but I can guarantee that your first stop will be Bahrain. I'll be going with you, and that will give you an entrée into any of the other countries you need."

"You're the best. I'll add you and Khalid to my gigantic entourage roster. What about Oren, Jakob, and Leah?"

"I believe that Mossad will be present."

Considered this. "Wow, you have fake Bahraini passports for them, don't you?"

"I like to keep my friends close, and safe, since they keep *me* safe. Besides, as the religious summit has said and you have confirmed, we're about to enter into a new world order where Mossad will be a friendly comfort opposed to the strange new beings coming here to hide or hinder."

"Well put. Keep me posted, I doubt anyone's getting much sleep tonight."

We hung up, and now it was time to contact Olga. Olga normally preferred personal visits. Considered options and called her granddaughter, Adriana. "Grandmother says that she will be pleased for us to join you in the Large Situation Room, if you would be so kind as to send escorts."

"Wow. I swear that Olga is the most amazing person I know."

"She said you'd say that and wanted me to remind you that she pays attention to everything. And to tell you that she and I will, of course, not tell your husband or anyone else why you want to go to the Middle East first. We are fully invested in getting rid of the Mastermind and all of his cronies sooner as opposed to later."

"Again, wow. Um, do you two know that we have more aliens on the way?"

Received a few moments of silence. "No, but it makes sense. I will let Grandmother know."

"Do, because some of them are coming to hide, some to help, and some to destroy. So, you know, business as usual for all of us. I'll revel in knowing something Olga didn't for as long as it takes for you guys to get here. I'll send Len and Kyle and a couple of Field teams to get you two. You want an obvious car or stealth?"

"Stealth for tonight, I believe. Obvious will be for later."

"Gotcha, and see you soon."

Sent Chuckie and Jeff a text, telling them that I needed Olga and Adriana picked up pronto. Got a confirmation text from Chuckie that this would be done immediately and the strong suggestion to get my butt into the LSR before the Romanians arrived.

Decided there was no more stalling I could get away with. Used hyperspeed to get to the room in less than three seconds. Opened the door at human normal speeds, just in case we had someone who wasn't aware that I was enhanced in there. By now I couldn't remember who knew what and had stopped trying to remember.

My timing was great, as I opened the door just in time to hear people yelling at each other.

CHAPTER 45

THANKFULLY, a quick scan of the room showed that no one in here was doing the shouting. The TV screens were live and showing a variety of religious and other protests going on. The shouting was coming from a Club Fifty-One True Believers and Church of Hate and Intolerance rally on one screen, and several different screaming protests in what were clearly Middle Eastern countries. Frankly, there were protests going on all over the world, it looked like.

"You're just in time," Jeff said as I took my seat next to him. "Paul's on speakerphone, by the way. He's the one who told us to turn on the TVs."

"I hate this show. Let's find a *Love Boat* marathon."

"I wish. The hackers are also listening in. I have them on mute, however. They'll text Chuck if they have something key." Jeff heaved a sigh. "Raj, turn it down, please, I think we all get the gist."

While Raj complied, took a look around the room. Everyone from earlier in the day was here, along with extras like the Chief Usher, Antoinette Reilly, which made sense since she would be intimately involved in planning my FLOTUS World Tour. I wasn't stressing her out every minute of every day anymore, but I was pretty sure I was still causing her pain on an hourly basis. There were a ton of other important folks here as well. Nice to be popular.

The Secret Service, K-9 squad, dogs, and sorta prisoners weren't in the room. Had no idea where they were, but in this room wasn't it. Maybe Jeff had sent them to hang out with Hacker International over at the Zoo, which was what we called the second building of our Embassy Complex.

Wherever they were, it was good they weren't in the LSR,

because I wouldn't have had a hope of getting in if they'd been here. Basically, the room—the extra-large room we were using because we had so many people—was packed. Wondered if I should sit on Jeff's lap to make a seat available, then decided that was a question I should never voice aloud unless I wanted to give Antoinette a heart attack and hear everyone else tell me I wasn't acting appropriately for my station, which was never in both cases.

"Paul," Raj said when the sound was finally turned off for all the screens, "this definitely makes your points, both of them."

"Figured it was easier to show you than to try to explain it," Gower said from the speakerphone.

"Which points were?" I asked Jeff quietly.

"That I'm staying here and you're starting your tour in the Middle East and leaving, most likely, tomorrow. Don't play like you don't know—Paul told us he'd already spoken to you."

"Wasn't trying to hide anything." Well, not about that. "I just wanted to be sure we were on the same page and all that." Chose not to focus on flowers and instead to worry about whether or not the kids should be coming with me. It was a legit concern and something Jeff would expect to pick up from me emotionally.

Wisely, as it turned out. Jeff squeezed my hand. "I think we'll have to leave the decision on the kids to your mother and uncle, baby."

There were so many people in here that I'd missed him, but my Uncle Mort was indeed in the room. The fact that I'd missed him was just a testament to my lack of observational skills, since he was in the Military Corridor. Colonel Marvin Hamlin, Colonel Arthur Franklin, and Captain Gil Morgan were with him, and they weren't the only ones.

I was kind of surprised to see Lt. Col. Sergio Gonzalez here, in from Home Base, aka Area 51, and Colonel John Butler, too. Butler was now an in-control android, but under the circumstances, couldn't argue about having the additional military support, and presumably Gonzalez had felt it was worth it to bring Butler along. That Hochberg wasn't sitting with them was only due to the fact that he was sitting with the rest of Jeff's Cabinet, who were all bunched together.

In fact, Alpha Team and Airborne were sitting together, along with Christopher, Doreen, and the others from our Diplomatic Mission. The Planetary Council were together, with White next to Alexander and Doreen, or as I was fast coming to think of it, bridging the gap. Meaning we were aligning according to groups. Just like the rest of the world. This boded.

People were talking amongst themselves, mostly about what we'd seen on TV. Nudged Jeff. "Did you request that everyone sit according to party lines?"

"No."

Chuckie, who was on Jeff's other side, leaned over. "Humans are tribal," he said softly, "and right now, every human in this room is frightened and huddling with their tribe."

"You're not."

He grinned at me. "You're my tribe, Kitty."

"You're part of Hacker International's tribe, too."

"They're huddling in their tribal location," Chuckie said with another grin. "I'm not. I'm huddling with my smaller tribe."

"What am I, chopped liver?" Jeff asked.

Chuckie laughed. "No, I include you in the Tribe of Kitty, Jeff. And, apparently A-Cs are tribal, too."

"And just as frightened," Jeff agreed. He heaved a sigh. "I don't want us reacting out of fear or hatred. I want us going forward in the way I know we can—as representatives of the best Earth has to offer."

Jeff hadn't been speaking loudly and there was a lot of noise in the room, but A-Cs had hearing far superior to humans. White made eye contact with us. "That is the correct goal, Jeffrey. World cohesion, greeting the new horizon bravely and compassionately."

"Then we need to do our best to help and support," Jeff said. "And convince the rest of the world that they want to do the same."

"That's the religious summit's stated goal as well," Gower said. "Not sure if we're going to manage to actually achieve it, but at least everyone here is willing to work for that goal."

"Everyone? Really?" Mom asked. "I find that shocking, honestly."

Gower chuckled. "Well, seeing aliens arrive outside of Pueblo Caliente today gave those of us pushing for unity a boost."

"Do the other religious leaders know we have more aliens coming?" Chuckie asked.

"No. I didn't know until Kitty told me. I'll ask Alpha Team why they kept that from me later."

"We didn't want you distracted," Reader said. "And that's because you're the one who told us to not distract you."

"I didn't get that memo, my bad."

"Your timing was good, Kitty," Gower said.

"Paul is my favorite."

Sent Stryker Dane, the Head of Hacker International, a text telling him to put the best hackers in the world onto my newest craze that was right up their Conspiracy Theory Alley—find all of the triangles in the world that could be alien landing sites. Asked for specific focus in the Middle East, but didn't tell them where. Not because I was trying to be coy, but because I wanted to see what they found without my influence.

Stryker's response was suitably enthusiastic. Apparently I'd finally given Hacker International a job they were excited about. Go me.

Len and Kyle came in now, Kyle pushing Olga's wheelchair. He placed Olga in between White and Alexander, while Adriana stayed standing, just like Buchanan, Siler, Wruck, and the boys, once Olga was situated. Meaning the guardians were doing their own form of tribal cocooning.

Olga looked around the room, then smiled at me. "Interesting times."

"And it's a Chinese curse for a reason." Quickly shared with the room that I'd already contacted Mona and that we were on schedule for me to hit Bahrain first. "I'm not sure how much time we'll have to give to that region, but I think Russia and its neighbors need to be next on the hit parade."

Olga nodded. "We will ensure that you're meeting with the appropriate people and that they're properly appeased for being chosen second."

"Regionally second," Gower said. "Logistically, we have no idea until we know what the Bahraini Diplomatic Mission can arrange for us. Plus, I've got the rest of the religious leaders of the world to wrangle. We're in agreement that it's the Middle East first, but beyond that, how long we're in the region is up in the air."

"Speaking of things up in the air," Chuckie said, "we can't take forever. We have ships arriving in less than a week."

On cue the com went on. "Excuse me, Mister President," Walter said, sounding stressed. "But we have a situation."

"Is it the same situation that it's been all day?" Jeff asked. "Or is this a brand-new situation?"

Walter cleared his throat. "Ah, both?"

"More clarity, Walt, less panicking."

"Yes, ma'am, Chief First Lady. The first of the alien space-craft is within our solar system."

CHAPTER 46

THE ROOM THREATENED TO ERUPT. Humans liked to talk a lot when they were panicking, and though A-Cs were normally quiet when thinking, they were a lot more like humans when they were frightened. The noise level was intense and getting higher every second.

"Enough!" Jeff bellowed. No one could bellow like my man. The TV screens and curtains shook and everyone stared at him. Everyone also shut the hell up. "No one will be speaking other than me, Kitty, Chuck, or Walter. If one of us asks one of you a question, by all means, reply promptly. Otherwise, if you want to panic, leave this room right now. I don't need the emotional stress, and panic won't solve anything. Clear minds, calm emotions, and silence right now. Period."

The room went still. Noted that Uncle Mort and Mom both looked quietly impressed. Yeah, Jeff was an amazing leader.

Crossed my fingers and sent up a prayer that our first arrival wasn't going to be the Faradawn Treeship. "Which one, Walt?"

"The ship Mister Wruck identified as being from the Sirius system, the Roving Planet of the Themnir."

"How close are the others?" Jeff asked.

"Unsure, but they still appear to be behind the Themnir ship."

"Walt, can we tell what part of the world they're heading for?"

"Not yet, Chief First Lady. They're near Neptune at this time. But I have more data coming in from the Alpha Centauri planets, because they're tracking as well."

"So it'll be a little while," Chuckie said, "but not what we were hoping for. Hours, not days."

"Will something called a Roving Planet even attempt to land?" Jeff asked Wruck.

Who shook his head. "I don't know. The Turleens may have an opinion."

Muddy stood up on the conference table. It was the only way he could be seen or heard. "Because the Themnir are coming to seek refuge, they will request a landing. They will most likely be heading for a large body of water—it will be difficult for the Roving Planet to land on flat ground. It's possible, but we," he nodded toward Mossy and Dew, "have discussed it and feel that water is the most likely choice."

"What are the odds they'll go for the Bermuda Triangle area?" I asked him. Mouths opened. Put up the paw. Mouths closed. "Per the Turleens, that's a standard landing site. So is the area where the Planetary Council landed as part of our pre-wedding festivities. Basically, we should start looking at any major triangular area as a potential alien spacecraft landing site. But, the only person who gets to talk next is Muddy. The odds, in your opinion, of the Themnir going for the Bermuda Triangle?"

"Very good. It's a known landing site and would put them near to where you are, which is their goal."

Hoped he was right and that the Themnir weren't headed for the Persian Gulf. Felt the need to race off, but knew we had to handle as much as we could before I left for the other side of the world.

"We could have a problem if they're presumed to be landing in international waters," Chuckie said quietly to Jeff.

"Why?" I asked.

"Some countries will consider that 'claiming' the new aliens will give them an advantage."

"Will one of those countries be the UK?" Jeff asked now. "I mean that question seriously—they're our ally."

Chuckie shook his head. "I have no idea, we're in brand-new territory. Countries have betrayed each other for far less than what we're about to experience."

"It will not matter," Alexander said, breaking Jeff's no speaking until spoken to edict. "We are on this planet, and, as an emperor, should the need arise, we are more than willing to announce Earth as part of our empire."

Uncle Mort chuckled. "I like your moxie, son, but that won't fly here, and it could cause problems, too."

"Frankly, wherever they land is going to be an issue," I pointed out.

Muddy was still on top of the conference table. He stomped

his foot and everyone looked at him. "I see I must repeat this again. I would greatly appreciate if all of you would listen to me this time." The entire room went still again, this time focused on the Turleen. "Every single ship and every being on those ships are all coming to meet with the same two people." He nodded toward me and Jeff. "The King and Queen of the world."

Mouths again opened. Put up the paw. Mouths again shut. The FLOTUS Paw In Action. Oh well, there were lamer superhero powers. "Muddy is choosing his words quite carefully. Before you all freak out at us, Jeff and I are really clear that we're not the King and Queen of anything, let alone Earth. However, we literally have a galaxy full of hurt heading toward us. So, in the interests of my getting on my world tour faster as opposed to slower, we're all going to stop worrying about policy and who 'owns' what newly arriving aliens. They own themselves. Period."

Jeff nodded. "They're either coming to ask for asylum or to attack. Those coming to ask for asylum will have that granted."

"You can't make that decision, Jeff," Hochberg said worriedly. "Congress has to approve."

"Oh, so glad you brought that up, Fritzy." Looked back at Alexander. "*Now's* the time to go all We Are Emperor Alexander, dude. For the rest of the room, I'm going to point out Jeff's cousin, Emperor Alexander, sitting with the Planetary Council from the Alpha Centauri system, and share that they have more firepower than we want to contemplate. They can use it to help us, or they can use it to force us to cooperate with the Greater Galactic Community."

"I vote for helping us," Chuckie said dryly. "If my vote counts at all in this monarchy."

"Dude, of course it does. Jeff gave you permission to talk freely and everything. And I'm perfectly willing to play nicely with others. They just need to keep to our timeline."

Alexander cleared his throat. "I wasn't trying to 'take over,' Kitty. I was saying that I was willing to make an official announcement."

"Want to explain that?"

"Of course. Per our royal lines of succession, despite Jeff refusing the crown on Alpha Four, the bloodline is still that of our royal family. Technically, Jeff would be the King Regent of Earth, since this was the planet he chose to remain upon. That is how we refer to all of you on Alpha Four. And based on how our royalty works, that makes you the Queen Regent, Kitty. Jamie and Charlie are the Princess and Prince Regent. All of Alfred's line, and Stanley Gower's, and my late aunt's, have a claim to our royalty and all the rights and such contained therein. Hence what I was saying was that I'd share the fact that, since we have a King Regent on Earth, Earth is, therefore, considered to be part of the Annocusal Royal Empire."

Let that sit on the air for a moment while I enjoyed Jeff and Christopher's totally shocked looks. They matched most of the rest of the room's quite nicely. "I thought that the rules said that if someone said 'no way, José' that they were out of contention. And that Alfred, Stanley, and Terry being banished here removed them from the royal line."

Alexander shook his head. "Per my great-uncle? Yes. Per Councilor Leonidas, who reviewed all of our royal history once I was put onto the throne, King Adolphus was a traitor to our people and our world, and therefore any decrees he made against another member of the Royal Family are null and void. The entire Martini, Gower, and White families, including the former and current Supreme Pontifexes, are all Alpha Four royalty of some kind, either by blood or by marriage. Alfred is the most direct descendant in the bloodline, but remains a Royal Prince since he officially abdicated once relations between Alpha Four and Earth were normalized. Therefore, Jeff, as his only son, has the strongest claim."

"Ah, I refused the throne on Alpha Four," Jeff pointed out. "We all did, me, Christopher, Paul, and Michael."

Alexander smiled at us. A little nervously. "Yes, you did. However, that does not affect this situation, as it was interpreted by our laws as a specific refusal of the Alpha Four throne only. In other words, should you wish it or it becomes necessary, you actually can say you're King Jeffrey and Queen Katherine of Earth."

CHAPTER 47

THERE WAS UTTER QUIET in the room. Could understand that. Galactic royal politics was confusing as hell. And even more surprising. I was, frankly, almost as surprised by this as I'd been when I'd first discovered Jeff was royalty. Nice to know that I wasn't so jaded that things like this still threw me. And everyone else, based on the expressions of most of the room.

Chose to be the one to break the shocked silence. "Wow. Well, that's a handy thing to have in our back pockets should we need it. I'm saying these next words as the First Lady, though. Someone needs to call Congress into an immediate emergency session. Anyone not in town can be whisked here via a nice team of Field agents and the nearest gate. Anyone refusing to show up within the next, oh, let's call it two hours, will be considered a traitor and tossed into jail."

"That's a tad extreme," Antoinette said, voice loaded with disapproval.

"*Is* it? Oh, I'm sorry, I thought an absolute tonnage of aliens were arriving, with an armada of deadly killers right behind them. My bad. I'm sure we have all the time in the freaking world. Let's all call it a night, sleep in, and hang by the pool tomorrow, what say?"

The room went still again. Quieter than it had been when Muddy had stomped his foot or Jeff had bellowed or Alexander had shared that the Royal Family was going strong on Earth. Apparently everyone was waiting to see if we were about to get into a Girl Fight. Wondered that myself.

Antoinette actually tried to stare me down. I was impressed. She folded fast, but still, gave her props for trying. "I apologize for speaking out of turn."

"Whatever and as if I care. I do that all the time. It isn't that you spoke, it's what you were trying to say that was the issue. And, I'm going to channel Muddy and say that you need to listen, really listen, to what I'm about to say."

She locked eyes with me again. "I'm listening."

"You have no freaking idea of what's coming. But I do. Many of us in this room do. And you will stop worrying about protocol right now. In what I'm going to bet is less than twelve hours, all of Earth's precious protocols are going to be shattered, potentially forever."

"You're talking about our constitution, our laws," Antoinette said.

"I'm talking about our survival. When the Themnir arrive, our world will be changed forever. Because, unlike the last couple of invasions, these aliens don't plan to leave. We will either become a nation of aliens or we will likely perish. If we had the luxury of time, sure, we'd follow all the protocols. But we don't."

"You don't know that."

"Oh, but I do, I really and truly do. Unless we all work together, faster than we ever have before, what's chasing the people fleeing here for protection will destroy us. Ergo, I'm going for more than a tad extreme—I'm going Full Monty Extreme, and if you don't like it, then it point-blank sucks to be you, because I refuse to allow your clucking over meaningless crap to be the reason I, my husband, our nation, and our world aren't ready for the biggest test we've ever had."

"And in this test," Jeff said, "failure means the death of every living soul on this planet. So, should anyone else feel that Kitty's overstating things, you can feel free to get the hell out. I want solutions and actionable plans, not roadblocks."

No one moved, no one spoke. Wondered if everyone was taking my sales wisdom to heart or if we'd just scared the crap out of them. Kind of hoped it was the latter, but was unwilling to bet on it.

McMillan cleared his throat, breaking the tense silence. "I'll send out the call to the Senate."

"And I will send the call to the House," Nathalie Gagnon-Brewer added quickly. "I have more influence as Secretary of Transportation than I did as a Representative." She looked at the other Cabinet members, who all nodded and said they'd help with calling all the various congresspeople.

"I'll get the military on high alert, but with the admonition that we cannot fire on these people," Uncle Mort said. "However, we'll need to have Jeff involved in all of that, because we're going to have a lot of pushback."

"Tell them that it didn't work when the Z'porrah invaded the last time, and it won't work now," I suggested. Of course, it hadn't worked because of ACE. Had no idea if ACE could or should do that again—he'd been harmed by all he'd had to do, and I didn't want him that near to his version of death again, let alone risking Jamie.

Jeff nodded. "Whatever we need to do, Mort, let's make it happen, because I don't want us firing on innocents."

"I don't want us wasting firepower we're going to need the moment the Aicirtap arrive. With the Z'porrah fleet coming merrily behind them."

"Kitty's point is the key one," Chuckie said to Uncle Mort. "Make sure you make it clear that we do have enemies arriving, they're just coming a little later than the friendlies who are fleeing from them."

"Guy, Thomas, and I will also make calls," Lillian Culver said. "I can guarantee that you'll have a full Congress before midnight."

"We will contact the Cleophese," Bettini, the Head Spokespenguin for the Shantanu, said. "If they are willing to come, they will make formidable shock troops. However, it will take them time to arrive as they cannot travel as the rest of us do."

"Even one Cleophese would be a huge help. More would be wonderful." Terrifying, since they looked like Cthulhu and his pals, but they'd helped us repel the Z'porrah from the Alpha Centauri system and that meant they could do it again.

"We will have the rest of our system on alert and ready to fight," Alexander said. The rest of the Planetary Council nodded. "Our ships can arrive quickly so we can hold them until such time as Earth is prepared for support to arrive."

"And that is why I like to work with all of you."

"However, you can't leave the Alpha Centauri system unguarded," Chuckie said. "Because the Z'porrah could easily make a detour and take over your system if all of your fighting forces are here, protecting Earth against the Aicirtap." He jerked. "Oh. Oh no."

He and I looked at each other. "Crap. That's exactly what they're going to do, isn't it?"

"It's a sound strategy," Uncle Mort said. "Meaning that we can't actually have the backup just discussed. The Z'porrah taking over the Alpha Centauri system is no more desirable than them taking over ours."

Looked at Wruck and the Turleens. "We need a rundown on all the races that are coming. Full workups, starting with what they look like, what they eat and drink, how they reproduce, what their political structure is, who they like and who they hate in the Greater Galactic Community, and anything else you can think of, specifically which of them can and are willing to fight, and how they do so. John, I don't care if your data is out of date—it's still more than any of us on Earth have."

"Translated into every language we can," Chuckie added. "Because we'll need to advise the other world leaders of what's going on and they'll need the same information."

"We can do that," Dew said. "We have a star manual that already has most of this information in it."

"There is one issue," Muddy said. "As soon as the Themnir land they will request to meet with you. And you will not be together."

"Means we can meet more of them as opposed to less of them, because we know they're not all going to land in the same place. We call that a win-win. And before you argue that one, Muddy, trust me when I say that I need to get to the Middle East."

"Will the Themnir have anyone else on their ship?" Chuckie asked Wruck.

"Unlikely." Wruck sighed. "I'd hoped they wouldn't be the first ones to arrive."

That got the room's attention. "Why?" Jeff asked, Commander in Chief Voice on Full.

"Not for any bad reason," Wruck said. "Only . . . to humans . . . well . . ." He looked at the Turleens for confirmation.

Muddy nodded. "I agree, but hopefully they can adapt."

"Well what?" I asked. "And adapt to what, whom, or how?"

Wruck heaved a sigh. "To humans the Themnir will look like giant slugs."

CHAPTER 48

LET THAT ONE SIT on the air for a bit. "Excuse me?" I asked
finally.

"Humanoid slugs with limbs," Wruck confirmed.

Couldn't stop myself, I had to ask. "Squishy limbs?"

"Slimy, too," Muddy said. "They are a very peaceful race
dedicated to the arts."

"Oh. Good." Risked a look around the room. Sure enough,
every human and Earth A-C now looked shocked-to-horrified.
We were really batting a thousand on the shockeroonies tonight.
"Um, yeah, John. I get why you were hoping they wouldn't be
the first to arrive."

"The Faradawn resemble willow trees and similar and are
quite a lovely race, but the Themnir are very decent people,"
Wruck said, sounding like he was going to try to start selling us
on why our cousins should consider the Themnirs' great personalities and overlook that they weren't pretty on the blind date he
was setting them up on.

"I'm sure that we'll manage to treat them as we treat all races
we've met," Jeff said, clearly in agreement that our cousins
should marry the nice Themnirs instead of pinning their hopes
on the pretty but flighty tree people.

"Well, the giant walking honeybees are coming, too, right?
That's what the Lyssara are, correct?" Risked another look. Apparently honeybees were right up there with slugs in terms of
what our assembled folks wanted to get up close and personal
with.

"Yes," Wruck admitted.

"I'm sure they're great, too," I said quickly, before he could
try to fix up those dead set against dating a giant slug with a

giant bee person as their alternative. "The Planetary Council has been met with what I'd be willing to call casual acceptance. I'm sure these others will be, as well."

"I wouldn't say that, necessarily," Alexander said carefully.

"It's easier for us, we look like giant cats," Felicia the Feliniad said.

"And giant dogs," Wahoa the Canus Majorian added.

"And we Iguanadons are like your lizards," Jareen the Reptilian said. "The Shantanu are penguins and King Benny is an otter, two animals I've come to understand humans find completely adorable. Lakin is a Hawkman and so might be considered attractive by humanity. However, not everyone on this planet thinks lizards are great. Trust me when I say that I've had my share of people looking at me and then running away."

"Okay! So sometimes it takes humanity a while to warm up to people who look different from us. But overall, we've managed it."

"With limited exposure and success," Queen Renata of the Less Pissed Off Daily Amazons said. "I am quite happy that my daughters and I are able to shapeshift into what humans find acceptable."

"It doesn't matter," Mom said. She said it in a way I was used to—her "I'm done listening to you whine, you will do what I said and you will do it now" voice. I'd heard this voice a lot growing up, and it was a voice you did not argue with.

Showing their intelligence, the Planetary Council subsided.

Mom glared at the room. "In a few hours humanity is going to be reminded, once again, that we're not alone in the galaxy. Despite having been attacked by hostile aliens and subsequently saved by other aliens, having a contingent of visiting aliens on the planet for the past several weeks, and learning that we've had aliens living here for decades, most of humanity has chosen to do what they always do when faced with something difficult to comprehend or accept—ignore it."

Chuckie snorted a laugh. "That's so damn true."

Mom shot him a fond smile, then turned back to the rest of the room. "The issue isn't that we have aliens that look like giant garden pests coming. The issue is that only the people in this room are aware of what's coming. So, we solve that issue by doing exactly what Kitty said to do—get Congress and the rest of the Washington Political Machine to do some damn work for a change, no offense meant to present company."

"Oh, none taken," McMillan said with a laugh that was shared by the rest of Jeff's Cabinet.

"We'll have Jeff here," Mom went on, "looking amazingly Presidential, standing guard against the invading hordes, and have Kitty go around the world to share why cohesion is in everyone's best interests. Anyone not excited by those plans need not worry. By my guess, within a few hours things will have changed again and we'll have to adapt again. And, the mere fact that we're all sitting here—alive and well, despite what seems like constant invasion and world domination attempts made by aliens and our own homegrown lunatics—is proof enough for me that the people who need to handle this are the exact ones who are doing so."

"In other words, I'm here to look good while Kitty does the actual work," Jeff said, easily at nine on the sarcasm meter.

Mom shrugged. "Your words. We each play to our strengths, Jeff." Mom looked at Antoinette. "You have a choice. You can work with the First Lady to get her very complex and fast-moving tour arranged, and accept that most of your plans will be shattered immediately if not sooner, or you can stay with the President, assisting him with the various protocol intricacies that are going to hit him from all sides."

"Ah . . ." Antoinette seemed at a loss.

"I won't be offended if you choose to help the President," I told her. "At all. Nor will I be pissed off if you decide you're helping me. If you want my vote, though, I say you stay here with Jeff, because what will be coming at me I'm used to, but what's heading for him is new territory for all."

Jeff and Chuckie both shot me suspicious looks. Might have sounded far too confident about what was supposed to be a diplomatic mission.

Antoinette saved me, though. "Honestly, I think I should be going with you."

Saw a couple of jaws drop in the room. "Why so?"

"What's coming for the President is indeed something none of us have experience with. However, I have a great deal of experience with what you're going to be doing. I believe I'll be more of an asset with you than with the President. In this instance."

"Huh. Well, welcome to Team Diplomacy, Antoinette. We're probably leaving at dawn, based on how things are looking."

"My first suggestion would be that some of the Planetary

Council members who don't look like humans should go with us. As well as one of the Turleens. And, if they land before we leave, one of the Themnir, as well." The entire room stared at her. Had to give it to Antoinette—she had the moxie when it mattered.

"Again, why so?"

She smiled at me. "I believe that the representative from Beta Thirteen is correct—humans are afraid of many things that don't look like us or versions of animals we find cuddly. So, let's allow these leaders to meet the aliens we already know are our friends, cuddly or not." She shrugged. "It's what we would have done if President Armstrong hadn't been murdered. The turmoil caused by the attack that killed him and so many others hasn't allowed us time to do this before now."

I was all for this, and not just because I hadn't gotten to spend any real time with Jareen or the others, half of whom had been in my wedding. Basically, Antoinette was asking for us to bring some major butt-kickers along. Butt-kickers I knew would be all for helping me enact Mission: Stop The Mastermind Permanently.

"Awesome spin, you're definitely hired." Looked at Mom. "You okay with that?"

She nodded. "I am, and I agree with the Chief Usher's assessments as well."

"Then let's get the world party started. We're burning moonlight and have no time to waste."

"You just want to be gone before the Themnir get here," Jeff said to me as the rest of the room leaped into action.

"You don't know me."

"Hah. I know you too well." He took my hand. "Just promise me that, when things get bad, you'll call me or send me an emotional signal. I don't like you going into action without me, baby, you know that."

"I have no idea what you're talking about."

Jeff laughed. "And you say that I'm the one who can't lie."

CHAPTER 49

JEFF WAS GOING TO BE addressing Congress in their emergency session. His entire Cabinet were going as well, along with Mom, Raj, Chuckie, and Serene. He also had the lobbyists, Muddy and anyone from the Planetary Council who weren't on my team, plus the majority of the military, including the flyboys. So, basically half of the room.

The other half was with me. Thankfully we were the Loud and Proud Contingent, because stealth was out of the question.

We'd coordinated as much as we could with Gower, then he'd gotten off the phone to do his own kind of wrangling. My gigantic entourage was busy prepping—making copies of the Turleen's star chart, doing translations, and doing whatever Antoinette and Vance felt was necessary in terms of where we were going. Chose to leave most of this to them—I'd do what they told me when it mattered, but otherwise, I was focused on my real job, which was finding and stopping Cliff.

I'd been given one member of the military—Butler. "I'm the most expendable," he explained. "And I've been able to download information as well. I have comprehensive military knowledge, and can speak and read every language in the world now."

"Wow. John, that's kind of awesome."

He gave me a sad smile. "Not as awesome as being fully human, but there are perks. This is my first important mission since . . . my transition. I hope to reward your faith in me."

Didn't think about it, just gave him a hug. "You did that yourself. I helped and Chuckie and the others helped, too, but the manual override was all you."

He looked surprised, but hugged me back, very gently. "Thank you. I'll do whatever you need. By the way, Mister

Reynolds told me to be aware that you probably have an agenda that isn't being shared with the general group and asked me to tell you to please include me in whatever, and I quote, insane commando idea you're planning."

"Gosh, duly noted." Would have said that I hated that both Jeff and Chuckie knew me this well, but reality said that if they already kind of knew, then I wasn't lying to them. Moral quandary solved.

Jeff grabbed me and we stepped out of the LSR for a few moments. We spent the time making out, which was fine with me. "Come back to me safely," Jeff said, as he stroked my face. "That's all I'm asking. I don't care about the rest of the world if you're not in it."

Leaned my head on his chest and let his double heartbeats soothe me. "I'll do my best, Jeff. I promise."

"Then everything will turn out just fine." He kissed the top of my head. "Your mother feels that, under the circumstances, the kids need to stay here. And by here I mean in the Embassy, under lockdown, with their full security details with them twenty-four-seven."

"I'll take the Worst Mother of the Year hit on that, because I think they'll be safer here than with me."

Jeff heaved a sigh. "I'm not sure if anyplace will be safe. If the Aicirtap are what Muddy's said they are, we're in for a world of hurt."

"We'll handle it. We always do." Looked up at him. "So, technically, you really are the king of the world. Did you know your dad abdicated?"

"No one tells me anything, my parents least of all, so no." Jeff managed a small grin. "You chose well, baby, when you put Alexander on the throne. I do know that."

"Chose even better when I picked you."

"I feel exactly the same way."

We spent a couple more minutes making out. Then duty called and we went back into the LSR. Jeff and his team took a floater gate over to Capitol Hill. The room seemed normally full now.

"You need to get some rest," Antoinette said to me. "You look tired, and I'm sure you are. You're the face of this entire operation, so do yourself and the mission a favor and catch a few winks."

"I want to see my children before we leave. They might be up, they're having a slumber party."

"I've already contacted their nanny. They're all in bed asleep, even your ward, but the nanny will wake them when I call her to tell her that we're ready to leave. You'll see them then. Right now, you need to focus on you."

Couldn't argue because I was exhausted all of a sudden. Considered asking for Chef to bring me a dessert per Algar's instructions, but decided I'd rather just get to my room.

Headed off and upstairs. But I stopped midway up. "I know you're there."

Siler appeared next to me. "Did you hear me breathing?"

"No. I just know how you roll. I don't need babysitting." Started off again, this time with him visible next to me. "Per Antoinette, the kids are asleep but we can see them in the morning, right before we leave. I assume you want to go over with me."

"I do. But I mainly wanted to mention that the empire in *Star Wars* started similarly to this. Since it's a reference I know you'll not only get but embrace."

"Yes, I know. And I also know that it's not going to be easy or smooth or anything else. What I also know is that no one on this planet is going to declare me and Jeff their sovereign lords, Alpha Four's policies or no, so I don't think we're at the same risk as they were in the movies."

"I think that if Muddy's correct, five or six shiploads of aliens are going to be declaring you their rulers."

"*If* Muddy is correct about that. I'm not saying that he's lying or even wrong, but he has an agenda. He wants us to stop the Aicirtap before they destroy his system. He also wants us to stop the Z'porrah from uplifting already sentient races, based on what happened to the Aicirtap. Having met some Z'porrah personally, I can't argue with that mindset."

"And the Turleens want to come to Earth if their planet is destroyed. I know. But . . . can you trust him?"

Thought about it. "Yeah, I can."

"What makes you so sure?"

Shrugged. "He reminds me of Richard. And you."

"Ah. I'll take that as a compliment."

"You should. I've almost never been wrong about who I could trust." Of course, I'd been wrong in a big way when we'd first gotten to D.C. But why mention that now?

"Malcolm mentioned that you've been wrong before. But the person who fooled you was a pro at doing so. And you weren't in your element."

"Of course you know about that. Look, if the Turleens are lying about the Aicirtap we'll know fast. However, if they're not—and John Wruck doesn't seem to think they are, and neither does Jeff, and he can read them by now—then we only know about what's coming behind the refugees because of them."

"I'm more concerned that you and your husband are about to become the rulers of this world."

"I'll take Jeff as a ruler over at least half of the actual rulers we have right now."

"No argument about that. However, it's going to create a backlash we may not be able to survive."

"If it happens. You're assuming that Jeff and I are going to toss on crowns and say that everyone has to listen to us. We aren't."

"But you are," Siler said patiently as we reached my rooms. "You're going on a world tour to basically tell all the leaders what you told Antoinette—what's coming is so terrifying that we need to join together or be destroyed. But there can only be one leader in a situation like that and, once the battle is won, will that leader give the control back to the ones who used to have it?"

"I know what I want to say, which is yes, but I can see a lot of scenarios where that would be worse than just keeping hold of the reins. But, since I have you as my Jiminy Cricket, and, frankly, the Turleens looking like the real thing, I'm probably good."

He didn't look convinced. "Just remember that many times it's easier to take control than to give control up."

"And often the enemy of my enemy is my friend. Sometimes they're a worse enemy. And sometimes you feel like a nut and sometimes you don't. I have to go give the world a Coke and a smile. And I need to do it at hyperspeed."

"Basically, yeah." He didn't look comforted.

There were Secret Service agents in the hall. Opened my room, pulled him inside, and shut the door. Expected to hear through the Secret Service Grapevine before sunrise that I was having a torrid affair with Siler.

"Look, this is a between us only right now statement. I could not care less about getting the rest of the world on board—the aliens are coming whether they like it or not. I'm going to the Middle East because I point-blank know that's where Cliff

Goodman's hiding out. I'm positive that the Casey Thing was actually a badly completed clone. And that means Cliff's back in the cloning game. My plan, my real plan, is to take him down, permanently, before he can capture, sway, or compel any of the new aliens that are coming here to hide into becoming his next cloning targets, particularly the ones Muddy already identified as the Z'porrah's next targets, the minotaur people called the Q'vox. Now, are you in or are you not?"

Siler stared at me, as a slow grin formed on his face. "I knew I'd chosen my allegiance correctly. In, one hundred percent. I'll reassure Malcolm and Wruck that there's more going on and that they'll approve, but won't tell them anything beyond that until we're on-site. I think Butler is already aware that you're going to be doing something more than diplomatic."

"Yeah, he told me as much."

"Good. At least half of your team are fighters, too. And with the Chief Usher along, you actually have someone who can be diplomatic if needed."

"Vance is coming, too. He'll handle all the real FLOTUS stuff. I'll handle what really needs to be done."

Siler laughed. "Or, as you all call it, routine."

CHAPTER 50

FASTEST FAKE QUICKIE in the world over, Siler left and I dragged over to the bed. Broke down and got undressed since I was in FLOTUS clothes and they weren't nearly as comfortable to sleep in as a concert t-shirt.

Dumped my clothes on the floor—O-dark-thirty was soon enough to put them into the hamper. Got into bed, my head hit the pillow, and I was out like a light. My second-to-last thought was that I hadn't eaten anything that would help me have weird dreams where I could more easily talk to ACE. My last thought was that I was finally too tired to care.

Had no idea how long I'd been asleep but someone shook me gently awake.

"Is it time already?" I mumbled, keeping my eyes closed.

The shaking continued.

Managed to drag my eyes open. There was no one there. Groaned, rolled over, and put the pillow over my head.

The pillow was removed and the gentle shaking continued. My brain mentioned that it was possible that I was asleep and, if that was the case, maybe this was ACE trying to reach me.

ACE? I thought in my mind. Is that you?

Nothing but the shaking.

Rolled onto my back and opened my eyes again. This time, there was someone there. Mephistopheles was sitting at the edge of my bed, shaking me awake.

"Are you kidding me?"

The Fugly of My Nightmares smiled at me, always a weird combination of terrifying and nice. He still looked like a huge, blood-red faun, complete with curling horns coming out of his forehead, fingers that ended in claws, and bat wings. "Do I have your attention?"

"Oh my God, yes. I wanted to talk to ACE."

"I'm sure you did. I want to warn you."

"About what? There's a lot going on."

"There is. The Turleen is correct."

Waited. That appeared to be his entire contribution. "Um, yes? You woke me up or whatever this is for that? Muddy's right? Or did you mean Dew or Mossy or a Turleen I haven't met yet?"

"Muddy. He is correct. The Z'porrah's uplift will bring nothing but agony to any race so graced with it."

"Good to know. I really didn't doubt it."

"What has been done to the Aicirtap has been done before."

Waited again. Again, Mephistopheles seemed to have shot his entire wad. "So, am I supposed to guess or know what you're talking about or what? Seriously, as dream clue-givers go, you're usually better than this. Though, admittedly, you're always as obscure as possible."

"That's in the rules. Obscurity is required in order to have the visitation."

"Gotcha. It's guessing game time, then, is it?"

"It is."

Heaved a sigh and sat up. "I really hope I'm actually still asleep and getting some kind of rest. Okay, when was the bad uplift done before?"

He gave me the "really?" look. "Think about it."

Did my best. "I got nothin'. They sure didn't uplift humans."

"No, the Ancients did that." He stared at me. I stared back. He winked at me. Slowly.

"Are we starring in a remake of *The Sting* or *Ocean's Eleven* or something? If so, I didn't get the script and I have no idea what you're so cleverly trying to impart. Words would help me an absolute tonnage."

He heaved a sigh. "Just ask the Ancient or the Turleens about the Cettans and the Uglors."

"The who and the what?"

"They were two races that were dependent upon each other. The Z'porrah gave them the uplift they thought they wanted. It was not what they expected."

"When did this happen?"

"Approximately three hundred years ago. In time as you'd understand it."

"Gotcha. I'll be sure to ask about ancient galactic history during the downtime we won't be having."

"Ask them as soon as possible. It's relevant to your interests. And mine."

And with that he disappeared. Thankfully without a puff of sulfur or doing some icky slow fade. Just one moment sharing confusing clues and then the next, gone.

Flopped back onto the pillows. Couldn't tell if I was asleep or awake, but either way, now was the time to try for ACE again. Tried to concentrate, but all I got was the blackness of dreamless sleep.

For a while, at any rate. Heard a faint voice that sounded quite far away. Calling my name.

ACE, is that you?

Yes, Kitty, ACE is here.

Relief washed over me. It's so good to talk to you. Are you okay?

Yes, Kitty, ACE is okay. Jamie is okay, too. ACE has been . . . busy.

Doing what? Can you tell me?

Jamie is very powerful. So are many of the other children. ACE must teach them and ACE must watch them closely so they do not . . . interfere inappropriately.

Is that what you're doing, training and watching over the kids?

Yes, but ACE still watches over Kitty and the others, too. And ACE can do more. Just not all the time. He sounded hesitant.

I know. It's okay. You shouldn't do all for us, we've had that talk many times.

Jamie does not agree.

Ah. Um, is she fighting you?

In a way. Not unpleasantly. Jamie is a good girl. Lizzie is a good girl, too.

Are the other kids good, too?

They are.

Silence from ACE. Had no idea where he was going with this, so focused on the first issue I was worried about. Should I bring the kids with me on my world tour?

They would like to go. ACE has been . . . discussing it with them.

Interesting. Jamie and Charlie?

All the children who are special, like Serene and Naomi and Abigail are special.

Are. He was speaking as if Naomi was still alive. Of course, for ACE, she was. She was a superconsciousness now, too. Is Naomi safe?

As safe as the rest of us.

So, not safe at all. Great. Which kids are special besides Jamie, Charlie, and Patrick? Becky is, I assume.

Yes, Becky is very special. All the children in the Embassy Daycare are special in some way.

There was something in his tone that made me replay this sentence over in my mind a few times. Considered what he'd said earlier. Are you talking to Lizzie, too?

In a way. Jamie loves Lizzie very much. Lizzie is the big sister Jamie wants.

Why does she want a big sister when she is the big sister?

It is a natural thing. Many children long for a younger or older sibling, depending. In Jamie's eyes, Lizzie can do no wrong.

That sounds dangerous.

It would be if Lizzie were not the person Lizzie is. However, Lizzie is Lizzie, and that means Jamie has chosen Jamie's hero wisely.

Hero. Well, why not? Lizzie was honestly a hero, after all. And better to hero worship the kid who'd stood up to evil when she was eleven than the kid who'd turned to the Dark Side as fast as possible. Um, there are kids hero-worshipping Stephanie out there, aren't there?

Yes. Jamie would like ACE to make them think differently. But ACE cannot and will not. And Jamie is learning why this must be so.

Is this something I can do anything about right now?

No. What is coming is more important and what Kitty goes to do is more important.

So, back to the question of bringing the kids along. Should I?

ACE does not believe it will be necessary. If Kitty needs ACE, or Jamie, or Charlie, or Lizzie, they will be able to help Kitty. Said with finality.

Decided ACE was done with this particular part of our conversation. But I sure had new things to worry about, which was nice, since I didn't have enough of that going on right now.

We have aliens coming. The first ship will be spotted by most of the world soon. And we can't have these aliens attacked. At least, not the ones coming here for protection.

What they flee is terrifying. Said utterly calmly.

Terrifying because of what they are or because of what they'll do to us?

Terrifying because of what they have become.

Are the Aicirtap evil?

No more or less than humans or A-Cs are evil.

That leaves wide range for interpretation. The Turleens think that the Aicirtap want to eat all of us.

They do. Now that they have been newly uplifted, they believe that the rest of the sentient races are to them as cattle are to humans.

Who were the Cettans and the Uglors?

They were the example. But people forget. ACE sounded sad.

Did you watch over them in any way?

No, ACE is much younger than that. But ACE learned much when ACE was . . . exiled. ACE is happy to be home with Kitty, protecting Jamie, watching over Earth. Earth is ACE's home and ACE will not desert Earth. Ever.

You're going to have to protect us from ourselves again, aren't you?

ACE fears this will be true, yes. Jeff will do Jeff's best, just as Kitty will do Kitty's best, but some will not listen. ACE cannot do all that ACE would like. And even less than Jamie would like.

You do a ton for us already ACE. Jamie has to learn that no means no.

ACE cannot stop the Aicirtap from coming to Earth.

That's okay, ACE. That's not your job. Not really.

But ACE is here to protect.

I know. But you're restricted by the Superconsciousness Council and also, even if they were all gung ho for you to protect us from everything, that would ultimately destroy you. And you matter, just like everyone else. You have a right to exist and be happy and safe, just like everyone else. And I don't want you doing something that would harm you.

There is always risk. Kitty knows this.

Yes, but I don't want to lose you, ACE. I don't want you harmed, especially permanently, any more than I want Jamie or Charlie or any of the other kids harmed.

ACE knows Kitty and Paul would like ACE to return to Paul. But this cannot be.

We know. People just like to wish for things, even things they know they can't have. And Jamie is safe with you and vice versa.

ACE was quiet. Not a good sign.

Um, she *is* safe with you and you *are* safe with her, right?

Others are watching. Watching ACE and Jamie. Watching Kitty. Watching . . . others.

Knew he meant Algar. Decided not to say that aloud, so to speak. We're interesting, I guess. How much risk does all this watching create for us?

Much is happening here. Much more recently than has happened over time. The galaxy has taken notice of Earth.

That sounds foreboding.

Earth is about to take its place in the galactic community. ACE knows that Kitty knows this. But others do not. How Earth deals with all that will come will determine much. And ACE cannot help too much or ACE will doom Earth.

Because the other superconciousnesses would feel that we weren't worthy or something like that?

Yes, something very like that. So ACE is limited in what ACE can do. Jamie is learning this, but still does not agree.

I understand, but you're right. Can you prevent us from launching nukes at friendly aliens or each other?

ACE can do that, yes. That is what Kitty calls self-preservation. ACE cannot keep Jamie safe if the Earth explodes in nuclear warfare.

Was always impressed by the way ACE spun his way through the morass of superconsciousness red tape he was stuck in. If you can keep us from launching the nukes and such, that's plenty, ACE. It's more than any of us can do, and it's vital to everyone's survival.

What if the missiles are aimed at the Aicirtap?

The big question. And the one I didn't have the answer for. Can the Aicirtap be saved? Unuplifted or something?

It is . . . possible, yes.

Then we have to try to save them, first. Muddy says they were kind and fun and friendly before. If we have the chance to save them, to at least give them the choice of being saved, then we have to try.

And if the Aicirtap will not accept the help? If the Aicirtap refuse to be retrograded back to what the Aicirtap used to be? Then what will Kitty do?

Whatever we have to in order to survive and protect our world and our allies' worlds from being destroyed. And that does include the nuclear option, unfortunately. I'd offer a pacifistic choice, but cows are pacifists and we eat them.

Yes, Kitty's analogy is good. Kitty's analogies are always good.

Let's hope. And if there is an option that doesn't involve killing the Aicirtap, we'll try it. The Neutral Zone might be out there, right?

Potentially, everything is out there, as ACE knows Kitty now knows.

True enough.

Kitty should look for the way to save the Aicirtap.

Um, okay. Where should I look?

In the obvious places. Once again, said with finality. Clearly that was all the hint I was going to get.

Will do. When push comes to shove, will we do what we should, rather than what we want?

ACE trusts Kitty and Jeff and the others to do their best. And Kitty is still ACE's most beloved penguin.

Not Jamie or Paul?

Jamie and Paul are both ACE's favorite penguins, too. But none are more important to ACE than Kitty. Kitty protects those who need it, even if they are not Kitty's friends. Kitty thinks right. Never doubt that—Kitty thinks right.

I hope I do. You're still the best decision I ever made, ACE.

And asking Kitty for help is still the best decision ACE ever made.

Together forever, ACE. I promise you that. Together forever.

Felt the warmth in my mind that was ACE's way of hugging me. And then it was gone.

CHAPTER 51

THE REST OF MY SO-CALLED SLEEP was filled with weird dream fragments that I thought I'd remember but were whisked out of my clear memory by each dream fragment that followed.

Saw a lot of people who'd died in the line of our duty and many of them were talking to me, but nothing they said stuck. Just hoped I'd remember whatever when it mattered.

Felt someone shaking me again. "Oh my God, Mephs, are you back for round two?"

"Huh?"

Opened my eyes to see Mahin standing there. "Huh right back atcha."

"Good morning. I drew the short straw and won the job of getting you out of bed."

"So much is explained. I'd say nice to see you but I'd be lying. I can't remember, are you with Jeff or with me?"

"With you," she said as she pulled me up into a sitting position. "I'm from Iran. You're going to my region. I'm going with you. Duh."

"Right, right. Makes sense. Sleep brain just couldn't remember."

"Antoinette says you have an hour to get ready and see the children. How long you take to get ready is inversely proportional to how long you get to see the kids. Her words, not mine."

"Please let Pierre know that I'll be over really soon and would love some coffee."

Mahin grinned. "He's already got you covered."

Took a hyperspeed shower. I was good enough with hyperspeed now that I could dry off fast, too. Hair still took a normal amount of time, though, especially if I was going to blow-dry it. Decided the Banana Clip Look was what I was going with. Looked like I'd taken time with the 'do, required the least amount of drying time, and was the best look for action. Getting a triple first thing in the morning said winning in my book.

The Elves had my FLOTUS clothes out and lying on top the bed and my large rolling suitcase packed and sitting at the foot of the bed. Once I was dressed, Mahin took my suitcase and went off to tell Antoinette that I was prepped and ready to go, and in twenty minutes, too.

Looked for my purse but it wasn't where I'd left it. Checked in the closet, to discover I also had a brand-new snazzy rolling purse/briefcase combo, which my purse was sitting on top of. Checked the rolling purse—in addition to interesting things like a laptop, an extended life battery charger, goggles, rope, a lot of clips for my Glock, and more, I had an Aerosmith t-shirt, jeans, socks, and a pair of Converse in there. I also had a bathing suit and swimming goggles. Clearly Algar wanted me to be able to change for action without raising too much suspicion. Hoped this was a portal like my purse, just because extra portals were never a bad thing.

Checked my regular purse. Another pair of goggles were in there, as well as my Glock, my iPod, my portable speakers, my earbuds, and the usual crap I carried at all times. Harlie, Poofikins, and several other Poofs were in there, too, snoozing. Poofs On Board was never an issue.

Looked around the room. "Peregrines please report."

The room was filled with beautiful feathers in a moment. Not all the Peregrines were here, but a lot of them were, including Bruno. Knew without asking that Lola was with the kids, because she was the Peregrine Nanny To The Stars.

"Bruno my bird, what's the good word?"

Got some squawking, feather flapping, floor scratching, and then a pointed head cock.

"Gotcha. I agree—I think you're all needed here, protecting my family and friends and so forth. I'll have Poofs with me, and I have a suspicion I'm going to be in the water again, which is not your element."

Bruno nodded, then squawked again.

"No, I agree, I don't think I want the ocellars or chochos along, either." Ocellars were fox-cats and chochos were pig-dogs, both from Beta Eight. Ostensibly, all the animals lived on the first floor of the Zoo. They'd all moved into the White House with us, however, and part of the residence section was devoted to them and their A-C caretakers. Right now, however, all ocellars and chochos were on duty at the Embassy, protecting all the kids, along with other Peregrines and Poofs.

Gave all the Peregrines fast scritchy-scratches between their wings, then grabbed my purse and the Rolling Action Arsenal and used the gate in my bathroom to go to the Embassy. Didn't have to calibrate it, because all White House Complex gates recalibrated for the Embassy, on the correct idea that this is where we'd all want to go.

Exited in the basement, which was standard operating procedure for all A-C homes and such, which I had long ago put down to the fact that aliens were weird. Left the rolling bag and my purse near the gate, took my phone, and went upstairs and into the kitchen, to find Pierre serving food to my dad and Siler along with the kids.

Trotted over and gave Dad a hug and a peck, did the same with Lizzie, then gave Jamie a huge hug. "How was your slumber party?"

"Oh, it was fun, Mommy." She gave me a kiss. "I wish I was going with you on your trip."

Hugged her again. "I do, too, sweetie, but Nana Angela said you needed to stay here in case Daddy needs your help."

Jamie looked unhappy. "But you need us, Mommy." Said firmly and as fact.

"This isn't a trip for children," Siler said using a Father voice.

Lizzie shot an annoyed look at him. "You know I speak the languages. I should be going with you guys."

"No," he said firmly. "You're needed here."

Lizzie grimaced and appealed to me. "You know I can help."

"Me, too, Mommy," Jamie said, with a hint of petulance. "Even Charlie can help."

"I know that Lizzie is an asset, and Jamie-Kat, you've saved the day more than once, and I'm sure Charlie can do his part. I also know that I'm going to be racing around the globe and Daddy is going to be dealing with political things that are going to take all of his focus, and we need to know that the three of you, and all the other kids, are safe."

"There are, like, fifty Secret Service, Field, and P.T.C.U. agents around all of us all the time," Lizzie grumbled. "The interesting stuff is going to be where you two are going."

ACE's hero worship comments seemed remarkably helpful right about now. "Lizzie, I know that it's not nearly as cool to stay home rather than be going along with the diplomatic mission to listen to all the blah, blah, blah political stuff. I get it. But Jeff and I have a lot riding on everything we're about to do and say."

"So?" Lizzie asked. "We know how to behave." Jamie nodded. Charlie gurgled. I struggled for a nicer option than "because I said so," with limited success.

Dad cleared his throat. "I know that you're quite the capable young woman, Lizzie. And Jamie and Charlie are, of course, amazing. The three of you make us all proud every day. But . . . Nana Angela and I didn't want to bring your mother into our worlds until it was necessary. And even after your mother proved herself to be extremely capable and all that we could have hoped for and more, there still isn't a mission she goes on or a job she does where we both don't worry about her."

"Why?" Lizzie asked. "Kitty's totes on top of things."

Dad nodded. "She is. But she's our only child. Jeff is, therefore, our only son-in-law. And that makes the three of you our only grandchildren. But it wouldn't matter if we had ten children and fifty grandchildren. We love all of you and worry about all of you, and all those 'in the family,' such as your Uncle Charles and Uncle Christopher and Aunt Amy and little Becky, as well. And your father, Benjamin, too. Benjamin and Kitty need to be able to do the jobs they've been assigned without having to worry about the three of you."

"But—" Jamie started.

Dad shook his head sternly and she stopped. "There are no buts, Jamie-Kat. I don't care how amazing and competent your child is. That child is still your child, and you love them more than life itself, and you would do anything to protect them. And your parents are going to places where they need to be one hundred percent focused on the jobs they're there to do. Not on protecting the most precious things in the world to them. That's why you're staying here, with me and Pierre and the others. Not because you're not the best in the world, but because you are."

"And Lizzie, before you argue again, keep in mind that Jeff is about to handle the most intricate and important political moments in the history of our world, and know that he, also, has to know that the three of you are safe and secure, that you're somewhere he knows is protected, somewhere he knows he can run and find you immediately in case of danger."

"But I'm only your ward," she argued, but with a lot less passion.

Snorted. "Right. You're also like the eldest daughter we share with your dad. Both of us will feel a lot better about leaving our younger children here without us if you're with them, too. Because you'll be the most competent protector in this building once your dad and I are gone."

Lizzie heaved a dramatic sigh but I could tell she was flattered. "Fine. As babysitting goes, I'm always up for hanging with Jamie and Charlie. Besides, that way you know where we are if you need to call us in for backup."

Jamie beamed at her, petulance gone, presumably because Lizzie had chosen to stop arguing. Also possibly because of the backup comment, which Siler and I both had the brains not to react to. "I'm glad you're staying with us, Lizzie. It's always more fun if you're with us."

Charlie gurgled at Lizzie and floated the salt shaker to her.

"Charlie agrees," Jamie said.

"Good to know, and thanks for the salt, Charlie." She sprinkled it on her eggs.

Pointedly didn't make any comments. Maybe Charlie guessed that Lizzie wanted salt, or maybe she put it on to make him feel good. Jamie could just be doing the big sister thing and "translating" her little brother's sounds. Or she could be reading his mind or emotions. Or both.

"Kitty, darling," Pierre said, possibly to fill the silence, "I'll have your plate ready in a jiff."

Gave Pierre a quick hug. "You're the best."

He whipped my plate down as I picked Charlie up and gave him his hug and kisses. "Mommy's missed you, too, little man."

Charlie gurgled at me. He was eight months now and I knew the toddler phase was just around the corner. At least, I hoped it was.

Jamie's teeth had come in at four months, she'd become verbal almost immediately after, and started toddling around then, too. By the time she'd hit Charlie's age she'd seemed like a child several years older than she was.

But Charlie was behind her, with no signs of catching up. Despite my prep, he hadn't given the least indication that his teeth were coming, he wasn't talking or even giving it much of a try, and he didn't seem interested in walking. He was all about crawling, so there was that.

He was also all about lifting things with his mind. The best reason no one had given for why all the kids should stay home while I went around the world was that Charlie wasn't really controllable in terms of what he lifted and when he chose to do it.

"Don't worry, Mommy," Jamie said, as I put Charlie back into his highchair and sat down between them. "Charlie will be just fine."

Dad raised his eyebrow. "Are you worried about him?"

"Just normal mother worries."

"Everyone goes at their own pace," Dad said reassuringly.

"Charlie lifted everyone at the slumber party," Lizzie shared. "So, he's way ahead of everyone else on that skill."

"Oh. Um, great." Tried not to worry about that, or the idea that his teeth were going to come in while I was out of the country and Jeff was in the middle of negotiating the most important event in world history. Shoved the image of Jeff buckling in agony from feeling Charlie's pain out of my mind—maybe teething would be easier this time. Whenever it happened.

Dad thankfully turned the conversation to the list of who was going with me, and by the time we were done doing roll call for my gigantic entourage, breakfast was done and Antoinette was texting me to advise that we were leaving in five minutes.

Hugged all the kids, Dad, and Pierre again. Then Siler and I headed back down to the basement.

"It'll be fine," he said when we were downstairs.

"What will be?"

"The kids. They're talented above the norm, but you'll handle it."

"I want to worry about Charlie, but I can't do that and do the job that needs to be done right now."

"Then don't worry about Charlie. Or Jamie or Lizzie. The best thing you can do for them right now is what you're planning."

Heaved a sigh as I grabbed my purse and the Rolling Action Arsenal. Put my purse on top of the rolling purse and wrapped the straps around the handle. Why make it harder on myself? "I'll try."

"Ready for action?" Siler asked, as he calibrated the gate.

"As ready as I'll ever be."

"Good." And with that, he grabbed my rolling bag and pushed me through the gate.

CHAPTER 52

STUMBLED OUT into the White House Residence Entrance Hall. Buchanan was waiting there and he steadied me. "Why so shocked, Missus Executive Chief?"

Siler and my purse and rolling bag came through now, and he grinned at me. "Oh, the expression on your face." He handed the bag's handle back to me.

Took it. "What the literal hell, dudes?"

Siler shrugged. "You hate going through those. We're on a schedule. It was faster to do it this way than be as nice about it as Malcolm tends to be."

"Wow. Remind me to hurt you later." Looked around. There were a tonnage of people here, including Mona and her entourage. "We're gating it from here?"

"Yes, because we'll need a large floater gate to take everyone as fast as possible," Buchanan said.

Len, Kyle, and Adriana joined us. "Grandmother is going to stay here. She and Grandfather will be sleeping in the Lincoln Bedroom."

"I'm all for it. Why so, though?"

"To ensure that those who need to know are quite clear that we are on America's side in all of this."

"Works for me. Adriana, boys, I want the three of you sticking really close to me."

Len and Kyle exchanged a look. "What about the Secret Service?"

"We'll deal with them as we have to."

Buchanan nudged me. "Someone saw reason." He nodded toward the crowd. Francine was here, dressed pretty much like me, along with Colette.

"I look at it as whoever insisted on Francine coming along knows me very well."

"That would be Mister Reynolds," Len said.

"As I said. And it's a smart plan even if I was the best-behaved girl in the world. By the way, where are the K-Nine guys and the sorta prisoners?"

"They're here, in the underground section," Kyle said. "Due to everything that's happened, we didn't want to release them or put them somewhere they could be hurt or taken. They were there for first contact with the Turleens, there are people who would want to get their hands on them."

"They're fine," Buchanan added. "Being treated well, all of them. The dogs are getting spoiled by every White House staffer who's in their general vicinity."

"Good to know." Wouldn't have minded Prince coming along for this part of the mission, but reality said that he was safer where we had him. Besides, who knew how the various dignitaries we were going to see would react to a huge German Shepherd arriving along with the rest of us. We were literally an invading horde as it was.

"Attention please!" Antoinette shouted. The room quieted. "Thank you. We're about to travel to Manama, Bahrain. We will be arriving inside the Al-Qudaibiya Palace. It will be early afternoon there. There is a possibility that food and drink will be offered to you. Please accept it graciously and do nothing to insult our hosts. This first stop is vitally important because it will set the tone for the First Lady's entire tour."

Some Field agents arrived, carrying cloths.

"All female members of the party, including the First Lady, need to don and wear traditional headgear. We have hijabs for everyone. We also have kufiyahs for any men who would feel comfortable wearing them."

Took a gander while everyone started taking the headscarves and putting them on. All the women took hijabs, of course, but only Khalid, Oren, Jakob, and, interestingly enough, Siler, took a kufiyah.

Mona put her hijab on then brought mine over. It was iced blue. Even when going to an Arab country I couldn't escape "my" color.

Mona smiled at me as she helped me put it on correctly. "It will enhance your eyes."

"Glad I didn't bother to do much with my hair." Noted that

Francine was wearing the same thing. The positives of being less recognizable in the hijab could only help the cause.

"Any men, alien men who do not look human in particular, who are not dressed in conservative suits will need to wear a thobe with a bisht over it," Antoinette shared now. "Yes, it will be warm. However, these are the prices you pay to achieve international diplomacy. Alien women who don't look like humans will need to wear an abaya over their clothes. Otherwise, as long as you dressed appropriately for a workday at Capitol Hill, you should be fine."

King Benny was the obvious target of the long robe and ornate outer cloak combo, and I couldn't blame Antoinette for it, either. King Benny wore boots, his fur, and a loincloth-type thing, and that was about it. Sure, he might not cause an uproar, but why push it?

Mossy was the Turleen going with my team, and he was in the robes as well. Jareen, Felicia, and Wahoa all opted to wear abayas, though they didn't cover their faces. Queen Renata, Rahmi, and Rhee all shifted to look like fully human women in conservative business suits and put on hijabs, though clearly unwillingly.

Trotted over to them. "Just remember that while this is kowtowing to a very male-dominated society, we need these people to pay attention to what we're saying, not how we look."

They all nodded. "We will behave appropriately," Queen Renata said.

"Great. Princesses, don't look so down. First off, you *are* princesses, so expect some special treatment once that's clearly stated. Secondly, I promise there will be more going on. You guys have your battlestaffs with you, right?"

Both princesses brightened right up. "We do indeed," Rahmi said.

"They never leave our sides," Rhee added. Couldn't prove that by me. I literally never saw them carrying their staffs—the staffs were just in their hands when they needed them.

"And we had to do similar just a few weeks ago, after all," Queen Renata said. "Including wearing clothing that is not . . . natural to us."

"Speaking of that particular dog and pony show, where are Drax and the rest of the Vata? I thought they'd be coming with me."

"It was decided last night that they and your five main pilots would be in the Vatusan ships," Queen Renata replied. "All of them. Just in case things go . . . badly."

We had four Vatusan ships on the planet. One was what I considered our version of the S.H.I.E.L.D. Helicarrier, which was what I figured the flyboys were in, since it required five at the controls. Four of the Vata had come in two ships, and Drax had come in a ship he flew himself.

The Vata had organic metal plates in their temples that allowed them to communicate with electronics, which was why it took so few to fly large spaceships. The flyboys used helmets linked into the helicarrier in order to do the same thing. Basically, with four Vatusan ships, we had decent backup. Not the same as having the Cleophese or the Alpha Four fleet, but still, a lot more than nothing.

"That was some good thinking. Who came up with it?"

Queen Renata smiled at me. "I have learned much from my time with you. As have my daughters."

"You three rock."

"Drax has also alerted Vatusus of what is transpiring on Earth. His world is prepared to come to assist us if he feels that the need is great enough. He also asked me to remind you that he is also royalty and, therefore, stands ready to toss his royal weight around as you and Jeff see fit."

"Now, that's backup we can use. I'm really glad all of you handled this while I was sleeping."

Queen Renata hugged me. "You needed the rest. The rest of us are here to assist. The weight of all our worlds rests on your and Jeff's shoulders. We all know this. Just as we know that you two will always find a way to save the day."

"Wow, no pressure."

Antoinette was getting everyone into formation for our fun walk through the giant floater gate, so we had to separate, as the Amazons weren't going in next to me. Got moved up next to Mona. Looked around. Jakob, Oren, and Leah, our friends from the Israeli embassy who all happened to be Mossad agents, were scattered throughout our crowd.

Len and Kyle flanked me and Mona with Alpha Team behind us, but we weren't really at the front—my Secret Service detail, Manfred, and the rest of my permanently assigned Field protection detail, along with Butler and Mona's bodyguard, Khalid, were going through the gate first. Couldn't spot Siler, Buchanan, or Wruck, so assumed Siler had hold of the other two and they were all blending. Chose not to ask why—they always had their reasons.

Of course, Wruck could have shifted to look like anyone, so whether he was in the crowd or with the rest of Team Tough Guys, I couldn't be sure.

A woman stepped up next to me, moving Len over. As she did so, she took my rolling bag, and therefore my purse as well, from me. Turned to see who was shoving in and tell her to get her mitts off my stuff.

"Well," she said before I could speak, "this is another fine mess you've gotten us into."

CHAPTER 53

"CAMILLA, what kept you?"

Was surprised she was here, but I shouldn't have been. After all, I'd asked for her by name. I'd just asked what seemed so long ago in terms of experience that I'd forgotten she was coming along.

She snorted. "Oh, just the usual crap you royals create in your wake. Your husband requests that you behave, Mister Reynolds requests that you not do something we'll all regret, and your father-in-law, also known as Prince Alfred, says to do what you do best and not let the turkeys get you down. So to speak. I take direction from all three of them, but you get to guess who has the most authority as far as I'm concerned."

Camilla was that rarest kind of A-C—one who could lie believably and at the drop of a hat. Alfred, being a good father, had assigned Camilla to protect Jeff and his family the moment I'd gotten pregnant with Jamie. As with Buchanan, who'd been put in place by my mother with the same directive, there wasn't a day I wasn't grateful for Camilla's service.

She didn't hang out with the rest of us all that much. The Official Liars had their own club, similar to *Fight Club* in that you could only find it if you knew about it and its first rule was that you didn't talk about it. But since we'd been moving higher and higher up the political food chain, with more and more chaos circling around us, we'd seen her with greater frequency.

"Alfred is my guess and my favorite."

"Got it in one, though I never had a doubt."

"I'm flattered. But what's up with the 'you royals' bit? Did Muddy talk to you or something?"

"No. *I* talked to *him*. He's right. And I heard about Emperor

Alexander's sharing reality with all of you. He's right, too. Time
to play up the fact that your husband is royalty, Queen Katherine. I'm your lady in waiting, by the way, so expect me to be
glued to your royal side for the duration."

"Gotcha. What do I call you?"

"My name works. No one will pay attention to the servant."
She looked over at Mona. "Isn't that right, Ambassadress?"

Mona laughed softly. "Queen Katherine, your servant appears to have forgotten her station."

"Wow. You're all so much better at this crap than I am."

"We are." Camilla looked around and waved her hand in a
way I knew was a signal. Rahmi and Rhee zipped over. "Your
other ladies in waiting need to stay near you as well, Queen
Katherine." Clearly Camilla was allowed to change the plan as
she saw fit.

"You're enjoying this title thing a little too much. You know
I'm going on this tour as the First Lady, right? You did get that
memo?"

"I know that royalty has a lot more cachet where we're
headed. So, however the Ambassadress refers to you, you go
with it, including if she refers to you as the First Lady and as a
royal queen by marriage in the same sentence. Am I clear?"

"Crystal."

Would have said more but the floater gate shimmered into
view and the first line stepped through. Mona put her arm through
mine. "I understand these are unsettling for your stomach. I don't
care for them that much, either. So we'll suffer through together."

"Works for me."

Would have liked to have kept a hold of my rolling bag, because it would have given me something to clutch with my free
hand. But I didn't have to think about it long, because Camilla
took my hand and gave it a squeeze. "Just focus on me and
Mona and you'll be fine."

We stepped through. And it was pretty damn horrible, because Bahrain was far away from D.C. I wanted to close my
eyes, but knew the worst thing in the world would be to step out
in front of whoever we were going to be seeing with my eyes
squeezed shut. Basically had a death grip on Camilla's hand and
was clutching Mona's arm to me for the entire time.

Wasn't quite as long a trip as it was to Sydney Base, but I was
holding my breakfast down with all my might by the time our
feet hit the floor in Bahrain. And we were definitely in Bahrain.

We'd landed in a large room that had high windows with yellow drapes, some very official-looking carpet with what might have been a royal crest pattern, and a lot of chairs placed around the room, backs up against the walls. There was a man in every, single seat. They were all in traditional dress and, based on what little I knew, were likely all sheiks or high-up government officials. Not one of them looked inviting or happy to be here.

We'd exited the gate in the middle and there were no chairs or tables or anything else. Well, there was a Bahraini flag at one end, standing next to the comfiest-looking chair in the room. Took a wild one and guessed that the flag was next to the king. We were facing him, and I really focused on not throwing up.

He was sitting, but he didn't look very tall. He was also a little chubby, though on the cute side of chubby, like a teddy bear. He was wearing robes over a military uniform loaded with medals, the kufiyah he was wearing resembled a red and white checkered tablecloth, and he was also sporting a really 1970s moustache. Focused on his eyes—presumably gingham was a sign of royalty in this country, and maybe he was a huge *Magnum P.I.* fan.

Camilla and Mona moved us forward so the next people could come through. Then Camilla let go of my hand, though Mona didn't release my arm.

Mona waited until the man I was now certain was the king nodded to her. Presumably he nodded once our people were in the room, because it was a good minute or more of waiting. She walked us forward. Then she let go of my arm and curtseyed. "Your Majesty, thank you for seeing us on such short notice."

The king looked at me. No one had bothered to tell me if I was supposed to bow or curtsey or whatever. My first move, for what would literally set the stage for this entire endeavor, and I had no freaking idea of what to do.

And now I was unintentionally having a staring contest with the King of Bahrain.

"Well, woman?" he said as we stared at each other. "Why do you stand there unmoving?"

I'd been a feminist all my life, well before it had become cool again. Rage nudged in and mentioned that while I was representing the United States I was also, clearly, representing my gender here. At least based on that greeting. And, I still had no idea of what I was supposed to say, though I had less worry about it now.

For whatever reason, what Camilla had relayed from Alfred—to do what I did best—registered, along with what Muddy and Alexander had been imparting. What I did best was not kowtow to anyone, no matter how important they thought they were. And the Queen of the World curtseyed to no one.

She also didn't have to wear a hijab.

Keeping eye contact with the king, I removed the hijab, ignoring the quiet murmurings from around the room. Folded it neatly. Then handed it behind me, still looking at the king.

Thankfully, Camilla took the hijab so I didn't have to drop it on the ground. Then I walked closer and pulled myself up to my full height, so that I was definitely looking down on the king.

And then I ensured that I did something else—I channeled Mom's Voice of Authority and everything I'd ever learned in the dreaded Washington Wife class, including how to speak as if I'd actually paid attention in the Washington Wife class.

"I am Katherine Sarah Katt-Martini, the First Lady of the United States, the Queen Regent of Earth for the Annocusal Royal Family of the Alpha Centauri Empire. My husband's lineage goes back tens of thousands of years. His ancestors were exploring the stars before yours had learned to read or write. You will address me as either Madame First Lady or Queen Katherine, and you will never, ever speak to me disparagingly or in that tone of voice again, or I will gladly declare war upon your entire region."

"You would set the U.S. against us for so minor a slight?" another man in the room asked.

Didn't look at him. Kept my staring contest with the king going. "No, you utter fool. Not war from the United States. War from the stars. I will ask Emperor Alexander, he who *I* put on the throne, to avenge this insult in a way that ensures that no one else will ever dare be rude to any one of my people ever again. Now, you have exactly one second to decide what happens next."

CHAPTER 54

THE KING STARED AT ME for a very long moment. Then he nodded and rose from his seat. He wasn't much taller than me. "You are all that we have been told and, it seems, much more. It is an honor to meet one so well versed in politics and power." The king bowed to me.

Nodded my head in return and felt the entire room relax behind us. The king offered his hand and I took and shook it. Heard gasps. Knew enough about Arab culture to know this was an incredible rarity.

"You wish to speak with me on matters of great urgency," he said after we'd stopped shaking paws. "I would like to offer your retainers refreshment."

"We would be most grateful for it."

The king's mouth quirked. "If your people would be so kind as to humor us again?" He nodded behind me.

Turned to see that every single person in my entourage, including Mona—heck, including Antoinette—had removed their hijab, kufiyah, or robes. Managed to keep a poker face, but only because Chuckie had spent years teaching me how to do it. Wondered if Jeff could feel how much I loved everyone with me right now. Kind of hoped he could.

Made sure I had full control of my voice before I spoke. "The apology has been accepted."

Mona nodded and put her hijab back on. The rest of the team did likewise. I actively chose not to. No one complained.

Turned back to the king. "I want assurances that the Ambassadress and her family and diplomatic mission will not be . . . reprimanded in any way for her support of my undertaking."

His lips quirked again. "No, we would not want to bring your anger down upon us." He waved his hand. "Leave us, all of you. I wish to speak to Queen Katherine privately."

This was a wrinkle I hadn't been prepared for. However, I was also really good at rolling with whatever came along, so I didn't argue or question.

The room emptied slowly. The king had to continually keep on telling people to go away. Guards in particular, both his and mine. But finally we were alone in the gigantic room.

"Now," he said, "we can speak freely."

"I could speak freely in front of everyone who came with me."

"And I could not. Would you care for any refreshment?"

"I won't say no, but we can't actually be alone if you're having servants bring in snacks."

He chuckled. "And now I hear the real person."

"Oh, I can go right back to being Queen Katherine if you make me."

"Good." He offered his arm. "I have a private study. It will be more comfortable there." His eyes twinkled. "And the snacks are there already."

Figured I had no real options and, besides, I honestly felt I could take him, without using super strength or hyperspeed. Took his arm, and we headed off through a door behind his cushy chair.

"What shall I call you when we are in private?" he asked as he ushered me through the door.

"Well, if we're being relaxed and friendly, Kitty is my preference. What do I call you?"

Realized that no one had told me his actual name, and I hadn't bothered to look it up. Would have complained about my staff not prepping me correctly, but perhaps they'd anticipated that Mona would tell me his name. Perhaps she'd told them she'd take care of all that—it would make sense, since she was the one with the most knowledge of the king and the situation here.

She hadn't shared anything, and she'd had time to. Plenty of time, really. So, did that mean Mona had expected this outcome? She wasn't stupid, and she knew how I rolled. Presumably, she knew how her king rolled, too. Meaning she hadn't told me his name, or what to do on purpose, so that exactly what had happened would—he'd be a jerk and I'd get pissed and be myself, versus the version of myself Antoinette wanted.

I'd have questioned whether or not Mona had done this by accident or design, and if she'd done it to make me look bad, but she'd removed her hijab, presumably after I'd removed mine. She'd been first for sure, since the others didn't put their garments back on until Mona did. So she'd led the way in terms of removal for certain.

The risk to her for doing that—of being that disrespectful to her king in her own country—was much higher than any risk I had. Meaning everything she'd done was intentional, and this was the outcome she'd been betting on.

"I'm rarely that casual, but in your case, I sense it will be in my best interests. Please call me Raheem."

We entered a much smaller room, with even comfier looking chairs and settees. It had tables, and those were loaded with food and drink, and there was also a fully stocked tea cart standing near to these tables. But there was only service for two.

"You always planned to speak with me privately?"

"Oh," Raheem said, as he helped me to one of the two cushiest chairs in the room, which were the two next to the food and tea cart, "only if you were what I was expecting."

"What was that?"

"Not the usual political wife." Bingo. Mona had set this up, the entire thing, betting on him pissing me off and me acting like the person she knew. It was nice to know I chose my friends really well. "Tea?"

"Please. Milk or cream and more sugar than you'd think I should have." He chuckled again as he poured the tea, added the milk and six sugar cubes, then handed me the cup and saucer. I waited until he'd made his own cup and seated himself before I took a sip. "Delicious. Thank you, it's perfect."

It was. I was impressed. Either he'd researched my sweet tooth or he was just lucky. Or he "got" me. It did happen occasionally. Hoped that this was one of those times, because I needed this man's help.

"I'm pleased you find it so. Sweetmeat?" There was a set of tables between our two chairs. The bigger table was the one with all the food, the smaller table was clearly where we were to put our china.

"Sure." Put my cup and saucer down onto the little table. He used a very expensive pair of silver tongs to put some cookies and candies and other sweets onto a small, beautiful porcelain plate. It was trimmed with what I figured was real gold and it was so fine that the plate was almost translucent. Really hoped I didn't drop it, but then again, the thick carpeting would probably ensure it didn't break. Yeah, there was a lot of wealth in this region. Actively reminded myself that now was not the time to channel Dad and have a Proper Distribution of Wealth discussion. "But I'd like to know—why the unpleasant greeting if you were planning to wine and dine me, so to speak, five minutes later?"

"Ah," he said as he filled his own pretty plate. "As I said, this was only if you were what I was expecting."

We each ate something now, though I waited to start until he'd taken a bite. The food was delicious. Different from what I normally got at the Romanian embassy, similar to what I'd been served at the Bahraini embassy, nothing like what we served normally. None were better or worse, but I could certainly get used to this. Clearly it was good to be the king. Contemplated asking him to have his people send Chef some of these recipes, then decided we hadn't been friends long enough for me to go there.

"This is wonderful, thank you," I said as I cleared off the majority of my plate and he poured me another cup of tea, complete with putting in the milk and sugar again.

He smiled. "I'm pleased you are enjoying my humble offering. I have seen you on television. When will Code Name: First Lady be released?"

"Wow, not you, too. I hope never. Time is a factor. I say that even though, frankly, I'm willing to sit here all day snacking on delicacies and drinking really excellent tea. We do have the fate of the world to consider, however."

"I needed to verify that my intelligence about you was correct. And while we do need to hurry, I would like to hear what is going on, particularly because the religious summit has moved to this region. I would also like to know why you chose Bahrain as your first stop. And please don't tell me it's because of your close relationship with the Ambassadress. I am aware of your friendship. However, this is a great honor that you've bestowed upon us. The expectation would have been that Israel or possibly Saudi Arabia would have received you first. But you are here, and there is a reason why. And it's not a reason you've told anyone else."

So he was smarter than the average teddy bear. Good and good to know.

"Oh, I've told a few people. But yes, you're right. I have two missions. The first is to share this news—alien ships are coming to seek asylum on Earth. Six of them, containing various alien races, most of which no one on Earth or from the Alpha Centauri system has ever encountered. We need to accept these people and offer them safe haven, and not just because it's the right thing to do. But also because the entire galaxy is watching us and waiting to see how Earth will handle her biggest challenge to date."

He was quiet for a moment. "It was only a matter of time, I suppose. Is this why your people are leading the religious summit?"

"In a way. Call it us being forward-thinking versus prescient."

"I see. What are these aliens seeking asylum from?"

"That's the key question. The answer is another alien race, called the Aicirtap. A race that's been altered into a frightening version of themselves by our world's biggest enemy, the Z'porrah. This race will destroy Earth unless we can repel them."

"What of those aliens who want asylum? Will they destroy us?"

"Not intentionally, at least to our knowledge. Interestingly enough, however, that question relates to my second mission. The one only a handful know about."

"I'm listening."

"I have reason to believe that Clifford Goodman, who we call the Mastermind, the man who tried to literally kill half the world a few months ago, is hiding out nearby, most likely in Dubai. He has a wealthy benefactor or someone with money who's helping him. I want to find him."

"What will you do if you find him?"

Considered all my responses. Decided to go with the truth. "I plan to make him really most sincerely dead."

The king stared at me for a few long seconds. "You mean that."

"I do."

He smiled. "Good. I will be happy to offer you whatever assistance you need."

My turn to stare. "That was a lot easier than I'd expected."

"I'll make it even easier. I know who his benefactor is. And I will gladly share that with you, because I consider his benefactor to be as dangerous as Goodman himself, but said benefactor is someone I cannot touch. At least, someone who cannot know that I work against him. And yes, again, we know of Goodman, of what he did and why. There is no extradition to the United States from our countries. But accidents happen, especially to criminals in our countries illegally."

"Works for me. We've never had these conversations should anyone ask, though I may need to take notes so I don't forget anything. We also need to move fast. The first alien ship will likely land soon, and near the U.S. One of the ships, however, I'm certain is going to land in the Persian Gulf. When, I'm not sure, but we probably have less than a day or two, max, before it arrives."

"Why do you worry more about that ship than the others?"

Definitely a smart teddy bear. "Because that ship contains some people who, for us, resemble minotaurs. Our intelligence tells us that they're normally Ferdinands. However, when roused, they're considered close to unstoppable. And if given the same alteration that the Z'porrah gave to the Aicirtap, they will become weapons of incredible mass destruction, and that means we're doomed, because what we'll have to do to stop them and the Aicirtap both will result in us having to destroy our own planet."

Raheem cocked his head. "By 'Ferdinands' are you referring to the children's book, *The Story of Ferdinand*, and/or the Disney cartoon, *Ferdinand the Bull*?"

"I am, as a matter of fact! And I'm incredibly impressed that you understood that reference."

"We do read in this country," he said dryly. "My mother read that book to me when I was a child."

"No insult intended."

"None taken. You fear that Goodman will find these gentle bulls first, and do similar to what the Z'porrah intend to do."

"Yes. It's his kind of evil plan, he wants to make us all pay for him losing so badly and publicly, and our intelligence also suggests that he's doing frightening things with cloning."

Raheem nodded decisively. "Then we will begin immediately. Normally I would urge us both to greater speed, but with the level of intricacy we will need to map out we will have to take more time than we would prefer in order to ensure success and safety."

"Think the religious summit will give us the time?"

He chuckled. "If not, we will know immediately. While we plot and plan, may I suggest the cucumber sandwiches? They are truly excellent."

"I sense the beginning of a beautiful friendship."

CHAPTER 55

KING RAHEEM AND I had a long conversation. I did indeed need to take notes. Fortunately, he had the means to contact people and Camilla was allowed to bring my rolling bag and purse to me. Then she was required to skedaddle.

She was required to come back several times, take things away, and give us things in return. During these exchanges the king barely looked at her. Clearly Camilla had been right—being a servant meant you were totally anonymous.

Some of the king's retainers had been called, and my gigantic entourage was moved into a wing of the palace. This was one of the big things Raheem was helping us with—we would appear to be in Bahrain even when we weren't, because not everyone in the entourage was expected to go to every event.

And he was indeed setting up events. Due to the nature of what was happening, it was a fairly easy thing to request that all the top people in the region meet up. Dubai was chosen as the city, and the Burj Khalifa was chosen as the meeting place.

Thanks to Gower's influence with the religious leaders, they were now coming to Bahrain and would also be in the palace, though the religious leaders were put into a different wing than my team, and Raheem had many palace guards assigned to keep them in check. Also, the various Muslim leaders had managed to get their squabbling flocks to play nicely with each other, which I was willing to count as a miracle. Doubted we'd luck into a similar miracle back home, but a girl could dream.

Israel was also included in this regional meeting, which made it even more fraught with tension and excitement than normal. Raheem, however, had insisted, in part because there would be so much focus on the Israeli leaders and their people that it would give me more cover. Everyone had agreed that no hostilities would be allowed, and the U.S. in the form of my husband had shared that, should anyone be harmed or even jostled, the U.S. would interpret that to mean that the jostlers wanted to have the U.S. send shock troops over via gates. Raheem felt that this threat would support the clerics' edicts. Really hoped he was right.

About two hours into this there was a knock. "Come," Raheem called.

Vance opened the door. "Your Majesty, I apologize greatly for this interruption. However, I need to confer with the First Lady for a few minutes on a private matter of extreme importance. May I remove her from your presence for a short while?"

Raheem nodded. "Yes, you may." Raheem helped me up and handed me off to Vance. Contemplated taking my purse with me then figured that would be rude.

"What's up?" I asked as we were leaving the room.

Vance looked worried. "Madame First Lady, we have a situation."

"What situation is that?" Tried not to worry. Failed.

Vance closed the door behind us. "The situation that you're really not good at this," he said in a very low voice. "Don't speak." He walked us quickly through the large room we'd arrived in and out into a wide hallway. Then he trotted us down that hallway quite some ways away. "We're going to be speaking at a whisper in case there are bugs, which you should assume there are."

"God, did Chuckie give you some kind of Paranoia Lecture?" Though I spoke softly as requested.

"No, I just understand how things work. At any rate, we're in a part of the palace that Buchanan feels is not wired too well for sound, ergo, we're going to stand here and speak very quietly to each other about 'matters of state' that require your immediate attention. To clarify, I'm going to impart classified information so that you're not flying blind. Blinder than you normally fly, I mean."

"Wow, you're really reminding me of what I think of as The Old Vance."

"And you're reminding me of The Old Kitty. Stop acting like a ditz. We don't have time for it."

"Sorry, you just threw me with the situation thing."

"Moving on because, much as I love bantering about things

like this with you, I want you to know who's where before we watch the show, because I expect all hell to break loose as soon as the Themnir are actually seen by everyone."

"Makes sense, all of it, and works for me."

"I feel so proud. All your things are in the nicest suite in our part of the palace. Francine is rooming with you, is in those rooms now though no one on the king's staff knows this, and she won't be seen again until you two do the switch."

"What switch?" I asked as innocently as I could.

Which clearly wasn't successfully innocent, because Vance shot me a really snide look. "There isn't one person with us, other than the Chief Usher, who believes for one moment that what you plan to do is sit around shaking hands while speaking passionately on behalf of immigrants of all kinds. No one doubts that you're capable of it, other than, again, the Chief Usher, but we all know you."

"Who leaked the classified intel?"

Vance rolled his eyes at me. "Mona and Siler confirmed what the rest of us suspected when we were all alone in the gigantic suite you'll be sleeping in and after Malcolm, Len, and Kyle searched that room for bugs and removed or neutralized them all."

"Um. Wow. Okay. Nice to know the team knows me."

"Once again, everyone *but* the Chief Usher, and she's being indoctrinated in a very severe way by Malcolm, Siler, and Mona."

"Mona? Really?"

"She's representing as the person the Chief Usher has the most in common with out of our entire contingent. They're bonding, which is good, because Antoinette is completely out of her element. I have no idea why your mother approved her coming along."

Thought about it. "To get her indoctrinated fast, would be my guess."

"I can buy that. Okay, back to housing. Colette is in the gigantic suite with you as well, and so are Camilla, Mahin, Abigail, Lorraine, and Claudia."

"That seems like a lot of people in one room."

He heaved the sigh of the long-suffering. "It's a five-bedroom suite. And I wasn't using hyperbole when I called it gigantic. You have your own bedroom with its own bathroom, Francine and Colette are sharing, so are Mahin and Abigail, same again with

Claudia and Lorraine. Camilla has her own room. Again, all with their own bathrooms. The room is essentially circular and the gigantic sitting room is in the middle. This ensures that you're surrounded by women and therefore nothing untoward can happen. This was arranged so that everyone, our host included, will not have any reason to complain about our impropriety."

"Gotcha. Is everyone else in nice rooms, too?"

"Yes, actually. The king is definitely giving us the honored guest treatment. All rooms have had bugs removed or neutralized. If the king complains, I'm sure you can handle it."

"I doubt he will. He's on our side at this time."

"Let's hope that continues. Paul Gower is on-site. He's staying with the other religious leaders, a wing away from us. He's staying there in part to run herd on the rest of them and in other part so that no one can have hysterics about two men sleeping together in the same bed with intent to love each other." Vance's sarcasm meter was definitely at eleven.

"Wise. We'll worry about being offended by the people not helping us. Right now, King Raheem is our golden teddy bear and I want him to stay that way. Have we determined which team Abigail's going to be on yet?"

The four Gower siblings were hybrids. Hybrid females were rare and always talented above the norm. Hybrid males had the same likelihood for being talented as the full-blooded A-Cs. Michael, for example, hadn't had any talents other than being charming and smart and athletic enough to become an astronaut. He was the rarity of his siblings, though.

In addition to being the Supreme Pontifex, Gower was a powerful dream and memory reader. Naomi had had this talent, too, but she had been able to not only read dreams and memories, she'd been able to alter them as well.

Abigail, the youngest Gower, was a reverse empath—she felt thoughts as emotions. So if someone near her was thinking angry thoughts, Abigail felt angry, and so on. She was also able to manipulate the gasses that were natural to Earth that the Field agents used to alter human memories, but she didn't need an implant to do so.

Naomi and Abigail had worked as a team frequently and had learned how to create shields together—shields that could hold off bullets or bombs. They were the reason that any part of D.C. was still standing after Operation Destruction. But doing this had burned out both girls' powers, which was why Naomi had taken so much Surcenthumain during our raid on the Gaultier Underground Cloning Facility in order to get her powers back and protect everyone.

That plan had backfired, as so many of our plans liked to. But after our trip to Beta Eight, Abigail had come home with all of her powers back and all of her sister's powers as well. And probably more besides. Meaning she was now one of the most powerful A-Cs on the planet. And someone who could tell what everyone was thinking via her own emotions as well as alter their dreams and memories *and* create shields was someone you wanted on your team.

These days, Abigail and Mahin had become besties—Abigail had found a replacement sister, and only child Mahin had found a person who felt like a real sister to her. Mahin was also an earth bender, for lack of a better term. If it had dirt in it or on it, or just was dirt, she could move it. The girls worked together a lot now and were a formidable team. Meaning that whichever team Abigail was going to be on was likely the team Mahin was going to be on.

"Sorry, Abigail and, therefore, Mahin are with Team Subterfuge. Under the circumstances, we figured it's more important for them to be protecting Francine, Abigail in particular. It also gives Francine someone who speaks Farsi, as well as various dialects of Arabic, which I'm sure we'll hear while we're doing the dog and pony show."

"Who's going to be translating for me?"

"Colonel Butler, as I know you know. Stop being a sore loser—you currently have the best gig in this palace. I know what you've been scarfing down all afternoon because I verified that there was nothing deadly to you in the food."

"I don't have food allergies."

"I know. I'm just nosy. By the way, nicely done with the king. I honestly had no idea how that was going to go."

"Did Mona give you any idea of what she was planning?"

"No, but it worked, so hurray. Back to logistics. Mona is, of course, staying with Francine. That means that so are Khalid, Oren, Jakob, and Leah."

"Can't argue with that. I want to argue with it, but I can't. What about my Secret Service detail? Are they clued in?"

He snorted softly. "Beyond clued in. The moment we'd cleared the rooms of bugs, Evalyne asked Malcolm to tell her what you were really planning to do."

"They have to stay with Francine."

"They do, and they're clear on it. The six who came with us are your normal detail, the six most loyal to you, and are also fully aware that, when it comes right down to it, they can't actually protect you. However, they're also clear about what's coming and what's at stake, and because Evalyne is willing to break the rules, the rest of them are as well. Right now, we sent them to be with Paul, because you don't need them here and he truly might."

"I don't want any of them hurt, but yeah, Paul might actually make them feel useful and them being willing to go along with the plan is a huge win. I hate having to lie to them."

"They know. They're all willing to take a bullet for you, same with Jeff's detail. And not because of your positions and their jobs, but because of who the two of you are. Pretty much you've weeded out most of the bad agents already and the rest working the White House detail are droolingly loyal."

"That makes me feel all warm and fuzzy." It did. It was nice to have confirmation that we hadn't made these poor people hate us for constantly making their jobs close to impossible to perform as they were used to. If Surcenthumain wasn't such a risky drug, I'd have suggested giving it to our details, just so they could feel more involved with the team.

"Good. We've done the same thing for your Centaurion protection detail—they're with the Supreme Pontifex."

"I'm glad they're with Paul, but they could be really helpful with what my team will be doing." In addition to Manfred, I'd asked for the two teams of Field agents we'd rescued from Stephanie's Haunted Asylum Lair to be assigned to me, in part because I hadn't been able to keep any Field teams around long on my security detail, since they were as annoyed with how hard I was to protect as the Secret Service, but a lot less willing to put up with it. These two teams seemed willing to go for my kind of gusto, however, and I had hopes that they'd continue to work out.

"They could be, and Daniel, Joshua, Lucas, and Marcus have all fought to go with you as well. But Malcom and Siler both feel that the people on Team Subterfuge will easily face as much risk as those on your team. And Team Subterfuge will have the most humans as well as the most who have literally no combat experience. In other words, we're keeping the A-Cs because we all want to survive this."

"So touchy. Fine, fine. Who *do* I get?"

"In addition to Butler, you're 'stuck' with Alpha Team, Buchanan, Wruck, and Siler."

"What about Len and Kyle?"

"You mean the two bodyguards assigned to Queen Katherine since she arrived in Washington, D.C.? Those bodyguards? Those bodyguards who need to be very clearly seen with Queen Katherine at all times? Them?"

Heaved a sigh. "Gotcha. The boys will be bummed, though." Had a thought. "Um, where's Adriana?"

"Good question and I'm glad you asked. She's doing what she does best."

"She does a lot of things really, really well. Is she in the country?"

"Yes, but no longer in the palace, and she's taking direction from Camilla and Malcolm, who are coordinating Team Commando. As in, you will get to find out when it matters."

"Touchy much? Okay, how is Camilla going to do anything, since she's identified as my lady-in-waiting?"

"Two good questions in a row, I'm impressed."

"You could be fired if you're not careful."

"I know where the bodies are buried, I'll risk it. At any rate, part of my reason for going to the kitchens was to ensure that I found out, too late gosh darn it, that there was food ingested by the princesses that will not agree with them. Rahmi is going to 'take ill' and stay in the royal suite Renata and the princesses have been assigned to. Then she'll shift into Camilla and be there with Francine. Rhee is also going to feel poorly and stay in the room with her sister. She'll be going with you."

"What about Renata?"

"She'll be with Francine."

"Not arguing. One Amazon is a lot better than none. What about Richard?"

"He's more problematic. Because he was the A-C's former religious leader, it makes sense for him to stick around and help Paul. However, Richard is insisting on going with you. We haven't found a workaround that we like."

"Who's 'we'? I'll wager Richard already suggested this—his presence decreases Paul's authority. So, as a good retired Pope With Benefits, he needs to hang out in the palace, or wherever we're going to say Team Commando is, so that Paul's authority isn't questioned during this delicate time."

"Wow. I see why you two partner together so well. That is almost word for word what he said. Malcolm wasn't thrilled with it."

"Malcolm would prefer to do all this by himself or with just Siler and Wruck along. Tough cookies, we're going with Richard's excuse and he's with me. So, Team Commando is a team of thirteen, I think that's probably enough."

"Per Malcolm, it's more than double the number he'd like to be rolling with."

"As I said. Per me, I want everyone already listed in my Baker's Dozen plus players to be named later."

"I know, and so does he."

"Starting with my Reptilian Soul Sister."

Received an eye roll. "Yes. Jareen voiced her opinion, as did Wahoa and Felicia. However, we had them come along to show that aliens are nice, and if they're off kicking butt with you, then they cannot do that. I realize everyone would like to leave the cute and cuddly work to Bettini, King Benny, and Mossy, but, trust me, those three are needed as well. With Team Subterfuge. Period."

"You truly live to take the fun out of everything, don't you?"

"That's me." Vance heaved another sigh. "I heard from Stryker."

"What's the good word?"

"He has news for you on the search you had him and the rest of them doing. News he won't share with anyone but you, because all of the hackers are lunatics of the highest order."

"No, they'd think this entire place was bugged, too."

"Hilarious. It *is* bugged, so perhaps they're not lunatics but truly paranoid for all the right reasons. Stryker's also aware of what you're planning, because he knows you. Not specifically, mind you, but his guess was good. He wants you to talk to him before you roll anything."

"Why?"

Vance shot me the "really?" look. "Because he's thought things through."

"What things? As in, what are you trying to tell me not at all clearly?"

"Oh, nothing much. Other than, you know, one of the people you're likely going after with intent to exterminate is Chernobog's son."

CHAPTER 56

CHERNOBOG WAS THE NAME of the world's greatest hacker. Thought to be a myth Russian hackers used to scare their kids into behaving, we'd discovered that not only was Chernobog real, but the greatest hacker in the world was an old lady who looked like Everybody's Grandma.

She'd been working against us, which was why we'd been hurt so badly during Operation Infiltration. But we'd found and captured her during Operation Defection Election. Circumstances had caused her to flip to our side, and us saving her life while also faking her death—and giving her the greatest setup a hacker could want along with a cadre of loyal sycophants in Hacker International as part of the package—had made staying with us and staying loyal to us something Chernobog found more than acceptable.

Olga had known her back in their heyday in the KGB. They'd been frenemies and then enemies, but age and circumstances had now made them friends.

"What does Olga say?"

"I anticipated that question and with Adriana gone, I had Malcolm contact Olga, since you seem to think that he and Mister Joel Oliver get her clues the fastest."

"They do and MJO is probably pretty busy right now."

"He is. He's on the Coast Guard ship with your husband and the others, getting ready to get the story of a lifetime. Which, all things considered, is impressive, since he's already gotten every other scoop that matters." Vance was an MJO fanboy of the highest order. I found it to be one of his more endearing traits, and Oliver certainly appreciated the love, since Vance had been fanboying at him long before the A-Cs had been outed to the world.

"Okay, so what did Malcolm get from Olga?"

"That you need to call Chernobog."

"Really? That's it?"

"Yes. Be sure to do it the moment you're back in your room."

"Will do. Anything else I need to know?"

"No, but we need things. None of us look like natives. Team Commando needs papers to travel back and forth between the countries we all know you're going to make them travel through. Yours cannot show you to be the First Lady or we're all dead. By the way."

"Gotcha. I'll ask Raheem for help with that. What else do we need?"

"Raheem? I'm impressed. Sleep with him if you need to, because your team needs transportation of all kinds."

"And scuba gear, too. You can run the idea of me sleeping with Raheem by Jeff. Let me know how that conversation goes."

"Ha ha ha, this is me laughing at that idea. And I truly don't want to know why you want scuba gear and am ever so grateful that I'm vital to Team Subterfuge. At any rate, ask your new bestie for whatever he can give us and be sure you have enough for that baker's dozen, and extra oxygen tanks. As a reminder, your team can't be officially known to be doing this."

"Right, we have to do it *Mission: Impossible* style."

"Stop sounding jazzed about it."

"Can't, sorry. Okay, text me with whatever we need."

Got a shot of the "really?" look. "Texts can be hacked. So, no. Have Camilla do information transfer."

"Gotcha, M."

Vance grinned. "I'm happy to be the spy who stays in the warm and does the paperwork. People rarely die from that."

"Don't say things like that. It's tempting fate."

"Duly noted. So, I'm going to get you back to *Raheem* so that you can continue whatever the two of you are doing in there aside from eating your weight in finger foods."

"We're plotting, actually. He's on our side. And you're just jealous."

"Guilty as charged. At least in terms of the foodstuffs and opulence. By the way, assume that he went through your bags and planted bugs."

"He's the king, why would he do that?"

Vance shook his head at me as he took my arm. "Why does anyone do that?"

I didn't answer, mostly because we'd taken all the time Vance had asked to have and more. We hurried back to the private room, Vance knocked, opened the door after Raheem had told us to enter, and handed me back off. "Please remember that the landing will be happening reasonably soon," Vance said to both of us. "We will send people to collect you when it's time."

Vance left and Raheem helped me back into the comfy chair. "Is everything alright?" he asked politely.

"It is." Well, in for a penny, in for the whole piggybank, right? "My team is, ah, fully aware of both of my missions."

Raheem's lips quirked. "And here you thought they were not. That saves time. Good."

"Let's see if you still think so after I go over what we need."

More talking, more planning, lots of helping, done as fast as possible. This was good. Camilla was getting a workout in terms of running back and forth getting information and giving it in return.

Alpha Team coordinated the setup of Field agents and floater gates to get the various important personages to their assigned meeting spot as well as getting the religious bodies into the palace. By now the Themnir ship had been spotted by every country that was paying attention to space, and the world was waking up fast to what was coming.

Technically, these meetings were going to be my Big Moments as the First Lady. However, Raheem had agreed with my assessment, which was that aliens requesting permission to land was going to overshadow anything I might say and prove my point at the same time.

Raheem had given me access to any number of things he possessed, including speedboats, a yacht, a plane, and a whole lot of cars. He'd requested that we not try to destroy any of the things we were borrowing, but also shared that a wrecked car or even a sunken yacht was a small price to pay for saving the world. Clearly he'd read up on how we tended to roll.

Raheem also chose not to take offense when I checked my phone several times, though he did mention that he hadn't bothered to plant any bugs, which either meant that Vance and I had been overheard or Raheem was just clearer on how things rolled than I was. Fifty-fifty for either or both.

Phone checking was proven to be a good thing near the end

of our tête-à-tête, because Chuckie shared some important news, which I shared in turn. "The Themnir have just requested permission to land."

"How close to us are they?"

"Near Mars."

"They all seem to travel so much faster than we have yet achieved."

"Well, Alpha Four has given us plans for ships. And we have other aliens on the planet who are also assisting."

"Ah, yes, Prince Gustav." So he'd met or heard of Drax. Not a surprise, since they'd done that whole Aliens Are Our Friends tour. "I was impressed with all the royalty that came from afar to visit us."

"That was the goal."

Raheem chuckled. "I'm sure it was. I will now go do my part of our work while you do yours. I wonder, though . . . is your double up to this level of subterfuge?"

Francine was a troubadour, so yes she was. But I considered the question as if she wasn't. "Well, first off, Mona will be with her the entire time, and I feel confident she can steer Francine toward the right things to say. Also, per what we've discussed, Francine's main job is going to be shaking hands with various royalty that you're going to introduce her to, and then you're going to do most of the talking."

"Yes. However, if someone makes the mistake of being rude . . ."

"I'll make sure she's clear to really act like me in all ways." Francine had a lot of sass, and we'd spent plenty of time together—I knew she could channel her Inner Kitty in all the ways necessary. Just hoped none of them would be necessary.

"Excellent. I'm relieved that you had the workaround for the necessary paperwork. Creating that for one is time-consuming enough. Creating what will be necessary for all of those going with you . . ."

The workaround was that King Raheem would provide us with all the official seals, inks, paper stock, and printing plates for us to create "real" Bahraini IDs, and Centaurion Division would get into the fake ID business, using his supplies to create legitimate papers and passports and all other forms of ID to show that everyone on Team Commando was actually carrying the right documentation to prove they were a legal Bahraini citizen, Adriana included. Myself, too. Myself especially.

"I appreciate you giving us all the items necessary for us to pull this off in a timely manner." Hyperspeed was, as always, a good thing, and gates were a blessing, especially if I wasn't the one going back and forth using them. And while printing couldn't be sped up, having access to all the right materials meant that the A-Cs had created the necessary IDs in about five minutes.

He shook his head. "Your people are amazing."

"But, ultimately, they're still just people. Like the ones coming here. The good ones and the bad ones."

"Yes. Good luck with your mission. I will not be able to do much if things go wrong."

"I know. Like the State Department, you'll have to disavow all knowledge of what we're doing and who we are. I think the world is going to be focused on what's coming, more than what I'm doing, though."

"Let us both hope."

CHAPTER 57

AROUND FIVE IN THE EVENING one of the many servants knocked, was allowed entry, then stuck his head in the door. "Your Majesty, the televised landing is beginning."

Raheem nodded. "We will join everyone shortly. Please ensure that our visitors are seated immediately." The servant nodded in return and left.

This information hadn't come as a surprise, since I'd just heard from Chuckie again. Getting the nuclear nations of the world to back down from readying their launch codes had seemed like a near thing, despite Jeff, Uncle Mort, Mom, and Olga having been on the phones with most of those who we didn't want pushing buttons down, but they got it done. Mostly.

Surprising absolutely no one, North Korea ignored everyone's requests and warnings. Their nukes launched, fizzled, and fell right back down onto their own missile silos where they didn't explode but did ensure that all North Korea would be doing was digging out for a little while. Sent up a mental thank you to ACE as I shoved one last tea sandwich in my mouth while I packed up my notebook and such.

Raheem chuckled. "I love to see a Western woman with an actual appetite."

"Yeah, you had me at the tea service."

He laughed, stood, and helped me up. I grabbed my purse and rolling bag, took his arm, and we headed out to join everyone else to watch the Themnir land and be greeted.

We walked arm-in-arm, me rolling my bag and purse along, and I actually got to look around a little, since we weren't having whispered conversations in the halls. The palace was ornate and airy at the same time, loaded with opulent furnishings. And yet it managed to be rather welcoming. "It's a beautiful place."

The king smiled. "I'm glad you find it so."

We reached the theater to find some of the king's guards and Len and Kyle waiting for us. The guards held the doors open for us while Raheem continued to escort me into the theater. This Queen Regent gig did have its perks.

Unsurprisingly, the king had a very nice theater with comfortable seats. There were also less comfortable seats, and they were in the back half of the theater. Noted that those from my entourage who were considered important had the cushy seats, meaning all the aliens, Queen Renata, Rahmi, and Rhee included. Thankfully, Mona was also in a good seat, as was Antoinette, with White in between them.

Mahin, Claudia, Lorraine, and Colette had good seats, too. Bummer for Francine, but presumed she had a TV of her own. Or, rather, that we did in my supposedly gigantic suite. This was really like an actual movie theater, much more so than what we had at the White House.

Those who were thought to be on the servant side of the house were in the less comfy chairs, meaning Camilla and pretty much anyone considered to be my security, Reader and Tim included, though I didn't see Wruck in the room. Len and Kyle were required to stand in the back, along with Raheem's guards, the better to tackle or shoot attackers, apparently.

Other than the security personnel, none of the men who had been in the conference room when we'd entered the palace were here. Presumed they were at the Burj Khalifa already. Either that or they had their own theater. Really, both were quite possible.

The king and I had the best seats, and I had enough legroom that the rolling bag and my purse weren't in the way. The theater was large and ornate. It was really like a Golden Age movie theater, complete with gilding that I hoped was paint but was probably real gold on the various moldings, columns, and cornices. Was really glad again that Dad wasn't with me on this excursion—there was no way he could have handled all the wealth being casually displayed everywhere.

"Where is the religious contingent?" I asked Raheem.

"Somewhere else, where nothing we say will affect them and vice versa. They have their own viewing area, never fear. And palace guards are there with your security teams to ensure that nothing untoward happens."

Chose not to ask if they were with the others who'd been in the arrival room before, or if there were three or more theaters in the palace. Took some real self-control, but I managed it.

Theater or not, there wasn't a lot of time to request popcorn and a Coke, as the screen went live just as Raheem and I got seated.

It was early morning on the East Coast, but it was a sunny day. All the better to watch the new aliens arrive.

There was Mr. Joel Oliver in all his glory, reporting live at the scene. He'd tidied up a bit from how he'd dressed when I'd first met him, but his clothes were still baggy enough that I couldn't tell if he was muscular or if the baggy was there to hide a slight pudge. He'd refused to shave his beard once he'd been accepted into the legitimate media and he wore his hair in an unruly style to, presumably, show that he was still a maverick.

Didn't pay a lot of attention to what Oliver was saying. It was the usual blah, blah, blah about how this was an historic day for all of Earth-kind. He was being very careful to not use the words "human" or "humanity" or even "mankind" and was instead using the word "people." Wasn't sure if he'd come up with that spin alone or if he'd been briefed on what to expect, but I was all for the effort.

The camera moved to Jeff, who was standing at the bow of the ship, hair and suit jacket ruffling in the wind. He looked beyond dreamy and totally presidential. Or like he was starring in an action movie. Both, really. Missed him tons right now. Sure, we hadn't been apart all that long, but that didn't mean I wasn't ready to jump his bones at this exact moment.

Had no idea if he'd picked up my lust from halfway across the world or if someone had said something that made him turn, but Jeff looked over his shoulder at the camera and smiled a very sexy little smile. Then he turned back toward the descending spaceship.

The camera panned over the others on board—Muddy and Dew were there, along with Rohini, who was representing for the Shantanu since Bettini was with my massive entourage, Lakin, Wrolf and Willem covering the Canus Majorians, and Arup representing for the Feliniads. Realized that Vance was right—we needed to keep our part of Animal Planet with Francine so as to keep humans reassured that Aliens Were A-Okay.

Uncle Mort was there, too, but there weren't many other humans or A-Cs. It made sense that Hochberg wasn't on the boat—as Vice President he needed to be back in D.C. But I didn't see a lot of other people I'd have expected to try to get into the picture, for good or bad.

The camera panned away from the deck of the ship and had us looking upward again. The Roving Planet was even more impressive when it was entering Earth's airspace. It still looked like a giant Death Star Atomizer to me, but to see it compared to the boat Jeff and the others were on—the largest Coast Guard cutter on the East Coast, the USCGC *Hamilton*—was to truly realize the magnitude of what was happening. The cutter was to the Roving Planet as a Poof was to a blue whale.

And blue was the operative word. Closer up, the neon blue of the spinning rings was even brighter and prettier. The round ship on the inside of the rings was a lighter blue. Realized my FLOTUS color matched the Themnir's ship. Hoped this was a good sign but didn't bet on it.

"It's a pity the President does not have a yacht to entertain these visitors," Raheem said.

"President Carter sold the one we had way back when. He felt it was excessive."

"I'm sure he did." Apparently Raheem had a sarcasm meter he'd been hiding, because he was easily at eight on the scale.

"I'm sure the *Hamilton* will be fine." I wasn't. Had no idea how many Themnir were in this ship, but even if it was nominally staffed for its size, there was no way they could all fit on the cutter.

"How do you plan to move these visitors?" Raheem asked, obviously reading my mind. Or merely doing the same math that I was. "I cannot believe that all who are coming will fit onto that one small ship."

Refrained from asking if Raheem thought the ship was small because he had one that was larger or if it was just that the Roving Planet was so gigantic in comparison to the *Hamilton* that there was presumably no way that everyone in it could fit on the cutter. Decided not to ask, since I shared his concern.

"The Roving Planet is really not that much bigger than Drax's helicarrier," Vance, who was sitting on my other side, said quietly. "It's the layout that makes it look larger."

"Well, that and the spinning neon propulsion system. Wonder if it turns off and, if it doesn't, how it's going to safely land in the ocean." Looked at Raheem out of the corner of my eye.

He smiled at me. "Feel free to discuss whatever is necessary. This is both historic and something you'll be having to discuss with many others shortly. If your people feel that they need to brief you on anything, they should feel free to do so."

"We—well, really I, tend to talk a lot while we're ingesting information."

Raheem was really trying not to laugh. "So my intelligence has shared with me. Please go ahead, I'm sure I'll find it most educational, especially if I get to add in as well."

"Absolutely," Vance said.

"Frankly, I'm curious," Raheem said. "Where is the military? Other than the Coast Guard, I mean."

Realized he was right—there was no evidence of any other ships or aircraft. Felt worry hit—it was one thing to not have Jeff with a lot of other people nearby. It was another to allow an alien ship to land without some sort of protection for the President in evidence.

Vance did a quiet cough. "There's protection. It's just cloaked."

Relief washed over me. "The Vatusan ships?"

He nodded but we all stopped talking because the spaceship was almost down. Everyone was silent now, as the world watched Earth's first out and proud alien arrival.

It took a few minutes, but the Roving Planet finally landed gently on the Atlantic Ocean. And it was clear that the landing was gentle, because the cutter wasn't swamped and there were no large waves created. The ship bobbed a bit more, discernable due to the handheld cameras bobbing, but that was it.

The spinning neon bands stopped spinning and collected together as if they were the equator for the Roving Planet, settling in neatly. Eight bands, each of slightly larger diameter, radiated out like Blue Saturn's Rings. Once they were aligned together, they stopped glowing, seemingly turned off.

And there the giant mini-world was, just, sort of floating in the water, about halfway submerged. How it wasn't sinking was beyond me. Possibly the rings acted as a flotation device when they were together and around the ship in this way, because they were sitting on the water.

"Nicely done," Raheem said, while Oliver did the speculation without information so near and dear to so many journalists' hearts. Said speculation sounded a lot like what I'd been thinking, right down to the flotation device idea. Nice to see that

Oliver and I were in tune. Raheem's next question wrenched me right back to the right here and right now. "What will these, ah, people be like?"

Mossy moved from his seat and came to where we were. "I believe that I have the most information about the Themnir, and I think you would prefer that I not shout while I share it." Vance moved like he was getting up but Mossy put his hand up. "No need. I'm fine with standing right now."

"Thank you," Raheem said. "We appreciate your consideration."

Mossy turned to the screen. "Your concerns about a military escort are, as you will see, of no actual worry. The Themnir are extremely pacifistic."

"And the Greeks gave the Trojans a lovely horse as a gift, a gift which contained many soldiers who were not pacifistic," Raheem pointed out.

Realized he had an extremely legitimate concern. We were trusting that the Turleens, Wruck, and any number of other people were correct in their assessments and not all working together in some sort of gigantic Take Over The Earth conspiracy.

Sure, Algar and ACE had pretty much said that Muddy was right on with his intel, but they didn't always tell me everything. In fact, they never told me everything. They gave me fiddly little clues that I had to work out and hope I'd guessed correctly.

And my husband was essentially alone, a sitting duck for whatever the Themnir might choose to throw at him. My analogy from earlier came back to me. Cows *were* pacifistic, but they could certainly kick a man to death if they were roused.

Focused on not panicking because there wasn't a lot I could do right now. Christopher was with Jeff somewhere, and Chuckie too, I was sure, and no matter what, they weren't going to be faster than the Flash or smarter than Batman. And Jeff was Superman—he'd handle it, whatever "it" was going to be.

A ramp opened from the side of the Roving Planet. Held my breath. Here it was, good or bad, the official First Contact that all the world was watching.

"Here they come," Oliver shared from the deck, sounding excited beyond belief. "The world waits in breathless anticipation!"

The first Themnir started down the ramp. And everyone in the theater gasped. Gasps of shock and horror.

CHAPTER 58

WRUCK AND MUDDY had not exaggerated the Themnir's appearance. The Themnir really looked like slugs, giant slugs, only they had faces of a sort, arms, and legs. Four stout legs, which they needed in order to drag the latter half of their body along.

They walked or slid or whatever they called it in a sort of bobbing serpentine gait. The kind of gait that said, if they were in a Disney movie, they'd be the characters that were happy with their lowly lot in life because they had the sunshine and flowers and such, and their particular song would win the Oscar.

The gasps from the room had been because, no matter how many times someone told you the people coming were giant slugs, the sight of a slug that was taller than Jeff really gave humans and A-Cs and, from the sounds, everyone from the Alpha Centauri system, pause. Was certain I heard a little gagging, but it was contained.

The people on the cutter were having no less fun. Either the cameraman had jumped or was really trying out for a job on the camera crew of the next Jason Bourne movie. Even Oliver looked thrown when the camera finally, shakily, focused on him. "And," he said haltingly, "the first emissary of the Themnir has shown himself. Herself. Itself." Oliver managed a weak chuckle. "We'll be finding out shortly, I'm sure."

"Ah," Raheem asked slowly, "these are the people we've been expecting?"

"Um, yes. I left out the little details about them, but yes, these are the Themnir, as accurately described."

"They're leaving a trail," Vance said quietly, clearly trying his hardest to channel his years of time spent hanging out in the

Washington Wife class and not sound totally icked out. With limited success.

"They probably don't do it on purpose."

"They do," Mossy corrected. "The trail, as you call it, nourishes the ground as they walk over it. The Themnir are one with their planet. The Roving Planet has an interior that is appropriate to the Themnir's ways of life, so they nourish it as well."

"Will that work on Earth like it does on their home planet?" Reader asked from the cheap seats. The no shouting rule was totally out the window, it was clear, because Raheem was obviously trying hard not to act totally repulsed and had thrown any kingly propriety out the window.

"We'll be finding out," Mossy said. Clearly the Turleens liked the Themnir, because I could tell Mossy wasn't happy with our reactions. Time to cowgirl up and take one for the team.

"I'm sure they're lovely people. And, frankly, they're not firing at us. I don't even see where weapons would be on their ship. They look kind of . . . fragile, really. It's clear why they were coming for protection." And, frankly, if the Aicirtap were giant beetles of some kind, then the Themnir would look like a delicious delicacy to them. All soft squishy bits, not even a shell to have to crack.

The cutter was moving carefully into position so that the ramp from the Roving Planet would be able to sit on the bow. It would be bumpy, but the Themnir would be able to exit their ship and come onto the *Hamilton*.

Eventually, at any rate. The *Hamilton* got into place with the ramp tied to it, and the line of Themnir were still making their way down said ramp. Couldn't tell if they were that slow naturally, if they were being really hella careful so as not to fall into the ocean, or if this was some weird kind of official greeting that took forever, but was really hoping it was one of the latter two options.

"We're not sure if the Themnir fear our reactions," Oliver, echoing my thoughts, said in a hushed voice, "or are merely being cautious so as to not fall into the salt water. Ah, ocean."

Yeah, slugs were harmed badly by salt. Had a feeling this race wasn't going to be settled in Utah. Unless, you know, we were going to treat them like we'd treated the Native Americans. Made a firm decision that we would not. Made a mental note that, when Jeff had a spare second, he needed to focus on fixing what we could of what humanity's forebears had done to said

Native Americans. Perhaps we'd try that next week, once our little alien immigration and invasion problem was solved.

Jeff and Muddy were having a conversation that wasn't being broadcast. Muddy nodded, then he altered into his dirigible form, flew to the first of the exiting Themnir, all of whom were still slowly moving down the ramp, changed back, and spoke to the Lead Themnir. Said Themnir nodded its head, or the top part of its body, or however they chose to describe where they had two antennae sticking up.

"The Lieutenant General of the Turleen Air Force has just consulted with the President and is now acting as emissary to the Themnir," Oliver shared.

"Really, that's Muddy's title?" I asked Mossy.

"As you would understand it, yes."

"You and Dew have equally impressive titles, don't you?"

Mossy managed a tight smile. "Every Turleen here has what, to a human, would be an impressive title. We do understand how you work—probably more than you think we do."

"Oh, no. I'm getting the really clear idea that the Turleens know a lot about everyone. You have one of the most impressive spy networks I've ever encountered, and I totally mean that as a compliment." Clearly Chuckie and Serene were going to want to have a private sit-down with our Turleen Contingent and get some awesome tips and training ideas.

"Thank you. I think."

Would have said something, but we had action on the screen again. Muddy turned and nodded to Jeff. Who leaped up onto the ramp and strode up the walkway.

"What is he doing?" Vance asked, for the room, presumably. I certainly wanted to know.

Jeff joined Muddy and the Lead Themnir. There was a conversation. The Themnir bowed to Jeff. Jeff bowed back. More conversation. Then Jeff shook the Themnir's hands in a sort of joint double handclasp. More conversation. Then Jeff did something no one saw coming.

He put his arms around the Themnir and did the French version greeting, where you kiss each other on each cheek. And they both did the cheek-kissing thing.

My first reaction was a form of revulsion and the desire to say that lips that had touched slug slime would never touch mine. Shoved that one away fast, because not only was there no way in the world I wasn't going to kiss Jeff again, but it was a xenophobic reaction and I wasn't proud of it and I didn't want to keep it around.

My second reaction, though, was pride. My husband had just greeted an alien that was, at first blush, repulsive to his entire world, and he'd greeted that alien as a beloved and honored friend.

"I see why your Emperor chose your husband as King Regent," Raheem said quietly. "He is an impressive man."

"Yes, he is, isn't he?"

Jeff turned, smiled, and waved to the camera. He didn't look slimy, which was a relief on any number of levels. No, what he looked was, for want of a better term, Kennedy-esque. As if, finally, the President was someone you could once again not only respect and admire, but who was going to give you hope, hope that he'd lead you toward being the best you could be.

"President Martini has greeted the Themnir as welcomed guests," Oliver shared. "And our new lives as a planet joining the Greater Galactic Community begin."

Jeff had Muddy and the Themnir wave, too. Muddy waved normally. The Themnir waved with their arms and their antennae. Focused on the way Disney would draw them. In other words, I looked for the cute and cuddly. It was hard to find, but it was there.

Muddy flew back to the ship and had a conversation with someone I realized with relief was Alexander. Alexander nodded and then did what Jeff had—leaped up onto the ramp and went to join Jeff and the others. Muddy stayed on the cutter but moved out of the camera's view.

More talk, more obvious greetings. Once again the bow, the handclasp, and, to Alexander's great credit, the kissing on both cheeks. This time, the room seemed to handle it better. Did not look forward to when I had to do that for the first time. Knew it was coming and would be soon, too. Also knew, without asking, that Raheem was looking as forward to that as I was.

"Emperor Alexander, representing all of the Alpha Centauri System, also greets the Themnir as welcomed friends," Oliver shared. He walked to the ramp. Whether because he'd been told to stay on the boat or if he just wanted to delay the greeting by however many seconds, Oliver stayed on the cutter at the end of the ramp.

Muddy was back on camera. He put his fingers to his mouth and gave an impressive wolf whistle. Other Turleens appeared in dirigible form. They flew over onto the Themnir's ramp and lined it, Space Turtle next to Space Turtle all the way on both sides. Then Muddy moved out of camera range again. The Themnir sped up.

"So, they fear the ocean," Raheem said.

"Makes sense. Even if salt isn't a problem for them, who wants to fall in? They might be buoyant and able to swim, but right now isn't the time to find out."

"I'm talking to the Major General of the Turleen Air Force, Dew Lakes," Oliver shared. "Major General Lakes, why are the Themnir visiting Earth?"

"The Themnir are, as you can see, non-aggressive people," Dew replied. "They are fleeing our home system of Sirius for the same reason that we Turleens have come to request Earth's aid and allegiance. A common enemy is approaching."

"Uh, Kitty?" Tim called from the back. "Was mass panic the plan?"

"I've been with you guys, remember? I have no idea if this was rehearsed or if Dew is off-script."

"She is not," Mossy said. "At least, she is not off *our* script. You all seem to think there is the luxury of time. There is not. Your planet needs to be ready as fast as possible."

"Well," Raheem said with a little chuckle, "all of this should make all the meetings we're going to be having go a bit more smoothly."

Looked at him. "How long before one of your counterparts starts accusing Israel of coordinating this?"

"I give it less than five minutes, honestly. However, we do have some sway with that." Raheem raised a hand and one of his guards came trotting down. "Please tell our religious guests that Queen Katherine and I will want to address them immediately after this televised event is over. Ensure that none of them leave the room, even if that room must be locked from the outside."

The guard nodded to Raheem and raced off. We were all quiet for a moment. "Wow, you're going to lock them in?"

"If necessary." Raheem shrugged. "I will blame faulty door locks. We cannot have a lack of unity, just because these visitors are . . . unappealing to us, at least at first glance. If what the military man with us just said is correct, we have little time." He nodded to Mossy.

"I'm a Brigadier General," Mossy said. "And yes, there is almost no time. Certainly none for needless, petty delays."

"You've been here a lot, and yet I still don't think you 'get' humanity. We're totally freaking into needless and petty. It's one of our 'things.'"

Mossy shrugged. "And yet, your husband is not. And he leads the world."

"Not really and not yet."

"America is still the world leader," Mossy said. "Act like it."

"Wow, I totally prefer hanging out with Muddy. He's folksy."

Mossy shot me a snide look worthy of any Vance could do. "He is. He's far more diplomatic. I'm far more focused on saving the galaxy."

"In other words, Mossy's just like you," Vance said. "It happens," he said to Mossy. "You get two of the exact same personalities in the room and at first they fight. She'll warm up to you, I'm sure."

Mossy shrugged. "I don't care, in a personal sense. In a general sense, Earth is at the center of what will be the biggest battle this side of the galaxy has seen in at least a thousand years. I don't care if the Queen Regent and I spend the entire time snarling at each other as long as, when it's over, we've won and our planets and people are not destroyed."

"What Bossy Mossy said, and that's me giving you a nickname, meaning I like you. Sort of. At any rate, we need to know what in the world Jeff's plan is for what to do not only with the Themnir but their ship."

"I already know," Reader said, having removed himself from the servants' section and come forward. "Chuck just gave me an update. Per Muddy, the five who are on the gangplank are going to be escorted to the White House. The rest of the Themnir are staying on their ship. Until they know we're going to be able to beat the Aicirtap back, they want to keep the majority of their population inside their escape mechanism."

"Can't blame them. How many Themnir are here?"

Reader took a deep breath and let it out slowly. "Their entire population. Every last one of them."

CHAPTER 59

"**H**OW? I mean that seriously. How can an entire planet full of beings be in one ship, even a ship that size?"

Mossy took point on this one. "The Themnir's home planet is truly more of a small, lush moon. It's incredibly moist, with a lot of foliage and the small things that live in lush, abundant foliage. I would assume that the Roving Planet is packed to capacity, but the Themnir are able to go into a form of suspended animation."

"Similar to what you Turleens do?" Hey, wanted to show I'd been paying attention.

"In a way. However, we are still able to fly ourselves around obstacles, avoid anomalies, avoid collisions with others of our kind or other ships or asteroids and the like. It's something we can do innately, and it's a focus for all of us, so the ability is improved over time. For the Themnir, their suspended animation is far deeper. They will be sleeping in layers."

"Layers of what?" Tim, who'd also abandoned the cheap seats, asked.

"Layers of themselves."

Looked at the screen. The camera was focused on the Roving Planet again, as the ramp slowly closed. Did some higher math calculations in my head, only because Chuckie wasn't around to do the heavy lifting at this moment. "It's very possible, based on their size in comparison to the ramp. I can see that you could have tens of thousands in there. Packed like canned sardines, but if they don't really notice, it wouldn't be a problem."

Everyone stared at me.

"What?" I asked finally. "You all staring at me had better not be in shock because I don't sound like a moron."

"It's not," Reader said. "We're not actually staring at you, girlfriend." He nodded his head toward Raheem, who was on my right.

Turned to see that one of Raheem's guards, the one who hadn't left to go lock up the religious types, was holding a semi-automatic pointed right at Raheem, who was still in his cushy seat and therefore had nowhere to go. The gun was shaking, though Raheem was not. He looked calm. Annoyed and disappointed, but calm.

"Your Majesty," the guard choked out, "you cannot allow this. You are listening to this . . . this *Jewess* about allowing those . . . *things* to come into our lands? You would imprison our ayatollahs and imams and allamahs so that they will acquiesce to worship a God other than our own? You are a traitor. To Allah, to your people, and to all who have served under you."

It was dark in here but my eyes had adjusted ages ago. Could see Len and Kyle out of the corner of my eye—their guns were out, but they didn't have a clean shot. Vance was still sitting on my left, and Reader and Tim had stood near and in front of him. Vance wouldn't have a gun and Reader and Tim couldn't pull theirs without the gunman shooting.

Mossy, however, was standing in front of and between me and the king. And my stuff was between me and Vance and, due to turning to see what was going on, I'd shifted so that I was facing the guard. And my mouth was opened slightly because I'd been planning a snarky comeback.

Had no idea how well Turleens heard, but now was the time to find out. "I go low," I said as softly as I could, not moving my lips, while I revved myself up. "You go high. Now."

Launched myself at the guard's legs using a hyperspeed boost. At the same time, Mossy shifted into dirigible form and slammed into the guard's arm. Turleens apparently had great hearing, one definitely for the win column.

The gun went off, but the shot hit the ceiling. The guard was on his back, and I straddled his chest while Mossy turned back into turtle form and wrested the gun away. And then I did a ground and pound that would have made Tito very proud.

"Listen, you religious jackhat, reality is here and it's not going away!" Slammed my fists into his face with each word. "Who you worship doesn't matter anymore because there is no more human against human action that's going to be able to be allowed, you moron!"

He managed to flip me off of him. Just barely, but still. Not a problem, though, because he staggered to his feet with his legs apart. I was on my feet a lot faster, hyperspeed again being the best thing in the galaxy.

I sent a massive kick right to his very personal region and he buckled. "We have to join together or we'll be destroyed. Sorry that intel is coming from a *Jewess*," slammed a double fist into his face that slammed him into the wall, "but you'll just have to live with it, you sexist, racist, misogynistic, xenophobic, traitorous idiot." Slammed a kick into his body for every word as said body slumped to the ground. "Or not." Picked him up and rammed him against the nearby wall. Realized why Jeff liked this move—you got to hold onto your enemy and just bash the crap out of them without actually hurting yourself.

Someone cleared their throat and I stopped, dropped the now extremely unconscious guard, and turned to see who was so clearing, while Len and Kyle ran down and slapped cuffs on the guard just in case.

The throat clearer was Raheem. "I am beyond impressed. I would firstly like to thank both you and the Brigadier General for your timely protection of my person. And then I would like to hope that someone taped that performance, because all I will need to do to convince any who have doubts is to replay that and I'm certain that, after they finish wetting themselves, they will see reason."

"We didn't and they won't," Reader said. "However, the First Lady is right. We don't have the luxury of infighting anymore." He looked back at the screen, where the cutter was moving away from the Roving Planet and Oliver was interviewing Jeff, Alexander, and the Themnir representatives.

We all listened for a bit. No one was saying anything of actual interest to anyone in this room—it was all the usual political and diplomatic type of chat I'd been sick of since my first week in Washington. The Themnir representatives had either studied up on our ways, or bureaucracy and political-speak were galaxy-wide traits. Bet on the latter, honestly.

"The Themnir sound sloshy," I said finally. "And Mossy, before you start, cool your protective jets. They do. We need to accept that they're different and how they're different before we can accept them *as* different and then accept them for themselves. It's how we work."

"It is," White said, finally deigning to join the party. "And, frankly, if your guard's reaction is any indication, Your Majesty, we should head to wherever the religious leaders are with much haste."

"Yeah, even with Paul, my Secret Service detail, and my Centaurion detail, I'd imagine the side of nonviolence is in the minority." The Israeli Prime Minister might have Mossad agents with him, but the three I knew we could rely on were in this room with us.

Raheem nodded. "I would suggest we have guards remain to ensure that my former employee does not wake up and try to cause more problems."

"We'll do that," Lorraine said, indicating herself and Claudia.

"With pleasure," Claudia said. Almost pitied the guard if he woke up. The girls sounded as pissed as I felt.

Raheem looked a little concerned. "Trust me," I said as I took his arm and sort of tugged him up and toward the door. "One of them is more than enough."

Len poked his head out of the door, then looked at us over his shoulder. "No one's outside. I realize only one shot was fired, but the king was in this room. Where are the other guards?"

"The room is fairly soundproofed," Raheem said.

"If Jeff was here I'd test that theory, but since he's not, let's assume that things are going down and be pleasantly surprised otherwise." Ignored Tim and Reader's coughs and White's chuckles. "We need to go in protective formation, gang, with King Raheem in the center."

"Why?" Rahmi asked. "We can go far faster than they can see."

"I don't think the king wants to toss his cookies." Had a thought. "Hang on, though." Went to my rolling purse and checked inside. Nothing appeared to have been moved but something sure had been added. There was a bottle of the Hyperspeed Dramamine that Tito had created. And a small bottle of water. And some zip ties and a gag. "Thank you," I said under my breath.

Gave a pill and the water to Raheem. "Take this. It will mean that we can take you with us using hyperspeed and it won't make you sick." He looked a little uncertain but did as requested.

Gave the zip ties and gag to the girls. "Let's just truss him up and leave him. I think we're going to want you two with us. Len, take back your handcuffs, in case we need them later." Went back and grabbed my purse and rolling bag. No way I was leaving them anywhere.

"Yeah." Reader looked around the theater again. "Your Majesty, who runs this room? As in, why aren't the lights on?"

"Or, to put it another way," I said as I made sure all the humans were with an A-C or one of the Amazons, "we need to assume that we're going to exit into a fight of some kind."

CHAPTER 60

"THE LIGHT CONTROLS are internal to the room," Raheem said, as he indicated where we could turn them on. Reader did so. Yep, there was light.

"What about the video feed?" Tim asked. "I didn't see you using a remote control in here."

"No, but in this case, I requested that the feed be set up and that the operators leave their posts, so that all of you could speak without restriction."

"You rock, but I have to agree with the others on this one—a shot was fired and no one's come running or even sauntering over to see if all's well. Either they're all watching on a different TV somewhere—which is always a possibility given the magnitude of what's going on—or they're taking the world's religious leaders hostage. Or worse."

"Assume worse," Reader said. "It's always a safe bet."

Put Antoinette with the king. "You two are to keep your heads low and stay in the middle. Lorraine and Claudia will be with you. You do what I say when I say it, and if we're separated, you do what Lorraine and Claudia say when they say it. Clear?" They both nodded.

"I've contacted Manfred," Tim said, looking at his phone. "Things are heated, but no one is attacking anyone else. Yet. He feels that's only because the Secret Service and Centaurion agents are there, by the way."

"I'm in contact with head of the Centaurion detail I assigned to the Burj Khalifa," Reader shared. "Things are tense, but we have enough Field agents there that everyone's behaving themselves."

"So maybe nothing's going on and we're all just jumpy after the guard's attack," Mahin suggested.

A worry nudged. "Colette, see if you can reach Francine."

She texted. Waited. No response. She called. "Hey, it's me, call me the moment you get this." Colette looked worried as she hung up. "She's never unresponsive."

"Perhaps she's using the restroom," Antoinette suggested.

"Or, perhaps someone snuck in and found the 'First Lady' alone in her rooms." Got the "huh?" look from several people, but not all. "Francine is my double," I explained for the confused. "The world knows I'm here. Our greatest enemy, therefore, knows I'm here."

Reader nodded. "Cliff wouldn't come himself, he'd send someone. And that someone probably wouldn't know you well enough to notice the differences between you and Francine."

"I assigned guards to the rooms," Raheem said.

"So either they're hurt, doing their jobs, or flipped out like the dude here. We won't know staying in here."

"Let's roll out," Buchanan said briskly. "I'd suggest we go alone," he indicated himself and Siler, "but I know Missus Executive Chief would object. We're in the lead," he said to me. "You can be right behind me, but you're not going first." He motioned to Butler, who moved next to me. White went to my other side.

"Fine. Where's Wruck?"

"He was scouting the palace the last time we saw him," Siler said. "You want me to try to reach him?"

"No. I want to hope he's with Francine in some way." Because if he was, then he was going to get into Cliff's latest lair or at least be able to help her. I didn't want Francine hurt, and though I knew she was a trained A-C CIA operative, she'd be alone if Wruck wasn't with her, and alone with our enemies was never the best place to be.

We headed off at hyperspeed, though we were walking, not running, mostly because every woman was in heels and none of us felt like breaking an ankle right now. Still, it was faster than normal walking, and we reached the wing where our rooms were quickly. There was no one in the halls.

"This isn't normal," Raheem said. "And I don't mean the speed. We should have passed many people by now."

"We call that boding," I shared over my shoulder. Turned back so I didn't trip, even though White and Butler both had a hold of me. "Everything we're planning is going to be screwed up if Francine's been taken," I said softly. "In addition to the worry about her being taken in the first place."

"We'll adapt as we have to," White said, sounding as worried as I felt.

"Malcolm, are we in every room in this hallway?"

He stopped walking, and therefore so did the rest of us. A-C's had such good reflexes that they couldn't operate human machinery—fast stops were something I was pretty sure only I worried about.

"We are. I know what you're thinking. You all stay here and on high alert." Buchanan grabbed Siler, who blended. They disappeared and went into each room. They were back quickly.

"Nothing out of place that we can tell," Buchanan said. "Looks like everyone's things are in there, unmolested. No people in the rooms, which isn't a surprise."

Lorraine and Claudia zipped off and did the same search. They were back just as fast. "We just wanted to be sure," Lorraine said, to the "really?" looks Buchanan and Siler were shooting them. "But you're right. We checked every room before we came to the theater and nothing looks moved from what we saw."

"Professionals can toss a room in just a few minutes and you wouldn't know," Oren pointed out.

"However, we're going to assume that your underwear isn't what they were after," Buchanan said, sarcasm meter at eleven and rising.

We all moved on and quickly reached the cul-de-sac at the end of the hallway where the royal suites were. To find bodies littered about. We stopped and Buchanan and Siler checked every body. "All dead," Buchanan said grimly as he examined the last body.

"Mine, too." Siler shook his head. "Whoever did this, they're professionals. Every hit is from the rear."

"Some of these were guarding us outside the theater," Raheem said, sounding ill.

"Meaning they were lured away, which would have been easy to do." Wave a gun around and run away and watch most of the guards run after you.

Considered who was in the Crazy Eights these days. Cliff, the LaRue and Reid clones, Casey Jones, Chernobog's son Russell Kozlow, Darryl Lowe, Nerida Alfero, and Nigel Kellogg.

There was no way in the world that Cliff was doing this particular raid, and it was unlikely that he'd have the LaRue and Reid clones do it regardless of what ages they were now or what powers they'd acquired along the way—they were necessary to too many other things and the only two people Cliff likely honestly cared about.

Kozlow, Lowe, and Nerida were all hybrids, all children of Ronald Yates and their respective mothers. Lowe was an air bender and Nerida was a water bender, but neither one was a trained assassin. Neither was Casey, who was a full human.

Kozlow and Kellogg, on the other hand, were both trained killers. Kozlow supposedly had no powers other than the ability to affect magnetic fields in a small way, but he'd been enough of a danger to be on Israel's Most Wanted List and had been locked up for years before our enemies broke him out of prison in order to get Chernobog's help. Kellogg was a human and the guy who'd almost murdered Mrs. Maurer during Operation Defection Election. He'd been caught by Prince when he was trying to murder Jeff. And his MO was to attack you from behind.

"Nigel Kellogg is my first guess for who did the killing. I'm also willing to bet that he was assisted by Russell Kozlow, and yes, Vance, I'll call Chernobog really soon."

Buchanan, Reader, Tim, Len, and Kyle all had guns drawn. Siler grabbed Buchanan then blended, and they disappeared. Saw them going into the rooms at hyperspeed, but only because I was watching the doors.

Lorraine grabbed Tim, and Claudia took James, and they did the same thing, albeit without being invisible.

"Don't even think about it," Len said to me and White.

"Spoilsport."

The six of them were back fast. "No one and nothing in these rooms, either, other than everyone's personal items," Siler said. "No sign of Francine, though. Or Wruck."

"Which room is mine?"

Was led to the room at the end of the cul-de-sac. Vance hadn't been kidding—this place was like a movie suite—one where you had to be a gazillionaire just to hope to spend one night. "Wow, this is amazing and gorgeous," I said to Raheem. "I'm going to feel all shoddy when you visit us and stay in the infinitesimally smaller Lincoln Bedroom."

He beamed at me. "However, the invitation is what matters most. And the congeniality of the hosts."

Saw Mona out of the corner of my eye. She looked pleased. Well, at least something was going right.

Looked around. "You know what I don't see, and what I assume you guys didn't see in each room?"

"What?" Buchanan asked.

"Signs of a struggle," Tim answered for me. "Every room we saw looked normal." The others who'd searched agreed that the rooms hadn't been messed up in any way beyond the normal things that they'd all done earlier, like unpack a couple of things and wash their hands.

Trotted through the place. Never thought I'd find someplace that made both the Embassy and the White House Complex seem small, but here I was. Went into the room Colette confirmed she and Francine were sharing. It looked normal. "So, where's the ransom note?"

"None of us found anything that would indicate a note was left," Buchanan said. "And we were looking for one."

"So, are we supposed to think that I just took a stroll? Would no one notice that I was gone?"

Vance shrugged. "It's you. Would anyone assume you'd just stay put, even if you were told to?"

"No. But then why leave dead bodies in the hallway? That's kind of a sign that things are amiss."

"To create panic," Leah suggested. "The knowledge that something is very wrong."

"Maybe . . ." Something was bugging me about all of this, more than just the dead guards and Francine being missing. Wandered through the rooms and found the nicest bedroom. The room was pristine, so if Francine had been lounging somewhere, hanging out, she hadn't been doing it in the room chosen as mine. My stuff was here, such as it was. One lone rolling bag. "Did you guys search this?"

"We opened it," Siler said. "It was undisturbed."

"Hmmm." Hoisted it onto the bed and opened it. It certainly looked neat. Not that I had any idea of what had been in here prior—I didn't pack my own bags often anymore. That's what the Elves were for. Had a thought and stepped back from the bag.

"What is it?" White asked.

"No one touch that right now, and that's an order."

"Okay, why?" Reader asked.

"You know, way back when, during Operation Fugly, Christopher and I went to my apartment to get some of my stuff. Which ended up being the only stuff I'd have of my old life that wasn't at my parents' house, because not only was there a rattlesnake in my bed, but there was a bomb in my apartment." Really wished we'd brought Prince with us. Realized it wasn't a hard thing to get him here. "Um, I want Prince sent to us via floater gate."

"We don't need a bomb dog," Siler said. "We're all fast enough."

"Possibly, yes. Probably faster than a cobra or whatever horrid venomous snakes are native here. And no one tell me, I don't need or want to know. However, I don't want Raheem's palace destroyed. Nor do I want whatever message Cliff's henchpersons left for me destroyed."

"You're kind of assuming a lot," Jakob said.

"Yeah, I am. This is my skill. I may be the First Lady and the Queen Regent because of my husband, but I'm Megalomaniac Girl because of me. And I'm telling you that this reeks of a setup of epic proportions right now."

"A bomb set off in your suite, with you nowhere to be found, would be highly suspicious," Leah said.

"I could be around and it's still suspicious. In fact, it would be better."

"What do you mean?" Buchanan asked. "They've taken Francine, thinking she's you."

"Have they?" Considered things. "Wruck was with her, I'd bet. Because he knows these people far better than we do. And it's a perfect way for him to get back inside."

"What?" Siler asked, sounding shocked. "There's no way he's turning on you, Kitty. No way in the world."

"Oh, I don't think John's a traitor. I think he's braver than almost anyone realizes, and he's also far smarter than he lets on, and I'm not insinuating that he makes anyone think he's stupid. However, he spent decades digging in with the bad guys to try to find LaRue, end her, and usurp from within."

"You think that whoever took Francine knew it was your double, not you," White said.

"Yeah, I do."

"Then why no signs of struggle?" Colette asked.

"Because we aren't the only ones who made plans. I'm betting that Wruck and Francine had a talk about what they'd do 'if,' and then 'if' happened. Why struggle and risk being hurt?

Why struggle at all, when you're already Wruck's 'captive' who he's bringing in to Cliff in order to get back in with the old gang?"

"But why leave twelve dead bodies in the hallway?" Leah asked. "That makes no sense."

"Sure it does. It lets us all know something's wrong. And all those guards are Bahrainis. Meaning it's easy enough to insinuate that Francine wasn't kidnapped and instead shot them all and then escaped off into the city to wreak more havoc."

"Who would believe that?" Mahin asked. "Why would you, if they think it's the First Lady they've taken, or Francine, if they think they have your double, want to do anything negative here? You came here to gather everyone together as one."

"I did. And all that it will take to light the powder keg that the Middle East always is would be for the U.S. mission to blow up any part of one of Bahrain's palaces." Considered things some more. "Crap. We need to ensure that there isn't a bomb or a snake or both in my luggage. And at the same time, we need to get everyone out of the room where the religious leaders are."

"Why?" half the room asked.

Managed not to heave a sigh, but only because I was revved up on rage and fear. "Because that room is going to blow at any minute."

CHAPTER 61

TO MY TEAM'S GREAT CREDIT, no one argued. Not even Raheem. Definitely a smart teddy bear. No one panicked, either, which was also a positive.

Tim was texting and Reader was on his phone, calling in Field agents to arrive via a floater in these rooms. But the person who walked out of the floater first wasn't a Field agent. Well, not anymore.

"Tim says you guys need the Flash and told me not to strain myself until I arrived," Christopher said as soon as he was solidly here. "What's up?"

"Nostalgia for Operation Fugly." Pointed to the bag on my bed.

"Fantastic. Snake or bomb? Or both?"

"See, this is why Megalomaniac Lad called you. Both is my guess, but who knows? Poisoned darts and such are always a possibility, too."

"Do you care what happens to your clothes and stuff?"

"Wow, Amy's really made you a hell of a lot more thoughtful. No. The Elves can just get me more stuff. They might have a challenge recreating all the people, though."

Christopher nodded, then went to the suitcase. "You all should leave the room, just in case."

Field agents started arriving in the general living room area, so it was easy enough to tell the others to go with them. Reader had to tell them what to do anyway. We moved most everyone out, and I literally had to shove Buchanan, Len, and Kyle through the door, but White and I remained. It was his son, and this was Jeff's cousin. The two of us weren't leaving.

"Dad, you shouldn't be in here."

"Son, I've outrun explosions and so has Missus Martini. We're staying. Just in case."

"Call us worrywarts. There's always a possibility that I'm being overly paranoid, but be cautious."

Christopher nodded, then went to town. My stuff was flying through the air because he was pulling it out and tossing it so fast. He got to the bottom of the case in seconds. "Huh."

"What?"

"How are you with rubber snakes?"

"If they're lifelike they still scare the crap out of me. Why?"

Christopher turned around. He had a very lifelike rubber cobra in one hand and a round black ball that said "Bomb!" on it. "Someone knows us far too well."

"It's Cliff, as if there was any doubt. Was there a note in there of any kind?"

Christopher handed the fake bomb and rubber snake to White, then he searched every inch of the suitcase, including ripping out the lining. "Nothing."

"Then it's in the snake or it's in the bomb."

They both looked at me. "Why are you sure there *is* a note?" Christopher asked. "These two things seem clear enough."

"Yeah, the old, I know what you're terrified of and I also know how we almost got you way back when ploys. But I think there's a note because Cliff is a freaking lunatic and if we've found this, then we know we're not exploding or being snake bit, but we don't know anything else. Like, he doesn't know for sure that we know he's here."

"He might," White said slowly. "If John is, in fact, a very canny triple agent. Or if King Raheem has been lying to you."

"Raheem might have been. Without an empath to be sure, all we have is my gut. Which says he was not."

"Daniel and Marcus both were reading him and he gave off no signs of betrayal. And also gave off the right mixture of emotions to indicate that he wasn't wearing a blocker or an overlay."

"Then he's what we think he is unless he's an android."

"Let's hope not."

"Let's be sure." Opened my rolling purse. "I think I have an OVS in here." Sure enough, one of the handheld models was sitting right there.

Trotted into the other room. "Pardon this, but under the circumstances . . ." Wanded Raheem. Wanded the rest of the people in the room for good measure. Per the OVS, they were all organic enough that they couldn't be an android or a fembot. This was because Butler was gone, along with all of Alpha Team, Mossad, Buchanan, Siler, the Amazons, Jareen, Felicia, and Wahoa. Presumably to go save the day and get the religious leaders out of the deadly room they'd been locked into. Good thing I was rolling with a million people.

"Camilla, come with me. The rest of you, please continue to stay put."

Camilla returned to the bedroom with me. We showed her the snake and the bomb. "You seriously think something's inside those?" she asked.

"I think the possibility is there. I want to ask you your thoughts on King Raheem."

"You want to know if I think he's in on whatever's going on?"

"Yeah."

"He shook a Jewish-American woman's hand in front of every minister this country has. I think he's potentially as crazy as you, but if he's setting you up, he really likes to live on the edge. I'd assume someone's already put a contract out on him as we speak."

"That fits with everything that's already gone on. So, what do you know of Ali Baba Gadhavi? And not the guy from the stories, though he does have forty thieves and all that."

"The gangster?" Camilla gave me the hairy eyeball look. "He has more like four thousand thieves. But what the hell . . . oh. Really? Dammit, that's going to make things harder."

"I haven't made the leap," Christopher said.

Camilla sighed. "Ali Baba Gadhavi is a notorious Indian gangster, and he's been hiding out in Bahrain for decades. He's who's funding Cliff?"

"Yeah, per Raheem. And, to add to the intrigue, this can't come back on Raheem."

"The king has other worries. Let me again mention that he broke Islamic law by shaking hands with you and we'll take it from there."

"He's seen the saucers, so to speak."

"Yes. Let's hope he and the rest of us live to see the rest of them. Cliff's well-funded if he's now considered part of G-Company." We all stared at her blankly. "What the media calls his crime syndicate. Gadhavi is running his own version of the mafia."

"Do we have a hope of getting Cliff, then?" Didn't want to

have come here with all these people and plans only to have no hope of achieving either one of our missions.

"Yes, because while Gadhavi might be funding Goodman, there's no way they're hanging out together. It just means that Cliff will have a lot of toys I'm sure we won't like. Speaking of which, there's a third possibility for what's going on with Francine and John that you may not have considered."

"You mean aside from John using Francine as his cover to get back inside with Cliff, or Francine being kidnapped—either as 'me' or as herself—and John going along to protect her and, again, re-infiltrate Cliff's Crazy Eights?"

"And other than John being as captured as Francine, yes."

"We hadn't considered that one. Thanks for the extra worry."

"I have a theory other than that one, was what I meant." Camilla was giving me a look that indicated she thought I needed a nap. "There's a good chance that Adriana contacted them."

"Why would she have contacted either one?" White asked.

"Well, not John, but Francine is a very high possibility. Malcolm and I sent Adriana off to scout hours ago. Because of what was going on, the moment we were in these rooms, I told her to contact Francine if she found anything, as Francine would be the only one likely to be alone and not compromised with visitors who weren't part of our team."

"Well, that's good in one sense. But why not leave us a note?"

"Saying what? We're off on a secret mission, will call soon?" Camilla's sarcasm meter, like Mom's, went well past eleven. "Either they thought they'd be quick or they plan to contact us at another time."

"So if that option is the case, why are all the guards dead?" White asked.

"What?" Christopher barked. "Who's dead?" Right, he'd come into the room via a gate and had immediately done the luggage search.

White filled him in at hyperspeed while I put my fingers in my ears and hummed Lit's "Hard to Find" to keep from hearing White and thereby getting sick. White nodded to me when he was done. "So, what I've been thinking about while trying to avoid barfing or passing out from Richard's smooth vocal stylings is this—what if Francine and John left before Cliff's goons ever got here? Francine has hyperspeed—none of the guards would see her if she didn't want them to."

"John could have merely shifted to look like another guard and told the others he was escorting her elsewhere, too," White said.

"But does it make sense for what we know?" Christopher asked.

Camilla nodded slowly. "Cliff's men—and I agree with Kitty that it was most likely Kellogg and Kozlow—think they're coming to get you. They kill a bunch of guards, then get into the rooms and they're empty. It's not hard or time-consuming to carefully remove a bag's contents, leave moronic joke threats, and then take off."

"Cliff's way of telling me he knows where I am."

"A dozen dead men outside your door isn't easy to explain, either," White added.

"So, how do we determine which of the many options we have for Francine and John is the one that's really happening? Colette texted and called Francine. There was no answer."

"Huh." Camilla put her head outside of the room. "Colette, how many rings before your call to Francine went to voice-mail?"

Colette joined us. "One. Oh. You think she turned her phone off? Why? She's always available." Colette's eyes didn't quite meet everyone else's.

A-Cs trying to lie were always interesting. Other than the rare natural liars like Camilla, troubadours as a class had the least issues with it. And yet Colette was betraying signs of lying. Then again, it was her big sister in danger.

Considered options. We didn't have a lot of time to waste. Either the others would be back soon with, please God, news that all the religious leaders and those with them were alive and well, or we'd be pulled into action.

Camilla was a vault unless she felt it was necessary to share intel. White might have made the same assumptions I had. So that left Christopher. Who'd been the number two man in Centaurion Division for over a decade and who had, along with Jeff, kept the worst secrets in the world to himself.

"Colette, you know as well as I do that there's plenty of times a troubadour will go into a form of silent running. I want you to search the rooms to see what fiddly little clue Francine left to tell you, and Manfred, what's really going on."

"What do you mean, Kitty?" She'd recovered from the lapse that worry had given her. Colette looked completely confused, and I could tell she was trying to use her talent to make me think I was wrong. However, I'd realized that once you knew, really knew, what the troubadours were doing, it lessened their effect.

Heaved a sigh. "Colette, I *know*. I've known for a long time. Camilla either knows or she's guessed. And Richard and Christopher are both trustworthy. They can keep the secret, especially because it's in all our best interests. We're going to have to tell Jeff soon, anyway. Might as well be sooner as opposed to later."

"Tell him what?" Christopher asked.

"That Serene's running the A-C's version of the CIA, very competently, I might add, and she's doing it with every troubadour you guys have."

CHAPTER 62

CHRISTOPHER'S JAW DROPPED. "You're kidding me."

"Nope. All those people you shoved aside? Yeah, they're all awesome and finally getting to serve their people and country in the ways they've been longing to."

"Son, really, you didn't realize?" White sounded surprised and a little amused.

"How long have you known, Mister White?"

"Oh, not as long as you, I'm sure, but it dawned on me that we had a tremendous number of troubadours who were not only available at the drop of a hat, but were well versed in everything every standard Field agent knew without ever going through training. I took the logical leap. I'd assume Charles has taken that leap as well, and probably your mother. Whether they've shared the fact that they know with Serene, however, is any-body's guess."

"I figured it out the moment I realized that Serene wasn't a ditz," Camilla said. "Pretty much when Raj came on board and was accepted as an important member of your team, I figured it wouldn't be long before he and Serene were running this. Jeff doesn't know?"

"No, he's been a little busy. So has Christopher." Hey, might as well throw him that bone. "Anyway, back to the matter at hand. Colette, we know you're in the A-C CIA. So, what sign did Francine leave?"

Colette shook her head. "Serene and Raj never told me that you knew."

"Secrets are best kept silently," White said.

"True dat. But whatever. Again, your sister, clues, what have we got?"

"Hang on. I didn't look. And before anyone yells at me for that, I'm your press secretary because I'm not that great at fieldwork."

"Christopher won't be yelling at anyone, and you know the rest of us aren't going to bawl you out."

She managed a laugh. "Fine. Be right back." She zipped off.

"If there is no sign from Francine, does that mean that we have to discard Camilla's more positive option?" White asked.

"Probably. I mean, they have to have ways of letting each other know that they're doing a mission or kidnapped or whatever. Right?" I asked Camilla.

"It would make sense, and I'm sure Raj would think of it even if Serene didn't. And yes, I know he's her number two. And he's now Jeff's number two. Be happy he's loyal."

"Always am."

Camilla cocked her head at me. "You didn't ask me for confirmation of his loyalty. Why?"

"Aside from the fact that you'd just said it? Because Raj has had plenty of opportunities to screw us over and has never taken them. It's why I'm not worried that Wruck's gone to the dark side for real. Or Siler. Too many opportunities not taken."

Colette returned. "I think I found it. There was a blank piece of paper under the lamp in our room."

We all stared at her. "And?" Camilla asked finally.

"Sorry." Colette handed the notepad-sized piece of paper to me. The seal of the President of the United States was on it, but that was it.

"Not following you. Does this indicate that Francine is on a mission for His Majesty's Secret Service?"

"Well, yes. I mean, why are you asking if you already know?"

"Wow, I'm good. Okay, are we sure there's no invisible writing on it?"

Camilla took the paper from me and sniffed it. "No smell of lemon, so doubtful unless they're all equipped with vials of invisible ink."

"We're not," Colette said. "If you find a piece of Embassy or White House letterhead sitting on the desk or nightstand, it means the operative is on their assigned mission. If you find it somewhere it shouldn't be, it means the operative is on an impromptu and likely unsanctioned mission. We have other items if paper would be suspicious, but they all work like this."

"Okay, then, thank God, it's Camilla's scenario that's the most likely."

"That makes the snake and bomb make more sense, too," Christopher said.

"How so?" White asked.

"If they have a hostage, then I'm with Kitty—where's the ransom note? They came equipped with these things—I mean, no sane adult is wandering around with a realistic looking rubber cobra just in case they want to leave it somewhere. I'm sure they had a ransom note with them, too. They sneak in, no one's here, so they leave these as a calling card, something to scare the hell out of Kitty when she was most likely alone. But I doubt they'd have left them if they'd actually taken her because they'd *want* us to know she'd been taken. I mean, maybe, but the snake and fake bomb are here for Kitty, not someone else. And, therefore, I think there's no note because Kitty, or Francine, take your pick, wasn't here."

"Sounds right to me. Says they're watching us and can sneak in and all that jazz. But there could still be a note. One for if I'm here, one for if I'm not. Have you searched the novelty items there for anything?"

"Not yet. I want to be sure there isn't something bad inside of either one."

"Wise," Camilla said. "We're talking about a crazy genius, after all."

"Take them to Dulce," White suggested, as he handed Cliff's "presents" back to Christopher. "Using a gate, please, son. We and Jeffrey both need you at full optimum."

"You want me back here once we know what's going on with these things?" he asked while Colette called for yet another floater gate.

"Stay near a gate, but beyond that, no. I don't want you here, doing nothing, when Jeff might need you."

"I'd like to go with you on whatever insanity you're going to be doing," Christopher said, without glaring. "I know you'll need me."

Felt his forehead. "Huh. No fever."

"What? I'm fine. Look, seriously, I think I'm going to be a lot more necessary to the team that's going to try to take down Cliff—and I know that's what you're planning, so don't try to say otherwise—than I am to the galactic party that's currently being thrown."

"Good point," I said as the gate shimmered into existence. "Look, go to Dulce. Have this safely examined and be sure they get every possible bit of information out of it. Even something small and seemingly insignificant could give us a lot to work with. Then call me or your dad. We'll determine at that time what to do. Okay?"

"Yeah, makes sense. Just . . . seriously, Kitty. I have a really bad feeling about this. I don't think Chuck and Jeff realize what you're really here for, but they both know you're up to something. If the Themnir hadn't arrived, I'm sure they'd be onto you, too. But it's more than that. This," he held up the snake and bomb, "stuff is crazier than normal. He's taunting us. That means he's ready for us. He wants you to find him. Never forget that. It's what he wants."

"Why?" White asked him.

Christopher sighed. "Because this isn't about us and never has been, Dad, that's why. We're just the means to the end. All of it, everything that's been done by Cliff—either what he could when he was an assistant or Apprentice and everything since he took over as Mastermind—is focused on one goal."

"Beating Chuckie and making him suffer."

Christopher nodded. "And now? Now Cliff wants to kill Kitty—as slowly and painfully as possible—and make Chuck watch. That's how he wins. Even if he dies right after, that's how he wins."

CHAPTER 63

CHRISTOPHER WENT TO DULCE and the rest of us looked at each other. "He's not wrong," Camilla said finally. "Maybe Francine being gone is a good thing. It means you'll have to do the meetings and we'll roll Team Commando without you."

"When pigs fly. And by that I mean our pigs, not aliens that look like pigs with wings. Our pigs. Just in case and all that."

"I agree," White said. "While I believe Christopher's concerns are correct, that's always been the end game. And we need Missus Martini's skills."

There was a knock at the door, then Mona ran in. "James just told us to get to where the religious leaders are as fast as possible."

Decided all my stuff could stay strewn about the room. Flipped my purse over my head so that it was securely on my person. Lowered the handle on the rolling bag and picked that up in my other hand. It was heavy but not unmanageable.

White took it from me. "I'll ensure that it's with us and never out of my control." He took my hand, Camilla grabbed Mona, and Colette led the way out of the room. The others were already linked up, other than Raheem.

Grabbed his hand. "Get us to where we need to go. You steer, Richard and I will provide the speed." We took off.

Hyperspeed being what it was, it didn't take us more than a couple of seconds of racing past the dead bodies in the hall, then through the beautiful, huge palace, to get where we were going. I'd never find my room again without a map and a guide, and we needed to tell someone to take care of the corpses, but we reached the area to discover that where we were going was bedlam.

There were people outside of this room—mostly ours but some that appeared to be palace guards. There were many more people inside this room, and most of them were shouting and yelling at each other.

Turned out the religious folks had not been sent to another theater. Instead they were in yet another very large room with chairs all around the walls, though there were also chairs set up in the typical rows you saw at any conference around the world. The room was easily as big as the LSR, maybe bigger.

There was a ginormous screen at the end of the room. It was, I realized, actually eight big screens put together, similar to how Imageering did it, where the screens formed one larger screen but could show different feeds as needed.

Realized Imageering probably *had* done it—noted several A-Cs who weren't dealing with screaming religious folks. They were dealing with the equipment, protecting it from flying objects, of which there were more than a few, as well as keeping the screens upright and functioning. To my knowledge my team hadn't requested this, but the Supreme Pontifex got whatever his little heart desired, so I figured Gower had asked for the setup.

All the chairs in the middle were facing the display. Most of the people weren't looking at the screens, which currently only showed a single feed in Extra Giant Size. Jeff and the Themnir weren't back to shore yet—not a surprise considering where the Themnir had landed—so we had a close-up of Jeff's face. Nicest thing I'd seen in what felt like ages.

Couldn't hear what Oliver or anyone else onscreen was saying, however, because of all the freaking out going on in here. Raheem waded in and attempted to get things under control, with limited success.

Managed to find Reader, though I kept hold of White, too. "What in God's name is going on?"

"Appropriate choice of words, girlfriend. There were indeed bombs in here. We found them and deactivated all of them, just in time, too, so good call on your part as always. Then, you know, instead of anyone saying thank you they started accusing us and each other of setting this whole thing up merely to get everyone in one place and kill them."

"The illogic of the person or persons behind this plot being *in* the room at the same time has not been forwarded?"

"Oh, it has. Several times. They aren't interested in logic. They aren't killing each other only because I've kept the Field agents here." Noted that a lot of our people were having to physically stop others from fighting.

And these were the religious leaders. God alone knew what those over at the Burj Khalifa were doing. "Do we have people over at the meeting with the Heads of State of the region?"

"Oh, yeah, we do." Reader sounded pissed and resigned. "No bombs there, so there's that. Otherwise? It's the same thing only worse, because no one who could be a calming influence—like you or Paul—is there. To the point where I had to send your Secret Service *and* Centaurion details over there in order to keep the peace."

The mere fact that Reader somehow thought that I was a calming influence was proof enough that things were out of control, let alone the reassignment of staff. "Did we do a video feed between the two locations?"

"We did, at Paul's request. He'd hoped that the religious side would positively influence the political side."

"Wow, he really hasn't been paying attention, has he? Who's controlling the feeds?"

"We are, mostly."

"Great, I want to see what's going on in the other meeting. Can we get it on split screen?"

While Reader sent a text, because it was too loud to make a call, White pointed to the screen. "There's more."

We looked to see that the screen was no longer one big image. Instead there was Jeff in one corner, and shots of every ship we'd been expecting filling five other slots, Z'porrah ship included. Sure, they were shots from space, taken from the space station most likely. But most of the ships were close. As in, near the moon close.

The last two screens showed what I was pretty sure was the Heads of State meeting. It was filled with Middle Eastern people, men mostly, all looking formal, and all also fighting. "Well, at least we can see what's going on. And vice versa?"

"Yes, they have the same screen setup there. Doesn't matter, really, though. Looks like everyone else is almost here." Reader's voice was tight. "I thought we had more time."

Considered this. "The aliens can see us. Radio and TV waves carry, per everyone in the Alpha Centauri system, and they're all more scientifically advanced than we are. They were waiting."

"For what?" Reader asked.

"To see how we greeted the Themnir," White answered.

"Exactly. We didn't fire on the Themnir and we didn't attack them in horror. We allowed them to land and then Jeff and Alexander greeted them as if they were old friends. So everyone else sped the hell up to get here as fast as possible."

"All our planning seems to be for nothing, though." Reader sounded stressed. "We need more time."

"We don't have it." The feed had switched the meeting room image to a single screen so as to have the last screen of the eight show what was the Persian Gulf. "What are they saying?"

"That the Faradawn have requested to land in the Persian Gulf," Butler said from behind us. "That's what some of the arguing is about. But only some."

Heard a lot of curse words along with "Death to America" and "Death to Aliens" and similar. Sounded like a Club 51 True Believers rally. Raheem was up front, under the big screen setup, but he was getting shouted at, too. Basically, as with any diplomatic type of mission I went on, this was an unmitigated disaster.

Reader was right—we didn't have time for this.

Headed for the front of the room, still keeping hold of White, Reader and Butler both following us. Got there then let go of White's hand. Grabbed one of the A-Cs working the media stuff. "You know who I am?" He nodded. "Great. Then I need a lectern and podium and a teleprompter that's showing me what's on the screens that will be behind me. I also want to ensure that anything I do or say will be broadcast to the others receiving the feed from this room. And I want that done at the fastest hyperspeed you guys have."

The A-C grabbed one of the others and they raced off.

"James, get to Paul and make sure you're ready to get him and our people out of here if I give the signal."

"What signal is that?"

"Oh, you'll know it when I say or do it."

"Oh, you don't know what the signal will be. Gotcha." Reader gave me a shot of the cover boy grin. He looked a lot more relaxed all of a sudden. "I'm better with our form of routine."

He went off and I took my bag from White. "Let's see, might I have somehow put a cordless microphone in here?" Algar was good to me—sure enough, there was a cordless mic. Didn't have to ask if it was wired or tuned to the right channel.

Closed the bag and handed it back to White. Ensured the mic

was on, then tapped it. Hard. Could definitely hear something. Good. Always nice to be right, or at least right-ish.

"I heard the microphone thump in the feed from the other room," White said. "You should be transmitting to both."

"Good." The A-Cs returned with the setup I'd asked for. Appeared to be working. Well and good. They also gave me a little Bluetooth to slip into and over my ear. Did so. Presumably this would let whoever was at the controls give me intel. We'd used similar at the end of Operation Epidemic, after all.

"What shall I do to assist, Missus Martini?"

"Mister White, could you please take the currently only sane leader in the region and ensure that Raheem is in the room but extremely safe? Probably within Animal Planet and Friends, since they're all in the room and apparently having an effect of some kind on the crowd. Keep Mona with him, too." All our non A-C aliens were literally shoving people in the back of the room into their seats. I approved of this action.

"I can and will. Your Majesty, if I may?"

The king looked worried. "They are not above ordering everyone's death."

"Oh, Raheem, never fear. Death is coming, whether they order it or not. We're just deciding how fast we die and by whose hand. You know, democratic style." For, as far as I was concerned, the last time until this was over, one way or another.

"What shall I do?" Butler asked as White hustled Raheem to relative safety.

"Oh, I'll need you doing translations. For me and for them. Are you up to that?"

He smiled. "I can talk as fast as an A-C now. But your translation chip should ensure I don't need to translate for you." Realized he was right—I'd understood all the nasty stuff being shouted earlier, after all.

"Okay, awesome, and no need for that speed level unless we need to get them to stop rioting. None who I need to get through to can hear at that speed."

"Understood. I can also project as if I were holding a microphone."

"It's always nice when bad things work out and end up good, isn't it?" Well, no time like the present. Turned and faced the bedlam. Took a deep breath and channeled Jeff and Mom both. "ENOUGH!"

CHAPTER 64

MY BELLOWING wasn't up to Jeff's standards, but I held my own. Butler had an impressive bellow, too. He was translating not only my words but my tone and volume level. The room started to quiet. "I meant it," I bellowed again. "Sit down, all of you, and SHUT UP!"

One of the many men wearing a kufiyah stayed up and shook his fist at me, as Butler repeated what I'd said in a variety of languages. Or at least I assumed he did. Just as Butler had said, the universal translator was working on all the foreign languages in the room. For me and presumably everyone else from Centaurion Division who had them, at any rate.

Looked at the small screen in front of me, which now had a shot of the Heads of State room on it. They were acting no more mature and statesmanlike than the people in here. "That goes for you in the Burj Khalifa, too!"

Checked to see where the camera was that was feeding from this room into the other. Spotted Tim, waving at me, near to what sure looked like a camera set up in the far back. All my team was back there with him, as well, some protecting the camera. Okay, I was playing to the cheap seats. Noted a couple of floating camera drones as well. Wasn't sure if they'd always been in here or if the A-Cs doing my AV work had brought them. Decided not to care. If they were weapons, there were enough people who could shoot accurately in the room, myself among them.

Time to get the quieting to go down to silence. "You will all quiet down and stop this ridiculous posturing and all the other crap, and you'll do it now."

"Why should we listen to *you*, woman?" someone who was

probably representing one of the many Islamic factions shouted. Of course, there were plenty who were here clearly representing the Judeo-Christian viewpoints, and they looked no more likely to do what I said and as if they agreed with this man's question. In fact, most of them were nodding in support of this man's question. A common enemy tended to make you join forces.

The Queen Regent Speech wasn't going to work in here, though I noted the Heads of State room was quieting far more quickly. Many of them had been in the room when I'd arrived in Bahrain, so that might have been why. Or else the Secret Service had gotten fed up and pulled their Big American Guns out and mentioned that a weapons malfunction wasn't impossible.

Looked at the people in the room. Really looked at them. And realized that I was going to have to tell the truth, because we didn't have time for any kind of diplomacy.

"You all disgust me."

Interesting. This got a lot of shocked looks. Especially once Butler finished running through all the languages in the room. An android translator made a lot of sense—no wonder George Lucas had used one.

"Look at yourselves. I mean, really look. You're the people who lead the hearts and minds of the majority of the world. And you can't even be in a room together for more than fifteen minutes without acting like the worst examples of humanity we have." Paused to let Butler catch up again.

Pointed to the screens behind me when he was done. "Do you see those ships? Do you? They see us, they see you. And let me tell you something—they aren't coming to Earth for any reasons you've told yourselves. Least of all because of who you say God is or isn't."

"Have received images of what all the aliens seeking asylum look like," a voice I recognized said in my ear while I did my next translation pause. Serene was running the show. "Faradawn ship also says that they have images of the Aicirtap and what they've done. Will wait for your cue for when to display."

"In fact," I continued, "the only religious leader in this room who's never led with hatred at any time isn't a human. He's an alien." Well, half-alien, but that wasn't important now. Gower was an A-C in mind, thought, and action far more than he was a human.

"And his people came here to help us. And, because they were here, others came to help us, too. But before you all start feeling warm and fuzzy, or ready to shove all the aliens off the planet, let me remind you that this isn't *Star Trek*. No one, none of the new aliens currently on Earth or heading toward us with intent to land and stretch their legs, tentacles, or whatever, are coming because we're *evolved* or *civilized*. None of them are coming because we're *compassionate* or *kind*. They're not coming because we're scientifically advanced enough to equal them. Because we are none of those things, the people I'm addressing in this room in particular."

This was earning me a lot of nasty looks. Whatever.

"No, *I* came here to appeal to all of you. To ask you to put aside the ridiculous fights you perpetrate among all your flocks. The fights over skin color, country of origin, who someone loves, what gender gets to be important or not, and, most of all, what each one of you calls God and God's laws. I came to ask you to stop, for one whole damn day, to stop being the petty, manipulative, mean-spirited, nasty pieces of work humans are. I wanted you to be something better. But you can't, can you?"

"Have made contact with Z'porrah ship," Serene said in my ear. "They are asking for clemency, just as the others are. Jeff has agreed. Their ship will be landing with the Vata ships guarding it. They're referring to Jeff as the King Regent. Every race has referred to him that way."

Butler was done, so I continued. "But you know what? That's alright. Because it doesn't matter now. The aliens are coming and we are not going to stop them. We are going to let them in. And nothing you do will stop that. For a variety of reasons. But here's the main one.

"All the aliens in all these amazing spaceships, they're coming to Earth not because we're good, or smart, or kind, or compassionate, or anything positive. They're coming *because* we're those nasty pieces of work. They're running to us for protection, just like someone would run to a warlord for protection—you don't have to like the warlord or think he's any good as a human being, but if he keeps you alive and protects you from the other people trying to kill you, he gets your loyalty.

"Think about that. We have six ships full of alien lifeforms fleeing to us, to Earth. Asking us to protect them. This is our real introduction to the Greater Galactic Community. And all you people can do is argue about whose ancient, multi-translated book or set of rules is the right one. All you do is complain that someone is 'other,' whine about slights committed by others long dead but clung to as if who said what to whom a thousand years ago matters today. Well, guess what? Humans breed true. Truer than dogs or cats. There is almost nothing different about any of us at the DNA level. We are *one* race with minor external differences to make us interesting. Want to see different, gang? Let's see how 'other' the people in this room you want to hit or blow up or whatever look to you in a few moments."

"Pictures going up now," Serene said. "Teleprompter will share the race names for you."

"Let me share who's coming to visit, the star systems they claim as theirs, and the names for their ships. You've already seen the Themnir, Sirius, Roving Planet." Interestingly, the reaction to the Themnir was just mildly negative this time. So there was hope. A sliver of it, but a sliver was better than nothing.

"You've also seen the Turleens, Sirius, and you've also seen that they are their own spaceships." Didn't mention that we had one in the room. Several people knew because Mossy had shoved them into a sitting position by flying up and standing on their shoulders.

A giant, humanoid honeybee hit my teleprompter. The reaction was the general gasp and pulling back thing humans did when faced with a six-limbed giant insect. "Lyssara, Tau Ceti, and they call their ship a Comb, it's not a Borg ship."

What looked truly like walking, living trees came on next. Mostly willows, but there were some other pretty tress represented, too. And yet, they were still humanoid. The life in this galaxy was fascinating. "Faradawn, Tau Ceti, Treeship."

A humanoid butterfly crossed with a fish was the next colorful entry. It was pretty, but not something you'd want to snuggle up to. "Khylida, Tau Ceti. Q'vox, Fomalhaut, both in the Faradawn Treeship." The Q'vox really did look like giant minotaurs, emphasis on giant. A picture of a Q'vox standing next to a Turleen and a Themnir popped up, presumably for us to be clear on the size differentials.

No time to admire the new people, or listen to the murmurings of the crowd, because there were more new people coming on. Something that looked a lot like Sandy the Superconsciousness and His Fun Pals more than a human hit the screens. It was somewhat in the shape of a manta ray, or a man, depending on the moment, and definitely fit the cloudlike and ethereal yet solid enough description Wruck had given me. "Vrierst, Upsilon

Andromedae, and their ship doesn't have an official name, so we'll call it as we'd see it and say it's a Manta Ray." This actually earned me some nervous chuckles. Hoped this meant the reality of our situation was coming home to roost.

Our next picture came up. Finally, some cute and cuddly in the form of some people who really looked like large golden lemurs, complete with prehensile tails, three long fingers and one equally long thumb on all four paws, triangular ears that moved around a lot, and bright, black eyes. "Draea, Yggethnia, Jewel of the Sky." Pretty name for a ship that still looked like a giant hand trowel to me.

Another cute and cuddly one. Two in a row. Didn't expect it to last. "Aschaffen, Yggethnia, Jewel of the Sky." These looked like tall humanoid sloths with silver hair or fur, extremely large, lavender eyes, three fingers and one opposable thumb on their hands and four toes on their feet, all of which had long claws that were like a sloth's. Or a bear's.

"Yah!"

Had no idea who in the audience shouted, but couldn't blame them. "Nemmen, Tau Ceti, Faradawn Treeship." These looked like rat-sized cockroaches. That walked upright. Wouldn't have thought that we'd hit a race that would have made the Themnir look attractive, but the Nemmen had that sewn up, six hands down.

"We have many more," Serene shared. "But there are less of them than these others. The remainder are refugees and for the most part, per the Faradawn, the very last of their kind. Refugees with no homes anymore are mostly on the Faradawn Treeship, but some are on the Jewel of the Sky."

"There are more, and we'll show you their pictures, but I think you get the general gist. For every race that looks like the A-Cs, there's a race that doesn't resemble us at all." Pictures flashed onto the screens. Mercifully I saw no snake people, for which I was truly thankful.

Looked out over the audience. "Now, look at the people in this room, the people around you. The other humans. And ask yourselves if we really need to spill more of our own blood in the name of God, or if we can stop that."

"But you're letting these aliens come here," someone shouted from the audience. Not nastily, which was a shocker, but with fear in his tone.

"We are. Because the reason these people are running to

Earth—running to the people so busy killing and doing terrible things to each other for the stupidest reasons that they haven't bothered with things like world peace, solving the hunger crisis, curing deadly illnesses, or achieving long-range spaceflight—is because what's chasing them is terrifying. More terrifying than us."

A picture came onscreen now. The other pictures had been put up one small screen at a time, so that there were eight pictures filling the screen. But this one was a single, eight-frame view. It was a side-by-side picture, the before and after shot.

Before was a humanoid scarab beetle, a very pretty kind of electric blue with green highlights. Nothing most humans would want to snuggle with but otherwise along the lines of the Lyssara—it wasn't threatening unless you were afraid of bees or bugs. And if you were, you could still see the face, make out that there was something more there than just an insect.

But the after picture told a different story. Overall it was now a sort of dark, iridescent blue and three times the size it had been, all bulky muscle underneath a chitin shell that looked a lot thicker than it had been originally. Where it had had pincer-like hands originally, it now had metal claws that would have made Edward Scissorhands jealous, particularly because the claws moved like fingers.

Its face was altered, too. A mouthful of serrated teeth, sharp, pointed horns coming out from the top of its forehead, and bright, crazy red eyes. And now, to put the icing on the cupcake, it had wings.

"This is one of the Aicirtap. They were pleasant and peaceful and friends with every alien race you've seen so far and many you haven't. Until they were uplifted by our enemies, the Z'porrah, and turned into killing machines. They eat their victims. Alive. And every alien whose picture you just saw, along with everyone on Earth, they now consider their food."

New images came on now. War scenes. Horrible war scenes. Scorched and destroyed earth, any buildings in rubble, half-eaten bodies strewn about, blood everywhere. But no dead Aicirtap. Dead other beings, and lots of them, but no Aicirtap bodies.

"Some of the alien races on the Faradawn and Jewel of the Sky ships have no homes anymore. They're the last of their races. Some still have home planets they can't reach or fear for. Every alien race that's about to land here considers themselves refugees of some kind."

The Q'vox were possibly the worst, because they were so huge and looked so mighty. And they were so horrifically dead, faces, if there were faces left, twisted in terrible agony. Like our people would be dead if we didn't get it together.

"Now, it's up to all of you. Do we offer safe haven to these people who have nothing left and nowhere else to go? Or do we turn them away, like we've all done to our own people, our own *race*, time and time again? Do we let the Aicirtap come destroy us and the people who've come to us for protection? Do we keep on squabbling with each other until the Aicirtap arrive and eat us? Or do we act like the warlord, or possibly, like something better, the something better we can be, and protect our world and those who've come to us for help?"

Stopped speaking and waited. To see what our world was going to pick.

CHAPTER 65

A MAN IN THE AUDIENCE stood up. He was old and I was pretty sure he was an ayatollah. "Who is their God?" He pointed at the screen. "Who do they follow?"

"Why does it matter?"

"Do they fight a holy war?"

"Why does it matter?"

"Are the others their enemies?"

"At one time they were all friends. And I ask again—*why* does it *matter*?"

He and I looked at each other. Another stare-down. Lucky me. Wasn't confident with someone like this—had to bet he'd won a lot of stare-downs in his day. And there was no way in the world I was intimidating him.

Could see the teleprompter in my peripheral vision. Pictures of what the Aicirtap had done were flashing by. Wasn't sure if it was going to be enough.

Finally, he nodded. "They will eat us regardless of the God we worship, or the God they worship. Even if it is the same God."

"Yes."

"Who will lead?"

Oh, fantastic, another question likely to start the arguments up all over again. Couldn't give the same response, though, because it definitely mattered.

The picture on my teleprompter changed, to a picture of me and Jeff. Winced inside. I was on a Harley and Jeff was leaning out of a helicopter to pull me off. In other words, it was the scene I knew had broadcast to the world, the scene that pretty much ensured that Hollywood wanted to make Code Name: First Lady. Had no idea what Serene was thinking.

"Have lost control of the feeds," she said urgently. "I'm not sure who—"

"They will." The voice that interrupted Serene wasn't mine, and it wasn't from someone in the room. It was from someone in the Heads of State room. Hadn't remembered the audio feed was two-way. The voice was also familiar.

And so was the person who stood up. "I am Gustav Drax, Prince of the planet Vatusus, youngest in the line of our monarchy that has lasted for ten thousand years and will last for ten thousand more. I have met most of you. In this fight there can be only one leader. And it must be the leader who has already successfully repelled the strongest force in the galaxy from this part of the galaxy not once, but twice."

Drax had his hair pulled back into a high ponytail, showing the organic metal plates in his head. The lights in them were blinking. So he'd used the natural Vata ability to mentally join with electronics to take over the feed. Not a surprise, really. For all I knew, what ACE had done was give the suggestion via subtle means to the Vata here on Earth to control and prevent the nuclear launches worldwide. I hadn't thought of asking them, either, but maybe Jeff or Chuckie or someone else had.

Of course, if Drax was here, who was flying his ship? And, the other question was, where was his ship parked? In the U.S. or somewhere here in the region?

"They did not work alone," someone in that room pointed out.

"No," Drax agreed. "They did not. However, they led, and it was their leadership that ensured victory. I have heard from my father, the King of Vatusus. The Z'porrah fleet is on the move, traveling toward Tau Ceti, Sirius, Yggethnia, Alpha Centauri, and Earth. Spies are certain the Z'porrah plan to overtake this part of the galaxy by force, using the Aicirtap as their shock troops."

This created a lot of panic in both rooms. Heaved a sigh. "SHUT UP!" My bellow was getting better, practice making perfect and all that. Butler's was as well and he had to bellow in a variety of languages. He was the android for the job, though. The rooms quieted. "Gustav, you again have the floor."

"Thank you, My Queen Regent." Uh oh. Here it came. "Some of you stare at that title, and some of you have already heard it. Because of who the President of the United States is, he and his wife, the First Lady, are considered the King and

Queen Regent of Earth by the Alpha Centauri Empire. That makes Earth a part of that empire. And for that, more than anything else, you should be grateful."

"Why?" the old ayatollah, who was still standing, asked.

"Because this fight cannot be fought alone. And the Vatusan fleet will not come at the request of some mere elected official, or a petty king of a small land. And in comparison to Vatusus, all your lands are small." Drax got a lot of sneering contempt into those words.

"Why will they come?" the old ayatollah asked.

"They will come if another world leader they respect requests it. And my father respects only two on this world." Another picture of me and Jeff, this one a little more professional, taken at Jeff's inauguration party, popped onscreen.

Drax waited for a few long, theatrical moments. Really, he was impressive when he wasn't trying to be sneaky. "Choose your allegiance. You align with them, you join Centaurion Division as one cohesive fighting force, and I can promise that Vatusus will rally their forces, and the forces of other allies in our part of the galaxy, and they will come and intercept the Z'porrah and drive them away. If you choose your usual human ways, Vatusus will wash their hands of Earth and never offer assistance again. So say I, Prince Gustav of the Vata, for my father, King Varian the Twentieth of Vatusus."

Drax nodded, then sat down.

"I have control again," Serene said in my ear. "No idea what picture to put up, if any."

The old ayatollah was still standing. Looked at him. He was acting as the Voice of the Crowd, meaning whatever he did or said next was probably going to be what the majority agreed with.

"Per your Supreme Pontifex, your husband does not crave rule."

"He doesn't. He's a natural leader, but becoming the President was never his goal. It just sort of happened." Oh well, in for that whole piggybank again. "He didn't ask to be the Annocusal King Regent of this planet, either. But when the time came to choose a new Emperor of the Alpha Centauri system, he refused the crown and chose Earth as his home."

"And therefore, to his people, he is King," the old ayatollah said.

Considered how to reply. But Gower answered before I had to. "No."

The room turned to look at him, as did the camera, so I had a view of Gower in the room and on my teleprompter. Didn't see Tim, Reader, Lorraine, or Claudia anywhere but couldn't risk obviously looking around the room to find them.

"How do your people see him?" the old ayatollah asked. The floating cameras were doing their job. The video feed was switching back and forth between him and Gower.

"American Centaurion has three leaders. The Supreme Pontifex, the Head of Field for Centaurion Division, and the Head of the Diplomatic Corps. Those leaders answer to the President of the United States, which is our home country. Jeff has been the Head of Field and the Diplomatic Corps, Kitty the Head of the Diplomatic Corps as well. Now that they're the President and First Lady, American Centaurion answers to them. Just as we always have."

Gower looked around the room. "But we've been here, long before many of you knew we were, hiding in plain sight, doing our best to protect this world from the threats against it, most of which you have no idea of because we kept them from you. And now you know what's coming." Pictures of the Aicirtap's devastation came onscreen.

"American Centaurion will not turn away the refugees, because we were once refugees and, unlike humans, we remember. If we must house them in our Bases, then we will do so. And we will do what the man who's led us for over a decade says to do." Now Serene put up Jeff's picture.

"Whether you want to call him President, King Regent, or merely what he'd prefer, which is Jeff, American Centaurion will follow his lead."

Thought he was done, but Gower went on. "However, the rest of the aliens, both here and arriving shortly? They don't actually follow Jeff's lead." This got the rooms murmuring again. Fantastic. "Hush," Gower said in a normal tone. Everyone shut up. Well, he *was* the nice one.

"The aliens follow the lead of one person and one person only. And they're coming to ask for help from one person and one person only. The person who repaired our alliance with the ruling Annocusal Empire of Alpha Centauri. The person who has, so far, repelled not one, and not two, but actually three alien invasions. The person who stopped a multiplanet civil war. The person who saved a planet not their own, filled with sentient life, from destruction.

"The person who forged the alliance with the Vata, the Turleens, the Reptilians, the Feliniads, the Shantanu, the Lecanora, the Canus Majorians, and the Free Women." As he listed their planets, the representatives in the room here and the Heads of State room, which was now onscreen, stood up. Hadn't realized it, but Renata had gone to the Heads of State room somewhere in there.

"The person who forged an alliance with the Cleophese." At this, a picture of the Space Cthulhus appeared. Taken somehow during Operation Civil War. Presumably to show the size of the Cleophese as compared to the spaceships. The gasps in the room shared that they were impressed. Or terrified. Probably both. "And the person who repelled beings so powerful as to be gods to us, who made them leave and leave us alone." Thankfully, no pictures of Sandy or the other Superconciousnesses, and, extra thankfully, none of them stood up in either room.

"All these aliens and more give their loyalty to one person on this planet, and one person only." Gower pointed. At me. "Her. The aliens follow her. And if you want to live, you'll follow her, too."

Then he sat down. And, once again, it was time to see what was going to happen.

CHAPTER 66

ALL HEADS TURNED toward the old ayatollah, who was still standing. He was, by now, clearly the spokesperson for the entire religious body, whatever differences they had notwithstanding.

He turned around and looked at me. I looked right back because I was always up for a stare-down regardless of where or when or with whom.

"What would you have us do?" he asked me finally.

Well, for this, I actually had an answer. "Welcome the alien refugees and allow them to live where they can survive best, whether on Earth or one or more of the planets or moons in our solar system, none of which we 'own,' before anyone starts complaining. Gather every fighting force we have as fast as humanly possible, probably under Centaurion Division because it has the most experience with dealing and fighting with aliens, and get them prepped to fight the Aicirtap. And stop fighting amongst ourselves, because this is our *Brave New World* and we either go forward together, as one race, as one planet, or we're all going to die. Not necessarily in that order."

The ayatollah seemed to be considering this. Did my best to look calm and in control because, despite Gower's speech, I didn't feel confident that whatever happened next was going to go our way.

"Who do you call God?" the ayatollah asked now.

Oh goody, another tough question. This wasn't a time to be flippant. "I've met beings who, as our Supreme Pontifex has said, are so powerful compared to us that they're like gods. But they aren't. I've met the people who influenced our evolution

and how we think of God, both good and bad, and they aren't
gods, either."

It wasn't enough. Remembered a conversation I'd had with
ACE so very long ago now. And what he and Algar both had told
me.

"What I know is that God is vast. And God gave us Free Will
so that God would not have to do it all. God isn't one thing, or a
man or a woman or a creature. God is too vast for us to understand. But I do know this—all these people who look so different or so similar to us, all these stars with all these planets in just
this galaxy alone, all of this life—it didn't happen just so that we
could spend our lives killing each other in the name of whatever
part of God we want to claim."

"Who do you call God?" the ayatollah asked again.

Pondered my response. "Everyone. Everyone is part of God.
Even the Aicirtap. Even the Z'porrah. But I don't call on God to
help me. I call on myself and my friends, family, and allies. God
isn't there to help me, to help us. We're here to help ourselves
and each other."

Once again, the stare-down. This man loved the stare-down.
Perhaps, in another part of the multiverse, we were friends and
did this for fun. Right now, it was getting on my nerves. But that
poker face Chuckie had trained me to put on when needed was
doing its job, because I could see myself in the teleprompter and
I looked cool, calm, and collected.

"The Lyssara Comb has set down in the landing area between
Animas, Hatchet, and Chiricahua Peaks," Serene shared. The
screen split, so there was a shot of me, one of the ayatollah, one
of the Heads of State room, one of Alexander, Dew, and the
Themnir heading off the cutter finally, and the other half of the
screen was given to the Lyssara.

A bunch of giant honeybees walked out of what looked like
a hole in their ship. The Comb had a ton of holes, but apparently
this one was the exit one. They were all carrying little flags.
Little American Centaurion flags. And they were waving them
wildly in all four hands, while looking around like tourists at the
desert surrounding them.

Couldn't help it. They looked cute and kind of silly. I snorted
a little laugh. Got the Inner Hyena under control, but just barely.

The ayatollah noticed, of course. He cocked his head at me.
"You wish to laugh? At so serious a time? Why?"

Shrugged. "Because I'm a human and it's funny. They're

waving the flag that, a day ago, was the biggest concern and scandal my husband's presidency had to deal with. And now? Now it's just cute that these aliens who don't seem to know us all that well," or who knew us very well, but I chose not to add that, "are waving yesterday's Flag O' Controversy with so much excited gusto. Yesterday this would have been a disaster. Today? Today who cares what flag anyone's waving? What matters is—will we all see tomorrow, flags or no flags?"

The ayatollah did something that shocked the hell out of me. He smiled. "Agreed." Then he bowed his head to me. "I will follow you. Not as First Lady or Queen Regent. But as yourself. I will follow you and I will tell all those who follow me to do the same."

Someone else stood up. The Pope. "I will follow you. Not as First Lady or as Queen Regent, but as yourself. And I will tell my flock to do likewise."

One by one the rest of the room stood up and pledged fealty, while the Lyssara waved their flags and Jeff appeared onscreen now, presumably having gated over to greet the next arrivals. The world's religious leaders pledged while Jeff hugged, clasped, and did the French greeting with the honeybees. Decided that, despite everything else, I still had the better gig.

At last the religious leaders were done. The screen shifted to give us a half screen of the Heads of State room. They all stood. One who was sitting near Drax spoke. "I speak for everyone here. We, too, will follow you. We accept that our world is changing forever, and we all choose to greet it boldly and with honor."

The screen shifted to another room. This one looked like it had every head of state for the rest of the African continent. Another screen came up, this one covering Europe and everything around Russia. A third screen showed the rest of North and all of South America's leadership. And the last showed the rest of Asia—every Pacific Rim country, China, and, interestingly enough, the Australian Prime Minister.

It was Costello who stood and spoke. "Madam First Lady, it's good to see you, even at a distance. We've concurred as well, and all of the Asia-Pacific countries are with you. To save time, the other country summits have asked that I share that they, too, are unanimously with you." His lips quirked. "Well, other than North Korea, who has not joined any of the summit meetings and who insists upon standing apart."

"Shocker on North Korea. Thank you to everyone else."

"And now I'm asking the question I'm sure is on everyone's mind," Costello said. "Where do we go to get prepared for the Aicirtap's arrival?"

"Any country that has an American Centaurion base in it should have their able-bodied and willing fighting forces head there for training. Any country that doesn't needs to go to the nearest country that does. I believe I see Centaurion personnel in all the various summit rooms. They can assist with logistics and physical transfers as well. Beyond that, I've been a little busy getting all of you on board, so we haven't crafted finalized battle plans. We'll ensure that you have them as soon as they're confirmed."

Costello nodded and sat down. So did everyone else. Before I could speak again, though, the screens lit up once more, this time with eight shots of different cities around the world, rotating through. Most of them had people in the streets holding signs that said "One World" or "Let the Good Ones In" or similar. Many were naming the aliens, although most of the signs were spelled wrong, which wasn't surprising. I only knew the proper spellings thanks to Serene. There were plenty of anti-alien signs, but they were vastly outnumbered and at least half of them were anti Aicirtap, spelled in a variety of ways, some of them even right.

"You've been live to every media outlet in the world since you started," Serene shared in my ear. "Surprise. Alpha Team left your meeting already because I knew this was going on around the world well before anyone else in the summit meetings did. We've already coordinated all Worldwide Bases. They're ready to take in both refugees and new recruits. The Science Center is prepping weapons the Faradawn and Turleens feel are effective against the Aicirtap."

Decided it was time to paraphrase *Ghostbusters*, *Stripes*, and David Bowie, especially if I was live to the world. I mean, why not, right?

"Okay, everyone. Let's channel all our basic human nastiness and use it for galactic good. It's time to get ready to show these scary monsters and super creeps how we do things in the bad part of the galactic town. Now, let's get it together faster than we ever have because it's never mattered as much. Remember that no matter what, what humanity does best is kick the crap out of people we don't like. So, do what I do, say what I say, and make me proud."

This speech wasn't really worthy of a Standing O. And yet, thanks to the old ayatollah leading the way, I got one. It was a crazy old universe, when you got right down to it.

CHAPTER 67

POLITICAL DRAMA over for the moment, had Butler use his military uniform and android strength to get us safely to Raheem and White—who thankfully still had hold of the rolling purse—and then to get the four of us out of this room and back to my suite.

Under the circumstances, we didn't use hyperspeed. Still had no idea where I was in the palace, in no small part because the rest of the team that were here, Gower included, came along with us, so I was busy having everyone verifying that our other team members were all okay and where we expected them to be.

Unfortunately, we'd forgotten to have anyone remove the dead bodies in the hall. Shocking me to my core, they were still there. I was far too used to dead bodies disappearing and new dead bodies being put in their place. "Oh. Right."

"It slipped my mind," Raheem said, sounding regretful. "I am a terrible king."

"It's the end of the world as we know it and a *lot* was going on. You can be forgiven for forgetting. I forgot, too. We all did. But no one forgot intentionally."

Other guards were called, as well as maids to clean up the blood. Thankfully we hadn't been gone too long, so the smell wasn't too bad, and there weren't a lot of flies, either, but the maids got to deal with all that as well. Buchanan and Siler guarded the bodies and the maids, and also confirmed that the bodies were the same ones as before. Yeah, they weren't used to this level of normal, either.

The rest of us went into my rooms to find that Francine and Wruck were not back. Neither was Adriana. And no one had any texts or calls from them, either.

No one had cleaned up my room, either. Chose not to make a joke about bad service because I wasn't sure that Raheem would take it as such and I didn't want to hurt his feelings.

Shared that I wanted to freshen up and went into my incredibly spacious bathroom. Checked it all, just in case Kellogg, Kozlow, or one of the other Crazy Eights had left a present. Thankfully there was nothing.

Didn't really want to freshen up. Wanted to relax. Of course, I'd chosen the bathroom instead of just closing the door to the bedroom. Closed the toilet lid, sat on that, and heaved a sigh.

"You did an amazing job," Serene said in my ear. I'd forgotten about the Bluetooth, which I was still wearing and that we hadn't disconnected.

"Thanks. I feel exhausted and revved up at the same time."

"I'm sure you do."

"Where are you and where's Jeff?"

"I'm in Los Angeles. Jeff's at the Science Center with the Lyssara."

"I thought you were with Jeff when he was addressing Congress."

"I was. Then we discussed it and decided that someone needed to investigate just what Amos Tobin was doing in Los Angeles. Christopher didn't have time to do a full search. I did."

"What did you find?"

"The usual. Nothing that relates to what's going on right now, so it can wait for a quieter time. But it was convenient to be here when the aliens' ships started coming in for their landings, and also to ensure that what we wanted broadcast went out."

"It could have gone really badly."

"I knew you'd make them see reason." Serene laughed. "You were able to get through to me when Club Fifty-One had me drugged out of my mind. I knew you could reach a room full of frightened men."

"Love your confidence and super glad it was rewarded. Oh, by the way, more than just I now know about your other organization." Caught her up quickly on who knew what, and what had gone on that she'd missed. Also told her about Francine and Wruck being gone, and our Best Hope Scenario, as well as the far less positive possibilities.

"Francine's been trained to think like you," Serene said when I was done. "So that in case she has to impersonate you as you'd planned for her to do on this trip, she'd be able to fake it longer. She isn't you, no one is, but she's close. So I'm not too worried. I mean, I'm worried, but she's a very competent agent. We've had her in the field for several years. And we both know that John is more than competent."

"Yeah. Doesn't mean I'm not worried about them. And Adriana. When are the rest of the ships landing?"

"The Treeship takes a while to lower into the atmosphere. They expect to land near to dawn. Dawn for the region you're in, not for the U.S."

"That many hours?" Dawn here was probably about ten hours away, give or take.

"They're doing a water landing and apparently there's something in the Persian Gulf they need to connect with, just like you figured. They'd prefer to do the final portion of the landing in daylight."

"So, we have until dawn, which will come early, to find and stop Cliff and the Crazy Eights."

"I'd tell you to rest and deal with them another day, but I saw all the different aliens coming, too. And I've been in communication with every ship, the Treeship in particular."

"Why wasn't NASA Base involved?"

"They were. We're linked via our internal systems. I'm not at Tobin's several media outlets here now, Kitty. I'm at Los Angeles Base."

"L.A. has a Base? Wow, nice to know that I got my 'learned something new daily' requirement in before midnight. No one has ever mentioned it or taken me there. And before you say it, I did finally read the gigantic Books of Boredom and I don't recall anything as interesting as a base in Los Angeles."

"Well, you're not an imageer, nor are you married to one. This is the smallest of all our Bases. It's here because we need it, though Christopher always preferred to use East Base as his main headquarters after Dulce. He came here occasionally, when it made sense to be on the West Coast, but he doesn't care for Southern California, so he avoids L.A. Base for the most part."

"Oh my God! That's where you're running the special division from! No one thinks about it, and who fits into the Home of Hollywood better than troubadours?"

She laughed again. "Right you are. At any rate, I have other agents I can send, if you need them."

"I'd love to do a gigantic raid, but we'll lose every bit of goodwill and acquiescence if any of us are caught sneaking around this area."

"And somehow your logic says that it's okay for you to do that? Wow, and they call me the crazy one."

"Oh, not where you can hear it." We both laughed. "It has to be us, the ones already planned for, because we're the ones with the papers. Technically we're all set. I just don't feel ready. I thought we had at least another day. We don't."

"James was saying the same thing earlier. I don't know why you two are so thrown by this. The timelines are always moving on us and you always adapt. Are you not feeling well?"

"It's not that. I can't even say why this particular situation is throwing me."

"I can. It's because you're hoping to finally put an end to the Mastermind. And once you do, we'll be able to close that chapter of our lives."

"I miss the Dingo and Surly Vic." Hadn't had that thought in my head before I blurted it out, but realized it was true—I missed the two top assassins in the world who'd become my uncles by choice. I missed them because one of Cliff's top lieutenants, Annette Dier, had killed them. Or, rather, they'd sacrificed themselves to save me from her attack.

"We all do," Serene said softly. "They were . . . much more than their profession. They did bad things, but never . . ."

"Crazy things. They didn't kill people for the fun of it or to prove they were better than someone else. They killed for money, but they had honor while doing it. And I just . . . I don't have anyone left like that to talk to. And I miss it. And them."

"Talk to Benjamin. Or John."

"Siler's great, but he's not the same. We have a different relationship."

"What about John?"

"He's with Francine, we hope. So no luck there right now."

"I'm doing my best."

"Yeah, and it helps a lot to talk to you like this, when it's just us. But you don't have the same life experience or worldview. Maybe you will in a few years. But you don't right now."

"I know who does. Hang on, I'm going to transfer you. Keep the Bluetooth with you. It's got a tracker in it so I can find you if necessary, and I can turn it on remotely and silently, too. It's already paired to your phone."

"Wow, nice tech."

"Thank Gustav, it's his design. Hang in there, Kitty. I'll talk to you later."

"I will do. Serene, who are you transferring me to?"

"Hello?" A woman's voice. One I knew well. Probably the voice I knew best in the world, really.

"Mom." Felt a huge wave of relief wash over me. And also felt a little dumb. But then, that was why you had a team—because when you were dumb, one of your teammates remembered that your mother had written the book on counterterrorism for you.

"Kitty? Are you alright? That was some performance you put on today. Your father and I are incredibly proud of you."

"Thanks, Mom. How are things there?"

"Oh, you know, same politicians, terrorists, and crackpots, different day."

Snorted a laugh. "Yeah, I feel you on that one." Couldn't figure out what to actually say or ask. It wasn't as if my mother didn't know what I did. She encouraged it half the time. More than half, really.

"Kitten," Mom asked gently, "what is it? What's wrong?"

"I'm afraid." As with what I'd said about the uncles, I hadn't had this thought in my head before it came out of my mouth. But it was the truth.

"Is that all?"

"All? Wow, you're not up on the latest pick-me-up sayings, are you?"

Mom chuckled. "Everyone's afraid, kitten. What is it, exactly, you're afraid of?"

"Right now? Kind of everything."

"Since when?"

"Since we have the end of the world staring at us."

Mom snorted. "We have that all the time. Since the day you met Jeff you've been averting the end of the world."

"You've done that, too."

"Longer than you. Still doing it, too."

"Yeah, I know. I'm just . . . I'm just not sure if anything we're planning is even close to right. And before you say that none of our ideas go according to plan, you didn't want Naomi to go with me when we raided Gaultier's underground cloning lab. And you were right. If she hadn't gone, she'd still be alive today."

"But, based on what you've told me, the rest of you might not be. And, if you recall, I wanted you to go, and the others. Just not her. And while I might indeed have been right, every plan has to be able to change on the fly due to changing circumstances."

"Yeah. Mom, I need to tell you what I'm planning to do or, rather, what we were planning to do, which I now don't know will work, and I also need to hear if you think it's a good idea or not."

"Well, you only need to tell me if you aren't planning to find Cliff Goodman's hideout and kill that bastard and all of his cronies once and for all."

Let that sit on the air for a moment. "Um, am I that transparent?"

"To me, yes. To Serene, too, as far as I can tell. To everyone else? Somewhat. I have an edge over the others, though, in that I'm your mother and I know how you think. I'm also the Head of the P.T.C.U. and we've been looking for Goodman since he disappeared. Middle East was all we've found, though. I assume you've got better intel?"

"I do." Time to flip on my Recap Girl cape and fill Mom in on what had gone down. "But we still don't know where he is," I said as I finished up. "And I don't know how to get out of whatever Heads of State stuff Francine was supposed to be handling."

"Well, if he's funded by G-Company . . ."

"What?"

"Hang on for a moment." I so hung on for more than a moment. "Huh. Talk about hiding in plain sight. You were ready to search the countryside for him, I imagine?"

"Yeah, I mean, Raheem has no clear idea of where Cliff is, he just knows that Ali Baba Gadhavi—and Raheem swears it's his real name and not assumed for business, so to speak—is funding him, and that Cliff's definitely in this area. Presumed close to where we are right now, but nothing is confirmed."

"Oh, it's his real name and he's close alright." Mom sounded pissed. "And, if Adriana did her job right, I'd assume that she, Francine, and Wruck are close by, too."

"What, are you saying they're in this palace? Raheem isn't setting me up, is he?"

"Oh, no, he's not. And no, they're not. Based on Cliff's new benefactor being Gadhavi, though, I'm about ninety-nine percent certain they're in the Burj Khalifa."

CHAPTER 68

"YOU'RE KIDDING."

"No," Mom said. "Believe me, I wish I was. G-Company owns several floors of that building. Not officially, of course, but they have at least one full residential floor and one full corporate floor, as well as other sections scattered throughout. I'll send you the intel we have."

"Why haven't the others checked in then?"

"I don't know. The hopeful spin would be that they're too busy."

"And the realistic spin is that they're captured or compromised in some way. So, um, I guess the State Dinner, which is supposed to happen unless it was called off, is the way to go."

"Maybe. It's a gigantic place and there's a lot of ground to cover. Plus, it's Goodman, so you know that he's got a backup location somewhere close by, in case he and Gadhavi have a falling out."

"Yeah, I do know Cliff, and what I expect him to be doing is trying to figure out how to take over G-Company. Which would be our newest definition of 'bad news' and therefore what we cannot allow to happen. And he's probably waiting to kill everyone once the State Dinner starts because we'll all be in one place. Crap. That's his plan, isn't it?"

"Most likely. Go get 'em, kitten."

"Thanks, Mom. Um, any words of advice? Aside from the fact that the State Department will disavow all knowledge of us if we're caught?"

"You're not the Impossible Missions Force. You're the First Lady and, apparently, the Queen Regent. It's hard to disavow you, but I'll curtsey when you're home."

"Makes you the Queen Mother, Mom, no curtseying necessary."

"Good to know. Tell Malcolm to let me know the moment he thinks you need backup."

"Malcolm wants to do this with only him and Siler."

"I'm sure he does. He and Kevin are my best agents, but still, neither one of them has your skill set."

"Yeah, my ability to mind meld with the Crazed Evil Genius Society is consistently stellar."

"We all serve in the best ways we can. Some ways are conventional, some are not. But as long as the good guys win more than the bad guys, it's worth the effort and sacrifice." Her voice softened. "Just be sure you aren't what's sacrificed, kitten."

"I promise, Mom. Cliff and his team are going down, not me or my team."

"Good. Leave Gadhavi and G-Company alone. Don't engage with them unless you're forced to. There are too many of them and now isn't the time."

"Will do, Mom. Love you, and love to Dad."

"Love you, too, Kitty."

We hung up, and I wasn't scared anymore. I was pissed and worried and excited, but not scared. However, I had no plan at all now, since all our prep seemed to have been cancelled out.

Left the bathroom, left my stuff all over the floor, and trotted out to the main area. Buchanan and Siler were inside with the others now, and Alpha Team was back onsite, too.

"We're trying to determine next steps," Reader said to me.

"Originally there was going to be a large dinner," Raheem said. "What are your thoughts on that?"

Our relaxed, three-hour combination tea and planning session seemed so very long ago. Checked Mr. Watch. "My God, it's only six thirty in the evening?" Good. That meant the dinner could still be on.

"Time flies when you're having fun," Vance said, sarcasm meter around eight on the scale. "But if the dinner was planned, is it wise to change or cancel it, Your Majesty?"

Raheem shrugged. "Under these circumstances, Queen Katherine can say or ask for whatever she wants."

"Oh, Queen Katherine wants to go to that dinner and she wants everyone on Team Commando to go to that dinner, too." Shared the intel I'd gotten from Mom and her assumptions about the same.

"We should just have the P.T.C.U. raid it and keep you out of it," Buchanan said the moment I was done.

"Per your boss and my mother, you're going to need me and my special skill set."

Tim's phone beeped. "Uh oh."

"What?" half the room asked.

"Jeff's on his way here. With the head Themnir and head Lyssara and any other aliens who've landed already or will land shortly. They're going to be coming to the State Dinner. Apparently someone invited them."

Raheem shook his head. "No one should have done that. The dinner was set up to honor Queen Katherine, only, and no one other than those already here were invited. Give me a moment to verify who did not follow my instructions." He got onto his phone and started speaking rapidly, as he stepped into one of the other rooms. Butler followed him, though he stood a polite distance away.

"So that means Chuckie's coming, too, right?"

Tim nodded. "I'd assume so. My text came from Chuck."

"Why'd he contact you and not me?" Reader asked. "I'm not mad, I'm just curious."

Tim's phone beeped again and he snorted a laugh. "Because I'm the Head of Airborne. He's telling me that the rest of my team will be in the helicarrier, cloaked, hanging out in the Persian Gulf."

"Do they know the Treeship is landing there?"

"Yes, and they're going to be there to assist if needed. But they want to remain close to the President, and under the circumstances, they're right. But that means that Chuck will be here for sure."

Raheem returned and he looked worried and furious. "No one from my team will claim responsibility. They insist that no one invited the President, nor have any of them heard from him or his secretary or anyone else from the White House."

Looked at Butler, who nodded. Nice to have him verifying that Raheem wasn't lying to us. It also wasn't hard to guess what was going on. "None of your people invited Jeff. Cliff invited Jeff. It's a trap."

"And every leader in the Middle East and every religious leader in the world will be at this dinner," Lorraine said.

"For all we know, other world leaders have been invited,

too," Claudia added. Which earned looks of horror from the entire room.

Raheem got back on his phone and trotted out of the room again. Butler remained at his Listening-In Post.

"Invited and able to come are two different things," Mona pointed out.

"Not with us," I countered. "If they've been invited, they'll all use gates to get there, and there won't be any delays or issues with that, because they're all with Field agents doing their best to accommodate these people and make them continue to be happy and play nicely with others. Wow, Cliff's amazing."

This earned me the room's full attention. "Excuse me?" Mona asked, clearly speaking for everyone.

Mossy rolled his eyes. "Seriously?" Okay, Mona wasn't speaking for everyone. "There is no way in the world that your enemy could have planned to attack the State Dinner because it was only planned in the last few hours *and* the likelihood that the summits were going to dissolve into the usual human bickering was high, so there would have been no *need* to attack it. Things worked out far better than anyone could have expected, so he had to regroup and form a new plan, which he's done far faster than we've formed our new plan. She's impressed by her enemy's abilities. That's not a bad thing—it's far better to realize when your enemy is superior to you, so that you can look for their weaknesses, than to consider yourself invincible and discover that belief to be untrue."

"Mossy, I sincerely feel this is the beginning of a beautiful friendship. What he said. All of it. The Treeship is landing at dawn and I guarantee Cliff knows it. If he's in with the Indian Mafia, and he is for certain, then he's got access to their spy network, so he knows when the ship is landing and everything else that's going on. He has the same amount of time we do to stop us, only he has the luxury of knowing that if he misses here, he still has all those aliens, the Q'vox in particular, to capture and clone. And he has the Aicirtap coming, too."

"He'll be eaten just like the rest of us," Vance said.

"I doubt he believes that, and I refuse to believe we're going to get eaten by them. Well, as long as we win. If Cliff succeeds in killing all the world leaders, that means he has a plan for how to deal with the Aicirtap and the Z'porrah, too."

"He will have no need to deal with the Z'porrah," Raheem said as he returned, "if what Prince Gustav promised happens."

"It won't happen if Drax is killed," Reader said.

"Cliff will just figure out a way to tell the Vatusan Royal Family that we killed Gustav and that will be that. I don't care what Cliff's plan is to handle the Aicirtap. I care that we stop him tonight, before he can kill everyone he wants to, which includes my husband and everyone in this room. We'll worry about the Aicirtap tomorrow, when, the way our luck runs, they'll show up."

"I agree with Queen Katherine," Raheem said, "in no small part because I called the restaurant in the Burj Khalifa where the dinner is planned. We always had the entire restaurant reserved, but now we have every seat accounted for and more besides. Per the restaurant manager, they expect over two hundred and fifty people. And at least half are there already, possibly more. And more are arriving. And the restaurant believes that my staff requested this."

"Every head of state plus the religious leaders fits that headcount, yeah. And, again, this was Cliff. It's not hard to fake a restaurant hostess out, no offence intended to anyone who might have done that kind of job in the past. It's just, why *would* anyone at the restaurant question this? You'd reserved the entire place and we just all sang "We Are The World" together—that every freaking leader in the world other than North Korea's is hanging out having a Coke and a smile together makes total sense. Sure the restaurant may be having to scramble, but this is the highest-profile reason to scramble there is. I expect the food to be amazing. If any of us get to live to eat it."

"How would you kill that many people?" Rhee asked, potentially to get me back on topic. "A bomb?"

"A bomb puts the entire building at risk," Reader said. "I doubt his benefactor is going to appreciate that."

"He may not care," Rahmi pointed out. "Besides, a self-contained bomb would work."

"If he owns property there, he will care," Mona said dryly.

"I agree with Mona, and besides, bombs are messy and still have a chance of not getting an A-C. And there's always a chance that the A-Cs will get to the bomb or bombs before they can explode. We've done it before." Jeff had certainly done that before.

"It's a meal," Jareen said. "Poison would seem obvious."

"But it's uncertain, and you can't count on it getting everyone." Definitely had experience with that one, and I knew Cliff remembered that particular failure. "Poisoned gas would be more effective, especially if you have everyone locked in. How high up is the restaurant?"

"The one hundred and twenty-second floor," Raheem replied.

"So jumping to safety is out of the question. I know what floors G-Company controls and which ones they only control part of. Interestingly enough, Floor one hundred and twenty-one is one of theirs."

"So, what do we do?" Raheem asked. "Evacuate? They're bringing the leaders in via your gates. Can't we just take them out the same way, immediately?"

"Why are they bringing everyone in that way?" Antoinette asked. "I thought it was policy not to use them all the time for non-Centaurion personnel."

"But this is a world event where the world has changed," I said slowly. My brain was really nudging. "The agents are using gates because it's the safest way to transfer personnel and they're all Field agents and this is what they use to get places all the time. It's less difficult and dangerous than dragging humans everywhere at hyperspeed and, besides, they're coming from all over. But that does mean we can get them out just as quickly . . ." My brain shared what was bothering it.

"What?" Reader asked. "I know that look."

"He'll have something that's going to prevent our using gates. They already figured out how to create floater gates. Not as good as ours but good enough. If he's letting them congregate he's going to get them all in and then he'll close the trap."

"Sounds like time for evacuation," Siler said briskly. Buchanan nodded.

"Wait." Tim waved his hand. "Jeff's already there, along with Chuck and the aliens and anyone else you'd think would be there other than Christopher and Serene. I'd asked Chuck to keep me advised of their schedule. I was hoping to have time to tell them not to go, but he'd told me they were there after they'd already arrived."

Looked at White. "Call your son. We're going to need the Flash. Tell him to take a gate." Looked at Colette. "Call Serene, tell her to stay where she is and send over whatever we're going to need in order to infiltrate the tallest building in the world, which undoubtedly has some of the best security in the world." Looked at Siler and Buchanan. "If we try to evacuate now, they'll lock it down. Cliff has the two main people he wants to kill."

"Aside from you," Tim pointed out.

"Aside from me."

"Our mother is still there," Rahmi said in a small voice.

"So is your Secret Service detail," Lorraine shared.

"And your Field team, too," Claudia added.

White looked around. "I presume it's a safe bet that if the person is not in this room with us right now, they are in the Burj Khalifa's restaurant."

"Raheem, what legitimate reason can you give for why the two of us and Mona and anyone expected from our entourages are late? Needs to be a damned good reason or Cliff will see through it."

Tim groaned. "It's worse. Per Chuck, the only world leaders missing are King Raheem, you, Kitty, and the Australian Prime Minister." He looked up from his phone. "That makes no sense."

"It might." Serene hadn't told me how to work the Bluetooth, but she'd sure felt I could reach her on it, so I tapped it. "Serene?"

"Here, just got off with Colette." She sounded tense and ready for action. Good. "I told Christopher what to get from Dulce that you'll need, I think, for what Colette says you're going to be doing. I have these kinds of supplies stored in various places."

"Great thinking. I need you to put me through to Tony Costello, the Australian Prime Minister."

"Okay. Huh. Uh, why, just out of curiosity, do you need me to call him for you?"

"What do you mean? I need to warn him to stay home."

"Too late for that. He's in Bahrain. In the same place you are, as a matter of fact."

CHAPTER 69

SHARED THIS NEWS with the others. "Why is he here?" Reader asked, echoing Serene.

Gower jerked. "He's here to help Kitty. He considers himself her friend, and he knows how often she gets into, ah, difficult diplomatic situations."

"You mean how often I blow it with the bigwigs, Paul, we all know."

"I do not," Raheem said. "You are the most competent and commanding woman I have ever met."

"Raheem is my favorite. However, Tony doesn't see me in quite the same light." Because during our first meeting I'd accidentally flipped him off in Australian, caused hot coffee to be spilled on him and his wife, and fallen and knocked myself into another universe. Tony didn't know all about the last one, but he sure knew about the first two.

Other Me had saved the day, and she'd thankfully left me a note filled with information so I'd know what I'd supposedly done. And one of those things she'd done was to forge a very strong bond between our family and the Costellos.

"Tony's coming to help me because he knows I've done what I'm good at already. The rest? This is supposed to be a Washington Wife Extravaganza, and I am not the girl for that job."

Saw the light go on for both Vance and Buchanan. "He's not wrong," Vance said. "So how did he get into the palace?"

"He's with Field agents, right Serene?"

"Yes. They took a gate. He's waiting for someone to call the king to allow him in."

"Super. Okay, Raheem, you need to have them let the Prime Minister come here. Insist he bring the A-Cs along, don't allow him to allow them to leave." Raheem made the call, this time not even bothering to step away.

"So, we can save one whole world leader?" Abigail asked. "That seems underwhelming at best."

"And you know that's not my whole plan." Looked at her and Mahin. Raheem got off the phone. "Raheem . . . how often does this area get hit with haboobs?"

"I'm impressed you know the word. Often enough. And the Prime Minister and his escorts are on their way."

"I'm from Pueblo Caliente, Arizona. We get haboobs all the time. Serene, would a haboob affect a gate transfer?"

"I doubt it, but it's possible. I can ask Walter or William. I believe they'd know."

"Make it so, Number One."

She laughed, and I could tell I was on hold. Silent hold, not that some music right now wouldn't be a great thing for me. Maybe once we had some semblance of an effective plan in place.

"What do I tell Chuck?" Tim asked. "He's starting to get suspicious based on what I'm asking him."

"You can't tell him the truth," Gower said quickly. "If you do, he'll try to find and stop Cliff himself."

"Which will mean that Cliff gets Chuckie and probably Jeff, too."

"Technically, he has them already," White pointed out.

A gate shimmered into view and Christopher arrived, carrying a big bag. "Serene says that we're going to need everything in here. She also said we were at DEFCON Worse. I assume that means it's the usual end of the world as we know it."

"Right you are, Christopher. Mister White, the speedy talking again falls to you. Just, please do it in another room with the door closed."

White nodded and he and Christopher stepped into the nearest room, which happened to be mine. Oh well, hopefully they wouldn't step on all my clothes.

"Clothes. Those of us doing action duty are going to need to change, women especially. I'm actually packed for it, but how about the rest of you?"

While the Jeans and Sneakers Roll Call was sounding off, Serene came back on my line. "Per William and Walter, a haboob of enough ferocity, size, and speed would mean they would route anyone using a gate to a different location, first."

"So, like changing planes because your flight doesn't go non-stop?"

"Somewhat, yes. It's also similar to us evacuating from any other natural disaster. When there are earthquakes in Southern California, many times we can't use the gates here to leave because they're being too affected by the shaking. It's one of the reasons this base is small and normally runs with a skeleton crew."

"Gotcha. So, a natural event would mean we can use that as an excuse."

"Yes. But there isn't one I see on any weather service maps right now. But, if you can create a haboob, Jeff would understand why you're late, because you can't go outside in that, and in order for you to arrive on time anyway, you'd have to take a gate, and William could believably tell him conditions were too bad to bring you in."

"We'll do that!"

"Kitty, one thing—William and Walter both said that whether it's real or made by Mahin, they truly can't safely transport anyone through it."

"Not to worry. We're going to go over, then create the haboob. Jeff just isn't going to know about it."

"Sounds good. I've told them both what's going on, and they've told Missy to put the Embassy onto high alert lockdown with all shields up. The Romanian Diplomatic Mission is inside our Embassy, and Walter's advising the Israeli and Bahraini Missions to pull their people in and go into lockdown as well. William is running gates for your team now exclusively, and Walter's going to Dulce to help him. There's still plenty of security over at the White House, but all gate transfers and all shield controls for the White House Complex have been given to Missy as well. Trying to keep this with as few in the know as possible."

"Wise, but the action isn't happening there so much."

"If Cliff kills all the leaders of the world, especially right when aliens have arrived, you get anarchy, Kitty, and you get it immediately, because this kind of event will create utter panic. Once you roll, I'm going to be locking down every Base worldwide, and families have already been pulled into the nearest Bases, P.T.C.U. and Secret Service families included. And I've ordered that we move the Vice President and any Cabinet members into the Bunker. I had Senator and Missus McMillan moved to the Bunker as well. Secret Service has confirmed that every-

one who should be in the Bunker is. Other than you, Jeff, and
Chuck, and they're not happy that you three are at the center of
this, but that's why we have chain of command separated."

Let the reality of all of this settle for a moment. Serene was
right. And if I focused on all of this, I wouldn't be able to func-
tion. So, I wasn't going to focus on it much longer. "Good call.
Am I keeping you on the line?"

"Yes. Though I'm only going to be live to you. Make sure
everyone's wearing a Bluetooth from the supplies Christopher
brought over, though—I can track and connect with everyone
that way and as needed. Put on the watches, too—they'll func-
tion as a way for the team to communicate with each other and
additional tracking should someone lose a Bluetooth. Oh, and
yes, you can listen to music. I sent over a special Bluetooth—
wear it in your other ear. It'll let you play music without having
to use earbuds that can get caught on something. And you'll still
be able to hear what's going on around you. It's synced to your
phone and your iPod both."

"Wow. You think of everything."

She laughed. "I know what to ask Gustav to create. He's
good with things that aren't weapons, too."

"You could weaponize all of this."

"We could. We might. But not today."

"Works for me." Dug through the stuff Christopher had
brought and found the device. It was easy, since it was marked
"For Kitty." Put it in my left ear. No music, but I hadn't turned
anything on yet. Wondered if I was going to be put onto the
Algar Channel, but knew I couldn't depend on that.

There was a knock at my door. Siler and Buchanan answered
it, guns drawn. To find who we expected outside—a Field team
and Tony Costello. The Field team was something of a shock,
though.

"Jennifer, Jeremy, what are you guys doing here?" Jennifer
Barone-Gaekwad and Jeremy Barone were a brother-sister team
of Field agents. Jeremy was the empath, Jennifer was the imageer. They'd come onto our team during Operation Destruction.
"I thought you guys were with Jeff."

"We were," Jeremy said. "He asked us to help Prime Minister
Costello when he found out about the summits."

Gave them both hugs, then hugged Costello. "Thanks for
coming."

"Well, I figured you could probably use another person for

support." Costello had entered the room with a typical politician's smile on his face, and he'd kept it on while I was hugging
everyone. But, as he looked around the room, the smile faded
and his eyes narrowed. "Kitty—what's going on? And don't tell
me nothing. This isn't a group prepping you to swan into an
important all-world dinner. This is a commando team getting
ready to strike."

"Wow. Tony, you're good. First off, we're all thankful you're
a cool guy and were coming to help because, right now, only you
and King Raheem are safe." Tossed on the Recap Girl cape and
brought Costello up to speed as fast as possible. "So, we have to
save everyone but in a way that Cliff doesn't realize that we're
doing it."

"I like the idea of the commando raid while a dust storm of
that magnitude is going on," Costello said. "But I don't like the
idea of you being in that team."

"Neither does anyone else," Buchanan said.

"Other than my mother. Who, as of right now, gets the deciding vote."

Costello chuckled. "True enough. So, what can I do to help?"

"You're going to be our cover. I want you and King Raheem,
along with everyone else who isn't going on the raid, to stay
here. You're going to be communicating with Jeff. First, I'll
want you to send him a text right now, telling him that you've
done exactly what you first intended—you decided to surprise
me and come help King Raheem escort me, so that I'd have you
by my side to tell me who to smile at and who to be imperious
with, both for leaders from your region and for those that you
know from outside of your region, as well."

"Got it. Then what?"

"Then, you're going to be the one to say that I spilled stuff
all over myself because I'm nervous, so I'm having to change
clothes, and, therefore, jewelry and shoes, and fixing my hair."

"Will Jeff believe that?"

Half the room snorted. "Oh, he'll believe it," Vance said. "It's
a common occurrence."

"I'll hurt you later, Vance. Then, you'll be the one who tells
them the truth, and potentially gets them evacuated."

"You're sure gates won't work to get everyone out?" Costello
asked.

"I'm sure that if we try one everyone in that restaurant is
going to die."

Costello didn't look convinced.

"This is her skill," Siler said. "This is why she and all the others are still alive. It's why Jeff survived long enough to make it to the White House. She knows how the psycho megalomaniacs think."

Now Costello looked a little horrified. Yeah, Other Me had represented the classy side. Hadn't known I had a classy side, but apparently if I was married to Chuckie it came out. Something to ponder at another time, once we were all alive and Cliff was not.

"It's a gift and a curse. I'm not a psycho, though, so there's that."

Costello shook himself. "You know, I want to argue this. And then I remember what happened when this madman tried to kill half the world. I saw you on that motorcycle and I saw Jeff lean out of a helicopter to grab you—you both were far more natural doing that than doing any political thing I've seen. I can believe it. And I know you both came out of Centaurion Division, meaning you're both military trained."

"Exactly. So, I need to change, and so does anyone else who's on Team Commando. Camilla and Malcolm: other than Abigail and Mahin, who are musts, you choose the team. Remember that, per Serene, Walter, and William, once we go over and start the haboob, we can't leave, and no one else can come in, so choose wisely."

Buchanan looked at Camilla and shrugged. "Don't put too much effort into it. She'll just add or subtract whoever she does or doesn't want anyway."

Camilla barked a laugh. "Or, as we call it, routine."

CHAPTER 70

TROTTED INTO MY ROOM. Considered things and opened the closet. Sure enough, there were clothes hanging up, and they weren't for any woman in this country. Apparently Algar had chosen to "hang up" the important clothes out of the Rolling Arsenal. Had no complaints.

Pulled on the black jeans, black on black, lightweight long-sleeved Aerosmith t-shirt, black socks, and black shoes waiting for me. The shoes weren't my usual Converse, but appeared to be both flexible and non-sliding. Chose not to complain. The black on black shirt was reminiscent—Algar had equipped all of us with our favorite band shirts in black on black for the raid on Gaultier's underground cloning lab.

My throat felt tight. "I hope you just think this is cool, as opposed to you warning me that we're going to lose someone we love while doing this." There was no reply, but I hadn't really expected one.

Did a fast count in my head of who was in my suite while I dressed. Realized that we were missing people. Checked the rolling bag—it no longer had any changes of clothing in it, but instead was loaded with Raid The Tall Tower things. Decided it had better come along with us.

Put my purse over my head, dragged the bag out of the room, and looked around again. "Um, where the heck are Len and Kyle?"

Those out and ready all looked around. "I thought they were here," Tim said. "Weren't they with us when we went to the meeting room for your multimedia presentation?"

"They were, but I can't remember seeing them since we left my suite." Ran through what I could remember of the room and the chaos and what I'd noted while I was essentially on stage. Couldn't recall if I'd seen the boys or not.

"I don't remember them coming into the room," Gower said slowly. "Not that I was paying a lot of attention."

"No one was," Reader said, sounding worried and pissed. "So, what's happened to them?"

Thought about it. "Adriana." Got the room's attention, including those of the gals who were coming out after having changed. Every one of them was in black jeans and a black on black long-sleeved t-shirt. Algar liked to stick to a theme. "Adriana is used to working with the boys. If she needed backup of some kind, she would know I'd be too busy."

"Why didn't she contact me or Malcolm?" Camilla asked, sounding pissed.

"You want my honest assessment?"

"Yes," Buchanan said. "We do."

"She doesn't trust Camilla."

This earned me a lot of shocked looks. But Tim nodded. "Camilla's been a double, triple, and quadruple agent when she's had to be. I can see why that might be something Adriana wouldn't trust."

"Um, yes, but that's not exactly what I mean. Adriana knows Camilla's on our side." Did not know how to say this without hurting Camilla's feelings.

But Camilla beat me to it. "No, it's not that. And I know why Kitty's not saying what it is aloud. My team and I were captured and we weren't able to escape. If Kitty and her team, which included Adriana, hadn't come looking for us, we'd still be captured. That's why she doesn't trust me—the plan of mine she knows the best was an utter failure."

"You did your best," Rhee said loyally. Camille shot her a fond smile.

"Not to sound negative at a time like this," Mahin said, "but Kitty's plans fail all the time."

"And Adriana saves Kitty half the time," Abigail added.

"But her grandmother is training Kitty, just like she's training Adriana," Camilla said patiently.

Mouths opened. Put up the paw. Mouths closed. The FLOTUS Power had its uses.

Camilla snorted a laugh, then continued. "Olga is *training* Kitty—never think she isn't. She's doing it because Olga likes Kitty and wants her to survive and continue to save the world once Olga dies. Kitty's *expected* to fail because she's not fully trained, that's why Adriana backs her up, and vice versa. I'm already trained. I'm not expected to fail."

"Makes sense," I said, since these were my thoughts as well. "And she wouldn't contact Malcolm because, as far as her mission went, he'd confer with Camilla."

"So, why call in Len and Kyle?" Reader asked. "They don't have a better track record of not getting captured."

"Olga's training them, too. And perhaps she's training them a little more openly than she's training me."

"What do you mean?" Lorraine asked. "The boys are with you all the time."

"No, they aren't, and normally when they're not with me, they're visiting Adriana at her embassy. So, perhaps it's not just hanging out eating cookies and drinking lemonade and shooting the breeze. Perhaps what they're all doing is training as a team."

"Sounds right to me," White said, as he came out, also wearing black jeans and a black on black long-sleeved t-shirt. My jaw dropped. He smiled. "As you pointed out so long ago now, I understand why changing what we wear can be a wise and useful thing." He looked at Tim, Reader, and Christopher. "You boys should see about changing, too."

"Our luggage is in our rooms," Reader pointed out.

"I contacted the Operations Team and asked them to supply us here, due to what's going on." Well, it wasn't a lie—I'd told Algar what we were doing and asked for his help. "So, treat the closet in my room like you treat the closets at home."

"You're the only one who talks to the closets, Kitty," Christopher said. "The rest of us just figure that it's not requiring brilliance to know that we're going to wear what we always wear."

"Humor me. And get changed. Doctor Strange and Nightcrawler, too." Grumbling, the five men went into my room. "John, you should change, too," I said to Butler. He nodded and joined the other men in my room. Without argument. Androids on my side rocked. "Camilla, you too."

She looked thoughtful. "No."

"Pardon me?"

"I'm going to work under two assumptions—one, that Adriana is right to keep me out of this, and two, that something's going to go wrong, because it always does. That means you need people here who can either rescue you or assist you."

Considered this. "Makes sense on the second one. I don't think Adriana thinks you're incompetent, by the way."

"But she doesn't think my skill set is useful for whatever she's doing, or she'd have called Malcolm, told him her concerns about my abilities, and then let him handle me. But she didn't. And before you argue this, understand that the moment you became friendly with the Romanian Diplomatic Mission I was investigating them in ways that you don't know about."

"I thought you were working for Chuckie on stuff then."

"I was. I can and do multitask all the time. And while I answer to Charles and Jeff, and you, just as Malcolm takes his *real* direction from your mother, I take my real direction from the person who truly employs me."

"Alfred."

She nodded. "Royals aren't nearly as trusting as the ones you know here, Alfred least of all, considering what our people went through before being exiled here. Despite how it seems, Alfred trusts no one until they've been thoroughly vetted."

"By you and the other Liars in existence?"

"Yes. His only blind spot is his family, and that weakness has been over-exploited by now. He's accepted that we're going to find traitors in his family line, and not just among those who married in. Blood will out, and all that."

"Yeah, there's a lot of Ronald Yates and King Adolphus out there, isn't there? And not just in Stephanie." Though she had the blood of both, and I needed to remember that because she'd clearly inherited all the ruthlessness both of those men had.

"There is, but they aren't our problem right now. So, I'm staying here, guarding those also staying. So, who's staying with me, King Raheem, and Prime Minister Costello?"

"Any and all members of the Planetary Council are staying—no arguing, gang, we can't have you guys risked at a time like this. Paul is staying, same thing, dude, before you argue with me. You're the only religious leader who's safe, you're in the exact same boat as Raheem and Tony. Vance, Colette, Jennifer, and Mona, for sure I also want staying here. Jeremy's coming with because it's useful to have an empath along. Go change, by the way."

Jeremy trotted off. Gower looked resigned, Animal Planet looked disappointed and pissed, Vance and Colette looked relieved, and Mona nodded. "But I feel that you will need help from my security team." She looked at Khalid, Oren, Jakob, and

Leah, all of whom were sort of hanging back, presumably lest Raheem realize that three of them were Israelis versus Bahrainis.

Shook my head. "Right now, truly, we have only two world leaders who are what we can laughingly call safe. I want your security team with you."

Mona didn't look convinced, and she also looked a little worried. Raheem noticed. "I will appreciate both our loyal guard," he nodded at Khalid, "and also Mossad staying with us." He gave them a nod, too. "And yes, I know you're Mossad. And I also know that if you're with the Ambassadress, then you're not my enemies."

All five of my Middle Eastern Contingent looked shocked by this reveal. Costello chuckled. "It's going to be an interesting night, isn't it?"

"Oh, Tony, you have no idea."

CHAPTER 71

DECIDED TO KEEP RAHMI AND RHEE with Camilla, too, which earned me no complaining at all from Rhee and a tremendous amount of it from Rahmi.

"Look, if you guys could still make shields, I'd have you along in a New York Minute. But since we're talking about it, any luck with your mother fixing the issue?"

When they'd arrived, the princesses had been able to create shields that repelled and/or surrounded people. That had been a nifty skill we'd employed during Operation Sherlock. However, it had turned out that it wasn't a skill so much as a device—jewelry they wore that allowed them to create and manipulate the shields.

Unfortunately, the jewelry had gotten broken, years ago now—during a training session, to add insult to injury—and without the right supplies, supplies from their home planet, nothing anyone had tried had been able to fix them. Most of us rarely thought about that ability these days, but under the circumstances, figured it wasn't a bad idea to ask.

Rahmi shook her head. "Our mother did not know of our . . . clumsiness and so did not come equipped to refurbish our tools." She stood up straight. "However, a true princess of the Free Women is ready to fight with only her bare hands." She sounded proud, but her eyes were pleading.

Broke down and decided a shapeshifting Amazon wasn't overkill but thinking ahead. "Fine, Rahmi, you're in." She managed not to squeal and jump up and down, but I could tell she wanted to. "Mossy, I'd like you to come, too, if you're up for it."

"I was going whether you asked or not," he said with a grin.

"I figured. The rest of you, don't even think about it. No one appears to be as mobile as the Turleens and he's the smallest and my bet is that we're going to need small somewhere along the way."

Buchanan shook his head. "Half of these should stay here as well."

"I'd agree, only that tower is huge and we have no clear idea where all of the Crazy Eights may be. That they're there is likely. That they're together is not."

Jeremy came out, dressed for our kind of success. We all matched now, everyone in black jeans, black on black long-sleeved t-shirts, and those flexible and non-slip shoes. We looked like a bunch of commandos, or like we were a troupe about to go out and do some hip-hop for *So You Think You Can Dance*. Rahmi shifted to match us. Mossy didn't bother. Presumably he'd be our stage manager if we landed on TV. Everyone dug through the bag Serene had sent over and ensured we were all equipped.

"Why are you bringing that extra bag?" Christopher asked as we finished up, all of us putting on the communicator watches and goggles and clipping gas masks to our pants. The goggles were the fancy kind, and I sincerely hoped they'd work for us like the ones we'd used during Operations Epidemic and Mad-house, because we were going to need all the help we could get.

"It's got more supplies, and it's mobile and smaller than the bag you brought over." And Algar wanted me to have it.

"I've been carrying it, Son," White said calmly. "It's fine. And a useful weapon, too, if necessary."

Checked Mr. Watch and Mr. New Watch, which looked a lot like an iWatch. Chose not to ask Serene about it at this precise time. They both shared the same time, 7:15, so I had that going for me. We'd only spent about forty-five minutes on this. Which was too long. "Tim, Tony, have you heard anything, good or bad, from Jeff or Chuckie?"

"Impatience from your husband," Tony said.

"Suspicion from Chuck," Tim replied. "And I'm running out of ways to be vague that won't tip him off that something's really wrong. And I'm also not sure I shouldn't tell them that something *is* wrong."

"I point out that the moment Cliff knows that they suspect something, he's going to stop waiting for me and just roll his latest Death to All But Metal campaign. Camilla, take over the Chuckie wrangling, would you?"

"Oh, it's what I live for."

Serene pinged in my ear. "Kitty, you need to hurry. There appears to be some sort of dust storm starting near your target location."

"Crap. Okay, gang, we're rolling right now, a haboob we didn't create is forming. Camilla and Tony, do your best to keep Chuckie and Jeff respectively misinformed but prepared in some way. Do your best to have them explaining why I'm late out loud to people, because I'm sure Cliff's listening in and he needs to be reassured that I'm just making an entrance versus coming to get him. And good luck with that."

"It's all conjecture at this point," Buchanan said to those two. "But still, conjecture based on history."

My goggles shifted and I had a schematic of the Burj Khalifa in front of me, though I could still see everyone else, too. Looked for where to go and found it. "Serene, we're ready, get us a floater gate over to the Burj Khalifa, Floor One Hundred and Twenty-Four."

"Why above the restaurant, not below?" Mona asked.

"The most likely gasses being used will be heavier than air," Siler answered for me. "So we need to be above them in order to ensure that we aren't affected."

"And this deck is open-air and currently closed for maintenance."

"Go fast, all of you," Serene said. "That storm is about to hit."

Shared this with the team as the floater gate shimmered into view. "Silent exit, just in case," Buchanan admonished.

White grabbed my hand and we went through first and fast, but not yet furious, the others coming after us. The gate left us out on what was indeed an outdoor deck. It was all glass and shiny metal, and the theme was sleek and rounded geometric shapes.

There was an overhead structure that was another rounded geometric with metal slats that wouldn't really block the sun. But it looked cool. We'd landed on a beautiful wooden floor in front of an all-glass revolving door. There were glass walls that were at least twelve feet high all around, and even some comfortable chairs scattered about. The deck curved around to both the right and left from where we'd landed.

The heat was intense but not as bad as I'd been expecting. It felt like home, really. My home, Pueblo Caliente, not D.C. And there was something else, too. Wind.

"It shouldn't be windy, not as much as we can feel right now," White said softly, as the last of the team stepped through and the floater gate disappeared. "Not with the height of the glass."

"Serene said a haboob was forming. I'd assume it's having help. Abby, Mahin, you're with me and Mister White. Malcolm, we'll take the exterior, at least until we have to take cover."

Tim tried the door. It revolved without issue. "I have a bad feeling about this," he said.

"So it's a typical mission. You guys find a way for us to get in and around without being spotted. Everyone remember, speak softly, use the wrist communicators sparingly, just in case, and if it's one of the Crazy Eights, aim to kill."

While Buchanan and Siler divided the rest of the group into teams, White, Abigail, Mahin and I stepped off a bit and conferred. "What's the best place to draw sand from here?"

"The opposite side from the sea," Mahin said, sarcasm meter at only about four on the scale.

"Thanks for that." Looked around. The view was breathtaking. The sun was just starting to set and lights were coming on, and we were so high up it was like we could see forever. But, as with all the cool places I went while working, I had no time to actually enjoy it. Because we were looking at water, ergo, we were on the wrong side of the building.

The four of us moved off quickly but cautiously. Despite being a hybrid, Mahin didn't have hyperspeed. She'd been the person who'd made us realize that not all hybrids were even close to alike, particularly anyone sired by Ronald Yates. And while any one of us could have just grabbed her and run, we had other hybrids in the Crazy Eights and we weren't sure if they could see people going at hyperspeed or not.

We slunk around and I noted a couple of the "Closed for Maintenance" signs. They looked slightly wrong, in part because they were in English as well as Arabic. "I don't think that the people who actually run this tower closed this floor off." Looked at Mr. New Watch. "How do we use these? I mean that seriously."

White tapped a button. "Malcolm, Missus Martini feels that this level is closed due to foul play."

"Affirmative," Buchanan said, voice coming softly through White's watch. "Have already found dead bodies. Throats are slit."

"Kellogg is on-site." White hit a button on my watch. Stopped talking into his and talked into mine. "That's another one of his moves."

"Agreed. Sending the Minister of Sulky Looks up to the top to verify who and what we're dealing with above us."

That was Buchanan's nickname for Christopher, seeing as I wasn't the only one who'd noticed his glaring. Controlled the Inner Hyena, mostly so that we wouldn't be given away to our enemies by my snickering. "Good plan."

My team started off again. At its base, the Burj Khalifa had the cross-section of a rounded Y. But up this high, most of that outline was gone and it was more like a giant, rounded arrowhead. There were wide sections of walkway that hugged the exterior glass walls, and interior walls that were also mostly glass because people came to this floor to look at the amazing view. There weren't a lot of corners, just curving walls, meaning we could come upon someone at any moment.

Which we did. He was in the spot I figured Mahin would have chosen, at the far end of this side of the deck, where the scene was all desert in the near distance. His back was to us, but I recognized his shape and stance—arms out, head tilted up.

We'd found our first Crazy Eight—Darryl Lowe, Air Bender to the Stars.

Pulled the others back so that he couldn't see us. "We've found Lowe." White somehow shared this via his watch without speaking into it. Decided he had the Communications Post from now on in. "Mahin, he's doing what we want essentially, creating a haboob. Can you help him do it?"

"Do we want that?" Abigail asked. "If Cliff wants a haboob, maybe it's because that's when he plans to kill everyone—when there's no chance that help can come."

"That makes far too much logical sense to be ignored." Dug into my purse and found my Glock. My iPod was there, too. Hit play to see if the earpiece worked like Serene had promised. "Hot Shot" by Shaggy came on. Worked for me.

Wasn't enough to let me know if I was on the Algar Channel or not, though. However, I wanted to get rid of the Crazy Eights, and I was willing to start with Lowe. He'd tried to kill far too many of us far too often for me to want to give him another chance.

Started to head back and had him in sight, when White put his hand on my shoulder. "Wait a moment."

"Why? Do you think he's going to give us intel or something?"

"No, I saw something, or someone. I don't believe he's alone."

Abigail concentrated. "I feel . . . supremely confident. But it's more confidence than I've ever felt from one person before. And before you ask, Kitty, think of how confident your Aunt Carla normally is. This feeling is easily ten times what I've felt from her."

"Wow, I don't think Aunt Carla's had an unconfident moment in her life. So, there are more people than I saw there?"

Abigail shook her head. "That's just it. I only feel *one* person."

"Okay, well, we can't dally. Let's move forward. Mahin, start revving up the earth bending prep. Abby, before we go, can you shield Jeff and the others in the restaurant?"

"No. I can't feel them at all. This one confident person . . . he's almost blocking me, it's so strong."

White still had my rolling purse, though he was carrying it over his shoulder. "You need me to take that?" I asked him.

He chuckled. "No, I'm secure enough in my masculinity to carry the bag. Besides, I'm not joking—I believe it will make an excellent blunt instrument."

"Then, let's get rid of our air bender once and for all."

Took the lead since I had the gun. Hunched down and headed out, hugging the inner wall. My music changed to "Double Vision" by Foreigner just as Lowe was in my sight again.

There were several chairs here. Walked slowly and quietly toward him, keeping my eye on the chairs so I didn't bump into one and alert Lowe to our presence.

Which was a great plan. What I hadn't realized, however, was that White was right—Lowe wasn't alone. There were people sitting in those chairs.

I froze as soon as I saw that the chairs were occupied. But it didn't matter—we'd been spotted. The people in the chairs stood up. Then they all turned around. Lowe turned, too. In fact, they all turned in unison.

There were ten Darryl Lowes standing there.

CHAPTER 72

"**O**H, HELLO," Lowe said. All of them. In unison. The unison thing again. This was, by far, the creepiest it had ever been. Resolved not to care about normal people talking in unison ever again in my life as long as I could ensure I'd never have to deal with unison like this ever again. "We've been expecting you."

Managed not to scream but only because I'd been focused enough on being quiet that I could control it.

Mahin and Abigail both gasped, but quietly. White didn't make a sound, but his expression shared that he was controlling himself.

"Um, nice to see you. All of you. Clones?"

Lowe nodded. They all nodded. "It's amazing how much more powerful I am now," all of them said.

Was fairly sure that the Lowe that was standing nearest to the glass was the original. But it was hard to be positive. For all I knew, the original was elsewhere. "So, which one is the real you?"

"This one," they all said as they all pointed to themselves. They all looked over my shoulder. "Oh, Mahin, how funny you are, trying to stop my storm. You can't, you know. Air is stronger than dirt."

"And paper covers rock, rock smashes scissors, and scissors cut paper."

All the Lowes stared at me. "You're stupid. You and Mahin both. You had your chance to join us and you threw it away."

"I feel all terrible about that, too. Mahin, what's our status?"

"He's right," she said quietly. "I can't stop it. The storm is now a storm of its own."

"Then we'll do it my way." With that, I aimed my Glock at the Lowe nearest me and used the rapid-fire technique Mom had taught me, and fired three shots into his head.

The less said about the blood splatter the better, but the Lowe went down. Moved the gun and shot the next-nearest one. Same thing—three to the head, body went down.

The rest of the Lowes just stood there. Well, not quite. They turned back to face the coming storm. And then they just stood there.

Went up to the next one and put three into the back of his head. Hit his neighbor next.

What I didn't want to do was miss, however. The blood and bodies and such could be cleaned up. But permanent destruction didn't say "saving the day." It said "acting like the Avengers fighting Ultron," and that was not the way we wanted to be perceived.

Maybe the glass was all bulletproof. And maybe it wasn't. But either way, a bullet or bullets ripping through the glass would be the definition of a bad idea. I didn't want to wreck this beautiful building, nor did I want to find out what happened when you were up this high and the twelve-foot glass walls disappeared. Perhaps nothing. Perhaps you were sucked off the platform. Chose not to find out.

"Two minutes until the storm hits you," Serene said in my ear. "And it's massive."

Decided I'd better hurry up. Shot another two dead, which used up my clip. Dug around in my purse for another, popped the old one out and put the new one in. Killed another Lowe.

It was creepy and gross and weird. At this point, I wasn't sure if I was killing anything for real or if this was all some bizarre stunt of Cliff's. If so, it made no sense, but crazy people didn't make sense all the time.

Killed the next three without issue. White was making sure they were really dead. Waited for them to reanimate in some way, but it didn't happen. Reached the final Lowe. He turned around and smiled at me. A really weird, really crazy smile. "Goodbye," he said. Just like the Casey Thing had at the police station.

"Bomb!"

White ran forward at hyperspeed and grabbed Lowe, who didn't resist at all. White spun around a couple of times then flung the body up. "Skeet shooting time, Missus Martini!"

Lowe sailed over the top of the glass wall. I had one shot and I took it. Hit the torso. Not a killing shot.

We all ran to the glass walls. The haboob was almost to the Burj Khalifa, but we were high enough up that it might not bother us. The body exploded just before it was lost in the dust.

"He was confident because the real Lowe wasn't where he could be caught."

"I felt all of them." Abigail sounded as grossed out as I felt.

"Are the rest going to explode, too?" Mahin asked.

White and I looked at each other. "Probably," I said. "But if not, we're tossing dead bodies off the side of the tallest building in the world. I don't know how we explain that." My music changed to "Bombs Away" by B.o.B. Meaning Algar was suggesting we toss the bodies. "Then again, the haboob may solve the issue for us. Better something on the ground we can clean up than blowing up this level."

White, Abigail, and I now all did the spin and toss thing, all at hyperspeed, while Mahin watched to see if the bodies exploded or not before they were in the dust storm and so out of view. Some of them did, some of them didn't.

"I had no idea I had the ability to toss a dead body over a twelve-foot wall. Go team."

"Do you think Darryl used all of his clones to create the wind that made the storm?" Mahin asked.

"I think if they were moving and talking as one, they might have been powering as one, yeah."

"That makes sense," Mahin said. "Because Darryl doesn't have the range to be doing this from afar, unless he's expanded his talent in the last few weeks."

"Why isn't the haboob stopping?" Abigail asked as we headed back toward the revolving doors. "If it was created, shouldn't it have died the moment he did?"

"The storm found its own life," Mahin said. "The winds were strong enough that it's fueling itself now. Probably not for too much longer, but long enough that we can't safely leave."

"Maybe, but we're above most of it up here, so we might still be able to get people out."

Abigail looked out one of the window walls. "Yeah, it's still raging but I don't think it's going to hit above about the hundredth floor. So, where do we think the real Lowe is?"

"He has to be nearby, in this building somewhere." Dropped my almost-empty clip out and put a full one in. Saved the clip with two shots left, though, because who knew, right? "Clones or not, there's no way that his range has become so massive in the time since we last saw him that he's somewhere else. Serene, do we have status on the restaurant?"

"It's being televised because Mister Joel Oliver is there with Jeff, so yes." Serene sounded tense, which was appropriate in this case. "Everyone's still alive." She didn't add "for now" but assumed she was thinking it.

White tapped on his communicator watch. "Christopher, what have you found?" There was no answer. White tried again. Still silence.

"Christopher's found a trap or a bunch of enemies and is too busy to talk, is what Christopher's found. Meaning we have to get off this deck and into the building. The issue is, do we go up or down?"

White was tapping away on his watch. "I have no idea," he said finally. "Because either the entire team is too busy to respond, or they're all captured. Or worse."

"Serene, are you still there?"

"Yes, but I can't raise anyone else. Nothing shows as malfunctioning but no one is responding to Bluetooth or watch communicators."

Thought fast. "They're captured, some or all of the team, and someone's reverse engineered the tech to spot where we all are. And that means they're tracing back to you."

"It'll take them a long while to manage it," Serene said. "I'm using Tobin's equipment."

"Well and good, but turn the tech off."

"What, yours?"

"Everyone's. Turn the watches and Bluetooths and whatever else off right now. Kill them, so to speak. The four of us need to get rid of our watches and earpieces immediately."

"But Gustav created all this," Serene protested. "How could they reverse engineer it so fast?"

"LaRue's clone would be my first guess. The Tinkerer is doing them a solid is my second guess. G-Company employs the best is my third guess. Take your pick, but we're off the line. Will call you when we can using our regular phones. Anyone calling in on whatever your Bluetooth line is should be immediately suspect. And put up the shield for wherever you are—just in case they've had enough time to break Tobin's scrambling code."

Took the Bluetooth out of my ear and the watch communicator off my wrist. Considered taking the music Bluetooth out, but my music changed to Billy Joel's "Leave a Tender Moment Alone," which seemed to indicate Algar wanted me to keep on feeling the special bond of his musical choices. Worked for me.

Was pretty sure the shoes weren't sturdy enough to stomp on these without hurting us. Put them on the deck and used the butt of one of the spare guns to smash them. The others handed me theirs and I did the same. Had a pile of formerly awesome junk shortly.

Scooped it all up and indicated White should open the big purse. He did and I found a bag in it. Dumped the remains into it, folded the top of the bag up, and dumped it into the big purse.

"Why are you taking that?" Abigail asked.

"I'm not willing to give any of our enemies, old, new, or yet to come, an extra edge. Serene couldn't reach anyone, either, by the way, though I'm sure you all guessed."

"So it's just the four of us?" Mahin asked. She sounded more than slightly freaked out.

"Apparently." White didn't sound freaked out, but he didn't sound happy, either.

The revolving door moved, but there was no one there. Siler shimmered into view. "The five of us."

CHAPTER 73

ALL FOUR OF US JUMPED. I only managed not to scream because I'd seen the door move. "Nightcrawler, was that drama really necessary?"

"Yes. Link up, fast." We did. White held my upper arm so my gun hand was technically free and Siler grabbed my left hand. Felt the tingle that meant we were blending.

Just in time, as another Darryl Lowe walked out through the revolving doors. He was carrying what looked like a stun gun, but he had a semiautomatic pistol on his hip. "They have to be here," Lowe said as Kellogg walked through the revolving doors now, too, also carrying a stun gun but with two semis on his hips. "I saw them clearly. My 'sister' is with them. But I think we should kill her, too."

So the cloning worked like it did for Multiple Man—he could see what his clones saw. Hoped he could feel what they felt, too, but didn't bet on it.

"No, the boss wants them alive," Kellogg said. "All of them. He has plans."

"Why hasn't he cloned you yet?" Lowe asked as they started off at a leisurely stroll, heading for where we'd just been. We followed, walking slowly and carefully.

"He said it's because my talents don't transfer the way yours do. Yours are innate, mine are learned."

Interesting. So they'd lost the ability to transfer their minds' knowledge back and forth. Good and go team. Nice to know our raid during Operation Infiltration had done some lasting damage to Cliff's side.

"Think we're going back to the States soon?" Lowe asked

now. Apparently this was just a day at the park for them. Or it was the first time they were able to talk alone.

Kellogg shrugged. "Don't care. It's better here. You ask me, the boss should stick with G-Company."

"He has bigger plans, you know that."

"Yeah, I've heard. Look, all I know is that we've spent more time locked up than not following his plans. We're finally in with a solid organization. I say we stay here, shut up, and just enjoy what G-Co had to offer."

"Yeah, I see your point." Lowe shrugged. "Well, we'll take care of the remaining problems and then worry about it tomorrow, right?"

Kellogg laughed. "Yeah. Tomorrow's definitely going to be another day."

Figured we had less than a minute before they realized we weren't where they expected us to be. Had a choice. We could find out what Cliff's plans were or we could kill these two right now. Figured I knew what Cliff's plans were, the likelihood that we'd get any intel we could use out of these two was slim to none, my gun was fully loaded and in my hand, and there was literally no time like the present. My music changing to "Shoot to Thrill" by AC/DC was also something of a clue.

Let go of Siler and pulled away from White. Moved into the position Mom had taught me—body straight, shoulders over hips, legs just a bit more than shoulder length apart. Aimed for Kellogg. Took a deep breath, let it out slowly, and shot to kill.

Hit him three times in his torso and one in the back of the head. As he went down, Lowe spun around and aimed his stun gun at me. Would have shot him but White pulled me aside and down. He had Mahin and Abigail down already.

Tried to get up to shoot again, but it turned out I didn't have to. Lowe's neck twisted around in a way human necks are not supposed to. Then Siler unblended and put three bullets into Lowe's head. He added two more into Kellogg's head, presumably because he believed in the double-tap. I didn't fault this at all.

"I wasn't expecting you to shoot anyone in the back," Siler said as we trotted over to him and he searched the bodies. "But well done."

"Yeah, that Old West honor thing sounds great, but in real life, you get better results if you choose to just kill the known, irredeemable bad guys the fastest and easiest way possible."

Lowe wanting to kill Mahin had been more than enough proof for me that he was a lost cause, and Kellogg was a hired killer who couldn't wait to move up in G-Company. Felt no remorse at all. Wondered if I should and decided this was a talk I could have with Jeff and Mom later. I first needed to assure that Jeff and the others all got to have a later.

"What happened to everyone else?" White asked.

"No idea," Siler said as he took their guns and handed them to me. Dropped said guns into my purse. Noted I had Poofs on Board, all snoozing. The Poofs who normally traveled with me, plus all the Poofs who belonged to everyone inside the restaurant. This boded. "I tried to reach James, got no response, and stopped trying. I was closest to you four, and on my way, I spotted these two," he indicated the dead bodies, "coming here, cheerfully discussing how much fun they were going to have hurting the four of you since they weren't allowed to kill you."

"Charming. Do we think this is the real Lowe? I mean that seriously." Filled Siler in on the Multiple Man situation.

"Kellogg was treating him like a real person," Siler said. "Barring both of these being clones and all of this an elaborate ruse to pass misinformation to you."

"Where's your watch and Bluetooth?" Abigail asked. "Kitty had us destroy ours."

Siler shot me a proud smile. "Well done." He reached into his pocket and pulled out trashed tech. White got out our Tech Trash Bag and Siler added his in. "The moment I couldn't reach the person who was supposed to be waiting to share intel back and forth, I figured we were compromised. You stay uncompromised longer if they can't take your teammate's tech and track you with it."

"Go team. So, where to now? I mean, now we have to save even more people and I have no idea what you guys were doing while we were skeet shooting creepy clones."

"I'd assume that some of the team is still loose. The Turleen went into the ventilation system immediately, and he never took any of the tech in the first place."

"He didn't?" Shockingly, I hadn't paid attention to that.

"No. Trust me, he doesn't think he needs any of us to effect whatever rescue he's planning."

"More power to him and all that. So, what about the others?"

"James, Tim, Lorraine, Claudia, and Rahmi were going down to the floor below. Malcolm, Jeremy, Butler, and I went up to the hundred and fifty-fourth floor, which is one of the ones you identified as being partly owned by G-Company. Christopher was checking all the floors going all the way up. We lost contact with him when he was around floor one hundred and fifty-nine. Jeremy, Butler, and Malcolm went to look for him. I stayed because I'd found something."

"What?"

"A diary written in English. I think it's Goodman's. It sounded crazy enough. There was some information that I figured we might be able to use, if we can decipher the crazy. Which I know will be your job." He pulled a small leather notebook out of his back pocket and handed it to me. "Put this somewhere safe, just in case."

Looked at White, who opened the big purse. Dropped it in, he closed the big purse. We were a well-oiled team. "So, what about the others?"

"James was supposed to advise me when they'd surveyed their floor and were ready to go down, and I was to let him know what we found up on my level. He didn't answer when I told him Christopher had gone out of communication. That's when I figured we were screwed."

"Sounds like Thursday, yeah." Turned my iPod off. Pulled my phone out, turned my music on, and slid it into my back pocket as "The Rescue" by American Hi-Fi came on. "Richard, I'm sorry, but we need to focus on the people we came here to rescue, not the captured rescuers."

"I agree," White said. "I truly trust that Christopher and the others will be fine."

"If not, we'll make them suffer for it," Siler said. "I promise you that."

My music changed mid-song to "Come to My Window" by Melissa Etheridge. Went to the nearest exterior window and looked around. As I did so the sun officially slipped all the way down. There were lots of lights I could see now, and the building itself was lit up. Didn't see anything else, but looked down to check if I could still see the haboob. And saw something else.

"Meanwhile, I have a crazy idea that just might work."

"What's that?" Siler asked.

Turned around and smiled brightly. "There's a window washing rig one floor below us."

CHAPTER 74

"NOT JUST NO, but hell no," Mahin said.

"How would we get into it?" Abigail asked.

"And what will we do when we're on it?" Siler asked. "Wave to everyone as they die?"

"Look, we have people captured. That means the remaining Crazy Eights know we're here. They're going to start gassing people if they haven't already." Refused to let myself get scared that Jeff and Chuckie and everyone else was dead already. Focused on being angry that—at the point in history when the world was finally joining together—a crazed madman was going to ruin everything.

"Missus Martini is right," White said calmly. "We need to adapt, and this adaptation makes sense."

"I also have more of a plan than just washing the windows to make up for splattering blood and gray matter all over this observation deck. I want Mahin to take some of the dirt that Lowe so nicely has sent this way and make a small whirlwind inside the restaurant, while Abby puts a shield around the people inside."

"Then what?" Abigail asked. "We can hold that for a while, but not forever."

"Then we have Serene send a floater gate that's on our window washing rig. We'll move everyone through that and immediately to the Science Center where we'll have doctors standing by and they can get treated."

"Serene?" Mahin asked. "The Serene we just hung up on and told to not trust any incoming calls? That Serene?"

"One and the same! Glad you're all with the program. Mister White, the Bag of Bigness, if you would."

White flipped the rolling purse down and I opened it up. All the climbing equipment was in there. Pulled it out and handed it to Siler. "I'd assume you have the most experience with this."

"I do, but honestly the hardest part is going to be getting over the twelve-foot walls of glass."

Heaved a sigh. "Well, as to that . . ." Handed him the spare guns. "Have at it."

White was looking in the big bag. "Just a moment. I believe we have something in here that will work more effectively." He pulled out a glass cutter set, complete with suction cups. He also pulled out five pairs of black gloves.

"I'm not going to ask why you have all this," Abigail said to me. "But if you want to share . . ."

Managed not to say that the Elves thought of everything, but only just. Also had to think fast to give a reply that wouldn't make everyone suspicious. Well, more suspicious. "We're burgling. It seemed wise to bring it along. I just forgot I had it. Creepy clones and losing two thirds of our team mysteriously put my focus elsewhere."

"I'll take it," Siler said. "And I'll also take the glass cutter stuff." We traded the glass cutter kit for the spare guns. Siler eyed everything. "We could avoid cutting the glass and go over if we get on top of that." He nodded his head at the geometric covering thing with the slats.

"I don't know which would be worse, or harder," White said. "Our people can repair the glass swiftly."

"I am not jumping up there and then over the side," Mahin said. "In the dark. Or in the light, either. At all. I am not doing that at all."

"Wrecking the tallest building in the world, Dubai's and the UAE's proudest landmark, and the winner of the Best Attraction in the World award coming right up," Siler said.

Actually, what he did first was to secure the lines we'd be using to get down to the geometric covering. It was set up perfectly for this. Chose not to point this out, since Mahin and Abigail were barely one with the plan as it was.

Once the lines were set and deemed safe enough, Siler cut out a two-foot diameter hole, just like they did in the movies. White had to help him pull the glass inwards, since it was very heavy. Chose not to mention that we'd tossed ten exploding dead bodies over with no concerns for who they might land on and yet were treating the glass as if it might be a problem should it fall on someone all those floors below.

While they were doing this I called Serene using my phone. Wasn't quite as convenient as the Bluetooth had been, but found the will to go on. She answered, we verified I was me and she was her, then I told her what we were doing and what we needed her to do. "And it's too late to tell us not to, because we've already cut the glass."

"I won't tell you that because we've lost the televised feed. Kitty, you need to be prepared—they may have already released the gas."

"Got it. It's likely I won't be able to call you to tell you to send the floater."

"You still have the music earpiece in? It looks like you do."

"Yeah. I figured it was safe in terms of tracking."

"It is because I set it up separately from the others. I can track you using it. How long did it take them to cut the glass?"

"Ten minutes probably. It'll be harder on the window washing rig, I'm sure, but we'll be able to kick the glass in so figure roughly the same time."

"Okay. When you've been stationary for ten minutes, I'll send the gate."

"It's going to need to be very precise."

"Walter will do it, then, we're still coordinated. Good luck."

Hung up and my music started again. Olivia Newton-John's "Don't Stop Believin'." This wasn't the "Don't Stop Believin'" I'd have expected, but Journey wasn't what I was hearing. Clearly Algar was telling me everyone was still alive. Listened to the lyrics while we pulled on the gloves and got ready. Seemed to be Algar giving me an Atta Girl. Chose to indeed not stop believing that we'd save everyone.

Perky ONJ song over, B.o.B.'s "Don't Let Me Fall" on as Algar's choice for hilarious background music, and we were ready to start down.

"Remember," Siler said, "we're walking down. You're going to lie on your stomachs and back through the hole, carefully, so you don't get cut on the glass. It's thick, so it should be okay, but we want to be safe."

Mahin snorted. "Right."

Siler ignored her. "The moment you're able to bend at the waist, I want you getting the balls of your feet onto the glass as soon as possible. It's not that far down, and I'll be on the rig first to catch anyone, but you don't want to go too fast. Not too slow, either," he added, looking at Mahin. "We're running out of time."

With that, he did exactly what he'd described. We had a long rope that was tied off around the base of the geometric covering thing. We had another, longer rope that was hooked through the slats on top of the covering, so that we could hold onto one end of the rope in each hand.

The idea was that we were using the hooked rope to get through the hole, and then would transfer and hold onto the stationary rope to get the rest of the way down. The four of us crowded on each side of the hole so we could watch Siler. The lighting on the tower was good, the lights aimed upwards, so we could see him pretty clearly. Naturally, he did this as if he was born to it.

Next we tied the rolling purse to the stationary rope and sent that down. Siler tugged that rope when he had the bag, and now it was the next person's turn. We sent Abigail next, because White and I could help her through the hole. "I think I hate you guys," she said as her head made it through the opening and my music switched to "Highwire" by the Gin Blossoms. Clearly Algar was enjoying himself.

Abigail didn't have all that much trouble, though. White held one of her wrists while she let go and wrapped the stationary rope around her hand like Siler had told her to. She nodded, White let go slowly, she grabbed the rope with her other hand, and she walked her way down to Siler. Looked easy peasey.

Mahin was next, mostly because it was going to take both of us to get her to do this in the first place and, again, we could help her. She was muttering in Farsi, and I realized that I could understand it now that I knew I could. "I didn't think you knew those words."

"I know those words and more and, right now, they're all for you. Everyone had better be alive and well but in mortal peril we're actually able to save them from, is all I can say."

Her head through, White did the same for her as he had for Abigail. Mahin took longer to grab the stationary rope, but grab it she finally did. She went down about halfway, then her foot slipped. She smacked into the glass but held on. Couldn't hear him, but could see Siler shouting to her. Mahin let herself slide a little, and Siler was able to catch her and get her onto the rig. Looked less easy peasey, but still, doable.

I and my purse were up next. White had suggested I send it down with the rolling purse, but I just felt safer with it around my neck. I was used to working this way, after all.

The purse did make it a little harder to get through the opening, but avoiding getting cut was a lot harder than it had looked. White holding onto me was a big help. "This is going to suck for you, Mister White."

"I'll be fine, Missus Martini, never fear."

Felt wind on my lower body, but chose not to focus on it and, instead, ensured that the balls of my feet were on the glass like Siler wanted. I was having a lot of issues managing this, with me doing The Bicycle more than actually getting my feet to stick, but I finally got kind of in the right position.

Once my head was through, I really noticed the wind. It wasn't pleasant. However, I had to let go of the one rope and grab the stationary rope. Let go and grabbed. And missed. Grabbed again. Missed again. Grabbed a third time and managed to get the rope in my hand. Wrapped it like Siler had shown, and nodded to White, who let go of my other hand.

Started to fall immediately. Because, as it turned out, I'd grabbed the rope I'd been holding originally, the one made to slide, not the stationary rope.

CHAPTER 75

I **FLIPPED OVER** almost immediately. Tucked my head so when my back slammed into the glass, the back of my head did not. One small favor.

The rope stopped moving. Due to the way I was hanging I could see that White had stepped on it. So, as long as he didn't move, I was good. This moment's definition of damning with faint praise.

I was now upside-down, with my purse trying to strangle me because of course it had slipped over my arm and now was only holding on because my chin was acting like a ledge. But not for long. Gravity was a bitch, we were rarely on close terms, and she was all about reminding me that my lower half was heavier than my upper half. My body slid around. Now I was right side up and about to have my right arm wrenched out of the socket, though my purse was now longer trying to fall off. No, now it was just hanging around my neck like the heaviest albatross necklace in the world. My music changed to "Hold On" by Smash Mouth. If only I could.

My wrist was wrapped up in the rope, which was good, because my fingers couldn't stay closed since the rope was cutting off circulation. I could feel the stationary rope—I was lying on it, meaning it was at my back. And of course, it was more on my right side than my left, meaning I was going to have to twist to grab it. Somehow.

I was too far up to let go willingly and not expect that I'd cause the entire rig to go down when I hit. However, as my wrist started to slide slowly through the rope, realized I didn't have a choice.

Someone's feet were right by my head. White was coming

down like he'd spent his entire life vacationing in the Alps. He had hold of both sides of the sliding rope. He got relatively even with me. "Hang on, Missus Martini. This is going to take split-second timing."

"I have no choice other than to hang, Mister White. I also have no control over when the rope loosens enough and I plummet to my and everyone else's death, but I give it no more than three seconds." Realized that the only reason the rope was still holding me up was because White was keeping it taut enough that I couldn't slip. Yet.

White didn't comment. Instead he let go of the sliding rope with his left hand, grabbed the stationary rope, let go with his right hand, and wrapped his right arm around me just as the rope loosened enough on my wrist that my arm fell down. Then we were sliding down the window, but White was controlling it, not gravity. Hyperspeed and White's über awesomeness for the win.

Saw him make the Grimace Face when he managed to stop us before we smashed into the rig. Siler grabbed me and put me down at hyperspeed, then grabbed White, while Abigail and Mahin grabbed me.

"Well, that was bracing," White said once we were all together.

"You continue to rock above all others, Mister White." Made sure my shoulder, elbow, and wrist were still in their respective sockets, while White did the same. Moved my purse back into its proper cross-body position as I checked inside. Everything, snoozing Poofs included, was in there just as if nothing had happened. Clearly riding via an Algar Portal was the way to go. Filed requesting a Personal Portal Pod on my To-Do List for later.

"Of all your plans, I hate this one the most," Mahin said.

"Give it time. I'm sure we'll do something much worse sooner than anyone would like."

"Hold on to the railings," Siler said, as he went to the control box. We started down, the window washing rig shaking all the way because that's how it had to be in my world, apparently, my soundtrack now going to "Shake, Rattle, and Roll" by Huey Lewis and the News.

The windows on the Sky Lobby level, and probably all the levels that weren't observation decks, were mirrored on the outside, so everyone inside didn't broil daily. Therefore, it was close to impossible to see inside. Did my best, but all I got was that there weren't people clustered around the window, so either no one had noticed our acrobatics or there were no people on this floor in this area.

The wind was really unpleasant as we went down. Wasn't sure if it was because we were so high up or because of the haboob Lowe had created or both. Decided it didn't matter. Was glad I still had my hair up in the banana clip. The clip was a trooper, too, considering everything it had been through with me today.

Reached the next floor down. The restaurant did indeed have the same mirroring, so we couldn't see in. Siler stopped us so that, once we cut the glass, anyone could safely step out onto the rig, to use the term "safely" loosely.

"Bigger cut now," he said. "Gas masks on first, though."

So much for the banana clip. And our goggles. Which I realized hadn't shown us anything once we got here. "Kozlow is definitely in the building." Took off the banana clip and my goggles and dropped both into my purse. "We may be going into poisoned gas," I whispered to the Poofs. "Take precautions and all that."

"How do you know?" Abigail asked.

"Our goggles aren't showing us anything. I don't even have infrared. Someone's affecting them in some way. I assume it's Kozlow using his power, such as it is."

"Then it's amplified by something," Mahin said. "Because Russell's powers are not strong at all."

"It didn't affect our communications," Abigail pointed out.

"Possibly because they wanted to hear what we were saying," Siler said. He handed me his goggles. Put them and everyone else's into the rolling purse.

The gas masks covered our faces and heads pretty fully. If I hadn't known who I was with, I wouldn't have recognized any of us. But we could talk and hear each other, so that was good. I also got to hear "I Saved the World Today" by The Eurythmics, which was nice.

White and Siler started glass cutting. Waited until they were about halfway through, then figured it was time for the rest of us to get prepped. "Mahin, get dust up here. Abby, get ready to start shielding. And can you feel anyone?"

"Yeah. Kitty, I'm freaking out! I don't know if I can do this."

That meant the people inside were still alive and likely panicking, so good news and bad news. Meaning Jeff was being attacked by poisoned gas and a haboob of emotions at the same

time. We had to hurry, but there was nothing we could do to
speed this up, since shooting at the windows would only cause
more panic.

Got as near to the window as I could and tried to look in. Saw
no one or a lot of someones. Couldn't be sure. Had to focus on
getting Abigail to calm down. My music changed to Linda Ron-
stadt's "Someone to Watch Over Me."

"Take a deep breath and think of Naomi."

"What the hell? You want me to remember how my sister
died? How is that going to help me?" Abigail sounded ready to
lose it.

"No. I want you to think about her as if she's alive and out
there somewhere, watching over you." Because she was. Maybe
Abigail hadn't realized how she'd gotten all her powers back
and received all of Naomi's, too. "Think of your sister and let
the calmness that was part of her personality calm you, too.
She's protecting you, I know she is."

"Deep breaths," Mahin said. "In with the good air, out with
the bad air."

Abigail nodded. Saw her chest moving as if she was at least
doing what Mahin had said.

"The dead watch over us, Abigail," White said over his shoulder. "Your sister, your brother, all your family before you are
with you now, helping you to succeed."

Finally saw her shoulders relax. White may have retired, but
once a Pontifex always a Pontifex apparently. "You're right, Uncle
Richard. The dead watch over us." She pulled herself up straight.
"And we avenge our dead. I'm good, you guys. And thanks."

"Almost there," Siler said. "Has anyone been keeping track
of time?"

Looked at Mr. Watch. It was 8:30. Had no idea what time it
had been when we'd started down to the window washing rig.
"No, because that would have been smart. I have no idea how
long before the floater creates."

"We'll handle it," White said calmly. "I assume we'll have to
help people to the gate, Missus Martini."

"You, me, and Nightcrawler. Mahin and Abby need to concentrate on their powers and stay out of the way of said powers
and the gate both." Plus, the girls were barely holding it together
as it was. Tossing them into the poisonous gas-filled room might
make them feel more secure than the window washing rig, or it
might send them over the edge.

"Get those powers revved right now," Siler said. "Mahin, we need to open as soon as you have your dust devil up here."

She put her hands out. A mini dust devil flew up to us. "It will be larger the moment the entryway opens."

"Then ready in three . . ." Siler said, as he and White started to lean against the large-person-sized doorway they'd cut out. "Two . . ." Picked up the rolling purse and flung it over my other shoulder. Grabbed the back of their pants, just in case. "One."

The men pushed hard and the glass moved inward. So did the three of us. "Jump," White said calmly as my music changed to Flo Rida's "Jump" and the "door" broke free of the window and shoved inwards. The three of us jumped as ordered. The men were on the floor.

I was, naturally, on the edge. And my two purses were heavy and pulling me backwards.

Always the way.

CHAPTER 76

TIGHTENED MY HOLD on their pants. Siler and White both stepped forward and pulled me along with them. Teamwork all the way.

Dumped the rolling purse well to the side so it wouldn't fall out and I wouldn't lose it and took a look around. What I was seeing wasn't what I'd expected.

There were five rounded domes that, frankly, looked like honeycombs. There were five Themnir slowly walking around the room pooping out large pellets. And there were a heck of a lot of people in gas masks fighting each other. One set in gas masks had Jeff and Chuckie—who were in what looked like airplane breathing masks—and one set was trying to get Jeff and Chuckie away from the other set. All of them were in black and there were too many to count quickly. Fantastic.

"Everyone else first," White shouted as Mahin's dust devil flew into the room and encircled everything. "Remember the goal."

Went to the nearest dome and knocked as "Hello Kitty" by Avril Lavigne came on. Algar was batting a thousand in terms of "hilarious" musical choices. "Hello? Good guys are here to do a rescue." Nothing. Knocked harder. "First Lady of the United States here. Are you guys alive in there or do I have to break this down?"

A hole opened at what looked to be about head height. Waved. Nothing. "I'm in a gas mask so I don't die."

"Prove who you are," a voice called. Was pretty sure that voice belonged to Raj.

"You joined our team during Operation Sherlock. If that's you, Raj. And if it's not, we're trying to rescue all of you and you're not exactly cooperating. Mahin's creating a dust devil to hide our escape and Abby's going to shield everyone." I hoped.

The dome lifted. It was indeed Raj. "Kitty?"

"In the gas-masked flesh. Stop talking, we need to get you all out of here."

Raj looked around. "The Themnir are handling the gas." He winced against the flying dirt. "How are you getting us out of here? The way is blocked and the elevators are shut down."

"We have a gate." I sincerely hoped.

"Great. Where?"

"Um, on the window washing rig that's hanging right outside. We came in through the window."

Raj nodded and turned around to face the people huddled near to a Lyssara. "It's definitely her, ladies and gentlemen. Follow me, please, quickly, but no pushing or shoving."

"They're landing in Dulce." I really and sincerely hoped.

Saw a shield shimmer around us, creating a tunnel that the dust went around, so it was easy to make it through. Decided no one was dying and I was hot in the gas mask. Took it off and clipped it to my belt. Saw Raj relax, as much as one could under the circumstances. Took the arm of the first person who came forward, who happened to be the old ayatollah who'd essentially helped me sell World Unity to everyone. "Glad you're okay, sir."

"I as well. May Allah and whoever else shower blessings on you."

Helped him to the window. Could see the floater gate shimmering at the back part of the rig. The girls were standing as close to the window side as they could. And they couldn't help him on, because they were concentrating and holding on themselves.

"Draw the Line" by Aerosmith came on. Knew what I had to do, and it was less scary with my boys in my ears. Did my best to plant my left foot and put my right onto the rig. Raj ran over and did the same on the other side of the doorway. We helped the old ayatollah to do the jump.

"Walk straight ahead," I told him. "Don't hesitate, head for the back railing."

"But there is nothing there."

Said the only thing I figured would work. "Have faith in God."

He nodded, then stepped forward as requested. He did the slow fade. Looked to help the next person, but everyone was hanging back. "Chop, chop, folks," I shouted. "Time's a wastin'. Movin', movin', movin', let's keep all you doggies moving. Like right now. Move 'em out, head 'em up, cut 'em out, ride 'em in, Rawhide. Keep the line moving *quickly*, people, you're the first set we're getting out. There are hundreds of people waiting. Move 'em *out*, Rawhide."

The *Rawhide* theme seemed to resonate for whatever reason. It earned a few chuckles, which somehow turned to laughter. Suddenly we were a fun party experience instead of a Terror Trip to Death. Whatever worked.

Was thankful Raj was here to help, because it was hard to keep my balance. The rig moved every time someone stepped on it and both Raj and I had to regroup more than once. Algar did me a solid and kept up a stream of Aerosmith, treating me to "Walking the Dog," "Walk This Way," "Get the Lead Out," and the "Dulcimer Stomp/The Other Side" combo. But finally all from that dome were through the floater, including the Lyssara.

White had gotten through to his group, which included Mr. Joel Oliver. "Good to see you, Madame First Lady," he said as he led his group over and White took my place.

"Good to be seen, MJO. I'd ask what the hell's going on, but I figure we don't have the time."

"Indeed." He smiled at me and then stepped through the gate. The rest of his dome fell into line. Noted that there were what looked like restaurant staff in this group, too. My music changed to David Bowie's "All The Young Dudes" and I got the hint. Time to move it.

Put my gas mask back on. "Remember, everyone out, even A-Cs. No one gets to hang out and try to help at this time. Abby, I need out of the shield!" Left Raj and White as soon as I saw an opening in the shield. Ran through and went to find another dome.

Found the one with Siler outside of it. "No one will open up to me," he said, sounding understandably pissed.

"Yeah, they're freaked. Go see if you can figure out who's who and get Jeff and Chuckie to safety." He nodded and went off and I knocked on the dome. "This is the First Lady. Open up, we're trying to rescue you and it's hard to do if you won't let us." Nothing. Knocked again. "Gang, seriously, time's wasting." Nada.

Had to figure there wasn't someone on my team in this dome. Decided they could wait for later, especially when "Next In Line" by Meese came on my airwaves. Left to search for another dome.

Found one after too much staggering around in the dust and far too much Themnir Poop Avoidance. Had to give the dust storm idea this—if Cliff or his team were watching, they wouldn't be able to see what was going on.

Knocked on this dome as "Slow Motion" by Lifehouse lit up my musical life while simultaneously sharing that Algar wanted us all to speed up. Managed not to mention aloud that I was moving as fast as I could, I wasn't the holdup, and if he was that impatient he could come down here and help. "First Lady Rescue Services. Open up, we're really behind schedule on this rescue mission."

Another peephole opened up. The Lyssara had some cool skills. "Identify yourself."

Excellent. Knew this voice, too. "Manfred, it's me, saving you yet again from a container you find yourself in."

The dome lifted. "Kitty?"

The shield tunnel surrounded us. Took off the gas mask. "Yes. Let's hoof it, gang. This is taking too long and I still have a lot of people left to rescue."

Manfred and I hustled everyone over to the window. His group seemed far happier to be moving quickly. Manfred spelled Raj with the Extreme Sports Straddling Competition, White gave Raj his gas mask, and the two of us headed off for the dome that wouldn't open up for me, Elton John's "Whenever You're Ready (We'll Go Steady Again)" providing this section of my theme music and proving that Algar, like ACE, was definitely willing to listen to my thoughts along with my words.

Raj managed to convince them he wasn't a bad guy, presumably because the Lyssara who was creating the dome recognized him, since the dome lifted without a peephole experience. Had Raj lead them and jumped away just before the shield tunnel started.

Found the last dome and did the knock and identify thing as "Agent Green" by Megadeth came on. The peephole opened and, thanks to the music, I was prepared for who was behind the dome this time—Evalyne, whose last name was Green and who asked for identification. "Aren't you glad that I don't ever listen to you guys? I mean, right now, not all the time."

"It's her," Evalyne said. The dome lifted and she grabbed me. "Jeff and Charles are in danger."

"Everyone's in danger." The shield tunnel arrived, I took off the gas mask, and we headed everyone toward the window.

"No, I mean they were singled out specifically to not die here with the rest of us. Some people in gas masks just like yours came in with guns. They killed the camera crew and took their equipment. Then they demanded Jeff and Charles, who went with them to avoid more bloodshed. But before they could leave, more people in gas masks came in and they all started fighting."

"Fantastic." Hadn't noted nor stumbled upon the dead camera team. More dead people caught in Cliff's crossfire. Realized I hadn't been really angry yet, just focused, but the murder of innocents seemed to get the old Rage embers sparking. We stopped near to the window and ushered everyone ahead of us. Phoebe nodded to us and took over leading the others.

"While that was happening, we got a voiceover from Cliff Goodman, sharing that we were all idiots and going to die a horrific death so that he could take over the world. He even cackled. Several times. He released phosgene, which is the deadliest gas in existence."

"Good lord."

"Yeah. We'd all be dead if not for the Themnir and Lyssara."

"Um, as to that—can you explain why we have Themnir poop all over?"

"Yes. They can absorb any gas through their skins and then excrete it into pellets that are coated so they contain the gas and are nontoxic as long as they aren't breached."

"So, no stepping on Themnir poop, I was already doing that, well done me. I'm going to assume that Siler is as careful because he's never struck me as a step-in-poop-indiscriminately kind of guy. How do the Themnir not suck up oxygen?"

"Well, it's how they breathe as well, so they bring in the good gasses and bad gasses at the same time, then their bodies separate the good, which goes to their lungs or whatever, and the bad, which goes to their alimentary tract or whatever they have. Their planet is very gaseous as well as lush."

"Amazing. And thank God Jeff chose to bring them along to this. Does Cliff know what's going on?"

"I think so—the dust didn't start until you arrived. And he was yelling at us for hiding from him. The Lyssara create those honeycomb shelters to protect themselves and their young from various predatory attacks and natural disasters. So, even if we hadn't had the Themnir, the Lyssara felt their combs would have kept the poisons out."

"Wow, go Team New Aliens."

"Yes. The combs don't protect against the Aicirtap." Evalyne shuddered. "There are three more spaceship Combs on the way. And those contain the last of the Lyssara."

"Fantastic. Well, at least, after this, I think they'll be welcomed here. You know, if we survive the Aicirtap and all that jazz. By the way, is it just me, or do you think Cliff is getting all his career advice from watching *Pinky and the Brain*, too? I mean that seriously—his plans are baroque and, quite frankly, seem to have been created by a crazed laboratory mouse."

Algar apparently agreed with my take on Cliff, as he treated me to the *Pinky and the Brain* theme song. Wondered if he was going to give me more theme songs. Wasn't like I had all of them ever written. Just the ones I liked. Which were a lot, as I thought of it. Chose to focus on the moment. Seemed like a wiser choice for my own personal sanity.

Evalyne laughed and hugged me. "I love working for you, even though most of the time you do my job for me."

"Yeah? Let's see how you feel about it when you get to make the window washing rig leap." It was Evalyne's turn to go.

"Remember that he'll have a backup plan," she said as she took Manfred's hand. "I have no idea what it is, Cliff didn't say anything about it, but if he wants Jeff and Charles, then he has something else planned." She swallowed. "We couldn't protect the President. He wouldn't let us."

"I know. Go back to calling him Jeff. Not because you're fired or anything, but because that's the better way to think of him. Because there's never going to be a time when he's going to say that his life is more important than yours. I won't say that, either."

She kissed my cheek. "That's why we're all willing to take the bullets for you two, though. Not just because it's our jobs. But because we all know you both mean that." White took her other hand and they sent her through the gate.

"We have the five Themnir still to rescue, so to speak, dead civilians somewhere whose bodies I want to get out of here, and I think we still have a fight going on that centers on Jeff and Chuckie. Mahin, I think you can stop the dust storm, but Abby, be ready with the shield. Manfred, Raj, Mister White, with me. Avoid stepping on Themnir poop, it's storing all the bad gas."

With that I turned and headed back to get my men, with the theme song from *The A-Team* playing.

CHAPTER 77

WHITE, RAJ, AND MANFRED were right behind me. With the dust settling it was a lot easier to see. The domes were all on their sides, and the Themnir were heading for the window and away from the fighting that was still somehow going on. Well, whoever was fighting was dealing with at least one A-C in the form of Jeff, so that explained why I could still see him and Chuckie.

Didn't see Siler anywhere, so either he'd taken off for some reason or he was blending.

"There is no more poisonous gas that we can detect," one of the Themnir said to Raj.

Didn't think about it, because if I did I might not do it. Threw my arms around its neck and hugged it. "Thank you for saving everyone." It was kind of slimy but not horrifically so. Hugged the other four Themnir, too.

"We were happy to be able to be of service in this way," the first Themnir said.

"Raj, Manfred, get them through the gates." It was likely going to take two A-Cs to move the Themnir—they were quite large and hella slow. "Once the Themnir are through, you two go as well."

"But you need help," Manfred protested.

"I need to know that the Chief of Staff is safely out of this. We still have a country and world to keep running. I have Mister White and the girls. I'm good."

White and I took off. He'd grabbed the rolling purse. "Are you thinking what I'm thinking, Mister White?"

"I think so, Missus Martini. But I do fear that we'll hit the wrong people."

"Look for band t-shirts, because everyone on our team is in one. If you can't tell, knock them all out and let the removal of gas masks sort 'em out."

We slammed into the mass of fighting, gas-masked people as Joe Jackson's "Look Sharp!" came on. Our gas masks were off and attached to our belts again, so we were easily identified. Meaning that Claudia and Lorraine didn't try to hit us and instead pulled their masks off so we could see it was them.

Them doing that meant that Reader and Tim pulled their masks off too. Sadly, the people who had Jeff and Chuckie were still wearing their masks, though Jeff and Chuckie managed to get theirs off as they spotted us. White and I waded into the fray, White wielding the rolling bag like a very mobile, large, and effective mace.

But there were easily twenty who had Jeff and Chuckie. Jeff looked tired, and Chuckie looked like he'd gotten hit a lot where it didn't show. And for every one that White or the rest of us knocked away, two more blocked us.

"Break off!" one of them shouted. The original language wasn't English, and I could tell, but beyond that, I didn't have a clue. Needed to learn more about how the Universal Translator worked. In the downtime. Whenever that might show up.

The larger group of thugs started dragging Jeff and Chuckie toward the stairwell. Chuckie managed a kick that knocked one of the people holding Jeff loose. White and I slammed through the thugs nearest to him and managed to reach Jeff. I pulled him away as hard as possible and we sort of flew out of the huddle. White was still slamming people with the bag, but they were blocking him from Chuckie.

"Thanks, baby," Jeff said as we landed and spun around to head back.

My music changed to "Duck and Run" by 3 Doors Down as the thugs produced guns and they started shooting at everyone. Grabbed Jeff and pulled him down. Bullets flew over our heads.

"Run for the window," White shouted, as he grabbed Tim and followed his own advice at hyperspeed. Lorraine grabbed Reader and did likewise. "Get through the gate!" White called to Mahin and Abigail.

Claudia was still trying to get to Chuckie. "Get out of here," Chuckie yelled at her. Right before one of the thugs slammed the butt of his gun against the back of Chuckie's head.

"GO!" Jeff bellowed at her as he and I leaped out of the way of more bullets. Jeff shoved me into one of the Lyssara domes, ran over, grabbed Claudia, and ran her to the window.

Meanwhile, did my best to get to Chuckie, who was definitely unconscious based on how hard that hit had looked and how his head was lolling. But someone grabbed me and flung me around a wall, just as bullets hit the air where I'd been.

"You don't like to listen to your husband much, do you?" Siler asked as he unblended. Him grabbing me had happened so fast I hadn't felt the tingling.

"They're going to kill Chuckie!"

"Not yet." Siler wasn't letting go of me. He looked around. "Really?" He shoved me farther away and ran out. He and Jeff were back quickly. Happily, neither one appeared to be shot. "You both have a serious death wish. Do you actually *want* your children to be raised by others?"

"My parents did a great job with me, so I'm not worried. But I do see your point, Nightcrawler. Jeff, are you okay?"

He pulled me to him and hugged me tightly, hearts pounding. "Yeah, baby, I'm okay, all things considered. I have no idea where they're taking Chuck, though."

"We need to rescue the rest of the rescue team first," Siler said. "Which includes your cousin."

White joined us. "The gunmen have all left. We have a cleanup team coming," he shared as a bunch of people in hazmat suits arrived. "They're taking the Themnir excrement and any dead bodies. The moment they're done, the gate is going to be gone."

"I'd love to tell all three of you to go and let me handle it," Siler said, "but I know what you'll say, so I'll save my breath."

"We need to get up to the floor where Christopher went dark, is what I'm saying. And I'm sure I speak for Jeff and Mister White, too."

"You do," White said. He grabbed Jeff and hugged him. "It's good to see you still alive and well, Jeffrey."

"Thanks, Uncle Richard, and I'll say the same for you, too," Jeff said as he hugged him back tightly. "All of you." He reached out and pulled me and Siler into the group hug. I was used to this, but I could tell it still sort of surprised Siler. But he went with it and hugged back.

"We need to get upstairs fast," I said once we broke up the group hug. "And we can't use the elevators."

"I have plenty of 'juice' left, Missus Martini."

"So do I," Siler said. "Mostly because I gave up trying to get into the fight and checked our exit options instead. There are G-Company troops in the stairwell going down, and I assume it's more G-Company thugs who have Reynolds."

"They fought really well," Jeff said. "As in, I couldn't get them off of us, and normally I don't have trouble with humans who aren't Centaurion trained."

"There were a lot of them, and I think they were using some sort of tech that made them stronger because I gave up due to not being able to make a dent, which I'm not used to. Kitty's right to not trust the elevators, I think they're shut down."

"Per Raj they are, yeah. And I think if they're off, then it's Cliff's side doing it. I don't want us stuck in a metal box that can plummet us to our messy deaths, call me crazy." On cue, Patsy Cline started crooning "Crazy." Algar was enjoying this entire raid far too much.

The last person in a hazmat suit came near. "We're leaving now. Are you sure you don't want to come with us, Mister President?"

"I'm positive, yes," Jeff said.

Watched the hazmat team leave. Reader and Tim stepped through just before the floater stopped shimmering.

"What are you guys doing here?" I asked.

"Our jobs," Reader said flatly. "In case you've forgotten what your jobs happen to be these days, which I'm really clear that you have."

"Claudia and Lorraine are handling things at Dulce," Tim said. "We came back to help you. Forgive us, we just can't help ourselves. It's in the job descriptions—help Jeff and Kitty even when they insist they can do it all themselves."

"Oh, it's always nice to see you two, stop whining."

"Also, Dulce shares that there was nothing in the rubber cobra, but that there was indeed a little note in the fake bomb," Tim continued. "It said 'Kill you soon, see you sooner.'"

"Really? That was it?"

Tim shrugged. "Cliff's insane, Kitty. I mean really and truly over the edge. It's no less stupid than putting children's toys into your suitcase as an opening salvo."

"True dat."

"I've checked in with Camilla," Reader said, ignoring me and Tim. "All's well at the palace, everyone remains safe, but no word from anyone still missing."

"What about Rahmi? Where is she?"

"I have no idea." Reader looked worried. "She came in with us. We hit G-Company thugs in the stairwell, but we were able to get through them easily enough. In fact, Rahmi slammed her staff through all of them, in the heart or head, depending, because she said she was following your rules and making sure they were really most sincerely dead."

"I'm so proud."

"Uh, yeah, that's one emotion that you could choose in that instance. I went with relief that she's no longer hating men you consider on your side and calling it good. But once we got into the restaurant and the fighting started I could barely keep track of who was who. The gas masks really make you anonymous."

"That's it." Everyone looked at me. Heaved a sigh. "She shifted to look like one of the thugs. She's going with them to protect Chuckie. She's the only one who has a shot at it, too, at least right now."

"I hope you're right," Jeff said. "Because I know whatever Cliff has planned for Chuck is going to redefine horrific."

"Then let's get the rest of the team here and get to finding where Cliff's hiding out."

"You don't think he's here, in the tower somewhere?" Siler asked as we headed for the stairwell.

My music changed to "God We Look Good (Going Down In Flames)" by The Exies. "Nope. There's always a risk of the poisonous gas getting into the general ventilation system. Cliff doesn't care who he kills, but he's attached to staying alive." Had a thought spurred by the musical choice. "Mister White, the Bag of Bigness, please and thank you."

White opened it up. I took out all the extra semiautomatics. Ensured they were all ready to go with the safeties off. Put two in my back pockets, kept the third in my hand, then opened the stairwell door going down at hyperspeed. Verified that everyone in it, and there were a lot of men there, were all carrying weapons and all looked like bad mofos. Sprayed bullets out of the first gun while I pulled the second and started the same with it. Emptied one clip, dropped the empty gun, grabbed the last pistol. Continued shooting until I was out of ammo. No one in the stairwell was upright any longer.

"Nightcrawler, if you would?"

He nodded and went invisible. Every head got a direct shot, including when he had to move bodies. He had to reload three times, which included him having a shootout with the couple of people I'd missed due to them hiding. Then he was back. "Good call."

"Yeah, hopefully none of them were good guys."

"They weren't. They all had G-Company tattoos visible."

"Great, my conscience is clear." Opened the door going up as my music changed to No Doubt's "The Climb."

Lots of dead bodies to wade through, which we did, while Reader called someone and requested dead body removal for both stairwells. Told him to have teams verify that everyone else in the Burj Khalifa was alive and not poisoned or shot to death or something and also requested a cleaning and repair crew for the observatory deck.

Once we were past the stairway morgue we were able to move at hyperspeed. Jeff took me, White had Reader, Siler took Tim, and we all headed up thirty-six freaking floors. Fortunately, my sadistic track coaches in both high school and college had adored making their teams do stair charges on a daily basis, so doing this was no big deal, since my career with Centaurion had ensured that I kept all my track and kung fu skills at optimum.

The positive was that we were all able to update each other in the time it took, because hyperspeed didn't make running up this many stairs easy, just faster. And Jeff was close to drained, so we weren't going all that fast, and I was providing most of our hyperspeed.

"Remember," White said as we neared our destination, "we're looking for Jeremy, Malcolm, and Colonel Butler as well as Christopher."

We hit a problem in the stairwell between Floors 158 and 159 in the form of two things, one of which was my music changing to "Just Stop" by Disturbed. Came to a screeching halt and made the others do so, too. "Something's wrong."

"What?" Jeff asked. "There's no one and nothing here."

"Right. That's the problem." Remembered the schematic that my goggles had shared with me while they were still working. "This section, floors one-fifty-six through one-fifty-nine, are communications and broadcasting. Christopher went dark when he hit one-fifty-nine. Meaning there was no one lying in wait for him between one-fifty-six and here."

"So?" Jeff asked patiently.

"So, there were a million G-Company thugs hanging out in the stairwells above and below the restaurant, lying in wait to catch anyone who might manage to escape and anyone who might be coming to rescue those trapped inside. The bad guys took Chuckie, and even if they took the elevator down instead of the stairs, no one called off the guys lying in wait. Ergo, if there were any here, they weren't called off, either."

"Maybe Christopher got rid of all of them," Reader suggested. "I couldn't answer Ben when he tried to reach me because we were engaged with the enemy." Hadn't heard anyone call Siler anything other than Benjamin, Siler, or Nightcrawler, if it was me. But Siler didn't act like this nickname was an unpleasant or even pleasant shock, and he didn't do the usual A-C Wincing At A Nickname thing, either. Interesting. Chose not to ask how often he was helping out Alpha Team these days, but it probably bore some research later.

"Christopher did not get rid of anyone, because not only are there no bodies left in the stairwells, but if he had he'd have then tried to reach his father to reassure said father that his only child was alive, well, and victorious. At that point, we'd destroyed our equipment. Meaning Christopher would have come down to find us and make sure his father was okay. He didn't come down and he's had plenty of time to do so. Therefore, he's captured." Or dead. Chose not to say that aloud because I refused to believe it.

"I agree with my partner," White said. "Caution needs to be our watchword, as rare a watchword as it is for us."

"Yeah, slow and steady, emphasis on slow. And weapons out, too. Figure we're going to have to shoot someone soon."

"Haven't you shot enough people tonight?" Jeff asked. "I mean that seriously."

"Are Cliff and the remaining Crazy Eights still alive? Yes? Then, no, I have not killed enough people yet."

We reached the doorway and Siler grabbed my shoulder just as my music changed to "Electric Worry" by Clutch. "Don't take another step and don't touch the door handle. Anyone."

"Okey dokey. Why not?"

"I think the handle's wired and, if I'm right, it's wired to send enough current through it to stop someone's breathing, if not kill them."

CHAPTER 78

"HYPERSPEED WOULDN'T AVOID the threat," Tim said. "You still have to make contact with the door to open it, no matter how fast you're doing it."

"Figure the voltage and current both are high to account for A-C speed," Siler said.

"A-Cs recover fast, so I'm betting Christopher's still alive. But that means he's definitely a prisoner." And we had to open the door without getting knocked out or killed ourselves. "So, we need to either disconnect the electric feed or use a form of insulation between our hand and the door handle."

"I don't think we can disconnect from this side," Siler said. "At least, not without risking getting hit with the current or being discovered."

"Insulating materials it is, then."

White moved me and Jeff back. "Three of us are still wearing gloves. I also have no rings on. Benjamin doesn't either, but his skills are more vital right now." Jeff opened his mouth to argue, but White shot him a very parental "because I said so" look. "He's my son, Jeffrey. And yes, I understand the risks."

"Make sure the insulation on your gloves wasn't stripped off when you rescued me."

White did the check. "Ah, good call, Missus Martini."

Siler took his gloves off and gave them to White, who pulled this pair on over the ones he already had on. Super strength was helpful here, because the gloves did not actually fit well this way. But they were finally on. "Silent entry, and speak softly once inside," Siler warned us all.

White handed Jeff the rolling bag, took a deep breath, let it out, then moved at hyperspeed and opened the door.

That there was indeed electrical current flowing was evident from the sparks that flew off the handle. But White didn't go down.

The rest of us ran through the door, Siler grabbing White on his way in. Thankfully, White's hand released from the doorknob.

We'd entered what really looked like what you'd expect a broadcast studio to resemble. Algar shared the theme from *WKRP in Cincinnati* with me. Started to wonder if he was feeling alright. "Feel Fine" by Augustana came on. Okay, he was just entertaining himself at my expense, so, business as usual for me and the King of the Elves.

This place was more filled with things than the other floors we'd hit, too. Lots of walls, desks, equipment I knew nothing about, the usual stuff I'd expect to see that might or might not be something a real broadcaster used but that every TV show or movie insinuated was part of a studio setup.

This particular studio was packing special extras—it came complete with dead bodies of the people I assumed had been working in here.

What didn't belong here were buckets of water. They were strewn everywhere that I could see. Not that I could see that much. As with so many places, this was a maze. On the plus side, the higher we got, the less floor space there was to cover, so we had that going for us.

"Everyone be on alert," I said softly, as White massaged his hand. "Nerida the Water Bender is up here." Meaning she was around to drown or electrocute anyone who made it through the door. Really tried not to worry about Christopher and the guys who'd come to check on him, but found it hard to do.

Siler checked the bodies. "No entry wounds, but signs of electrocution, so Kitty's right and we're in a hell of a lot of danger." Considering this was the first time since we'd entered the Burj Khalifa that Siler had expressed serious concern, felt myself get a tad tense.

Considered what our options were while The Eagles' "Take It to the Limit" came on. "Let me lead."

"Not just no, but hell no," Jeff said, optimistically using the growly man voice, which worked on me as it always did when we weren't in bed, which was not at all. At least he growled it quietly.

"I have no idea who else is here, but I can guarantee that

Nerida is, and I can also guarantee that she thinks she can beat me and wants a chance to prove it."

"She can beat you by electrocuting you," Tim pointed out.

"She lost to you on the train," White additionally pointed out.

"Not in *her* mind. In her mind I guarantee that fight was a draw. And she wants to *beat* me. As in, she wants to win and have me know she's won. That requires more than just shooting someone dead. Which means we'll all have more time if she sees me first than if she sees any of you first." They didn't look convinced. Went for an explanation that might get through. "She was pals with Stephanie as far as I could tell."

Siler nodded. "Yes, they were friendly." He sighed. "I think Kitty may be right."

"My wife is not going to be our shield," Jeff snarled. He was still keeping quiet but had to figure bellowing was on the horizon.

Heaved a sigh of my own. "Jeff, what do you think I was doing while you were at the restaurant? Hanging out getting a pedicure?"

"That was when I wasn't with you." He looked worried, upset, and protective, meaning I couldn't be mad at him for trying to throw himself in front of me.

"At least you're cute when the caveman comes out. A lot of people are depending on us right now, not the least of which being your cousin and my best friend. You can accept that we're going to do things in the way that gives us the best chance of success or survival, or I will have Nightcrawler do to you what I did to you when we first met and you were being a fatalistic jerk."

Jeff winced. "I don't need my head bashed, thanks."

"Good to know, Mister President. Don't make me regret letting you come along."

"I'd complain that I'm henpecked, but then I'd have to feel everyone laughing at me. And I can feel that all of you think Kitty's right." He jerked. "Huh. My blocks were on the highest level I could manage because of what was going on. I shouldn't be able to feel anyone, not even Kitty."

"Did you take your blocks down and forget?" Reader asked worriedly.

"No . . ." Jeff concentrated. "My blocks are still up. But I can . . . feel? But it's different. It's sort of muted. Like . . . like watching a mixed martial arts fight on TV versus watching it ringside, or being involved in the fight."

"Why ask why? Take the help as it comes. Who else can you feel here and where are they?"

"So now I get to lead?" Jeff's sarcasm knob was turned to about seven.

"No. You get to tell me where I'm going."

"Jeff, we're running out of time," Reader said, Commander Voice on Full. "Do what Kitty wants."

Jeff shot him a betrayed look. "Fine." He was concentrating again and he nodded. "I feel Christopher. He's angry and worried. But not about himself. He's worried about . . . Butler?"

"John is an android. Nerida dousing him with water could be a bad thing and getting zapped with electricity could be worse. Plus, Kozlow is probably up here, too, affecting what he can, and out of all of us, he has the best shot of hurting John."

"I have someone who feels very self-satisfied and anticipatory. Pretty sure it's a woman."

"Pretty sure it's Nerida. Where is she?"

"Near Christopher. There's also someone who feels bored, a little worried, and a lot jealous."

"That's certainly an emotion you'd know. What's he jealous of?"

"Ha ha ha, this is me laughing at your attempt to keep things light. He's jealous of the woman's abilities, Christopher's abilities, others' abilities. And he's really uncomfortable being here. Not here in this building, but here in this region. He's resentful for having to be here at all."

"That's Kozlow, for certain. He's probably worried that Mossad will find him again."

"Do you feel Malcolm or Jeremy?" White asked as Olivia Newton-John singing "Suspended in Time" came on. Algar was focused way more than normal on the easy listening selections right now. Possibly to keep me moving cautiously.

"No, but . . ." Jeff cocked his head. "He's waiting. But for what? Or whom?" He looked at me. "Oh. Yeah, baby, I think you need to lead."

"Who's waiting for me to make my move?"

"Mossy. He's here somewhere watching. He's ready to kill but not in an angry way. He's a soldier and he's identified his targets. But he hasn't killed them yet and I can't tell why."

"That's all you feel?" Siler asked, sounding worried. "Two people in addition to Christopher and Mossy?"

"Yeah, I don't feel Butler and he's a well-made android, one of Marling's, and he has emotions, so I can pick him up. And I don't. I don't feel Buchanan or Jeremy, either."

Refused to say that this could be because all of them were dead. Forced myself to focus on what I could do, which was kill Nerida and Kozlow as fast as possible. "Okay, no hyperspeed unless we're running away and running in a direction we've already confirmed as safe. One electrical booby trap merely indicates others are likely. Stay low, and everyone please look for traps."

"Spotting them is definitely not her strong suit," White said as he took the rolling purse back from Jeff. Was about ninety-nine percent positive White knew it was an Algar Portal and was ensuring that he or I had it under our control at all times.

"I'd be offended but it's true."

"Keep an eye out for cameras, obvious and hidden," Siler said. "If they're watching us coming then we don't have the element of surprise. They may already know someone's in here, so expect ambush, too."

"I don't get anything like that from either one of them," Jeff said. "But the emotions are coming through to me in such an odd way I can't be sure what I'm getting is accurate."

"Well, then we'll do what we always do—wing it until it works. So, lead on MacDuff. Hand signals from here on in unless we have to speak or one of us dies."

Jeff rolled his eyes. "Thanks for that." But he took my hand and gave it a squeeze. "Ready for silent running, baby."

I did go first, with Jeff pointing the way. We all stayed low, and everyone kept a wary eye out for traps. Neither found nor tripped any. Either no one had been expected to get through that doorway, they were hugely overconfident, or we were expected. Or all three.

This area was nice and state of the art and all that, but it wasn't nearly as sleek and beautiful as the other floors we'd seen and sort of messed up. Really hoped White was right and that the A-Cs could fix what had gotten wrecked fast.

This floor was another thick arrowhead shape, though less elongated than the observation deck level. Weaved in, out, and around the walls, furnishings, and office rubble to finally get to the section of this floor that was at the arrowhead's point. And it was here, as No Doubt's "Suspension Without Suspense" hit my airwaves, that we found the only people alive on this floor.

On the plus side, everyone we were looking for was here.

On the negative side, only one of those people was standing.

CHAPTER 79

ON THE PLUS SIDE AGAIN, Butler, Buchanan, and Jeremy were all present. They were each prone, sort of floating a few inches off the floor. They were all also surrounded by a faint, hazy glow.

Took Algar's musical clues to indicate that they were in some form of suspended animation because, on the negative side again, I couldn't tell if they were breathing or not.

Christopher was breathing. He was also standing with his legs spread apart, each foot and lower leg in a bucket of water. His arms were spread apart and tied to a very large circuit board. His neck was tied to it, too.

Based on the way we'd slunk into this area, Christopher was directly in front of me. A somewhat swarthy, Slavic-looking man was sitting at a desk to my right and Christopher's left. He had his feet up on the desk, was leaning back in his chair, and looked hella bored. I'd seen him plenty of times and fought with him more than once—I'd been right: this was Russell Kozlow. Remembered that I hadn't called Chernobog. Decided I'd worry about that later.

A woman was on the other side of Christopher, in profile to me. But I recognized her insipid nastiness. Definitely Nerida Alfero. Super, this part of the gang was all here.

Kozlow was playing with something in his hand. Had a feeling it was a kill switch, either tied to the circuit board or to the men in suspended animation, or both, which would explain why Mossy wasn't making a move, wherever he happened to be observing this from.

We still hadn't been spotted and to everyone's credit, we all stayed low and silent. Did my best to assess the scene. Got nothing, other than the feeling that Kozlow and Nerida were waiting for something. Us, probably.

Made the "stay put" hand signal that hopefully was clear to the guys. Then I stood up.

"Interesting setup," I said as I walked fully into this section. "I'd like to request "(Don't Fear) The Reaper" by Blue Öyster Cult. If you're cool enough to have that tune, I mean."

Kozlow shot me the "really?" look. Nerida went for derisive. "As if we'd give you anything you want?" Yeah, she said it derisively, too.

This was fine with me. I needed my rage going, and someone being a jerk while holding my friends hostage was a big help. Looked around the room. My Glock was in my hand and I was prepped for a sneak attack. Didn't see where Mossy might be. Also didn't spot the guys with me. Hoped that meant Nerida and Kozlow hadn't spotted them, either.

"So, let me get this straight. While other people are taking hostages and killing people, you two are just up here playing around?" Started to wander the room. Neither one of them tried to stop me. Made sure I walked slowly and looked where I was going as well as all around.

"Maybe you haven't noticed who we have here," Nerida said. My music changed to "Floaty" by the Foo Fighters.

Shrugged. "I noticed, yeah. Hey, Christopher. Wondered why you hadn't come down. I see you were all tied up."

This earned me Patented Glare #1. Good to see he was feeling okay.

"How did you get through the door?" Kozlow asked. He wasn't asking in a derisive or bored way. He sounded interested.

Waved my free hand—I was still wearing my gloves. "Insulation's an amazing thing. So, what's the plan for you guys up here? I mean, I assume you were the ones ensuring that Cliff's latest Crazed Madman Speech was broadcast downstairs and such, but it seems sort of weird to have you two sequestered up here by yourselves."

"There were reasons," Nerida said imperiously.

Couldn't think of what they might be. My music changed to "Open the Gate" by No Doubt. Put two and two together. "You're controlling access in and out of the building, aren't you?"

Kozlow nodded. Nerida shrugged. "Maybe we are. Maybe we aren't."

Needed a full answer, because if they were controlling Cliff's floater gate ability, I needed to know how and where and all the other pertinent details. But had no clear idea how to get this out of them without seeming to care about getting it out of them.

My music changed to "Sex and Death" by Motörhead. Chose to take this as a hint. "Oh, wait! Are you two a couple?"

Nerida made the "gag me" face. Kozlow glared at her. Not up to Christopher's standards, but then none were. "Never in a million years," Nerida said, making the "gag me" sound to emphasize her disgust with my suggestion. "We're siblings, remember?"

"Half-siblings, I think. Not that I'm a proponent of any form of incest." Didn't think Kozlow was interested in Nerida, but it was clear that she wasn't just doing the gagging thing because of the familial relationship, and it was also clear that his feelings were hurt by this. "So, why are you up here then, if it wasn't for nookie?"

"You're so focused on sex," Nerida sneered at me.

"Probably because I get to have it all the time."

"I've heard that those who talk about it the most do it the least." Nerida wasn't going to win the Comeback Award with replies like that.

Was between her and Christopher now, so able to look at the equipment. They had a lot of screens they were supposedly keeping an eye on. And none of them showed the stairwells.

This seemed patently ridiculous. Although, as I thought of it, not every high rise had cameras in the stairwells. Some did, but not all. Though I'd expect them in a building as massive and state of the art as this one. Then again, hadn't seen any on the way up and was pretty darned sure that Siler had been looking for them, even if none of the rest of us had thought of it.

So, no stairwell cameras made the electric current running through the door handle more logical. It wasn't there to just stop us—it was there to stop anyone. Maybe that's how all those people we'd found near the entrance had died, by coming into the room. We certainly hadn't found any bodies once we'd moved further into the floor.

"We're running communications," Kozlow answered. "The boss wanted someone he could trust up here."

The other screens weren't showing anything of interest. The restaurant in particular. The observation deck in other particular. The observation deck looked pristine and the restaurant still looked like it was filled with dust. I only knew it was the restaurant because I could just make out a Lyssara dome in there.

However, they also had a screen that showed the entry door from the stairwell. But they weren't acting like they thought anyone else was with me. Looked at the picture more carefully. The bodies looked as they had when we'd come into the room. But Siler had moved some of them, rolling the bodies onto their backs, in order to examine them. And he hadn't moved them back.

Realized what Mossy was likely doing in his spare time—altering the feeds so that the two up here weren't alerted to anything untoward elsewhere in the building. And he wasn't making a move because of the kill switch Kozlow had.

"Um, and so he picked Nerida? No offense," I said to her sweetly. Then turned back to Kozlow. "You, I get. Her? Other than planning to short out the entire building and possibly cause it to collapse, I'm not sure why Nerida is even up here."

Kozlow shot me the nicest look I'd ever seen from him. "I know. I told them her up here is a bad idea, but . . ." He shrugged.

"Yeah, no one listens until it's too late, right? Always the way. But seriously, I get the threat with Christopher, I mean it's obvious. But if he electrocutes, especially with what you have him attached to, I sincerely think you'll take out everything in this building. I don't know how you'd work access in or out if this place went down electronically. And I doubt Gadhavi would appreciate that. He has a lot of money invested in this place."

It was a long shot, but Kozlow nodded again, with more emphasis, and put his feet onto the floor. "Exactly! We're finally someplace safe and he wants to wreck it all." Knew the "he" Kozlow meant was Cliff.

"I didn't think you'd want to be in this region if you could help it."

He shrugged. "Yeah, not my preferred location. But you go where the work is."

"Why are you telling her anything?" Nerida sounded annoyed. "And we go where the boss says we go. Stop acting as if you have any other options."

Kozlow's eyes narrowed. "Mister Gadhavi would be happy to have me in his organization. With or without the rest of you."

Of this I had no doubt. Noted that the three guys in suspended animation had bobbed a little closer to the floor. Meaning, I was pretty sure, that Kozlow was the one controlling that. My music changed to "Give Thanks and Praises" by the Bad Brains.

This helped my mind give me a big nudge. Cliff thought he was all that and an extra-large bag of chips. LaRue and Reid were pretty damn full of themselves, too. Stephanie was in a class by herself in terms of hubris. Lowe and Kellogg, may they rest in eternal damnation, had been impressed with themselves as well. Casey was a supercilious bitch.

Meaning Kozlow was surrounded by people who were busy congratulating themselves about how awesome they were. He'd been in prison in Israel before he'd been released. With help from Mahin and a bunch of other people. Because he wasn't able to escape on his own. Took a wild one that the others weren't big on letting him forget that. Took another wild one and assumed that Cliff was spending his time ranting and preening and not giving his loyal soldiers any feelings of being necessary or important.

"I agree with Russell," I said conversationally as I did the lean and sit on the edge of the desk thing, meaning I looked casual but I was still on my feet and could push off with my butt if necessary. "I mean, whatever you're doing with my friends is pretty impressive. I'm sure G-Company would have uses for it."

"Yeah? It's not as easy to do as it looks," he said rather proudly.

Nerida snorted. "It's nothing. You can't even kill anyone with what you can do."

Rolled my eyes. "I'm sure you're not impressed with anything unless it's you doing it." Smiled at Kozlow, who snorted a laugh. "And just because something can't kill doesn't mean it's not awesome." This earned me a Happy Puppy look. "However, I honestly have no idea what you've done to them, and I've seen a lot of things."

"It's a form of suspended animation," he shared proudly. "They're surrounded by an electromagnetic field that essentially freezes them. They aren't dead, though," he added quickly, presumably in case that would make me unhappy with him. Which it would, so he was clearly smarter than Nerida. Not that this was a high bar.

"How can you control it and talk to me at the same time?" Ensured I sounded impressed.

"It's my talent," he said, almost shyly. "I have limited control of electromagnetic fields, and I can create them, too." He nodded at all the equipment. "Me being up here makes sense because I can draw power from the equipment."

"Wow, a lot of power?"

He shrugged. "Enough for what we need. That's why it's not difficult for me to have them suspended."

"How did you know they'd come here? What made you realize one of us might come up here?" Made sure to sound like I thought it was all Kozlow's idea.

"It seemed logical," he said. "And that way we'd have prisoners if needed."

"Because they're bait," Nerida said, in an Aha! Voice.

"No kidding." Turned and stared at her. "Bait for whom? Besides me, I mean?"

She seemed thrown. "Uh, for . . . whoever else is looking for them." She tried to stare back. She wasn't very good at it. Lots of blinking.

"I'm the only one. Whee. You've caught me. Sort of." Sniffed at her in my best Mean Girl impersonation, then turned back to Kozlow. "I sincerely don't know how you can stand being up here with just her to talk to."

He grimaced. "You get used to it."

"Do you? Wow, I wouldn't think that would be possible. So, is she up here merely to have buckets of water sloshing about in the worst place in this building for water to be, or is she doing something more than threatening Christopher, like helping with building access and escape and whatnot?"

"That's it," Kozlow said with a resigned sigh. "They made me carry in all the water, too, because they can't trust her not to spray it everywhere."

"No control? That's an issue for this kind of skill."

"Russell's 'suspended animation' field isn't strong enough to hold your precious Christopher," Nerida sneered. "If it wasn't for me, he'd have escaped already."

"Huh. Good to know."

Unlike Kozlow, Nerida wasn't holding anything that looked like a kill switch. She was also perfectly placed and really quite close to me. I didn't even have to move from where I was because I was braced against the desk.

"Don't you want to know why I'm not worried that you have your gun out?" Nerida taunted.

"Oh my, yes. Breathless with anticipation here."

She smirked. "Because, unlike Russell, I'm faster than you are. I only have to think about the water and it'll flow up his body and fry him."

Nodded and looked at Kozlow. "That's a scary thing, alright. Is she doing anything else? I mean that seriously. Is this literally all she's good for?"

"Yeah, and don't let her fool you. She's not as fast as she thinks she is," he said, glaring at Nerida.

She shot him a simpering sneer in return. Perfect. He was focused on her, she was focused him, and this was the expression I always thought of whenever Nerida was on my mind.

So I shot her through the head.

But I put two in her heart as she was going down because, I, too, believed in the double-tap.

CHAPTER 80

TURNED THE GUN ON KOZLOW. Hyperspeed being what it was, I had the gun pointed between his eyes before he'd done more than have his jaw drop open.

"Feel free to give me a reason."

"Ah, I have a kill switch," he said in a rather panicked and hopeful tone.

"Which is why you're not dead at this precise time. What does the kill switch go to?"

"The circuit board. It's not actually getting current right now."

"So, Russell, you need to ask yourself how much you want to destroy this building."

"I don't want to die. So if it's the building or me . . ."

"We'll ponder that. Dudes, are you still there or did you all get captured or something?" Kept eye contact with Kozlow.

"We're here," Jeff said, sounding annoyed. "Siler insisted on us letting you do your thing."

"Is that a complaining tone I hear? Why so serious and bitter? One more Crazy Eight down, one in my sights. I'm not seeing the downside to this at the moment."

"He wanted to be heroic," Siler said. "I felt that getting out of this in the easiest way possible was the better choice."

"Super-duper. Three things. One: Most of you get Christopher out of that ridiculous deathtrap he's in."

"Ah, I have the kill switch," Kozlow said in the way one does when trying to remind a superior of something key.

"And if you use it, you die. Any questions?"

"No," Kozlow said. He carefully turned the kill switch off and put it on the desk.

"Now, was that so hard? I knew you were smarter than Nerida. The second thing is that I want you, Russell, to explain to me how his team is using and controlling Cliff's floater gates or whatever you guys call them."

"He calls it fast transport. It works a lot like your floater gates."

"Why not use the term floater gate, then?"

"Honestly?"

"Do I look like I want you to lie?"

"No, you don't. Honestly, I think it's because that's the term you guys use and he refuses to sound the same. I'm not certain how close they are to your gates, though. Ours require clashing harmonic frequencies. I know how to get the right sounds and smash them together. We used to have more people who could do that, but they're all dead. So, right now, I'm the only one."

"Seriously? No one else has bothered to learn this skill?" Wondered if Cliff's brain had fried or something.

"It requires some talent," he said, rather modestly. "Nerida was right—my talent isn't strong, but it's specialized, and it's the right talent for this particular job."

"You're right—G-Company would be thrilled to have you exclusively on their team." Not that I was going to allow that outcome.

He blushed. He actually blushed, despite a gun barrel settled between his eyes. This guy hadn't heard a word of praise for years, possibly decades. "Thank you."

"You're welcome. And the third thing is that I want one of you to get my phone for me." It was in my back pocket and I didn't want to risk looking away and giving Kozlow a chance to try to grab my gun from me or similar.

"I have your phone," Reader said. "Since I'm allowed to touch your butt because I'm gay." He also took the kill switch, which action I totally approved of.

"No you're not," Jeff said.

"Says only you, Jeff. Who am I calling for you, girlfriend?"

"Chernobog."

At this Kozlow's eyes opened wider, but he didn't say anything.

"Put it on speaker?" Reader asked.

"Please and thank you."

My music switched off as the phone rang. It rang a few times but then she answered. "Hello?"

"Boggy baby, how're they hangin'?"

"Kitty? Why are you calling me? Was Stryker's phone busy?"

"Not sure if that's a hint that Stryker has intel for me or something, but no, I'm calling you directly. For reasons."

"Alright. What might those reasons be?"

"How much do you love your son?"

She was silent for a few moments. "I would prefer that you not kill Russell, if that's what you're asking."

"It's not possible," Kozlow whispered.

"In a way it is. But I want to know, how much do you love your son? I ask because I'm sitting here with him, and he seems far more thrown by hearing your voice than by the fact that I have a Glock with a lot of bullets still in the clip sitting on the bridge of his nose."

"I didn't tell him I was still alive, is that a sin?"

"Not sure. Ask my Mom what she thinks about it."

"She approves," Chernobog said dryly. "Telling someone—someone identified as working against those you've aligned with, I might add—that you're alive and well when the world needs to believe you dead is one of those big don'ts in spy craft."

"Why so testy? Did I interrupt another Hacker International Movie Night?"

"It's the early afternoon here, so no. Is Russell there?"

"Mother?" He sounded as freaked out as he looked. "Why didn't you tell me you were alive?"

"When should I have done that, Russell? When you were in the Pentagon's supermax prison or when you were broken out of it and trying to help the lunatic who put a contract out on me to destroy the world?"

"I'm your son!"

"Yes. Yes, you are. Which is why I'd prefer it if Kitty not kill you."

"You'd prefer it?" Kozlow sounded shocked and pissed both. "So if she kills me, what? You'll be a little sad and then move on?"

There was another pause. "Russell, during all the time you were not in prison, how often did you call me or visit me?"

"We were both busy. You said you understood!"

"Parents say that but they're lying," I shared. "Trust me on that one."

"Mother, I need your help!"

Chernobog heaved a sigh. "I'm sure you do. I helped you

recently. My price for participation with that lunatic Goodman's plans was your freedom from the Israelis, which set up a chain of events that culminated in a hit being put on my head and assigned to the best assassin in the world. And you didn't call me then, did you? You were out, working for the same people I was. You had time. But nothing. Kitty is a better daughter to me than you were a son, and she's not even trying to be. But I live with her, in a lovely suite, surrounded with luxury, working with people who admire me, given anything I want."

"Other than your freedom," I felt the need to point out. "Not that we don't trust you by now. And, no offense, but I kind of think of you as more of a grandmother *en residence*."

She snorted. "I'm 'dead,' remember? There is nothing more freeing and there is also no need to leave the building. Everything I want is here, and if I lack something, I contact Pierre, who gets it for me. And grandmother is perfectly acceptable. You're a good granddaughter, is what I'm telling my ungrateful son."

"They're all squatters," Jeff muttered. "Even her. Especially her."

"You . . . you're protecting my mother?" Kozlow asked, sounding even more shocked, if such were possible. "She's part of your *family*?"

"She's the only reason I'm alive," Chernobog snapped. "*She* brokered the deal with the Dingo to fake my death. Not you, Russell, her. So if she chooses to kill you, Russell, then I will have to mourn you. As I do every day, since you never call and you never write."

"Ah, in Russell's defense, he'd thought you were dead. Seriously, I'd thought you'd have told him you were alive somehow."

"Olga is here and wishes me to share that you tend to be far too sentimental. It's a failing. We both love you for it, but still."

"You *love* her?" Kozlow sounded ready to freak out or cry or both. Probably both.

"Figure of speech," I said quickly. "Okay, Boggy, good to know where you stand and all that. Does Stryker need me or were you just assuming that I'd have tried him first because I've known him longest and consider him the leader of the hacker pack, so to speak?"

"No, I assumed you'd try him first because you appear to really enjoy baiting him."

"That's me all the way, honestly. So, intel, yea or nay?"

"Yea. He has news on the alien landing sites you asked him to research. Shall I put him on now?"

"Um, sure. Either Russell's going into custody or into the morgue, so we can share whatever within his hearing." Waited while the phone changed hands. Heard a lot of bickering in the background. Yep, Chernobog was in the Zoo's Computer Lab.

"Kitty, you really have Chernobog's son?" Stryker asked by way of hello.

"I do. Say hello, Russell."

"Hello, who are you? My mother's new son?" Asked with extreme bitterness.

"Well, I think she thinks of me more as a nephew," Stryker said rather proudly. "Yuri, though, yeah, Yuri's definitely scoring the son treatment. I think it's because he's Russian and that makes her more susceptible to the charm he claims to possess."

"Proud of you for not saying that it's because he's blind, Stryker. That's some personal growth, that is."

"She says he's a better hacker because he can't see." Heard voices. "Oh, Big George, Ravi, and Henry all say that Chernobog thinks of them as nephews, too. But she likes me best of you guys." More voices, many raised. "No, we're not all equal to anyone. I'm Kitty's favorite, too, in case you aren't aware. I've known her longer than anyone around other than Chuck and Amy. And I'm still Chuck's go-to man, and don't the rest of you forget it!"

"Stryker! Focus, dude."

"Huh? Oh, right. But anyway, we have a ton to tell you about all the alien landing sites, but Ravi says that since his wife is in the Middle East, right in the middle of one of the triangles we should focus on that one."

"I'm one with Ravi on this thought. What about this one? The triangle points are three impressive buildings, two of which are quite old. Why so?"

"Builders were drawn to those locations, we're sure. They're over places where we have known Z'porrah power cube rooms. Same with every other triangle we could find. All points of the triangles have a Z'porrah power cube room under them."

"Interesting, especially since almost none of the spaceships we've seen so far are triangular, the Z'porrah's in particular. Any relevance for averting the end of the world as we know it?"

"Doubt it. But there's also a power cube room under the Persian Gulf, nearish to Kharg Island. I think it's connected to whatever the Treeship is going to land in or on in a few hours."

"Super, something to mull over in the downtime I don't have. Anything else?"

"Nope, other than that I think Chernobog would appreciate it a little more than she's saying if you wouldn't kill her son." Heard voices in the background again. "Nope, sorry. She says that it's up to you, a hundred percent. She just appreciates that you called to check with her first. Unlike some people. And that's a direct quote."

"Gotcha. Love to all, be home soon. I sincerely hope."

Reader hung up. My music turned right back on, yay technology. Now I was listening to "Flip, Flop And Fly" by Indigo Swing. Presumed this was a hint and/or encouragement.

"So, Russell, your mother is not on your side at this precise time."

"Because you've stolen her from me." He sounded jealous and defeated and more than a little sad.

It was stupid, because he was a killer—the Israelis hadn't had him locked up for stealing lollipops, after all—and he'd helped kill a lot of my friends and family. And yet, I felt sorry for him. If someone had me at gunpoint and was asking my mother what she wanted them to do, it would crush my heart if she'd said what Chernobog had. My mother would have said to let me live. No, my mother would have offered to take my place. Demanded to take my place. Begged, even, depending on the situation. And my mother didn't beg. But if I were in this situation, she might, if she thought it was the only way. Because she loved me.

Pulled the gun away from his head. He gaped at me. Heard Jeff grunt in a very annoyed way that I was, due to being me, very familiar with. Shrugged. "Dude, I can kill you any time, and my arm's tired. Plus, I have a bunch of men with me who will be more than happy to kill you if I don't feel like it."

"So, what are you waiting for?" he asked in a low voice.

"Honestly?"

"I'm dying to hear what it is, myself," Jeff said, sarcasm knob at eleven and threatening to go for twelve.

"Many things, really. But, first off, I want my friends out of suspended animation."

"Not Butler!" Christopher shouted.

"Um, okay, why not?"

"I think it's all that's keeping him alive."

CHAPTER 81

LET THAT SIT on the air for a moment. "Mind explaining?"

"Yeah." Christopher came over to where I was. So did the other guys. Meaning Kozlow was surrounded. Therefore, I could look at Christopher. It was nice to move my neck. "I took a hit when I touched the doorknob and woke up just like you found me. The others arrived pretty much as I was coming to."

"Why were all three of them zapped? Only takes one to open the door."

"They were all holding hands," Kozlow said. "The current traveled. The A-C and the human, they just dropped. But the other one . . . he's an android, right?"

"Yeah, he is."

"I hadn't intended to use suspended animation, but he was shorting out, herking and jerking everywhere. So, I gave it a try to see if I could get him to stop short-circuiting. It seemed to help. So, I put the others in suspended animation, too. In part so Nerida couldn't tie them up to more equipment. One set up that way was more than enough."

"So, let me be sure I understand this, but you did what you could to save the android?" He nodded. "Why?"

He eyed Jeff. "I'd lie, but why bother? The boss wants hostages, and an android is a great addition to any crew. I figured if things went badly, I could offer him to Mister Gadhavi."

Jeff was growling. "How noble."

"Look, I'm not on your side, okay? Stop acting like this is some sort of surprise, that I might not be doing everything for altruistic reasons." He shot me a look similar to the ones I'd given him when talking about Nerida as "Another Version Of

The Truth" by Nine Inch Nails came on my airwaves. "Is it only clear to you?"

"Potentially. Let's wake up the human and the A-C and make sure they're feeling extremely well. If they're not, we'll need Tito to gate it over here faster than fast."

"I already have him ready and waiting," Tim said.

"I need to stand up," Kozlow said. "I need to concentrate to not release all three of them at once."

We let him stand and moved en masse with him as he stepped over to the bodies. It was clear he was concentrating. Jeremy lowered to the ground and the glow around him disappeared. His eyes fluttered, then opened. "Where am I?"

Jeff helped him up. "Who am I?"

"Ah, the President? Jeff Martini? Don't you remember?" Jeremy sounded worried.

"How are you feeling?" I asked him.

"Like I've been trampled by elephants. What happened?"

"Tell you in a minute. Russell, well done. On to the next."

Kozlow concentrated again and Buchanan was lowered. The glow left him. But his eyes didn't flutter. "Time for CPR?" Jeff asked worriedly. Kozlow stepped closer and Jeff stepped in front of him. "Just what do you think you're doing?"

"I think he might need more than CPR." He looked at me. "I'm clear I die if he does."

I nodded. "Give him his chance."

Kozlow knelt down and put his hands on Buchanan's chest, in the same places a doctor would put the defibrillators. The way Buchanan's body bucked it was clear that Kozlow was acting as a human defibrillator, too.

But it worked. Buchanan coughed and opened his eyes. "What the hell?" He grabbed Kozlow by the neck. Siler pried Buchanan's hand off and I pulled Kozlow out of the way. "Let me at him," Buchanan growled.

"It's okay," Siler said soothingly. "We're in control of the situation."

"Malcolm, he just saved your life."

"After almost killing us? I think, at any rate." Siler and Jeff helped Buchanan up. He looked around. "Damn it. We got hit with electric current, didn't we?"

"Yeah."

"How's Butler?"

"As to that . . . Russell, how long can you keep him in suspended animation and what's your range?"

"I can keep him like that as long as I'm conscious, but my range isn't far."

"Call Dulce, we need a crash team here that can deal with John's situation. Not sure that's Tito."

"It's not," Tim said. "But I have that team standing by, too, and I've described the situation. When do you want them?"

"Russell, any issues with us using a gate of our own?"

"No. I'm the only one who can prevent it. And I won't," he added quickly.

"Smart man. Tim, right about now would be peachy, then."

A floater gate appeared and a set of Dazzlers with a gurney exited. There was just enough room for them in this area, but only just. Christopher and Jeff each took hold of one of Kozlow's arms.

The gurney had a metal pod-coffin-type thing on it, one with the top half of the lid made of glass, so you could see the head and torso of whoever was inside. It was blinking in various places on the inside as well. Hadn't seen something like this before, but assumed it had been created for Butler and probably our other in-control android, Mrs. Maurer's son, Cameron.

"We need to get him into the containment pod," the Head Dazzler said to Reader. Who looked at Kozlow.

"I can concentrate better when two big guys aren't trying to rip my arms off."

My music changed to Billy Joel's "A Matter of Trust." "Let him go," I said. Jeff and Christopher both shot me suspicious and worried looks, but they did let go.

Kozlow stepped forward. "Thanks." His brow furrowed and Butler lifted up slowly. The Dazzler opened the pod's lid. It totally made the swooshing sound I was expecting, too.

Kozlow lowered Butler into the pod. "Take him out now or wait?" he asked the Head Dazzler.

"Wait, if you can."

"Not sure if the pod will block me, but I'll do my best."

She closed the lid. Could tell that the suspended animation thing was still going on. The Dazzlers hit some sleek buttons on the outer part of the pod. "Now, please," the Head Dazzler said.

Kozlow nodded and the suspended animation went away. Held my breath as the lights inside the pod started blinking at a furious rate.

"If he dies . . ." Jeff growled,

"I know, I know," Kozlow said. "I die. Got it. Look I'm still concentrating, okay?"

"On what?" Reader asked him.

"On helping."

Could tell that most of the guys wanted to make a sarcastic remark of some kind, but Kozlow was ignoring them, and I could tell he was focused. Finally, the lights stopped flashing frantically and started going on and off in unison, and at a much slower rate. They seemed timed like breaths, lighting up when breathing in, fading out when exhaling.

The Dazzlers all relaxed. "Thank you," the Head Dazzler said to Kozlow. "He needed the extra boost."

"Will John be okay?" I asked.

She nodded. "We have to get him home and rebooted. But he should be himself soon."

"If any of his circuits," pointed to Kozlow, "will be useful, he'll gladly donate them."

This earned me a dirty look from Kozlow, chuckles from the four human guys, and blank looks from the A-Cs. "Ah, thank you," the Head Dazzler said, sounding confused. "We'll let you know."

"Check these two," Jeff indicated Buchanan and Jeremy, "before you go. Electric shock."

"Christopher, too. He was not only electric shocked but soaking in water for far too long."

The Dazzlers checked them all over, including using an OVS, which, under the circumstances, was wise. Once all three guys were given a reasonably clean bill of health, and they sprayed something on Christopher's feet and lower legs to presumably get him de-pruned, the Dazzlers took their android patient back through the floater gate, which then shimmered out of view.

My music changed to "Opportunities (Let's Make Lots of Money)" by the Pet Shop Boys, proving that Algar and I were on the same wavelength.

"Well, that was fun, and I'm hella relieved that John's going to be okay. Speaking of which . . . Russell, I have a question for you, keeping in mind that all that's gone on with John, Malcolm, and Jeremy just now merely means I don't kill you ugly and leave you for the maintenance crew to clean up."

"Okay."

"What do you think you can give me that would make me not want to kill you at all?"

"Huh?"

"Okay, it's more of a riddle. What would you *think* I'd want?"

Saw what I hoped was the light dawn for Kozlow. "What will you give me if I tell you? Going back to the supermax under the Pentagon isn't going to make me want to give you anything."

"It would mean you're still alive."

"It would mean they give me back to Israel, because with what I assume you want, I won't have any value left. They'll get what they can out of me about G-Company, and then I'll be tossed back to Mossad to be their new chew toy. If that's what you're offering, I'll choose you shooting me in the head right now."

"Oh my God," Christopher muttered, "this guy speaks Kitty."

"He might, he might indeed. Tell you what, Russell. You give me what you think I want to know, and if it's what I do want, then I'll tell you what's behind Door Number Three. Could be an all expenses paid trip to a luxury prison, or it could be death. Time to play *Let's Make a Deal*."

CHAPTER 82

EVERYONE WAS QUIET. Kozlow took a deep breath. "You want to know where Cliff is and what he's planning to do."

"I do, I do indeed. I want more than that, though. I want to know all of his hideouts, where he's got his doomsday stuff ready to go off if he doesn't check in or whatever, how many G-Company troops he's controlling, and if he has any other close lackeys beyond the three I can think of, which are Casey Jones, LaRue or whatever that clone is calling herself, and Leventhal Reid." Managed not to shudder when I mentioned Reid's name, but it took effort.

"He has Darryl and Nigel, too."

Coughed. "Um, how to put this? Not anymore."

Kozlow's eyes widened. "You guys killed them?"

Stepped closer to him. "No, Russell. *I* killed them. And all of Darryl's clones, too. Just like I killed Nerida. Just like I'm going to kill Casey, LaRue, Reid, and Cliff, not necessarily in that order. Like I'll kill you, if you don't manage to secure the best prize I'm offering."

"What is the best prize?" he asked quietly.

"You get to spend quality time with your mother."

"Are you insane?" Christopher shouted. "He can't move in!"

"He can and he just might, if he manages to be the level of helpful I'm demanding. Russell, this is a one-time only deal and the offer will not remain on the table for long. You'll get to live in the American Centaurion Embassy complex. You'll be restricted to a bedroom-bathroom-living room kind of hotel setup with no windows, and I'd plan on having the living room wall that's along the hallway be made out of really thick glass, so we can watch you from near and far. Your rooms will be reinforced with steel and whatever else they're using these days to make them inescapable." Why not? The Elves could pretty much do anything. "You won't be able to leave that set of rooms, unless you're under heavy guard, and even then it will only be to walk down the hall to say hi to your mother."

"Jeff, you cannot let her do this," Christopher said urgently.

Ignored him. "You will not be allowed any access to a phone or any electronics you might be able to manipulate. If we think you're okay with a television, you'll get that, but what you watch will be severely limited and monitored twenty-four-seven. You'll be monitored twenty-four-seven as well."

"How will you manage this? The State Department will want me and the pressure Israel will put on you will make giving me to them worthwhile."

"Oh, as to that, you'll be dead. At least as far as the world is concerned. Your mother has some excellent computer skills, in case you weren't aware."

"What about the torture?" He asked it as if it was an expected addition, the way you'd ask the hotel desk clerk if there was an iron and ironing board in your room.

"We don't do that," Jeff said.

Kozlow snorted. "Right. I realize you haven't been the top man for too long, but you can't be that naïve."

"A-Cs don't torture. Humans do. I'll torture you beyond your most terrifying nightmares if any of the intel you give us is wrong, or leads us into a trap. And if you think you'll just fool me, guess again. You'll be going with us, with a gun in your back, and with an explosive in your head."

"Kitty, I'm not allowing this," Christopher snarled. "Regardless of what you say." Prince came on my personal airwaves, singing "Let's Go Crazy." Nice to get Algar's approval.

Turned away from Kozlow and got right up into Christopher's face. "Cliff has Chuckie," I snarled right back, only I ensured that I sounded far scarier than Christopher. "I saved you first. Consider that before you speak again. And if you're *ever* insubordinate to me again in a situation like this I will rip your tongue out in front of everyone and then use it to wipe my ass. Is that clear?"

Christopher's jaw dropped. "Ah . . ."

"Say you're sorry, son," White said calmly. "Right now. You know better than to speak to her that way."

"I'm sorry."

"Mean it." I was still snarling.

"I . . . mean it, Kitty. I apologize. Sincerely." Christopher was looking at me like he'd never seen me before.

Nodded, then turned back to Kozlow. Shot him a bright smile and ensured my eyes were opened just a little too wide. "So, Russell, what's your pleasure? Door Number Three or a bullet through your brain right now?"

"They don't know how crazy you are," he said, sounding frightened and also impressed. "Or that you're really the one in charge. They have no idea. They think you're lucky and stupid, but not crazy and running the show. If you're serious about the offer, I'll tell you everything. I know where all the strongholds are, all the different doomsday plans, and where Cliff is right now. Which is where I assume your friend is, too."

"Russell, this could be the start of a beautiful jailer and prisoner relationship. You'll be rolling on G-Company, too, but they will also think you're dead, so no harm there, right?"

"Right . . . boss. No harm there."

"Good man. Christopher, take a lesson in how to speak to me. And, as of right now, Christopher, continue to stay silent because the sound of your voice is bothering me and if it bothers me any longer you'll be a dead man. Boys, insert the explosive. Just in case," I said nicely to Kozlow.

"Yeah, I understand. Cliff didn't take those out until you guys exposed him."

Interesting. Ensured my Crazy Killer Poker Face was fully in place. "Make it so," I snapped at Siler and Buchanan. "Now."

They both nodded and manhandled Kozlow out of this area.

"God," Reader said quietly, "I love watching you work."

"It's a gift and a skill." Looked at Christopher. "Your timing was excellent and so were your reactions. Seriously, you were great. We need to remember that for when we need to do it again."

He gaped at me. "What . . . what are you talking about? You . . . you were acting insane. Are you okay? Did they dose you with something?"

"I'm So Confused" by The Soul Rebels came on. "Oh." Looked to White. "I thought he'd caught on. I *know* you did."

White chuckled. "I'm your partner for a reason. And I know that Malcolm and Benjamin were with you all the way."

"I never had a doubt."

"I caught on, too, you know," Jeff said, sounding slightly jealous.

"Me, too," Jeremy said quickly.

"Caught on to what?" Christopher asked, sounding like he was more than lost.

Tim shook his head. "You were with her and part of the interrogation at the Pueblo Caliente airport." Christopher continued to look blank and more than a little freaked out.

Heaved a sigh. "Operation Drug Addict." Christopher continued to look blank. "I was acting, Christopher. Just like a troubadour." Wondered where Francine and the others were and hoped they were okay. If they were in the building they weren't making themselves known.

"That was an act?" Christopher now looked shocked.

"Yeah. I thought you'd figured it out and were playing along."

"No, I had no idea. Why would you do that, act the way you did? Threaten me the way you did?"

Heaved a sigh. "Because my audience respects crazy leaders with a plan and a willingness to kill their underlings if said underlings step out of line. He'd never have stuck around with Cliff otherwise once his exploding implant was removed, particularly since he shared that G-Company was respecting his skills. Which you heard. Hence why I thought you were playing along."

"No. I'm not an empath. I really think your idea is insane and shouldn't be done."

"My 'insane' idea is to get the one person out of all the Crazy Eights who has any reason to want to help us to do so. I have both a big stick and an even bigger carrot. What we need from him is huge, he is the *only* one we have a prayer of getting this intel from, and it's not something that we're going to get via the normal methods, because if the dude was asking that nonchalantly about torture, he's experienced it a lot and yet no one had a bead on Cliff until yesterday."

"But we have families living there. Kids."

"Your kid in particular, I know. However, he'll be in the Zoo, spending his time trying to beat out Hacker International for his mother's affections, in the most secure room the Operations Team can devise with help from a lot of humans who are sneakier than any A-C. And, since you weren't clear and you *don't* know, I wasn't making this up—Cliff has Chuckie and I came to get you and the others first. I am willing to do a lot to find Cliff and stop him from hurting my best friend any more than he already has, and if that means Kozlow gets to live the rest of his days locked up in the Zoo like our private attraction, then I'm willing to do it."

"Unless you have a better idea for how we find Charles that you can share within the next five minutes, son," White said. "Then I know we'd all like to hear it."

Christopher shook his head. "I don't. But, I do know that, whatever Cliff's doing to Chuck, it won't be pleasant." He heaved a sigh. "And yeah, getting Chuck back is worth the compromise, Kitty. Though I may have to sleep with one eye open for the rest of my life."

"As if I won't assign permanent Field teams to guard both Kozlow and the Embassy?" Reader asked. "More than there are already assigned, I mean."

"What James said, and dude, why are you such a drama llama all of a sudden? This kind of guard duty is what the Secret Service was made for."

Christopher might have gone on whining but Tim nudged me and pointed up. A small grate in the ceiling was opening. We all watched as Mossy dropped down from the ceiling to land on the desk in a catlike stance. Which was cute and kind of funny, though I knew better than to laugh.

"Good of you to join us. And thanks for guarding everyone."

"What do you mean?" Christopher asked.

"Mossy was watching over you guys. He was ready to shoot Nerida and Kozlow if he had to, but he was waiting, just in case. He also altered the feeds to any areas where our teams were, so that what they saw was boring nothing or a lot of dust, depending, meaning those two had no reason to kill any of you."

Mossy looked impressed. "I wasn't sure if you'd figured it out or not. Well done. Your newest recruit is an . . . interesting addition."

"You can whine about it with Christopher when we have time. Until then, we need to get prepped to save Chuckie."

Buchanan came back. "The 'implant' is in. Thank God there were staplers here. Nice to see you," he said to Mossy.

"You stapled him?" Christopher asked.

"No, Siler did. On the back of his head. Under his hair. He knows not to try to take it out because it'll explode if he does."

Jeff got a faraway look. "Yeah, he believes it. He's kind of . . ."

"Gullible. Yeah. I picked that up. Hence my Crazy Kitty

Routine. He wants what most people want—to feel needed and important. And he hasn't for a very long time, I don't think."

Jeff nodded. "Yeah. He's kind of excited about joining your team." He shook his head. "Only my girl."

"Only your girl gets the results we need," Buchanan said. "We have a location for where Cliff is. I think we need to focus on him first and then worry about finding his other strongholds, though the doomsday plans are also something of a must."

"Well, that means we have to keep Kozlow alive or we lose that intel," Christopher pointed out. "Please don't tell me that's going to be my job."

"No," Buchanan answered for me, "that will go to me and Siler. I have coordinates for the gates," he said to Reader.

"So how are we going in?" Jeff asked. "Sneak attack?"

My music switched to "Hero Of The Day" by Metallica. "No. I think we want to use our newest team member to the fullest and let him be a hero for a few minutes."

CHAPTER 83

"I DIDN'T THINK IT WAS POSSIBLE for me to hate a plan of yours more than I hate your moving Kozlow into the Embassy if he comes through like you expect," Christopher said as we stepped out of our floater gate outside of Cliff's hidden base on Kharg Island, in the Persian Gulf off the coast of Iran. "But, hard as it is to believe, I hate *this* plan even more."

"Blah, blah, blah. Fatherhood apparently suits you, but boy, is it cramping your kick-butt style."

"I agree with Missus Martini, son. Why so tense?"

"Oh, I don't know. We're just trusting someone who's been our sworn enemy for years with not only Chuck's life, but Jeff's, James', Tim's, Buchanan's, and Siler's. Why am I the only one who sees all the ways this could go wrong?"

"You're not," Mossy said. "You're just the one complaining about it the most."

"Mossy is my favorite, I'm just sayin'."

If Kozlow could be trusted, we had all the intel we could need for what to expect in terms of raiding this stronghold, including the fact that while I'd killed the original model, there were several clones of Nerida hanging about. Hers had been made with more autonomy than Lowe's, in part because her powers had been stronger than his.

Once we'd gotten the relevant info from Kozlow, we'd sent Jeremy back to the palace to brief Camilla and the others on what was going on, gather a variety of the supplies I'd requested from Raheem, and stand by.

Per Jeremy via Camilla, as far as our worldwide intelligence knew, we only had Chuckie, Rahmi, Adriana, Francine, Wruck, Len, and Kyle unaccounted for. We at least had a guess for

where Chuckie and Rahmi were, but the others were officially
M.I.A.

We'd verified that everyone we'd rescued from the Burj
Khalifa was safe and well, and had also gotten an influx of
weapons and ammo from Dulce sent to those of us still hanging
out at the top of the Burj Khalifa and not getting to enjoy the
view.

I'd even taken the time to fill my empty clips because I'd had
it. Despite hyperspeed and everyone's wishes to the contrary, the
various rescues and all the stuff with Kozlow and Nerida had
taken time, and the prep for our guerilla attacks had taken more.
It was after midnight when we finally rolled Mission: Trojan
Horse. Actively chose not to worry about what Cliff was doing
to Chuckie, as well as avoiding worrying about the others listed
as missing, but it took effort.

Once my strike team was in position, the other half of the
team would take a floater gate to where Cliff would expect them
to exit. During our prep time Kozlow had fixed all our goggles—
apparently his talent had been boosted by equipment in the Burj
Khalifa's broadcast level, and he'd been able to sort of short out
minor kinds of equipment. Not cell phones, but our goggles had
fallen under the level of what he could affect. And, happily, re-
pairing them was within his ability, too.

So, we were goggled up—though White and I still had our
gas masks, and Christopher had Buchanan's, clipped to our
belts. Christopher had obtained dry pants and shoes because the
Elves never failed to deliver, I had my purse, White had the
rolling purse, and Mossy had sassy Turleen attitude. We were
good.

We were also far fewer than anyone would have liked. However, in order to both impress Cliff and ensure that Jeff wasn't
going into the Lair of the White Jerk alone, the rest of the guys
kind of had to be with him.

Had stopped my music while we were planning, but my earpiece was still in my ear and it was time to go back listening to
the Algar Channel.

Christopher looked like he wanted to give me grief over this,
but wisely kept his mouth shut. Looked at my playlists, because
presuming Algar was going to help was not my wisest choice.
Of course, sometimes he was more helpful than others—found
an "Island Retreat" playlist that I certainly hadn't created. Hit
play because I was good at comprehending obvious hints.

Was rewarded with Frontline Assembly's "Search and Destroy." Which was nice, since our first part of the plan was to search the island to ensure that we weren't all in the biggest trap known to mankind.

Infrared was a blessing here, because this island had been ruined by bombing during one of the many wars in this region and it wasn't loaded with safe places to walk, let alone run. In the day it would be bad enough—in the black of night it sucked. A lot.

We took off at a slow hyperspeed trot, Christopher leading with White bringing up the rear, and me with Mossy, flying low and slow next to me, in the middle.

We did the outer perimeter first. And we found something within thirty seconds—a dead body. As Christopher turned it over, realized it wasn't just any dead body—it was Nerida. Or, I had to figure, her clone.

"What killed her?" I asked quietly.

"I can't see anything," Christopher said. "She looks unharmed."

"You shot the original," White said. "And Lowe's clones did what he did and said what he said."

"So, what, you think that it's really just like Multiple Man? If the original is killed, all the clones die? Russell said hers were more autonomous than Lowe's."

"That doesn't mean the basic structure and connection is different," Mossy said. "Let's mark where the body is and move on."

Move on we did, and we completed the outer perimeter of the island. No traps that we found, but we did find something else—a body every quarter mile or so. All the bodies were Nerida, all appeared to have nothing wrong with them, and all appeared dead and not in stasis.

As we checked the last body, my music changed to Pat Benatar's "My Clone Sleeps Alone." Reminded myself of two things—the first song had said to search *and* destroy. And we hadn't lived by the rule of the double-tap.

We were now all equipped with suppressors for our guns. Pulled mine and put a bullet through this clone's head. The body jerked as I did this, as if it was trying to do a sit-up.

"Why did you choose to make noise when we're sneaking around?" Christopher asked, seeing as suppressors didn't work in real life the way they did in movies.

"The body shouldn't have done that," Mossy said, before I

could reply. "A body dead that long shouldn't have moved in that way. That was a death throe."

We all looked at each other and the others pulled out their pistols. We'd found, with this one, thirty-nine bodies. "Okay, Kitty, let me rephrase. Great plan, let's go make more noise. My dad and I will go to the farthest point from here, split up, and start shooting. You two split from here and do the same. We know we can stop when we run into each other."

We all nodded, Christopher grabbed White and they took off. I went to the right and Mossy went to the left.

Had plenty of bullets in this clip as I ran at hyperspeed, shot a possibly dead body in the head, watched it do that death jerk, ran off again, shot again, and so on. Simple math said that I shouldn't have to do more than ten bodies before I ran into White or Christopher.

Only I hit eleven, and there was no sign of either one of them.

Ran on, got to number twelve. Did the shooting and kept going. If something had happened, I'd have a better chance of finding out what if I continued with the plan, such as it was. Reached number fifteen. Had to drop my clip and load in a new one. Also had to force panic away.

Kept on. Was definitely at the part of the island that Christopher and White would have gone to. No sign of them, no bullets in the clone heads. Fixed the latter, worried about the former, and kept on going.

Ran into Mossy at body number twenty-one, presumably because I was taller and therefore faster. My music changed to "Old Friend" by Rancid. Had that right. "I'm so glad to see you I'd be willing to not shoot this clone."

Mossy shot the clone instead. "I'm glad to see you, too. How many did you shoot?"

"Twenty, not counting the first one. You?"

"With this one, eighteen. So we've solved that problem and found a bigger one."

"This is how our luck goes. All the time. I mean, I shouldn't even be surprised that half of our team has already disappeared somehow. And yet, I am."

"Being able to be surprised is a good quality. Thoughts for how we search for them?"

"Together, potentially holding hands. I think we should go back a couple bodies and see if we can tell if they ever made it there. I didn't stop to look."

The area where I sort of guessed Christopher had considered his and White's starting point was near the now extremely defunct Kharg airport, so that's where we went. It was, like the rest of the place, a ruin.

"I wonder where the bathroom with the gate is," I said half-jokingly. "Wait. This was an airport. There would absolutely be a gate here."

"Wouldn't it have been ruined in the bombings that clearly happened here?"

"Maybe, maybe not. Christopher may have used it—superbeings showed up all over, after all. Maybe they went to check for it."

"Maybe." Mossy didn't sound convinced. "That seems more like what you'd do. Christopher doesn't seem to be someone who alters plans at a whim."

"I'm going to resent that later, Mossy, don't think I'm not. I have no other ideas. So unless you do . . ."

"Why yes, let's search through the rubble here as opposed to elsewhere."

We headed into the rubble of what had once been possibly one of the smallest airports in existence. And my music changed to "All My Friends" by Counting Crows. Considered this. Came up with nothing.

Mossy put his hand on my arm. "Listen," he said softly.

Did. Heard something, a low murmur. "Voices?" I asked in kind.

He nodded. I hunched down, gun still ready. He took point and we crept forward. Reached a still-standing wall. The murmuring was louder here. And there was a glow. Not a lot, but there was light with the voices.

Rounded the corner of the wall to find a man who looked Middle Eastern and who definitely had tattoos that indicated he was in G-Company standing there. He grabbed our guns before we could fire.

"You're finally here. We've been waiting for you. Impatiently."

CHAPTER 84

THE MAN TURNED and headed back to the others who were around a small lantern. But they weren't G-Company troops. And Algar's clues suddenly made a hell of a lot more sense. My music shut off of its own accord. Apparently Algar wanted me to concentrate fully or else he had nothing to add to the conversation. Put money on both.

I was looking at Christopher and White, who both looked fine. And several other people, one of whom was laughing quietly. At me, I was pretty sure.

Slid my goggles onto my forehead. "Adriana, what the hell?"

"Rahmi grabbed us," Christopher said to me. "She dragged us here before I could tell her what we were doing."

Looked around. "I don't see Rahmi. Anywhere."

The man who'd taken our guns grinned at me. "I'm flattered."

"I called it! You imitated a G-Company thug!"

"Mostly. When they took Charles, I shifted my body to look like a man's, but I knew that wouldn't last the moment I took my gas mask off. I ensured I was last down the stairwell, grabbed the man ahead of me, broke his neck, removed his gas mask and shirt, copied him, and was able to get through their rather makeshift floater gate just in time."

"I am so damn proud of you. Your mother is going to be, too."

Rahmi beamed. Well, Rahmi looking like a G-Company dude beamed. Same thing. In that sense. Then her, well, his, face fell. "We took Charles to Cliff. But I didn't see him and we didn't really get inside. Another man was waiting inside the entrance and told us all to come to the gate here and go back to headquarters. I slipped off and I don't think the others noticed, since there were over twenty of them to handle one man."

"Wait. If they have this gate, why do they need a floater at all?"

"This gate is broken," Rahmi said. "It can only go to G-Company headquarters. I found out by complaining a little about Cliff making us walk all this way to take this gate, and the others reminded me that it's a one-way trip. And you can't get here from there, either."

"Gotcha. By the way, Francine, John, Len, and Kyle, nice to see you and thanks for checking in."

"You don't check in with the President when you're doing a mission he'll have to disavow you for if you're caught," Francine said. She was in jeans and a t-shirt. And she was carrying a purse that looked a lot like mine.

"Are you impersonating me for this mission?"

"Well, three of us can," she pointed out. "But no. I only had clothes that matched yours for this trip. So I changed into this when Adriana called for backup."

"I want the poop and scoop, desperately, but we need to roll Jeff's part of the plan."

"Not yet," Christopher said. "That's what they're telling us." He looked at Adriana. "Please get her caught up and then finish what you were saying."

"Certainly. Mister White tells me that you've already figured out why I didn't check in with Camilla and Malcolm."

"Yeah. You know, Camilla's really damn good. We all have missions that go bust."

"At infiltration there are none better, I agree. But my mission wasn't to infiltrate. My mission was to find where Cliff Goodman was, not become his employee in order to find out his secrets and stop his evil plans."

"Gotcha. So, how did you get here? We only know because we sort of flipped one of the Crazy Eights."

"Grandmother already knew who Cliff's benefactor is."

"Why am I not surprised? So, she told you?"

Adriana gave me a good shot of the "really?" look. "Hardly. However, she's educated us about G-Company."

"By 'us' you mean you, Len, and Kyle, don't you?"

She smiled. "I do. Grandmother will be very proud of you. At any rate, I left the palace and remembered that G-Company had moved its base to Bahrain decades ago. Ali Baba Gadhavi is a very powerful man, and powerful men like to show off their power. He has little fear in this region. So, if I were the head of the most powerful underworld organization in this part of the world, where would I choose to ensure I had offices and one of my residences?"

"Damn, girl, you went straight to the Burj Khalifa? No stopping at go, no collecting two hundred dirhams?"

She grinned. "I did. Once there, however, I realized that I needed assistance. So, I called Francine, shared my mission with her, and asked for her help. That Mister Wruck was with her to guard her was a happy coincidence."

"I felt it was best to help Adriana," Wruck said. "You had plenty of protectors and, if we were successful, you wouldn't need them."

"No complaining coming from me. But I never saw any of you at the tower."

"We weren't there all that long," Adriana said. "I had Francine and Mister Wruck do a quick search for information about Mister Gadhavi as well as what he looks like."

"I shifted to look like him," Wruck said. "We were given immediate entry. When a person is that powerful, they can make others do things for them. So underlings took us to everyplace we needed to go within the tower."

"We struck gold." Francine shared. "Gadhavi keeps very good records on his key people, and he had a good folder on Cliff. Not only did we find details about what he's assigned to and for Cliff, but we found out where Cliff was living. Residence in the Burj Khalifa, office there, too, and also a residence in Manama."

"That seems like a lot for a guy who'd only joined the organization a couple of months ago."

"Yeah," Francine said, "that would be true for a regular person."

Adriana nodded. "But for the underworld, Cliff is something of a celebrity. But more than that—he's the heir to the Al Dejahl network."

"Giving myself the duh on that one. Knew he'd be trying to hook in with them, but him being the obvious 'owner' of Al Dejahl didn't occur to me. No wonder he got moved in and up fast. For all we know, Gadhavi and Ronald Yates were pals. For all we know, Gadhavi has known Cliff for years. And you found proof of all of this?"

"And more," Francine said. "We searched Cliff's office first, then his room. Nothing much in the office, but we found a list he had hidden in his room. It was a copy of a copy of a copy, and written in code."

"And you deciphered it already?"

"Oh, no," Adriana replied. "Chernobog and the others did that."

"You have Chernobog and Hacker International involved? They didn't say anything to me about this."

"They were told not to by Grandmother, who is at your embassy along with the rest of our mission right now. Grandmother is spending time with her old enemy and now dear friend. Grandfather is being entertained by your father and all the children."

"Gotcha. So what did they find?"

"Everything," Wruck said. "All money trails, which are all drained now. Listings of Al Dejahl strongholds, doomsday plans, and Cliff's plan to take over G-Company."

"Wow. So, once we rescue Chuckie and all that, we can take care of those."

Len shook his head. "We've done it already."

"Done what?"

"All of it," Kyle said. "Well, except for here. That's why Adriana called us in. She realized it needed more than a three-person team. We've cleared out all the strongholds but this one. Weapons are in Dulce's armory or destroyed. Data is with the hackers or in Dulce as well. Like John said, bank accounts are drained and various humanitarian organizations around the world have gotten donations from American Centaurion."

"We destroyed all the bioweapons," Len said. "He had every kind, too, each in a different stronghold."

"Yeah, he had some in the Burj Khalifa, too."

"Yeah, Christopher and Richard told us," Kyle said, "while we were waiting for you and Mossy to finish up and come find us."

"Mossy and I will laugh about this later. Potentially much later."

"We had no idea he was moving poisoned gas into the tower," Len said apologetically, "until we were already at a stronghold, and by then we knew you guys were rolling and it didn't seem like we could help. At least not as effectively as we were already doing."

"Can't argue, we're all alive." At least, I hoped Chuckie was still alive. I was antsy to get to him, but if the rest of the team felt we needed to recap—and Algar turning the music off indicated he agreed with the recap, too—then recapping it would be. "Where were the strongholds?"

"The UAE, Bahrain, Iran, Iraq, and Qatar," Adriana said. "And here, which is part of Iran, but Cliff thinks of it as his."

"Wait, how in the world did you all get all over the place in such a short time?"

They all stared at me. "Ah, floater gates," Kyle said. "We use them all the time."

"But we were lockdown worldwide and no one told me, Jeff, or Alpha Team about this."

"Ah," Adriana said. "Forgive me, but Missy is also part of the group. Grandmother and Chernobog spoke with her and she agreed that my mission was vital. She also agreed that not alerting you or the President was the right course of action, and since Alpha Team was with you and the President is the strongest empath known, they couldn't know, either. Since the idea was that you two would not be involved in this."

"Well, you know what they say about the best laid plans and all that. So, what about the doomsday plans?"

"The gasses can't release now, since we destroyed them," Len said. "So that's plan number one."

"You said you found the gasses in strongholds. But a doomsday plan means that the gasses are elsewhere, too."

Len nodded. "They were. We found them in various major cities and neutralized them as well." He grinned. "Kyle and I aren't as fast as A-Cs, but with a floater gate, it doesn't matter. And Francine has all the skills and then some."

She blushed. "You're a flatterer, Leonard Parker."

He laughed. "Only when it's warranted."

"So, how many doomsday plans did our least favorite crazed madman have set up or in the planning stages?"

"He had four," Kyle said. "The first was the bioweapons being released all over the world, presumably at midnight on New Year's Eve. At least, that's what the intelligence looked like to all of us."

"Nice to see he's really channeling the Joker. And Brain."

Len snorted. "I don't want to know who he thinks Pinky is."

"Len remains my favorite."

Kyle chuckled. "The second plan was a computer virus set to

take down financial institutions worldwide. That one was ready to go, big time. Chernobog and her team got that one neutralized, though."

"The third one you just foiled," Wruck said. "He really felt he had a winner with the whole idea of killing all the world leaders."

"How is that a doomsday plan? The summits literally just happened last-minute."

Wruck sighed. "He had a plan in place for this kind of world event. And options for whatever country would end up hosting, too. He adapted the doomsday plan to fit the current situation."

"Wow. He really is the Leader of the Lunatic Pack, isn't he? So, what's plan number four?" This question earned silence. "Gang?"

"We don't know," Adriana admitted. "He just calls it The Close Encounter."

"Fantastic. So, you just gated all the stuff back and forth to Dulce?"

Len nodded. "We treated everything like we've heard you all describe handling superbeings. We treated intelligence and weapons as you would people—took them to safety—and we treated the strongholds themselves and any bioweapons or similar as you would a superbeing—we destroyed them."

"Kitty, the copy of a copy Francine found, we found it everywhere," Kyle said. "In every stronghold and in his residence in Bahrain, too."

"We sent them back to the Embassy," Adriana said. "Grandmother says they are all the same, no differences, and Chernobog and her team agree."

"So, other than this last stronghold and The Spielberg Doomsday Plan, Cliff's got nothing?"

"Correct." Adriana smiled at me. "And we hear that you've taken care of half of his loyal team, as well."

"Yeah, as to that, didn't the dead clone bodies seem odd to you?"

"We didn't go around the perimeter like you did," Len said.

"I did," Rahmi said. "But at hyperspeed so as not to be spotted. They weren't down when I got here, so I had to avoid them spotting me. I saw all of them fall at the same time a little while ago. But I didn't want to risk being exposed as still being here. I haven't shifted out of this form in case we're spotted. I can then 'capture' all of you for Cliff."

"Rahmi found us when we exited our gate," Francine said.

"How did you know they were coming?"

Rahmi shrugged. "Being where they would exit was calculated luck—I was on the highest ground here, which is not that high, so I could see everything, and that's where Adriana's team landed. But I was waiting for you. Cliff took Charles. I knew you'd be coming for him. So I was keeping a lookout. I tried to contact Serene using the device she gave me, but it didn't work."

"Oh, yeah, we thought Cliff had control of our airwaves, so we destroyed from both ends."

She nodded. "Wise. And it gave me time to search for another entrance. I found what appears to be a secret path."

"Where does it lead?" White asked. Clearly this was where Mossy and I had come in.

"Directly to Cliff."

CHAPTER 85

"**K**ITTY, I think we can do this without risking Jeff and the others," Christopher said. "If we can get in without them knowing, then we can get Chuck and destroy this last stronghold."

"Which leaves that last Doomsday plan flapping in the breeze." There was something about the name—I knew I could make the connection for what Cliff's plan was, I just had to focus. But I didn't feel up to focusing. I felt up to saving Chuckie and killing Cliff and the others, but not focusing.

"It might be like his world leaders plan," Len said. "Something that requires a major event to happen, and then he'd have to do something. If he's dead, he can't do anything."

"John, you were in with these people for a long time. Did Cliff ever talk about any of this?"

"He talked about taking over the world all the time. Specifics, however, not as much. Those plans were limited to LaRue. And I was never close enough to LaRue to kill her, let alone to stop her. And once the clones of her and Reid were a part of the team, it was worse." He sighed. "If we're going to discuss those whose missions did not work, I'm the least effective of anyone here. I might have gotten closer to Cliff after the fiasco that was Operation Epidemic, but I chose to stay with you."

Hugged him. "And we're all glad. Just like Siler, you did more for us than you realize while you were undercover and you've been the greatest since you've joined with us, so no more beating yourself up."

"She just likes you because you used her name for it," Kyle said with a laugh.

"You don't know me."

"Speaking of knowing, if John had no clear idea of all of Cliff's plans, then why does Kozlow think he knows all of this?" Christopher asked. "At least supposedly."

Wruck shrugged. "Cliff had a large organization that, as of the end of Operation Epidemic and just earlier today, was down to seven people he felt he could trust. He might have wanted to ensure that they could make his plans happen if he were incapacitated."

"Kozlow said that Cliff had a bomb implanted in everyone's heads that he removed after Operation Epidemic. Did you have that?"

Wruck snorted a laugh. "Oh yes, they put that in. I took it out immediately. Shifting makes the removal of an item like that simple. It wouldn't have been easy if it had been created by my people or even the Z'porrah, but the level that humanity is at made it easy and safe. That was only for underlings, though. Stephanie, for example, had no implant."

"Huh. Cliff might think he's blown your head up." Wasn't sure how to use that information, but if I was going to, tonight was going to be the time.

"If he does, then he thinks he blew me up during Operation Epidemic. I doubt he's given me any thought since then. Thinking about others isn't Cliff's strong suit."

"So, does that mean Kozlow's playing us?" Christopher asked.

"Jeff didn't think so," I reminded him. "But, trap or not, Cliff has Chuckie. We need to go in the back way or knock at the front door, but either way, we have to do something before it's too late."

"Therefore," White said, "the question is—do we go with the plan that includes Jeffrey, or do we try to sneak in and take care of things without him and the others?"

My music came back to life and Jethro Tull's "Back-Door Angels" came on. Felt it was a clear sign. "We go in the way Rahmi found. And we go right now."

Everyone pulled their goggles back on and pulled out whatever big gun they felt they wanted for this particular raid. Stuck with my Glock—I was used to it.

Adriana turned off the light. "Mark this place and remember how to get here," she reminded us. "If things go bad, we can get to the Burj Khalifa this way, and it may be preferable to land there than stay here."

We headed off, Rahmi in the lead, Wruck bringing up the rear, humans teamed with A-Cs, but all of us moving at the slow hyperspeed which always sounded like an oxymoron but wasn't. My music changed to Alice Cooper's "Welcome To My Nightmare" and I realized I'd forgotten something. It might not be a big deal, but then again, it might.

Mossy was my trotting partner and he didn't need me in order to keep up, so I hung back to walk with Wruck. "John, who were the Cettans and the Uglors?"

He looked at me. "How do you know those names? The races have been extinct for several centuries."

"Someone mentioned them to me and said they were the example. But I don't know of what."

He heaved a sigh. "They were older races. Not as old as us, but far older than humanity. Their planets were neighbors in the same solar system, a solar system teeming with many planets, all with sentient life. The Cettans were flat beings, you'd think of them as looking like a pancake. Highly intelligent. The Uglors looked like fauns, and did not consider themselves as smart as the Cettans, but they were hearty and very strong."

I tripped over a rock and he caught me. "Thanks. Sorry, I'm listening, not looking."

"That's fine." He put his arm through mine as we started up what, for this island, was its highest hill. Not all that high, but we were definitely rising decently above sea level. "The others in the system achieved spaceflight, but these two races did not—the Cettans because they had no limbs, the Uglors because they didn't have the brain capacity."

"Did the other races help them?"

"To a degree, but mostly they left them alone. However, the Cettans achieved communications with the Uglors and taught the Uglors how to build a spaceship that would bring the Uglors to them. Once they met, a bonding between races took place. The Uglors wanted to learn and the Cettans wanted to teach. They both wanted to go to the stars. So, they created a matching ceremony. Uglor and Cettan would choose each other and bond. The Uglor would carry their Cettan in their arms or draped around their shoulders, and this way, both would reap the benefits of each other. Both planets became as one, with Cettans and Uglors living in harmony on both worlds. It was quite beautiful."

"What took the beauty away?"

"The Z'porrah." Wruck's voice turned angry. "The Cettans

and Uglors were the first to receive the Z'porrah's 'improved' uplift. They would combine to become fully integrated together. Stronger, smarter, larger. Able to protect themselves and their worlds, able reproduce as a combined being, versus as individual races. The Z'porrah made it sound like a paradise."

"So, they made the Cettans and Uglors an offer they couldn't refuse. I'm just betting that didn't go as planned." I was also getting a feeling that I knew where this was going, and why Mephistopheles had told me to ask about this.

"It did not. The combination worked, but at a terrible cost. The new beings that created were not what the two races had expected."

"So not a faun wearing a permanent pancake?"

"No, not at all. They turned into giants, into monsters. Still intelligent, still strong and hearty. But warped. Their minds were no longer bent on learning and travel but on rage and domination. And they were able to dominate. They created many things, mostly weapons. Within a generation the Superiors, which is what they named their new selves, controlled their entire solar system. They were branching out and starting to control nearby systems as well. And their rage was legendary. Their rage made them what they were, both good and bad. But mostly bad."

My music changed to "Story of My Life" by Smash Mouth. But I didn't need this hint.

"I think I know how this story ends. Their leader got into a murderous rage due to real and perceived slights, and threatened to blow up their sun if all the people in his solar system didn't kowtow to his demands. They didn't. And then that leader, Mephistopheles, followed through and destroyed their sun, and killed billions . . . including himself."

"Yes."

"But the Superiors' were a created race, something not occurring naturally, and therefore their souls, their essences, somehow survived. Mephistopheles landed here or was drawn here or, knowing the Z'porrah, was sort of aimed here. He made his perfect love match with Ronald Yates. And we've spent two or three generations here on Earth killing them, what we call parasites, and what you, I'd guess, call Surviving Superiors."

"Yes again. They were made to combine and they will combine with any mammal. You have not destroyed all the remaining Superiors, but I am grateful every day that you've destroyed all that have come here that you have found."

That we have found. "Um, are there more in-control super-beings hanging about on the planet?"

"There may be. There were a billion or more Superiors living on the two planets when Mephistopheles destroyed their sun. A billion have not been killed on Earth. They may be landing on other planets, or may still be traveling through space, headed toward Earth or elsewhere, searching for a new host. But they aren't all gone."

"That's why your religious text talks about them."

"Yes. Unlike this planet's religious books, we adapt ours as events in the galaxy change."

"Wise. Far wiser than us, but then we knew that already."

"Right now, I can't feel that we are wiser, honestly, or more effective. We seem to have failed in warning the rest of the galaxy against the danger of the Z'porrah's enticements."

No wonder Mephs had wanted me to get this intel, and also no wonder he hadn't wanted to tell me himself. "And now the Z'porrah have ruined the Aicirtap. Was there any way to reverse what they did to the Cettans and Uglors?"

"No, the combination was too well done, in that sense. As for the Aicirtap, who knows?"

"It's a new form of uplift, isn't it?"

"Yes, the Z'porrah are, at their cores, scientists. They are ever experimenting, ever trying new things." He sighed. "When we were friends, they were the ones who came up with the ideas for how to help the younger races, and we were the ones who came up with how to ensure that the souls, if you will, and the hearts and minds of those younger races were protected."

"I always knew you guys were missionaries, at your cores, I mean."

"Yes, we are. And they are not. But, in their way, they are now the missionaries and in our way we are now scientists. And neither side is as good at it as the other."

"Interesting and good to know." Would have said more but our line came to a stop as my music changed to "Depending on You" by Tom Petty.

"We're close," Adriana, who was in front of us, said. "Silence from here on in."

Wruck had me step in front of him as Rahmi led us through what looked like just more rubble but what, as soon as I really looked at it, was clearly a path, and a rather flat path at that. There were wide wheel marks in the dirt. Had no idea what they were wheeling in and out, but supplies seemed the obvious answer.

We reached a very old, crude elevator. Thankfully, there were stairs next to it, because not only would an elevator make noise—especially one that looked as ancient and rickety as this one—but hyperspeed meant we'd be faster in and out on the stairs, and far more quiet.

Wanted to get up near the front but it was too late now. Almost tripped again, but Wruck caught my shoulder and steadied me. Had to literally regroup because of this, too.

This put us even farther behind the others, but I was tripping far too much to go quickly. Was about to start down the stairs, but Wruck stopped me and indicated he'd go first. Wise. That way, when I tripped again, I'd hit him and he'd be ready for it and keep us both upright. My music changed to "Slow It Down" by The Goo Goo Dolls. Took the hint.

We crept down slowly, me staying close so that if I did trip, there wouldn't be a lot of momentum to my fall. We made it almost all the way down before I heard someone speaking. It was a voice I knew. A voice that sent shivers down my spine.

"So good of you to join us." It was Leventhal Reid, and he sounded exactly as he had when he'd been planning to rape, torture, and kill me in the Arizona desert. "We're just about to start the fun, so come on in and prepare to die."

CHAPTER 86

WRUCK FROZE and so did I. Reid was still talking. "Let's see, we have one, two, my goodness, seven of you. And look, Chuckles, your girlfriend's here to save you, too."

Reid thought Francine was me. Okay, the original hadn't known me well, this was a clone, that was her job, after all, and she was dressed like me. Chuckie would know the difference, but there was no way he'd share that or react to let them know. The others wouldn't, either.

Someone backed up to us. Mossy. Good. So we had the three of us not noticed. So far so not really good but at least we three were out. Was really glad we hadn't told Jeff to roll.

"And won't this be fun?" Reid went on. "We get to see the love triangle of the ages play out before us. We'll let your lady love choose which one of you gets to die pleasantly and which one gets to be tortured first."

"Leave my wife alone." Dammit. That was Jeff's voice. We'd taken too long and they must have figured we'd been captured, so had rolled their plan. Or else Kozlow was a lying sack. We'd find out shortly, of that I was sure. Was certain Jeff knew that was Francine not me, but he was selling it, so that gave us whatever tiny advantage we might be able to assume we had.

"Oh," Reid said in the scary, lecherous way I still heard in my worst nightmares, "I can't do that. She and I have so much . . . unfinished business."

"Enough," a woman said in a bored tone. LaRue, also sounding grown up. Fabulous. "We can play with the food later. Right now, we have to ensure that dear old Russell learns what happens to those who oppose us."

So, Kozlow had tried, and failed. That wasn't necessarily a mark against him. We were all failing right now.

"No, right now, we need to get the DNA for cloning." This was Cliff. I was pretty sure. But he didn't sound like he had the last time I'd heard his voice. He sounded kind of shaky.

"You already took mine," Chuckie said. "Why do you need anyone else's?"

Had to figure out how to see what was going on without being exposed. Mossy apparently had the same idea, because he took to the air and slowly flew back up the way we'd come. He returned shortly and beckoned to us. Followed him quietly and, for my part, very carefully.

My music changed to "Look At Me" by Sum 41. We were back by the elevator. There was a little alcove to the other side of it, and that's where Mossy led us. It was a tight fit, and if Mossy had been human-sized all three of us couldn't have done it. As it was, he had to light on my shoulder.

The rock went to chest height for me, but there was an overhang of rock right above us that made this a great little lookout spot. Because it was near the elevator, it meant that we could see the whole room, too, but someone in the room would have to look just right in order to see us. This was a sniper's dream location.

My music changed to "Keep Looking" by Sade. Assumed this meant Algar felt it wasn't sniper time yet and that I needed to examine the room. And what a room it was.

It was a long rectangle—we were at the corner, with a long side to our right—cut out of rock, so the acoustics were excellent. We were a story above the floor, and there were at least two stories' worth of space above. The décor was typical Mad Scientist About To Take Over The World Chic, complete with lab tables at the usual 120-degree angle so popular with the crazed lunatic set. And, naturally, Chuckie was strapped to one of these. Still fully clothed, which was a rarity, but perhaps Cliff was holding off on stripping him to the waist for some reason.

That reason might have been that he had a bunch of other people strapped up to different lab tables throughout the room. Chuckie was at the far end from where we were, but the others were closer, on the middle of the opposite wall. Sadly, those others were indeed Jeff, Reader, Tim, and Buchanan. Didn't see Siler and hoped he'd blended his way to some kind of safety.

Those four were strapped near something that looked a hell

of a lot like the android-creation equipment we'd found in
Stephanie's lab during Operation Madhouse, complete with a
wall of wires seemingly ready to go. But their tables also looked
like the cloning bays we'd destroyed during Operation Infiltration. Had an extremely bad feeling about this, made worse by
my music changing to Alice Cooper's "Clones (We're All)."

Chuckie was near a contraption that looked very like the
death ray machine I'd seen in Bizarro World. Really hoped that's
not what it was, because this machine had far more than one
nozzle on it. It was like four octopi had been attached to the cube
within a cube within a cube, all attached by pipes at every corner. The arms were all thick and wide, like Doc Octopus's, but,
thankfully, without pincers on the end. They just had a wide-
open hole, as if they were ordinary flexible pipes.

The Killer Octopus did not, thank all the Powers That Be,
have a glowing Z'porrah power cube at the center, though, so it
gave me a little hope that I wasn't going to see everyone turned
into little piles of dust.

Of course, the five guys strapped to the tables also had guns
at their heads, which was, presumably, why Rahmi and Adriana
hadn't shot the place up the moment they were spotted. And the
person holding the guns at the heads of my husband and friends
was Leventhal Reid. As in, there were five Reids, and each one
had a gun at the head of one of the five guys strapped down.

The others, including Kozlow, were surrounded by more
Leventhal Reids. There were twenty more Reids encircling the
newest captives. All of them brandishing semiautomatics. Had
no idea which one was the real one, or, rather, the Original
Clone, but, for me, it was like seeing my friends surrounded by
twenty human vipers while five other vipers loomed over my
husband and my other friends. Basically, this place was the
worst kind of snake pit.

Everyone's weapons had been taken away and were in a pile
that no one was going to get to before they could be shot. Noted
that Rahmi still looked like a G-Company thug. Had no idea if this
was going to help us or just make her the first person Cliff had
shot to teach everyone else "a lesson."

There was only one LaRue, interestingly enough, and she
looked as she always had to me, supercilious attitude and
bleached blonde hair included. Or at least only one that we
could see. Why ask why. And there was only one Cliff. But it
definitely wasn't the Cliff I knew. And another couple of reasons

for Chuckie and the others not being stripped to the waist presented themselves—jealousy and comparison.

Cliff was in a white suit and sitting in a motorized wheelchair, which explained the wheel tracks I'd seen. He looked flat-out awful. He'd been a good-looking guy, always dressed well, always wearing a high and tight haircut, and though he was about ten years older than me and Chuckie, he'd always looked young and vibrant. He looked young and vibrant no more.

He was sort of shriveled, a bit hunched, and his hair wasn't in a high and tight anymore. What there was of it was kind of long and stringy. His face was in profile to us and it was sunken in, as if he was a very old man.

He had a lizard on his lap, a large, fat Egyptian spiny-tailed lizard, if my memory of my natural sciences classes served. He was petting this lizard as if it was a cat.

To confirm my view that Cliff had chosen Blofeld as his new spirit animal, my music changed to the instrumental James Bond 007 theme. It would have been funny if everyone wasn't captured and in mortal peril.

The entire thing was very reminiscent of Cliff's lair in Bizarro World. What was missing, though, were banks of TV screens. Either they had no cameras set up anywhere or their reception here was next to nothing, because there was one TV screen and it was showing the Faradawn Treeship's descent. And that was it. Had no idea if the bank of surveillance equipment was in another room that a hundred LaRues were monitoring or if Cliff just hadn't had time to set that all up, but it was a lack that was working in our favor.

"Now that we're all here," Cliff said, rather pleasantly, ignoring Chuckie's question, "I'm sure you'd like to know what I'm going to do with you."

Sent up a fervent prayer that someone, anyone, would keep this guy monologuing. Had no idea if Francine could, would, or should. She looked like me, but didn't sound like me.

"Oh, we're, hah, dying to know," Francine said. Sounding just like me. Troubadour talent was amazing and, right now, possibly all we had going for us.

"I figured you might. And you're the center of it. Chain her up, we have something special planned for you."

"I'll bet." Francine sounded bored. "You look as bad as Casey did." She was damned good—clearly Serene's training was topnotch. "You a clone, too?"

"You wish I was," he growled.

"I wish you were dead," Francine said conversationally. "But I've heard you can't always get what you want."

"I'm going to get what I want," Reid said menacingly.

"Oh, blah, blah, blah."

Wow. Hoped Jeff wasn't having fantasies about a threesome with Francine right now, because she was doing an amazing impersonation of me. Then again, the only fantasies my team were probably having were of magnificent rescue.

Cliff cackled. Yeah, he was fully around the bend. "You put me in this chair! You're going to suffer as I have. Slowly, though not as slowly as I'd like. We do have a timetable to keep to."

Interesting. He thought Francine was me. The others mistaking us made sense. But I'd known Cliff for years and, epically good as she was, Francine shouldn't have fooled him. Others, yes, but not Cliff.

"Leave her alone," Chuckie growled. "You've got me. Why does anyone else have to suffer?"

"Because they love you," Cliff said, as if it was obvious. "And no one should love you. Ever." He rolled over to be closer to Chuckie while two of the Reids pulled Francine out of the pack and dragged her to a couple of iron rings on the floor. She struggled, but A-C or not, she wasn't able to shake them off. Remembered that the Reid and LaRue teenagers we'd met had indicated that they had A-C DNA spliced into their genes. Meaning they'd be stronger than any human and probably stronger than any single A-C other than Jeff.

"This is all your fault," Cliff said to Chuckie, sounding like a petulant child. "All of it. You've always thought you were better than me, and now, now I'm finally going to prove once and for all that you're not. I'm going to torture and murder the only person you've had who's always stood by you, your one true love, your best friend, and make you watch. Then I'm going to create androids out of those four," he indicated Jeff and the others. "And then, then I'm going to do something I'm really going to enjoy."

"What's that?" Chuckie asked, managing to sound bored.

"I'm going to use my new baby," he patted the Killer Octopus, "to turn you into a moron."

"Come again?" Francine asked, as the Reids chained her ankles to the iron rings. My music changed to "Listen Like Thieves" by INXS.

Cliff turned his wheelchair to look at her. "I'm going to zap your beloved's brain. We'll take him down a few notches. He won't get to be a gibbering idiot, because then he wouldn't remember. He'll just be too stupid to do anything about it. He'll be my toy for the rest of his sad, stupid life."

"That's not possible," Chuckie said. But I heard the fear, just a little.

"Anything's possible," Cliff said, turning back to him. "Other than her loving you more than the alien. That's not possible in this or any other world."

Patently untrue, as Bizarro World had shown. And I knew Chuckie knew it. But he looked frightened, hurt, and angry. So it was an act, and he was leading Cliff on to get more intel. At least, I hoped.

"You're lying," Chuckie said.

"I'm not. Trust me, I'm going to show you soon enough. Three hits and your IQ will be under a hundred. Far enough under that you won't be able to figure out how to escape, not that we'll ever give you the means or the opportunity. And you won't be able to figure out how to kill yourself to escape, either. But you'll remember that it's your fault all your friends are dead."

"How can you be sure of that?" Chuckie asked.

Cliff leaned closer to him. "Because I'll remind you every, single hour of every, single day."

CHAPTER 87

MY MUSIC CHANGED to R.E.M.'s "Imitation of Life." Wondered why Algar was telling me that there were clones here. I kind of already knew. Didn't need to hear a song about psychopaths, either, because I was quite clear that I was looking at half a room full of them.

"Earth is finally joining the rest of the galaxy," Jeff said, possibly to get Cliff's attention off of Chuckie. "Why are you so hell-bent on destroying that?"

Cliff cackled again, but he did indeed turn away from Chuckie. "Oh, I'm not going to destroy that. I'm going to watch this world burn and then I'm going to take my place as the ruler of the galaxy."

"Megalomaniac much?" Tim asked. "Some people start with successfully running a country or something first."

Cliff shrugged. "And some don't. Really, we need to get things rolling," he said to LaRue. "We do have—"

"A timetable to keep to." LaRue sounded bored and annoyed. "Do you say anything else anymore?"

"Someone undoubtedly has their part to play, too," Reader said. "Don't forget Cliff's other favorite phrase." LaRue snorted a laugh while Cliff glared. And squinted. That was it. His eyesight had been damaged along with the rest of him. He couldn't see Francine clearly enough to note the differences. Everyone was acting like Francine was me, so Cliff was assuming they were correct.

"The aliens coming next are going to destroy everyone," White said. "You won't be immune."

Cliff, LaRue, and all the Reids all chortled. "Yes, the ones coming will indeed help me destroy everything," Cliff said. "We're looking very forward to their arrival."

"I meant the ones these others are fleeing," White clarified, keeping the monologuing alive.

"Oh, we have that handled," LaRue said. "You all always aim so low." She shook her head. "You could have ruled this world. And all you did was cower in your underground buildings and help humanity." She got a lot of sneer into that sentence.

"We understand that you're not the altruistic type," White said calmly. "Though, honestly, I fail to see how you have a hope against the Aicirtap. You might be a Z'porrah spy or, rather, your original was. But you mean nothing to the Aicirtap."

The music changed again. To the Beastie Boys' "Rhymin and Stealin." Had no idea where Algar was going with this now at all.

"I'm a real person," LaRue said defensively. "So are they," she indicated the Reids.

"That's why you made twenty-five of him and only one of you?" Reader asked.

"More of me means I get to have more fun," the Reid who was likely to be the Original Clone said. He pulled Adriana out of the group. "I want this one. Every one of us wants this one."

"Sure," Cliff said. "I'll enjoy watching."

"Leave her alone," Buchanan growled.

"You wish," LaRue said. "I think we want to do whatever to the ladies first. So all their protective men can watch helplessly while Lev does what he does best to them. Repeatedly."

My body felt cold. Better than anyone here, I knew exactly what Reid wanted to do to Francine, Adriana, and, if he caught me, me. Rahmi, too, if she shifted to show she was a woman. And I could not allow that. But I had literally no idea of what to do.

"How did you make all the clones?" Adriana asked. "We destroyed your lab."

LaRue's eyes got wide. "You *were* there. I can't wait for Lev to rip you apart."

Adriana shrugged, as much as she could with the grip Reid had on her upper arm. "I still have no idea how you were able to create the others. Frankly, I didn't think any of you had the capability to adapt this quickly."

Cliff patted the Killer Octopus. "This has many settings."

"You've created a cloning ray?" Reader asked. "Pull the other one." Had to give it to my team—no one sounded as scared as they had to be in reality.

"Want to see it in action?" Cliff asked.

"I don't want to have my brain devolved, so not really," Reader said, sounding unimpressed.

"Oh, we'll show you. Russell, come to daddy." Cliff smiled in a way that was intended to be frightening. It was effective.

Kozlow walked toward him in the jerking manner one does when one is trying not to pee in terror. Okay, so my regular team wasn't showing how frightened they were.

Cliff took one of the nozzles on the Killer Octopus. My goggles adjusted their magnification so that I could see what he was doing as if I was standing right there. Sent a silent thank you to Algar.

Cliff was fiddling with some knobs. Unlike the Death Ray in Bizarro World, the Killer Octopus wasn't golden. It looked to be made out of ordinary steel. There were three large knobs, which also looked like steel, each with three smaller knobs under them. He fiddled with the left set of knobs, then turned the nozzle on Kozlow.

A stream of light came out of the metal hose and bathed Kozlow. At the same time, all the lights went out, the TV screen went blank, and a couple of backup lights went on, ensuring that the room now looked like the creepiest cave ever. So maybe that's why they didn't bother with cameras and screens—the Killer Octopus was taking all their available power.

Realized that "Rhymin and Stealin" was on repeat. Of all the songs to repeat, this one seemed the least helpful. Then again, Algar never repeated a song for no reason. Forced myself to focus on the music and think while Cliff kept the light hose on Kozlow, which was even harder because the machine was making a high, whining noise.

Considered the songs Algar had had on repeat during Operation Madhouse. One had been repeated due to its title. But one had repeated due to its lyrics. So, while Cliff indeed ordered the "traitor" from G-Company who'd had the nerve to help his enemies find his private entrance come forward to be "taught a lesson" next, I listened to the lyrics.

There was a form of chorus in this song. And when I listened, actually listened, to it, I got it. Because the chorus was "Ali Baba and the forty thieves."

Leaned up to whisper in where I hoped Mossy's ear was. "You stay here. You'll know when to shoot."

He nodded and sat on the ledge. It was precarious, but he was too short to stand on the ground and be able to see.

Pulled Wruck's head down. "It's showtime. We need to get out of the alcove."

Wruck nodded and stepped out. I followed. As I did, my music changed to "Invisible Touch" by Genesis. So I neither jumped nor screamed when Siler appeared. He had a couple rifles. Figured he'd taken them off the pile downstairs. "What are you doing?" he asked softly.

"Creating the distraction." Looked at Wruck. "Give him all your guns." Wruck obliged. "Mossy's up here with you. I know I can count on you to shoot straight."

Siler nodded. "Go get 'em, tiger. Just be careful. I've been through the rest of the complex—anything living is not alive any longer."

"Clones?"

"Or what's passing for them."

Mossy waved at us and I went back over. He pointed down and I took a look. There were now two Kozlows standing there. They both looked ready to faint, presumably because Kozlow hadn't expected to be cloned but to be disintegrated. But one didn't look quite as right as the other. "The one on the right is the clone," Mossy whispered. "Whatever tech he's using for this, it's not from Earth."

The glowing light stopped and the lights came back on. Cliff fiddled with the knobs on the right. Then he turned back to face Kozlow. "And now, you'll get to see the other thing this can do." He turned the hose on the one Mossy had identified as the clone. The lights went off again, then a white hot beam shot out of the hose. And then there was no clone, just a little pile of dust. The lights dutifully came back on.

Everyone in the room gasped, even LaRue and some of the Reid clones, and there were a few little shrieks as well. Didn't stop to be horrified—I had work to do.

Backed out of the alcove and went to Wruck and Siler to continue whispering. "Nightcrawler, tell me what you found, right now. Just do it fast."

"Fifteen versions of Casey. Most of them looked like her, but some looked as bad as you all said the one who blew up the D.C.P.D. had. Didn't find her original, though. Did find young versions of what I'm certain were LaRue and Cliff. They didn't resemble Reid at all, but they looked just like those two do, in LaRue's case, and did, in Cliff's. Various ages, none younger than nine, none older than late teens."

"You killed them all?" Wruck asked.

Siler nodded. "Quickly and painlessly, which is more than they were doing to the other things I found."

"Which were?"

He heaved a quiet sigh. "Infants. I think they were already starting to clone Reynolds in the time since he's been taken. All of them looked alike and, due to whatever process they're using, they looked like him now, versus how I presume he looked as a child. And the other 'children' were torturing these clones. Horrifically. And they were enjoying it."

My stomach clenched. "What did you do with—"

"I put them out of their misery." Siler looked like I remembered the uncles looking—stoic and all business. "There is no way Reynolds would want these 'children' to grow up, if they even could after what was being done to them, and we have no way of knowing what Cliff mixed into them, either. We have enough monsters to deal with—we don't need any more."

My throat felt tight. "But they were innocent."

"And suffering," Siler said flatly.

"To kill evil is, many times, easy," Wruck said gently. "But to put something innocent out of its misery is much harder. But, all too often, it's just as necessary."

Jeff had said similar to me, at the end of Operation Confusion, when I'd had to destroy the Room of Hot Zombies, who had all included the mental signature of Wade, Walter and William's middle brother, as well as a ton of other murdered Field agents. Wade had begged me to kill them all before they became an unstoppable threat to everyone they cared about. Chuckie had been with me and White when we'd had to do that. And I knew without asking that he'd agreed with the others—the evil and the innocent were, in this case, both better off dead.

I didn't have to like it. But, as with everything and everyone else, I was going to have to avenge what Cliff's latest bouts of insanity had done. And I needed to do that right now.

CHAPTER 88

"YOU'RE RIGHT and I'm not berating you for any decisions made in the field. Either one of you." Siler and Wruck both relaxed a little. Would have reassured them more but my music changed to "Band on the Run" by Paul McCartney & Wings. I agreed—it was time to get our jailbreak running. And then some. "The Killer Octopus is a cloning ray, a brain devolution ray, and a death ray. Three in one, such a deal. Let's go get it."

"What is the plan?" Wruck asked, while Cliff explained how he was going to turn most of the people downstairs into dust piles and the team managed to keep him monologuing.

"Oh, sorry. Need you to shift into Ali Baba Gadhavi. You're about to make a house call."

Wruck changed. Normally he looked like an average, nice-looking American of Northern European descent. But right now, I was standing with a man of obvious Middle Eastern descent, kind of chubby, with a full beard, dressed almost exactly like Raheem, complete with a gingham kufiyah. Apparently the teddy bear look was in. However, this teddy bear had sharp claws and fangs, too. He wasn't giving off an air of friendliness, either. He radiated cool authority. Good.

Pulled my goggles off and dropped them into my purse. Still had a lot of Poofs on Board. "Poofies, stay silent, avoid the nozzles, but Kitty and the others could use your help." The Poofs sort of looked at me sleepily. Possibly there was help there, possibly not. Couldn't take my purse with me, though—that would be a total giveaway. Took it off with great reluctance, took out as many clips as I could fit into the back pocket that didn't have my phone, shoved some in my front pockets, and handed the purse to Siler. "Guard this and the Poofs, please and thank you. In between killing bad guys."

"I loosened the restraints," he said. "All five on the slabs can get free if no one notices."

"You rock." Put my gas mask on. I was unrecognizable with it on, unless you looked at my chest. So far, hadn't seen any G-Company thugs who were easily spotted as girls.

"Hang on," Siler said. He pulled his shirt off. Managed not to gape. Or stare at his chest. Much. Not that anyone could tell, in the gas mask. Had the realization again that I really worked with the hottest guys in the world. "Put this on, it'll be loose and should hide, ah, that you're a woman."

Nodded, since there wasn't a good way to whisper in the gas mask. Pulled on his shirt as suggested. Definitely baggy on me and therefore it was going to be good enough. Gave Wruck the "go" sign, which he got after the third time. Almost no one ever got my hand signals right off the bat for whatever reason. Had no time to be bitter, but made a mental note to put it onto my schedule.

Wruck and I headed down the stairs again. We weren't going to have the element of surprise for long, but hopefully it would be long enough. Happily, Cliff was still monologuing, this time about how he could control the aliens.

"You see, I can alter how much or how little autonomy a clone has," he said as we reached the bottom of the stairs. "The example clone had no autonomy, which was why it made the same ridiculous faces as Russell." My music changed to "Summer Nights" from *Grease*. The one with the "tell me more, tell me more" chorus. Managed to control the Inner Hyena, but it took great effort.

"What about memories?" Adriana asked. "Does it share the same mind?"

"In a way," Cliff said. "We lost the capability, thanks to all of you. However, while memory doesn't go along with the package, ability does. Depending on the level of the clone, it can be as effective as the original. Or it can be a puppet. It depends on what we need."

"Why do you even need DNA if you have that machine?" Christopher asked. Prayed Cliff wouldn't share what he was doing. Or what he had been doing before Siler took care of the horrible business.

"Oh," Cliff patted the Killer Octopus, "this is for fast work that doesn't matter. To make really good clones, and to splice all of your DNA into those clones, we need a much slower and more effective process. But don't feel left out—we'll be taking more DNA from you, too."

"Yeah," LaRue said. "We lost what we had when you people destroyed our labs."

Did my best not to consider the fact that the A-C genetics LaRue and the Reid clones had in them was Christopher's. If we managed to pull this off, that DNA would never be replicated by anyone other than Christopher, ever again.

One of the Reids came running in from the other room. "They're all dead!"

"What?" Cliff asked. "Who?"

"All the others! All of them!" He grabbed LaRue and dragged her into the other room.

She screamed like a banshee. Then they both ran back in. "Kill them all," LaRue shrieked at Cliff. "Right now! They destroyed all the young ones, yours and mine!"

"Not all the good ones," Cliff gasped, eyes bugging out.

"Every one, *and* all the clones of Casey you had hanging around, too," the Reid clone confirmed, sounding angry and freaked out. "And the ones we were starting of him," he sneered at Chuckie, who went pale. So much for the slim hope that no one else would know what Siler had had to do.

Cliff looked around and he looked furious. "Which one of you did this?" he snarled at the prisoners.

"Ah, we're tied up or surrounded," Jeff said. "Who in the hell do you think did whatever? One of your people, obviously."

"Casey could have," Tim said quickly. "I haven't seen her around here."

"She's on a mission for me!" Cliff screamed, spraying spittle. "One of you must have slipped by us!"

"Or she's betrayed you and gone for better employment," White suggested.

"Could have been someone from G-Company," Reader offered as an alternative. "I don't know that their leader would like what you're doing here."

Nudged Wruck. "Take that as our cue and let's roll."

He nodded and stepped into the light. "What is going on here?" Wruck boomed out as we walked into the room. The voice didn't sound like his. Hadn't realized that he could alter his voice just as the troubadours could. "Clifford, I want answers and I want them now!"

Cliff, LaRue, and all the Reid clones gaped. It was kind of nice to see them all speechless for once. Didn't expect it to last but, still, it was a small rarity and I enjoyed not hearing them.

"You!" Wruck pointed to Rahmi. "What are you doing here?" He strode through the clones and hostages—shoving the hostages away from the clones but in a manner that seemed random—and grabbed her arm, which, of course, looked like the Head Dude was grabbing the Insubordinate Lackey. Wruck dragged Rahmi over to me while the rest of our people who weren't strapped down moved closer to the pile of guns. "We'll deal with you later."

"How did you get here?" Cliff managed to ask.

"You would question me?" Wruck snarled. "I own you."

"You don't talk to me that way," Cliff snarled. "We're equals."

"You are my subordinate. At best. And I will teach you a lesson to ensure you never forget it." Wruck strode toward Cliff.

And Cliff aimed the nozzle he was still holding at Wruck.

CHAPTER 89

BODY-SLAMMED WRUCK out of the way and made sure I was out of the way, too. Due to where we were when this happened, Wruck and I hit into some of the Reids and took them to the ground. My luck being what it was, lost my hold on my Glock and watched it skitter away from me.

The nozzle sprayed and the lights went out, only the backup ones didn't come on. Had no idea if Siler or Mossy had helped make that happen, but it meant that I was in great shape because the gas mask was infrared.

Thankfully Rahmi leaped the other way, so what the ray ended up hitting was the elevator. Apparently the death ray portion was able to turn more than a person to dust. No one was going to be leaving via anything but the stairs now.

This also gave the rest of the room the impetus to take action. True to what Siler had told me, the five guys who were on the tables leaped off. Chuckie was nearest to Cliff and he kicked the nozzle out of Cliff's hand, then tackled him, knocking the wheelchair over and Cliff out of it, and thereby leaving the Killer Octopus unmanned.

Wruck, meanwhile, shifted again and turned into himself. Or, rather, a version of himself. He was taller than I was used to, and looked a little less average and a little more unformed. Not unattractive but somehow beautiful in a way that was hard for a human to describe. Remembered how he'd told me that the Ancients looked like humanity, all of humanity. I could see it now. It was as if every feature and body type was there, even though he didn't look like A Multiple Man. He looked like himself, only more so. And he glowed, just a bit. And, he had wings.

This was what the Anciannas race actually looked like—like

our biblical descriptions of angels. Would have said, "Told you so," to the room, but we were all a little busy.

He didn't register for LaRue, not at first, not until he was right in front of her. But then her eyes opened wide and I saw the recognition hit. "You! You can't be alive. There are no memories that say you are."

Wruck grabbed her by her throat. "All my memories tell me you're a traitor."

Meanwhile, Jeff was trying to get into the fight and Christopher, White, Reader, and Tim were trying to keep him out of it, which was requiring all their strength. Meaning they were ignoring Francine.

Len and Kyle were not, however. They ran to her and started working to get her out of the shackles. Of course, a key would help with that. Had no idea where the key was, other than somewhere here.

Rahmi shifted to her own form and produced her battlestaff. Then she went to town on the Reid clones. Buchanan and Adriana were back-to-back, near Rahmi, fighting Reid clones as well.

My music changed to "Cloning Technology" by Fear Factory. Took the hint and ran to the Killer Octopus. Sure enough, it had a power cord. Unplugged it. The lights came back on. Not what I was hoping for. Had to get this out of here and away from Cliff's control. Tried to move it. It was hella heavy and didn't budge.

Noted that Chuckie was pounding Cliff, snarling about a variety of things, not the least of which were about Cliff threatening me, threatening his friends, and being the reason Naomi was dead. Cliff was in that crazy state where the adrenaline's going strong, though, and he was snarling right back about all of Chuckie's perceived personal attacks against him, so it was something of an even fight at the moment.

Cliff's pet lizard had been kind of thrown when the wheelchair went over, but it waddled back, hissed, and attacked Chuckie.

Grabbed it to get it away from him. Now the beast was attacking me. Tried to get into its mind. Couldn't. Knew there was a mind there, but it was a locked door to me. Held onto the lizard with both hands, keeping it at arm's length, and contemplated a few things—I'd been able to connect with a freaking great white shark at a tenser time than this, the Turleens came here all the time and camouflaged themselves to look like tortoises and such, the Mykali had been here for ages and we'd decided they were sea slugs and not sentient, and Mossy had said that the tech in this machine wasn't from Earth.

Held the lizard a little tighter. "You're not just a pet, are you?"

It tried to grow, I could feel it. Fought against it, but it burst out of my hands. In its place was a very large lizard, one that made the Reptilians look extremely small and cuddly. One that looked very much like a larger version of the lizard it had been while, at the same time, being a smaller version of a T-Rex only with, sadly, slightly more useful arms.

It roared at me and grabbed at my face. It got the gas mask and ripped it off of me, but it wasn't my head, so I counted that in the win column. I backed up. And hit the wall.

"It's her!" Cliff screamed as he saw who I was. He looked at Francine, squinting madly, then back to me. "That's the real one! Kill her! Kill her now."

Might have happened. But I heard a different kind of roar.

The Poofs were large and in charge. This wasn't a typical foe for them, though. There were six Poofs and one Alien Rex and the Poofs were having to really work at it. Would have helped them, but noticed movement out of the corner of my eye.

Spun to see Leventhal Reid aiming a gun at one of the Poofs.

Wasn't sure if this was the "real" Reid or not and didn't care. He was threatening my pets, my protectors, my Poofs. He was not going to be allowed to do that.

My rage spiked and I remembered what I'd told Jeff, Chuckie, and Reader not all that long ago—the only reason Reid could hurt me before was because I wasn't enhanced. Those days were long gone. He might have A-C in there. So what? So did I. My music changed to Mötley Crüe's "Goin' Out Swingin'" and I waded in.

"I remember you," Reid said as I kicked the gun out of his hand and the bullet fired into the ceiling. "You tried to kill me when I was younger."

So, this was the Original Clone. The others couldn't have that memory since they'd lost the ability to share those. And the original had been a well-made clone, literally Reid reborn. My stomach clenched and I froze.

Managed to talk. "Yeah and do you remember why?"

"I do. We're going to have so much fun." He smiled the Typical Reid Smile, and it was still chilling and terrifying. And I knew that was what he wanted—to terrorize and therefore control me. He was back, fully back—truly the only person who'd ever made me want to beg for mercy. And just like before, I had no weapon. Just like before, he could kill me before anyone else could save me. "You only made it last time because your man saved you. That won't happen now. Everyone's too busy. It's just you and me." He reached out and stroked my cheek.

He really shouldn't have said or done either. As my music changed to "Never Again" by Discharge, I remembered something—victims needed rescuing. And that's what Reid liked to do—make other people victims. That's what Cliff and his Minions did. What all the bad guys did, really. Only I wasn't his or anyone else's victim. I'd never begged when he'd wanted me to the first time, and I sure as hell wasn't going to do so now. I was Code Name: First Lady and I did the saving. My rage went supernova. He was going down.

He tried to turn the caress into a slap, but I blocked it and batted his arm away. "Don't flatter yourself."

He lunged for me and I leaped back while throwing a front ball kick that, due to his position, hit his solar plexus. He hit the ground, but was up again by the time I'd landed. Dropped down and swept his legs, then did a backflip to get more space. Yeah, when I was this enraged, the skills worked at optimum.

He started fighting, boxing, really. Which was a good strategy against most women. However, I'd not only spent years being trained by Christopher, but I'd also had Tito, aka Mr. Mixed Martial Arts, advising me during fights for a long time.

Reid was bigger than me, but kung fu wasn't a martial art that depended on size and strength. And in MMA, if you weren't a striker, you did your best to take your opponent to the ground.

Dodged and blocked Reid's punches, then saw my opening. Tackled him at the waist and took him down. I was on top and he didn't appear to have heard the rule that you shouldn't let your opponent get you in mount. I was sitting on his abs, had my knees locked against his ribs, and my legs clamped against his sides. Then I started doing ground and pound, which meant I was hitting his face with my fists while he tried to get me off of him and block my punches at the same time.

He was not effective at either. And I was hitting him at the fastest hyperspeed I'd ever managed, so that his head was a double-end bag—the little boxing training bag you always saw boxers hitting repeatedly at head height in every training montage done in every boxing movie ever made—only his head had no place to swing to except the floor.

"You will not ever hurt any woman ever again." Each word punctuated with two punches. "Especially not me or any of my friends. Your evil leaves this world forever tonight or today or whatever time it is."

He was never able to reply, and very soon, he wasn't fighting me anymore. And soon after that, there wasn't much head or face left.

Part of me wanted to keep on pounding him until he was a liquid. But the other part reminded me that my friends and family weren't safe, particularly when Trik Turner's "Friends and Family" came on. Leaped up and looked around. More than half of the Reid clones were down. Jeff had apparently gotten the others to see reason, had broken free, or else they'd all decided that they wanted to hit something. He, Christopher, White, Reader, and Tim were all finishing off whatever Reid clones the others weren't handling.

Any time a Reid clone went down, the moment their opponent moved away, a bullet went into the head and then body. Siler was living by the Double-Tap Code. Which made sense that he was doing it this way because there were too many bodies in motion for him to be sure he wouldn't hit one of the team.

Wruck was literally rending LaRue limb from limb. The Poofs appeared to be holding their own with Long Armed Rexie, and someone was sending bullets into the Rexie, too. Figured this was Mossy, since bullets were hitting downed opponents at the same time.

Rahmi had used her battlestaff to free Francine, who was fighting a Reid clone along with Len and Kyle. All the clones appeared to have A-C in them, which was why it was taking the good guys longer to win.

And Chuckie was still fighting Cliff. Well, he was a human and while Cliff wasn't looking all that healthy, he'd been trained at fighting. And, realistically, Chuckie had a lot of rage to work out. Maybe he was taking his time and enjoying his work.

Saw my gun, which was getting kicked all over the room. Ran and managed to retrieve it without getting kicked too much, then ran back to Reid and shot him twice in the heart because the double-tap was not to be ignored, ever.

Then headed over to Chuckie.

Cliff was about dead, which was nice. He looked at me. "You've doomed yourselves," he gasped out. "I could have saved everyone."

"But you never intended to save anyone." Nudged Chuckie and handed him my gun. "Why hurt your knuckles any longer?"

Chuckie took the gun and stood up. "The queen always saves the king. She saves the other pieces, too, when she has to. And this is, once and for all, checkmate."

Cliff laughed the Dying Villain Laugh. "You think you've won? You have no idea. I always have more than one plan in place."

"Yeah? About that. We've ensured that your plans can't happen, or didn't you realize that our team destroyed all your strongholds and neutralized all your doomsday plans?" The Long Armed Rexie gave a death cry and toppled over. The Poofs didn't eat it, however, though Mossy and Siler sent a lot of bullets into it, just in case. "And your last ally just went down."

He smiled. "You can't stop the Close Encounter. Enjoy your pyrrhic victory—you all, like this planet, only have a few hours left to live."

"Then we'll spend them happily together, burning your bodies," Chuckie said. "Oh, and by the way? I've always been better than you, without trying. Because I always had the right person on my side."

He put his arm around my shoulders and I put mine around his waist. Then he shot Cliff in the groin once, the heart twice, and the head three times. Because Chuckie also believed in the double-tap.

CHAPTER 90

"**B**ODY BURNING SOUNDS like a good idea," Jeff said as he joined us. "You two okay?"

Nodded as we separated. "We both killed the people that hurt us the most. So yeah. How are you?"

Jeff shrugged. "I killed the original, human Reid. Killing some enhanced clones wasn't a problem—all I had to do was think back to what he'd wanted to do to you and killing them was easy." He reached out and pulled me to him. "I felt what you went through, baby. I'm proud of you for facing your biggest fear, getting through it, and coming out even stronger on the other side."

Couldn't help it, had to kiss him. Jeff obliged, of course. He ended our kiss just before I started grinding against him. Couldn't complain—we weren't exactly in private. "So," I asked when we ended our kiss far too soon, "are *you* okay? Do you need an adrenaline harpoon?"

"I feel fine, honestly. And no, I'm not lying. I don't need it at all." He shrugged at the hairy eyeball look I knew I was giving him. "Honestly, baby, the barrage of emotions is just sort of . . . there. I can feel it, I can access it, but they aren't hurting me."

"I'll take it." Perhaps the Powers That Be were doing Jeff a solid for once. Chose not to worry, question, or complain.

He looked around. "Kozlow's gone."

"We'll catch him."

"Let's hope, or else your mother's going to really give it to us."

"Cliff felt that his last doomsday plan was going to roll no matter what," Chuckie said worriedly as Jeff reached out and pulled him in for a group hug. "We need to figure out what that was and neutralize it."

"Maybe he meant the Aicirtap," Jeff suggested.

Thought about it as my music changed to "Same Shit, Different Drink" by Lit. "No, I don't think so. I mean, with a name like Close Encounter it clearly deals with alien arrivals. But he said that he could have saved everyone, and I think he meant the Aicirtap when he said that. But this was a separate thing."

Reader joined us as we stopped hugging. "What the hell is that lizard thing?"

"No clue, but Mossy might know. Not sure why he and Siler aren't down here."

"Oh, we're here now," Siler said, sounding a little tense. Turned to see him and Mossy walking with their hands up. A lot of G-Company thugs with guns were with them. So was Kozlow, and he was with the man Wruck had imitated—Gadhavi was in the house.

"Let me handle this, and I mean it, stay out of it," I said to the men with me. Pulled off Siler's shirt on the way over to them and handed it to him. "Thanks for letting me borrow that. Mister Ali Baba Gadhavi, formerly of India, now of Bahrain, head of G-Company, I presume?"

He nodded to me. "I understand that you have caused some . . . issues within my organization this past day. I don't appreciate that."

"Yeah? Here's what you might want to think about. Cliff Goodman, he who is dead on the floor over there next to an alien life-form none of us recognize, had plans, big plans. Many of which centered around taking over your entire operation. The way I see it, we just did you a huge favor."

"These are just words from a lying woman's mouth."

"Uh huh. Francine or Adriana, whichever one of you other lying women has the proof, trot it over here."

Francine joined us and pulled a thick ledger out of her purse. "You'll be particularly interested in what's on pages fifty-seven through seventy-two. There's more, but that will give you the gist."

Gadhavi flipped to the pages mentioned. He read a bit, flipped some more, read some more, and so on. His countenance got darker and darker. He slammed the ledger shut and looked up. "I apologize for my earlier words. You are indeed a woman of truth. I appreciate your removing this viper from my nest."

"Great. So, you can keep that, a little present from us." Had to figure that Adriana had sent this over to the hackers to be copied and if not, oh well. Trades were made when one was working at this level of diplomacy. "In return, we'd appreciate it if you'd choose to not be upset about our clearing out all of the remaining Al Dejahl strongholds, as well as removing all of Cliff's dangerous biochemical weapons and neutralizing most of his doomsday plans."

"Most?" Ah, so he was also an attentive bear. Hard to call him a teddy bear in person. Grizzly might have been more accurate.

"Yes, there's one we were just trying to decipher when your august presence arrived."

"Was that sarcasm?"

"No, not really. I enjoy sarcasm as much as the next girl, but in this case, meeting the head of G-Company is kind of a thrill."

He studied me. "You do not plan to try to arrest me?"

Snorted. "Hardly. We're not here on that kind of business. Frankly, with the way things are going, I'm betting that most of the underworld is going to have to actually step up and get involved in more than sex, drugs, extortion, gambling, and the rest of your pursuits. The world is changing, and you're going to have to adapt or die. People like you, who run huge, successful organizations, have a lot to offer."

He stared at me. "You mean that. I must mention that no one with you seems to be in agreement."

"Oh, I'm sure they're not. I'm just willing to see things differently, call me an out of the box thinker. However, the killing and drugs and the sex trafficking and the hurting and all that jazz would have to go. I'm just saying that we're all humanity, all Earthlings together, as we meet the rest of our vast galaxy. From here on in, this is going to be one world that's a nation of aliens. Adapt or die. I'm voting for adaptation, and, based on what little I know of you, I'm betting that you're going to go for adaptation, too."

"I have people quite dear to me whom the aliens saved this past evening. And I agree that the world is about to change." He nodded to me. "I will mull over what you have said. Use all the power here that you might need, and then please destroy this area as you see fit. We part as friends and, should we meet again, I hope that it will be as friends again." He looked at his troops. "Come. We have business to conduct." They nodded to him, took their guns off of all of us, and headed upstairs.

Gadhavi turned and started for the stairs. Kozlow stayed

where he was. Gadhavi turned back. "Why are you not coming, Russell?" So, Kozlow had moved up to first name status. "When you came to tell me what was happening here I told you that, were your words true, I would ensure that you never had to enter the United States again, and that I will protect you from any who sought to imprison you."

"I know." Kozlow looked at me then back to Gadhavi. "But I gave her my word."

Gadhavi cocked his head. "Interesting. You will go back with her, to a lifetime of incarceration, simply because you gave her your word?"

"Yes. Because I gave it to *her*, Mister Gadhavi."

Gadhavi didn't look convinced. Couldn't blame him.

"Someone very important to him lives with me. Trust me, if that wasn't the case, he'd be leaping at your extremely generous and kind offer. And I mean that. Many men in your position enjoy killing the messengers."

"Mohammed was a messenger. And, perhaps, as you so eloquently said earlier, the only thing that matters is that we go forward together, regardless of which messenger we have listened to for all of our lives." He bowed to me. "Until we meet again." Then he turned and headed up the stairs, the rest of his troops following him.

CHAPTER 91

"WELL, THAT WAS FUN," Jeff said as "It's Not Over" by Daughtry came on my airwaves. "You get to explain what just went on to your mother."

"No problem. Well, in the grand scheme of things, not compared to figuring out what the Close Encounter Doomsday Plan actually is."

Looked around the lab. There had to be something, something here, that would be the trigger, or Cliff wouldn't have thought this plan would still activate.

"I believe we can use the machine to, ah, clean up," Wruck said as he joined us, once again looking as I was used to.

"We'll need to plug it back in, but yeah, that's a good idea. It's not the same, killing a clone versus the real deal, is it?" Frankly, I felt great about it, but I hadn't spent decades trying to find and neutralize my enemy.

He shook his head. "But it was satisfying. The brain was LaRue's, albeit warped. She could no longer shift. She tried, I felt it, but she didn't have the ability."

"Glad you still do. Okay, um, gang, let's get the remains into piles for scary dust creating services."

"Only those with strong stomachs should clear out the other room," Siler said. Rahmi shrugged and went in there with him.

While the others started dragging the bodies in this room toward the Killer Octopus, stared at the giant lizard. "Seriously, what planet is that from?"

"None I know of," Wruck said.

"I don't know it, either," Mossy shared. "It was almost impossible to kill."

And the Poofs, which had gone small and disappeared the

moment Gadhavi had arrived, hadn't eaten it. And they were carnivores and tended to eat their kills. If those kills were organic. Normally the Poofs would have done cleanup here, too, but they were avoiding the clones as well.

"It's not a real thing, whatever it is. It's created. And, based on it being a giant dino-type thing that could also shift into a pet lizard, I'm going to spitball that it was created and snuck in here by the Z'porrah."

"Sounds like them," Mossy said. "And it could also be a new uplift that's changed the race so much we can't recognize it."

"It's always something. Zap it last, I guess."

"We could send it to Dulce for study," Jeff suggested, sounding less than enthusiastic.

"I think that would be wise," Wruck said. "It could help us prepare for attack."

Jeff sighed and trotted over to James. They plugged the Killer Octopus back into the wall. I took the time to look around some more. The TV was still showing the Treeship. Spotted the Vatusan ships around it, helicarrier included. They were uncloaked and shining lights on the Treeship and on the water, and they'd probably been doing that for a while, since I'd been able to see the Treeship on TV even though it was night. Well, early morning now.

"We should search for clues while we have time. Along with anything else of value to us." Some of the others nodded and wandered off, presumably to do just that.

Siler came out of the other room and went over to Jeff and Reader. "Let's see if we can move that in here."

Jeff didn't argue—knew he was reading Siler's emotions even if he was protected from them. Instead the two of them, helped by White and Christopher, all shoved the Killer Octopus toward the doorway between the two rooms. It had a long cord, so they were able to leave it plugged in.

Chuckie squared his shoulders and went into the room before the machine was in place. Heaved a sigh and went after him. You didn't let your best friend see something like this alone.

There was nothing to see, though, because Rahmi and Siler had the bodies piled up and under a tarp. Well, there was still a lot of fluid that didn't look quite like real blood around. Figured this would be similar to the blood Tito had taken from the Casey Clone and actively avoided stepping in it.

Otherwise, this was a combination cloning nursery, exercise

area, and mess hall, all in one. Had to hand it to Cliff—he'd made do with limited space. No TV in here, no books, no radio, no art. To call it Spartan would have been overstating the décor.

"Trust me," Rahmi said, putting her hand on Chuckie's shoulder as he bent to lift the tarp. "You don't need to see it."

"Were any of them . . . me?" he asked quietly.

"No," Siler said, as the Killer Octopus moved into place. "Leave it at that."

Chuckie nodded and stood up.

"Chuck, let's see if this thing is easy to handle or not," Jeff said gently.

Told Chuckie what I'd seen Cliff doing when he'd fiddled with the knobs, and Chuckie examined the machine before he did anything. "You and Rahmi should get out of the way," he said. "I have no idea how hard this is to control—Cliff being in a wheelchair gave him a different center of gravity."

Rahmi pointed. "We'll go search these other areas." There were indeed a few small rooms off of this one, which we trotted over to.

One was a bathroom that hadn't been cleaned in a long time, though it wasn't the worst I'd ever seen, seeing as I'd visited some bad ones in my time with Centaurion Division. Searched it as carefully as possible, including and especially for a gate, found nothing but gross, and finished just as the lights went out.

Waited out of range while Chuckie zapped the tarp and what it was hiding for a good long while. Finally, he stopped, the lights came back on, and we could see quite a large pile of dust on the floor in front of him.

There were two more small rooms, one of which was a walk-in closet with a lot of white suits along with other things, including clothes for kids. Chose not to think about it. Instead, we searched all the clothing, but found nothing of interest.

The last room contained cleaning supplies, which, considering the state of the bathroom, was a shock. Nothing relevant in here, either.

Moving the Killer Octopus back was harder than moving it to the doorway, because the four A-Cs were on the pull versus the push side. Rahmi and I helped Chuckie shove—after making sure the nozzle was in the off position—and we got the thing moved enough that Jeff and the others could get on our side and push it the rest of the way.

"Some genius," I said to Chuckie as he, Rahmi, and I caught our breath. "Who doesn't put wheels on a thing like that?"

He barked a laugh, then joined the other men to get ready to zap again. "I don't think we want to do as many at a time from now on. Just in case."

Rahmi and I went back in and searched the rest of the other room. "Not much here," she said when we were done. "I don't understand it. Based on what Adriana and her team found, I'd expected to find much more here."

"I think he kept more at the Burj Khalifa because it was safer, in that sense."

"Perhaps." Rahmi didn't sound convinced.

"Perhaps we'll never know."

She nodded. "Or perhaps we'll discover that Cliff had a more secure area we just haven't found yet."

We went back out and checked on the Treeship's progress. It was closer to the water.

Noted that we were missing most of the team, but they returned just as I was so noting. "Couldn't find anything outside," Buchanan said, sounding frustrated. "If he planned to launch something from this island, it's hidden beyond what any of us can discover."

Checked Mr. Watch. Somehow, despite feeling that we'd only been on this island for a few minutes, all of this had taken a hefty chunk of time—we were getting close to dawn. And we hadn't found a single thing that would tell any of us what the Close Encounter Doomsday Plan was.

Turned away from the TV and looked behind me. There was a whole bank of extremely old-fashioned computers on the wall opposite the one Jeff and the others had been strapped against. Several chairs had gotten toppled during the fighting, but the computer system appeared to be running.

The next, lesser pile of bodies from the many we had in this room was tested, with Chuckie again at the controls. While the Killer Octopus zapped a bunch of Reid clones and the dismembered portions of LaRue, we again lost the lights and the TV while the backup lights came on again this time. But the computer system didn't stop. Meaning it was on the main system and the backup generator both.

"Chuckie, let someone else have a turn with the new toy. I need you over here. And, seriously, dudes, we need to get the giant dead lizard over to Dulce before it starts to smell."

Reader took over Nozzle Control, Jeff manned the plug just in case, while Tim called for Rexie transport and Chuckie came to me. "What are you thinking?"

"That whatever the Close Encounter Plan is, it's tied to this ancient computer."

Wruck, Mossy, Chuckie, and I all stepped closer. Chuckie examined everything. "There's a timer. It shows seventeen minutes." As we look at what he was pointing to, the timer flipped to sixteen minutes.

The power came back on. Looked over my shoulder to see how the team was planning to move the Long Armed Rexie corpse in order to send it through a floater gate, when the TV came back on at the same time as my music changed to "Blues Before And After" by The Smithereens. The Treeship looked close enough to the water that I had to figure it was going to land in the next few minutes.

"When is dawn here?" I shouted to the room at large, as the next pile of dead bodies got zapped and we lost all power to everything other than the creepy lights and this computer system. "As in, is it within fifteen minutes?"

"Yes," Kozlow replied. "Almost exactly."

"Crap."

CHAPTER 92

"**R**USSELL, did Cliff have Nerida doing anything in the water of the gulf?"

"Yes, he had her put water mines around the dock and the island so that no one could arrive unannounced."

"So, he could turn those mines on and off?"

"Yes. Though I don't know how."

Anyone who'd know how was dead now, which was an irony was going to totally ignore. And Nerida had been powerful. Maybe not precise, but powerful. For all we knew, her clones had been placed near to every mine so that she could pull them out of the water as needed. Or send them deeper down.

Looked at Chuckie, who'd clearly made the leap along with me, based on the look of horror on his face. "Close Encounter is the doomsday plan for when aliens arrive. LaRue would have known about the landing area in these waters and, if not, the Z'porrah certainly do, and Cliff would have known that this day would come and come sooner as opposed to later. There's at least one mine attached to the structure the Treeship is going to try to connect to. Christopher!"

He zipped over. Explained what was going on. "Are you able to swim down there at Flash speeds?"

He shook his head. "I'm not confident. It's deep, meaning I'd need deep-sea diving equipment, equipment that I've never used before. Plus, we don't know where it is, other than under the area the Treeship is over. I can try, but we can't count on me."

"I could go with him," Mossy said. "However, the depth could prove an issue. But I am also willing to try."

"Call Jeremy, Raheem gave us scuba equipment." Christopher stepped away and made the call. Mossy went with him. "If he can't do this, we don't have time to find the bomb, and with Nerida dead, we have no one who can pull it out of the water."

"What are we going to do?" Chuckie asked quietly.

"Well, what I'm going to do is give this one to the smartest guy in the room, who thankfully still has all his brain capacity intact. Take it away, Chuckie."

"Thanks for that," he said with a laugh as he turned back to the computer and started to fiddle around. "I need help, Kitty. This equipment is potentially older than Richard."

"I'll choose not to take offense," White said from behind us. "Adriana shared that all of our computer team is fully aware of what's going on. You're on speaker," he said as he put his phone down.

"Chuck, it's Stryker. You have the whole team, including Chernobog and Olga, all on the line. Tell us what you're seeing, we'll get it solved." Chuckie started saying technical things very quickly and getting technical answers back just as fast, and without bickering. Clearly Hacker International was aware of the magnitude of the issue.

This was not quite as bad as hearing A-Cs talking at hyper-speed, but it was close enough. Stepped away and went over to Christopher and Mossy. Jeremy came through a floater gate carrying equipment at the same time.

Jeff joined us. "No," he said, as he took the equipment away from Christopher. "We can swim, baby, but we aren't a water race. Swimming in and running on water are one thing, but deep-sea diving is another. The pressure of the water will make it difficult for both of them to get back to the surface. If it takes them too long to find the bomb, then they'll be at even more risk. I can't allow it. And yes, I'll take the hit and the blame if we can't save these people any other way."

"Jeff, are you sure?" Christopher asked. "I can at least give it a try."

"This is an order," Jeff said. "No one's going down there, you least of all." He looked at Mossy. "And not you, either, so don't get any ideas." Jeff handed the equipment back to Jeremy. "Thank the king profusely for his generosity. Then get a lot of agents here to get that thing," he indicated the dead Rexie, "over to Dulce for study."

"The agents are on their way, per Commander Crawford's request," Jeremy said. "The Science Center is just preparing a room for the cadaver." He nodded to us and stepped back through the floater gate.

Leaned my back against Jeff's chest, he wrapped his arms around me, and we both stared at the TV.

"Thirteen minutes," Adriana called.

"The pressure isn't helping," Chuckie shared.

And neither were we. My music changed to "Fly" by Sugar Ray. Took the hint. Pulled out my phone and dialed.

"Commander, it's always so nice to hear your voice. How goes the offensive?"

"It's our usual, Jerry."

"That bad, huh? What can your favorite flyboy do to help?"

"Um, right now? Not let the Treeship land."

There was silence. "That's not possible," he said after a few long moments. "They're in final approach. If they try to take off now the Treeship will rip apart."

Took a deep breath and let it out slowly. "Okay, so Plan B is out." Filled him in fast on what was going on, including that we'd nixed the idea of swimming down there.

"Wise choice, Commander. I honestly don't think someone untrained in scuba would have a chance of survival, A-C or no A-C. Not even Christopher, not even with his speed."

"Ten minutes," Adriana called.

"Jeff agrees. I don't want to count our team out, but it's not looking good, Jerry. Can the helicarrier do anything?"

"Uh, pick up survivors. The Treeship can't allow anyone to beam in or out right now."

"They have beaming technology?"

"Yes, but it's useless at the moment. During landing, the Treeship is incredibly vulnerable, with all power focused on the safe landing. It's part of why they're heading for the landing site they are—it was made for ships like theirs."

"I'm officially done with the entire idea of us being in the boondocks. Apparently we're the vacation getaway of choice for this entire damn galaxy."

"Eight minutes."

"Jerry, anything? Any ideas at all? I'm really open to any-thing crazy that anyone wants to suggest, and I totally include the Vata in that. Oh, my God, we are so stupid! Is Tevvik there?"

"He is. Well, in his ship, I mean, but he's in the same vicinity.

I can transfer your call to his ship while still keeping you connected to me. Hang on."

"Seven minutes."

"You know, Adriana," Tim said, "that is getting *really* annoying. And it's not like Chuck and the others aren't aware that time's ticking away."

"She can count down if she wants to," Buchanan said in a very calm and also very protective way that suggested that Tim was about one syllable away from getting punched in the face. Reminded me a lot of Jeff.

"Uh, sure, okay, yeah, the pressure's probably what Chuck actually needs right now," Tim said. "I'll just go over and mop his brow or something." He shot me the WTH look as he skedaddled over to Chuckie.

Jeff leaned his chin on my head and sighed. "All the good stuff won't matter if we can't save these people."

"No, it won't matter if we can't stop the Aicirtap." Would have said more, but Tevvik came on the line. Shared what was going on as fast as humanly possible. "So can you connect to this machine and make it stop?"

"Let me try . . . ow!" There was a lot of cursing that the universal translator wasn't catching, probably because it related to Vatusan anatomy. "It's rigged. It's rigged against us. How could anything that old be set up to repel Vata?"

"Five minutes."

"It was set up by people who knew the Vata were here and also knew how to circumvent you. I'll say this for the now dead piles of dust—they were damned smart and cagy, and they were chess masters." Heaved a sigh. "Our enemy may be dead, but, as he said, he's about to get the last laugh."

"The hell with that," Chuckie snarled. "That bastard who spent his entire life trying to ruin mine is not going to win. Put the Vata on speaker, Kitty."

Trotted over and did as requested. Those not involved in cleanup came with us. Which was pretty much everyone, since cleaning up didn't matter at the moment. Put my phone down next to White's. "Tevvik, you're on with Chuckie."

"Can I just unplug this damn machine?" Chuckie asked. "Or will that trigger the bomb? Any guesses?"

"Something made to repel us is likely on some sort of kill switch," Tevvik said. "To me, that seems a given and the risk is too high to safely attempt."

The lights went out, the computer stayed on. Rahmi had taken over cleanup and was zapping another pile of clone bodies. "Why are you doing that?" I asked when she was done.

"Three minutes." Tim wasn't wrong, Adriana doing this was nerve-wracking. But I understood why she was—everyone dealt with fear in their own ways.

"Just because things look as if they are at the end doesn't mean that they are," Rahmi said calmly, as she unplugged the Killer Octopus. "I know you've been in similar situations and overcome them to be victorious. I see no reason to assume that this time will be different. You and Charles will figure it out."

"I'm tired of being in crazed mad scientist lairs, but you're right, we get out of them. I mean, during Operation Confusion, when we left the room of Hot Zombies we had the entire place folding in on itself on top of us. And Mister White, Chuckie, and I are still here to talk about it."

Chuckie jerked. "Oh my God, could it be that simple?" He looked around wildly and shoved Tim, who'd righted the best available chair to sit in, out of said chair.

"God, is it me?" Tim asked as Chuckie flung the chair in front of the obvious place someone would sit if they were managing this system, then flung himself into it. The system suddenly seemed far more active.

"V.A.R.I.S., this is Doctor LaRue Demorte Gaultier," Chuckie said.

"Negative," the computer said, in a computer voice I remembered. "Doctor Gaultier is a woman."

"Rahmi! Get over here!" Chuckie leaped out of the chair.

But Wruck beat Rahmi to the punch. He shifted into LaRue and sat down. "V.A.R.I.S., this is Doctor Gaultier," he said in her voice. "Well done."

"Thank you, Doctor. What may I assist you with?"

"Status of explosive devices in the Persian Gulf," Chuckie said, which Wruck repeated in LaRue's voice.

"All bombs ready to explode in—"

"One minute."

"– one minute," the computer echoed.

"Terminate the program," Wruck said.

"Cannot do that, Doctor Gaultier."

"No," Chuckie said. "Terminate Protocol Close Encounter."

Wruck repeated this.

"Forty-five seconds."

"Are you sure, Doctor Gaultier?" V.A.R.I.S. asked.

"Yes," Wruck said.

Nothing.

"We've achieved checkmate," Chuckie said and Wruck repeated.

Nothing.

Chuckie looked at me. "Kitty, there's got to be a code phrase to confirm. I think that's what it's waiting for. What do you have?"

"Thirty seconds."

Chuckie had guessed for Cliff. But the person who'd created V.A.R.I.S. was LaRue. Flipped my Megalomania Girl cape on and considered what LaRue would have used for a confirmation of cancellation. All I could come up with was what the LaRue in Bizarro World had said to me, roughly right before I killed her.

"Ten seconds."

"The only good Naked Ape is a dead Naked Ape."

CHAPTER 93

WRUCK REPEATED THIS, while everyone gave me looks that said they thought the Treeship was going down.

"Thank you for confirmation, Doctor Gaultier," V.A.R.I.S. said. "Explosives have been deactivated."

"All of them?" Wruck asked.

"Yes, Doctor Gaultier. All explosives in and around Kharg Island and all explosives on the underwater docking area have been deactivated."

The entire room let out its collective breath. Heard breaths being let out via both cell phones, too.

"Getting off the line," Jerry said. "Landing is commencing." My phone turned off. No music came on. Put my phone into my back pocket. Wished I had my purse—needed to get all these extra clips out of my pants.

"We're getting off, too, Chuck," Stryker said. "We're all watching the landing." White's phone disconnected and he took it back as well.

"Well done, V.A.R.I.S., thank you," Chuckie said. Wruck did the repeat. "And now, V.A.R.I.S., I'd like full printouts for all plans, missions, projects, and protocols, completed, currently active, and upcoming." Wruck repeated again.

"Yes, Doctor." The sound of printing started.

"How did you know what to say?" Jeff asked me, as we turned to watch the television.

"It was that or 'I'm the Queen of the World.' But when I boiled LaRue down to what her driving motivation was, it was hatred."

Rahmi had brought in a broom and dustpan from the cleaning supplies closet and was sweeping up the dead bad guy dust into a bucket. "Since when did you get so domesticated?"

She shrugged. "One day, when The Great Tito and I marry, I will have to share in the care of our home." Resolved that, no matter what, that marriage was happening as soon as possible. They'd had literally the longest engagement in history. Rahmi smiled. "I knew you would be victorious."

Chuckie turned around. "We wouldn't have been without you, Rahmi."

She cocked her head. "Why so?"

"If you hadn't said what you had, Kitty wouldn't have said what she did, and I wouldn't have made the connection. As with everything we do, it was a team effort. Your mother, sister, and fiancé will all be very proud of you."

She beamed at him. "Thank you, Charles."

"Time to watch a ship none of us could conceive of before last week land," Jeff said. "That's an executive order, folks. Let's join the rest of the world and see what no one on Earth ever has before."

We all clustered around the screen. The Treeship was huge and, as the sun hit it, it glowed in rippling shades of green and blue. It was beautiful and amazing and gigantic.

Chuckie and Wruck had the computer system turn the sound on for the TV, so we got to hear the announcer's commentary. Realized why Cliff had had the sound off—they were kind of vacuous. Until commentary switched to Mr. Joel Oliver.

Oliver was sharing the history of each of the races confirmed to be in the Treeship. We'd done this at a very high level during my Impromptu World Teleconference, but Oliver was going into far more depth. He also had Lyssara and Themnir as guests, voiceovers only, since all video was focused on the ship. They added interesting facts and tidbits as well, sounding buzzy and sloshy respectively. But it was cute and not off-putting.

The Treeship took an hour to safely dock. But it didn't seem like it. And Adriana didn't have to count down to anything.

"Six years ago, I'd have had to have all of Imageering hide this," Christopher said softly as Oliver announced that the Treeship had successfully docked.

Naval ships from all the countries that bordered the Persian Gulf and yachts owned by kings and princes in the region were all heading to the ship to offload the passengers. And no one was shooting at anyone else.

"Six years ago the world was different," White said.

"Not as different as it is now," Jeff said.

"The world is the same," Reader pointed out. "It's the people on it who are different now. And that's a good thing."

"Our brave new world," Chuckie said.

"The world you always told me was out there." Was next to Jeff, our arms around each other. Reached out and took Chuckie's hand. "How does it feel to never be wrong?"

"Well, as I keep on reminding you, I was wrong about where Hoffa was buried."

"Right, you know, finally tell me, where *is* Hoffa buried?"

Chuckie's mouth opened but everyone's phones started ringing. We all stopped looking at the screen and answered our phones. My call was from my mother.

"Hey Mom, amazing timing. Every one of our phones just started ringing."

"Because Walter just confirmed that the Aicirtap have entered our solar system."

"Crap."

"And they're moving faster than any of the other ships have so far."

"Does it get any better than this?"

"Yes. The lone Z'porrah ship has managed to stay ahead of the Aicirtap, but they're not sure that they'll make it to Earth before the Aicirtap overtake them. They are begging for help."

"That we have no way of giving them."

"Correct."

"So, they'll be the appetizer and then we'll be the main course?"

"It looks that way. You and Jeff need to get back to D.C. The President needs to be in the White House."

Mom and I said we loved each other and then hung up. Everyone else's calls had been short, too. "We need to get out of here," Reader said briskly.

"We can't leave this equipment yet," Chuckie pointed out. "We can't allow any of it to fall into enemy hands, and Kitty essentially promised Gadhavi that she'd blast this place once we were done."

"We need to move the Killer Octopus, too, and it's incredibly heavy."

Jeff, Reader, Tim, and Chuckie started mildly arguing about what to do. Realized my purse was still in the alcove. Trotted upstairs. No one appeared to notice. Yeah, we were all a bit preoccupied.

Retrieved my purse and found the Poofs snoozing. Relieved myself of the tons of clips I'd taken with me and realized that I had no idea where my Glock was. Chuckie had had it last, meaning he'd probably put it down onto the computer. Couldn't see the computer all that well from this alcove, so couldn't confirm that.

Put my purse over my neck and turned around. To find Siler standing there with a gun in his hand. Managed not to scream, but couldn't stop myself from jumping.

"Sorry," he said with a small smile as he handed me my Glock. "You're heading back to D.C.?"

"Thanks. And, well, we all got the calls. You did, too, right?"

"Yes. My call was from Lizzie. She's frightened. So are the rest of the children. The news has announced that the Aicirtap are coming within a few hours."

"So, I guess you're heading home with us, then, right?"

He looked at me. "Why bother?"

That wasn't what I was expecting. "Come again?"

"Why bother going anywhere? Why go lie to the girl I promised to protect from harm when there's nothing I can do to stop what's coming?"

He wasn't wrong. Had no idea what I was going to tell Jamie and Charlie, aside from how much their father and I loved them. Didn't want to say goodbye forever to my children. And I really didn't want some aliens who weren't even themselves anymore to hurt my children, especially not in the ways I knew they would.

My music turned back on. Elton John's "Answer in the Sky" was the current musical selection.

"The helicarrier—do you think it has the firepower to stop the Aicirtap?"

Siler shook his head. "If it did, Drax would have already told everyone to stop worrying."

The music switched to "Octopus's Garden" by the Beatles. Looked at the Killer Octopus. "We have the means to zap them all into dust."

"But not the time to create more of those."

"But there are four sets . . ."

"What are you thinking?"

"Four people, each manning a nozzle. Dropped into the middle of a group, able to zap at will."

"I don't even want to contemplate the odds. And it might

even work, except that the machine needs electricity to run, and a lot of it."

Pulled my phone out and called Drax. "Gustav, the amazing helicarrier, can it do spaceflight?"

"Of course, what do you take me for?"

"Just checking. How fast can it fly? And by that, I mean is it up to the level of the latest spaceships to grace Earth with their presences?"

"Vata ships are all extremely fast. If you're looking for a comparison, I believe the helicarrier is at least as fast as whatever the Z'porrah fly, probably faster."

"Super. How quickly can you alter an existing machine to have its own power source? It needs a nuclear level of power, but it would be nice if the machine didn't kill those wielding it." Described the Killer Octopus, how it worked, and how I'd like it to work in the very near future.

"I'll need to see it to be sure if it's able to be altered, but the Vrierst could assist."

"Excellent, make it so. And bring along any other aliens who might be able to help. Pronto." Gave him our location and we hung up. "Now the issue will be to move it. That thing is hella heavy."

"We were able to move it, though, since we have a lot of strong people," Siler said. "One of whom is being called back to his post."

Considered our options as Iron Maiden's "For The Greater Good of God" came on. "Screw that. Come on." Trotted back downstairs, Siler right behind me. "Chuckie's right. We can't leave this stuff lying around. Because we're not going to be killed by the Aicirtap."

This got me the room's attention. "How are we not?" Tim asked, for everyone based on expressions. "I'm not against survival, mind you, but I'm not seeing a lot of options."

Pointed to the Killer Octopus. "I am." The air near me shimmered and Drax walked through the floater gate. He wasn't alone. There were three Vrierst with him, swirling from manta to human, depending on how their personal winds were flowing. None of them bothered with introductions, they just headed for the machine.

"What's going on?" Jeff asked.

"We have something that can zap someone into dust as easily as it makes living photocopies and, apparently, devolves your

IQ. This is what Cliff was talking about when he said he could have saved everyone. He meant he'd use this machine. So, I want us to use it."

"Who do you mean by 'us'?" Jeff asked.

"Us. You, me, Nightcrawler, whoever else wants to handle the fourth nozzle."

"We can't allow that," Reader said. "Jeff is the President—"

Put up the paw. Reader stopped talking. Was starting to love this power. Meaning I had to save the world or I'd never get to use it again.

"The President needs to lead. And that means he needs to protect his people. But more than that, in this case, Jeff is the King Regent of the Alpha Centaurion Empire. And since the Emperor himself came to rescue us during Operation Destruction, I'd say that precedent has been set. The good kings, the ones people want to follow, lead. Period."

"Kitty's right," Jeff said. "If I go back to D.C. all that means is that they'll shove me into the Bunker. We all saw the pictures the Faradawn shared—I don't want to survive in order to see how anyone not deemed 'important enough' has been destroyed, since I already know it will be in one of the most horrible ways possible. If this is how we die, then it's a far better death than to cower in a metal room while everyone else dies."

"Then we're all going," Reader said.

"Nope. Because, as Chuckie said, I'm right. Always, I'm forced to add because now isn't the time for modesty. You and Tim need to stay here with Chuckie and ensure that we get everything useful, dangerous, or compromising out of here."

Rahmi zipped over. "We need to take that." She pointed to V.A.R.I.S. "Kitty, that's where everything we couldn't find will be."

"Rahmi's right, Chuckie, we need to save this version of V.A.R.I.S. John can tell her to listen to you. Rahmi and I are both listening to our guts and betting the computer is hiding more than you're going to get via the printouts."

"I agree," Chuckie said. "I want it at Dulce, though."

"No argument. After moving V.A.R.I.S. you guys need to ensure that you reduce this place to rubble. You'll all need help with that, meaning that A-Cs or those with hyperspeed have to stay."

"Christopher, you stay here," Jeff said.

This earned him Patented Glare #4. "Why?"

Jeff sighed. "You need to be with your family." Christopher started to protest and Jeff shook his head. "Your children need you here."

"Children?" Considered how stressed he'd been over Kozlow moving in and how adamant Jeff had been about Christopher not attempting the water rescue. "Oh, wow. Congrats! When's the baby due?"

"Eight months from now. Faster than we'd planned, but we're not complaining. But this wasn't how we wanted to tell everyone."

"But this is how it tends to roll for us. I'm with Jeff, you stay home. So to speak."

"You have two children, and Siler has Lizzie. Why are you three allowed to go?"

"Someone has to stay to take care of the kids if we don't come back," Siler said.

"Ah. Uh. Yeah." Christopher didn't look happy with the reality of this answer, but he stopped arguing.

Drax trotted over. "I have good news and bad news."

"Fantastic. We'll take the bad news first."

"This is not something that anyone on Earth could possibly have created, at least not without assistance, because the materials at the core are not from this solar system."

"Super. Is that it or is there more bad news?"

"More. The core is made up of a metal found only on certain worlds in the galaxy."

"Wow, and I'll bet none of them are in our neighborhood."

"No, they are not. Would you like the good news now?"

"I'd love some, yes."

He smiled. "One of those planets is Netu."

We all stared at him. "Yes?" I asked finally.

"Apologies. Netu is the Vrierst home world. They use large balls of this metal to power their ship. And they have spares with them."

Now wasn't the time to do a comparison between Drax and Wruck's views of what constituted our galactic neighborhood. Now was the time for cautious optimism. "So, we can stick a ball into the Killer Octopus?"

"Oh, no, that won't work. It's too unwieldy and, frankly, more than a little unstable."

"Just like the guy who created it." So much for cautious optimism. "So, um, where does this leave us?"

"The Vrierst and I have agreed. We'll have to manufacture something that's more mobile and easier for humans to wield."

"Wow, that sounds great. Only we don't have a few months to get things into production. We have, like, maybe three hours."

Drax's smile widened. "You forget, I am a weapons expert, a Prince of Vatusus, and I have plenty of my smart metal available. I'll have all the personal laser cannons you'll need within two hours."

CHAPTER 94

WHILE WE WAITED, Jeff, Reader, and Tim fielded "why aren't you here?" calls, the others helped or hindered with V.A.R.I.S. Relocation, and I was on a conference call with the captain of the Treeship, a female Faradawn named Othala, her chief engineer, who was a male Faradawn named Abralox, and Tevvik. Because the best weapon in the world wasn't going to work if we couldn't get onto the Aicirtap ships.

The Vrierst didn't have enough of their metal balls, called cryex, to power a large enough blasting weapon that could be mounted on the helicarrier. Or rather, they did, but only just enough, and if we used them all, then they had no way to escape, because ethereal and cloudlike though they were, they could be shredded, and the Aicirtap had already proved that with half of their people.

Tempting though it was to tell them that they needed to give us what they had and trust us, the fact was that if we weren't successful, we were going to have to load as much of humanity as possible onto the various alien ships that were here now and flee right along with everyone else. And the Vrierst ship had landed in the waters outside of D.C. and had room for refugees, meaning that we could evacuate the Embassy and White House to that ship.

So we were trying to determine if we could use, borrow, or recreate the beaming tech the Faradawn had. Abralox and his team were working with the other Vata to get this integrated somehow with the helicarrier. Didn't know if they'd manage it in time, but Tevvik assured me they were doing their best.

The gate system was getting the workout of its existence, sending people and materials all over the world, but those at the

Dome said that everything was holding up just fine. So one thing was going right.

Turned out that "all we'd need" was a dozen. Well, it was a lot better than none, or just one unwieldy one that four could use. Meaning it was time to pick the twelve people who were going to go in as Earth's shock troops.

Anyone without hyperspeed was out, so despite Adriana, Buchanan, Len, and Kyle insisting on going, they were vetoed.

"Right now those going are me, Jeff, and Siler. I need volunteers."

"I'm in, Missus Martini, and son, don't start. I'm going to protect all of our people, but my current and future grandchildren most of all. It will be up to you to manage our people's evacuation from the Embassy and White House—James and Timothy will be far too busy dealing with preparing troops for the fight."

Felt my stomach clench. "I refuse to allow the Aicirtap to touch Earth soil."

White smiled gently at me. "Well, that's why we're going, Missus Martini, is it not?"

"We're going too," Lorraine said, as she, Claudia, and Abigail stepped through a floater gate. She grinned at my shocked look. "You've been on with Jerry. He's not a tomb when you don't tell him to be. Our husbands called us and told us the plan."

"We're in," Claudia said. "And we don't want to hear it from you. We already had to crush Mahin, and learn some new Farsi curse words, by telling her that she had to stay at the Science Center. But, James, she's prepping to fight on the ground. So are the rest of our people."

"I am going," Rahmi said, as Rhee and Gower came through a different gate.

"We are, too," Gower said, indicating himself and Rhee. "And, Jamie, before you start, this is the best way I can protect our people right now, and you know it."

"We know," Reader said as he hugged his husband. "But we don't have to like it."

"Like has never had anything to do with what we've had to do," Gower reminded him.

"This is what we came here to do," White added. "To protect this planet that is the only home most of our people have ever known and the world that allowed us to stay when our own rejected us."

"Girls and Paul, you all wound me by thinking I'm not jazzed to have you all be a part of this show. But that only makes ten, and we need two more."

Another floater shimmered into view and Butler walked through it, along with someone else I hadn't expected, Cameron Maurer. "Your small but dedicated android strike force is here to help," Butler said. He nodded to Kozlow. "I hear you helped save my life. Thank you."

"You're welcome," Kozlow said. "Ah, sorry to ask, but where are those of us staying here on the island going once we've blown this place up?"

"Into the Vata ships. Per Othala, the Treeship is pretty full, and even though they're offloading their people, they can beam them back in, since everyone's tagged at a genetic level. They'll take anyone who's in the ships with them, but they won't have room for much more."

We didn't have nearly enough ships for evacuation of an entire planet. Meaning that, once again, we'd just have to be successful. Well, having two androids had to be a help, right?

"I've downloaded all military history into both myself and Cameron," Butler said. "Every tactic ever used in human or A-C history, and the Vata were kind enough to allow us to download their military history as well."

The download was important for Maurer, who'd been a career politician before Cliff and his cronies had gotten their evil talons into him. And it might be the thing that saved us, too. Yay for androids. Had to sort of thank the memory of Antony Marling again. He'd been the Head of the League of Crazed Evil Geniuses for a while, but he'd also really been an artist in his own weird, dark, twisted way.

"My mother says that she knows as long as you're leading we'll make it, Kitty," Maurer said. "She also said that she has everyone you personally care about either in the Bunker or with her, prepared to go in case of evacuation, the entire K-Nine squad included."

"I love your mother."

"I will be going with you as well," Wruck said.

"Sorry, Martian Manhunter, we don't have a weapon for you."

He laughed. "I am the weapon. And I can talk to those of my kind who are on the Z'porrah ship. Most of our people use their shifting ability to avoid frightening the locals, so to speak. Or else we use it to impress them. And, of course, to survive on alien worlds. It's time I showed at least some of our people how to use the power we have naturally for guerilla warfare. I've already had V.A.R.I.S. reprogram herself to listen to and obey Charles."

Wanted to tell him no, that he needed to stay here and stay safe and protect people, my family in particular. But that was what my team was doing—protecting everyone. And I couldn't ask him to be less or risk less than the rest of us. "Works for me."

My phone beeped. A text from Tevvik. The beaming situation was solved due to a suggestion from one of the Q'vox scientists who'd been called in. At least in a way. But it was something that could be done quickly. Shared that it needed to be done for thirteen of us, including two androids, and was thankfully told that wouldn't be an issue. If they could get the core of the devices to work, which wasn't yet a given. Chose not to share this last part.

"The Faradawn have come through in a pinch, so we can assume that we'll have beaming capability by the time the weapons are done. So, Colonel Butler, what's our plan?"

He looked like he was trying not to laugh, which was kind of cool to see—it meant his human side was really still there, because machines didn't usually have a sense of humor. V.A.R.I.S., for example, was a particularly dry Operating System. Maurer looked amused, too. Go Team Android and Android Repair. We had this.

"After reviewing all of three different races' military histories," Butler said, very clearly trying not to laugh, "and regardless of anything else and paramount to every rule, idea, or suggestion, the bottom line is this: Follow the leader who always wins and do what they say regardless of whether or not you feel their plan is correct or will work. So, Kitty, what's *your* plan?"

Everyone stared at me. I had nothin', because without the beaming tech confirmed, any idea of mine wouldn't work.

A Poof appeared before me. Mous-Mous, Jamie's Poof. It mewed at me, then coughed something up. A Z'porrah power cube. Picked the cube and Mous-Mous up. "Oh, I like where your head's at." Snuggled the Poof and got a mighty purr in return.

Mous-Mous then mewed again, this time angrily. Got the distinct impression that, even though Harlie was the Head Poof, Mous-Mous was one of the Top Poofs in Charge, because twenty other Poofs appeared, Harlie and Poofikins included. And each one of them barfed up a power cube.

My music chose this moment to start up again—Panic! At the Disco's "Victorious." I'd heard that on repeat long enough during the endgame of Operation Madhouse to know exactly what Algar meant. This time on the very first try. I *could* be taught.

Smiled brightly. "Well then, we're going to do what's always worked. We're going with the crazy."

CHAPTER 95

"I HATE THIS PLAN," Jeff grumbled. "Seriously, I hate it."

The strike team was in the helicarrier, with the flyboys at the controls. We'd left Drax on Earth, because we were going to need his ship to save people, in case my plan didn't work.

So we were all suited up in the excellent battle gear the helicarrier possessed. Maybe we were going to our deaths, but we were going to look totally badass while doing it.

"Stop complaining, Donnie Downer. I'd like morale to be high, spirits up, everyone focused on success sort of thing."

"Just sharing. And sharing that if these new pieces of tech don't work, we're dead before we start."

Jeff wasn't wrong to be worried. The Q'vox scientist's suggestion had been personal beaming tech. It was smaller, faster to create, and had the added advantage of being something the wearer, as well as the main controller in the helicarrier, could utilize. The Q'vox, being big, lumbering beings, used similar on their home planet to go long distances without killing themselves or it taking forever.

The issue had been that the Faradawn's beaming tech didn't "divide up," so to speak, and they'd been trying to figure out how to replicate it in time. The Z'porrah power cubes solved that issue.

Chuckie had had to spend some time explaining how the power cubes worked, since he was the one of us who understood them best. Due to a variety of factors, he'd ended up on the helicarrier with the rest of the team, just in case he had to use one of the spare power cubes to beam over to save someone. He was also running the main beaming control. Thankfully, we were all adaptable and he still had all his brain.

So the rest of us were wearing serious bling, since the power cubes glowed various shades of gold and bright white, and they were encased in the personal beaming contraption that made us all look like we were Flavor Flav wannabes.

No one liked the idea that the only thing allowing us to get to safety was, essentially, a target hanging right in the middle of our chests. But we had no time for better options.

Our guns, on the other hand, we were all jazzed about. They were the typical Drax design of totally badass cool, and they had three settings—devolve, clone, and dust. No one had had time to fiddle with the original design to remove either the cloning or devolving features. That was okay—we'd all just flipped the switch on our guns to dust and called it good.

We'd gotten prepped while the helicarrier rose up out through the Earth's atmosphere. Now we were all at the main operations area, hanging with Chuckie and the flyboys, watching our world fall away from us. Chuckie and the flyboys were also in battle gear, and the flyboys were wearing the funky helmets that allowed them to use this ship essentially as if they were Vata.

"We have clearance," Hughes said calmly. "Passengers and crew, brace for escape velocity."

"Seatbacks and tray tables up," Jerry said cheerfully.

"You may feel a slight pulling sensation," Walker added.

Joe and Randy had Lorraine and Claudia standing right by them, and they indicated that their wives should hold onto the restraints keeping the guys in their seats, which the girls did. Quickly.

The command area was circular and there were metal poles around and within it. White took hold of one and indicated the rest of us should follow suit. Jeff grabbed one and me just in time, as Hughes hit the gas or whatever the helicarrier's equivalent was.

I was too busy trying to get my feet back on the floor to care.

The "slight pulling sensation" was more like being sucked at by the biggest vacuum cleaner in the world and just as pleasant as that sounds. It was over relatively quickly, and none of us were hurt, but that was only because Gower had managed to grab Abigail and Rahmi caught Rhee.

"Really?" I asked once we were all back on our feet and steady again. "That's your idea of a warning?"

Joe grinned at me. "If we can't have fun with our jobs, why would we want to do them?"

"Other than that whole saving the galaxy thing," Randy added.

Walker nodded. "We just enjoy keeping things light and all of you on your toes."

"We weren't on our toes," Abigail pointed out. "In case you missed that."

Jerry ginned at her. "Oh, I make sure I never miss anything you do." She laughed and Gower rolled his eyes.

"We will now be proceeding to the main event," Hughes shared, sounding far more official than I was used to. But then again, he was the head dude whenever the flyboys were rolling, and that meant he got to joke the least in these situations. "Kitty, just want to say that if we get home and the American Centaurion flag is still an issue, a picture of you flying sideways is always an option for a new design." Relatively speaking, apparently, on that whole serious thing.

We had NASA Base on the line, and were, in fact, talking to Jeff's dad. Because the extra pressure was apparently something the cosmos felt we all needed. But Jeff didn't seem thrown by it, so decided not to worry. And it was nice to hear another friendly voice.

"Alfred, where is the Z'porrah ship?" Chuckie asked.

"They just passed Mars and have shared that the Aicirtap are right on their tails." He cleared his throat. "They've shared farewell messages they've asked us to get to their loved ones."

"Screw that. Matt, put the pedal down."

"You got it, Commander."

Felt the ship moving faster. "Will be to the Z'porrah ship in thirty seconds," Walker said.

Chuckie whistled. "Damn."

"We're in a new age, son," Alfred said. "Just ensure that all of you survive this to see it."

"Slow down once we reach the Z'porrah ship." Turned to Wruck. "You sure you're up for this, Martian Manhunter? Not only the risk, but seeing Ancients and Z'porrah both?"

"I am." He flipped his blast visor down. "Alfred, please advise them that I'll be boarding via unconventional means."

"Already done," Alfred replied.

Wruck went to Walker's station, which had the largest viewing screen. We basically pulled up alongside the Z'porrah ship by circling around them and matching their velocity, which was damned fast. But not as fast as we'd been going.

"See you on the other side," Wruck said. Then he touched his Beaming Bling and disappeared.

"John Wruck is confirmed to be on the Z'porrah ship," Alfred said a few seconds later. "Alive and well." And totally on his own now. No one had had a guess for what range the Beaming Bling might have, Z'porrah power cube or no Z'porrah power cube. And we knew it wasn't capable of interstellar transfers, or else LaRue wouldn't have based on Earth.

"Great. Matt, let's move it, we have a fight we're late for."

We swung back around and headed off for Mars. Would have totally been excited, but this wasn't going to be the trip where mankind stepped onto the Red Planet. This was the trip where we hoped to keep Earth from becoming a second Mars—all red and devoid of life.

My music turned on. "I Can Change" by Brandon Flowers. We were back to inscrutable clues unless Algar wanted me to change my plans, which seemed unlikely, since I was pretty sure this was exactly what he'd wanted us doing.

We started slowing down. "Aicirtap fleet in enhanced visual range," Walker said. He did something, and what he was seeing flipped up onto a large screen that lowered from the ceiling. Drax was one with the idea of impressive luxury extras.

What we saw was a lot of dark silver ships massed near Mars. They were relatively small, all things considered, and were yet another new design. They were rounded and kind of hunched, with a long nose, what kind of looked like a thick shell on top that might be the entry and exit hatch or might not be, four extended legs in the rear, two smaller legs that faced forward in the front, and a rounded engine on either side, sitting right above the back legs. There were strong lights beaming out from right next to the engines.

"You know what I don't see?" I asked, as my music changed to the Cherry Poppin' Daddies' "When I Change Your Mind."

Still had no idea what Algar meant. Possibly because I was tired and hungry. Despite checking in regularly with Mr. Watch, which shockingly wasn't working in space, time had jumbled completely for me. Not only could I not remember the last time I'd eaten—though I suspected it was when I'd been with Raheem—but my body had no idea what time zone it was in, let alone what time zone it was going to consider home when it cashed the check my adrenaline had been writing. And, despite the situation, said adrenaline wasn't recharged yet.

"Gun turrets," Chuckie answered. "I don't see torpedo bays, either."

"They just may be waiting to shoot at us," Hughes warned.

"Refugees share that the Aicirtap have been, ah, hands on," Alfred said.

"Maybe they don't shoot?" Jeff asked, sounding like he didn't believe any sentient race didn't use guns of some kind. Tended to agree with him.

"Muddy is with me," Alfred said. So that's where he'd gone. Interesting choice. "He shares that, before the uplift, the Aicirtap did not use projectile weapons of any kind."

"Interesting," Chuckie said. "That means they're all hand-to-hand. Meaning it's even more dangerous for all of you. Because they won't be shooting at you, where you have a hope of avoiding the bullets or lasers or whatever if you're fast enough. They'll be grabbing you, and I can guarantee, based on the pictures that we've seen, that they don't follow the Marquess of Queensberry rules."

"Huh?" Jeff said.

"They don't fight fair," I translated. "And they'll happily gang up on us." Meaning we were going to have to be really damned fast. Hoped the new weapons were up to it. But this was their first test, and if they didn't work, then our only choice would be to escape or go down fighting against a race that apparently really enjoyed their work when it came to rending and destroying other living things. Tried not to feel afraid. Failed.

The song ended, my music switched to The Fray's "How to Save a Life," and I heard a voice in my head.

Mommy, are you there?

Jerked. Jamie, is that you?

Yes. Why are you so frightened?

I can't explain it right now, sweetheart. The last thing I wanted to do was tell my little girl what was scaring me and why.

I think you need to have a snack and a nap.

Managed to control the Inner Hyena—I'd said this to her a lot and she was parroting it right back, with the exact same inflections I used. I'm sure you're right, but, sadly, Mommy has to wait to do either. Are you and your brother okay?

Yes. That's not why I'm talking to you. She sounded impatient.

Okay, then why?

Fairy Godfather ACE needs to tell you something, but he can't, because things are watching.

Things. That boded. Are they trying to hurt Fairy Godfather ACE or you?

They can try. She sounded just like me again—my little girl was ready to share that the cosmos could feel free to bring it.

Okay, well, I'll try to figure it out, then. I don't want you or Fairy Godfather ACE hurt, Jamie.

I know, Mommy. I don't want you or Daddy hurt, either.

Considered this statement. Um, Jamie, are you the reason why all the emotions aren't hurting Daddy?

Yes! Because Daddy needs to be okay right now.

I'm glad you're protecting him, but isn't that hard for you?

Not really.

Not really. Wow. Hoped she wasn't lying. Well, Daddy would agree that if it is hurting you, even a little, to protect him, that you should stop. Okay?

Okay, Mommy.

Promise me, Jamie-Kat. Mommy and Daddy want you protecting yourself, Charlie, and Fairy Godfather ACE more than us, and if it's a choice between you or us, you pick you. Promise me.

I promise, Mommy. She sounded angry.

I don't want to upset you, or for you to think we don't love and appreciate you, baby. It's just that we love you and your brother so much, you two getting hurt is the worst thing in the world to me and Daddy.

I know, Mommy. I'm not mad at you. I'm mad at the things. The things say it's cheating for any of us to help you, but the things are cheating, too, and I'm not going to let them. Because cheating like this is wrong. Now it sounded like she was talking to or at someone else in addition to or instead of me. You need to flip the switch, Mommy.

Um, that's what Fairy Godfather ACE wants to tell me? To flip the switch?

And that anything or anyone can be put back to how they were. If you have the right tool with you.

Could tell she was trying to give me clues in the way that ACE and Algar did—obscurely. Had to say this—she had it down. Though, had a feeling the obscurity was more on my side than hers—I was clearly missing the obvious.

The life you save doesn't have to be yours. The change you make doesn't have to be to your plan, Mommy. Well, not to most of it.

Um, okay, sweetheart. Mommy will think hard about all of this.

Okay, Mommy. Fairy Godfather ACE says you always think right. Love to Uncle Chuckie. And then the presence in my mind was gone.

She hadn't sent love to her father, or me. Only to Chuckie. Looked at him. Why only Chuckie? It was a clue, the biggest one, apparently, because it was making me think. Why would Jamie tell me to give her love to Chuckie in this situation?

Got nothing. Other than the feelings of failure and letting my daughter down.

Heaved a sigh and turned to look at the Aicirtap fleet. There were a lot of ships out there. Presumably all packed to the gills with beings that wanted to eat us all.

The music switched again. To Puddle of Mudd's "Change My Mind."

Started to laugh. "Oh, my great gods and protectors, I will give myself the most major of duhs on this one. But, don't worry, baby—my brain has finally chosen to join the party."

CHAPTER 96

"WHAT IS IT?" Jeff asked worriedly. "What are you talking about? You seemed out of it for a couple of minutes."

"I was, but I'm back." Considered next moves. Decided it was time to do what I did best—go with the crazy. Focused on the lead Aicirtap ship. "Wait for my next order." Touched my Beaming Bling and the helicarrier wasn't there anymore.

Instead I was at the command center of the ship I'd focused on. Didn't stop to stare at the Aicirtap all around me, who were all reacting to my sudden appearance by flapping their gigantic mandibles and pincers and such. Flipped the switch on my gun from Dust to Devolve. And fired at the first Bug Person I saw.

The guns were sporting self-contained nukes, thanks to the A-Cs, who had these lying around the Science Center like party favors. Meaning the shot was powerful and faster than the Killer Octopus had been.

Didn't stop to see what was going to happen, just spun and shot every Bug Person near me as fast as I could. The weapons had been created to fire as fast as an A-C could work the trigger, meaning fast. And adrenaline had done me a solid and shown up when I needed it—I was revved up as if I was at the height of my rage. But I wasn't angry. I was inspired.

Did a full revolution, hitting at least twenty Aicirtap. Then took a fast look around. The ship was set up for beings with multiple limbs and had a very insectoid feeling, which wasn't totally a shock. Had no idea if the flyboys could work the controls I saw, but doubted that I could.

My music changed to "Built for Speed" by the Stray Cats. It was nice to be back in sync with Algar.

Would have spent more time in perusal and/or rocking out,

but all the hints and what I'd hoped for was paying off—the Aicirtap I'd hit were shuddering and appeared to be smaller. Not a lot yet, but perhaps undoing someone else's evil work took time.

Time to zap again, since the rest of the Aicirtap I could see were converging on me. My adrenaline was at an all-time high, and it was like everything was in slow motion. Zapped, ducked, zapped, dodged, zapped, zapped, leaped, zapped, rolled, and on and on. Managed a very impressive run up the side of a wall then backwards somersaulting flip, while zapping every bug in sight. I was like a live-action ad for Raid.

Landed in an impressive catlike stance because no one I wanted to impress was around to see it. As near as I could tell, I'd zapped every Aicirtap if not on the ship, then at least that had come into the command deck area, or wherever I was.

The first one I'd hit stopped shuddering. It had been as Muddy had described—about three times bigger than Kyle. Now it was just Kyle-sized, so still a hell of a lot bigger than me.

It made noises for a while, then suddenly I could understand it. "Sorry, you'll need to repeat yourself, missed anything you said prior."

"What . . . what did you do?" it asked me. Couldn't tell if it was a male or female.

"I think I just turned you back into what you used to be. Hopefully still as smart as you used to be, but if not, apologies in advance."

It looked around as "Victim Of Circumstance" by Joan Jett & The Blackhearts came on. "Why are we in warships?"

"Oh dear. Um, this is probably going to sound like so much lying, but the uplift the Z'porrah gave you made you three times bigger and turned you into murderous monsters. You've torn up a great deal of this side of the galaxy."

"That . . . that is impossible. We are a peaceful race! Our ships are defensive, only."

As it said this, more Unzapped Aicirtap arrived. The Zapped Aicirtap all screamed. Yeah, that was the galaxy's reaction, too. "Sorry, gotta save you from yourselves." Zapped the newcomers using rapid fire. Got them all. Blew on the end of my gun. "I think I'm enjoying cleaning up this town. You were saying?"

"Why did you do that?"

"Um, to save you from your crewmates or relatives or whatever."

"No, I meant blowing on your gun."

"Oh, that. It's a human thing from the part of Earth where I was born."

"Earth! What is an Earthling doing out here?"

"Um, not sure you've been following me, but *you* are in *my* solar system."

"No," the Zapped Spokes-Aicirtap said. "That cannot be." It ran to look out. "What have we done?"

"Lots of horrible things. You need to do a headcount, right now. I need to know if I've hit all your crew or if there are more of you here."

"I have no idea." It turned back to me. "I remember . . . a terrible dream. A nightmare."

"It was all real. Someone needs to take me through your ship, fast. We have the rest of your fleet to try to save, and if I don't get back to my ship, my people are going to do their best to kill all of yours."

Wouldn't have thought a sort of humanoid beetle could go pale, but this one managed it. "No," it whispered. "Earth is bloodthirsty. The humans murder our kind every day."

"Um, on my planet your kind tend to be the size of my thumb or smaller, and they aren't sentient as you'd know it. However, the bloodthirsty part is right on. Take me through this ship, right now."

It obliged and we scuttled off. Well, it scuttled—the Aicirtap could and did walk on their hind legs but apparently if speed was required they went on all sixes, or whatever they called it. Every Zapped Aicirtap we passed was coming out of their terrible nightmare. All seemed distressed, many were sobbing, and some were wailing.

Turned out to be a good thing I'd seen *Alien* and *Aliens* and any horror movie you wanted to name, because there were plenty of Unzapped Aicirtap. Zapped them all, even the couple that were hiding in the cargo bay. Algar did me a solid and put one of my favorite songs to fight to, "Electric Worry" by Clutch, on repeat. This time I was fairly sure it was only for my enjoyment, as opposed to warning me about dangerous electrical currents.

Once the ship was cleaned—and we'd waded back through Aicirtap who were falling on me, begging me to either tell them their collective nightmare wasn't true or begging me to save the rest of their people—told the Zapped Spokes-Aicirtap to sit tight. "If weapons start firing, land on that planet." Pointed to Mars. "I don't think you can breathe there, but it'll get you out of the fight and identify you as the ship where all the Aicirtap are back to normal." I hoped.

"Wait," it said. "What do I call you?"

"Kitty. What's your name?"

"Ulzax. Are you a female or a male?"

"Female. You?"

"Female as well."

"Great, then, girl to girl, this situation really isn't your race's fault, in that sense, but that's not going to fly in a war crimes court. So, don't fire on my ship but get ready to have to fire on your own, because if the rest of your fleet reaches Earth, everyone dies. And that includes all of you."

She nodded. "We will do as you've said."

"Great." Considered what else to say. "I'll be back." Then I thought of Chuckie, because he was guaranteed to still be on the helicarrier, and hit my Beaming Bling.

Landed next to Chuckie right back in the helicarrier's command center, just in time to hear Jeff bellowing about demanding to be allowed off the ship. My music turned off.

"Chillax your face. I've got it under control."

Everyone stared at me. "Where the hell have you been?" Jeff asked, sounding freaked out and huffy. "None of us could leave. This equipment doesn't work."

"Oh, it works." ACE, Jamie, Algar, and/or Naomi were just ensuring that it couldn't work until I was back.

Everyone started talking. Put up the paw. Everyone, including Jeff, shut up. I had embraced the FLOTUS Power and now it was mine to use at will. Excellent.

"No arguing, no speaking, no complaining. Just listening and doing exactly what I say. The Aicirtap are salvageable. Change the setting on your guns to Devolve. We're all going to pick specific ships, one of us to a ship. Then, once you're there, zap any and all Aicirtap you see with the Devolution ray. I don't want dead Aicirtap, I want living ones. Search every inch of the ship—I found plenty in the obvious places but more than enough in the not so obvious ones, too."

"What the hell are you talking about?" Jeff asked.

"I get it," Chuckie said excitedly. "Cliff's ray works on the mind, and that's what the Z'porrah's uplift must have affected in the Aicirtap. The pituitary gland would affect size and strength, and messing with the mind can always affect the emotional centers. Did you actually devolve one?"

"No." He looked disappointed. "I devolved the entire ship full of them." Chuckie brightened back up. Turned back to the others. "And every one of them is distraught to hysterical over what's happened and is happening. They are to be rescued, just like the rest of the aliens who came to Earth for help. They came to us for help, too. They just didn't know it."

"Where do we aim?" Jeff asked, Commander in Chief Voice on Full, all freaked-out husband gone and replaced by the guy who'd led his people against much worse monsters wearing only an Armani suit and a hell of a lot of leadership and authority.

"It takes a direct hit anywhere on the Aicirtap, but if you can hit the head it's a faster return to normal for them. They have no memory of what they've done, by the way. Remembered as a nightmare. But since I told them the nightmares are real, they are, as I said earlier, pretty damn freaked out."

"They've murdered millions of people," Siler said. "You sure we should show them mercy?" Had a feeling I knew why he was asking.

I nodded. "Not all killers are evil. What they did was evil, but *they* aren't. If we're going to save the world, or the galaxy, or whatever, that means we have to try to save all of it. Even the parts we don't like, are afraid of, or have hurt us. We have to save it all. Or we're no better than the Z'porrah. Or what the majority of the Aicirtap are right now."

"And no better than Cliff or LaRue or Reid," Chuckie said quietly.

"Exactly. Secret Agent Man, you have to stay here in case one of us gets into trouble. My first ship was easy, relatively speaking, but there's no guarantee the others will be. And there are a lot of others. I took the lead ship, but we're spoilt for choice for where we go next."

"Count off," Jeff said, as he changed his gun's setting. Everyone else followed suit. "We'll be going from left to right, avoiding the lead ship. You count one, you choose the leftmost ship. Two, the one directly to the first one's right. And so on. Shoot to kill if that's your only option to survive. Otherwise, as Kitty said, shoot to save."

"Once you've cleaned your ship, return to Chuckie, and seriously, think of him because it'll land you right back here, versus on the controls the flyboys are using to keep us all safe. The flyboys will be able to tell you what ships are cleared. Pick the next one, moving right from the last where one of us went, lather, rinse, and repeat. If you're at the end, start from the leftmost side of the next line."

"Can we get the cleaned ships to move?" Gower asked. "If only to make it easier."

"Possibly. I suggested that the lead ship head for Mars, but only if things went bad, mostly because I didn't want their breaking ranks to cause the rest of the fleet to attack. So, um, as with most things, play that one by ear."

Gower grinned at me. "Or, as we call it, routine."

CHAPTER 97

"ANY OTHER QUESTIONS?" Jeff asked. There were none. "Everyone ready?" Everyone nodded.

"One," White said. He put his hand on his Beaming Bling and disappeared.

"Glad that's working again," Jeff said. "Next."

"Two." Siler went next. Then Maurer, Butler, Rahmi, Rhee, and Gower.

Lorraine kissed Joe. "Eight."

"Nine," Claudia said after she kissed Randy.

Jerry took off his helmet, got up, grabbed Abigail, and planted a kiss worthy of a sailor returning from WWII on her. "Kick ass and come home safely," he said when he ended their kiss.

"You know it, Studly." She winked at me. "Don't tell my brother that's his nickname. I think Paul still thinks I'm a virgin. Ten."

"You're up," I said to Jeff. "Shoot fast, move faster."

He kissed me. "Always do." He grinned at me, giving me a great shot of his Jungle Cat About To Eat Me Look. "Other than in bed. Eleven." Then he was gone.

Turned to Chuckie. "Someone needs to reach Wruck and let him know what we're doing. That's probably going to be you via Alfred."

He nodded. "I'm really proud of you, Kitty."

"Thanks. Always proud of you, too."

"Want to know where Hoffa's buried?"

Considered this. "Wait until I'm back."

"Why?"

Grinned at him. "Incentive." Looked at my next ship. "Twelve."

Once again, I was in the middle of a bunch of Aicirtap, and this time, Algar gave me a different fight song favorite—Tina Turner's "Steel Claw."

This ship was much like the first. Did my circular zapping technique first, then branched out. Got the first Zapped Aicirtap to take me through the ship. Zapped all available options. Gave some instructions, went back to Chuckie.

Everyone was on their second ship by the time I was back. Not a problem. It was a race, but the faster we went, the faster we all won.

My third ship was like my first two, and by now what I was doing felt routine. Didn't mean I was any less alert—the Unzapped Aicirtap remained a terrifying reality—but it did mean I felt more comfortable doing it.

Returned to the helicarrier. "The androids are on their sixth ship each," Chuckie said. "We've managed to get through to Wruck. The Ancients are still coming, just in case."

"Wise." Noted that a good portion of the Aicirtap fleet were heading down to Mars, the lead ship, or what I was pretty sure was the lead ship, included. "Are we sure that all those ships are cleansed?"

Chuckie did a fast count. "Yes, they tally correctly."

"Super." Chose my next ship, and went to it. My music changed to Iron Maiden's "Be Quick Or Be Dead."

Which, shocker, was prophetic. The people in here were aware that something was wrong, since the other ships were breaking ranks. So when I appeared, they weren't so much surprised as given a convenient target.

Zapped plenty of them, but I wasn't able to get the full radius around me hit. Which meant I had no breathing room.

Also meant I had to scramble and run, because there were a lot of the Unzapped and I was having trouble clearing the area.

Bent low and ran fast, zapping as I could. Fortunately, all these ships were alike and I'd just gone through three of them from top to bottom. Headed for the cargo hold, running as fast as I could, which was necessary. I had a lot of the Unzapped Masses after me.

Found what I was looking for—a small, high ledge that was difficult to access if you were a gigantic bug. I was going so fast I was able to run up the side of the wall and leap onto this ledge. Shoved in as far back, as hard, and as firmly braced as possible. Then started firing.

The good news was that I was in a sniper's position and the easiest things to hit were the Aicirtap's heads. The bad news was it looked like the entire crew was shoving into the cargo hold. And some of them in the back were standing on another's shoulders.

Which meant I had to fire at those in the back now, instead of those nearer to the middle. "Steel Claw" came back on, and it definitely was getting a double in both keeping me revved and reminding me of what I was going to face if I didn't hit every one of these people as fast as possible.

The ones in the back and middle started shoving forward, and I got a good shot of what ravenous hordes really looked like. And, as the Aicirtap in the front devolved, those who were now in full bloodlust ripped them apart.

I was seeing exactly what the Aicirtap could do in this "evolved" state, and it was beyond horrifying. And, oh joy, if they were in bloodlust, they needed more hits to devolve. Either that or my gun wasn't working anymore. Or both. Gave it even odds for both.

Was about to give up and change my setting from Devolve to Dust when I heard a sound. It was loud and sounded like a combination of roaring and growling, somehow deep and high-pitched at the same time.

It had an effect on the Unzapped Aicirtap. They turned away from me and toward the sound. The effect on the Zapped was quite different. They were crying in terror and trying to get as far to the back of the cargo hold as possible.

Took the opportunity and zapped the backs of the Unzapped. Got almost all of them. There were only three left—all the others were either doing the confused devolve headshake or scrambling toward me in terror—and no matter what I did, these three were all moving just before I pulled the trigger, meaning I was missing them. But the walls around the cargo hold were sure going to be stupid later. If we all got a later.

Something came into the cargo hold. It was a creature of nightmare, but not a Cleophese, in part because it was too small and in other part because it was less Cthulhu and a lot more Cujo crossed with Freddy Kruger, as siphoned through all the ravens in the universe. And it was twice as large as the Unzapped Aicirtap.

Whatever it was, it grabbed an Unzapped Aicirtap in either, well, chose to charitably call them hands. Maybe claws. Maybe beaks. It was hard to tell.

It slammed the two Aicirtap together and knocked their heads hard enough that they looked unconscious. Then it threw them in the air, toward me.

Shot both of them in the head with the laser, gun still set on Devolve. They landed just shy of me, on top of a bunch of the still-living Zapped, who promptly scattered out from under, though none of them were making a move toward the door, where the Creature was.

The last Unzapped Aicirtap was a fighter. Chose to think of it as a she, mostly because, so far, I'd only talked to Aicirtap females. She was all claws and fangs and fury, and if she'd been on my side I would have been excited, because the Creature didn't look like it was on anyone's side.

Had no idea of what to do. I could try to devolve the creature and the Aicirtap both, I could try to kill them both, or I could zap out of here and have the flyboys shoot it out of existence. None of these options seemed right, but I was going to run out of time, and the moment the Creature saw me, it might decide that the Aicirtap wasn't nearly as interesting or tasty. Because it was clear that a creature like this probably considered the Aicirtap food. The Zapped's reactions certainly said this was the case.

The Marine saying, "Kill 'em all and let God sort it out," crept up and waved at me. Devolution seemed the best choice, but if I devolved the Aicirtap before the Creature, then the Aicirtap was toast. And I had no idea what hitting the Creature with the ray would do.

My finger was on the switch, to flip it from Devolve to Dust when my music changed. Bruce Springsteen's "Brilliant Disguise" came on.

Took a deep breath, aimed, and fired.

CHAPTER 98

MY SHOT WAS PERFECT, hitting the Aicirtap right in the back of the head. As soon as the shot hit, the Creature let the Aicirtap drop to the floor. Then it headed for me.

Put my gun down.

The Creature looked sort of liquidy now. It turned into Wruck by the middle of the cargo bay. He smiled at me. "Thank you for not shooting me."

"Great disguise, dude. You scared the crap out of all of us."

"That was the idea. Jeff said that you were having problems. I told him I would take care of you. Transforming into the Aicirtap's most terrifying predator seemed the right choice."

"I do *not* want to visit their home world."

"I'm sure." He looked around and his expression was sad. "They killed their own people."

"Only because they were alerted by the ships moving out of formation. That was a bad choice, I guess."

"Per Paul, not yours. Everyone is having more difficulties with their last ships. I would like to request that the rest of you allow me, John Butler, and Cameron Maurer to complete the rest. It will go faster and, hopefully, with less bloodshed."

"You do not need to ask me twice." Jumped down. Naturally, because someone I'd like to impress was here, I slipped on Aicirtap blood and went down on my butt.

Two of them helped me up. Now that they weren't scary, their hands weren't razor-sharp pincers. They were just hands. I mean, hands that were pincers and all that jazz, but still, hands. And the Aicirtap were just people. People who looked like giant beetles, sure, but still, just people.

"Thank you," one of the ones who helped me up said.

"You're welcome." Really, there wasn't anything else to say.

Though, of course, as we moved through the ship, it was the usual comforting and sharing of the reality. For this ship, and presumably some of the others, the horror was compounded, though, as many realized they'd killed their own loved ones.

"The Z'porrah have a hell of a lot to answer for," I said to Wruck, as we reached the command area.

"They do. I would consider them the Founding Members of the Mad Scientists Club."

Snorted a laugh. "Dude, I can't tell you how glad I am I didn't hit you with the devolution ray."

"I'm glad, too." He sighed. "We Anciannas are also Founding Members. That's the problem when you're old and extremely evolved as a race—the urge to meddle is almost impossible to ignore."

Thought about Algar, about all the Black Hole Universe People. And the superconciousnesses out there. Some wanted total free will, some wanted constant meddling. "It's just like our religions. There's really no one right answer." Thought some more. "Unless it's just the Golden Rule." My music changed to ABBA's "People Need Love."

"Do unto others as you would have them do unto you. Yes, I believe that is the one truth that actually matters."

"Then let's get this problem solved and start spreading that message to the rest of the galaxy. I'm sure some know it and live by it already, and I'm equally sure some have forgotten it."

He chuckled. "I see you have some missionary in you, as well."

"I get that from my dad."

"What do you get from your mother?"

Laughed. "Probably everything else."

We hit our Beaming Bling and landed on either side of Chuckie. "Glad you're back okay," he said to me. "I think most of the others need the same rescue," he said to Wruck.

Wruck nodded. Grabbed his hand before he could touch the Bling. "John, make sure that you let the Beaming Bling show. Or one of the others is going to shoot you for sure." Because I doubted that any of them other than possibly Gower and White were rolling with Algar's Helpful Musical Hints.

"A wise idea." He shifted but this time the Bling was obvious. Then he touched it and disappeared.

One by one the others came back, while Algar shared Smash

Mouth's full "Get The Picture?" album for my listening plea-
sure. Wruck was apparently just beaming from ship to ship now.
Jeff was the last to return. "Wruck is with both Butler and
Maurer, both of whom came over to help me."

"How did they know where you were?" Hughes asked.

"They both said they saw the ship rocking."

"Do I want to know?"

Jeff grinned at me. "We'll exchange war stories later, baby."
At any rate, the three of them are going to finish the last ships
together. The androids are faster than all of us and they both feel
that they can survive heavier injuries than the rest of us."

"Are you hurt?"

"No." He looked at me and his brow furrowed. "Are you hurt,
baby?"

"Huh? Oh. No. I slipped in Aicirtap blood. Long, embarrassing story I'll tell you later."

Jeff came over and kissed me. "As long as you walked away
from it, it'll be a great story and potentially one of my favorites."

"Works for me. Where are the rest of the Ancients?" Didn't
see anyone else in the helicarrier.

The viewing screen lowered again. It showed a line of Anciannas floating in space between our ship and the now much
smaller Aicirtap fleet. And these were Anciannas, in what was
presumably their true form, all looking similar to how Wruck
had when he'd killed LaRue. And yet, I could spot differences
enough to know that they were each distinct beings. Huge, distinct beings, with their equally huge wings fully extended.

"Wow. If all the religious of our world could see this."

"They can," Walker said. "I'm beaming this back to Mister
Joel Oliver."

"Was that wise?" Jeff asked.

"Probably not," Gower said. "But it was necessary."

White nodded. "It's time our worlds stopped clinging to the
myths we've built up around our creations. Most of them seem
sadly incorrect."

"Not sure we want to say that to our world, let alone all the
others," Siler said.

"No, we don't," I said slowly. "Because they're not all that
wrong. The one certainty we have is that every being that is so
advanced from us as to be a god—so advanced that every human
would have no issue falling to their knees and professing undy-
ing loyalty and worship—have all said the same thing."

"What's that, baby?" Jeff asked. "They talk to you far more than the rest of this."

"They all say that there is a God. God is something so vast that we can't really comprehend it, but it's not a man or a woman or a host of gods. Or maybe it is and isn't all at the same time. Maybe this is how you move as a race from one level of sentience to the next. Not via some process that changes you into a monster version of yourself, but by realizing that everything you've believed is wrong, and yet right at the same time. And none of it matters unless you're doing the best you can, for the most people you can, as frequently as you can."

"Spoken like the First Lady," Gower said.

"No way," Lorraine said. "She's the Queen Regent."

"I'd call her the Savior of the World," Jerry said. "Because I've been paying attention."

"I'm just me, you guys."

Jeff pulled me to him and kissed me again as my music changed to "An American Girl" by Tom Petty & The Heartbreakers. "That's what they all said, baby."

CHAPTER 99

WRUCK, **MAURER,** and Butler finally returned. "All cleared," Wruck said. "There were casualties, but not as many as there would have been."

"Our whole team is still alive and in one piece," Jeff said. "I count that as a huge success."

"Are the rest of your people going to stay in space or are they coming into our ship?" I asked Wruck.

He smiled at me. "I'm with my people." He looked at the screen. "They are going to shepherd the Aicirtap to Earth." As he said this, the Anciannas all broke formation and headed to Mars. "By the way, Mars is like the world the Aicirtap come from. Very sandy."

"Will it need terraforming?" Chuckie asked, as Hughes relayed that we were all coming back to Alfred.

"Potentially. I think we need to determine what will happen to them first. As well as all the others. Some have no worlds left because of the Aicirtap and should probably have first choice in terms of relocation."

"It's the Z'porrah who should stand trial," Claudia said. "This was all their fault, not the Aicirtap's."

Thought about what Algar might say. "They had free will. They chose of their own accord. They were lied to, or maybe they weren't. We may never know. But they said yes."

"You want them on trial?" Jeff asked.

"I don't know. I don't know how you get justice out of a situation like this one."

"Commanders, we may have a problem," Jerry said. "The Z'porrah ship is not being allowed to land. And to follow the current conversation through, we now have Z'porrah who are going to look like really perfect fall guys for everyone."

"I don't like their chances," Joe said.

"Yeah, instead of Z'porrah, I'd call them Tomorrow's Martyrs," Randy added.

My music went to Motörhead's "One More Fucking Time." Had that right. Heaved a sigh. "It never ends. Chip, can you put the Z'porrah ship onscreen?"

"Absolutely Your Saviorship."

"Hilarious." Turned to Wruck. "You think these are the okay ones?" He nodded. "Great. I'd like Superman and the Martian Manhunter to come with me, please. The rest of the Justice League can stay in the helicarrier, heading home but paying attention in case we need help. In other words, Matt, make sure Alfred and the rest of the world know that Jeff and I are on that ship."

Looked at the Z'porrah ship onscreen. Then, despite every fiber of my being telling me that nothing but evil was inside of it, hit my Beaming Bling.

Had to give the Bling this—the transfers were amazingly fast and so much better than gates. Figured I should keep this one to myself lest I hurt Jeff's and every other A-C's feelings. I was inside Dino-Bird Central, looking at what I and pretty much everyone on Earth considered our greatest enemies, in less than a totally nausea-free second.

The Z'porrah had heads that looked something like a humanoid version of an eagle's, but with an impressive underbite. Unlike most birds, their eyes were more centered. As per every Z'porrah I'd seen, they were wearing what I thought of as Space Muumuus, with six large, painted talons sticking out from under each muumuu, and feathers sticking out of their long Space Muumuu sleeves. Knew that under the muumuus they looked like miniature Tyrannosaurus Rexes with wings. The likelihood that it was the Z'porrah who'd sent Cliff the Long Armed Rexie seemed very high.

The Z'porrah seemed thrown by my arrival. They all jumped. And then they all backed away, arms raised, feathers in front of their faces. This wasn't a reaction I was used to from this race.

Wruck and Jeff chose to show up. "She comes in peace," Wruck said.

"Presumably. Why are they terrified of me?"

"Perhaps it's the big gun you're brandishing," Wruck said with a chuckle.

"Whoops. Sorry, Dino-Birds."

Several of them put their arms down. "What did you call us?" this ship's SpokesDino-Bird asked.

"Dino-Birds. Since you look like a dinosaur crossed with a bird. Sorry," I said to Wruck, "but that really seems obvious. Are these, perhaps, the very slow of wit Z'porrah?"

He laughed. "No. They're just extremely frightened. Think of them, and the Anciannas with them, as missionaries of different religions who were out in a very remote area, trying to convert the natives. Their home churches haven't been in regular touch with them, they have more in common with each other, and so they started spending the off hours together. Sharing stories of their successes and failures, talking about home, recreating the friendship our two races had so long ago."

"Then the Aicirtap attacked the planets we were helping," the SpokesDino-Bird said. "We didn't even realize that our people were responsible." Could tell it was a male now. He shook his head and looked down. Something wet hit his talons, then the floor. Realized he was crying. "We couldn't save any of them. Two worlds filled with young life and several sentient life-forms that had such promise, all destroyed." He buried his beak in his feathers and sobbed. There was a lot of that going around.

Couldn't help it. Handed Jeff my gun, went to the sobbing Z'porrah, and put my arms around him. They were my height, so it was easy. "It's okay. Well, it's not, not really, but it's not your fault. You didn't cause this."

He cried harder. "We, all of our survivors on this ship, have longed for a return to peace with the Anciannas. Their survivors with us have longed for the same. We had hoped that, using the two planets, we could show that we were better together. And now . . ." He kind of collapsed against me, wrapping his wings around me, sobbing his little Dino-Bird heart out.

"This is La'fean," Wruck said. "He is the leader of these Z'porrah."

"I don't deserve to be," La'fean sobbed.

Looked around. The rest of the Z'porrah looked stricken and many were also crying, though not as dramatically as La'fean. "Do you all feel that La'fean isn't qualified to lead?"

The rest shook their heads. "He just feels responsible," one of the others said. Was certain it was a female. "He cared so much about our flocks. To have them destroyed so utterly and then to discover it was due to our own people?" She shook her head. "We all wonder if we should not just tell Earth to do to us what they will, because we've failed."

"No," Jeff said strongly. "Wars happen. Horrible things happen. But you're all something that I can guarantee my wife and I never thought we'd meet—Z'porrah who seem just like us. Not our enemies. Not filled with hate. And it's vital to our world and this galaxy that you prove that the Z'porrah can be peaceful and loving, not just to each other, but to everyone else, as well."

Thought about Christopher's concerns from however long or short ago it was—was this all an elaborate ruse to get a whole spaceship full of Z'porrah spies onto the planet?

My music changed to "Nobody's Fault," by Aerosmith. Figured Algar was using the biggest musical gun he had, since my view was that if my boys were saying it, it must be true.

"No one here is to blame," I said. "No one is going to offer themselves as martyrs, and no one is giving up leading their people just because they've had a really horrible week."

"Earth is still not giving us permission to land," a different Z'porrah said.

"Really. Well, I'd like the com then." Handed La'fean off to the nearest Z'porrah and went to the seat that was being offered.

"Would you like a headset?" this Z'porrah asked politely.

"Nope. I'd like this on speaker, if at all possible. And if there's a way to connect this to the helicarrier we came from that would be extra special. I'd like to connect to the helicarrier first and not have whoever on Earth we're chatting with hear the conversation."

He nodded as he fiddled with some buttons and knobs. "You're on with the helicarrier, secured line."

"Kitty, nuclear warheads are aimed at the Z'porrah ship," Jerry shared. "Aimed from the United States, Russia, France, Israel, the UK, China, Pakistan, and India."

"North Korea isn't joining the party?"

"I don't think they've dug out from under their last attempt."

"Good to know. Okay, I'm ready to go live to whoever's being a cranky pants."

The Z'porrah chuckled and did some more button and knob fiddling. "You're on with Earth."

"Hey there, who's on the other end of this line? Oh, and as a mention, the *last* time I asked that question, someone almost fired nuclear weapons at me. I believe that my reaction to that has become something of a legend. Trust me when I say that the legend probably doesn't do justice to how enraged I really was. *So*, choose your next words really hella carefully."

"Kitty? It's Fritz Hochberg."

"Fritzy! Why aren't you allowing the only nice Z'porrah, potentially in the entire galaxy, to land? Was them begging in terror while fleeing the deadly hordes not enough for you?"

"Ah, is Jeff there?"

"I am. My wife has the com. Consider *that* before you say anything else."

Hochberg cleared his throat. "Ah ha. Ha ha. We weren't sure what was going to happen when you two once again broke protocol and headed off to fight space invaders."

"Or, as we call it, Friday. That's us, rule breakers who have the nerve to not want to risk any of our people when we know we've got the best chance of success. We both feel really badly that we didn't just sacrifice thousands of our young people to fight a war we managed to circumvent without any bloodshed on our side."

"You're all unharmed?"

"Got it in one. I'm sure everyone will be happy to know that we're unscathed. And, funny story, we used the weapon that the Mastermind created to kill everyone on Earth to, instead, save the Aicirtap from themselves. The ones that are still alive are back to what they once were. And there was much rejoicing and all that. And their fleet is coming right behind us, being escorted by what I know you want to call angels but what are, in fact, Anciannas, or Ancients as we call them. Following me so far?"

"Yes. You want to allow the formerly invading hordes to land because you've made them nice people again?"

"Fritzy, that was amazingly succinct. Go you. So what's the holdup?"

"The rest of the world is a little . . . unsure."

My music changed. To Queen's version of "God Save the Queen."

Heaved a sigh. "I was trying not to do this. But if everyone's going to suddenly stop singing "We Are The World" and, instead, go back to singing "Every Man For Himself," then I am going to be forced to remind you that Jeff and I both have another rank. We're both quite happy to not shove that rank in everyone's faces. However, that stops when the rest of you are going to choose to be dangerously obstinate and stupid."

"We can't tell the rest of the world what to do, Kitty," Hochberg said worriedly, as Guns N' Roses sang "Rocket Queen" to me. Algar really liked the Queen thing. Clearly it was a hint. Was too tired to argue.

"America cannot, that's very true. So I'm not speaking as the First Lady. I'm speaking as the Queen Regent of the Annocusal Royal Empire, known on Earth as American Centaurion. And I'm just going to bet that our emperor is already on the line, calling up troops to hyperjump right over here and explain that we need to start, right here and right now, learning when to hold 'em, when to fold 'em, when to walk away, and when to run, while at the same time never counting our money while sitting at the table. Or have you forgotten what saved every world leader last night?"

"Ah . . . Kenny Rogers?"

"Not that I noticed." Maybe Kenny had been there. There'd been a zillion people, so anything was possible. My stomach grumbled. Now I wanted a roasted chicken with all the extra-large sides. And about a gallon of Coke. And then more chicken. Yeah, it'd been a long while since I'd eaten.

Jerry broke in. "American, UK, Israeli, and Russian missiles have disengaged."

"Good job, Fritzy. It's nice to know that you're not trying to assassinate the President. We've had enough of that for a good long while."

"I just needed to verify that Jeff was alive and well," Hochberg said huffily.

"Whatever. So, half the world has decided to trust us. That's nice. I know who the other half is, in case anyone on Earth isn't aware that I know that China, India, Pakistan, and France are still aiming nukes at this ship that I happen to be on. Really, France? That's how you're doing us?"

"France's missiles have disengaged," Jerry shared.

"That's better. For the last three, the last one of you to disengage is pretty much telling me that their leaders didn't appreciate being saved yesterday. Or else they think they're going to take over. The thing is, all those Aicirtap ships all do have weapons on board. I'd consider playing the cooperation game sooner as opposed to later. Big Queenie is watching."

"China, India, and Pakistan have all disengaged." Jerry said, clearly trying not to laugh. "They all did it pretty much at the same time."

"That's better. We're going to be landing the Aicirtap in the

Arizona and New Mexico desert areas, and before everyone there freaks out, on American Centaurion lands. The Z'porrah ship, however, is going to land on the Potomac. Get the area cleared of ships and such. *Now*."

"The Air Force and Navy are prepping for your arrival," Hochberg said.

"Good. I assume it's to greet us as opposed to try to shoot us?"

"Of course it's to greet and protect you! Why in the world would it be anything else?"

"Fritzy, let's just say that it's been a long couple of days and leave it at that."

CHAPTER 100

AMAZINGLY ENOUGH, there were no more issues with the remaining aliens landing. Possibly because Hughes had streamed the entire conversation I'd had with Hochberg to Oliver, who'd ensured that it broadcast to the world. Take that, Amos Tobin.

Jeff, Wruck, and I stayed on the Z'porrah ship, just in case. But nothing untoward happened. Once we'd officially landed and had given the Z'porrah their photo op, we coordinated with Colonel Franklin and had the Z'porrah move the ship to Andrews. But it had mattered, for everyone on Earth and anyone who might be watching from far away, to see that ship land in peace, and to see the Z'porrah exit the ship with us, without them firing on anyone or anything.

We had the Z'porrah going to East Base, because we didn't trust any of the humans to not try to kill them, and we trusted the other aliens on the planet even less. The Anciannas were going to join them there as well, in part to guard the Z'porrah and in part because they wanted the comfort of being with the people they had the most in common with.

The aliens from the Treeship were housing in the Middle East. Those who'd come in the Yggethnian ship were being housed in South America. The Vrierst were in Siberia because they wanted to be—apparently Netu was a far colder planet than Earth.

The Turleens were at Caliente Base, and the Lyssara were staying in their Comb that was in the Arizona-New Mexico desert as well. The Themnir had been invited to go to Australia, China, and to stay in the U.S. They chose Florida because of the weather, so NASA Base was housing them.

The Aicirtap were sent to Home Base, where they were going

to house as well, meaning Area 51 got to have its first official, sanctioned, and broadcast alien landing. A red-letter day for everyone, conspiracy theorists in particular.

Speaking of my favorite one, Chuckie joined us once the helicarrier was parked back in its nice spot at Andrews, just as we were sending the last of the Z'porrah off with their Field escorts and Wruck, who wanted to be sure that they and the Anciannas were settled safely. "I'll see you back at the White House," Wruck said as he nodded to Chuckie. "Call if something happens before then."

"Let's hope not," Jeff said. "I think we've earned a break."

Chuckie looked better than he had in a really long time. "This ship has stairs?" he asked as Wruck pushed a rounded disc on the outside of the ship then headed off with the last of the Z'porrah. The stairs folded back up into the body of the saucer, just like airplane stairs did.

"All of them do," Jeff said. "As it turns out."

"Apparently the Z'porrah's beaming in and out maneuver is totally done as a wartime thing to impress the natives and make it harder for projectiles to hit them." Looked around. "Where's everyone else?" We were remarkably alone.

"The rest of the team is heading home to shower and sleep." He chuckled. "They told me to tell you to take the high fives for granted."

"Why aren't you doing the same?" Jeff asked.

Chuckie shrugged. "I want to make sure everything's really over for the moment. I've heard from James—everyone's back where they're supposed to be, including all White House and Embassy staff who were along for this particular wild ride. He says to warn you that Antoinette is either going to resign or demand to go on every mission with you."

Jeff laughed. "Good to know."

"Oh, Kitty, James also wanted me to tell you that Tito and Rahmi's wedding is finally a go. Renata doesn't expect to be on the planet much longer and wants to see that happen." He was laughing at a private joke, I could tell.

"What is it you're not telling me?"

"Rhee's getting married, too. She asked for an exception to the ridiculously long engagement cycle they have, and since she's the younger sister, Renata was able to agree."

"I'm surprised in a way. I didn't think she was the marrying kind."

"Rhee?" Jeff asked. "Why would you say that?"

Snorted. "No, not Rhee. Camilla."

He gaped at me. "There's no way. I haven't picked up anything like that."

Managed not to roll my eyes, but only just. "Dude, Camilla has never done anything other than sneer at Hacker International, the flyboys, James, you, and, most significantly, Chuckie. A-C women like brains. So if I see an A-C woman who isn't drooling at a really brainy dude, I take the logical leap and assume it's because she's looking for a brainy chick."

"But . . . but I know the others who are—"

Put up the paw. He closed his mouth. "Camilla is a Liar, capital L. She's trained Rhee in how to hide things like this from you. It's probably been a great test for her. But at any rate, Camilla fooling you emotionally isn't the surprise. You not realizing what was going on is just you being inattentive. Don't try to sell it any other way."

"I knew," Chuckie said. "I mean, just like Kitty said, it was obvious."

"I refuse to discuss this any longer," Jeff said. "I just hope we all get to have some sleep before the weddings. Of which I expect a lot more," he added rather defensively.

"Yes, yes, Mister Empath Supreme, we know. Hooking up is happening."

Chuckie laughed. "Not for everyone, but facing the end of the world does tend to make people finally admit their attractions."

"Just like—" Jeff started.

Put up the paw again. "Later. We can gossip about all the love connections later." Looked at Chuckie out of the corner of my eye. He definitely looked better than he had since Naomi had died. He looked like himself again.

Chuckie kissed my cheek. "It's fine, Kitty. Jeff can talk about people being happy around me. I finally believe that I'll be happy again like that in the future. You two can both stop worrying about me."

"Oh, that's never gonna happen. If we love you, we worry about you."

"What Kitty said."

Chuckie grinned. "I'll take it."

We were heading for the gate that Andrews had in what it was now calling its Alien Craft Hangar, when Tim stepped through it. "There you guys are. Nicely done, Kitty."

"What?"

He grinned. "Centaurion Division has people lined up for recruitment in pretty much every country. Your speech about not wanting to send kids in to die when you could handle it yourselves has apparently made all those kids and anyone else who's ever dreamed of being in the military or going into space want to get in on the action. And their governments are encouraging it, particularly those governments who don't have nukes and who, therefore, feel that they're firmly on Big Queenie's good side."

"I'm going to regret giving myself that nickname, aren't I?"

"Probably. We're going to have to expand in order to train everyone. Just wanted you to know so that it didn't catch you by surprise."

Gave him a hug. "You're the best, Megalomaniac Lad."

"I am, it's true. You guys need to go home, take showers—trust me on that—eat some food, be with your families, and get some sleep. Oh, Chuck, Angela had your parents brought out here, just in case. They're at the Embassy along with pretty much everyone else who isn't at the White House."

"I'm definitely going to go home and shower and change, then, before I see my parents. I don't think it's good for them to see any of us looking like we do right now." Chuckie hugged me, did the man hug thing with Jeff, got a fist bump from Tim, then Jeff calibrated the gate for him and he stepped through.

"Think he'll move on now?" Tim asked.

"We can but hope, but yeah, I do. Where are you going?"

"Home. As in, the house you grew up in. My wife's waiting, and before you beat yourself up, she was at Caliente Base for the last day or however long it's been since we had to roll out to the Middle East. I want a home-cooked meal and to sleep in my own bed before the next round of crises hits. You know, tomorrow."

We all laughed, Jeff and I both hugged Tim, then Jeff again calibrated the gate and Tim stepped through to Pueblo Caliente.

"Embassy first, showers first, or White House first?" Jeff asked as he spun the dial on the gate.

"Kids first. Well, kids and pets, since they're basically a packaged deal these days."

"Looking like this? You sure it won't frighten them?"

"I'm sure."

Jeff concentrated. "Huh. Siler's already there. He must have gone straight to Lizzie."

"Good. It's where he belongs, with his daughter."

Jeff put his arm around my waist as he finished calibrating our gate. "We saved the world, baby. And the galaxy."

"No. We saved our children and everybody else's children. So everyone gets to see what a brave new world really looks like."

We walked through the gate. Resisted asking why we hadn't used our Beaming Bling. Sometimes it was better to just go with the routine.

We weren't in the Embassy. We were in the White House, in Jamie's room. She had Charlie on her bed with her, along with literally every animal, domestic and space-foreign, we had. The K-9 dogs were here, too.

"Mommy! Daddy!" Jamie squealed. Charlie did the Happy Baby Bounce.

The sea of animals parted for us so we could get to the kids. Jeff picked up Jamie, I took Charlie, and we both hugged and kissed the heck out of them. "You did great," Jeff said to her when the initial loving was over and he was passing her to me and taking Charlie for the next round. "I'm so proud of you for protecting your little brother."

Jamie smiled at him, then looked at me and smiled a different smile. She looked like Mom did, any time she and I weren't telling Dad something for his own good.

I laughed as I hugged her tightly and kissed her head. "Oh, our Jamie-Kat is the best girl in the world. In all ways. And," I whispered to her as Jeff gave Charlie a short airplane ride, "I'm so proud of you. You really are your mother and grandmother's girl."

Jamie hugged me back, just as tightly. "Yes, Mommy, I am. And I always will be."

Then we went in for one big family hug, interspersed with lots and lots of kisses, for what seemed like far too short a time. But it made surviving that much sweeter, and everything we'd had to do to save our alien nation worthwhile. It turned out that it was indeed good to be Big Queenie.

Available May 2017,
the fifteenth novel in the *Alien* series
from Gini Koch:

ALIEN EDUCATION

Read on for a sneak preview

"IT'S ANOTHER GREAT DAY on Good Day USA!" the perky morning show host shared enthusiastically. "Our first hour we focused on all the new alien races we've gotten to know over these past few months." The audience dutifully applauded. "This next hour is going to be even better, though, folks. We can't wait because we're just so excited to announce our next special guest!" More audience applause.

Didn't share any of their enthusiasm, but then again, I was the opposite of a morning person and was still wondering why I was awake at this hour. Also could not remember the host's name, which was because, in part, I was never up to watch these shows and, in other part, I was never up because I wasn't a morning person and therefore wasn't sure I currently remembered my own name.

She was pretty and Hispanic and that was all I was getting, because my brain didn't want to do any work beyond what my eyes were sharing. Was fairly sure her name started with a K, since that appeared to be a morning show requirement. My name started with a K, too. Perhaps, in another part of the multiverse, I was a morning show anchor. Though I sincerely doubted it.

Her handsome male cohost, whose name was also escaping me, nodded equally enthusiastically. He was perky, too. Obnoxiously so. "This is a guest everyone wants, who we're really proud to have been able to bring to our viewers first, because we go out of our way to start your days right! Don't we, Kristie?"

Bingo, and starting with a K. Now if I could only remember

his name. The dudes' names didn't seem to have a letter require-ment. Managed to remember that he was a former baseball player, so there was that. He reminded me a lot of the late Mi-chael Gower—big, bald, black, and beautiful, with definite cha-risma. The audience was clapping again. Was pretty sure there was a sign somewhere telling them to do so.

"We sure do, Adam!" Kristie said, still sounding amazingly perky. Hurray for the requirement on these shows to use your fellow hosts' names at least once every ten minutes. "You all know her as the First Lady of the United States. Coming out right now, here's Code Name: First Lady, Katherine Katt-Martini!"

Yes, that was me and, barring my being really lucky, I wasn't asleep and this wasn't a nightmare, at least, not a sleeping one. There were a lot of hells that politics had put me into, but none worse than this—being a guest on a morning talk show.

As the audience clapped themselves into a frenzy and I was gently shoved forward toward the stage by my so-called friends, I once again asked myself and the greater cosmos why anyone had thought this was a good idea. And also who hadn't shared with Kristie and Adam that I never wanted anyone to refer to me as Code Name: First Lady. Whoever it was would be receiving a very nasty talking-to whenever I got out of here.

Wasn't walking forward with the right amount of enthusi-asm, and I knew it, since the stage manager hissed, "Move it!" to me. So much for the idea that being the FLOTUS got you any respect backstage.

Either he'd heard the stage manager or he was used to some guests not being thrilled to be on the show, because Adam jumped up out of his seat, trotted over to me, and escorted me to mine, potentially earning my lifelong love and adoration. He settled me into my so-called chair that was a lot more like a barstool with a back. I wasn't tall, so it was a little awkward. Of course, Kristie wasn't that tall, either, and she was making it work.

"Missus Martini," she said, beaming and perky beyond be-lief, "thank you for joining us on Good Day USA!"

"Happy to be here," I totally lied. "And please, call me Kitty."

She and Adam exchanged thrilled glances. I sincerely doubted they were as excited as they looked. They were the top morning show in the country and they hadn't gotten there by being dull to watch. And on the morning shows, reactions were Broadcast with a Capital B.

"Thank you . . . Kitty," Kristie said, sounding as thrilled and perky as she looked. "Gosh, we have so many questions for you, don't we, Adam?"

"We do!" Perk, perk, perk. These two were the King and Queen of Perkiness. "Kitty . . . gosh, I can't believe I get to speak to you so informally, Kristie and I have been prepping questions nonstop since you agreed to come onto Good Day USA, and now that you're here, I'm so excited that I just can't remember half of them!"

Prayed that these two weren't going to expect me to provide both questions and answers, because, if so, this program was about to go way down in the ratings. But a response seemed expected. "Um, that's really sweet of you to say."

"Isn't she great, folks?" Kristie perked at the audience, as if I'd done an Oprah and just given everyone a car.

The audience applauded hysterically. There had to be a sign somewhere telling them to do so, but I couldn't spot it from my vantage point of trying not to look at anyone or anything while still appearing poised and confident. Was pretty sure I was failing at all of it.

"Kitty, what's it like to be a human and yet part of the American Centaurion population on Earth?" Adam asked, apparently having managed to remember at least one of his prepared questions. He'd traded perky for inquisitive. So at least there was that.

"It's great. The A-Cs are wonderful people."

"They're stronger and faster than us, aren't they?" Adam asked. "And better looking, too."

"Well, yes." The A-Cs had two hearts which meant they could move so fast a human couldn't see them, and they were also super strong. I felt that hyperspeed was the better of the two, but I wasn't going to complain about the extra strength, either. They also had extremely fast healing and regeneration, which was a huge bonus for those in active and dangerous roles. And, as Adam had said, they were, to a person, all gorgeous, representing every skin tone on Earth, and every body type, too, as long as the term "hardbody" was applied as well. "But I don't think you have anything to feel inadequate about, Adam."

This earned me wild applause from the audience and some women whooped their approval. Adam looked flattered and a little embarrassed. So, presumably I was doing okay. As long as they didn't ask if I had any A-C bells and whistles, we were good. Because I did and no one wanted me talking about it.

Due to the mother-and-child feedback that had happened when I'd been pregnant with and given birth to our daughter, Jamie, I'd reverse inherited the A-C superstrength and hyperspeed. I'd also gotten a talent, and one that wasn't normal for A-Cs.

Talents didn't go to every A-C, but they got talents far more frequently than would seem statistically normal. Jeff was an empath—in fact, due to being given Surcenthumain, aka the Superpowers Drug, by some of our enemies, he was likely the strongest empath in the galaxy. Empaths felt emotions, everyone's emotions, all the time. They had ways to block the emotions, but still, they were walking lie-detectors among other things.

Imageers had been more powerful before our enemies had introduced a virus that successfully muted their powers. Done, most likely, to prevent Jeff's cousin, Christopher White, from discovering who our late, great enemy, the Mastermind, had really been. Before that, though, imageers could not only manipulate any image but they could read them, too, the pictures making a copy of mind and soul, at least as Christopher had explained it.

There were also dream and memory readers, but that talent was extremely rare. The third most common power, however, was also the one that got the least amount of respect—troubadours. This power was all in the voice, expressions, and body language. In other words, perfect for actors and politicians, which was why it was looked down upon by most of the A-C population. Of course, what most of that population hadn't realized was that it made troubadours incredibly powerful and totally stealth.

However, my talent was none of these. My talent was being Dr. Doolittle. Thankfully there wasn't supposed to be an animal segment on today's show, because the chances of me having a chat with said animal would be high. I couldn't help it—animals liked to talk to me.

"What's it like to be married to an A-C?" Kristie asked, bringing perky back.

Well, at least these were softball questions, so I had that going for me, though I'd have rather been listening to Justin Timberlake bringing "SexyBack". But what I wanted and what I got were not always one and the same.

Of course, had to make sure I censored my reply, because, as far as I was concerned, the number one best part of being married to my husband was Jeff's bedroom prowess and regenerative abilities, and I knew beyond a shadow of a doubt that no one wanted me sharing that with anyone, let alone the largest morning show viewership in the world.

"Wonderful. Jeff is a wonderful husband and father, just like he's a wonderful leader." I was using the word "wonderful" too much. But this wasn't my element and six in the morning really wasn't my time zone, and despite everything I was still having trouble focusing. "I'm always proud of him because he always does what's best for his people."

"Do you mean that as for American Centaurion, for Centaurion Division, for the American people, or for the world at large?" Kristie asked, sadly trading perky for this show's version of hard-hitting. "He *is* the King Regent of Earth for the Annocusal Royal Family, who control all of the Alpha Centauri system, isn't that right?"

"That's right. And I mean for all of them. Jeff's always been focused on protecting the people of Earth when he was in and then the head of Centaurion Division, even before he became a Representative, let alone the Vice President or President."

Managed not to say more about the whole King Regent thing, in part because that made me the Queen Regent and in other part because Jeff was working really hard to ensure that the Earth governments remained at least somewhat stable. It was a very interesting time to be on Earth, but I didn't want to share that with the cast, crew, and viewership of Good Day USA if I could possibly help it.

"What's it like being Queen Regent?" Adam asked, destroying my hopes of the conversation going elsewhere.

"It's fine. I'm more focused on the duties of the Office of the First Lady and my family." Thanked Jeff's Chief of Staff, Rajnish Singh, for drilling that line into me. Of course, Raj had been the one who'd arranged this little shindig, so my mental thanks were only halfhearted. Raj was a troubadour, so to him, this wasn't a Stress Test of Horror, it was just a great way to keep Jeff's approval rating high.

Kristie and Adam both looked at me expectantly. Apparently more of a response was expected. "Um, sorry, but honestly, I'm a little nervous. This is my first time on TV."

This earned me huge belly laughs from Kristie, Adam, and the studio audience. "Oh, isn't our First Lady just a hoot and a half?" Adam asked the crowd.

I'd been told there were two large TV screens where the audience could see them, and also there was a smaller one in front of the stage, where the hosts and guests could watch whatever footage the show was airing, so that actors would know for sure what scene from their latest movie or TV show was being touted and therefore react accordingly. Hadn't spotted this before, but Adam and Kristie stopped grinning like the Joker and Harley Quinn and both looked ahead and sort of down.

Followed their lead, found the screen, and saw that it had images on it. Images of me.

There I was, in my pink linen suit, taking down what looked like a terrorist six years ago. The start of Operation Fugly and my new life, really.

"I'm just amazed you were so brave on the spot," Kristie said as everyone watched me slam my Mont Blanc pen into someone's back.

In real life that had been a superbeing and I'd put the pen into the jellyfish-like thing on its back, between its wings, into what I later found out was a parasite, at least as far as Centaurion Division was concerned. I'd discovered what it really was during our last fun frolic with world and galaxy-ending danger, but that wasn't important now. Ah, the good old days, when Christopher and the Imageering team were able to change images on the fly. Missed those days. A lot. I wouldn't be here right now if those days hadn't been taken away from us.

"I'm just amazed that anyone ever buys linen," was the only thing I could think of to say. "Seriously, I didn't sleep in that suit, it just looks like it."

This comment earned roars of laughter from the studio audience, Kristie, and Adam. Apparently my role was to keep it light and keep things funny. Go me.

The scene shifted. Now we got to see me giving the eulogy for Michael Gower, at the end of Operation Infiltration, which I still considered our darkest day. This wasn't a funny moment, and I was relieved that no one was laughing. We didn't stay on this too long, thankfully. But what we moved to made me cringe inside.

Sure enough, there it was, the impetus for all the Code Name: First Lady crap. I was on a Harley, Jeff was in a helicopter, leaning out to grab me off said Harley. It looked like an action scene out of any movie you'd care to name.

"So," Kristie said, as the screen went blank and she turned back to me, "as we've seen, you've been on television a lot."

"Not intentionally."

Adam chuckled. "I need to ask the question that's foremost on everyone's minds, Kitty. When is Code Name: First Lady going to hit the screens?" Well, at least he wasn't asking me about being Queen Regent anymore.

Hoped I had a poker face firmly in place. "I really think that's a joke, not something that's seriously being considered by anyone." This was a lie, because, sadly, I knew it was something that was being heavily pursued by at least one Hollywood studio.

We'd managed to keep Code Name: First Lady from being created only by applying a great deal of political pressure and using the old "for the good of the nation" speech a lot. Didn't feel like going into that here, though.

Kristie shook her head. "We know it's not a joke. And, let's be honest—it's what the people want, to see a movie about all you and your husband have done to protect the world." At this, the studio audience started cheering. Tried not to hate them a little. Failed.

"Well, I honestly don't know that it would be that interesting."

Kristie and Adam both snorted, then turned toward the screen again. Managing to once again not wince, I turned toward it, too.

This time they had my "get it together, you jerks" speech

from Operation Immigration going, when I was addressing the conclave of religious leaders and hadn't known I was going live to the world. On the plus side, I looked totally in charge. On the negative side, this was, admittedly, interesting. Chose not to ask why, if they had archival footage, anyone would want to see a dramatic reenactment, because I wasn't stupid and I knew why—it was fun.

We were treated to this for a while, then the picture changed again. This time, the video showed something recent. Very recent. As in, last week recent.

Jeff and I were sitting at the front of the General Assembly of the United Nations. Normally we wouldn't have been in there unless we were addressing the U.N. And, in that case, we'd have been waiting in a nice antechamber until it was time to go on. However, due to the circumstances that a whole bunch of aliens arriving unexpectedly had created for Earth in general and us in particular, there we were. Operation Immigration continued to pay dividends in putting me places I didn't want to be.

We were up front and center because the Secretary General had chosen the U.S. to get the prime seats at that Assembly. We weren't in delegates chairs but were sitting behind America's delegation, where support staff normally hung out. The chairs were far less comfy than the ones the delegates had, but that wasn't the issue. No, the issue was that my Official First Lady Color of iced blue matched the fabric of these chairs perfectly. So perfectly that it looked like my disembodied head was floating near Jeff's shoulder, my having been in a long-sleeved dress, versus a suit for this particular shindig.

The audience tittered and I couldn't blame them. Would have made a comment, but the sound was going and people onscreen were talking.

"It is a historic day for our countries, our world, and our galaxy," the Secretary General of the United Nations said, sounding really excited. Wondered if he'd gotten his start on a morning show. "Not only are we inducting several new sovereign nations into our ranks, but we are also officially joining the greater galactic community as Earth and the Solaris System become a part of the Aligned Worlds of the Milky Way Galaxy."

This earned a lot of applause both onscreen and from my live studio audience.

"After much worldwide deliberation," the Secretary General went on, after the applause in the General Assembly had died down, "the United Nations has reached a unanimous decision for who will represent Earth's interests within the Union of Aligned Worlds. I am pleased and proud to announce that Katherine Katt-Martini has agreed to represent Earth and all of our interests!"

Gini Koch lives in Hell's Orientation Area (aka Phoenix, Arizona), works her butt off (sadly, not literally) by day, and writes by night with the rest of the beautiful people. She lives with her awesome husband, three dogs (aka The Canine Death Squad), and two cats (aka The Killer Kitties). She has one very wonderful and spoiled daughter, who will still tell you she's not as spoiled as the pets (and she'd be right), and a fun son-in-law who doesn't seem to mind that his mother-in-law is just this side of crazy.

When she's not writing, Gini spends her time cracking wise, staring at pictures of good looking leading men for "inspiration," teaching her pets to "bring it," and driving her husband insane asking, "Have I told you about this story idea yet?" She listens to every kind of music 24/7 (from Lifehouse to Pitbull and everything in between, particularly Aerosmith and Smash Mouth) and is a proud comics geek-girl willing to discuss at any time why Wolverine is the best superhero ever (even if Deadpool does get all the best lines).

You can reach Gini via her website (www.ginikoch.com), email (gini@ginikoch.com), Facebook (facebook.com/Gini.Koch), Facebook Fan Page: Hairspray & Rock 'n' Roll (www.facebook.com/GiniKochAuthor), Pinterest (www.pinterest.com/ginikoch), Twitter (@GiniKoch), or her Official Fan Site, the Alien Collective Virtual HQ (thealiencollectivevirtualhq.blogspot.com/).

Gini Koch
The Alien *Novels*

"Told with clever wit and non-stop pacing, this series follows the exploits of the country's top alien exterminators in the American Centaurion Diplomatic Corps. It blends diplomacy, action, and sense of humor into a memorable reading experience."
—*Kirkus*

"Amusing and interesting...a hilarious romp in the vein of *Men in Black* or *Ghostbusters*."
—*VOYA*

TOUCHED BY AN ALIEN	978-0-7564-0600-4
ALIEN TANGO	978-0-7564-0632-5
ALIEN IN THE FAMILY	978-0-7564-0668-4
ALIEN PROLIFERATION	978-0-7564-0697-4
ALIEN DIPLOMACY	978-0-7564-0716-2
ALIEN vs. ALIEN	978-0-7564-0770-4
ALIEN IN THE HOUSE	978-0-7564-0757-5
ALIEN RESEARCH	978-0-7564-0943-2
ALIEN COLLECTIVE	978-0-7564-0758-2
UNIVERSAL ALIEN	978-0-7564-0930-2
ALIEN SEPARATION	978-0-7564-0931-9
ALIEN IN CHIEF	978-0-7564-1007-0
CAMP ALIEN	978-0-7564-1008-7
ALIEN NATION	978-0-7564-1143-5

To Order Call: 1-800-788-6262
www.dawbooks.com

DAW 160

Tanya Huff
The *Confederation* Novels

"As a heroine, Kerr shines. She is cut from the same mold
as Ellen Ripley of the *Aliens* films. Like her heroine,
Huff delivers the goods." —*SF Weekly*

A CONFEDERATION OF VALOR
Omnibus Edition
(*Valor's Choice, The Better Part of Valor*)
978-0-7564-1041-4

THE HEART OF VALOR
978-0-7564-0481-9

VALOR'S TRIAL
978-0-7564-0557-1

THE TRUTH OF VALOR
978-0-7564-0684-4

To Order Call: 1-800-788-6262
www.dawbooks.com

DAW 73

Celia Jerome

The Willow Tate *Novels*

TROLLS IN THE HAMPTONS
978-0-7564-0630-1

NIGHT MARES IN THE HAMPTONS
978-0-7564-0663-9

FIRE WORKS IN THE HAMPTONS
978-0-7564-0688-2

LIFE GUARDS IN THE HAMPTONS
978-0-7564-0725-4

SAND WITCHES IN THE HAMPTONS
978-0-7564-0767-4

To Order Call: 1-800-788-6262
www.dawbooks.com

DAW 170

Lisanne Norman

The *Sholan Alliance* Series

"This is fun escapist fare, entertaining...."
—*Locus*

"Will hold you spellbound."
—*Romantic Times*

To Order Call: 1-800-788-6262
www.dawbooks.com

DAW 29

Once upon a time...

Cinderella, whose real name is Danielle
Whiteshore, did marry Prince Armand.
And their wedding was a dream come true.

But not long after the "happily ever after,"
Danielle is attacked by her stepsister Charlotte,
who suddenly has all sorts of magic to call upon.
And though Talia the martial arts master—
otherwise known as Sleeping Beauty—
comes to the rescue, Charlotte gets away.

That's when Danielle discovers a number of disturbing facts: Armand has been kidnapped; Danielle is
pregnant; and the Queen has her own Secret Service
that consists of Talia and Snow (White, of course).
Snow is an expert at mirror magic and heavy-duty
flirting. Can the princesses track down Armand and
rescue him from the clutches of some of
Fantasyland's most nefarious villains?

The Stepsister Scheme
by Jim C. Hines
978-0-7564-0532-8

"Do we look like we need to be rescued?"

DAW 130